The Upright & The Wicked

Book One of The Children of Light Series

by Sarah Wallis

Book cover art by BenJ https://www.deviantart.com/winterkeep

1st edition 2026

Chapter One

Be angry and do not sin;
do not let the sun go down on your anger,
and give no opportunity to the devil.
- Ephesians 4:26-27 ESV

The forest seemed still, but there was little doubt of the wickedness there. Such an unsafe place to be caught in the middle of, yet precisely where Wes found himself. He was lost in his memories; thinking on things instead of focusing on surroundings. There was something about the trees crowding around him that made him feel pressed upon by unseen hands. It was as though he was slowly, gently suffocating. Thus Wes turned inward to his memories. Though it wasn't like those times when a memory spell overtook him, the results were much the same.

He knew he allowed the hour to run too late. The sun's journey, seeming too brief to account for the day, already reached the west. Darkness was falling, and Wes was sorely unprepared. He had not gathered those necessary things needed to make a fire, but instead spent the past hour recollecting on moments from when he first met his wife. Wes wandered around the forest; plodding his way through thick shrubbery and overgrown trees, while his mind lingered a distance away, in that farmhouse where he left her.

Ah, Ruth. She was so beautiful when she was younger. She lived in the same village as Wes once upon a time. A village that was no more. He was sad to see it go to the decay of time, but such was the way with all things. Time was a robber that never bore the shame of its sin. Wes recalled all that he admired about Ruth in those early days of their courtship. Her thick honey-colored hair drew his attention first as it was so different from his own wispy hair that often fell into his eyes, and was the color of mud. Her hair seemed to float in the breeze, and gently play against the side of his cheek. Wes shook his head. He sensed a miasma; a cloud of delusion in these woods. It instilled in him a desire to remember; to fall back into the past and escape the present. Perhaps this forest intended to claim him. For if he wandered around much longer, the night would do what the trees could not in the day.

A nudge to his back made Wes realize he was no longer walking. Ruth captivated his mind and stilled his feet. He pushed all thought away; fighting with his own memories, and turned to rest a hand against his mare's nose.

"The Lord will provide," he assured her and she snorted out her skepticism. Wes helped her over a particularly bad jumble of roots, and she stamped her hooves; anxious about the growing darkness. She spent her life as a plow horse, and knew the comforts of a barn at night instead of a forest full of lurking hunger. She need not worry, for their hunger was for him, but Wes wondered how she might react if he was forced to face one of the Fallen. This thought led to another, and Wes found himself thinking about his father-in-law. He wondered if the man ever interacted with the mare. Did she respond similarly to his mutated face? Wes stared blankly at the ground as shadows grew long beneath their feet.

He shook his head again in frustration, and removed his wide-brimmed hat to rub his fingers against his forehead. The woozy confusion of the forest was causing a headache to form. Wes pushed forward, focusing his attention toward the west, and helped his mare over a patch of some earthly debris his boot skidded on.

He kept an eye on the ground and its potential snares, but couldn't ignore the way the creeping darkness made his hair stand on end. He sensed a familiar wickedness approaching, something that took notice of him the night before, which only worsened the danger he was in. If only he could think clearly, he might be able to use what time remained to gather enough kindling to form a small fire. But he was so befuddled in this miasma, that he struggled to hold onto a focused thought. Wes looked around, and tried to recall which direction he wanted to go.

Then, as though Heaven sent, he beheld a glow of flame. He stumbled towards it, fighting against the mental trap that ensnared him, and was relieved to see it was not a trick of his mind or the forest. There was indeed a fire, sitting at the edge of a large clearing, and it was being tended by a solitary man. Even from a distance, Wes saw the mark of sin upon the man's face.

He was bent over his fire with a stick, poking at the embers in an effort to give them more life. Wood no longer burned the way it once had, or so the stories say. In his youth,

Wes recalled hearing of flames that were able to engulf entire forests in their wrath. Stories like this were often told by those men and women that remained from the Before. Those in his village would talk to anyone willing to listen about all that they had lost when the world fell apart in the Damnation. Ruth would often sit next to Wes, her hand in his, and listen to their tales about such wondrous things, Wes could hardly believe half of them actually existed. In his later years, he no longer doubted the stories of what once was, but it mattered not in the now.

Wes focused on the present, for he felt the allure of the miasma caressing against his delicate memories; rekindling their life. He crouched down, keeping his mare close behind him, and watched the man from a distance. He dared not walk into the firelight without warning for the other man may be armed in some way, but Wes had to risk an intrusion all the same for he had no other options than this fire. He glanced to the west in time to see the last of the sun slip behind the distant mountains. Any choice he had, faded with that setting sun.

Wes reminded himself that stumbling upon this man was no coincidence. The world they lived in never provided such spontaneous grace. Thus it had to be the Lord's hand that brought Wes to face this unknown stranger. If this opportunity was the Lord's doing, Wes had nothing to fear from it. He also had to remember that he didn't arrive unguarded and lacking teeth. He kept his revolver in a belted holster against his right hip and cared for it regularly. In its cylinder, it carried three bullets, and while they were the last bullets he knew to exist in this world, it was still an option. A last resort. It was not lost to him that the bullets might not even fire. Everything decayed. Everything crumbled to ruin. This was the result of their sins. For the Damnation was an end but also a beginning to something new for those able to adapt to the change.

Considering his options, Wes' hand rested on the grip of his revolver, and the feel of it in his palm soothed him. Reflexively, he released the strap that held his gun in place, and while the soft sound barely permeated the night, the man abruptly stopped using his poking stick in the fire. He calmly placed it across his lap, and lifted his head to examine the forest around him. The fire snapped; tiny sparks bursting in a rain of light, as the men waited through the stillness to see what might happen next.

Wes' mare snorted, impatient from standing still for so long, and the man shifted his gaze to stare into the bushes where Wes was lurking.

Perhaps he has the second sight like dear Ruth.

The thought had an instant effect, and Wes had to fight with his own mind as it manifested bygone visions of his wife's youthful smile; her laughter; her promises to always be his. It was remarkable how clearly he was able to remember her lovely face long before it was marked with the legacy of her sins. All the memories were overwhelming. This damnable forest and its witchcraft miasma were trying one last time to claim him.

Frustrated, Wes squeezed shut his eyes, and clenched his teeth. The moment the sun left the sky, the forest's spell strengthened in its effort. He needed to get away from all these wretched trees, and the hungering Fallen lurking beneath them. He yearned to step into the light.

"Do ye have a gun?" The man called over to him, and Wes opened his eyes. The man had black scales spread like leathery skin over his hands and arms. Similar scales covered the man's forehead and extended down one side of his face. He was surely wicked, but no more than the many others Wes encountered in the past. All the same, he pulled the brim down on his hat to partially hide his face.

"I do," he called out over the distance between them. His voice was hoarse; his throat dry. He did not remember when he last allowed himself to eat or drink. Even so, he used words very little in the days before he left his homestead. Before he promised Ruth he would soon return. Wes ran a hand against his chin and felt stubble forming there. Ruth never favored him with a beard. If she saw him like this, surely she would...

Wes shook his head. The miasma again.

"Are ye fixin' to shoot me with it?" The man spoke again, breaking through the cloud of haze and confusion in Wes' mind. Oddly, the man did not seem surprised that Wes carried a gun even though such a thing was very rare. Could he possibly have a gun as well? Perhaps a bullet or two?

Hungry greed welled up in Wes, but he was able to quell the desire with practiced efficiency. Wickedness was always just out of sight trying to entice him to sin. Wes was not a thief, nor a killer. He also wasn't a liar.

"I don't intend to, no," Wes said, then waited while the stranger considered their circumstances. At last he nodded, and gestured Wes forward.

"Come into the light, friend. What little there is. My eyes aren't so good and I want to take a look at ye."

His eyes fail him, yet he was able to see me.

Wes tightened the slack on the tether he held, and urged his plow horse forward. They approached the fire together, breaking free from the shackles of the forest that oppressed them, and Wes instantly felt clarity return to his mind. He tried to keep his head low as he peered over at his new host, but the moment the firelight reached his face; dancing playfully upon it, the man's eyes widened and Wes knew he failed.

Reflexively, he tucked his chin again, and let the brim of his hat conceal what it could, but whether this stranger's eyes were keen or not, the firelight let him see what Wes wanted to avoid him seeing. He shifted uncomfortably, feeling the strength of the oppressive darkness surrounding them like claws to his throat, and forced himself to walk into the conversation he didn't want to have.

"Yer skin," the man said, then trailed off. There was a hint of wonderment in his voice that made Wes wince.

"I still carry the mark," he retorted, and walked his horse over to a tree at the edge of the clearing that had a low branch to tie her tether on. He would have to let her graze in the morning as long as he didn't get pulled back into the forest's spell. He realized by the light of the fire, that the stranger brought him out of the thickest part of the woods and to its edge.

"I can't remember the last time I saw such a face as yers," the man went on, and amazement was still laced through his words. This was not the first time Wes received such a reaction. When the Damnation fell upon them, the burden of their sins came with it. Those from the Before talked about days when everyone looked like Wes: faces that carried no mark upon them. Everyone appeared sinless whether they were truly that way or not. It was those people who remembered the Before who succumbed to their madness first. They could not stand seeing the mark spreading over their skin.

In truth, everyone bore the mark of wickedness upon their bodies; it was the nature of mankind to find appeal in the voice of sin, and while the sickness sometimes manifested in unique ways, for most people it started in the hands. Black scales formed on bare flesh, and often turned it brittle so that it cracked and oozed. It spread out from the hands over time; sometimes jumping to the face, and the scales often formed strange sweeping patterns. While the sin sickness always affected the skin first, this was only the start of a painful decline that twisted the body and turned the insides into rot.

The effect was slow for some, and moved more quickly for others, but as the body broke down, the mind soon followed. Madness always came before dying, and while death was inevitable, the Fallen spent their final days wandering the night. They were always hungry; always seeking; always desiring.

The man who sat before Wes, had hands that curled into tight knotted fists. They were festooned with lumps and warts, and oozed watery black fluid from painful cracks in the skin. The man didn't seem to notice the pain though, for he merely stared, astounded, at Wes' unmarked face.

"I carry the mark, friend," he said, cautiously trying to offer assurance to the man. "I am not as pure as you think." Wes stripped away a glove, and lifted his hand into the dimming firelight to show the man that it was covered in scales. Both of his hands were black far beyond the start of his wrists. When the stranger stared with no immediate reaction, Wes took the opportunity to reach over, gently pluck the stick from his lap, and turned his attention to tending the fire before it faded any further. The man watched Wes' hand as he worked, and soon he seemed to relax. He let out a nervous laugh and shook his head.

"It is as ye say. No flawless skin. No bringer of light. What a sight though. A face untarnished; as pure as a newborn. Remarkable."

"I'm not a Messiah," Wes said flatly. He stabbed at the fire, urging it to give more light.

"I beg yer pardon, and offer ye some hospitality. I can give ye a smoke, if ye yearn for it." When Wes nodded, the man rummaged through his belongings and produced two thin cigars rolled in oiled tobacco leaves. Feeling inspired, Wes returned to his horse, and rummaged through the pack he had tied behind her saddle until he was able to produce a small wedge of dry cheese, and brought it to where the man was sitting.

"In exchange for your flame, and your company," Wes said, and offered the wedge to the man before taking a thinly wrapped cigar in return. He stuck it between his teeth, and lifted the ember tip of his fire poker to light it.

"I thank ye, and while I don't have much to offer, I can break what bread I have with ye, friend." Hearing the man speak of breaking bread caught Wes' attention and he looked at his companion across the fire.

"Do you know the Word?" he asked, and the man's distorted face broke into a grin.

"I ain't sinnin' for the joy of it. The Lord knows my heart is his."

"The Lord knows all those that serve him," Wes said nodding, and knew he shouldn't be surprised that this man was a brother in the Word. God placed them both on this path it seemed. Realizing this, Wes felt compelled to rejoice with celebration. He went back to his pack, pulled out another parcel for an offering, then returned to his new companion.

"Let us break bread together in his name," Wes said, and opened a leather parcel so he could remove two strips of sun-dried venison jerky. The man gasped at the sight of salted meat.

"Truly, ye must be Heaven sent," he marveled and that wonderment returned to his voice. It was no wonder, considering their circumstances.

"God might have brought us together, but I don't come from Heaven. The Lord has blessed me with a well stocked homestead. It's by his grace that we have this food."

The man laughed, and rubbed his hands together in anticipation. He tried to be cunning, but Wes noticed the way he kept glancing at the pack on the mare's flank. Wes suspected the nature of this man's sin was that of a thief.

"Well if that be so," the man said with an easy smile, "then let this be a Jubilee." He turned to his own pack and pulled out a bundle wrapped in parchment paper. Gently opening it, he presented to Wes two round oiled cakes that gave off the sweet fragrance of corn. The smell overwhelmed him, and Wes gasped as his legs gave way beneath him. In an instant, he fell through reality, and into the deep hole of a memory spell.

Wes stood on the porch of his small homestead, and looked out over a field full of sweet corn; ready to harvest. Ruth's singing came to his ear, and he looked over to where she was hanging bed linen out to dry. Past her, little Peter laid on his back and threw seeds from the old maple tree up in the air so he could watch them spiral back down to the ground. His laughter was the sweetest harmony to Ruth's melody. The memory was so strong, it felt overwhelming. It stung Wes' eyes, and burned in his nose. He leaned into the moment; savoring the sounds and the smells, for he knew when he stepped off the porch, his life was going to change. He knew it was the last time he would ever be that happy, and because of that the memory was so bittersweet. Perhaps if he pleaded with the Lord, Wes would be allowed to remain in this moment forever, and never have to face the moment that followed. He wouldn't have to endure another goodbye. He clung to the memory for far longer than he should. His throat swelled from the effort, and Wes felt like he was suffocating in his own longing.

"Friend, return to me," the man called and Wes opened his eyes. He had dropped to one knee without recollection and stared blankly at the cigar which fell from his mouth and went out in the dust. His hand shook when he reached to retrieve it, and Wes pulled down the brim of his hat to hide his glassy eyes.

"Are ye unwell?" the man asked, mildly concerned.

"A memory spell," Wes said hoarsely. He cleared his throat, and searched for his canteen.

"The past haunts us all," the man said with a knowing nod. He too must endure the distortions of time. The Damnation spared nothing from decay.

"I'm Wes. Tell me your name."

"Gad," the man replied. He was a burly fellow, squat and wide but with broad shoulders and corded muscles in his exposed forearms. He was dressed like a laborer and maybe did work for hire. Wes judged him to be in his 50s, but it was hard to be certain. Ages also seemed skewed. Wes knew he didn't look his age of fourty-two.

"Well met," he said at last, and tugged at the brim of his hat in greeting.

"Sit. Please, join me in this Jubilee," Gad said, gesturing at the spot across from him and the fire.

"Not yet. I have one more thing for the offering plate." Wes took a long draw of water; unwilling to quench his thirst on his final offering, then went back to his pack where he removed one of two bottles housed there. The bottle was about the size of his fist and half full with an amber colored liquid.

"For our Jubilee," Wes said, then offered the bottle over to where Gad sat with eyes wide. He whistled long and slow through his teeth, and Wes fully understood why. Not too often one gets offered pure whiskey. The Damnation made all things a scarcity.

"The mark will not spare us tonight, friend," Gad said and his large joyous grin looked sinister with his black teeth and scaled face. "Let us break our bread, and have this Jubilee."

Whiskey loosens the lips of all men, and the two huddled around a small fire in the heart of a cool fall night were no exception. When Wes learned that Gad recently spent time in the capital, he insisted on knowing more. There was no need for Gad to clarify which capital, for there was only one. It was a place that did not boast a name for it didn't need to. The capital was just the capital as far as either man knew it to be, and if it was ever named something else, that name was lost to time. In the desolation of the Damnation, the only city that still existed to illuminate the night was the capital. Though it was still many miles away, Wes knew he would be able to see the glow of it from even this distance without the firelight blinding him to it.

When he admitted to Gad that the capital was where he intended to go, the man took delight in having Wes' ear. He spun riveting tales of his adventures there, and filled the night with information about the great city.

"The center of the capital houses the Divine Hall, where Old Father governs the nation," Gad said as he examined the thin line of whiskey still resting at the bottom of the bottle. "No one ever sees the fellow, but everyone seems both in awe of the man and in fear of him. There was some talk of prophecies, and visions, but it all sounds like witchcraft to me. I also heard that he has demons whispering the secrets of the world into his ear."

"Nonsense," Wes muttered, and puffed thoughtfully on the butt of his cigar.

"Everything requires some sort of paper," Gad continued as he waved a clawed hand around in the air. "Permits to do this, licenses to do that. Everyone is askin' to see this paper or that paper before ye are allowed to do anything. It drove me near to madness."

Gad chuckled as though he made a joke, but Wes never considered madness to be funny.

"Do they know the teachings of the Word?" he asked, and Gad shook his head sadly.

"Neh, friend. Oh they worship something, but it isn't the true God. Neh, they have their idols, but I suppose we all yearn for something that takes our eyes off of God." Wes appreciated that Gad was so forthcoming, and while the man's teeth were black, his tongue was not. He wasn't a liar, even to himself.

Gad went on about the best places to find women in the capital, and the best places to find drinks. He told a story of how the city guard drug one poor drunkard out into the street, and beat him with long thin clubs for suggesting that Old Father relied too much on his Elders to lead. They beat him so severely, he fell asleep and never woke up again.

"Died a week or so later, or at least that's what some say," Gad concluded, and smiled fondly for the memory of it. "We all had such a great time that night."

When the tales dried up, and Gad declared that he shared all he could about the place, Wes asked more pointed questions about the people that lived there. He tried to sound casual, asking about what people did for fun, how they dressed, and if there were a lot of travelers going in and out of the city. He then leaned over, tossing the nub of his cigar into what remained of the fire, and asked the only question he wanted to know an answer to.

"Do you remember seeing a tall old man with a long gray beard in the company of a teenage boy?" Gad glanced up at Wes, immediately noticing the shift in his questions, and a sly look came over him.

"Is there a man that needs killing, friend?" There was a sudden hunger in Gad's eyes, and he watched Wes intently. If there was a man that needed killing, maybe there was money involved in the deed. Wes shook his head though, and rebuffed his companion's greed.

"The man that needed killing is already dead," he found himself admitting, and knew the whiskey was talking for him.

"Well then," Gad said, visibly less intrigued. He puffed in a breath that filled his sunken cheeks. "No need to venture into that wretched place if ye don't have business there. I barely got out alive myself after stealing some tomatoes from Old Father's garden."

"Old Father," Wes repeated, sounding out the words. It was a strange title for a man of power. That was unless this 'Old Father' was taking ideas from the Word. Wes heard of the man in his past. He knew that this father carried no other name, but has ruled over the capital for almost a decade. From what he heard, much has changed in that time. Some for the better, but much of it for the worse.

"Aye, Old Father," Gad continued, and his eyes danced with firelight. "I heard he was ill. I'll not weep when he goes to his beyond." He stared at the licks of flame for a moment, then lifted his eyes back to Wes.

"When he got sick, they stopped having all those whore parties. The cooks had no one to cook for, and the crops rotted right there on the vine. Never crossed their minds to share with us desperate mouths wailing in the streets. When I took matters into my own hands, the guards chased me into the shadows, and nearly cost me my life. No compassion among that lot; no sir." Gad spit, and the gob sizzled in the fire's few remaining embers. One last offering to their Jubilee.

"Thieving has cost you much, it seems," Wes observed, and Gad narrowed his eyes.

"Yer not so different than I. I saw yer hands, I did. Ye have been tempted by the voices too, I know. Voices that convince ye the stealing isn't so bad. That the food is just going to go to waste anyway. They drove me half mad, they did." Wes nodded solemnly. He had heard those voices too, when he had his hands around his father-in-law's throat. He lifted his head, and looked to the west. The night hour was waning. Behind him, his mare snored softly through the pre-dawn. The last dregs of whiskey were tested and taken down to the final drop. Wes knew he should wish Gad a good night and bed down, but the drink tested his tongue, and he ventured one more question.

"Brother in faith, speak truth to me. During your time in the capital, and with all those people you encountered, were any of them a young lad with sandy blonde hair, deep blue eyes, and a scar running down the side of his face, here?" Wes took the tip of his thumb and dragged it along his face from his left eye to the corner of his mouth. Gad studied him; his eyes like dark coals in the fading firelight. The question left him suspicious, and Wes wondered if he went too far; revealed too much.

"We try not to remember faces in the capital, friend," Gad said at last. His words were careful but still rang true. "I offer ye a word to the wise. If ye do not heed my warning, and go to that place where all sinners dwell, yer best to keep yer mouth shut. Don't look people in the eye, and don't ask questions. Everyone has reasons not to trust." Gad leaned over conspiratorially. A smile stretched the scales on the right side of his face. "And stay away from the alleys, friend. Don't get chased into the shadows."

"Do the Fallen dwell there as well?" Wes asked, stunned.

"Oh yes, there are monsters in the capital, friend. No matter where ye rest yer head, there are Fallen huddled in the shadows, yearning to remove it from yer neck."

"All the same, the hour grows late," Wes said, and moved to lean against the tree next to his horse. He made himself busy to avoid Gad's gaze for he didn't want the other man to see how unnerved he was. If there were monsters in the city, was the boy even safe?

"I'm sorry I could not help ye find who yer lookin' for," Gad said to Wes' back. "But I thought ye said the man that needed killing was already dead."

"I don't need to kill this one, friend," Wes replied softly. "I need to bring him home."

Ruth writhed in bed; held captive by her dreams. As this was often the case, Wes rose from their bed as he always did, and moved to sit in the adjacent chair where he could observe her. He learned to not remain near her during these restless nights as she would often strike out at either him or herself. It was easier to restrain her if he needed to when he wasn't in bed with her.

Wes quickly realized though, that this dream seemed different. He could tell this wasn't one of those dreams where she was wandering through a hundred futures, or deciphering an unraveling past. Something else drew her attention and tormented her soul. Wes tried to wake her in the past when she got this way, but she slept so deeply, he could never break her out of it. When he accidentally hurt her the one time in trying, he refused any further attempts. He found that it was better to just console her when these episodes were over and she was able to recognize him again.

Ruth moaned, and Wes waited to see if she was about to wake, or fade back into her dreams. For a moment, her face was calm. She looked like she was at peace. Wes reached out with a tender finger, and ran it down the length of her hair.

Ruth suddenly sat up, her eyes wide in terror, and let out a shrill scream. Wes sprung to his feet, responding with practiced clarity, and reached for her to soothe her.

"Easy! Easy, wife!" He said as he tried to calm her, but Ruth seemed unaware that Wes was even sitting there. As soon as she exhausted the air in her lungs, she drew in a deep breath and screamed again. Wes reached for her, pulled her into his arms, and tried to soothe her but still it seemed as though she could not be reached. He never saw her like this before. Even her worst nightmares never terrified her like this.

"Ruth, you must calm down! Please tell me what torments you so." Wes held her tightly, keeping her from harming herself in her fit, and rocked her back and forth while she wept. She smelled of lilac flowers. She always smelled like the start of spring.

Eventually her crying subsided, and she simply stared off into the shadows while Wes continued to rock her back and forth in his arms. Back and forth. Back and forth, until the night gave way to day, and the birds greeted the morning outside their window.

"Ruth, talk to me. Tell me what happened. What did you see?"

"My father," Ruth eventually said, and her body tensed reflexively.

"What about him?" Wes asked, stroking her hair. Ruth's breath came in short bursts, and he could feel her heart thrumming against his skin.

"Oh, Wesley. My father is dead!"

"Is this such a great loss to mourn over?" Wes asked, feeling no sadness over that man's death.

"You don't understand. You don't understand! Lord, father is dead. So what will happen to our poor Daniel? Wesley, don't you see? Our son is lost to us now!"

Chapter Two

For behold, the Lord cometh out of his place
to punish the inhabitants of the earth for their iniquity:
the earth also shall disclose her blood,
and shall no more cover her slain. -Isaiah 26:21 KJV

Wes awoke to his plow horse nibbling at the brim of his hat. He swatted her muzzle with the back of his hand to jolt her away, then pushed himself up to look around. Gad was gone along with his fire, leaving Wes alone once more. He already knew nothing was stolen, for his horse would have made some noise if Gad went for her pack, and he would have been an utter fool to try for the gun on Wes' hip. Besides, if the man was so careless with his thieving, the Lord would have surely given him over to his nature long ago. Madness awaited all that sinned uninhibited. All the same, they shared a nice conversation, and Wes appreciated being able to talk to someone who wasn't trapped in the prison of their own mind.

Ah, Ruth. Hold on for me.

Wes put Gad out of his mind, for he did not expect to see the man again. He rose, brushed off his dusty trousers, and shrugged into his black trim jacket. The garment was a relic from another time, passed to him from his father, and one of the nicest things he owned alongside his black gambler's hat. He had them packed away for years; no longer willing to wear them after he stopped attending church, but thought them appropriate for this journey so he didn't look like a bumpkin when he entered the capital. Daniel would not be ashamed of him this time.

The sun was a few hours above the horizon, and Wes was relieved to see that he was indeed at the edge of this befuddling forest. He examined the landscape before him, which thinned out quickly, and led down into a large open grassland with rolling hills dotted by clumps of low trees. A smooth ride for his mare to endure. Breathing in the crisp autumn air, Wes closed his eyes and took a moment, as was custom every morning, to give up a quick prayer to the Lord.

Thank you, God, for giving me another day. Please look after Ruth, and keep Daniel safe until I find him. Help guide me to him Lord, and I pray you steer him away from the city's alleyways.

Any other living situation had to be better than that. Wes just hoped he'll be able to find the lad since Gad recommended he not ask the locals for help. He tried to imagine what Daniel might look like after all this time. Would he be hard to recognize? Would he still resemble his mother the way he used to?

These concerns lingered in his mind as Wes tended to his mare, allowed her to graze, and got her ready for a day's ride. He knew he needed to make the most of his remaining time in the day, and put some distance between himself and these trees. Climbing into his mare's saddle, he kicked her into a light trot, and picked his way out into the open plains. As he went, Wes turned his head and peered back at the forest he was grateful to leave behind.

The trees were dense, and many shadows still remained unaffected by the sun. Somewhere, in those deep spaces beneath the tangle of trees, Wes could still feel that evil presence that targeted him. Somehow, he knew that it was still there, watching him intently. Making up its mind. Wes would not be intimidated. He urged his mare to go a little faster in the open fields. Soon they came upon a narrow path that was once a major roadway, and Wes took advantage of the flat surface to make up any time he lost in the forest. With how sparse the shadows seemed in the terrain around him, Wes imagined that creature would be hard pressed to catch up to him. It had nowhere to hide from the sunlight. Of course, there would always be the Fallen lurking in the darkness hungering all around him, but he hoped that particular monster lost interest in him over time.

Wes studied the expanse of grassland that stretched before him toward the capital, and estimated he had a few more days of travel before he reached the city limits. That meant contending with the night. The sinners and the wicked avoided the fire, for any kind of light was painful to endure. This was why Wes wore gloves. Even his own sins were shamed in the cleansing light of day. Wes didn't know the exact reason for this, but assumed it was a mercy from God, and for that he was grateful. Without the hindrance of the light, the monsters would have devoured humanity decades ago.

Wes led his mare along the old weathered trail headed west, and when she started to pant from the effort, he eased off of her, and allowed her some relief while they both continued on foot. When she relaxed, and the pep returned to her gait, Wes would climb back into the saddle while he listened to her groan, and urge her forward at a faster pace. She voiced her objections, but was resigned to her situation. She knew he wouldn't push her, being that she was a plow horse and unfamiliar with this kind of exertion, so she trusted him to only take her as far as she was able to go. Wes pressed knees into her ribs when the small trickle of a trail opened up into something wider and covered with a smooth stone, and on they went; switching back and forth between riding and walking, and followed the sun's path towards the west.

All around them, the world was quiet, and the stillness of the day brought about memories that skimmed the surface like fish in a lake. They appeared in Wes' mind one moment, then in the next moment they vanished back into the shadowed depth of the past.

Wes remembered how once, when he was a boy, a man came into his village half mad with the sin sickness. For hours he stood in the middle of town, and cried out for the loss of the sun. This frightened Wes, for he knew the sun rose in the east and set in the west as it always had since the time of the Word. But the man insisted the sun did not remain in the sky as long as it used to. He swore that the days have gotten shorter. Wes was skeptical at the time, but the years were unkind, and time decayed alongside everything else. As he stood, he had no doubt of the truth in the man's words, and while some days were longer than others, it seemed that every day was just a little shorter than it used to be.

"The sun has turned her back on us," the man of his youth cried out in his mind. "In time, she will stop rising all together! We are all doomed to despair at the face of eternal night!"

The man was chased out of town of course, but it mattered not. Wes had nightmares because of his tales. Even before it grew apparent that time was unraveling, he was haunted by the thought that the sun may one day stop rising. Was there no end to the misery of this world?

Wes nudged his knees into the side of his mare, and she picked up the pace of her plodding. Time passed by the course of the sun, and onward they went until he could no longer ignore the impending night. They did not cover as much distance as he wanted, but there was little that could be done. A small way off, he saw an area that looked promising.

"Alright girl, go over there," Wes said, as he urged his mare to step off the trail and into the grass. He could hear her panting; exhausted from all the travel, and so Wes slid off of her to relieve her of some burden. He guided her toward a formation of rocks that jutted out of the earth in a way that he could put his back to them as a defense against the night. He slowed his pace to allow his horse to graze, and gathered anything that might burn along the way.

By the time they reached the formation, he had managed to acquire a decent amount of tinder. He secured his mare by her tether to a thin scrub tree, and returned to the fields to get larger branches to offer for his fire. Once he set up camp and had his fire lit, Wes tended to his mare: removing her saddle and brushing down her fur. She snorted her gratitude, but her attention was on the long prairie grass.

With everything done, Wes settled in front of his fire, prepared to wait out the long night. With nothing to distract himself with, his mind drifted, and thoughts of Ruth and Daniel came to him along with all those regrets that still haunted him from the past. He sometimes wondered how much of his life would have changed if he had given over to his temptation and killed his father-in-law.

Jethro was a tall man. Lean and sinewy, with gnarled bones and jagged teeth. Wes did not trust him an ounce or a pound, but he was smitten with the man's daughter, and sadly, dear Ruth was loyal to her father. Wes gained employment working the fields of Jethro's farm just for the chance to be graced by her company. He was captivated by Ruth since they were children, but quickly learned during his time of employment that she was just as enthralled by him.

Jethro was the tyrant of his farm, and worked Wes ragged for little pay. At night in those early days, Wes would collapse in the hayloft exhausted from the effort, but Ruth was always there tending to him: salving his blisters, and rubbing the ache from his muscles. He often fell asleep on her lap, while she gently stroked the hair at his temples. Over time, Wes grew stronger from the labor, and was eventually able to keep up with the work that Jethro placed upon him.

When Jethro saw that he was too strong to be dominated in this way, he shifted his tactics and focused on Ruth instead. The man developed a quiet cunning that Wes was too naive to notice being that he was just a boy of seventeen. He had not yet learned this new form of deception, but Jethro's deceitful nature was not overlooked by God. The more he schemed, lied, and manipulated his daughter, the more his sin spread over his arms and face.

Jethro beguiled Ruth, and insisted she tend to him instead of allowing her to fulfill her desire to be a wife. Months spread out into years, but the two of them never stopped yearning for each other. Eventually, he convinced Ruth to confront her father, and he was so proud when she stood before the wicked man and demanded she be allowed to marry. Wes saw anger burning in Jethro's eyes, and thought the man would refuse her, but then a smooth smile spread over his lips and that cunning came into play again. He actually rejoiced at her declaration, saying that he wondered why it took them so long. He was more than willing to give his blessing for them to get married.

"But perhaps not right away," Jethro said with an apologetic smile. "Maybe wait until summer, so that we have harvest to provide a great feast for our guests." When summer came and the harvest grew, Jethro shrugged helplessly.

"Time is a burden upon us all, and bringing in the harvest took too much of it away from us. Why not delay until the fall, so that the work will be finished and we can celebrate in our leisure." By then, Jethro's entire face was covered in scales and his tongue was as black as coal. It made him resemble a snake and Wes thought of another serpent that once sat in a garden tempting Eve. Much like that serpent, Jethro was very good with his words, and when he spoke the things he said always seemed to make sense. Wes could not find objection to all his reasoning, but before they knew it, a year passed them by.

He grew desperate to make Ruth his wife, and when he told her as much, it took little effort to convince her to marry him without her father's blessing. He just had to remind her how desperately she wanted to be a mother. Wes took some of his meager wages, and offered it to their church preacher so that he would say the words that allowed them to be called husband and wife.

The moment was rushed and filled with nervous laughter, but Ruth was radiant and Wes never felt more in love. When Jethro learned what they had done, he was furious. It wasn't the act that enraged him, but the fact that he didn't have the control he thought he had over his daughter. Thus it was Ruth that felt the brunt of his outrage. He called her a desperate whore, and accused her of betraying him. Wes barely kept his temper under control hearing the man saying such things, but when Jethro struck Ruth across the face with the back of his hand, his restraint shattered. Wes threw himself upon the vile man, and gave over to the seething hatred that had been growing inside of him for years. He overpowered his father-in-law easily, pinning him down, and suddenly his hands were squeezing Jethro's throat. He heard the voices for the first time in that moment. Hungry, gleeful voices in his mind encouraging him to do more. He barely heard them at first, nor did he notice his fingers darkening and turning black.

Jethro's face turned red as he gulped for air, and Wes found so much joy in it. He grinned wide and menacing, for he was delighted by the other man's suffering. His anger grew into a burning inferno, spreading inside him outside of his control, and the voices within him swelled to a roar. He was encouraged, he was revered, he was praised for succumbing to his sinful nature. They urged him to not stop; never stop; just keep squeezing, squeezing, squeezing.

Wes screamed out his rage, feeling the full pleasure of his violence, and lost all sense of himself as he gave over fully to his longing to squeeze the life from this man. But a small part of him registered the feel of fists pounding against his back, and the roar in his ears was not quite loud enough to mask Ruth screaming for him to let her father go.

"Please stop! Wesley! Don't kill my dad!" Her words sobered him instantly. Blinking, he looked down, and realized that it was his hands that gripped Jethro's neck. It was his mouth grunting with each fevered breath he took. Wes let go of Jethro, and stumbled off of the man as he stared in horror; knowing what he was willing to do. What just happened to him?

"That's it," Jethro wheezed as he coughed and slowly sat up. He rubbed at his neck, and laughed. "Now you are fit to be called my son."

Jethro did not stop laughing for a long time. The more miserable Wes looked, the more he laughed. When he eventually quieted down, a pleased smile remained on his face. Jethro had conceded the battle, but as far as he saw things, he had won the war.

After that night, Wes avoided Jethro as much as he could. As for Jethro, he seemed to be rather chummy towards Wes. He sat on the porch, watching his son-in-law work the day away, and if Wes ever glanced at him, Jethro would smile, and wiggle his fingers in a wave. It was a reminder of Wes' own fingers that were forever stained black, and while Wes didn't attack Jethro again, the anger he felt toward his father-in-law never left him.

This tension put Ruth in the middle of the two of them, causing her a lot of heartache and strain, but everything changed when she announced that she was at last with child. Because of her second sight, she already knew that it would be a boy.

Jethro lit up at the idea of a grandson, and again shifted his personality from cunning smug ruler, to humble joyful grandfather. Wes was no longer fooled by these changes, but Ruth sadly was. At least back then, she so wanted to believe that her father could be redeemed. Wes on the other hand knew to no longer trust the blackened tongue of his father-in-law. A liar's tongue. He grew to despise liars because of that man, and his sweet words that carried no more weight than the air they were breathed upon. He detested Jethro all the more for his sweet nature, and the voices in his mind urged him to do harm to the man over and over again. Wes' hands turned black; the sickness spreading along with his scrutiny.

"Why, Ruthie! What a joyous occasion!" Jethro crooned. Wes just scowled. He was so consumed by his hatred that he did not give any thought to the fact that he would soon be a father. It didn't occur to him that he was about to have a son that would need his protection against all that was wicked in this world including his own grandfather. Instead, Wes spent every waking moment seething, and allowing his anger to grow. Jethro must have sensed this, for he never stopped smiling. He never stopped wiggling his fingers in senseless greetings.

"A grandson," Jethro mused aloud from his perch upon the porch in earshot of Wes working. "What a joyous thing. Have you thought of a name, Ruthie? No? Why, surely, you will grant me the honor of naming him." Of course Ruth could not refuse her father. For her heart was pure, and she couldn't see the decay of sin upon his face.

Wes would not allow himself to grow angry with her, although his thoughts tempted him to. She endured so much growing up in a home without a mother, and yet somehow she found the Word and the Lord. It was a wonder Jethro did not draw her into wickedness along with him. It just showed how special Ruth truly was.

Jethro was allowed the naming, and Wes let him have his prize. And when Ruth at last felt the pains of her labor, the reality of the moment overtook his heart and cleared his mind. Jethro could not hold a candle to the light of the Lord's blessing upon Wes that day, for at last he was a father as well.

And so, Daniel was born. Wes' first son.

Wes laid awake, and looked upon the clear open sky. The stars seemed immeasurable, and while Wes often thought of Daniel in these quiet moments, that night he thought only of Ruth.

Ah, Ruth, you have suffered so. How much more will the Lord place upon your shoulders before it is deemed enough?

Wes thought about the night after they married, and recalled how Ruth's skin glowed in the moonlight when they slipped out to be alone in the fields. Her large green eyes, her beaming smile, and that honey colored hair. Her hair was so beautiful then. He wished she never started to pull it out.

"Stay with me, Ruth," Wes said to the stars. "I'll bring Daniel home to you."

He refused to think about what Ruth said to him regarding their son on that wretched night when Jethro died. She could not stop herself from telling him of everything she had seen. It left her mind broken.

The mare snorted in her sleep, and Wes turned his attention away from the sky to look out into the darkness. It was a dangerous time to be lost in his own mind. While the night seemed to be still and unmoving, Wes knew he was not alone. He tried to open his senses; feel how much of a threat was hidden in the dark, but he did not have the second sight, and his perception was lacking. He knew that the one with the desire to pursue him was not among the watchers, and for that he was grateful. Beyond that, he only knew that something existed outside the firelight, and that it yearned to bite into him and watch him bleed.

When at last the birdsong came, announcing an end to the night, Wes allowed himself to sleep. He only rested for a few hours, for there was always work to be done, and when he woke again, the sun was not yet visible in the sky. He took a moment to stretch the ache from his muscles, say a quick prayer, then checked on his mare and reached for his bow. He wanted to allow her some time to rest before another push toward the west and thought he might get lucky with a bit of hunting.

Wes always found comfort in keeping busy. Anything to distract him from his own thoughts and worries. Working with his hands also eased his loneliness, which never fully left him since Ruth stopped talking. Stringing his bow, Wes slung his quiver over his shoulder and looked to the east for the crest of the rising sun. All around him, he could just make out the dull shapes of the terrain, and noticed a cluster of shrubs that were a short distance away. If anything was alive in this wilderness, he would find it there. With the Lord's blessing, he will fill his stomach on this day.

Chapter Three

Yet when I hoped for good, evil came;
when I looked for light, then came darkness.
The churning inside me never stops;
days of suffering confront me.
I go about blackened, but not by the sun;
I stand up in the assembly and cry for help.
-Job 30:26-28 NIV

Wes peered into the darkness, and listened to the crackle-snap of his lowly fire. Two days passed since he left the forest, and while he pushed both himself and his horse as far as they could go during that time, it seemed to be not far enough. The Fallen that had taken interest in him had caught up to them somehow. How the thing was able to track him down in the open grassland like that baffled the mind, and Wes had to admit he was impressed by its diligence. What caused this creature to pursue him so doggedly? His mare snorted softly beside him; her tether tied with little slack to the tree he leaned against, and Wes reached up to stroke her nose. He needed to keep her close so she didn't try to run if she got spooked. She already seemed uneasy and for good reason.

"Pleeeaaassseee," the word was like a whisper in the wind. It was so faint, but Wes knew its source. Out there, cloaked in the full dark of night, he could feel her. He suddenly knew that the presence was in fact female, just as he knew she was only a few feet away from the edge of his firelight. He didn't have the second sight, but he could sense her hunger. He felt her eyes upon him, and knew she was examining his unmarked face. He felt her desperation. He heard the hoarseness of her voice in her whisper. He could smell the stench of her in the night breeze.

Wes squinted into the darkness, trying to make out her form, but the firelight blinded him to such things. Knowing that madness lied in the paranoia of the watched, he focused his attention back to his fire, adding kindling to embolden the flame, and stopped trying to seek her out. Let her come to him.

His hands reflexively reached for the two weapons he had positioned next to where he sat. On one side, his fingers brushed his remaining bottle of whiskey, left uncorked and propped up carefully so as not to be spilled. On the other side, his revolver sat snugly in the holster secured to his leg. Three bullets left. He did not know how many it would take to gun down this sinner, and he hoped to not find out. Wes lifted his hunting knife, sliding it cleanly along the end of a sturdy branch, and shed away another splinter of wood to hone its crude point.

"Pleeeaassssseee."

Wes hefted the rough spear, getting a feel for its weight, then placed it next to the fire to be used later. Lord willing, he will have time to ready it.

Give me strength, God. I will not fear.

"Ssssiiirrrrr."

He took a small swig of the whiskey to steady his hands. Then pulled out his revolver to ensure the cylinder was poised with a bullet at the ready. All of this was just as much show as it was preparation. He thought briefly about stringing his bow as well, but didn't see the threat in it. He encountered enough of these monsters in his past to know that it took much to penetrate their large hulking black bodies. They could also endure many wounds inflicted upon them as though they didn't feel pain like they should.

Wes knew that his best chance for survival lay in the use of his fire and his spear. For fire cleansed wickedness from whatever it touched. The dull painful burn of his hands and wrists reminded Wes he was no exception to this reality. It was something he could not fully ignore but grew accustomed to. The wicked ones that roamed the night were not as fortunate.

A rustling sounded in the darkness out of sight, and Wes looked up to scan the perimeter of his firelight. There seemed to be a constant battle between darkness and light, as the glow of the flame ebbed and flowed against the night that surrounded him. Was the darkness gaining ground? Was his circle of light shrinking around him? No. It was nothing more than paranoia tempting him to madness. Wes lifted his stick again, and decided to work the tip finer with his knife. Any task helped clear his tormented mind.

"Pleeeeaaasseee."

Wes ran his blade against the branch slowly; shaving away the chaff; refining the point of his makeshift spear.

"Sssiiirrrr."

He sensed the night was waning, yet she did not make her move. Would she allow this to stretch on another day? He doubted she would come so close, just to turn from him and flee.

"I will not go to thee," Wes called out, growing restless from her hesitation, "If you hunger for my blood, you must brave the light."

His horse stamped the earth, suddenly unsettled, and Wes warily got to his feet. Animals had their own form of second sight as a way to survive the darkness. His mare's anxiety must mean...

Movement caught his eye, and Wes faced her as her body separated from the darkness, and she edged into the firelight.

"Pleassse, sssiirrr," the creature hissed much louder than before, and Wes winced from the grating sound of her voice. The noise was that of a shovel scraping shale, or the scream of high winds through leaf-bare trees. It immediately put Wes on edge, and added credence to his foreknowledge on the depth of danger he found himself in. Wes knelt down and plunged his makeshift spear deep into the red-hot coals at the bottom of his fire. He could not allow his fear to stupefy him.

"Pleasssee heelp meeee." As the creature's body was revealed in the firelight, Wes noted the distortion of her legs; twisted in the wrong direction, and with cloven hooves like a goat. They were covered in glistening scales that oozed and dripped black bile onto the earth. The blackness of her sin sickness seemed to ignore those parts of her that once drew men's favor, and the nature of her sins were laid bare to Wes.

Why is a whore of Babylon pleading to me?

She bore her nudity without concern, and those once desirable parts of her sagged and swayed as she lurched and staggered closer to him. Her stomach writhed and bulged as though pregnant with worms, and her hands were contorted into black shriveled claws. No part of her was spared from the mutation of her wickedness, including her face.

She might have been beautiful once, but her sin disfigured her face to resemble that of a pig. Her mouth sagged open, showing yellow jagged teeth, and her thick tongue lolled, gray and festering, as fat tendrils of brown mucus dangled from its tip. Her eyes were fully black, and sunken into her skull under a pronounced brow. She stared at Wes intensely as she panted through the labor of her moving. It defied sense how she was able to catch up to him, let alone talk in the state she was in. Wes glared back at her just as fiercely as he watched her drag her body closer.

"You will only find pain and death here. Fade back into the Hell from which you spawned, and live to see another day," he demanded, but she did not seem to hear him. What madness drove this woman forward? He originally thought she sought him out because of his face, but he saw a hint of desperation in her black eyes, and grew to doubt this possible truth. She was obviously suffering from her deformities; the human body never survived for long after the transformation, but her contorted face also lent to a deeper despair. She seemed to be struggling against her own spirit.

"Pleaaassseee," she groaned, and dragged her bulk closer to Wes. A pocket of sap caused the fire to pop, and the extra burst of light splashed embers over her body. She lifted her head and wailed with the sound of two voices; the one an echo of the other. Hearing it filled Wes with a paralyzing dread. He heard stories telling of the twin voices in the damned, and knew it to be the worst circumstance a human soul could endure. Not only was this woman on the verge of madness, but housed a demon as well.

Wes was definitely in a lot of danger. It was no wonder he could sense her so clearly if she had a demon tucked away inside. Maybe if he wasn't so caught up in his day dreaming, he might have realized this warning for what it was. The fact that he survived as long as he did was only by the grace of God. He dare not hope for that good grace to last much longer. Next to where Wes stood, his mare stamped, snorted, and jerked at her tether.

"Leave now, or I will make you leave," he warned, and heard fear in his voice. Little chance of this threat swaying a demon. Three bullets, a spear, and a small bottle of whiskey, against a demon. Wes bent and picked up the whiskey first.

Lord, if it suits your will, see me through this night. Ruth, Daniel, I love you both.

The creature edged forward; keening and pleading with Wes, but unable to explain why. She clawed at her face with her ruined hands, and groaned in pain from the firelight. She seemed to be struggling with herself for one moment she staggered toward the darkness, then she'd stop and push forward toward the fire again. If this woman was combatting the demon inside of her, the vile thing might not be as strong as the ones he's heard about. Wes might still live to see another day. The pig snout lifted to the sky as she let out a long, anguished groan, and thick drool fell upon her naked flesh. She snorted the mucus from her snout, and a gob of it landed squarely in the fire with a soft hiss. Wes glanced at the flame, but it was in no risk of going out.

"Pleassse! Pleeeaaasseee!" She swayed back and forth under the weight of her conflicted spirit, and drug her body close enough that her scales sizzled from the fire. Deep in her throat, the demon wailed in pain, and Wes coughed as the smell of her cooking flesh caused his throat to seize with revulsion.

"This is madness!" Wes sputtered, and jabbed a finger toward the encircling night. "You will die if you try to reach me. Go back into your darkness. Hide away while you still have time before the sun." Why did he pity this creature all of a sudden? Why did he seek to help her?

The heat of the fire caused the scales on her legs to split open, and the trickle of black bile turned into an ooze that splattered uninhibited throughout the dust. The smell of it reached Wes' mare, and she screamed in horror. Her fervent desire to free her tether grew into a crazed panic. Wes covered his face with his gloved hand, willing himself to endure. He needed the use of his mouth if he stood a chance, and it would do him little good to vomit while this monster sliced open his stomach.

In spite of all she endured, the monster dragged her body even closer to him. Her hooves scraped the earth, her gnarled hands clawed at her body and her face, and Wes noticed blood had joined the splatters of bile in the dust. Killing her would be a mercy.

"Pleeeeeassseee, helllppp" she moaned, almost like a sigh, but she was within reach of him, and Wes had no desire to die.

"I'm sorry." He brought the whiskey bottle to his lips while pulling his spear from the coals. He shifted so that he stood across the fire from this strange wailing woman, held the flaming tip of the stick aloft, and pursed his lips to spew a thin spray of whiskey onto the flame on the spear. A plume of fire flashed intense light between them, and both demon and woman screamed from the pain.

She collapsed to the ground, writhing in anguish, and lifted a smoldering hand toward him. Wes was astounded. Why was she doing this? Even after he attacked her, she made no effort to strike out at him. Yet he dare not misjudge her. She housed a demon and if she gave over control to the presence within, Wes knew it would be his death.

"Leave this place! Don't make me hurt you further!" Wes shouted and his voice shook in his desperate pleading. He had no desire to kill this woman, but her madness was like a chasm between them.

"Please," he whispered; an echo of her plight. "Please don't do this."

She lifted her head, and looked at him with black haunted eyes that conveyed a glimpse of the woman she once was. Then she reared up with a quickness he did not expect, and growled her defiance at the firelight. Wes saw her authority slip, and as the demon seized control, a lust for blood overtook her eyes. She lunged for him, and Wes lifted his spear.

Twisting the stick in his hand, he brandished the smoldering point. As the woman grabbed for him, he dropped beneath her claws, and plunged the spear deep into her side. The creature screamed out in chorus with her demon, and her hooves skidded against the earth. Her clawed hands raked the sky as she scrambled to pivot and retreat, and one claw caught Wes across his upper arm before she was able to stumble out into the night.

"Lord!" Wes gasped, and clutched his arm. The scratch instantly burned as though he doused it with fire. He dashed over to his pack and grabbed the canteen slung there. He had little time to respond, and knew that if he was not quick, he would surely lose his arm if not his life.

Wes stripped off his jacket, then jerked up his sleeve to expose the angry looking slash on his arm. It was not deep, but that mattered little. He poured water over the scratch, then found his bottle of whiskey and poured a dose of that on it as well. Blood oozed lazily from the break in his skin but it would not be enough. He plunged his hunting knife into the fire. After a few seconds, he removed it, allowed it to cool a bit, then brought the knife to his wound and deepened the ragged cut. Blood oozed around the blade, raining fat droplets upon the earth, and Wes hissed through the pain. It was nothing compared to what that woman was feeling. This night would surely be her last, but he still needed to find her in the light of day. He dared not risk leaving her alive to fester and run the risk of her hurting someone else.

Wes gritted his teeth, and groaned when he poured more of his whiskey over the open wound. He tried to not cut deeply, knowing he'd be unable to stitch a wound so high on his arm by himself, but he had to make it bleed. It was the only way to get the sickness out of his body. It was the only way he might still survive.

Wes looked up, trying to see which direction the creature fled, but it was no good. The darkness swallowed her up and consumed her. Dawn was not far off, as the birds were already starting their morning song, and she would be her weakest in those brightest parts of the day. Wes examined her black blood mingling with his own upon the earth. If she continued to bleed this way, it would not be difficult to find her.

Suddenly feeling dizzy, Wes stumbled over to his horse, trying to use her tether to lower himself to the ground, but the dizziness overwhelmed him and he collapsed into the dust alongside his fire. His head whirled from the taint of the demon scratch, blood loss, and the many days of little food and little sleep. Wes rolled onto his back, and stared at a sky that was fading into gray. By the grace of God, he survived the night. Soon dawn would come, and with it, the need for killing to be done.

Wes thought about the twin voice of the woman and the demon within her. He previously assumed that he never encountered a demon possessed before, but as he sank into the abyss of sleep, he realized that he had in fact heard a demon once, when it echoed the words of his father-in-law.

Chapter Four

And he said, Lay not thine hand upon the lad,
neither do thou any thing unto him:
for now I know that thou fearest God,
seeing thou hast not withheld thy son,
thine *only* son, from me. - Genesis 22:12 KJV

When Daniel was born, Wes was still fairly young. His hair had grown long that year, with tufts of it curling around his ears, and his face was thinner by the jaw. Ruth often remarked on how Daniel was handsome like his father, but Wes always thought the lad resembled his mother.

Either way, Wes knew nothing about being a father, and was astounded at how small Daniel was when he was newborn. Every time he saw that tiny child wiggling helplessly in his mother's arms, Wes would be seized with an intense fear of failure. He avoided holding his son, but with Ruth's insistence, he agreed to place a calloused finger into Daniel's soft supple palm. When his son's fingers closed around his, gripping Wes' finger in his tiny hand, Wes couldn't help but feel amazed. God's miraculous power to create was made apparent in this infant child.

Jethro made sure to warn Wes of the many ways he could fail as a father. The pitfalls; the mistakes that caused a lifetime of damage; the failure to protect and provide; Jethro was a master in his craft of manipulation, and as Daniel grew older, it seemed the safer option to let Jethro take care of him. He raised Ruth, afterall, and she was as radiant as the sun. Surely, Daniel was in more capable hands under the care of his grandfather.

Wes recalled watching as Jethro bounced Daniel upon his knee, and sang to him. Daniel would giggle and beam; never seeing the monstrous features of Jethro's face for what they were, and Wes thought the interactions endearing. Harmless. The sharp edge of all memories fade, and Wes somehow forget just how wicked Jethro could be. He stopped seeing the sin on his father-in-law's face.

A rift started to form between Wes and his son; something that pained him greatly though he didn't know what to do about it. When he saw how happy everyone else was, especially Ruth who had to endure so much strife, Wes thought this was how things were meant to be. Everyone was so full of joy; everyone except for him. That was until Daniel got hurt.

Both Wes and Ruth assumed that Daniel was with Jethro that morning. They were both busy at work, Wes in the fields and Ruth in their home, and were unaware of Daniel climbing into the hayloft of the barn. He was barely four years old, and would have been fine on his own if he hadn't tripped and lost his footing. When he fell from the loft, his screams made a chill of dread travel the length of Wes's spine. All of his fears of failing his son were realized.

They found Daniel unharmed by the grace of God, but for a long cut that ran down the side of his face. He rolled around on the barn floor, unfamiliar with the intensity of pain, and his blood smeared across his face; his clothes; the ground beneath him. Ruth immediately stepped in and calmly scooped her boy into her arms. She took him into the house to tend to his wound, and the moment she was out of sight, Jethro turned on Wes.

"Where were you? Why weren't you watching the boy?" Jethro shouted; seething in fury, and it was in that moment that Wes heard a second voice that seemed to echo his. A voice that was deep inside his throat but distinctly different from Jethro's. The utter indignation in Jethro's eyes paralyzed Wes within his self doubt. Was this his fault? Sure, he had assumed that Jethro was caring for Daniel, but he never actually checked. He was overwhelmed by his guilt and it never occurred to him to ask where Jethro even was that he wasn't with the boy. He was far too consumed by his own failure.

Daniel eventually recovered from the injury, but carried a scar that ran down the side of his face from that point on. It was a constant reminder every time Wes saw it, that he wasn't able to protect his son. He burned with shame and over time, grew to hate himself for it. Instead of finding a way to cope with these bitter feelings, Wes just avoided Daniel entirely. The distance between them grew into a chasm, and Daniel took to following Jethro everywhere he went instead.

Wes despaired over the lost opportunity; the loss of connection with his son, and a dark jealousy for Jethro bloomed inside of him. He told himself that the situation was better for everyone else even if it wasn't for him, and he quietly convinced himself that he wasn't meant to be a father. He wasn't good at it. Jethro filled the role better.

The only time he doubted this, was when he found his son rubbing black ash on his pure skin so he could resemble his grandfather. He suddenly wondered if Jethro was another danger Wes failed to protect his son from. He didn't know what to do about this. So he did nothing. He said nothing. He was a coward. He was not fit to be called father.

Wes avoided Daniel after that encounter, but still shared a bed with Ruth and him at night. Daniel laid between the two of them, curled tight against his mother, and in those solitary moments of longing, Wes would study the features of his son's face. He would lean in close to smell the grass and the sun in his hair. For hours he would watch Daniel's small chest rise and fall. Occasionally, Wes ran a knuckle along the softness of his cheek. He felt like Daniel was a precious flower, destined to wither if Wes ever tried to pick him.

Then Jethro suddenly announced one day that he wanted to leave their farm for destinations in the West. He planned to rejoin old friends he expected to find in the capital. He didn't think he would return soon if at all, and while the news was a shock to each of them, Daniel took it especially hard.

"Please, go on tending to the farm without me. I am getting up in years and don't think I can make this journey more than once. Just consider me gone for good."

Wes did not know what to make of this sudden announcement from Jethro, but he recognized the old cunning in the man's eyes. Reflections of their past bubbled up in his mind, and Wes remembered Jethro's wicked nature. The Holy Spirit was working in him that day, but Wes didn't see it for what it was until it was too late. All he saw was an opportunity for him to finally connect with his son. In spite of his growing unease, Wes started to hope again.

He should have known that it was never Jethro's intention to let the boy go. Daniel worshiped his grandfather, and Jethro savored the affection. When he announced his leaving, Jethro already knew the lad would join him, even if Daniel remained naive. The boy was tormented and withdrawn all the days leading up to Jethro's departure. He helped Ruth pack provisions for her father's journey, but was quiet throughout the process. He helped Wes prepare his stallion for Jethro as a gift to aid on his journey, but was indifferent to his fathers attempts at conversation. Jethro went on and on about how great a family he had; how wonderful they were to give him so much. He must have found the whole thing very amusing, knowing he was about to take their only son.

When the day came for Jethro to depart, Daniel did not come out of the hayloft to say goodbye. Jethro called into the barn, wished him well, then tipped his hat to his daughter and Wes before mounting their stallion, and riding out of the homestead's clearing.

After he left, Daniel still refused to come down from the hayloft. Ruth tried to reason with the boy long after his grandfather departed, but Daniel refused to speak to her or to Wes. Eventually she gave up in frustration, and returned to the farmhouse to prepare their dinner. With her gone, Wes stood in the barn entrance for a long time in silence.

"I know he meant a lot to you," Wes eventually called up to Daniel; trying his best to connect with a son he felt he hardly knew. "I hope that you and I can get to know each other just as well."

Eventually they convinced Daniel to come inside if only to avoid the dangers of the night, but he would not join them in their bed. Instead, he placed one of Ruth's woven blankets on the floor next to the fire and fell asleep there. When Wes woke the next morning, the space Daniel had occupied was empty. He got out of bed, waking Ruth in the process, and they both went outside to check on their son.

Ruth was crying before they even reached the barn; her second sight telling her what she didn't want to believe. Daniel had left them some time in the middle of the night. She was certain Jethro had returned, and alerted him while they slept.

Ruth sat on the porch, crying and calling out for her son, while Wes entered the barn to make sure it was empty. He wanted to believe Ruth was wrong. Please, God, just this one time let her be wrong. But when he climbed the loft his worst fears were realized as he immediately saw the short message his son scratched into the floor boards with a knife.

YOU ARE NOT HIM.

Those words hurt Wes in a way he did not think was possible. He fell to his knees, and let his fingers feel the grooves of the letters carved into the wood. A permanent and final testament given to him by his son.

Wes woke to the sun high overhead, beaming down upon his face. He sat up suddenly, recollecting all that occurred the night before, and peered up at the sky to try to gauge the time of day. He suspected four or five hours had passed, but it was hard to judge with the shifting time.

He got to his feet, went to retrieve the bow he tucked behind his horse's saddle, but stumbled as a wave of dizziness overtook him. He reached for his mare to keep from falling again, and she snorted her indifference towards his plight. Wes rubbed at his eyes, trying to clear his vision, and as the world came back into focus, he realized that his mare was staring at him with new wariness. He glared at her, and she tossed her head in feigned indifference. She didn't want him to know she was concerned. Somehow, she must know that he still hated her.

When the dizziness subsided, Wes untied her, and led her to a nearby stream. He filled his canteen, and allowed her to drink her fill, then tied her off there where the grass was still a little green so that she could graze. Wes checked to make sure his knife was secured in its sheath on his leg, and pulled his bow free from behind her saddle. On his hip, his revolver rested as it always did; an extension of his body. By the Lord's grace, he will not need bullets to finish this job. He hoped that monster was already dead.

Wes returned to where the fire still gave off small lazy tendrils of smoke, and examined the black blood she spewed upon the dirt. He followed the trail out of camp, and continued down the zig-zag path it formed through the grass and brush. The trail led him north, and went for some distance until Wes noticed a large outcropping of rocks that leaned and allowed a shaded area underneath. This had to be where she fled.

If she found a cave, I dare not follow.

He had to deal with her though. He couldn't risk leaving her alive to seek vengeance on him or hurt someone else. If he was unable to locate her, or she retreated into the darkness of a den, he needed to race toward the capital and hope he found safety in numbers there. He hoped then that this monster would leave him alone, and he can do what needed to be done to keep his promise to Ruth.

As Wes cautiously approached the outcropping, he felt the scratch on his arm burn with increased intensity. He must have failed to eradicate all the poison. He needed to examine it more closely when he was able, but Lord, did it burn. He tried to put it out of his mind. He dared not be distracted when he was so close to something so deadly.

Wes crouched down closer to the earth and made an effort to camouflage himself among the brush. He did not expect to surprise whatever lurked ahead, but refused to be an easy target either. He also avoided all shadows longer than his arm no matter how faint. No reason to take careless chances. Before going further, Wes prayed silently.

Lord, see me to the end of this day, and to the days beyond.

He pulled an arrow from his quiver, and rested it against his bow with the fletching knocked in the cord. He wouldn't pull it taught until he saw something to aim at, and while he knew an arrow would never kill her, he hoped to catch her legs with a good shot so she couldn't charge at him. He then planned to get in close, and finish her with the knife. It was going to be a messy business, and Wes prayed again, asking for her to already be dead.

Wes' eyes followed the spatter of blood as it arched toward the outcropping, and vanished under an overhang of rock. The space beneath it was deeply shaded where the rock plunged at an angle into the earth. The area was dark and hidden away from the sun, but it wasn't a cave, thank the Lord. Wes could also see that the space was only large enough to house one of the Fallen. She had to be alone.

Will this truly be so easy?

Wes strained to make out the creature in the shadows, but could not discern her shape. He knew she was in there though, for the blood splatter trailed into the shadows and didn't come back out again.

Wes stepped under the overhang, and into the shadows beneath. He was slow and careful, always alert for signs of attack, but none came. He allowed his eyes to adjust to the gloom, and he was soon able to make out the form of the creature wedged tightly against the rock wall. She laid motionless in the dust, and as he approached her, she didn't move from where she was.

Wes let out the breath he was holding. Surely she must be dead. He returned his arrow to its quiver, and slung his bow over his shoulder so that the string ran diagonal across his chest and secured the weapon against his back. Taking another step closer, Wes pulled his six inch hunting knife from its sheath.

"...please...help..."

Wes stared at the creature, dumbfounded. She was still alive, and strangely, she was still begging him to help. Her black eyes were open and watching him warily, but she made no effort to move. His makeshift spear was still jutting out of her side. She must not have the strength to remove it.

Maybe she's asking for me to end her suffering.

Wes stepped forward, lifting the blade in his hand to bring it across her throat, but then movement caught his eye. He thought at first she was trying to lift her leg, perhaps in an effort to fend him off. But no...it was something else. A small part of her body seemed to...break away. It stood, then turned, and a pair of clear blue eyes peered up at him.

Wes gasped, and in his shock, the knife dropped from his hand. He stepped backwards but tripped, stumbled, and fell hard to the ground. All the while, he never stopped staring at those blue eyes as clear as a summer sky. Blue eyes in the dirty face of a young boy, staring defiantly up at him. Wes could not believe what he beheld. His mouth worked to find words. His ears rang from the buzz of incoherent thoughts jumbled in his mind.

"P-Peter?" He managed to stammer, and the moment the name was said, Wes was lost to his memory.

The sweet smell of corn, ready to harvest. Ruth, his beautiful wife, hanging clothing on the line to dry. She was singing. He was sure it was a church hymn but the words eluded him. And there was Peter, his youngest and last, laying in the grass. Peter, who laughed as he threw maple tree seeds into the air so that they spiraled down to land on his face. Wes smiled as he drew in the moment. He knew it couldn't last, but Lord how he wanted it to. This last time of glimpsed happiness. This bittersweet goodbye. If only he could step off of that porch, into the yard, and pull his son to him; hug him tightly, and never let him go. If only he had more time to tell his son how much he loved him, before all turned to darkness in the unraveling of time. Maybe then his anguish would heal. Maybe then his agony would end.

Wes came out of the memory spell with a jolt. He sat up, aware of the danger he was in, and snatched up the knife he left discarded in the dirt. He turned to confront the creature again, but was relieved to see that she had not moved. Indeed, his spear had hit true. She was dying. She continued to watch him, but Wes looked away ashamed.

This whore of Babylon, with a demon inside of her, somehow harbored a child that she did not devour. It defied everything he knew about the nature of the wicked in this world. She must have astounding resilience to fight against the madness inside her. What has she sacrificed to protect this boy from her sin?

"Please," she whispered, "Help...me... help...my...son."

Tears burned in Wes' eyes, but he quickly blinked them away. What had he done? He tried to warn her. He tried to make her leave him be, and yet she persisted. He would not have speared her if she had not attacked him. Her actions were suicide!

“Why me?” Wes implored. He needed to understand. For this boy, with his chestnut hair and clear blue eyes, looked identical to Peter. This fact brought with it a special kind of madness that invited Wes inside.

“You...know why,” she said, and the weak smile she offered him was horrifying on her grotesque face.

“I would never have harmed you if I had known,” Wes said, desperate to justify his taking of a mother from her son. He thought of Ruth and despaired. Tears threatened him again, and Wes squeezed his eyes shut. Peter’s smiling face came into his mind. The sound of his laughter... Wes fought to hold on to reality as a memory spell tried to swallow him once more.

It was so painful to remember all that he lost. But of course this sinful woman wanted Wes to help her son. She must carry the second sight. She must know that this boy was a window to the past for Wes: a portrait of his youngest child. She must know that Wes would do anything to protect this boy no matter the cost.

The woman nodded at him slowly. Affirming what he already suspected, she seemed to be at peace. It made sense why she risked so much to pursue him. He was her son’s best chance for survival.

“The...madnessss...” she whispered, her voice raspy and dry, “it...haunts...me. I’m... so... so... tired. Pleasssee...take...the...boy.” She never was hunting Wes. She followed him to beg for his mercy. On the brink of madness overtaking her soul, on the cusp of a demon forcing her to hurt and kill the only thing she loved, Wes was placed in her path. It had to be by the hand of God.

“I will take him,” Wes assured her. Children were rare, and so few survived to be as old as this one. He appeared to be five or maybe six. The same age Daniel was when he vanished that night. He was older than Peter, but so much his twin all the same. That didn’t matter as much as the woman might think though. He would have taken the boy whether he looked like Peter or not.

The woman blinked, her black eyes damp with tears, and tried to work words out of her mouth but they would not come. Wes could sense her longing, and unspoken words passed between their gaze.

Please, sir, her eyes silently said, *please take him now. Don’t let him see me die.*

Rising to his feet, Wes stepped forward and reached for the boy. Immediately, the lad recoiled. He clung to his mother. His hands were already black with her blood.

Wes could see that she didn’t have much time left, she was fighting to just breathe life into her collapsing lungs, and he knew what she wanted him to do. He reached out, lightning quick, and snatched the boy away before he was able to dodge Wes again. The child screeched in frustration and despair. He struggled against Wes, but he was not strong enough to break free. Slinging the boy over his shoulder, Wes realized how thin the child was. He barely weighed anything at all.

Wes stepped back, out of the hollow, and into the sunlight once more. The boy cried out again, the brightness stinging his eyes, but stopped fighting against Wes' grasp. Instead, he turned and looked longingly back to where his mother lay.

"I will do what I can for him," Wes called to her. He wanted her to at least have peace in this moment, when she spent so much of her life struggling. He could not see her anymore, the sun masking his vision, but he hoped she was smiling; knowing her effort was not in vain. The Lord gave his mercy to the wicked as well.

Resting his free hand against the boy's back, Wes started toward the south where his mare waited for them, and as he walked, the child cried wordlessly for his mother. His voice would be the last thing she heard as her life drained out of her one breath at a time.

I know you aren't Peter, lad, although I wish you were. But the Lord has brought us together for a reason, so let's see what he wants us to do about it.

Chapter Five

Thus says the Lord, your Redeemer,
the Holy One of Israel:
"I am the Lord your God, who teaches you to profit,
who leads you in the way you should go."
-Isaiah 48:17 ESV

Wes thought it best to put some distance between the lad and his mother before dealing with the state the boy was in. Not only did he look terribly underfed, but he was also wearing something he outgrew years ago. It had no sleeves and only extended mid-thigh, which was not suitable for the weather they were in and would only get worse as autumn slipped into winter. Wes needed to bathe him for the first time in what might be years, and find something suitable to dress him in, but first, he needed to get away from the area and the lad's mother. He carried the boy back to where his mare still grazed.

Every inch of the boys' exposed skin and bare feet were covered in streaks of dirt. His hands were black from his sin along with his mother's blood, and his matted hair covered his eyes and hung down his neck in tangles. Black blood smeared over his face and was streaked with tears. One look at him, and Wes' mare immediately started to back away.

"Be calm," Wes warned her, but as soon as he placed the boy on her saddle, he immediately tried to slide back onto the ground again. Wes caught him at the waist, and hoisted him back up onto the saddle again, but the boy immediately tried to slide off once more.

"Be still!" Wes shouted, at the boy this time instead of the mare, and the lad shrank away from him. He slumped in the saddle and started to cry, which in turn caused the horse to stamp her hooves and tug at her tether. Her eyes rolled, her anxiety over this change evident on her face. Wes closed his eyes, and tried to calm his irritation. He did not recall Daniel being so difficult at this age. He took a moment to soothe his horse, then pointed a finger at the blubbering boy.

"Don't move," he ordered sternly, then went about securing his pack and bow. He cast a few challenging glances towards the boy, silently warning him not to try to climb off again, but the child didn't even look at him. He just bit at his lip, snuffling through the wake of his tears, and smeared his face with a dirty arm. Wes' mare was not so easily resigned. She continued to tug at her tether as her eyes rolled wildly. The way she was acting...no. Wes would not allow himself to remember that one memory he would give anything to forget.

"She smells your mother on you. It's scaring her," he explained when he noticed the boy growing uneasy. He stroked her nose again, knowing this was the quickest way to soothe her, and took her tether into his hands. Wes knew that if he allowed her too, she would run. She has done it before. And this boy would not be able to hold on. He would fall. He would get hurt. He shook his head. There was no time for grief in the present. Leave that to the faltering past.

Wes gripped the lead firmly, aware that she might try to jerk it from his grasp, and started off toward the west. He looked up at the boy, and while the lad tried to scowl, his lower lip quivered, and tears still clung to the corners of his eyes. Wes sighed. He shouldn't have lost his temper.

"I didn't mean to shout at you, lad. But I cannot have you running back to your mother. She is not there anymore, do you understand? God has taken away her light."

The boy said nothing, but struggled not to cry again. Wes thought to distract him as they walked.

"Tell me your name." he said, but again the child said nothing. He just stared straight ahead, not meeting Wes' eyes, as tears rolled down his face; one after the other. Thinking that the lad might be seeking silence to grieve, Wes let matters be, and reticence swelled between them. He was not surprised that the boy didn't want to talk to him. He had to be scared, not knowing what his future held, and also heartbroken over the loss of his past. Wes turned his attention back to the road, and appreciated the tranquility of his surroundings.

The rolling grassland was still, without a breeze to stir the air, and Wes watched the sun travel lazily through the sky. To the north, low rolling hills seemed to keep step with his pace, and to the south, the land stretched far off before it was broken by the distant mountains. Directly ahead of him, Wes saw the small trail spiral out of sight and further in the distance was the ridge of the mountain that overshadowed the capital. The city itself was out of sight, resting lower in a valley, but Wes knew it was there and would still see the glow from it at night.

Over time, the sun slid into that familiar spot cresting the horizon, and Wes knew it was time to look for a place to build a fire. He scanned his surroundings for such a space, and after some time, he found a break in the terrain where a stream cut into the earth. Wes pulled at the lead, guiding his horse off the trail they were following, and toward yonder water.

Thinking this an opportunity to catch him off guard, the mare abruptly jerked her head, trying to pull the rope from his hand. Irritated, Wes turned with the intent of giving the animal a firm smack to her rump, but noticed the boy was watching him intently. He let his hand fall without fully understanding why, and returned his focus toward their destination instead. It was so much easier to deal with Daniel.

Next to the stream, Wes found a copse of trees overhanging the water and brought his horse to rest nearby. He tethered the horse while being mindful of the shade, for he didn't know what might lurk there, then reached for the boy.

As soon as he was placed back on the ground, the boy tried to run again.

"Your mother trusted you to me and I intend to see you're safe," Wes growled as he grabbed hold of the boy's arm and pulled him closer. Immediately, the child turned and struck Wes' chest with his fist. When Wes didn't retaliate, the boy gave over to his anger and grief. He bared his teeth through his sobs, and pounded small fists against Wes over and over again. The assault wasn't painful, and Wes understood the lad's anguish all too well. He made no effort to fend off the boy, and soon he grew too weak to keep fighting. The child let his hands fall in defeat, and gave over to his despair once more. He threw back his head, and sobbed with long groans of anguish for his mother. Wes knelt down before him, and pulled the boy into a hug while he cried and cried. He wailed wordlessly against Wes' chest, and the longing he had for his mother was thick like condensation in the air.

"I know, I know," Wes said as he stroked the boy's filthy hair. "I'm sorry she is gone. I'm sorry I hurt her the way I did." He would not make excuses for his actions. He knew first hand that this would do nothing to mend the boy's heart. The boy's tears slowed over time, and eventually stopped completely. Exhausted as he was, the boy fell asleep in Wes' arms. He felt so vulnerable. So fragile. Wes lifted him carefully, and laid him out gently in the grass where the late sun would warm him. Let him sleep for a spell. Wes had firewood to collect anyway.

"Hold still!" Wes snapped, yet again furious with this wretched boy! The tainted scratch on his left arm burned from the strain of struggling against the thrashing of this feral beast. He was also soaked from trying to clean the boy which wouldn't have happened if the little monster had just cooperated! He acted as though he never had a bath in his life! Considering how hard Wes had to scrub him, he might not have.

Wes used a bar of soap and his horse's brush to scrub the boy pink, and as he worked, he noticed that all the black of the lad's hands and face washed away in the stream. Beneath all the blood and layers of grime, and in spite of the cruelness of the world and the circumstances with his mother, this child somehow managed to remain free of all sin. He was completely pure from head to foot. Wes had not seen such a thing since long before Daniel was born.

He wanted to know how this miracle was even possible, but the boy refused to speak to him. He screeched and screamed instead. He thrashed, and bit, and hollered, and whined, and punched. After receiving a fist square on his jaw, Wes had enough of this wild boy. He grabbed him by the back of his neck, forced the lad over his leg, and placed three solid smacks against his bare backside.

Wes thought discipline would reach the boy since shouting at him failed, but noticed the child flinch when he released him. He backed away from Wes a few steps, and stood shivering with an expression that was more confused than chastened. He didn't understand why Wes struck him.

His reaction was completely different from Daniel or Peter on those occasions where either he or Ruth delivered punishment through spanking. Seeing his innocent confusion had Wes feeling ashamed and he vowed to himself never to strike the boy again. It didn't improve the situation anyway, for as soon as Wes tried to tackle his hair with the horse brush, the lad kicked him hard against the flat of his shin.

Wes growled and dunked the boy fully into the stream. He then pulled his naked body up out of the water and tossed him roughly onto the shore where a saddle blanket was laid out for him. The boy coughed and sputtered, but recovered quickly and cast a fiery glare at him. Wes had to admire his strength considering how fragile he seemed and how vulnerable the changes in his life made him, but didn't reveal his growing respect for the lad.

"I'm going to have to cut off that hair," he announced instead, and the child absently reached for his head. There was no saving that mop even if Wes dedicated hours to the task. He climbed out of the water, clothes heavy with their soak, and reached for the boy. When the child jerked away from him and made to struggle again, Wes slung his naked frame over his shoulder like a sack, and snatched up the saddle blanket. He trudged further inland to where he had a fire burning, and threw the blanket down near the warmth of the burning logs. He then pulled a squealing boy off his shoulder and plopped him down on top of it.

"You sit there!" Wes snapped, pointing a finger at the sulking boy. "Moving is *not* an option for you!"

The boy glowered, but to Wes' surprise he listened. He slumped his shoulders, hugged his knees up to his chest, and turned his attention to the fire. Wes returned to the water and scrubbed the boy's tiny outfit as best he could. The entire thing was filthy and the top was stripped down to the threads, but there was a thin piece of elastic around the waistline. Wes used his hunting knife to cut away the top, and fashioned crude underwear out of the rest. When he returned to the fire, the boy had wrapped the saddle blanket around his shoulders and sat quietly looking miserable.

Wes dug through his pack, and retrieved the few articles of clothing he had there. He only brought an extra set of clothes for the occasions where he washed what he was presently wearing. He laid out a pair of brown canvas trousers and an old gray-striped flannel shirt, then returned to rummaging in his pack until he found a small packet containing two needles and some thread. He cut the bottoms off the pants from below the knee, and used the thread to cinch up the waist.

The boy stopped scowling over time, and took to watching Wes work with unveiled curiosity. Satisfied with the pants, he did much the same with the shirt; cutting the bottom off and trimming up the sides, and eventually he had something that the boy might be able to wear.

The effort took the remainder of the day, and it did not escape Wes how much time the boy was delaying his journey. All the same, there was comfort in dealing with these simpler tasks. For while Wes was anxious to get to Daniel, he was also terrified to see him. With a final few stitches added to hold up the rolled sleeves, Wes lifted the garment to examine his work.

"I am not good at this. You need a woman's touch for such things. But I think this will work for now. At least it will keep you warm." He checked to make sure the crude underwear were dry, then invited the boy over. He hesitated for a moment, but then got to his feet and came over to let Wes help him into his new clothes. He examined his billowing shirt and bunched up pants with a pride that Wes thought was humbling.

"I still want to know your name."

The boy said nothing.

The sun sank in the west, and the distant capital cast its glow against the mountainside. Wes barely gave his destination a glance. His focus was on the lad who was walking around the fire and getting a feel of the new clothing against his skin. He seemed uncomfortable, but when he saw that Wes was watching him, he smiled. It was a wonderful thing to see.

"I don't have anything to cover your feet with," Wes said apologetically, and acknowledged the way the boy examined his dusty old boots then looked down at his own bare feet. He wiggled toes in the dust and Wes lifted his head to examine the night. Darkness fell all around them without him noticing, but the hunger it harbored was not lost to him. The wicked were unfurling their wings for this was their hour to roam the barren earth. He felt their longing; their desperate need to taste untarnished flesh, and had to wonder how the boy's mother was able to protect him for so long.

As he mulled over these thoughts, Wes stepped away from the fire, and stripped out of his jacket, vest, and shirt. He used his canteen to wash cool water over the cut on his arm. The thing stung all day; a minor annoyance, but after wrestling with that child, the sting grew into a deep and nagging ache. When he turned toward the fire to take a look at it, Wes whistled long and slow through his teeth. The cut was red, and it felt warm but not hot. He hoped this was the worst it was going to get. He hoped to be back to normal in a few days.

Wes heard a whisper carried slowly by a budding breeze and lifted his head to look off into the trees where the darkest shadows provided a dwelling place. He glanced over to the boy, who still sat with the blanket draped over his shoulders, and dressed quickly in case he needed to act. He might have imagined the sound; that urgent raspy voice.

Wes sat down next to him, and the lad tucked his legs into the shell of his blanket and moved his body to face the other way. His face glistened in the firelight. He'd been crying again. Wes noticed his small toes were peaking out from under the blanket, and leaned over to tug the covering over them.

"I don't want to see you cold," he said with a smile, and the boy turned to stare at him for a long time. He looked so small, cocooned as he was in the saddle blanket. Was Daniel this small on the day he left the farm? It was hard to believe. Wes got up, and went to the other side of the fire to rummage through his pack.

"You must be hungry and thirsty. I have some bread and a little jerky. I refilled my canteen and the water is cool. Will you take offering from me?"

Wes glanced over his shoulder and saw that the boy was still staring at him. Curiosity was plain on his face but the moment he was discovered, he quickly turned around again. He said nothing and neither did Wes. He simply waited, allowing the boy an opportunity to concede a small amount of trust, and absently wondered how things might have been different if he had been this patient with Peter; with Daniel as well. It hurt to think about the time he wasted when he thought he had all the time in the world. He fought against the pull of despondency.

The boy abruptly stood up, drawing Wes out of his mind, and marched over to where Wes was kneeling. He sat down next to Wes, and stared up at him with eyes the size of the moon itself. Those clear blue eyes had a sudden strangeness about them; a thoughtfulness he lacked a second before. For a moment, he looked well beyond his years. Then he lowered his gaze, focusing instead on the pack Wes still held, and leaned in to examine the contents inside.

Wes handed the boy his canteen, then reached into his pack to produce a bundle of jerky along with some hard biscuits. The boy watched the fire while he ate everything that was offered to him. He even hummed in appreciation at the tastes of what was given. It wasn't much in the way of food, but he seemed to appreciate the offering all the same.

"Tomorrow, I will go hunting and try to find something to put weight on your bones. With the Lord's blessing, I'll find something worth killing."

Another day of delay. Another day Ruth must wait for her Daniel.

Wes put the thought out of his mind, and smiled down at the boy. Now that he was clean, he didn't look so much like Peter the way he did before. The resemblance was still there, but the set of his nose and the way his cheekbones angled were not quite right. Still, it was uncanny how closely they resembled each other, and while Daniel looked like his mother, Peter always resembled Wes. This boy could pass as Wes' nephew if not his actual son. The thought made him feel uneasy, but before he could dwell on it, the boy picked up a stick from the dwindling pile of kindling Wes collected and scratched letters into the dirt in front of his uncovered toes. B-E-N-J-I.

"Benji?"

The boy nodded.

"Is that your name?"

The boy nodded.

"Benji. Is that short for Benjamin?"

After a moment, the boy nodded again.

"Why couldn't you just tell me your name? Why won't you talk to me?" Wes asked, but Benji just stared at him. Either he could not speak, or he chose not to.

"Well Benji, your name comes from the Word. Do you know what that is?" When the boy shook his head, Wes turned to his pack and reached inside. He stretched his hand down to the very bottom where a small leather bundle rested, wrestled it out, and placed it carefully on his lap. The leather was oiled to protect its contents from rain, and when he untied the cord that held it together, it fell open to reveal a delicate cloth underneath. It was a cloth that Ruth tied in her hair on their wedding day. Wes peeled this away as well to reveal an old weathered book.

"This, Benji, is the Word of the Lord. This book has been passed down through my family, and while some of the pages are too worn to read, it's still the most precious thing I own. Look, right there in this book is your name. Benjamin. See?"

Wes tapped a page in the book of Genesis, and Benji leaned over his hand to examine the name in the dim firelight. Benjamin.

"If your mother gave you a name from the Word, that must mean she was a follower of the Lord. She must be saved, which explains how she was able to protect you for as long as she did. If she's saved, then she will be waiting for you on the other side of the veil."

Just like all of mine are waiting for me. Right, Ruth?

Benji said nothing to this. He only stared at his name.

"Did your mother ever read to you from the Word?" Benji shook his head.

"Do you want me to read to you about the Benjamin in this book?" The boy lifted his head to peer up at Wes, and again that strange sage-like expression fell across his face. He watched Wes, calculating whether it was safe to trust him, and Wes waited; again feeling patience was the best approach. After some time, Benji nodded.

"Very well", Wes said and carefully turned the delicate pages of this ancient book. Wes thought it strange that the boy spelled out Benji and not Benjamin. If his mother truly was a follower of the Word, he had to wonder if she gave her son the original name the boy of the bible was given. When he was first born, his mother named him Ben Oni. Son of my sorrow. A fitting name for poor Benji.

"If your mother did find her salvation, and went to her return, I'm sure she wants you to join her there someday. It's possible for you to see her again. I would like to show you how." Wes tilted his book so the firelight illuminated the pages, and he began to read.

Benji leaned over him, trying to follow along with the words, but soon he grew tired, and laid his head upon Wes' leg. Eventually his breathing slowed as he drifted into sleep.

Wes closed his book, and looked at the distant glow of the capital. Feeling a sudden sinister presence, Wes' attention shifted to the copse of trees nearby. Again the whispers invaded the silence from the unyielding darkness under the trees. The voices were much louder this time. Much clearer. They called to him with earnest yearning carried through the stillness of the night.

"Unburden yourself, stranger."

"Release the child to us."

"Be free of the flesh."

"Vanquish the light."

Wes closed his mind to their siren song. They would not steal away what was his. He had a child. An actual healthy child, not taken with sickness. Never will he give this gift to the evils of the night. He's already lost too much to the cost of sin.

Chapter Six

Now will I rise, saith the Lord; now will I be exalted;
now will I lift up myself. Ye shall conceive chaff,
ye shall bring forth stubble:
your breath, as fire, shall devour you.
And the people shall be as the burnings of lime:
as thorns cut up shall they be burned in the fire.
-Isaiah 33:10-12 KJV

Daniel was the first to be born, but he was not the last. Ruth had a yearning for motherhood that kept her wanting. When Daniel left them for Jethro, she was determined to replace him with another. She thought that this would mend the hole he left in her heart. She found herself pregnant shortly after, and Wes gave her a daughter. Ruth named her Rachel, for her mother taught her to protect her children with names from the Word, but Rachel did not live to see spring.

So Ruth tried again. Determined, she laid with Wes passionately, tempting him at all hours of the day, and he could never deny her. Again, she was able to conceive and gave birth to another daughter. This time she named her Abigail, but the child's breath was hoarse and her cough wet. She did not live to see the sunrise. Ruth grieved for Abigail more than the other. Even more than Daniel who she prayed for the Lord to return to her every night. She thought herself cursed. She thought God had forsaken her. She formed a bitter resentment, and listened to neighboring women speak of witchcraft as a solution to her problems. Instead of seeking understanding, she stopped praying altogether. She turned her back on God in her anger, and sin spread from her hands to her wrists.

Seeing how distraught she became, Wes prayed twice as much as before. But he did not pray for a child. He prayed for Ruth. He prayed she stopped pursuing this obsession to conceive, fearing it might kill her. He didn't want to have another child, feeling he wasn't meant to be a father, and when his two daughters died he secretly worried that he might be responsible. Perhaps the Lord felt him ungrateful for the blessings he was given, and took his daughters home to heaven where they could be better loved. While he struggled with guilt, Ruth burned bundles of dried herbs in their home, and whispered to a little statue of a woman that she carried around in her apron pocket.

Wes tried to help her conceive, but his heart really wasn't in it anymore. Every time they failed, she would go off to be alone and cry. She went half mad with her yearning, always talking to that foolish little statue she carried around, but she was finally rewarded when the day came for rejoicing. At last, she was pregnant again.

Ruth attributed this new blessing to the idol and the herbs. She would meet with the neighboring women, talking in low voices that Wes could not hear. On more than one occasion, a vial of liquid passed from one of the women to Ruth and she would slip it into her pocket. She drank these concoctions, whatever they were, and smiled at her little woman statue at all hours of the day.

This fourth child she carried didn't last long enough to come out of her fully grown. They saw the tiny thing, lying motionless on their bloodied bed, and the light went out behind Ruth's eyes. She wrapped the child in a cloth and placed it in a small wooden box that she once used for trinkets from her mother. The child remained there, tucked away on a shelf, never to rejoin the earth.

Ruth stopped trying to get pregnant after the loss of this last child. Her anger towards the Lord seemed to overtake everything else and the blackness of her sin spread up her arms. She did not care. She hardly ate, and Wes could not remember the last time he heard her sing. It was as if she gave up not only on trying to conceive, but on life entirely.

Wes tried to explain to Ruth that this was how things were with everyone. She did not shoulder this misery alone. Children were often stillborn after the Damnation, and if they managed to enter the world breathing, many of them did not live long beyond that. Their small bodies could not endure the weight of this world. Life itself was too heavy to breathe in.

Only a small few grew beyond three years of age and even less made it to adulthood. Wes knew this was a hard thing to hear, especially for Ruth, who grew up believing that faith the size of a mustard seed could move mountains according to the Word. Ruth and Wes surrendered their lives to the Lord, but that did not mean they were an exception to the world's tragedies. Ruth's tears were only added to the well of grief shared by so many women over their lost sons and daughters.

The more Wes tried to explain this to her, the more Ruth distanced herself from him. So it was truly a miracle when she somehow became pregnant again. Ruth did not rejoice in this revelation. She was convinced that this one would also succumb like the others had. She did not whisper to her statue. She did not drink her potions. She did not pray to the Lord.

When she gave birth to their second son, Ruth declared that he would not survive the night. She stayed up with him for three days without sleeping. She sat in the dark, and stared at the baby, waiting for him to take his last breath.

"If I look away, God will steal him from us. God is a thief of all the joy in this world. He takes everything that brings happiness and keeps it for himself."

Wes did not have the heart to rebuke her. As time passed, and the boy grew older, Ruth slowly began to heal. The light came back into her eyes. She started to pray again, although not nearly as often as she used to. She dared to believe that this last child was God's form of a peace offering to her.

One morning, Wes woke to the sound of Ruth singing again. She smiled as she held their son closely. Their little boy was always reaching for her; loving her; needing her. He called out to her.

"Mamamama."

She would kiss him on his nose, his cheeks, his belly, his toes. When he turned a year old, she was ready to name him.

"We will call him Peter, for his strength," Ruth decided. "He is the cornerstone to our new foundation." Wes worried over the naming, but he held his tongue. He did not want to take Ruth's joy from her. It took her so long to believe she could be a mother again, and he wanted her to have that happiness. As for Wes, he did his best to be a better father for little Peter, while he silently prayed that his son would remain healthy for Ruth's sake. God must have heard his prayers, for Peter remained happy and healthy up until the day that he died.

Wes fell asleep at the first signs of dawn. The sleep was restless, fitful, and filled with the faces of his past. When at last he awoke, the sun was high in the sky, and he heard Benji crying again. Wes sat up, and his head swayed with a spell of dizziness.

Something is wrong with me, Ruth.

"Benji..." He said hoarsely, and tried to work moisture into his mouth. He felt like he was in a fog. The area swam in and out of focus and Wes fought to stay awake. As clarity slowly came back to him, Wes grew aware of a searing pain that radiated from his arm. That burdensome scratch. It must have festered. He reached for and found his revolver still secured to his leg. He undid the belt, and slid the holster and gun off of the strap. Then he used his teeth to help cinch the belt around his arm above the cut, and he secured it in place. It might help to slow the infection coursing through him. Laying next to him, the saddle blanket laid in a crumbled heap, vacant. A short distance away, Wes heard Benji continue to cry.

"Benji," Wes tried again. Lord, his mouth was dry. He rubbed at his eyes and looked around, then finally spotted the boy huddled near the stream. Wes rose to his feet, staggered a little, then stumbled down to where Benji sat staring into the water. Wes cupped the stream into the hand of his affected arm and noticed how the color was deeper than the other hand. There was nothing more he could do about it for the time being, and instead focused on slaking his parched throat.

Benji, noticing he was no longer alone, scrubbed at his eyes and bit his lower lip to stop his crying. Wes glanced over at him, then past him to the copse of trees that lay a few feet beyond. They needed to make distance between themselves and those trees, but Wes also needed to find something to feed to the boy who looked like he was half starved. Not to mention Wes was pretty sure Benji's mother caused him to get a sickness he might not survive. Which direction should he go? Nothing left to do but trust in the Lord.

Wes pulled at some of the long grass nearby and separated a few of the stems. Benji, watching him with slight curiosity, momentarily forgot about his despair and his mother. Instead he leaned in, and watched as Wes broke three stems at three different lengths and held them up.

"This long one means we leave this place, and use the daylight to gain some distance. This middle one means we stay here and I try to find us something to eat in those trees over there. This small one means I drink the rest of my whiskey and you use my hunting blade to cut away the sickness from my arm." Wes lifted his sleeve to show Benji the angry cut on his arm. It was a lot more red than the day before, the redness growing around the cut, and radiated heat as well. Benji shied away from the sight of it.

"Let's hope we do not draw the short straw," Wes agreed. He tucked the three lengths into his hand and made sure the tops of them were even when he poked a small portion of each one out from his fist. "Now, Benji. Let us pray."

Benji watched as Wes bowed his head, then followed along. Together, the two knelt facing one another with their heads bowed, and their eyes closed. All around them, everything was quiet as if waiting to see what would happen next. Perhaps the Lord will hear them, when the rest of the world was so silent.

"Lord, help guide us on the right path. Help me to do what is right for this boy and to protect him. I leave the choice to you, God. Guide Benji's hand to choose our way." Then he lifted his head and smiled at the lad.

"This is where you would say 'amen'."

The boy said nothing.

Holding up his hand, he showed the three stems of grass to Benji.

"Draw our lot, lad," Wes instructed, and so Benji did. The stem he drew was the long.

They traveled for the rest of the day, and as they went, Wes felt that they had made the right choice. He loosened the strap on his arm just a little, and still held his revolver tucked in the pocket of his jacket. He walked for a while, but when weariness caused him to stumble, he climbed onto his mare behind Benji and they rode on together. Some time later, they came across what appeared to be a recently abandoned homestead. Wes thought it would be a good place to stop for the evening. He did not go near the house itself, as it was getting late, and the shadows were dark within it. Fortunately, he located a stone fire ring with a pile of logs and kindling already placed nearby.

"The Lord has blessed us!" Wes declared, relieved that he did not have to collect wood before building a fire. His arm was aching, and he needed to cleanse the wound. He also found the remains of a well, with water still in its belly, and an overgrown garden bed nearby.

"Help me, lad. See if we can find some food here." The sun grew low, with shadows all around them, but hunger drove them forward. Soon, Benji called out and Wes joined him to see that the boy found some old yellowing pole beans still on their withered vines.

"Well done, Benji! Very well done!" Benji smiled and Wes couldn't help but feel proud of him. For a moment, they shared a warmth that Wes always yearned to have with Daniel. Then they both looked away from each other, and felt a little ashamed.

"I think those that love us would want to see us happy," Wes offered but said nothing further. He knew Benji needed time. He also struggled with his own past. They continued on, picking a few handfuls of beans in silence.

They put the beans in Wes' small cook pot full of water to soften, and he added a few pieces of jerky to give the broth flavor. Benji watched it cook over the fire intently, and when Wes declared it ready, he gulped down the first mouthful before it could burn his tongue. Wes wasn't sure he even paused to chew.

Wes ate slowly, focusing more on keeping pressure against the cut on his arm. Pressure helped to ease the pain. Earlier, he brought cool water up from the well in a bucket, and ran it over the cut repeatedly to bring down the heat of the skin. It helped a little, and the redness was slightly improved. Wes hoped this was an indication of healing.

He eased the arm back into his jacket, and glanced down at Benji who stared blankly at the fire. His misery was plain upon his face, but Wes would not try to console him again. The boy had every right to grieve for his mother.

Wes understood grief well, and knew that it was sometimes easier to live inside his own memories. He sat down quietly by Benji's side, while they both dwelt on moments in the past. Wes realized he could not remember things as well as he once had. Small holes were forming in his recollection, and prior to her decline, Ruth told him that this was happening to her as well.

"Maybe you will be spared," she told him once, "as you lack the second sight. The holes in your memory might be all you'll ever notice. As for me, I see a dozen sunrises and two dozen sunsets. All possibilities of the past are spread out before me like the uncertainty of the future. I'm starting to lose track of reality." Wes dreaded the thought. Everyone keeps saying that the past was unraveling, but to actually see it playing out in his mind terrified him. He glanced down at Benji, and wondered if he noticed any of these changes.

"Come, stranger, let him go."

Wes lifted his head to examine the darkness at the edge of the firelight. He sensed there was something beyond it. Something watching them; whispering to them.

"Give him to us."

"Vanquish the light."

"Benji, bring me the good book. I will read you more of the Word." Benji rose quietly, and went to Wes' pack. The mare was no longer bothered with being close to the lad since Wes got him clean. He still needed to deal with Benji's hair, but everything in its time. Wes wanted to avoid getting kicked or bit again.

The boy returned with the book cradled in his hands, but rested it between them, and lifted his head to study Wes. His stare was intensely focused, and Wes felt nervous under his scrutiny.

"What is it?" he asked, as he glanced into the darkness. Was this about the whispers calling out to them? Benji took Wes' hand in both of his and brought it to his chest. Then he lifted the hand to Wes' lips.

"What?" Wes asked as he pulled away. This strange new charade baffled him. Instead of explaining, Benji simply repeated the action: putting Wes' hand against his chest then lifting the hand to touch Wes' lips. Already on edge from the spectators in the night, Wes snapped at Benji in frustration. "Can't you just talk? Tell me what you want!"

The boy said nothing. He stared at Wes with an unreadable expression, then stubborn determination furrowed his brows. Benji reached out again for Wes' hand so that he could place it on his chest, but Wes had enough of all this guided touching. He originally assumed the boy was mute out of grief or possibly shock, but this charade had gone on long enough. He jerked his hand out of Benji's grasp.

"Are you stupid? Just say what it is you want!" Wes regretted shouting immediately after the words left him. It reminded him of those times he yelled at Peter for not wanting to ride their horse, and how rotten it made him feel afterward. He thought of Daniel, and how his horrible parenting formed a rift between them. He kept making mistakes. Over and over again.

Benji's face darkened, and his expression conveyed the depth of hurt and frustration he was feeling for not being understood. He stood up abruptly, gave Wes a defiant glare, then stomped off to crouch down at the edge of where the firelight touched the earth. As soon as Benji moved, Wes felt things stir around them. Forms shifted, and soft groans of excitement formed a chorus in the darkness.

"Benji, come here," Wes called nervously as his eyes darted around; trying to make out shapes in the night.

"Yes! Yesssss!"

"Come here, boy."

"Vanquish the light!"

"Devour the bringer of light!"

Benji did not move from where he sat on his knees; his legs splayed out beneath him. He acted as though he could not hear Wes, or the voices of those hungry monsters that were closing in. He was far too close to the darkness. Something could easily reach into the light and snatch him away. One moment he would be there, the next moment forever gone.

Wes could wait no longer. He sprung to his feet, and lunged towards the boy. Benji turned in time to see Wes bearing down upon him. He cowered as his head sunk below his shoulders, and he leaned away from the firelight. Wes grabbed hold of his arm, and yanked him to his feet to pull him back to the fire. Wes' hand completely enclosed the circumference of his frail arm. Lord, but he was so thin.

As he moved, Wes heard a low hiss and turned in time to see the shape of a monster fading back into the oblivion of the full darkness. He was mere inches away from where Benji was sitting. Wes turned on Benji, both furious at the boy, and terrified for him.

"You cannot do that again! You must stay near the fire! Do you understand me?" Benji turned away from Wes and squeezed his eyes shut. He put his hands to his ears, trying to block out Wes' shouts. He grabbed Benji's wrists, pulling them away from his ears, and gave him a quick jerk for good measure.

"You need to listen to me, Benji. You need to understand this. You can not go out into the darkness. You will be killed in an instant. Do you understand me?"

Benji screamed, a shrill high pitched noise, and struggled against Wes' grasp. He was angry, but also fearful of Wes, and he babbled out a jumble of incoherent words. Wes tried to get him under control, but Benji was desperate in his struggle, and managed to break free from his grip.

He backed away from Wes, and for a horrifying moment, Wes was certain the boy was going to run directly into the darkness.

"Benji!" Wes cried out, panic plain upon the name. But Benji just dropped down onto his knees next to the fire, covered his ears again, and rocked back and forth as he keened softly. Tears leaked through the lashes of his tightly squeezed eyes.

Wes sighed. This was all such a struggle. He considered how tempting it would be to abandon this responsibility, and was ashamed for feeling that way. The familiar self loathing returned to him. Yet again, he was unfit to be a father. No, he didn't want this to turn out the way it did with Daniel. He needed to do better. He needed to try harder. Wes knelt down beside where Benji sat slumped, and gently rested a hand upon the boy's back.

"I'm sorry I yelled, lad. I will try to do better. I was just worried about you. There are so many things in this world that want to take you away from me. They will surely hurt you if they get hold of you. It scares me to think of you getting hurt." Benji lifted his head and looked up at Wes with complete surprise. His innocent expression showed how touched he was, and all of Wes' irritation melted off of him like snow.

"Can we try again?" He asked and raised his hand to offer it over to Benji. Benji made quick work of drying the tears off his face with his sleeve, then shifted to face Wes fully. He took Wes' hand and brought it up to his lips.

"You want me to say something?" Wes asked with sudden understanding, and Benji smiled. Such a sweet boy smile. Wes' couldn't help but smile back at the lad, and his grin was large enough to pull at the corners of his eyes. Then Benji brought Wes' hand to his own chest, before returning it to Wes' lips. He released Wes' hand, then leaned forward, and tapped his own fingers against Wes' mouth.

"Benji? Is that what you want me to say?" Wes asked, and the boy clapped in victory. He tapped his chest, then leaned forward and placed fingertips against Wes' lips.

"Benji," Wes said and Benji nodded. Again the boy tapped his own chest, then returned fingers to lips.

"Benji," Wes repeated, his lips sending vibrations through the boy's fingertips. Benji leaned closer, and stared at Wes' mouth, intent on watching how it moved. Again the tapping, from chest to lips.

"B-e-n-j-i," Wes said slowly, sounding out each letter in the name. Benji withdrew his hand, and looked at his palm as though he expected a secret to be revealed there. His mouth fumbled as his lips tried to mimic the things that Wes did. He failed, but at least he tried. He wanted to learn which told Wes that he did not choose willfully to stop speaking, he just never learned how to start.

"Here," he said uncomfortably, and tried to distract Benji from this charade, "let me read to you from the Word."

He reached for his book, as Benji settled in beside him to look over his shoulder. Wes unwrapped his bible and opened it to Genesis, then an idea struck him.

"Benji, do you know how to read?" Benji shook his head.

"Your mother didn't teach you?" Again, Benji shook his head. "But you wrote your name for me in the dust."

Benji looked up at him and shrugged as if to say *I only have one trick, Mister, and you saw it.*

Wes sighed and scratched the stubble on his chin. It would have made things easier if they could communicate with writing. This strange language of grunts and gestures, kicks and screams were nothing more than a pointless guessing game.

"There is so much you need to learn," Wes sighed, suddenly overwhelmed by the vastness of it. How was Ruth able to teach Daniel all those years? When Wes tried to teach Peter, he failed in the most devastating of ways. Did he really think he was capable of teaching this boy to read? Benji would be better off learning from a mother or father. Not a useless vagabond like Wes.

"Unburden yourself, stranger."

"You don't want to deal with a boy like this one."

"So violent. So broken."

"Vanquish the light."

Benji tapped fingers against the book resting in Wes' lap, and Wes shut out the whispers from the night's shadows. He had a lot to teach the boy if they were ever going to communicate with one another. Putting aside his worries, Wes opened the Word and read.

Chapter Seven

Why wasn't I buried like a stillborn child?
Like a baby who never lives to see the light?
For in death the wicked cause no trouble,
And the weary are at rest. Job 3:16-17 NLT

When birdsong hinted at the coming of day, Wes rose from where he sat, easing Benji off of his lap, and stretched his weary muscles. Years within the homestead caused him to soften, and he was unaccustomed to the earth. He tested his arm, and thought the coolness of the night helped it to feel better. His dizziness seemed to lessen as well. He took advantage of the renewed vitality to sling his saddle on to his mare, and string up his bow. The horse stomped about, unhappy to have the saddle on her back again, but Wes made soothing noises, and ran a hand down her nose.

"Just a short ride. You'll get another day of rest out of me, be certain of it."

Wes looked down at Benji, and thought about how close he came to losing him. The night seemed more active, now that Benji was with him. Creatures lingered and whispered to him up until the early birdsong. Benji would disappear from his life in an instant if Wes was careless. The idea terrified him, especially considering how weak he felt already from the work he did that morning.

Sighing, he lifted his head and looked to the horizon where the capital sat nestled against a backdrop of mountains. What was he going to do with Benji once he got there? There was no way for him to keep him safe inside the capital. It seemed like evil was drawn to the lad, and if Wes was spending all his time fending off monsters, he would not be able to locate his son. Maybe he could hide the boy away somewhere before he entered the city, but what assurance did he have that Benji would remain safe? He dared not take risks with the child, but hoped an opportunity would present itself as he drew closer to his destination.

When he looked down at Benji, Wes marveled at how he came into his life. Why didn't this opportunity occur when Wes was still with Ruth and Peter was still alive? He shook his head and frowned. He was dwelling on lost things again. The past was like a dark cavern he often wandered into, and struggled to find his way out of. He feared losing the memories he had, but also feared being pulled into them.

Without cause, Benji woke abruptly and opened his eyes to see Wes scowling at him. He sat up, confusion painted upon his face, then looked around. Confusion quickly turned to recognition, which then turned to sadness. Benji lowered his head, and stared blankly at his open hands.

"Get a drink, and ready yourself, we need to take a short ride," Wes said. Benji rose to his feet, brushing off his makeshift clothes, and retrieved the canteen. Wes strapped the quiver onto his back, slung his bow over his shoulder, and reached for the lad to lift him up into the saddle. Benji looked up at him, and gestured with his hands like he was opening a book, and running his finger along an invisible page. A small smile twitched the corners of Wes' mouth.

"We have to make use of this sunlight. But I will read to you tonight, lad. You can trust me on that." The boy stared at Wes; his expression flat and his eyes full of that sage thoughtfulness. Then he tapped his own chest, and brought his hand to place fingers against Wes' lips.

"Benji," Wes said, impatiently. He was now familiar with this charade. "B-E-N-J-I, we need to get G-O-I-N-G." Benji's lips moved and twitched, but asking him to speak would be the same as asking him to strip and clean Wes' gun. Benji lifted his hand, tapping fingers against Wes' chest this time, and then brought those fingers to Wes' lips.

"What are you on about now? You are asking for my name?" Wes tried to be patient with Benji and his desire to speak, but he had things to do while he had light to do it in. Tasks needed to be done.

Oblivious to his impatience, the boy simply nodded.

"Wes," he said, his lips moving against the boy's fingertips. "W-E-S". Benji's lips twitched and quivered.

"Wuh."

It was a start.

Wes' eyes caught a flicker of movement and he looked off in the distance behind Benji. Something was bedding in the bushes yonder.

"Come, lad. Up on the horse you go."

"Wuh," Benji said again, practicing the word, and allowed Wes to put him on the mare's saddle. Wes climbed up behind him, and pressed his knees into her side indicating a light trot.

"I had hoped the Lord might bless us with some game today, and it seems that he is smiling upon us." Wes pointed to the bushes where he saw movement a moment earlier. "There is something bedding in yonder bush."

Benji nodded, as he stared with intense seriousness into the bushes ahead. When they got to be about fifty yards off, Wes pulled at the mare's reins and brought her to a stop. He slid off the saddle, and lifted Benji off in turn.

"Here," he said and placed the mare's tether in Benji's hand. "I need you to hold her here. She will spook our dinner if we let her get much closer. Watch me, lad. You might learn something."

Benji nodded, his eyes sharp and alert, and Wes turned his attention back to the bushes. He thought for a moment that Benji might use this opportunity to elope; to take hold of the horse and flee back in the direction of his dead mother, but then he felt the boy's small fingers wrap around his hand and squeeze it. They felt so cold and fragile. The only thing keeping him alive was Wes.

Wes moved away from Benji slowly, and slid his bow over his shoulder with fluid movements. There was nowhere for him to take cover in this open expanse of wilderness, so his best approach was to look like he belonged. Every step he took was smooth and slow. Every placement of the foot started with toes and rolled to the heel so as not to make a sound. Wes floated forward as though carried on the breeze, and Benji kept silent without being told to do so. He was a good lad.

Forty yards away, and Wes slowly pulled an arrow out of his quiver. He was a tree swaying in the breeze. He was blades of grass dancing in the sun. He was not a man trying to place an arrow in the breast of an animal and claim it for his dinner. Slow, fluid, and forward he went.

"Wuh!" Benji called to him, and Wes dropped a hand behind his back, out of sight of the bushes, to make a gesture with his fingers as if to shoo the boy away. So much for keeping quiet. Sudden movement drew his eye, and again Wes saw something in the bushes. Something brown and definitely full of life. He slid forward still.

Thirty yards away, and he might dare take a shot, but the closer he got the better chance he had. Before him, the bushes seemed to part, and a large bird stepped out into the open. It was a majestic male turkey, with his chest puffed out, and his tail feathers spread. He lifted his head, and looked directly to where Wes stood. Wes remained frozen in place, and prayed that Benji stayed quiet this time.

The turkey studied him for a long time, both of them motionless where they stood, then at last the bird turned his head and stepped more fully into the open. Behind him, another head emerged from the bushes and a second turkey stepped out. This one was smaller in frame and obviously a jenny. Wes slowly moved his leg forward. His muscles ached from this unfamiliar strain, but Wes hardly felt them. All his focus was pinpointed on that line of birds. When they all emerged, there were a total of six.

Twenty five yards away, Wes noticed a jenny on the end of the line, slightly smaller than the others, and with a lame leg. She had a foot that curled underneath, and limped with every step. She hung back from the others, seemingly ignored, and Wes doubted the jake would ever give her the time of his day. If Wes was to take any of them, the lame one would impact them the least. Slowly, he pulled back the string of his bow as he lifted it to rest alongside his cheek. His injured arm burned from the strain, and Wes' heart sank a little. He had really hoped that God saw fit to free him from this burden.

Twenty yards away, and Wes aimed his loaded arrow at the jake in the front of the line. He then slowly drifted to the left until he saw a clear shot of the lame jenny. Hesitation fed no hunger. Wes immediately released the taught bowstring, and launched the arrow cleanly through the sky.

There was so much to remember with bow hunting. The curve of the arrows fall, the distance in relation to the height of the aim, the accountability of wind; of scent; of fatigue on the arm. Yet in some miraculous way, all these things sometimes fit together in perfect unison to launch an arrow deep into the breast of a lame turkey. The twang of the bowstring alerted the other birds before the jenny was even struck, and they dashed back into the bushes in a blur of movement and fear.

Wes watched each of them slip out of sight, and marveled at seeing actual turkeys roaming these wicked wilds. If turkeys were able to survive in this dismal place, maybe humans still had a fighting chance as well. He looked over his shoulder, and saw that Benji was watching him. He had not moved from the spot he was told to stand in.

"Did you see that?" Wes called to him, and the boy nodded vigorously. Wes lifted his bow triumphantly and let out a shout of joy. "We will eat like kings tonight!"

Benji broke into a run, dragging a reluctant mare behind him, and as soon as he got close, he dropped her tether all together and leaped at Wes. Feeling his energy and excitement, Wes caught the boy in the air, and spun him around as they both laughed. The joy they felt was universal to the starving who were about to be fed. Benji whooped and squealed and when Wes set him down, he danced about pumping his fists in the air. Then, suddenly realizing what he was doing, he dropped his hands and put distance between himself and Wes. He looked down, ashamed, as he stared at his empty palms.

"You did well," Wes said, giving the boy's arm a sympathetic squeeze. "I'm sure your mother smiles upon you today."

Benji ducked his head to hide his secret joy, Wes never saw a boy look so proud. They approached the turkey together, and watched as she gave a final few flaps of her one wing. Wes' arrow found her heart. It was an excellent shot that killed her moments after impact. Her flapping made Benji nervous though, and he shied back a little when he saw it.

"It's alright. She's good and dead, lad. That wing is just her body not wanting to believe this truth." Benji reached out and took Wes' hand in his own as he examined the bird apprehensively. Wes could not comprehend the jumble of emotions this caused him. He cleared his throat uncomfortably, and released Benji's hand to examine the bird. He grabbed her lame leg and lifted her off the ground.

"I hope you're hungry," he said and flashed Benji a grin. Then he shoved the jenny into his arms. She looked as large as Benji. "She shouldn't be too heavy for you, lad. Hold on to her while I put you up in the saddle. It's high time we get back to camp, so we can work on cooking this bird."

Wes spent the remainder of the day showing Benji how to clean a turkey. They plucked the feathers while Wes explained the many ways that they could be used. He lifted the straightest ones up to the sun, and showed Benji how to split them for fletchings. The lad might make arrows one day. He might.

Wes showed Benji how to cut open a turkey, how to dismember the head, and how to remove the chitlins and all other potential fox bait. Everything seemed important for him to know. Benji might want to learn how to trap one day. He might.

Wes showed Benji how to preserve the feet, how to dry the meat, how to cook the bird in a bed of coals, or over burning logs. He showed Benji how to best cut up the bird once cooked, to ensure all the meat was removed from the bone. Benji might need to do this on his own one day. Even if he stayed with Wes always, it was still good for him to know. It might turn out to help him in the future. It might.

In truth, Wes couldn't seem to stop himself. Benji was so silent and attentive; his eyes bright and focused on every word, that Wes just kept teaching him more of what he knew. He used to daydream about having moments like this with Daniel, and even Peter one day. He thought it was so important to teach his children all that he knew.

Wes seemed to be thinking a lot about his two sons since Benji came into his life. There was always the danger of a memory spell, but there was also comfort in the remembering. Wes knew there were things in his past he had already forgotten. He couldn't remember the sound of Peter's voice. He did not remember Ruth's favorite hymn she always used to sing. He tried to recall it in specific moments from his past, but the thoughts turned thin like muddy water leaking from his cupped hands.

There have always been memories that faded with time. This was a part of the life the Lord gave him. But then there were these other memories that felt different to Wes. He knew somehow that these memories were specific to time unraveling. They were just out of sight; just beyond reach, and every time he strained for them, they turned thin in his mind. In those places full of muddy water, the holes in his mind were small, but seemed to be growing. Peter was not dead but a few weeks. How could Wes already forget the sound of his voice? Only the present remained intact. The here and the now were still a constant sequence. Would this always be the case?

Wes put the thought out of his mind, and focused on cutting up their turkey. He placed their portions on wooden platters he recovered from the empty farmhouse. As he worked, he could feel the deep ache in his arm increasing in intensity. He constantly soothed it with cool water from the well, but that only lasted so long, and every time he looked at it, the thing was progressively worse.

Already stripped of his jacket and vest, Wes wiped the turkey juice off his hand, and pulled up his sleeve to examine his arm. Benji gave a small whimper when he saw how angry the cut looked. The edges of it had curled back; opening the wound up like an overripe fruit. The hot redness on his skin spread beyond the size of his hand, and Wes realized his whole arm was swollen. Even his fingers were starting to swell, and they felt tight when he flexed them.

"It's alright. It's alright." Wes soothed, but he did not think it was alright at all, and his tongue burned from the lie. He considered drawing lots again, but after the short time he spent with Benji, he did not think the boy was capable of cutting into his arm; even if it might save his life. Wes stared at the wound for a moment, worry crippling him to inaction, then he covered it again with his sleeve.

"I hope you're hungry!" Wes smiled weakly at Benji whose face was marked with concern. "But first, you must eat this."

He lifted his knife, and stabbed something lumpy and brown on his plate. He held it out to Benji as an offering. Benji plucked the morsel carefully off the blade, then timidly popped it into his mouth. He immediately grimaced, and turned to spit the thing out again, but Wes reached out with a hand to block him.

"I know it's not the most pleasant thing to eat, but that's why I gave it to you first. Your body needs that gizzard boy, and if you know what's good for you, you'll eat it." Benji managed to swallow down the gizzard, then opened his mouth wide and stuck out his tongue to prove it was gone. Wes smiled, patted the boy's cheek, then handed over a platter of cooked turkey.

After his first apprehensive bite, Benji ate ravenously. Wes was not sure if this was due to how hungry he was, or how delicious the turkey tasted, but he found himself cautioning Benji to slow down or he might choke.

I'm like a nagging mother. Right, Ruth?

When at last every bone was picked clean between them, Benji laid back against the rolled up saddle blanket and sighed. Under his ill-fitting shirt, his belly bulged. Perhaps Wes should have restrained him, knowing how it might cause him to get sick from eating so much after hardly eating at all. But it was hard to deny the lad, seeing how much he liked it.

On a whim, Wes rummaged through the remains of the turkey carcass until he located the turkey's collar bone. He pulled it free, wiped it clean, then handed it to Benji.

"It's called a wishbone," Wes explained with a shrug. "My father told me of it when I was a lad like you. I can't remember everything he said, but I recall that you are supposed to break it while you pray. Then the Lord will better hear your prayer, and see it come to pass. I don't know how the bone of a bird could possibly accomplish such a thing. Now that I mention it, I realize how silly it sounds. I can get rid of it for you."

Wes reached to take the wishbone back, but Benji pulled away from him; cradling the bone to his chest.

"Alright," Wes said, getting to his feet. He moved to lower the bucket down into the well. "Suit yourself then." As he worked, he glanced over and saw that Benji was smiling as he examined the bone in his hands. What a strange boy he was.

As Wes took to washing out his wound again, easing the pain a little in the process, he looked out toward the horizon where the glow light illuminated the landscape. The capital was just out of sight in the valley, yet still so many miles away. He wondered what Daniel was doing in this moment, over there in that distant place.

"Benji... do you see those lights over there?" Benji came over to stand next to where Wes knelt, and together they looked out upon the sea of distant lights. "Everyone calls it the capital. It's a vast city full of people, including one specific person that I am trying to find. There will come a time, very soon I reckon, when I will need to go there, and I can't take you with me."

"Wuh!" Benji in his alarm, turned and grabbed hold of Wes' hurt arm. Wes winced but managed to not let the boy see how badly that hurt him.

"Listen to me, lad." Wes pulled Benji's hand from his arm and held it in his own. "You can not go with me. It's far too dangerous. I will find you some place safe outside the city, but don't try to chase after me. Do not ever go into the capital. Do you understand?" Benji turned away, not wanting to meet Wes' eye. Wes reached up and gave the boy's ear a firm tug. When Benji turned back to glare at him, he held fast to the boy's neck and peered sternly into his eyes. "Do you understand?"

Reluctantly, Benji nodded, then looked back at the city in the distance.

"I'll do what needs to be done there. Then I will return to you. You must wait for me through days and nights so you'll have to keep a fire lit at all times. I'll show you how when we get closer."

If we get closer. If I don't step through the veil this very night from the state my arm is in.

Wes lost himself in his worry for a moment, and did not know Benji stepped away from him until he returned holding the leather parcel containing the Word.

"You want me to read to you again?" Wes asked.

The boy nodded earnestly, and Wes couldn't help but smile. Such a good lad. He took the book from Benji, but set it to the side. "If you want me to read to you, there is something you need to do for me first."

He got to his feet, and wiped the flat of his knife on his pants.

"You better hold still, Benji. It's past time we cut that hair."

Chapter Eight

I also will do this to you:
I will even appoint terror over you,
wasting disease and fever
which shall consume the eyes and cause sorrow to the heart.
And you shall sow your seed in vain,
for your enemies shall eat it. -Leviticus 26:16 ESV

When Wes opened his eyes, his body was consumed with pain. He did not remember falling asleep, but at some point in the night, he recalled opening his eyes and seeing Benji sitting next to him, tending the fire. His hair, cut short, stuck up every which way upon his head, and he rubbed at his weary eyes, stopping occasionally to yawn. Wes didn't think the boy slept at all.

Groaning, he rolled to his side and managed to find his feet. When he stood, he staggered a little, and Benji was at his side, trying to steady him. Wes knew he was in a bad way. No longer could he hope that he might find God's grace in healing. No longer could he focus on the better moments as a sign that he was improving. He was not improving. He was surely dying.

It didn't matter. There was work that needed to be done. Wes stumbled over to the well, and Benji remained beside him. He assisted to retrieve a bucket of water, but Wes didn't care to see the state his arm was in. Instead he plunged the whole thing into the bucket as deep as he could, and rested his head against his shoulder. The effort of getting up and walking just a few feet left him exhausted and Wes panted as the world swam in and out of focus before him. Directly in front of him, Benji sat staring as fear filled his eyes with tears.

"Stiff upper lip now," Wes mumbled. "Don't let your mother see you crying like that. You know she isn't well." Wes closed his eyes and lost himself to sleep. Later, when he heard birdsong, Wes lifted his head again. The pain in his arm subsided, and with it his mind cleared. He blinked grit from his eyes and saw that Benji had not moved from where he was sitting.

"Benji," he whispered; his voice scratchy and dry, "I must teach you something new this morning."

It was a lesson he never wanted to teach again. Knowing he had to, did not lessen the mix of despair and dread that he felt. Wes took a deep breath, letting it out slowly, and closed his eyes. He gave a quick prayer for strength. Then he clenched his teeth and pulled his arm from the soothing water. He looked to Benji who's eyes were two full moons filled with worry, then reached for his hat and clapped it upon his head.

"I need to teach you how to ride my horse."

Wes spent the morning showing Benji how to get up onto the saddle of his mare, then how to get back off again. He made Benji practice this over and over until the boy growled in exasperation. He also showed Benji how to stroke her nose the way she liked it, and how to inspect her hooves to prevent her from getting lame. Wes' arm throbbed through the whole of it, but he focused on the pain so that he could ignore the sadness squeezing his heart.

He reminded himself that things were different this time. Benji was not Peter. He knew this needed to be done before the infection took his mind from him, but it was still hard all the same. Fortunately, Benji was a quick learner, and took to all that he was taught after only a few tries. Satisfied that he had the hang of things, Wes nodded up at Benji, then lifted the reins.

"Now I will show you the way to get her to move. You don't need to speak to her so that is good. Just lead her with your knees and with this." He put the reins in Benji's hand, and showed him how to guide the mare with his knees. He led his horse around, and directed Benji on how to turn her left, turn her right; how to get her to stop. It took most of the morning, but Wes was not so focused on the time he was wasting. Not anymore.

I won't be keeping my promise to you after all, Ruthie.

Wes hesitated on what he was about to say, but when he glanced over to Benji, the boy was already staring at him. That same odd expression on his unreadable face. Wes cleared his throat.

"Benji...If something happens to me, I want you to get on this mare and ride to the east. Just keep going in that direction, away from the city, and maybe, the Lord willing, you will find someone like me. There are good farmers to the east. Good people. Even so, be cautious lad. For there is so much evil in this world. Hopefully someone will take you in. Keep you safe. It will have to do...it will have to do..." Wes touched his left arm gingerly. He could feel the heat of it through the fabric of his shirt. He didn't bother to put on his jacket, as it felt too tight on his arm.

"Wuh," Benji called as he slid off the horse like he'd been doing it his whole life. Emotion returned to his face, and he looked up at Wes with his large worried moon eyes.

"It's alright. I'm just being cautious." Wes' tongue burned. It would surely turn black if he kept lying like this. "It always feels better at night. The sickness quiets down and doesn't hurt so much when it's not in the sun. The pain subsides, but still the infection spreads. I just wish I could do more for you..."

I think you would have really liked this boy, Ruth. He's such a good lad.

The boy's fingers touched his lips, and Wes opened his eyes. He hadn't realized that he closed them. Why was he on the ground? His head was foggy and his vision clouded. He shivered from a sudden chill in the air.

"Wuh."

"What is it, Peter?"

The boy stared at him for a moment, then pulled at his arm to help him up.

"Alright, alright," Wes said, finding his feet. Lord, he was tired. When did he last sleep? Where was his jacket? Fingers patted his chest and Wes opened his eyes. His thoughts cleared, and he saw Benji standing next to the mare.

"Benji? What are you doing?" Benji tapped the mare's flank, then walked over and brought his fingers up to touch Wes' lips.

"I can't tell you her name."

"Wuh."

"Because she doesn't have a name. I never bothered to name her."

Benji looked confused. He turned and looked at the mare, then walked over to her, patted her flank, and returned to place fingers on Wes' lips again.

"Benji, she doesn't have a name." The world around Benji seemed to shift and tilt. In the distance, trees swayed upon the earth. "I never named her."

"Wuh." Wes lifted fingers to his forehead and realized the skin there was dripping with sweat.

"Why? Because she's just a stupid plow horse. I never saw a reason to name her back then, and now..." Wes lifted his bleary eyes to look at Peter, then looked past him to the horse. Sensing his stare, she turned to face him, and gave him a knowing wink. "Now, I hate her."

Peter stared at him, utterly confused. Then his hands moved in a flurry of fingers dancing against his chest, his mouth, the horse's chest, Wes' mouth. Wes restrained his hands to stop them from fluttering.

"Listen, Peter..." The boy yanked his hands free of Wes' grasp. He was suddenly angry, but tears also filled his eyes.

"Wuh! Wuh!" Wes was too tired to make sense of this anymore.

"If you want her to have a name, then I reckon you can go ahead and give her a name. I don't care anymore." Wes turned from the two of them, and stumbled back towards the farmhouse. It looked different from what he remembered. Was Ruth still in there sleeping? Was Ruth still in there alive?

Wes slumped against the well, and sank his arm back into the bucket of water, drenching his shirt. His mind cleared, and his pain subsided. He used his good hand to splash water on his face, then sought out the position of the sun. It was late afternoon already! Where had the time gone?

"Benji!" Wes called out, and immediately the boy was at his side. "We need to work up the fire again and get ready for the night. The sun's path is growing short. The nights devour the day like the wicked vanquish the light. We don't have enough wood to survive total darkness. We won't be able to manage it!" The world tilted, and Wes felt himself pitch to the side; the bucket spilling out beneath him. He panted, finding it hard to breathe, and hugged the bucket for support. Benji watched him for a long time, his face unreadable. Then he got up, and went to collect more wood for the fire.

Wes watched the boy work, and as the sun got lower, the pain ebbed into a low ache. His mind cleared fully, and he was able to get to his feet with only a little dizziness. He walked over to a large fallen branch, and broke it up into a more manageable size for burning. When Benji saw that Wes was helping, he made hand gestures towards the garden. Wes nodded, and Benji went to forage for more leathery beans.

It seemed to Wes that a strange new form of communication was forming between the two of them. Benji made his gestures, and Wes knew exactly what he was trying to say. He doubted it would always be this easy between them. If only Ruth was there to spend some time with the boy and teach him properly. Such things were no longer possible. Wes felt conflicted between the reality of his situation, and what he longed for his situation to be. Being around Benji made him profoundly yearn to see Daniel again.

He's barely thirteen!

Ruth said that once. Thirteen was that strange place between child and adult, when a boy needs his father to show him the ways of a man. Wes wondered what Daniel looked like. Did the scar on his face fade over time? Would he have even recognized Wes if they met again? If he did, would he talk to Wes, or simply walk away?

When Jethro died, Ruth lost the will to eat. Wes pleaded with her, seeing the way her ribs jutted out under her dress, but it did little good. Eventually he took to feeding her since she wouldn't feed herself. He asked why she was doing this. He asked if she wanted to kill herself. She acted as though she did not hear him.

She was so lost in the second sight, it was as though she was in a constant memory spell. Her father, dead over a week, haunted her every night from beyond the veil. He told her all about what became of Daniel. How proud Jethro was of him. How the boy did not even understand the depth of his own wickedness.

"He's barely thirteen!" Ruth cried out in her sleep as the phantom of her father beguiled her. "Why do you find such joy in his destruction?"

The descent into madness did not take her long. She would often sick up any food Wes managed to get in her. She fought to stay awake; terrified of her dreams, then collapsed exhausted at all hours without warning. He woke to her weeping in the middle of the night while she begged for him to go bring Daniel back to her. Then, as he packed his things to leave, she demanded he not leave her; terrified to be without him.

Ruth blamed herself for failing Daniel; Wes' own insecurities reflected back to him in her words. She said that her father hid the truth from her somehow, tricking her to believe that Daniel was happier without them in his life. This deception ended with his death.

"If only you could see our son as I see him in my dreams," she ranted in the night; her eyes wide and crazed as they reflected the moonlight. "Nothing hidden from me now. Nothing! I see it there...the monster...it sleeps inside him. It sees with his eyes! Yes! It talks with his tongue! Oh Lord, our sweet boy...oh...oh... Wesley! Wesley! He's a dragon! A horrible, disfigured dragon! Oh, Daniel...no! He's not our son! He's not our son!"

She tore at her clothes and pulled out her hair. She rolled about the floor, and screamed in agony. She mourned in a way Wes did not think was possible from her, and it terrified him.

This is a window into Hell, and Ruth is lost somewhere inside.

Through all this turmoil, little Peter became an afterthought to both of them. He would reach for his mother, desperate for her attention, and it was as though he wasn't even there. In some rare moments, her mind would clear. Ruth would sit, with her youngest son cradled in her arms, and kiss away his tears. Then in an instant, she would fall into sudden trances. One moment she might be talking to Peter or cleaning their home, the next moment Wes would find her standing with her face slack and eyes vacant. She'd remain in one place without moving for hours. Her mind would slip away without warning, and sink through holes formed in this web of reality; falling back into her private torment. Her vision grew cloudy due to her not blinking. Phantoms danced across her dull eyes, and anguish bled from her heart.

She pulled out her hair until large bald spots formed on her head. Her remaining hair grew thin and brittle. She took to whispering under her breath, and held her lady totem close to her lips. She scratched thoughtlessly at her skin, producing scabs on her arms and legs and all over her face. Black scales overtook her face, and the scales on her arms cracked open; oozing watery blood.

The last time she spoke to Wes, was the day they lost Peter. Nothing brought her back after that. While he previously thought it difficult to keep up with her care, it quickly grew to be impossible. She soiled her clothing without knowing, and sat in it for hours until Wes was able to tend to her. Between bringing in the harvest, caring for their animals, and constantly checking on an invalid wife, Wes had no time to reflect on what he needed. He had no time to grieve.

He watched helplessly as Ruth's cheeks hollowed out, and her eyes sank into their sockets. She started to resemble a skeleton covered in oily skin. Her new appearance horrified Wes and haunted his dreams. She was no longer his wife. She was just a creature that breathed, and existed. Still, losing her terrified Wes. He kept reminding himself that she was still so young. She could overcome this if she would just try!

"Stay with me, Ruth. Don't go! Don't go." Her mind took residence in a place Wes could not reach. He dribbled water or broth into her mouth with a spoon, and Ruth would swallow it down reflexively. She never woke up again. She did not move, she did not cry. She didn't make a sound but to breathe fast and shallow through her baby-bird mouth. Days passed, and Wes went half mad isolated as he was in this cocoon of loss and suffering. It was then that he decided to bring Daniel back home to her. This gave him purpose. Finally, he had something to do.

Wes traveled to the neighboring farm, and implored them to look after Ruth so that he could retrieve her son, and bring him home to her. He offered his meager lot of chickens, and his single pig in exchange for her care. When their oldest daughter agreed to help him, he could not stop himself from hugging her in profound relief. Secretly, he knew that Ruth would probably not survive till he got back home, but he could not stand by and watch her die anymore. Perhaps she would hold on long enough for him to bring Daniel back. She already survived longer than he thought possible in the state she was in.

Wes knew he was running from her, but also knew he was running towards something he was afraid to face. The day he left, he felt like he was being freed from a prison. He tried to not think about it, for guilt already consumed him over the death of his youngest son. There wasn't room for any more. He told himself that he had no choice. He needed to bring Daniel home. And if Daniel refused to come, Wes would find a way. No matter what laid before him, Wes left his home determined he would return with Daniel at his side.

"Keep an eye on things," Wes said as he reached and clumsily ran a hand over Benji's chestnut hair. Lord, but he felt exhausted. And so cold! He moved closer to the fire, and savored its heat on his face. "Wake me if something happens."

"Wuh." A word that conveyed the depth of his worry. Benji did not like to be alone.

Wes closed his eyes, and immediately felt his mind spinning, swimming, drifting. Sleep took hold of him in seconds.

Then he felt Peter tapping at his arms urgently. Wes lifted his hat, and squinted up at his son who was leaning over him, with a worried expression on his face. In his hand, he clutched a wishbone of all things.

"Whadissit?" Wes asked hazily. Everything looked blurry; unfocused. Why was he shivering?

Lord, he was *so* tired. Nothing else mattered but sleep.

"Wuh!" Peter said.

He sounded scared.

A sound.

A noise.

A voice.

A whisper.

Wes opened his eyes again, not realizing that he closed them.

His gaze slid all about as he tried to locate the source of the sound.

Whispering from all directions. Were they the ghosts of his dreams?

Wes closed his eyes again.

Peter shook him, less gently than before, and pain shot down Wes' arm. He hissed through his teeth and lifted his head.

"Wha...whaissid? Isstirred." Peter swam in and out of focus. Then his son lifted a stick in his hand, and used it to draw letters into the dirt where Wes could see them.

He looked at them, blinking, but his mind could not comprehend their meaning.

E-V-E

"Wha dis? Ye wanta nameda horsse?"

For some reason, this made Peter angry. He used the stick to swat Wes on the leg.

"Hey! Hey hey hey, don't dotha now. Don..." Wes swallowed. When was the last time he drank something?

He opened his eyes.

The boy was shaking him.

The boy was crying.

The boy looked scared.

In his hands he clutched a broken wishbone.

"Getda Word, lad. I readja dabook." Sleep overtook him again, and with it visions of a painted sky. At first Wes thought it was the orange glow of the evening sun, but then he looked down into the valley, and saw the capital laid out below him on fire. Every inch of it burned. The screams of its residents reaching his ears, from so many miles away.

Chapter Nine

But you are not in darkness, brothers,
for that day to surprise you like a thief.
For you are all children of light, children of the day.
We are not of the night or of the darkness.
- 1 Thessalonians 5:4-5 ESV

"It's alright, Peter, she will not hurt you." Peter clung to his leg the moment they approached the plow horse, but Wes urged him forward. The boy was well into his second year and Wes thought to teach him some simple skills with the horse that he could build upon as he aged. But Peter always seemed apprehensive to try anything new. The mare was especially challenging to him, as Peter avoided interaction with all of the animals in their homestead.

"I am going to place you in the saddle. There you go. No, don't cry. You need to hold on here. Yes...like that. Now, hold on, I will walk her around for you."

"No, daddy!" Peter cried the moment Wes let go of him. He immediately tried to get off.

"No! No...don't try to get down without my help. Never try to get on this horse or off of her without my help. You could fall. It's not safe without me. Here...let's just sit on her for a spell. You can touch her fur. Yes, Peter. See? There is nothing to be afraid of."

Urgent hands clutched at his arm, and Wes jolted awake. How long had he been asleep? The world spun the moment he tried to sit up. But it was still dark, and the pain was dull. Wes rubbed his palms across his eyes, then placed his father's hat on his head. He glanced around, then looked down at Benji, and was alarmed to find that the boy looked utterly terrified.

"What is it? What's wrong, lad? Did you hear something?" The moment the words left him, Wes realized they were no longer alone. A form walked out of the darkness and took shape in the firelight. Wes reached for his gun.

"Now, now, no need for that. Not for one such as me." The man was lank and tall, and riding atop a young brown stallion. He had sharp dark eyes, and black hair that feathered out by his chin, complimenting his thin mustache and goatee. Wes was amazed at how pale his face looked. With his high cheekbones and harsh nose, the man resembled some ghostly bird. His face carried the mark upon his forehead, but the scales themselves appeared to be...painted. They were painted in a way that matched his pale skin.

Wes could not help but gape, for the man appeared to be wearing some sort of fancy suit as if he were a preacher man, but the cloth was all white. White jacket, white gloves, white vest, white button down shirt, white brimmed hat with a strange flat top, white pants, and a white pressed cravat. Even his shoes were polished white. With how fancy he looked, there was no mistaking that this man was from the capital. He looked completely out of place in this wilderness.

"Greetings, traveler!" The man called down to them and raised his hand in a wave. "Do you mind if I share your firelight? I got caught off guard on my way east and found myself out in this damnable darkness."

Wes frowned up at the man. He slept long enough to know that the sun had not just left the sky. How was it that this fellow seemed able to navigate the darkness without a light source, and come out unscathed? Wes' mind felt fuzzy, like he was coming out of a memory spell, but he was certain the man was lying. It was too dark to see the color of his tongue, but it mattered not. For it wouldn't change Wes's answer. No matter the nature of the man, Wes would not send a stranger out to fend for his life in the full darkness of night.

"You're welcome to stay," Wes said and the man's lips stretched into a smile.

"Wonderful! So kind of you, sir!" As the man climbed down from his horse, Wes examined the scales that fanned out on the man's forehead with dumbfounded fascination. He had never seen someone actually paint their sin as a way to camouflage it. It didn't occur to him that such a thing was possible. If the brim of his hat was set the right way, the man would look like his face was untarnished like Wes. And why all the white? Did it mean something? It was an odd choice of outfit for miles of dusty wilderness. The man approached, and Wes peered up at him from under the brim of his hat. He was tall and rail thin, like a skeletal specter with a pale death mask for a face.

"Why are you out so late at night, stranger?" Wes glanced down at Benji, who pressed up against him and clutched the hem of his jacket. He could feel the boy's little heart thrumming in his chest. Benji's stare did not waiver from the man in white.

"Ah, well, you see I am on urgent business from the capital. My paperwork is in order if you care to inspect it." The man lifted a gloved hand, poised to extract whatever documents he carried from an inner pocket of his jacket. Wes ignored the gesture.

"Urgent business from the capital. Are you employed by the Father's men?" Wes tried not to sound eager for information. The man shared his smile too freely to be trusted, and his eyes were black from lid to lid. Wes sensed a wickedness in him far greater than his face seemed to reveal. The cunning in his eyes and on his smile reminded Wes of Jethro, who was riddled with sin sickness the last he saw the man. It was an anomaly he couldn't explain. Something was wrong here.

"Ah, but sir...did you not hear?" The man did not sit, and his smile did not slip. "Old Father is dead." Wes hesitated. He felt Benji trembling and placed a protective arm around the boy. The man's black eyes took in the exchange, and his lips peeled back to add teeth to his uncanny smile.

"You have a good boy there," he said softly. His words were careful and calculated. They hinted at more meaning than what was said, and Wes felt a pang of unease.

Benji grabbed onto his left hand, causing needles to shoot up his arm, but it faded quickly. Wes welcomed the pain, for it helped his head to clear. He dare not lose consciousness in the presence of this man. He offered a thin, unfeeling smile, and gestured towards the fire.

"Come join us by the firelight." Wes made sure to indicate a place directly across the fire from where he was sitting. "There is a well over yonder, but I regret that I don't have food to offer you."

"Oh, not to worry, not to worry," the man said, as he tied off his horse. The animal seemed indifferent to all of them. The man pulled open a saddle bag, and extracted a canvas sack along with a bundle of wooden legs. He glanced over at Wes, his smile never leaving him. "As you can see, I brought plenty of my own. Does...the boy want some?"

He wiggled the sack invitingly, but Benji did not make a move towards it. Such a good lad.

"He must not be hungry, stranger. Eat your own, and honor our fire."

The man stepped forward, and lifted the bundle of legs. He flicked out the bundle with a practiced flourish, and it gave shape to form a three legged stool. The man then placed it on the ground back where his horse was tied, and faced them over the fire while he hugged along the darkness. His pale face: like a specter among the shadows.

Wes and Benji watched as the man opened his sack, and extracted parcels of steamed vegetables, chunks of bread, and morsels of roasted meat. The smell was intoxicating as neither Wes nor Benji ate anything since the turkey they had the night before, but both didn't move from their place. The man picked at his dinner, smiling at them through each bite, but he only ate a little of his spread. When he finished with his meal, he dabbed at his lips with a folded cloth.

"My, what a fine meal, but I am quite full. Are you sure you don't want any?" The man lifted an eyebrow in their direction, but Wes shook his head.

"Ah well. The animals will find it then." He tossed the remainder into the dust and closed up his sack. Benji looked over to the bread laying on the ground, then went back to observing the man in white.

"What is your name?" Wes asked and narrowed his eyes. He didn't like to see food wasted, even if he didn't trust it enough to eat it.

"They call me Chancy. Elder Chancy among the court, but we are all friends out here. Charmed to make your acquaintance, mister..." His speech was as fancy as his clothing.

"Wes."

"Mister Wes. Pleasure to meet you sir." Chancy tipped the brim of his hat with a gloved hand, and glanced down at Benji, but Wes didn't offer his name. Instead, he leaned over to feed another thick branch into the fire. He wanted to get a better look at this pale skinned fellow. Chancy reached into his coat pocket to pull out a flat long tin. He squeezed his hand and the top popped open on a spring. A row of neatly rolled cigars were held within.

"Do you care if I smoke, sir?"

"Seek his will in all you do," Wes replied. A test to see if the man had some understanding of the Word. For even the wicked should know the nature of what they betray. If the man knew the verse, he gave no indication. He just smiled that same smile, and extracted one of the cigars from the tin. He then pulled out a different metal box, much smaller than the first, peeled back its lid, and held it up to his cigar. With a flick of his thumb, a small fire appeared from the box and Chancy touched it to the cigar tip as he puffed it to life. Wes was stunned by this new trickery.

"You practice witchcraft," he accused, but Chancy just chuckled, and shook his head.

"Not at all, not at all. It's just a relic from the past. Some of us city folk still have a few of these laying around. It's called a lighter."

"A lighter," Wes repeated and looked at the box resting in the man's gloved palm.

"Would you like to see it?" Chancy asked, holding it up between them. Wes couldn't help himself. He let go of Benji, and got to his feet. Then he moved to the other side of the fire and approached the strange man in his strange clothing.

"Wuh!" Benji called out to him. The word laced with anxiety.

"I'm just looking at it. I'll be alright, lad" Wes said. Chancy watched calmly as Wes approached him, but relented the lighter when Wes reached for it. Seeing it up close, he realized that the metal of the casing had precise scroll-work scratched into it as a type of decoration. Wes marveled at it. The only relics he's ever seen in his life were his father's revolver still carried on his hip, and the other relic from his father-in-law that he kept tucked away in his pack. He wondered if the capital was full of relics like this. He handed the lighter over to Chancy, who slid it smoothly back into his jacket pocket. His black eyes then shifted over to Benji.

"What is your name, boy?" He asked. Benji lowered his head, and cupped his ears with his hands. He seemed to shrink into himself like he wanted to hide. Wes did not fully understand why Benji was so afraid of this man, when he recently lived with what became of his mother, but he didn't doubt the lad had his reasons. He had to also admit, he didn't like the way Chancy said the word 'boy'. He spoke the word slow and drawn out as though he was savoring the sound of it.

"He is none of your concern," Wes said, as he returned to his place next to the lad. Benji settled in close to him again, and Wes watched Chancy from across the fire. There was a stretch of silence between them, and in the stronger firelight, Wes could see something tucked away deep in Chancy's eyes. Something dangerous and hungry, like a wolf. When Chancy smiled, the wolf did not go away.

"So, not my concern. Is he your son, then?" Wes hesitated to respond, and Benji lifted his head to look at him.

"No...he is not. But he is in my care. I look after the lad."

"Ah, I see," Chancy ran fingertips along his mustache to smooth it down. "Well here's a thought. Perhaps I could entice you to release your burden to me. I would gladly take charge of the boy for you. We have great opportunities in the capital for such children like him. How much would it cost to buy him?"

Benji sat up, as he stared in shock at the man in white. Then, slowly, he turned his gaze on Wes. The fear in his eyes said more than words ever could. Benji must know that Wes cared for him, even though it's only been a few days. His fear must be due to Wes' sickness. Having to choose between a wicked man and a sickly one was not a choice any child should be forced to make. But when he really looked into Benji's eyes, Wes realized these weren't the thoughts that haunted him. Somehow he knew that Benji's fear was because he thought Wes might not want him anymore. Considering how sick he was, maybe caring for a child was just too much of a burden to undertake. Wes refused to let Benji live in this fear for another second.

"I'm not interested," he said flatly. No amount of money was enough to give this child over to slavery. Benji seemed to relax a little, but the fear didn't fully leave his eyes.

He's been through so much, Ruth. It must be hard for him to trust.

"Such a pity," Chancy said as he examined Benji thoughtfully. He licked his lips with a tongue the color of ink. A liar's tongue. Wes scowled at him openly.

"Maybe you will reconsider," Chancy went on, unaware of Wes' disgust. His hands darted about as he spoke, and his cigar carved out zig-zag trails of smoke through the still air between them, "when I tell you that we will keep him safe in the heart of the capital. I assure you, we can place the boy in the most opulent surroundings. He will never know hunger again. He will receive the best education. We can dress him in the finest of clothes."

Chancy's black eyes shifted as he took in the whole of Benji's bedraggled outfit.

"A few pairs of shoes as well. The long and short of it, Mister Wes, is that we can give this boy his best opportunities. He will benefit greatly from our...guidance."

Again that hunger flashed across Chancy's wolf eyes, and he offered Benji a small private smile. His tongue slid along the seam of his lips. Not only was it black, it was forked like a snake.

"I am not interested, and he is not for sale," Wes insisted with a voice as hard as a stone, but Chancy seemed unconvinced. He looked away from Benji, and instead examined the night.

"Have you heard them yet?" Chancy asked casually. When Wes did not respond, he turned his black eyes upon the other man. "The whispers of the damned?"

"I have," Wes said cautiously. His eyes narrowed while he considered this new angle.

"They long for him. They want to tear his flesh right off of his bones while he screams in agony. Can't you feel them, Mister Wes? Can't you feel how desperately they want to taste the flesh of your wayward child?"

"Speak of this no more or you can leave this firelight right now!" Wes covered Benji's ears and glared at the man. The nerve of this wretched being to say such things in front of a child!

"I understand. It's as you say," Chancy conceded, head bowed, and hands raised in supplication. Then he lifted his eyes and stared at Wes with such an extreme intensity. "But should you happen into the capital, sir. Please reconsider my offer. It would be a simple writ of sale. Seek out the guards, request a property exchange with the Elders. I can write you a voucher right now. Your boy is worth his weight in silver. The exchange will keep you comfortable for at least a year, perhaps even..."

Wes stood and in an instant his revolver was in his hand. Chancy immediately ducked his head and held his arms up in surrender.

"Okay! Okay, Mister Wes, please! I will not speak of it again. I swear."

"I'm sure you do," Wes spit out through clenched teeth. "That liar's tongue probably swears a lot." Wes glanced down at Benji and saw that the boy was riveted. His moon eyes transfixed upon Wes' gun. Wes quickly returned his revolver to its holster, and sat down next to the boy. He glared across the fire to where Chancy sat with his fancy white clothes and his stupid little stool. Anger bubbled inside of him in a way he had not felt since he had his hands on Jethro's throat. Something about this man brought out Wes' own sin. If Benji was not there witnessing the whole exchange, Wes might have pulled his gun's trigger.

Silence stretched on between them as Chancy puffed nervously at his cigar and Wes glared at him from across the fire. Benji relaxed next to Wes, and after some time, he took to drawing letters in the dirt. E-V-E. He wrote the word, brushed it away, then wrote it again. E-V-E.

Wes knew he might not have another chance like this one to find out about the city he was about to enter. He considered the other man, and Chancy smiled at him nervously.

"Tell me about the capital," Wes said at last, breaking the silence between them.

"What do you want to know?" Chancy asked, perking up at the change of subject. Wes was not deceived by his feigned politeness, for the wolf never seemed to leave his eyes.

He knows I'm sick, Ruth. If he wasn't such a coward, I would surely be dead.

"Tell me about the Father."

"Old Father is dead." Chancy spread his hands in a helpless shrug. The wolf inside him was an opportunist. This man played the long game. He would wait and bide his time until a moment presented itself. Wes would not give it to him.

"As you said." Wes said patiently. "So who has replaced him in command?"

"Why, the Guardian Son of course." Chancy's face remained placid, but a twinkle of curiosity entered his black wolf eyes.

"The Guardian Son." First Old Father, then the Guardian Son. Surely this wasn't Jethro and Daniel. How could Jethro gain power over a whole city? But of course, Wes knew how. He knew how cunning Jethro could be. Was it possible?

"Have you...met the Guardian Son?"

"But of course!" Chancy lifted his chin proudly. "I am an Elder! A direct member of his High Council!" Strange for a man of such high esteem to be sent out into the wilderness on an undisclosed errand. Wes considered, then decided to take a risk.

"Tell me something, and answer me true. Does this Guardian Son have a scar that runs down the length of his face?" Wes used his thumb and slid it along his face from the corner of his left eye down to his mouth. Beside him, Benji watched their exchange intently, his face expressionless. Chancy furrowed his brows in confusion.

"No...he doesn't have anything like that. Not a single scar on his body." Seeing that there was no cunning in Chancy's eyes, Wes chose to believe him.

So it's not our Daniel, Ruth. Praise the Lord.

Wes quietly fell into his thoughts, as he tried to remember exactly how Daniel obtained the scar that marked his face. The past was unraveling, but Wes was sure if he thought hard enough, he would be able to remember. Thin as muddy water. Wes yearned for his water bucket. His arm throbbed to the beat of his heart.

"Well, if you'll excuse me," Chancy said and abruptly stood, "I plan to retrieve my bedroll, and lay down for the night." He stubbed out the remains of his cigar, and folded his stool away.

"Very well," Wes replied. "I reckon I'll keep watch." It was Chancy he planned on watching.

Benji brought the saddle blanket over and laid it next to Wes so that he could use Wes' lap again as his pillow. Chancy pulled a bedroll off of his horse, and gave them a small smile when he returned to the fire. He unrolled the bedding far back from the flames, then removed his hat and jacket to use as a pillow for his head.

"I want you to know, I meant no disrespect with what I said earlier."

"Good night, Mister Chancy,' Wes said, concluding their conversation. Chancy nodded, the smile not leaving his lips, and laid down to sleep. Wes stroked Benji's hair absently as he glared at the other man intently. Even though he seemed to be sleeping, Wes did not believe it was so. Either way, the threat of this other man seemed to strengthen Wes. His head was clearer than it had been in days and he felt stronger too.

Chancy made clear to Wes how much danger Benji was truly in. It would be so easy to take advantage of a child who lacked the words to cry for help. It made Wes realize how vulnerable Benji was, and it scared him. He didn't know if he could endure losing another child to this wretched world.

Chancy shifted, and for a brief moment his face seemed to shimmer before Wes' eyes. For just an instant, his face was as black as the night that surrounded him, and took on the shape of something monstrous that Wes could not identify. Before he could comprehend what he was seeing, the face shifted back to the pale skin he had before.

Wes rubbed his eyes. Was he seeing things again? He stared at Chancy for a while, trying to see past his pale face. The creature Wes caught a glimpse of coincided with the level of evil this man seemed to possess, but he was somehow able to wear a disguise in the same way he used paint to cover the scales on his face.

Suddenly a sound came from inside the night, and Wes jerked his head in its direction. He peered intently into the darkness, and watched as a figure cautiously stepped into view at the edge of the firelight. Its dark eyes glowed as the animal turned his head toward Wes. It was a coyote. How could this animal survive roaming the night?

Wes realized suddenly how quiet it was. There were no whispers; no beckoning calls for him to vanquish the light. Wes did not have the second sight, but he could at least sense the hunger of those sinners that lingered nearby. Strangely, Wes could not feel anything of the sort in the darkness around them. The only thing that was a threat, slept across from him and shared his fire.

The coyote sniffed the air, then crept forward while keeping his focus on the sleeping Chancy. The moment he could, he snatched up the meat that was discarded from the other man's meal and fled back into the night. What was it about Chancy that made a coyote prefer the evils of the darkness over the safety of the firelight? Wes stared at the other man for a long time, but that strange second face did not appear again.

Chapter Ten

No sooner are they planted, no sooner are they sown,
no sooner do they take root in the ground,
than he blows on them and they wither,
and a whirlwind sweeps them away like chaff.
- Isaiah 40:24 NIV

"Sadly, I must part ways with you sir, for my destination lies in the east." Chancy smiled as he placed his hat just so upon his head. He rose before sunlight, having only slept a few hours, and collected his things to depart with little flourish. Wes was doing the same, as he dared not stay in place another night when someone so dangerous knew where they were.

Wes already felt the burden of the injury to his arm, as though his body knew of the coming sun, but it seemed lesser somehow. He dared not hope that he was improving. He looked into Chancy's black eyes, and touched the brim of his hat. He hoped to never see this man again.

"Safe travels to you." When Chancy climbed onto his horse, the animal brayed and woke Benji. He sat up, rubbing his eyes, and blinked up at the wicked man. Chancy gave him a smile and a wink, then with a wave turned his horse and trotted off in the direction of the sun. Wes frowned as he watched Chancy go.

Surely he can't be so wicked if he is able to travel in sunlight. Right, Ruth?

When Chancy was all but out of sight, Wes went to the well to let the bucket down for water one last time. Benji was at his side without asking; hauling the bucket over the edge of the well for him

"I can get it. You don't need to nurse me," Wes said, feeling annoyed. He removed enough clothing to expose his arm and examined the cut. It seemed as red as the day before. It was not any better, but did not seem any worse either. The swelling might have improved, he could not be sure. Wes flexed his fingers slowly, then noticed Benji watching him. He looked worried, and Wes wondered if he was afraid of encountering Chancy.

"It's not safe for you to go east anymore," Wes said and glared in the direction the other man went. "Maybe you could take the mare north…" He trailed off when the sun broke over the horizon and swept across the two of them. The sting of the light was like fire on his skin. He quickly cleaned the wound with water and tried to dress. Benji remained silent, while Wes shrugged into his jacket and looked at his mare. Then he felt fingers on his injured hand, and looked down to see Benji staring at him.

"Wuh."

"It's not so bad. See? The swelling has gone down in my hand."

"Wuh." Wes sighed. Lord, he felt tired. There was too much to do and it all needed done at once.

"We have to put distance between us and this place. There will be no food for us today. We don't have time to hunt for it. Help me with the horse." Wes managed to lift the saddle onto her back, and Benji helped to buckle the straps in place. When Wes finished securing his pack, he noticed Benji revisiting their spent fire. He picked something up, and brought it over to Wes; revealing two parts of a wishbone.

"Oh, it's broken. That's too bad," Wes said indifferently, but Benji was not finished. He stepped forward, grabbing at Wes' jacket, and stuffed the broken bones into his pocket.

"Wuh."

"Oh. Sure, I can hold onto that for you." Benji placed a hand on the pocket and closed his eyes. He bowed his head and started to pray. Wes should have never told him about that stupid superstition. His impatience grew by the second, but he didn't want to discourage Benji from praying, so he remained where he stood and waited.

Wes examined Benji's placid face, calm and lost in prayer, and found himself focusing on every feature in hopes that he will not forget them. He did not want any memories of this boy stolen by the thief of time. When at last Benji opened his eyes, his prayer completed, Wes quickly looked away and pretended to inspect his horse.

"We have spent enough time here," he said without meeting Benji's eyes. "Get up on the mare."

Benji rose and did as he was told. He got onto the saddle with no assistance, and Wes smiled a little, seeing how well the boy did.

He thought of telling Benji about Peter, and what happened to him. He thought of telling Benji about Daniel as well, and how things went wrong between them. But what would the point be of burdening this child with all his grief? It might cause Benji to think less of him. Benji might grow to be ashamed of him.

Instead, Wes climbed into the saddle behind Benji and reached for the reins. With how restless she was, it did not take much to urge his horse into a gallop. They rode on in silence, putting distance between themselves and Chancy. As time passed, Wes drifted into his memories. The further west he rode, the more his mind thought back to the east.

Wes tried to show Daniel the way of the Lord when he was young, but as he got older, Jethro convinced him that prayer was a form of weakness. If a man was strong in his household, he didn't need to ask for anything from the Lord. This sounded sinful to Wes, but Jethro was always so glib. It was hard to dispute his words. Wes would try to object to his father-in-law's teachings, but Jethro would say things to confuse him, and cause him to question his own understanding of the Word.

Jethro explained to Wes that if the boy prayed, or showed any weakness, he was revealing the true nature of his heart. This allowed for others to take advantage of him, thus Jethro was simply protecting him from the world.

"The Word tells us that a man needs to be the rock upon which his house is built," Jethro said to Daniel, "If the man is weak like the shifting sand, well then...what will become of his house?"

When Wes confronted Jethro, insisting the things he taught Daniel were untrue, Jethro looked confused.

"You wish me to go against the teachings of the Word? I thought you were a believer."

Wes would not be swayed. He found the verses in the book and showed Jethro that the foundation of the rock referred to the Christ. Jethro grew angry at Wes' attempts to correct him.

"You look for excuses to explain away your own weakness, but God knows the true nature of what you are, and so does your son." When he said these words, Daniel sat next to him listening.

Thinking on these things as he rode west, brought out a fury in Wes he could not fully understand. The anger he felt carried such intensity, it made him want to strike at something. He wanted to kick his horse into a full run, and let the chill of the air cool the burning of his face. His anger boiled inside of him, and in his mind's eye, all Wes could see was the shame on his son's face when he looked up at Wes.

He's ashamed of me.

"Daniel's going to grow up to be such a fine man," Jethro crooned as he smiled with tar stained teeth. "A rock to build a house upon."

As time passed and they continued to travel, Wes was convinced his arm was feeling better. He was still exhausted; his sleep restless over the past few nights, but he was certain the pain was subsiding. The swelling in his hand was also improving. Wes prayed that the Lord was healing him.

Benji made a noise, and Wes brought his mind back to focus. They faced a large highway that ran perpendicular to them, and as they approached the road, Wes gestured for his mare to stop so he could examine it. The hard packed dirt showed patches of stone slab from a time before knowing. Tracks from horses, men, and wagons going to and fro littered the path.

Wes looked to the north, and saw the road extended straight on into a series of rolling hills where it disappeared from sight. To the south, the path stretched out, then took a sharp turn to the left and continued on toward the west. It seemed to lead directly to the city in the distance, and while the tracks were a testament to the many feet that traveled before him, the extent of highway Wes could see was completely barren. Perhaps this meant that no one wanted to leave the capital under the rule of the Guardian Son. Perhaps this meant they weren't allowed to.

"We will take the highway for now," Wes decided, pointing to the south. "If we spot anyone in the distance, we can step off the path until they pass us by." Benji did not respond. Instead, he seemed to be staring off towards the north, his face flat, and his eyes distant. Wes urged his mare forward, turning her south onto the highway. They only went a few feet in that direction, then Benji suddenly came out of his spell and tried to grab hold of the reins.

"Benji! Stop that now."

"Wuh!" Benji yanked at the reigns and the mare whinnied and stamped her feet about; confused by her instructions.

“Benji, I need to go south. See? It goes west again, just up ahead. Stop trying to take control of the horse!” Anger surged up in Wes again like a white hot iron, and he fought to push it away. Benji jerked at the reins, insisting he take control, and for a brief second Wes considered slapping the boy. But he managed to wrestle his emotions back under control with a growl of frustration.

“Benji! Do as I say!” He shouted, and Benji abruptly swung his leg over the mare's neck and slid off of her. As soon as his feet touched the earth, he took off running in the opposite direction. Wes stared at him in outrage and shock. The nerve of this child!

“Benji, get back here!” Wes yelled after him, but Benji did not even slow. How dare he disobey? Wes was utterly furious. He squeezed the reins so tightly that his hands shook. What had gotten into that boy? Then his arm started to ache, and with the pain came an element of clarity. Wes stared at his shaking hands and realized just how angry he had become. What had gotten into him? He lifted his head, and saw that Benji had stopped running, but was walking briskly up the highway. He didn’t even glance back.

Foolish boy. Foolish foolish boy. It will be dark soon! In an hour or two the sun will set and Benji will find himself in the night with no food, no fire, and a whole host of evil wanting to tear him apart. Then Wes remembered what Chancy said about the damned, and a cold sobriety tempered the storm of anger inside of him. He turned his mare around, and galloped north to intercept the boy. It only took him minutes to reach the lad, and he drove his horse to step in front of Benji to block his path.

“Benji, we need to go south. I need to go to the capital.” Benji looked up at Wes, and he could see hurt and anger in the boy's eyes. His jaw was stubbornly set. His mouth was drawn down in a firm line, and he lifted his hand to point toward the north.

“Benji...”

“Wuh!” Benji dropped down, knees to chest, and used his finger to draw a word in the dirt.

E-V-E.

“I don’t know what that means. Are you talking about the Word?” Wes asked, thinking of Genesis. Benji let out a growl of frustration and slapped the letters, obscuring them in the dust. Then he stood up once more, and pointed up the highway running north.

“Is this about the horse's name again?” Wes asked dumbly. Benji screamed at the sky. He smacked his own head repeatedly with splayed hands. Then he turned from Wes, and stomped up the road again.

"Hey! Where are you going?" Wes called after him but Benji did not stop or turn around. What on earth was this boy doing? Anger threatened to well up in him again, but Wes forced it away. He closed his eyes and offered a prayer up to God.

Lord, you can not take this burden from me, but you can help me carry it.

Benji went north, and Wes followed behind him. After some time, he conceded to whatever destiny the lad had in store for them. While he longed to get back to his own task of retrieving his son, he thought they might at least find a safe place in these hills for Benji to hide away in while he's gone. Wes urged his mare forward, and rode up alongside the boy.

"Alright, we will do this your way. Up in the saddle with you. Show me where you want to go." Benji smiled, and all his frustration was forgotten. Wes helped him up onto the saddle, and Benji pointed at the road before them. To the north they went. Over time, small structures came into view, dotting the landscape and set back from the road.

They remind me of our homestead, Ruth.

Wes considered approaching one of them for he was desperate for food, but then thought about the risk and consequence. If anyone still lived in any of these homes, they might see Wes approaching. They might think he's a threat. They might have a shotgun or the like, passed down through the generations. They might shoot and ask questions later.

Wes decided against trying, and just kept following Benji's lead. The boy never wavered from his determination to continue north. Wes did not know where they were going, but it seemed like Benji certainly did. He barely noticed the homesteads when they came into view.

As they rode on, they started to climb higher and hills rose up all around them, blending into mountains. The structures also became more plentiful; dotting the low rolling hills with small homes and rough cut barns. Seeing the sun sinking in the west, Wes reconsidered approaching one of these homesteads after all. He did not see any trees among all the brush and rock. There wouldn't be much for him to burn if they were stuck camping in the open.

"Benji, it's getting late. We need to consider..." Wes looked back the way they came and his words trailed off as he took in a full view of the capital with its lights stretched over the distant valley below. It was sprawling and massive.

"How am I ever going to find him in all that mess," he muttered to himself, and Benji turned to look at Wes, then out toward the city. Wes watched him closely.

"You know that I need to go to the capital, but do you understand why?" Benji shrugged, his eyes transfixed on the lights. "Well...I'm looking for someone. My son Daniel. I want to bring him home to his mother. She's...she's not doing so well, and..."

Benji turned his attention back to the road ahead, and pointed to the north. Wes sighed, and pushed his mare forward. For some reason, Benji didn't want to know about Wes' intentions. He puzzled over this as he glanced again to the sky.

"Benji, we need to make camp. I need time to find something that can burn in this place." Benji shook his head, and pointed again. His face was set in that same stubborn expression.

"I understand you want to keep going," Wes said, trying again, "But the hills are high here. We are at the mercy of their shade. We must stop to build a fire." He might as well be talking to himself. At the base of the hills, not far from where they rode, Wes could see the shadows already forming, stretching, reaching out fingers of darkness. Why was he taking direction from a child? Benji was leading them onward to their graves.

Wes looked around, trying to find a place that would potentially offer them some shelter in the night, but the terrain grew uneven; full of dips and peaks making it impossible to locate homesteads that were tucked out of sight from the road. The expanse of earth around them was rocky, showing only loose shale and sparse shrubs. The further they went north, the worse their situation seemed to be.

"Benji," Wes tried again, and the boy shook his head. His expression reflected his determination. Their horse snorted, noticing the shadows stretching long, and Wes could sense her unease. She must feel something that Wes could not. Dark things lingering, and waiting for the night. The mare tossed her head about, voicing her objection in her own way, and Benji leaned over to place soothing strokes on her neck. The gesture made Wes think of Peter; so fearful of horses. He caught the scent of sweet corn ready for harvest.

"No," he said aloud, shaking his head, and squeezed shut his eyes in an effort to push away the memory spell. He did not have time to get lost in the recollection. Suddenly Benji pulled the reins from Wes' hands, and jerked on them to bring the mare to a halt. Wes looked around for a potential threat, but when his eyes fell upon the path before them, he was baffled with what he saw. The road was empty as far as he could see but for a rocking chair that seemed to appear out of nowhere. A woman rocked back and forth upon it, and when she saw Wes was looking at her, she offered him a friendly wave.

"Hello, brother! It's about time you showed up here!"

Chapter Eleven

We know that everyone who has been born of
God does not keep on sinning,
but he who was born of God protects him,
and the evil one does not touch him.
We know that we are from God,
and the whole world lies in the power of the evil one.
-1 John 5:18-19 ESV

"Careful, lad. We don't know what this is about." Wes urged his mare forward at a slow walk, and studied the woman sitting before him. She was very old, judging by her long iron grey hair, and weathered features. Dark in complexion, she was also short and round, but sturdy. Wes realized she only had one arm, for the blue cotton blouse she wore had the right sleeve pinned up to keep it out of the way. It was too dark to make out the details of her face, but Wes could see the glint in her eyes. She peered up at him as he approached her, and nested a pipe between her teeth as though the spot was meant just for it."Howdy." Wes said cautiously.

"Howdy, brother." Her voice was low and hummed in a way that made every word sound like a song. She smiled and her teeth all but glowed against her dark skin.

"You were expecting me sooner, or so you say," Wes said and the woman nodded. He suspected the second sight, but decided to share the truth anyway. "I'm sorry to disappoint you. We did a little sightseeing along the way."

The woman threw back her head and let out a hardy laugh. The rocking chair bucked under her girth, lifting her feet off the ground for a moment, but she leaned forward again, bringing her feet squarely back down to the earth, and pointed a finger at him.

"I suspected as much from you, but not from him. Not from the boy." Wes tilted his head to catch sight of Benji's face, and noticed him wearing a satisfied smile. Sassy went on, her laughter fading into deep chuckles like the distant rolls of thunder. "I'm glad you made it, brother, and just in time too. Now, come down here where I can get a better look at you. My eyes aren't what they used to be."

Wes slid off his horse, who brayed nervously at the encroaching darkness, and reached for Benji, but the boy slid down gracefully on his own. The woman rocked patiently in her chair as she watched them approach her, and as they got closer, Wes noticed that her brown skin also had a crown of black scales running along her hairline and spreading into her hair. Her hands were also black with scales but not beyond the wrists.

"What a handsome pair you are," she declared and pulled her pipe from her teeth. "Just what I expected to see. Lean and fit. Healthy boys, the both of you. Now, come on over here and help me on up out of this chair." Wes helped her to her feet, even though the effort sent bursts of pain radiating down his affected arm. As soon as she was upright, she grabbed hold of the hand Wes offered her, and turned it over in her own.

"Still swollen, but a bit better I see." Wes pulled his hand back as though she had burned him. Exactly how much did this woman know? He glanced down at Benji, but again the boy just stood with that satisfied grin on his face.

"Don't mind him, he just likes being right."

"Who are you? How do you know all of this?" Wes demanded. The woman bent to retrieve a gnarled cane tucked in alongside her chair, then hobbled toward Benji; showing the stiffness of her age. She wasn't much taller than the boy, but twice his width.

"Help me with my shawl, lad. I grow cold in this twilight." Benji immediately brushed past the woman to retrieve a shawl draped over her chair, and she used the opportunity to inspect him more closely. When he returned to her, she disguised her curiosity with a sudden interest in brushing the dust from her tan-hide skirts. Benji draped the thick woven shawl around her shoulders, and the woman smiled at him.

"That's a good boy. Such a sweet lad you are. Gather up your horse now, sonny, and as for you brother, I ask that you take up my chair. The hour grows late, and we must be on our way."

"On our way where?" Wes asked, for his instincts made him wary. His eyes remained intent on shadowed places. This might be an ambush. Men or wicked things might lie in wait to spring a trap. If Chancy was willing to buy Benji for such a high amount, what would stop this woman from selling him for the same? "I reckon we're going to stay right here."

Benji looked at Wes as though he just sprouted horns, but the woman only chuckled. Her whole body shook with her laughter; even the quiet ones.

"Brother, I understand. Who am I to you but some strange woman with a walking stick. But I reckon those shadows over yonder are full of all kinds of nasty little things, and I am not interested in letting them sink their claws into this young lad. So I ask you kindly, to reconsider trusting this old woman and her walking stick. Besides..." She hobbled closer to Wes, and spoke in a low humming voice. "Those nasty things aren't the only wicked that's here tonight. You got a dark seed in you, brother, and it's starting to grow. An angry seed; rooted in deep."

A cold chill raised the hair on Wes' head, and stilled the words on his tongue. Exactly how much did this woman know? When she spoke of an angry seed starting to grow...was this related to Wes' sudden short temper? Certainly not. He was just frustrated. Tired.

"Bring that mare over here, boy. We must get on with it while we still have light to live by." She hobbled off the road, and into the wilderness. Benji picked up the mare's tether, then gave Wes a small shrug as he followed after her. Where exactly was she leading them? Seeing no other option, Wes picked up her rocking chair and slung it across his back. He caught up to Benji, and followed behind the woman as she hummed to herself and hobbled along. There was no doubt she had the second sight. She might even be stronger in it than poor Ruth. Wes did not completely discredit the possibility of an ambush, but this woman's friendly nature was inviting, and she was difficult not to like. He felt like he wanted to trust her.

"Tell me why you are doing this. Why are you helping us?" The land before them stretched out with crags and dips but the woman took a sure path clear of pitfalls. They both followed closely behind her.

"Why?" The woman asked, pausing her song, "Because it's what the Lord wanted me to do."

"Are you an angel then?" Wes asked skeptically, and the woman let out a guffaw of laughter. Wes glanced around nervously. She was so loud, and it was getting so dark.

"No, brother Wes, I am not an angel. Like you, I am simply a child of God. That means I have a duty to serve him, and what the Lord wants right now is for me to take care of you and your boy there." Wes tried not to look startled at hearing her say his name. Could the second sight reveal so much? Indeed, it must.

As they walked along, Wes scanned all around them for potential signs of threat. The sun was just a sliver above the mountains, and everything carried the burden of long dark shadows. Were those whispers he heard? Did he see movement over there?

"How much farther are we going to go? There is nothing out here," Wes complained, and the woman gave a low hum.

"Your eyes deceive you, brother, for you hide away from the spirit. But your boy can tell you, salvation is upon us." Wes glanced over at Benji, and Benji in turn looked up at him. Wes let the question linger in his eyes:

Is this woman crazy or do you know something I don't?

Benji just stared at him. Whatever that meant. Wes lowered his head, shifting the cumbersome rocking chair off of his neck, and when he looked up again, he was startled to see that he was standing directly in front of a small crude cabin, its windows aglow with firelight. There was no fathomable way this structure was not visible from the road they were just on, yet somehow he did not see it until that moment.

Is this witchcraft, Ruth?

"Welcome to my home. It's now your home as well. Come inside and see."

"Are you here alone?" Wes asked, hesitating a few feet away. This might still be a trap. If there was witchcraft at play, Wes would be powerless to protect Benji from it. He looked at Benji, worried over their situation, and Benji laughed at him. He actually *laughed*. The sound pulled at Wes' mind, and he felt himself starting to drift back to that place where Peter laid in the grass laughing at...

"I'm not alone," the old woman crooned in her low hum voice, and her words brought Wes back from his thoughts. "But you'll see for yourself soon enough. Here, lad, tie your horse over there. The window will cast light upon her, and quell her nightmares."

Benji did as directed without hesitation, and after the mare was safely tethered, he all but frolicked as he returned to Wes' side. Wes looked to the sky one last time just as the last of the sun was swallowed up by the mountains, and let out a heavy sigh. No other options; not anymore.

"Right this way," the woman called as she opened the door to her home, and gestured for them to follow her inside. Benji barreled in after her; running through the door, and into the soft glow of light within, but Wes took more caution. He stopped at the threshold, lowered the rocking chair from his shoulders, and looked around the small cramped space.

The area was illuminated with a fireplace, and a few candles that were positioned on a narrow wooden table along the wall. On the wall opposite the table, a small bed was tucked up against the corner. A loft hung over the fireplace, half concealed behind the chimney and was cloaked in shadows. Every wall seemed covered in sacks, or drying herbs, or skinned pelts. It was cramped with the three of them but not unreasonable. In fact, it reminded Wes a lot of his own homestead, and for that reason he immediately felt safe.

"Sanctuary," he whispered to himself, and the woman placed a hand on his arm.

"Indeed it is, brother, the Lord watches over us. Now get on in here, and close out the night."

Wes stepped fully into the cozy cabin, and absently put a protective arm around Benji as he took in the room. The warmth of the place draped itself on Wes, and made him more aware of the persistent cold ache that lingered in his bones from so many nights sleeping on the ground. He hated how much he felt his own weakness, and shook his head in frustration. He was still scowling when his eyes met the old woman's, but she just smiled.

"Come,"she gestured, "bring that chair over here by the fire. Then you sit down while I fetch you something to eat." Wes set the rocking chair in an open space next to the fireplace, then decided to occupy a chair alongside the table. He didn't want to settle in by the fire for he surely would be asleep in seconds. He dared not leave Benji unguarded like that. Yawning, he removed his hat and jacket to help endure the warmth of the room. He rubbed at his face, savoring the chill of his fingers on his closed eyes, then felt Benji's hand on his arm. He looked up to see the boy staring at him."What is it?" he asked and Benji used hands to touch fingers to chest, fingers to lips, pointing fingers toward the woman, then across the room, then back to Wes, and all over the place. Gestures and finger waving and earnest looks, and it all seemed too overwhelming. Wes jerked his arm away from Benji's grasp, and felt an intense swell of frustration.

"I don't understand you!" He snapped, and Benji recoiled in surprise.

"It's names he's after, brother," the woman said as she spooned soup into a wooden bowl. "He wants our names."

"If that be so, it's a valid request. You know my name, will you tell me yours?"

"They call me Sassy," the woman said with a smile. She set aside one bowl and lifted another.

"Sassy," Wes repeated. Benji studied him for a moment, then moved to place fingers against Wes' mouth but Wes quickly shooed him away. "And who is it that calls you that?"

"You'll see soon enough," Sassy replied vaguely. Wes studied at her dubiously, then gestured towards Benji.

"Do you know his name?"

“Of course,” Sassy said as she hobbled over to them. She placed a bowl in front of Wes full of steaming stew, then set the other one in front of the lad. “I’ve heard all about Benji.”

Wes cupped the bowl in his hands, and the heat it radiated stung his fingertips. Benji lifted his own bowl up, and brought it hungrily to his lips.

“Stop that now,” Wes scolded, and Benji looked up at him with his lips still pursed to slurp in the first bite. “Say your prayers, and bless your vittles. This is the way of the Word, lad.” Benji carefully placed the bowl back on the table, and bowed his head as Wes taught him to. He closed his eyes in silent prayer, and Wes joined in to add a prayer of his own. When he opened his eyes again, he noticed Sassy was still standing by the fire next to her pot of soup.

“You aren’t joining us?”

“Neh, brother, I ate before you came. But there is still plenty, so have your fill.” Wes examined the soup in his bowl dubiously, but Benji was already slurping it down, so he relented and did the same. He drew in the hearty broth, finding it full of root vegetables, and some dried strips of meat. All in all, it tasted wonderful, and he fought to restrain himself from gulping it down like Benji. He peered over at the woman again.

Sassy took a stick from her stove, and used it to light the tobacco in her pipe. She puffed at it a little, then satisfied with the burn, hobbled over to her rocking chair. Wes scrutinized her as he ate absently from his bowl.

“The Lord asked me to look after you,” Sassy said at last, her eyes still upon the fire. “And *she* asked me to trust you with our secret. No sense hiding it anyway, when the boy already suspects the truth. You have a bit of the touch don’t you, lad?”

Benji smiled as he spooned more soup into his empty bowl. Sassy leaned far back in her rocking chair, then stretched her arm out to tap the end of her pipe against the wall alongside the fireplace. Immediately, the wall shifted and revealed itself to be a small pocket door. It opened, and out stepped what appeared to be a giant.

Wes let his eyes trail up until he took in the full length of a towering man who seemed a good foot taller in height than him. His skin was the deep brown of spring mud much like Sassy’s, and like Wes, his face was unmarked by sin. He nodded towards Wes in greeting, then smiled broadly at Benji. When he smiled, Wes could tell that he wasn’t a man at all, but instead a boy. A teenage boy of fourteen or maybe fifteen. He had a strong broad nose, wide shoulders, and tight curly hair shorn close to his head. He stood proud like a young bull ready to challenge anyone who tried to tame him, and black scales darkened the backs of his hands. Wes stood in greeting, but felt a little unsteady on his feet.

"This is Solomon," Sassy said to Benji, "who you sensed was hiding, I suspect." Benji nodded, looking pleased with himself, and Wes studied him for a moment. This seemed to confirm Sassy's suspicions that the lad indeed had the second sight.

"Ah yes, I thought as much," Sassy said as she settled back and looked into her fire. "But what you didn't sense was his sister." Benji froze, then a look of knowing fell over his face as a small girl stepped out of the area behind the pocket door, and into the light of the room. She was vastly shorter than her brother, slighter in frame, with long curly hair dressed in braids down the length of her back. Like Solomon, her face was free of any sickness, showing only signs of sin on her fingers. Her face was soft brown like cooked honey, with a hint of rose on her cheeks. She appeared to be around eight in age, but her eyes carried an awareness far older than her years. She dismissed Wes with a passing glance, then took in Benji with sudden intensity. She seemed strangely angry, and Benji grew nervous under her scrutiny.

"She's stronger in the touch than anyone I've known," Sassy proclaimed, "You saw her before, didn't you, boy?" Benji ducked his head, visibly uncomfortable, and Wes felt compelled to defend him.

"What are you saying?" he asked even though he was wary of the answer. Something was occurring beyond his understanding, and that always made him uneasy. A coolness blossomed in the pit of his stomach. He reached for the table to steady himself.

"Your boy has already met my granddaughter, brother, long before you rode up on me today. Tell him your name, girl." Wes felt suddenly dizzy. He reached out for the chair, and sunk back into it. He clung to the table. The small girl with her flawless face dipped her head in greeting. Her voice was soft like a whisper when she offered her name.

"Eve." The coolness Wes felt in his stomach spread down his body into his feet. His ears rang, and the room seemed to tilt around him.

"Wuh?" Wes felt Benji reach for him. The boy's small hands fluttered nervously against his arm, but Wes seemed unable to move. His eyes felt so heavy all of a sudden. Everything felt so heavy.

"Ah. The herbs are setting in." The voice came out of the darkness overtaking his vision. A name came to his mind: Sassy. Sassy drugged him. An ambush after all.

"Wuh!" Benji sounded more frantic. He sounded scared.

Wes felt his body hit the floor hard. The bowl he used shattered alongside his head. He must have fallen out of the chair. This could not happen! He needed to protect Benji! He needed to get up! He needed to...

Chapter Twelve

Stand fast in your enchantments and your many sorceries,
with which you have labored from your youth;
perhaps you may be able to succeed;
perhaps you may inspire terror. - Isaiah 47:12 ESV

When Wes woke, his mind felt hazy, but realization slowly swept through his consciousness, and with it came dread. He sat up suddenly, saw that he was in a bed, then dizziness overtook him and he collapsed back upon the pillows. Distant foggy memories came back to him:

Solomon and Benji dragging him into the bed.

Benji pulling off his boots.

Sassy spooning broth into his mouth.

Benji crying, curled up beside him.

Sassy cleaning his wound, scraping it with a knife, then packing it with cobwebs and herbs.

Eve singing to Solomon and Benji by the fire.

Sassy opening her windows, the sunlight burning against his skin.

All of this confirmed what he already felt in the stiffness of his body, and the spinning in his head: he's been asleep for a long time.

Wes tried to sit up again, more slowly than before, and his head seemed to tolerate this shift of orientation. Moving around, he quickly realized he was completely undressed, and extra bedding was tucked between his legs. Did this mean he messed himself? Exactly how long has he been asleep?

He recognized the tiny cabin, and he was laying in what he imagined to be Sassy's bed. A quick scan of the room allowed him to locate his clothes which appeared to be cleaned and folded neatly on one side of the table. On top of the pile, lay his father's hat.

Wes scratched a beard; much thicker than he remembered it to be, and slowly swung his legs onto the floor. His head lurched, and a black curtain swept across his vision, but then it faded a moment later. He waited, shivering a little as a light breeze brushed his bare back, and listened to the sounds around him. He heard Sassy singing outside in her low humming voice.

"Gonna get me a chicken, gonna get me a pot, gonna get me a hatchet which I have not got..." He hoped Benji was nearby. He ached with a dull worry that he knew wouldn't go away until he saw that Benji was well. If the boy was safe, everything would be alright.

Wes lifted his left arm to examine his wound and winced from the effort. Everything felt stiff and unused, so he turned his head gingerly to better examine the cut on his arm. He was pleased to see that all of the swelling and redness were gone. The wound was still healing, but closed; with a puckering scar that would never fully mend. He was grateful for the care, but he wasn't sure it was needed. He was doing better, and healing on his own.

Regardless, I will say thanks to Sassy, and give praise to God.

He tried to stand, but his legs went limp, and he fell back onto the bed. Wes shook his head, trying to expel his dizziness, then heard someone outside. He looked up in time to see the door swing open, and Sassy hobbled into the room with her song upon her lips. When she saw that Wes was sitting up with a blanket draped across his lap, her song cut short, and she gave him a wide toothy smile.

"He has risen!" Sassy proclaimed with her hand in the air. "Hallelujah!" She was holding a couple skinned rabbits which she tossed upon the table next to Wes' clothes. Then she hobbled closer to inspect his arm.

"How ya feeling, brother?" She asked, and Wes shrugged uncomfortably. He's not used to sitting around naked like he was. Not to mention that Sassy drugged him, and he didn't fully understand why, so he was apprehensive to trust her. Sassy went from inspecting his wound, to studying his face. She then slid over a chair, and sat down to face him. Wes sat up a little, trying to pretend his nudity didn't bother him, and matched Sassy's scrutiny.

"You don't seem to trust me much, do you, brother?"

"No, I reckon I don't," Wes agreed.

"Well, I don't blame you! If I were you, I might not trust me a whole lot neither. But I'll have you know, it was for your own good."

“You drugged me,” Wes accused but Sassy shook her head.

“I helped you sleep. But sure as day, you needed it.”

“I was doing better,” Wes argued, “the infection was fading.”

“So you think!” Sassy chuckled through her smile. “That wound ain’t ever gonna heal, not fully. The only reason you aren’t dead right now is ‘cause of that boy of yours. He’s what led you to me, and got you saved instead of you rotting out there in yonder ditch.”

“The swelling was going down before we came here,” Wes insisted stubbornly. “The pain was improving.” Sassy’s smile fell away, and she leaned in closer to Wes.

“Brother, this ain’t about no wound. There was a wickedness festering inside of you. Truly, some of it is still in there, for none of us could fully yank it out. One day, it’s going to return and turn your thoughts to anger. Eventually, it will take your life. Tending your wound wasn’t enough to get the darkness under control. If not for Eve and that boy of yours, you’d be dead right now, but he is strong in the prayer.”

“Prayer?” Wes did not expect this. Sassy nodded.

“Where else would you go to root out an evil seed, but the Lord? That boy might be able to pray away the devil himself, and he prayed over you for days.”

“Days...if he prayed over me for days, how long have I been asleep?”

“Five sunrises,” Sassy proclaimed and Wes stared at her in utter shock.

“How is this possible? How did I sleep so long?” Then, after a moment of thought he added, “Where is Benji?”

“You slept so long because all your energy was spent on fighting to get that seed inside you under control.”“Where is Benji?” Wes asked again. If Sassy was some kind of medicine woman, she would have no problem drugging someone as trusting as Benji. Maybe that big fellow Solomon carried him off to be sold to a man with a white suit and a large smile.

“Still don’t trust me,” Sassy said, then stuck out her pink tongue at him. “In spite of this.”

Wes pressed his lips together humbly, and looked away from her. She certainly had a point for she lacked a liar's tongue. Sassy got to her feet, then pulled a knife from the hem of her tan skirts and took to cutting her rabbit carcasses into chucks for the stew pot.

“Benji is a good lad,” she said over her shoulder to him. “A bit quiet, but good nonetheless. No need to worry, brother. He is quite safe. Solomon and Eve have the boy out in yonder forest. They are foraging for whatever they can find. Showing the boy what’s good to eat and what’s poison. He’s so hungry to learn, and he will learn much from them both.”

There was hidden meaning in her words, but Wes could not discern it. His mind felt fuzzy again. Fatigue looming up within him.

"I've been trying to teach him to read," Wes said as he pressed the palms of his hands to his aching eyes. "Trying to teach him the Word."

"Oh, this I know. It has been a long time, brother, since I held the good book in my hands. But the boy, he showed me your copy. I hope you don't mind me looking at it."

"Not at all," Wes said, then yawned. He leaned over, propping on his elbow, and covered himself better with the blanket.

"I've been reading to him from it some, and Solomon's been showing him his letters. He's old enough to remember being taught by his mamma so he's good at the teaching."

"Solomon's mother...where is she?" Wes relented to laying down fully, with his head on the pillow. If he closed his eyes, the room might stop spinning. Sassy's words carried to his ears, and it sounded like a lullaby.

"My daughter Mora. She is no more. Sin took her years ago and... just what do you think you're doing? Oh, no, brother. No sleep for you yet. It's time to build that strength back and that means getting you on your feet. Come now, up and out of bed with you. I'll help you dress, then you need to eat."

She hobbled over to him, and before Wes could respond, she reached down and yanked the blanket off of him. The sudden coolness swept the lethargy from his mind, and Wes sat up immediately. He glared at Sassy as he hugged himself against the cold. He hoped the heat in his cheeks was interpreted as anger, but of course Sassy was not fooled so easily.

"Why so bashful, brother? Who do you think wiped your bottom and changed your bedding these past five days? Sure wasn't one of the children. No, sir. There isn't an inch of you that I haven't seen."

"I am not used to being so exposed," Wes confessed, and had to admit to himself that he liked this woman. He decided he would trust her.

"I know, Wes," Sassy said, and her smile was genuinely caring. But then she flashed her teeth again and gave one of her rolling chuckles. "But I count myself lucky, all the same. I have very fond memories of you now that I'll never forget even when time steals all the others away."

Her chuckle turned into a hearty laugh, and Wes ducked his head to hide his burning face. He changed his mind, he did not trust her in the least.

Sassy encouraged Wes to his feet, and handed his clothes over one at a time from the pile. He dressed, taking his time so he didn't fall, and noted his shirt sleeve was clean of blood, with the cut stitched shut.

"Thank you," Wes said to Sassy, lifting the shirt in appreciation.

"Thank Eve when you can. Now stop your gawking and get them clothes on." Wes did as he was told, dressing in everything including his jacket, and finished by placing his hat on his head. Sassy made no comment about the lack of sin on his face, but of course she was used to that considering Solomon and Eve. Either way, he preferred to keep his forehead covered.

"Now you eat," she commanded, and gestured to one of the table chairs. Wes stumbled across the room, still feeling his legs were weak like blades of grass, and sank into the chair as Sassy placed a bowl in front of him filled with soft oats and honey.

Wes took a tentative bite, then a moment later realized the bowl was empty. He saw enough of his body when dressing to know how thin he has grown. Sassy dished more into his bowl, and he didn't need her warning to know he should pace himself. Yet the second bowl vanished almost as quickly as the first.

"Are you feeling better, brother, or do you need more rest?" Sassy asked and Wes shook his head.

"I'll be alright,"

"Well, if that be the case. Come with me. We have work to do. First we have to wash all this bedding. Tell me, brother, what do you know of tanning leather?"

Wes spent the remainder of the day helping Sassy with her chores. She sat in her rocking chair, brought outside by one of the children, while Wes used her skinning knife to remove the fat from a rabbit pelt. He listened to Sassy as she rattled on about her daughter and grandchildren. She talked of how proud she was of Solomon, and how he became a better man than his daddy who ran off and left them behind.

"The only thing his daddy gave him is his love for music." She also talked about Eve who was more contemplative but with a fiery temper. "Eve thinks carefully about her choices, knowin' the consequences of brash decisions made in anger. She sees much with the touch and always has a wondrous story to tell." The more she talked about her grandchildren, the more Wes worried about Daniel and more so about Ruth. He's been gone for almost two weeks because of this unexpected detour. Surely, she must be dead. This bothered him, even though he knew it might happen when he left, for he felt that he failed her. He worried that she died wondering why he was taking so long to return. Wes sat quietly, only half listening to Sassy rambling on, while he took comfort in the simple rhythm of meticulously running the dull knife down the length of rabbit fur.

"Well done, brother. Very nice," Sassy said as she looked over his shoulder. "I hope to make some boots for your boy, might take a week or so but this helps me greatly. Ah, speaking of the children, here they come now." Wes looked up, and saw three heads bobbing off in the distance where the forest's edge gave way to the sparse grass and shale. He could hear one of the children laugh, the sound carried on the breeze, and it made him nervous. It made him think of Peter. He lowered his head and returned to his work without comment. Sassy watched him with that knowing expression on her face.

"You're afraid to love that boy," she observed.

"I have lost much," Wes admitted, but she seemed to already know. She did not ask for an explanation.

"You will have more to lose, I regret to say," Sassy proclaimed, "But he is safe. As long as he remains here, nothing can harm him. You need not worry about giving him your heart."

"What choice do any of us really have, when it comes to loving children?" Wes asked with a dry chuckle. Of course Benji held his heart. The boy was a gift from the Lord as far as he was concerned. But Sassy's words worried him, even though he already knew he had more to lose. Silence stretched between them, as Wes listened to the sounds of the children coming closer.

"I killed his mother," Wes said without realizing the words were forming on his lips. He didn't want to kill her, but that did not stop the spread of sin up his arms. "She was a whore of Babylon. I thought she meant to attack me and in the end that was what she did, but I still regret the role I played in her death." Wes returned blade to fur, and focused on fleshing the rabbit hide.

"Please. That's what she kept saying to me. Please sir, help me. And I drove a burning stick into her ribs. When I caught up to her the next day, that's when I saw her son. All along she was just asking me to look after him. I couldn't refuse her."

"Of course," Sassy responded.

"But how will I keep him safe? Have you seen how the night hungers for him? Have you heard their whispers? And that man...Chancy was his name. The way he looked at Benji..."

"The world is full of the wicked," Sassy said solemnly. Her knowing tone spoke beyond her words. Wes focused fully on working the rabbit skin. He didn't want Sassy to see the wetness in his eyes. She rocked slowly in her rocking chair, and examined her unlit pipe.

"So what do I do, Sassy? You claim he is safe here, but can you be sure? Is he safe in yonder woods as well? Do we have to shut him away from all the darkness of this world for the rest of his life? I don't know how to protect him like this. I am terrified that I will fail him."

Sassy chewed on her pipe stem and thought for a moment. Then she lifted her head and looked out to the children still distant but coming closer.

"You can't avoid failing him. But you can try not to. He's still fragile. Easily broken. So pray for the Lord to keep him safe, brother, and if things go wrong, pray for the strength to pick up his pieces."

The laughter of children came again, closer than before. Wes turned from Sassy to seek out Benji, but then suddenly his vision went blurry. The world seemed to fade before him, and in an instant all went dark.

Wes staggered, then found his footing and opened his eyes. He was standing on the porch of his homestead. Realizing where he was, Wes smiled and lifted his head to examine the crop of his sweet corn, ready for harvest. He could hear Ruth as she was singing. He recognized the song, but when he tried to focus on the words, the whole melody seemed to slip through his open hands. It mattered not.

What did matter was Peter. Wes looked beyond Ruth to where the laundry billowed in the wind. Behind the bedding, he could just make out a pair of bare feet belonging to a small child laying in the grass.

His small child.

His Peter.

Peter was laughing, and Wes tried to draw the sound into him like warmth from the sun.

Peter laid in the grass, and laughed as he threw maple seeds up into the air, to let them fall on his face. In that moment, Wes felt pure happiness. In spite of Daniel running away. In spite of all the loss of the other children Ruth tried to rear. This place and time was what he held on to. He clung to it desperately, even though he could already feel it slipping away.

“Come back to me, brother.” Sassy’s voice was at his ear, and Wes opened his eyes. He looked up at her, and saw a knowing expression on her face. Looking around, he realized he fell from where he was sitting and laid on the ground. He pushed himself up and sat in the dirt as he brought a shaky hand to his head.

“Sorry, I...” Lord, but his mouth was suddenly dry. Sassy stood, and went to a well where she worked the crank to bring up a bucket of water. Soon she returned with a ladle full, which Wes gulped down greedily.

“You were caught up in the past,” she declared.

“A memory spell,” Wes agreed. In the distance, he could see the children strolling through the fields. Eve had her apron pulled up into a makeshift basket and the two boys carried limp forms of fallen animals at their sides. Benji had Wes’ bow slung over his shoulder.

“Ney, brother,” Sassy went on. “More than what you say. Far worse than a spell. This memory holds you captive. You hold it captive as well.” Wes glanced up at Sassy, then turned back to the children. His eyes met Benji’s and in an instant the boy broke into a run.

“It was the last time I saw my youngest son alive,” Wes admitted as he watched Benji run towards him.“Ah,” Sassy sighed. She returned the ladle back to the bucket and sought out her chair. “Peter was his name, was it not? Tell me how he died.”

“It’s not something I like to speak of,” Wes said quietly. He gnawed at his lower lip absently as he watched Benji: thin legs kicking out to the side as he ran. He would not cry over this.

“No sense in outrunning your grief, Wes.” Sassy’s voice was as somber as his own. Her sing-song words sounded like a prayer. The children whooped and hollered. Overcome by emotion, Benji started to cry.

“He...he fell from that horse over there,” Wes said in a rush. Wanting to get the whole explanation done and off his tongue. “She got away from him and he lost his grip and...he fell hard and... hit his head. He didn’t wake up again.”

"A horrible accident," Sassy sighed, "yet you blame yourself."

"Of course I blame myself!" Wes snapped, turning to glare at her. It was not Sassy's fault though. It was not even the mare's fault although he still hated her for it. All the blame rested on his shoulders alone. "Peter was terrified of horses but I kept trying to push him. He would never have gotten on that horse if I hadn't shown him how. He would never have tried to ride her on his own except he wanted to impress me. He wouldn't have tried to impress me if I hadn't..."

Wes realized he was shouting and pressed his lips together to stop the words from coming. Without the words, tears came instead. Furious, painful, bitter tears that burned his eyes as he fought to blink them away. Then suddenly Benji was there, standing in front of him, face wet and streaked with dirt. Wes' weakness was laid bare before the lad. He ducked his head, and looked away ashamed. He let the brim of his hat hide his face.

Benji knelt down in front of where Wes was sitting and used the cuff of his sleeve to dab at Wes' tears. Wes tried to shoo him away, embarrassed, but it only made Benji more determined. He lunged forward, and wrapped his arms around Wes, pulling him into a hug. Benji cried without abandon, as he clung to Wes. He rubbed his runny nose and dirty cheeks all over Wes' shirt, and Wes forgot about trivial things like pride, and weakness. He wrapped his arms around the boy's small frame, and leaned over to place a kiss on his head. Benji's hair smelled of grass and sun.

"We all bear the burdens of the choices we make, brother," Sassy said as she looked down on Wes. "Your choices have some heavy burdens, but they also brought you here. They brought you to Benji."

It does not change those things I wish could be undone. But if I can reunite with Daniel, these two boys might be enough to balance out the cost.

The other children left to tend to the fire and prepare their findings for dinner. Sassy gathered up the rabbit skins Wes had fleshed out, and went to cover them in salt. Alone with Benji, Wes gently pushed him away, and used his own sleeve to clean his dirty face.

"You're such a mess," Wes laughed. He noticed the clothing Benji wore seemed to fit him much better. Wes was taking in the new trim tan shirt, and supple leather pants when Benji tapped his small chest, then placed fingers on Wes' lips.

"Benji," Wes said against the fingertips. "B-E-N-J-I." Then Benji put fingers against Wes' chest and returned them to his lips.

"Wes," he responded, understanding the rules to this charade. "W-E-S." Benji let his hand fall into his lap, and leaned in to rest his head against Wes' chest. He closed his eyes and smiled.

"I'm sorry to worry you," Wes said. "I know I've been asleep for a long time."

"Wuh."

"I remember you laying with me. I remember hearing you cry. I'm really sorry that I scared you."

Benji said nothing. His eyes remained closed.

"Sassy said that you prayed over me. That it was your praying that helped me to recover. I'm grateful to you for that."

Again Benji said nothing. Wes tilted his head to look at Benji's face, and realized that he fell asleep right there sitting on his knees and leaning against Wes. He must be utterly exhausted. Wes held Benji up as he maneuvered to his feet, then he scooped the boy into his arms, and turned toward the cabin.

"He's hardly slept for days," Sassy said, and Wes jumped a little at being startled. Considering how slow she moved, she could sure be quiet when she wanted to be. She stood in the path leading to her home, with Solomon and Eve standing in the doorway behind her. She looked over her shoulder at them, then gestured for Solomon to come forward.

"Take the boy inside and lay him down. Look after him a spell, and keep an eye on our dinner. Don't let the pot get too hot or the rabbit will go tough. We'll be back soon enough."

"We?" Wes asked, and let Solomon gently lift Benji out of his arms.

"Yes, brother," Sassy said, and looked at him with an intensity that unsettled his nerves. "Eve and I must take you to a place near the woods. A place where the veil is thin. There's work to be done there today, and a wrong that needs fixing."

Chapter Thirteen

Don't you know that when you offer yourselves
to someone as obedient slaves,
you are slaves of the one you obey-
whether you are slaves to sin,
which leads to death, or to obedience,
which leads to righteousness? -Romans 6:16 NIV

"What is this 'wrong' that you're talking about?" Wes asked as he followed Eve and Sassy towards the forest. Sassy made the pace, moving in her slow meandering fashion, with Eve skipping alongside her. Her braids bobbed and swayed on her back.

"You and I have work to do, brother Wes," Sassy said over her shoulder. "We need to mend the rift you have caused in your past."

"That makes complete sense," Wes said sarcastically, then glanced at Eve. "And why is she with us?"

"Eve is strong in the touch. She can see past the veil." Wes stopped walking. Sassy took a few more steps then turned to look at him. Eve, still beside her, did the same. Her young face was a stark contrast to her all-knowing eyes.

"What wrong needs fixing that rests beyond the veil?" That same strange feeling of things outside his understanding, ran fingers up Wes' skin, and made him shiver.

"You'll see soon enough. Just up here, in the shade over there. We need to pray."

Sassy turned and continued her course, but Eve kept looking at Wes. Her dark eyes carried depth but Wes could not discern what they conveyed. In spite of his unease, Wes was curious about what this all meant. He relented to the desire to know more, and continued following Sassy. As he walked, Eve fell in beside him. She hummed to herself as she plucked blades of grass to weave them into a wreath.

The sun was still high, and while the forest loomed over them, the shadows weren't deep. At the base of the trees, there was a half circle of six stones that looked large enough to sit upon. Sassy approached one of them and eased herself onto it carefully.

"These legs aren't what they used to be," she said as she smiled up at Wes. "They went by the way of my eyes. Everything gets sacrificed to time."

"Sassy, what are we doing that requires prayer? I don't understand." Wes looked around warily which was in his nature to do. There was always a threat, he just needed to find it.

"We have to fix what is broken," Sassy said as she plucked at her skirts to make them fan out around her legs.

"What exactly is broken?" Was this about the cut on his arm again? He thought Sassy had addressed all that.

"It's you, brother Wes. You are what's broken." Eve parted from Wes' side and took a seat next to her grandmother. She placed her small wreath of grass atop her head.

"Come and sit for a spell. We must talk, brother, then you have a choice to make."

"A choice," Wes said dubiously, but he stepped forward and decided on a flat top rock on the other side of Eve.

"Your wife." Sassy pulled her pipe out of her pocket, looked into the cold bowl, then stuffed it away again.

"My...Ruth?" Wes stared at Sassy, confused. What was this all about? He no longer found it surprising how Sassy seemed to know things about him that no one should know. But surely Ruth was dead by now. Surely she was beyond the veil. Slowly, Wes shifted his gaze to Eve. She looked back at him, and smiled. Her smile was as warm as the sun.

"Listen to my words, and you'll know," Sassy said, then let out a sigh. Wes felt suddenly wary. Something within him knew this was not an experience he wanted to endure. He chose to trust Sassy, and Eve was just a little girl, yet somehow they both filled him with fear. He could just turn around. He could return to the cabin, collect Benji, and leave.

But he owed Sassy much for the way she cared for him and Benji. She told Wes that Benji would remain safe as long as he stayed there, and already Wes could see how happy the boy was, being around other children. The least he could do was to see this through, even though it scared him so.

"Alright," Wes relented, and Sassy seemed to relax. "Tell me what is going on."

"You are broken inside," Sassy repeated, "for you have grabbed hold of a memory that you will not allow to fade."

"The last time I saw Peter alive," Wes said and she nodded.

"You cling to that memory. It's too vivid. Too strong. You have used it to shield yourself from reality. You are unable to grieve for the boy, and you are unable to let him or his mother go."

"I don't want to forget him," Wes said, feeling defensive. What was wrong with wanting to hold on to the last memory he had of his son? The thought of forgetting that moment in time terrified him.

"All memories fade with time," Sassy replied. "They all aren't forgotten fully, but the brightness isn't quite so bright. The colors, not so sharp. The fading to dullness allows the memories to be easier to endure. Both those that are good and the ones you want to forget."

"There are many I want to forget," Wes admitted.

"But not this one."

"No, not this one. It's far too important to me."

"That may be true, brother, but it is also profoundly sad. You don't want to simply remember that moment. You are trying to relive it. You want to remain in it. Or perhaps change it."

"I would give anything to change it," Wes said and his voice faltered. It took effort to swallow against the sudden clenching in his throat.

"The past is unraveling," Sassy said and her voice seemed to change a little. It softened, and took on more of a humming quality.

"The past is unraveling," Eve repeated, in the same sing-song way of her grandmother. Wes looked between the two of them with increasing apprehension.

"But time will never go back. Only forward."

"Only forward," hummed Eve.

"What is this?" Wes asked. He felt as though a spell was being cast upon him.

"Memories are crumbling all around us, as the unraveling gets worse. One day, you will forget your wife. One day, you will forget your son."

"Never!" Wes snapped as he got to his feet. He felt appalled. How could she even suggest such a thing? He turned to walk away. He was done listening to this nonsense.

"Please, brother. Please sit with me. For your wife depends on your understanding." Sassy looked up at him, her weathered face showing lines formed from deep concern. Wes hesitated, then glanced at Eve. He watched her pick up something from the ground. It was a maple seed. She threw it into the air and watched idly as it spiraled to the ground again. Wes sat back down.

"Listen, brother, and listen well," Sassy said in that same strange voice, and beside her, Eve hummed low and slowly. "You have a memory so consuming, it draws you into it. You can smell it."

"Amen," said Eve.

"You can hear it!"

"Amen."

"You live it through over and over again!"

"Amen."

"It holds you captive, brother Wes, and just so, it holds dear Ruth captive as well." Eve parted her lips, and her hum turned into a wordless song.

"You have kept her prisoner in this memory, brother Wes. She can not escape from your grief. And oh, she is suffering."

"Suffering," Eve sang, her eyes closed in prayer.

"For as long as you hold her captive, she cannot die. Her body wastes away, but she cannot die."

"Cannot die."

"Release the memory, brother Wes. Release your wife's spirit. Let her go beyond the veil. Let her be free."

"Free," Eve sang. She swayed side to side. Sassy closed her eyes and started to hum.

"But...you said I will forget Ruth. You said I will forget Peter." Wes' eyes darted back and forth between them as he tried to make sense of what was happening. Ruth was still alive?

"Yes, brother. We all forget with this unraveling time. But you must forget."

"You must," said Eve.

"It is the only way to save your son."

"My son?" Asked Wes, truly perplexed. Sassy opened her eyes and looked directly into his.

"Your son. The only way to save him is to forget your past."

"Forget the past," said Eve.

"Face your own demise."

"Demise."

"Then take Daniel home."

"Home," sighed Eve. She hummed her song once more. Wes thought for a moment, his eyes upon his open hands resting in his lap. Then he looked up at Sassy.

"You said my memory holds Ruth captive. Am I holding Peter captive as well?"

"Hard to say," Sassy said. Breaking off from her song. "He rests on the other side of the veil."

"I cannot see him so well," Eve sang. Her voice sounded angelic. "I have tried."

"And if I somehow...release this memory. Does that mean Ruth will die?" Wes asked and Sassy closed her eyes as she hummed low and mournful.

"Her spirit is broken, brother Wes. She is suffering so. You must release her from this torture. You must let her go." Wes was stunned. He never would have imagined that he possessed the power to hold Ruth's spirit captive in this world. The imprisonment of her suffering was another way he failed her.

"You said I should bring Daniel home. To save him."

"You *must* take him home," Eve interjected. "Must!"

"To save him," Sassy agreed. "And to say goodbye."

"I promised Ruth I would bring him home. I told her to wait for us. I told her..." How many times did he speak to Ruth in his mind? How many times had he told her to stay with him; to avoid going beyond the veil where he couldn't reach her. He has been holding onto her beyond what any soul should endure. He's been holding her captive, and didn't even realize it.

Wes fell silent, and stared down at his hands once more. After some time, Eve reached out and slipped her small hand into his. He looked up at her, and she smiled sympathetically.

"Your eyes do not want to see, brother Wes. Your ears do not want to hear!" Sassy half spoke and half sang. The music of their words seemed almost hypnotic. She was right. None of this was something he wanted to hear. "Ruth is suffering greatly, brother. She wants to go. She wants to return home to the Lord. But she is held here by your longing. You don't want to let her go."

"I thought she was already dead," Wes admitted, feeling rotten for disregarding her death like he did.

"The way she suffers, she yearns for death."

"How awful," Eve whispered. Wes closed his eyes. It was one thing to assume Ruth stepped beyond the veil while he was unconscious, it was quite another to willingly let her go. To stop clinging to a memory he was not ready to forget.

"It was the last time I was happy. The last memory I have of Ruth, when she wasn't sick with the madness. The last memory I have of Peter alive. Sassy...I don't want to forget the sound of my son's laughter." Wes knew already the choice he had to make. For how could he let Ruth suffer for his own sake? But he was terrified of forgetting his son. His wife. There was no doubt in Sassy's words. If he released this memory, he would surely forget them both. He tried to remind himself that this would save Daniel somehow. He imagined how this opportunity might allow him to reconnect with his oldest son. He had no doubt on the choice Ruth would want him to make.

"All things are possible with God, brother Wes," Sassy said softly, and Wes looked over at her. This gave Wes something to hope for. Surely God would help him to remember his wife. Surely God would not allow him to forget his youngest son. He would find Daniel. He would bring his boy home so that he could say goodbye to his mother. Time would not rob him of those things most precious to him.

"Alright. I reckon I'm ready then." Wes said as he closed his eyes. He bowed his head. He knew that it was time to let his memory go. Eve's hand tightened in his. In spite of her hand feeling so small, it carried a strength he did not expect.

"We must pray," Sassy said in her sing-song voice and Eve's humming began anew. Sassy soon joined her, humming a harmony to her melody, and the sound cast a spell on Wes. Holding Eve's small hand, he felt a chill run through him. His nose burned. His eyes stung with more tears. He felt as though he could not catch his breath.

"What is this?" he gasped, opening his eyes to first look at the girl and then to her grandmother.

"This be the Holy Spirit," Sassy said, cutting her song short. "Now shush up and listen. For there is more than just your memory that holds dear Ruth a prisoner, and I need to focus. Sorcery is at play, brother. The capital and their wickedness is inside her. Her father haunts her regularly."

So Ruth's father still haunted her dreams. Wes had hoped she was spared this torture when she fell into her deep stillness, but this must not be the case.

Oh, dear Ruth. What all have you endured?

Wes felt like he was riding through a storm of sensation. He gasped and panted as the Holy Spirit ran all along his skin. It made him feel cold and hot at the same time. It overwhelmed him with emotion that choked his words in his throat. He could feel his presence grow detached and distant. It was as though he was merely observing the moment instead of being a part of it. He felt so far away, and yet anchored by the warmth of Eve's small hand.

"Father in heaven, hear our cry and know our longing. We seek to mend this poor soul, for brother Wes is surely suffering." Sassy bellowed out her song, and Eve hummed along to her prayer.

"Lord, while brother Wes has suffered so, your Ruth; your dear daughter in Christ, oh yes, poor dear Ruth has suffered so much more."

"Much more," echoed Eve.

"Lord, we know that Ruth's father is not your doing. He remains on this side of the veil to do the work of the wicked one."

"The devil at work," hissed Eve. Wes could feel the spirit swell within him. It seemed to be too much to contain. He drifted; churning in the abyss, then rose. Higher, he floated, then felt as though he were over all of them. He could see them from a distance, yet still felt the warmth of Eve's hand in his own. Was any of this truly happening? Wes struggled to remember how to breathe.

"Lord," Sassy sand, "we pray that you help Ruth to find her way to you. End her suffering, silence the torment from her earthly father, and help her find peace with you, Oh God."

"Bring her home," Eve sang.

Wait! Slow down! Wes wanted to cry out, this is happening too fast! It's too much to endure! But his voice would not come. His body seemed paralyzed where it sat, and yet he knew while his mind floated overhead, his body shook with his silent sobbing.

Ruth! Peter! I'm so sorry!

"We pray to you, Lord," Sassy called out.

"How we pray," Eve replied. Her hand felt like fire.

"Hear us, Lord. Hear our prayer," Sassy called out, her song a low rumble, "and rid the burden from this pure suffering woman. Let Ruth be free of her father."

"Free," sang Eve.

"Let her be free of her suffering."

"Free."

"Let her be free of brother Wes' memory!"

"Free!"

"Oh Lord, I pray, let our sister come home!"

"Let her come home," Eve sang, her voice delicate and small.

"Let her come home," Wes managed to whisper through his tears. He felt himself sinking and rising all at once. Just when he thought he could no longer stand the sensation, it started to fade from him. He no longer floated over his own head. Chills stopped rolling along his skin. The abyss of emotion faded from his mind. Eve's hand slipped out of his, and Wes opened his eyes.

The world suddenly seemed clearer to him. The colors were sharper; the greens of the trees revealing layers and textures he never noticed before. The sounds of the woods carried depth that traveled far into the shadows within. Sounds of animals, of insects, of the plants themselves whispering to one another. Wes wanted to cover his ears for all the noise. And his body! Oh, how it ached. He felt the pain in his joints far greater than he knew possible. He tasted the metallic tang of blood in his mouth. He felt the pulse of his heart through the headache throbbing his temples. He felt the tears wetting his cheeks and the cool of the fall air upon his skin. But under all of the increased sensation, inside his mind, Wes felt an utter and calming peace. Complete and perfect peace. It was unlike anything he felt before.

"What is this," Wes gasped as he closed his eyes and pressed his hands to his ears. He tried to shut out the intensity of the world around him, and wondered if this was how Benji sometimes felt.

"Give yourself a minute," Sassy said. Wes looked up at her and struggled a moment to sort her words out from all the other noises assaulting his ears. "The world will right itself soon enough."

"I have never had prayer like that before," Wes admitted. He still felt like he couldn't catch his breath. Sassy nodded her understanding. Of course this was something she had already known.

"Tis the touch that does it. Some from me, but mostly from Eve. As I've said, she is very strong. There is only one in this world that might be stronger. She sees all the futures and the many threads of the unraveling past. She sees beyond the veil, brother. What she can sees is chaos." The very idea of this overwhelmed Wes. He knew all about the veil from the Word. He knew that it was, among many things, a curtain between the world of the living and the place beyond knowing. To be able to see both the world of the living and the world of the dead was beyond his comprehension. He stared at Eve with new respect.

"How can you stand it?" Wes asked, a bit breathless. Eve just gave him another sweet smile.

"It's all I've ever known."

Chapter Fourteen

Thus says the Lord: "Cursed is the man who
trusts in man and makes flesh his strength,
whose heart turns away from the Lord.
He is like a shrub in the desert,
and shall not see any good come.
He shall dwell in the parched places of the wilderness,
in an uninhabited salt land.
-Jeremiah 17:5-6 ESV

Sassy insisted on a Jubilee. Perhaps it was to celebrate Ruth's life, or perhaps it was to distract from her inevitable death. It mattered not. The children were overjoyed at the prospect, and while Sassy rolled the dough for honey cakes, the three of them entertained Wes by acting out their day of hunting. Benji played out the part of a terrified rabbit, while Solomon stalked him through the bushes. Eve cried out as the fatal arrow was cast from his imaginary bow, and Benji collapsed dramatically onto the floor. Wes couldn't help but laugh. Perhaps Sassy's Jubilee did him some good.

While they gathered round the small table to eat, Benji stood beside Wes for lack of chairs, and laughed at Solomon's story about a time he got caught in a bramble patch. Seeing the way Benji lit up around the other children, Wes knew that this was the best place he could leave the lad when it was time for him to go. The idea of leaving Benji behind hurt his heart, but there was no better place for him to be.

That night after dinner, the children laughed and talked in the loft overhead, while Sassy and Wes shared a smoke by the fire. Wes took such joy in hearing how happy Benji was. He recalled a time when it used to make him apprehensive to hear a child's laughter, although he could not fathom why. With so little joy in this strange land, it was an inviting sound to hear. Wes closed his eyes and smiled to himself, savoring his full belly and warm company.

"It sure does me good to hear those children chattering away up there," Sassy said to Wes. Her pipe gave off lazy tendril of smoke as she clutched it in her hand. "They haven't spoken this much since their poor mother passed. Years, it has been. That boy has been a blessing to them both."

"You don't mind him being here," Wes said curiously, and looked over to Sassy. Her weathered face smiled with Wes' same contentment.

"Not at all. He is always welcome here. Same as you, brother Wes." Wes thought on this as he stared at the low burning fire.

"If that be so," he said after some time, "perhaps he can stay when the time comes for me to leave."

"It is as you say, let him stay here. But you must leave soon, there's little time to waste. You must find Daniel. You must take him home."

"Have you seen Daniel?" Wes asked, hopeful. He studied Sassy closely. "With your second sight?"

"Oh yes," Sassy said, and turned to meet his eye. Her expression betrayed nothing.

"Is he doing okay? Is he safe?" Wes asked, turning to face her fully. Anxiety and excitement swirling inside him at the mention of his son's condition. Sassy hummed, and puffed at her pipe. After some time, she responded.

"He is like a shrub in the desert."

"I don't understand," Wes said, and Sassy shook her head.

"I can not see clearly what Daniel endures, but I know he is alive and healthy."

"Ruth said he looks like a dragon. Is this true?" Wes dreaded to hear the answer, and again Sassy hesitated to respond. She watched Wes for a moment, then she looked back to the fire with a sigh.

"I think you must see these things for yourself. The only way you can protect your son is to stay with him."

"I hate to leave him behind," Wes said glumly. Sassy's talk of protection reminded him of his commitment to Benji instead of Daniel, but she seemed to understand all the same.

"He'll be safer here," she said softly so that the children would not hear.

"I know this, and I already told him that I couldn't take him into the city. I can't keep him safe there."

"Benji is convinced he has some purpose in yonder city. That stubborn boy wants to remain by your side, but even he has to admit it's too dangerous."

"Then why do I feel so wretched," Wes sighed. "It's hard enough for me to say goodbye when I'm not so conflicted. Am I a coward for wanting to sneak away while he's asleep?"

"You ain't foolin' him none," Sassy said with a chuckle, "I'm sure he knows exactly what you plan to do, but you leaving early is as good an idea as any. I doubt we'd see the back of you if he's right there crying, and begging you to stay."

"I need to look over my mare and get her ready to ride. I reckon I'll leave the morning after tomorrow."

"The morning after tomorrow," Sassy agreed, and hummed at her hidden thoughts. Wes fell silent for a spell, and thought about how much Benji changed over the past few weeks. He remembered that boy who stared at him from beside his dying mother. A boy half starved, filthy, and unwilling to trust. He remembered every moment that they shared which seemed to bring both of them closer to accepting one another. Even in the past few days while Wes slept, Benji seemed to have grown. He looked healthier, cleaner, and taller. He was definitely thriving around the other children. Wes could not begin to thank this strange old woman for all she has done for them both.

"Sassy," Wes began, but she immediately waved her hand dismissively.

"No thanks needed, brother Wes. The Lord called me to you, and I'm grateful he did." She pointed up to the loft with the tip of her pipe. "That boy up there is really special. Strong in the touch, though he don't know it yet. The things he might be able to do...if Eve is right about him, that boy may be the answer to everything."

"I don't understand," Wes said, but Sassy revealed no more. She shook her head, and pointed above them, indicating that these were not things she thought the children should hear. Overhead, he heard Solomon humming a song, and Benji trying to repeat the sounds. His voice sounded unsteady, but he was getting the hang of carrying a tune. Wes was amazed at how Sassy's grandchildren were able to find ways to include Benji even though he couldn't speak. This was a better place than any for him to grow up in. Wes glanced over to his new friend.

"Sassy, if I don't come back..."

"Stop speaking nonsense," Sassy said, jabbing her pipe in his direction. "But I must give you a word of advice."

"Go on."

"There is sorcery in the capital." Sassy's mouth turned down in a grim line. Her eyes were hard as she peered intently at Wes. "Old sorcery that has worked into the very bones of the place. Centuries of evil have ripped open a wound in that city and it will never heal. But the Lord will still hear you, even there. Keep him close to your heart, and return to us. You must return. Without you, I fear what will become of the boy." She looked up to the loft with a shake of her head. "I already fear he will do something foolish when he discovers you have gone."

"Can you see the future, Sassy?" Wes asked and she let out a disdainful laugh.

"I used to often see what was true, but no more. Nothing is certain in these dark times. Everything is unraveling. Everything is dying away. There is only the here and the now. This is what is true. The past matters no more, and the future only matters tomorrow."

"Aye," Wes sighed. He felt the weight of what he must do. He was suddenly reluctant to seek out his son. Considering all that was at stake, he would rather remain at that fire forever, and listen to Benji learn how to sing.

"The day after tomorrow," Wes declared as much to himself as to Sassy. That would be the day he left Benji behind.

"Best get your rest while you can," she said around the stem of her pipe. "For you will get little of it in the days to come. I'll mind the wee ones while you're sleeping." Wes rose to oblige the woman, but did not think sleep would come so easy. As soon as he sat upon her bed though, the weight of his worry, his loss, his heartache, his destiny all pushed down upon him and Wes slumped under the pressure. He pulled his boots off, placed his hat on top of them, then sought out the pillow. The last thing he saw before sleep took him, was Sassy flipping through his book, silently reading different passages of the Word.

Wes had a dream unlike any he had before. It was so clear and vivid to his mind's eye, he might have mistook it for reality if he was impressionable. He was sitting on the sloping grassland of his homestead; overlooking his field which was barren and fallow. The harvest long since done. The air was crisp with the chill of late autumn, and the sun warmed him from overhead in a cloudless sky.

Wes turned to look at his home placed at the top of the hill, and thought that it seemed strangely hollow. It appeared lifeless, vacant, an apparition from a distant past. There were no candles in the windows, and the blackness within caused the building to resemble a skull.

Wes turned away, unwilling to think further on what that meant, and instead focused on the field before him. In the distance, he noticed crows circling about. Some of them were landing in the field and some were making lazy circles in the air. What were they doing out there?

Wes was so focused on the birds, he did not realize that Ruth was suddenly there with him. He felt her touch, but was not alarmed by it. He knew it was her before he was even aware of the knowing. Ruth leaned over his shoulders, and wrapped her slender arms across his chest. Her hair; soft and long, brushed against his face. It did not seem thin and brittle anymore. She must have stopped pulling it out.

He wanted to turn and look at her; to drink in her face and her smile, but he also feared that she might resemble the woman he left behind. She was so gaunt and frail, he barely recognized her. Her body stank as it fed on itself, and her eyes, half open, were clouded over and empty. It's been two weeks since then, and he could only imagine how much worse things have gotten while she was alive.

Wes closed his eyes. He wanted Ruth to be as she was: when she was young and imagining the life they were going to live, and all the children they would have one day. Knowing this to be a dream, could he not remember her in that way? He was not so sure. It was so long ago.

Wesley.

Her voice did not speak, but Wes heard her in his mind. It has been a long time since he last heard Ruth's soft drawling voice say his name. Wes shivered; feeling the weight of nostalgia and longing for the woman he once had.

"Oh Ruth, I miss you so." Wes did not miss the Ruth he left behind, but the Ruth that once was. Truly, he missed Ruth for far longer than the two weeks he's been gone.

All is well now, Wesley. Thanks to you, all is well with my soul.

Wes felt the words more than heard them. Before he could respond, he felt Ruth pulling away. Her arms slid off of his shoulders, and her hair no longer brushed against his cheek. Wes felt a surge of panic. He should have looked at her when he had the chance. He might forget the finer details of her lovely face.

"Wait!" He called as he sought for her, but Ruth was already gone. The hill behind him was vacant. All that remained was that old farm house, with blackness in its windows, and its porch stairs resembling a skull's broken teeth.

Chapter Fifteen

For your waste and desolate places,
and the land of your destruction,
Will even now be too small for the inhabitants;
And those who swallowed you up will be far away.
- Isaiah 49:19 NKJV

The following morning, Wes took time to brush down his mare and prepare her for departure. She seemed more content than she has been since leaving her old life on the farm. After so much time passing, she probably thought this was her new home. He put a comb through her mane, and took the time to examine her teeth and feet. She certainly could use a fresh shoeing, but none of her hooves held a stone or something else burrowed in that might lead to infection. He also used the little neetsfoot oil Sassy had and oiled his saddle.

With this all done, Wes felt satisfied that she was ready to ride. He turned to see what he might find to eat from the morning breaking of bread, and realized that Benji was watching him.

"Whoa, lad. I didn't see you there," Wes said uncomfortably, but Benji only glared at him. He jabbed a finger in the direction of the mare, patted Wes on his chest, then tried to touch fingers to his lips but Wes was too tall for him to reach.

"I don't want to talk about this right now," Wes said, and moved to push past the boy, Benji intercepted him and blacked his path again.

"Benji, I need to..." Wes began, but Benji opened his mouth and yelled.

"Aaaah!" The sound startled Wes and he was taken off guard. Benji grabbed his jacket and yanked him forward so that his mouth was low enough to reach. Again, the boy pointed very sternly toward the mare, then jabbed Wes painfully in his chest, before placing his hand upon Wes' lips.

Wes stared at him, and Benji stared back at Wes. He knew exactly what Benji wanted to know, and of course the boy was not blind. He knew that Wes was readying the horse to ride. But when faced with this conversation, Wes could not bring himself to have it. He could not tell Benji goodbye.

"Look, I'm really hungry and I just want to..."

"Aaaah!" Benji shouted again. He stomped his foot and pressed his fingers more firmly upon Wes' lips. Wes gently pulled the boy's hand away, and straightened.

"That's enough, Benji," he said firmly. "I've already been clear about my intentions with you. I'm going to the capital, but I'm not leaving today."

He pushed past Benji again, and this time the boy let him go. He could feel the lad's eyes on him, watching him as he ducked his head to enter the cabin, and hated how rotten it made him feel. Sassy was sitting at her table, stripping beans into a bowl, and glanced up at him when he entered. She nodded in her strange understanding.

"He'll be alright," She said. "Fetch yourself some bread. I left it warming by the fire. Got some honey here too. Give it a little drizzle." Wes did as he was instructed, and waited for Benji to join them. The boy did not come. He finished his breakfast then fell into shucking beans with Sassy. He found himself glancing towards the door more than once, and Sassy gave him a sympathetic smile.

"Let's get you ready to go while we have the chance to do so."

They worked together to pack provisions for Wes' departure. He took some food and herbs in case his wound got worse. He decided to leave the Word with Sassy, so she can share it with the children. He also decided to leave his bow behind. Such a weapon did little good inside a city, and Benji seemed to be taking to it. In spite of his shorter draw, he managed to pull the string back far enough to sink an arrow into a treed squirrel. With time, Wes was certain he would do more.

Soon after the pack was sorted, Solomon strode in with a large groundhog for the cook pot which delighted Sassy. When he returned outside, Wes could hear singing from both him and Eve, but nothing from Benji. It was obvious the boy was upset, but Wes tried not to worry.

When he thought about the mistakes he made with Daniel, or those other more grave mistakes he made with Peter, he could not find comparisons to learn from. It was hard to find similarities between his two sons and this boy he was fostering as his own. What if he was making a mistake again? He wouldn't even know until it was too late to change anything.

Maybe he should look for Benji and talk to him. He could explain the situation again, and convince Benji to understand. Wes felt a hand on his arm, and turned to Sassy. He had not realized he got to his feet, and was staring at the door. She smiled up at him, and shook her head.

"He will come to you soon enough. Give him time to sort things out in his own mind."

Wes focused on any work that needed done, and the day marched onward. Before he knew it, the sun was finishing its journey across the sky. Seeing how dark the day was growing, Wes grew nervous with it. He kept looking to the door with every passing moment.

Eve entered just as the sun was setting, and Wes watched the doorway as she passed through, but no one was behind her. What was that foolish boy doing? He knew it was not safe to be in the dark like this! Wes thought of those whispers that called out to them while they were huddled by their fires. If anything so wicked was close by, they would not hesitate to snatch Benji away. Thinking about this had Wes on his feet. He was about to head out the door, when it opened on the edge of twilight, and Solomon strode in with Benji on his heels. Wes sighed in his relief, and sank back into his chair. Benji glanced over at him, their eyes meeting, then he quickly looked away again. He didn't appear to be angry, but seemed strangely hurt instead.

"Sorry if you worried, brother Wes," said Solomon in his deep baritone voice. "Been working on singing with Benji. Eve and I have been teaching him how." Wes looked over to Benji but still the boy would not meet his eye.

"Is that true, Benji," he offered, and the boy shrugged sheepishly.

"I might not know a whole lot about the world and the things in it," Sassy said to no one in particular as she examined her fire, "but if this were the last night I be spending with someone I care about, knowing I might not see them for a spell, I would want to celebrate it." Smoke curled around her face as she puffed thoughtfully on her pipe.

Solomon nudged Benji, who frowned down at his feet. Eve put her arm around him as well, giving him a gentle squeeze. After a moment of reluctance, Benji looked up at Wes, and gave him a small smile that would soften the devil's heart. As though on cue, Solomon lifted his head and broke into song.

"I'm just a poor Wayfaring stranger
traveling through this world below.

There is no sickness, toil, nor danger
in that bright world to which I go."

Benji lifted his head as well and opened his mouth. A soft single note came out of his throat, which then shifted to another note, then another still. Wes realized quickly that Benji was singing a harmony to Solomon's melody. He gained confidence with each note.

I'm going there to see my mother
She said she'd meet me when I come
I'm just going over Jordan
I'm just going over home.

As they sang together, Eve joined in with her brother. Their voices united like the heavenly host, and Wes was mesmerized by the song.

I'll soon be free from every trial
this form will rest beneath the sod,
I'll drop the cross of self denial,
and enter in my home with God.

Seeing all the effort Benji put into not only learning how to sing, but learning how to harmonize with his friends, Wes couldn't help but be proud of this child he barely knew, yet yearned to call his son.

I'm going there to be with my savior
Who shed for me his precious blood
I'm just going over Jordan
I'm just going over home.

Solomon led the children to the conclusion of the song by repeating the last chorus, then the three of them took a rehearsed bow. Sassy slapped hand against knee in applause while she hooted and cheered. Wes clapped his hands as well, unaccustomed to the gesture, then Benji leaped upon him in a wild embrace. He was filthy, sweaty, radiant, and laughing. He shone brighter than the sun. Wes couldn't remember the last time he saw a child so happy.

"That's enough now," Sassy announced, as she got to her feet. "Let us join for dinner."

Benji shared Wes' chair, and leaned close to his bowl, as his moon eyes took in the portion of stew Solomon spooned for him. The stew was savory due to the beans, and full of hearty hog meat. They said their prayers, Benji not needing to be reminded for once, and all tucked into their vittles with great appreciation. As they ate, Wes took in the moment they shared, and valued it for what it was: the start of a new family. This naturally reminded him of all the loss in his old family, and gave him an idea. After he recovered

Daniel, and they returned home to pay respects to Ruth, maybe Wes could bring his son here. They would need to expand the place, but Sassy could use the extra help, and perhaps this could be a new home for them. A less painful home that they could start over in.

Benji finished his stew with a final long slurp from his bowl, then wiped his mouth on his sleeve. He hopped off of Wes' lap, and walked over to where Sassy was sitting. He tapped his chest, then tapped Sassy on her hand, and placed his fingers upon her lips.

"You're welcome," Sassy said against his fingertips. Benji studied her mouth intently as she spoke. She pulled his hand away from her lips, and leaned close to him conspiratorially. "If you children get washed up, maybe brother Wes will read you a story before bed."

All three children dashed over to the wash basin, and Solomon poured water from a pitcher into it. They all brushed teeth, washed faces, and Eve helped to comb Benji's cropped hair.

I never thought to tend to him this way, Ruth. He needs a woman to look after him properly.

When they finished with their cleaning, they each stripped away their outer clothing, and stood shivering in their small-clothes.

"It gets hot in yonder loft due to the fire," Sassy explained to Wes as she tossed another log into the flame. "Go on up with you then. Settle in and wait for brother Wes to read from the Word."

All the children clambered to get to the pocket door and the ladder it contained. Wes smiled at the energy these children always seemed to have. They wanted to race between moments, not realizing the journey itself was a moment as well. Wes stood, stretching the ache in his limbs, and snatched up his book which rested on the edge of the table.

"Alright," he said, as he strolled over toward the fire for its light. "What should I read this evening?"

"David and Goliath!" Solomon bellowed down from overhead.

"Noah and the flood," Eve said softly, her small nose poking over the edge of the loft railing. Wes looked to Benji who was watching him intently beside them. His face, blank of expression.

"Well, lad? What do you say? Will it be floods or giants that entertain you this evening?"

Benji furrowed his brow in thought for a moment, then lifted his hands, and waved them over his head dramatically.

"Looks like a giant to me," said Sassy, never looking up from her pipe.

"Alright, everyone to bed. Listen well, for I'm going to tell you all about a boy named David, and how he stood up against a giant for the sake of his king."

Sassy was slumped in her chair dozing while the fire burned low. Wes eased his boots off quietly, and laid back on her bed for the last time. His eyes were heavy, and the warmth of the fading fire lulled him into sleep almost instantly. Then he felt small hands reach for him. Wes was in a place of half sleeping, half waking, when something wormed its way under his arm, then tucked icy toes against his side. Dreams swirled through his mind, pulling him deeper into his sleep, but Wes heard the sound of crying and reached for his boy laying next to him.

"Hush now," Wes mumbled and wrapped his arm more snugly around the child. "Don't cry."

The boy's body shook as he softly wept and rubbed his face against Wes to wipe away his tears. Wes swam to the shallows of his dreams, and floated along the shore of waking.

"Hush Peter, hush," he whispered. His hand stroked his son's hair, and after some time, Peter's tears seemed to lessen. His shaking subsided. "Mamma will wake up soon, Peter. Just wait and see. Wait and see." Sleep pulled him under again, while he held his son in his arms.

Wes opened his eyes, and took in the dimness of his surroundings. The sun had not yet risen, but he knew it was time to go. He was surprised to find that Benji had crawled into bed with him at some point in the night, and carefully untangled himself from the boy. As soon as he moved, Benji seemed to overtake the entire bed with arms and legs sprawled about. It was hard to separate himself, and Wes stumbled as he shifted his weight to step onto the floor. Fortunately, he caught himself before he fell into the table, and woke the entire house. Wes slid into his boots, slipped on his jacket, and placed his hat on his head. He then hoisted his pack onto his shoulder, much lighter without his book inside, and reached for the door.

Wes glanced over his shoulder, and watched Benji continue to sleep peacefully. He looked so innocent, lost in his dreams. Wes was grateful for the night they shared, knowing that Benji wasn't upset with him, but also vaguely remembered him crying, though it might have been a dream. Still, it was hard to leave, knowing Benji was going to miss him, and Wes wondered if it would be better to delay another day. Perhaps he could spend a little more time with the lad.

"If you don't go now, you won't go at all." Wes looked up to the loft, and found that Eve was watching him. Her face was placid and revealed none of what she was thinking.

"Am I doing the right thing?" Wes asked as he glanced over to Benji sleeping. He kept his voice soft, but just loud enough to reach Eve's ears. Her face did not betray her emotions.

"You are doing what must be done."

"Can you see the future, Eve?" Wes asked. "For Sassy can not."

"I see many futures," Eve responded. Wes couldn't fathom this strange child's existence. He shook his head in frustration.

"Then explain how I can save my son."

"Which son do you speak of?" Eve asked with a wry smile, "For Benji is now your son just as much as Daniel is."

"How do I save Daniel?" Wes amended in low whispers. "I know you said I should take him home, but then what? How am I supposed to know what to do so I don't mess things up somehow?" Eve's smile looked sad as she stepped away from the loft railing.

"You'll know what to do," she said softly, "take him home brother Wes."

Wes frowned at this, glanced over to Benji one last time, then stepped out into the start of a new day. The cold of the morning brought sharpness to his senses, and Wes turned his focus to the tasks at hand. He saddled his horse, secured his pack, and filled his canteen. He climbed up onto his mare, and with a deep breath, started back towards the highway. Wes only went a short distance when he heard a sound of despair coming from within the farmhouse. He knew right away that it was Benji, waking up and finding he was in the bed alone. Benji knew what this meant. They both knew that this had to happen. Still, Wes kicked his mare into a full gallop, fleeing the possibility of having to face this goodbye. Goodbyes were always hard for him. It was hard when Daniel left them, it was hard when he ran away from his ailing wife, and it was especially hard on that day when he realized that Peter was gone.

After Jethro took to tormenting Ruth, and she lost herself to her despair, Peter was cast to the winds. He was so small. So precious and fearful. He clung to his mother, but it was as though she was no longer there. He wandered about, not knowing what to do. He mourned from the loss of love his mother once showed him, and while Wes tried to help the boy, it was hard to replace her. A child that young needed their mother, and Peter was barely weaned. Meanwhile, Wes was also grieving as he watched Ruth waste away before his eyes.

Fearing Ruth might die, and that Peter would not be strong enough to cope with it, Wes thought it best to push the boy a little. He wanted Peter to be stronger, the way Daniel was. He wanted Peter to not cry all the time, and not be fearful of everything new. He thought if he pushed the lad the way Jethro did with Daniel, that Peter would be able to pull through if Ruth did not recover.

When he found Peter crying over his mother, Wes told the boy to stop with his tears. He told Peter what Jethro once said to Daniel: that tears were a sign of weak men and that Peter needed to be strong for his mother. He needed to be strong like Wes.

He took to explaining to Peter all the things he would need to learn to carry on the farm when Wes and Ruth were no longer there to care for him. Peter followed him all around, while Wes explained how to tend to the crops, how to mix dough and how long to let it rise, how to clean a chicken pen, how to safely store eggs, and yes, how to ride a horse. Wes was convinced that Peter learning to ride the mare would be the best way for him to grow less fearful of all the animals. He would be stronger for it.

He thought the mare was safe for Peter to learn on, and she certainly was as long as Wes was there to guide them both through everything. Peter would be fine with Wes there to show him how to get up in the saddle, how to collect the reins, how to get her to walk and slow her if she got too fast.

But Peter was always afraid of the mare. Even after coaxing him to sit on her, his fear never lessened. Perhaps he had the second sight like his mother. Perhaps he knew what was to come. Wes had plenty of time to speculate perpetually.

But not on that day in late summer, when Ruth woke up suddenly, and got out of bed on her own. She made biscuits and eggs for Peter, kissing each of his rosy cheeks while he ate. God, Peter was so happy. He was just so happy to have his mother again it was almost too painful to endure. For this was not the first time Ruth deceived him, and Wes knew that it would not last. But he appreciated her in the moment, and leaned in to kiss the bony ridge of her hollow cheek. She smiled up at him; her thin face aging her, and focused her attention on washing the linen from their bed.

The memory of him stepping out onto the porch to see her hanging the linen on the line to dry was once so clear to Wes. She sang a hymn while she worked. He could almost recall the words.

Jesus paid it all,
all to him I owe.
Sin has left a crimson stain,
He washed it white as snow.

Wes should have talked to her. If he had, he would have known that something was wrong. One of many regrets that haunted him in the days to come. But she looked happy; truly happy, and Peter was laughing. A sound that Wes had not heard for weeks. He dare not interrupt them. He didn't want to break this spell. He wanted so badly to believe things would be different this time. That Ruth would be normal.

Wes looked out over his field, and saw that the sweet corn was ready for harvesting. Peter threw maple seeds up in the air, and laughed as they fell upon his face. The bed linen billowed in a slow warm breeze. It was such a lovely day.

Wes could smell the sweetness of the corn, and thought that if he went to pick a few ears for their dinner, Ruth would be happy for it. Surely, she would tend to the lad in his absence. She tended to him all morning. Wes stepped off the porch, and walked toward the field.

He wouldn't be long.

Twenty minutes perhaps.

Just a few ears of nice corn.

But the light went out of Ruth's eyes shortly after Wes left the porch steps. She stopped singing. Her face went flat. She stood rigid for a moment, then turned, and walked back into the house.

Wes could only imagine what Peter thought when he saw that he was alone. He often tried to envision what went on in his son's mind at that moment. Was he scared? Did he cry and think that his tears would disappoint Wes? Maybe he thought that it would impress his father if he could climb onto the mare all by himself, and ride down into the corn field. Wouldn't that just shock his boots right off?

How many times did Wes imagine all this before his mind shut down, and blocked the whole memory from his thoughts? He liked to believe that Peter was not scared when he made up his mind to ride that horse. He liked to believe that all of the last moments of his son's life were happy ones.

Wes had no understanding of how Peter managed to get on the back of that mare. She had no saddle on, alone in her stable as she was. But Peter managed it all the same. Then the boy spooked her somehow. When she saw her gate open, she took off running.

Peter tried so hard to hold on, but he was just so little. He wasn't yet meant to be strong. When Wes turned towards the sound of his son crying out, his hands full of the corn he just picked, his eyes beheld the moment when Peter could hold on no more. It was a moment he tried never to remember. He prayed so often to forget it. It was better to go back to the moment before. Go back to the laughter and the maple seeds; to the sound of Ruth's sweet singing carried across the breeze. When he was last happy. Truly happy. Let Wes remember that moment instead. Hold onto it and never let it go. But with that moment gone, and the break inside him mended, the subsequent memories return to haunt him anew. They crept into his dreams and his idle thoughts. A memory so vivid repeated again and again.

Seeing his son fall;

hearing the sound of his little head cracking against the stones.

Seeing his son fall;

hearing the sound of his little head cracking against the stones.

Again, and again, and again. Wes could not stand this memory. He begged to be free from it. It filled him with so much anguish, he felt like he couldn't catch his breath. He felt like he couldn't see what was in front of his eyes.

All he saw was his son fall.

All he heard was the sound of his little head cracking against the stones.

Nothing he knew in this dying world ever caused such pain as his own grief did. Without that joyous memory blocking their way, and without Benji and the others to distract him, nothing held the memory at bay. Wes ground his teeth as he fought to exile the thoughts from his mind.

He would not make these mistakes again. He had another chance with Peter. In Benji, he had another chance with his son. Benji's tears did not make him weak. Strength was found not in the suppression of sadness, but in growing from it.

The children you will have, After you have lost the others,
Will say again in your ears, 'The place is too small for me;
Give me a place where I may dwell.' -Isaiah 49:20 NKJV

After the fall, Wes took Peter into his arms and stared at his son's lips; willing them to part. Willing the boy's chest to rise. He stood for a long time, with ears of corn all about his feet, and prayed the Lord would bring breath back to his son's body. When the shadows stretched long, and the sun grew low, Wes carried the boy into his home and brought him to his mother.

Ruth stared at the window, but not through it. Her eyes were open, but distant and vacant. Her lips, parted slightly, quivered with words unspoken. She was talking to her phantoms again; either the idol in her hand, or the tormentor in her brain.

"Ruth," Wes said, and he did not recognize his own voice. It sounded weighed down and heavy. It sounded like the voice of an impostor. Not the father of a lifeless child. "Ruth, Peter is dead."

Slowly, as though steering a plow through uncut ground, Ruth turned her head towards her son. Her eyes shifted into focus, and she beheld the boy crumpled in Wes' arms. She reached for him, her hand stroking his soft fine hair, and then she shook her head.

"Neh, husband. He is warm. He still lives. Put him to rest now, for he's just sleeping."

"Ruth! Look at him! He is broken! He is dead!" But already her eyes glazed over once more. He could see deep within her gaze, the true pain of understanding. But Ruth was not willing to face it. She would face it in the days to come, but in that moment, Peter was still warm in Wes' hands. He remained warm far longer than Wes thought he would. Wes left Ruth where she sat, and returned to his porch where just a short while before he stood happy.

He sat down on the steps and remained in the dark for a long time, holding his dead son, while he hoped that something; anything would come out of the night, and take him. Just grab him and rip out his throat. Let the world steal away his breath the way it stole his sons. Give him this mercy, and ease his wretched pain.

But nothing came for him. Not a sound stirred the night. When at last the sun brushed against the horizon, Wes stood, retrieved a shovel, and took his son down to the edge of the field to bury him for the Lord.

Chapter Sixteen

The city is left in ruins, its gates battered down.
Throughout the earth the story is the same-
Only a remnant is left, like stray olives left on a tree
Or the few grapes left on the vine after harvest.
-Isaiah 24:12-13

Fleeing from one dream, Wes landed in another. He sat outside his home, on that same familiar slope of grassland, and looked out upon the crows loitering in his barren field. Was there something laying on the ground that drew the birds in? He couldn't be sure.

Wes peered up at the cloudless sky, and let the sun warm his face. He closed his eyes, and breathed in the crisp late autumn air. Winter felt just beyond his reach. A hint of lilac blended with the smell of decaying leaves, and Wes felt Ruth wrap her arms around him. He dare not open his eyes, fearing he might dispel the illusion.

"I was thinking of Peter today," Wes said to her, and the name stung like an open wound. Ruth squeezed him in a sympathetic hug. "I can't stop thinking about that day...when I saw him die. I keep seeing him fall off that stupid horse. I keep hearing the sound his head made when it struck the stones. Lord help me, I wanted to slaughter that horse for what she did to our son. But I needed her to bring Daniel home to you."

Wes rubbed his eyes with the heel of his hands. Ruth's hair brushed his cheek. Her arms felt as though she stole the heat from the sun. How did she smell like summer lilacs on the cusp of winter?

"I thought you were gone from my life, Ruth," Wes said. "After that prayer we did...I can't remember the details but... I thought I was setting you free. Letting you go home to the Lord. Yet here you are, trapped in the past."

This isn't the past, Wesley.

The voice was in his mind and not in his ear. Her arms, so slender and yet so strong, slid away from his shoulders.

"If this isn't the past, what is it?" Wes asked. He opened his eyes, and looked out to the crows in his field. He reached for Ruth, but her arm burst like a bubble on the water. Gone in an instant. Not even her scent remained. Wes peered over his shoulder at the vacant farmhouse on top of the hill. An empty skull, devoid of life.

As was his way, Wes looked to the sky the moment he woke. He squinted at the sun, and determined he still had a few hours until nightfall. Time to move on. Wes rubbed the sleep from his eyes, and slowly got to his feet. He glanced over to his tethered mare, and she lifted her head to blink at him in calm recognition. The ride to get there was hard, as Wes fought to outrace his remembering. It was only when they reached this ridge that he allowed her to rest, and by then she was panting; utterly exhausted from the drive. They slept through the afternoon, and Wes prepared himself for what he would face in the night.

He put his mare out of his mind, and took a moment to stretch the cold from his muscles as he surveyed the area. From his vantage point on the mountain's ridge, he was provided a full view of the capital in the valley below.

His mare pushed her nose into his hand, and Wes stroked it absently, while he studied the layout of the city. He noted how the sparse wilderness flowed right up to the edge of the buildings, making the transition from one to the other jarring, and the capital appeared out of place.

It fanned out before him; a foreboding machine erected on top of a fossil from the Before. It was one of the last bastions of what still remained. The highway from the east led straight down the main street of the city which was lined on either side with rows of tall buildings. This central street extended about 500 feet into the heart of the city, where a large square indicated its center point. From there, narrow roads snaked out like fingers in all directions, and were lined with small earthly huts that must have been built after the Damnation. In the center of the city, facing the entrance to the east, was a cluster of massive buildings that towered over all the rest. There were four in total surrounding a vast central structure which fanned out like wax from a melting candle. He never saw anything like it.

Wes tried to focus on the task at hand, which meant finding Daniel. He reached for his pack, rummaged through its contents, and pulled out a scrap of cloth he brought along as protection against the wind. It used to belong to Ruth, and still carried the slightest scent of lilac. Wes plucked his hat off of his head, and tied the cloth to conceal his forehead. He didn't want to risk relying solely on the brim of his hat to hide his unmarked face. The more he was able to blend in, the safer he would be. Wes always kept his hands exposed, to show the sin that rested there, and he hoped that this extra measure would be enough to avoid any curiosity.

Returning his hat to his head, Wes climbed into his saddle, and used what remained of the sun to ride this final stretch into the city. As he rode, the sun sank, and the shadows stretched longer. Figures clad in black uniforms appeared on the uninhabited streets of the city. Wes watched them approach long poles in sequence running along the streets, to light small boxes suspended on them that were topped with glass globes. These lights lined the streets intermittently, spaced so that their small flames prevented darker shadows from forming. None of it was as bright as Sassy's little cabin, but it was bright enough. For as the day grew darker, more people stepped out into the street. Those in black uniforms got swallowed in a wave of dramatic colors and costumes.

In what seemed like an instant, the city came alive. Wes rode his mare down onto the highway, and had a good view of the activity that overtook the main street. So many voices shouting, talking, and singing. He could hear instruments playing; actual instruments! When was the last time he heard such a sound? He wondered what Benji would think of all the color and the music, if Wes ever dared to bring him there to see it.

All through the city, those strange metal boxes dotted the streets with light from a flame that did not use wood to stay alive. He wondered if they worked like Chancy's lighter: a clever creation from the Before. As he drew closer, Wes could see that most of the buildings along this main path were two stories in height, some of them three, and made from stone or a sort of brick. They loomed over the people walking between them but no one seemed to be bothered by it. All of them were illuminated with many windows, bright and inviting. Some were propped open, and women leaned out of them while they called to the people below; inviting them to come inside.

Wes brought his horse to the edge of where the wilderness changed over to the city, and climbed out of his saddle. He quickly took hold of the tether. The mare already seemed apprehensive, seeing the fray in front of her, but Wes was determined to stay the course. Right at the entrance, Wes noticed uniformed men dressed in black examining the crowds and while they didn't look in his direction, he had no doubt they were watching him closely. They made no effort to stop him, though, so he had to wonder if they were positioned to protect the people of the city, or to stop those trying to leave. He put it out of his mind as it was an issue for another day, and pulled his mare forward; entering the chaos.

He was immediately caught up in the cacophony of the city. He urged his mare into the throng, and was bombarded by noises, smells, and colors. Bodies pressed against him as people traveled about in a tight nest of activity. The air was warm and heavy with humidity, making it uncomfortable to breathe.

Wes was not the only one with a horse, so she did not draw attention, but it was near impossible to navigate through so much bustle while pulling her behind him. She immediately fought against him, and he knew if he let go of her, she would turn and run right back out into the night. Sadly, Wes did not see horse stables anywhere, so he pushed ahead, and doggedly dragged her behind him.

The buildings on either side of him advertised taverns, eateries, and shops, among other things Wes could not identify. The doors were propped open, in spite of the cold, and people funneled in and out of every opening. Music filled the street from half a dozen different places, and were drowned out by all the other discord.

Daniel lives in this place. He sees these things every day.

Wes pushed past the bulk of the taverns, and the street segued into shops with signs outside their doors. Shops selling food, tack, cloth, and all sorts of things. Wes marveled to think of all they had access to. One such store showed what Wes thought might be religious relics in their display window; including crosses and a variety of paintings of a young boy. He stepped up to the window and examined the pious child in the painting. Was this the Christ? Were their believers in this place?

A group of people stumbled past him, half drunk or otherwise distracted in their indulgences, and Wes acknowledged the strangeness of their attire. Some wore vast sweeping dresses with wide sculpted shoulders and elaborate head wear, while others wore hardly anything at all. Some even wore colored cloth too thin to conceal those things that it should. Wes turned back to the Christ child in the window display. If there were believers in this city, did they even number ten?

Wes' horse shoved her nose into his head to get his attention, and almost knocked his hat into the dirt. She stomped her hooves as her eyes rolled from side to side. When Wes followed her gaze, he realized what she was seeing that he wasn't. The colors and the music and the lights distracted from the reality that all the inhabitants of this city were cloaked in scales of sin. All around him, he saw black scales sweeping up arms and spreading over faces. Some of the scales appeared to be painted in different colors but none of them were powdered like Chancy.

"Easy now," Wes soothed, and stepped closer to his horse. Her eyes looked wild, and when a particularly wicked individual with a face that looked more insect than human got too close to her, she tried to throw a kick into his gut. Wes jerked her away in time, then fought to get her under control. He could not lose this animal when he brought her this far. Without her, the time to get back home would double. He needed to get away from all these people, and hopefully find a stable on one of the quieter side streets. Wes pushed ahead, focusing on the central square of town, where many roads fanned out from that point.

Lewd smells grew more prominent the farther Wes traveled into this Hell. Smells of urine, feces, food, alcohol, and decay all assaulted Wes' senses, and certainly his horses as well. The moment Wes tried to ignore the sights, it was the smells that overwhelmed him. His eyes watered as he stubbornly refused to divert from his path.

He saw a man stagger out of one of the taverns. He was already drunk when the sun only set less than an hour before. He stumbled down the porch, into the street, then dropped to his knees, and vomited out the whole of what he just consumed. All around him, people circumvented the scene without a glance. No one bothered to help him. When his retching subsided, the man stood, swayed in place for a moment, then staggered back into the same building he just vacated.

A little further along, Wes noticed a woman draped over a chair, unconscious on her porch. She had one let up on the rail, exposing herself to everyone walking past her, and in her hand she held a long pipe that had a narrow stem and small bowl. Her head lulled to the side; bent at an odd angle, as she snored softly through her gaping mouth. Wes quickly looked away, disgusted.

He knew this place would be bad. He knew it would be full of sin. But knowing such things was a lot easier than living through them.

Wes focused solely on the city square. Fortunately, the farther inward he went, the more spread out the area became. The street widened, and many of the buildings appeared to be affluent homes. He saw a fountain in the middle of the square, and behind it, those massive stone buildings were half concealed in darkness.

Wes' mare relaxed a little in the open space, but those tall buildings had Wes feeling unnerved. At least his horse wasn't trying to kick anyone anymore, or bite Wes' hand. He stopped a moment to stroke her nose, and looked around to see if he might ask someone on the location of a stable. He caught sight of a man and woman stepping out of one of those nicer homes, and was surprised to see they were both dressed all in white. They had on elaborate hats to match their elaborate costumes, and concealed their faces as they bent to light cigars. Wes took the opportunity to move to the other end of the street.

Chancy told him all he needed to know about those residents that preferred to wear white. He had not forgotten Gad's warning either, about challenging those in authority. No one else wore a scrap of white in the city. Wes knew who was in charge.

He moved on, but with the crowds thinning around him, so went the horses. People started to take more notice of him, their eyes glancing over him as they passed. Wes wondered if he appeared out of place because of how he was dressed in mostly black. It certainly wasn't because of his gun. He made sure the weapon was hidden under his jacket.

"Come join me, stranger!" A woman called out to him, her voice sweet and melodic. When Wes glanced in her direction, she lifted her skirt to reveal an inner thigh, covered in scales painted a deep shade of red. Wes quickly looked away, but was surprised at how unaffected he felt. Already he was growing accustomed to this city. He spotted a man walking towards the woman; apparently allured by her invitation. He did not stagger, and his eyes were not dull. Wes decided to take a chance.

"Excuse me, sir, can you point me toward a place where I can stable my horse?"

The man turned, surprised to be addressed in such a way, and stared at Wes. Then his eyes slid from Wes to his mare behind him. His expression softened, and a slow smile spread across his face.

"Why sure, stranger. Sure I can," the man began as he licked his lips, but Wes turned from him and walked on. The man's tongue was as black as coal. A filthy liar's tongue. He despised liars.

"You are looking for a place to keep your horse?"

Wes glanced to his side, then looked down. Next to him, a small girl peered up at him from under a hood. She fell in alongside him, as he continued into the square itself.

"Do you have any parents around that can help me, little girl?" Wes asked as he glanced about, then yelped in surprise as he felt the girl's fist land a solid jab in his ribs.

"I'm not a little girl! I'm sixteen years old, mister!" Wes was stunned. Sixteen? But she was so small! Wes faced her fully, and examined the heart shape of her fox-like face. Sharp green eyes glared up at him from within the shade of her hood. Wes rubbed a hand over his stinging ribs.

"I'm sorry, I didn't realize," he conceded, and the girl relaxed. Her glare softened, then she looked around, and grabbed Wes' arm.

"Come over here, out of the way of the street." She led Wes over to a tavern that had a large window flaunting its bar. On either side of the building, smaller side streets snaked out of sight in different directions from where they stood. Sitting against the building below the window, a small blonde girl wearing rags for clothes watched as they approached.

"Scram!" The fox girl snapped at her, and the younger girl vanished down one of the side streets before Wes could react.

"Did you have to be so mean?" He asked. When the girl looked at him, her eyes were as sharp as a blade.

"Out with it. Do you need a place for your horse or not?"

"I do," Wes replied. By the light of the bar, he was able to get a better look at her. Her rust colored hair was wild and curly, though she tried to conceal it within her hood. Her face was marked with her sin. Scales spread across her forehead and curved with the arch of her eyebrows. She made no effort to paint them or hide them under her hood, and Wes appreciated this about her. Her hooded tunic went to mid-thigh, and was a rich shade of dark green. She had tight pants tucked into soft leather boots laced to the knee. All in all she was a rather dashing sight, and pretty too, if she didn't look so angry.

"Do you have money?" She asked suspiciously, and Wes shifted his focus. He caught a glimpse of pink behind her teeth. A good sign.

"No," he said honestly. "But I have something of great value I can give you instead." As soon as he said this, her eyes widened with anticipation. It was plain to him which idol she worshiped.

"Show me." She said with uncloaked excitement. Her earnestness was a sign of her age. Wes looked around with an exaggerated expression, and then back at the girl in mock surprise.

"Right here? In the open?" He asked and her face darkened. She knew she was being teased, but his words gave her pause. She looked away from him, biting at her lip, while she considered the situation. He saw clearly the predicament she was in. They both knew it would be foolish to show anything of value out in the open as they were, but if she led

Wes somewhere secluded, he might hurt her. It might be a trap. She looked up at him, her eyes intense as she studied him, then she nodded to herself; her mind made up.

"Follow me," she announced, then slipped up the side street opposite from the one the small girl fled into. Wes took note of his surroundings to make sure he didn't lose his way, then followed after her. The girl kept a fast pace, trying to throw Wes off by forcing him to keep up, and while she was smart in her plan, he could see right through her cunning. She was overly confident, and terribly naive. Wes could not see futures as Eve does, but he knew that the future where this girl did not live to see adulthood was likely.

"Wait for me," Wes called after her, but she did not wait. Instead, she shoved past a drunkard and pitched the poor man onto his face. He seemed too drunk to care. On she went, without a glance back, and Wes conceded to chase after her, as she knew he would.

The girl weaved around people in her rush to get ahead, but the road was narrow, making it difficult for him to move about the way she did with a horse in tow. He tried to keep his eyes trained to the back of the girl's head, but she was so short that she blended into the smallest of crowds. He caught a final glimpse of her as she slipped from light into shadow. Then she was gone.

Wes stopped with a grunt, and considered the situation. They had not deviated from their course since she started him down this path, and he could not imagine she was trying to slip away from him after he saw the hunger for wealth in her eyes. This meant that the stable she was leading him to, must be somewhere on this street. Wes pressed on, absently patting his horse to keep her calm, and walked past people taking part in their own tasks of life.

After some time, the road opened into a clearing where it ended in front of a curving row of mud colored huts. The tip of the finger, as it were. To the right, a small alley yawned between two houses and revealed a depth of darkness that seemed to draw firelight into it. Wes stared down the alley for a moment, as something unseen wrapped chilly fingers around his throat. Then he shook his head, pushing the notion from his mind, and turned instead to the left. A crude stable was tucked away at the end of the row of huts, and a few other horses were already housed there. Outside one of the empty stalls, the girl leaned against its railing, and watched him with a smirk on her face.

Her little cat and mouse game was a demonstration for him. She wanted him to know that if he tried to hurt her, or take advantage of her in some way, she had the ability to get away from him. He respected the effort, but she needed strength to escape a man, not stealth. He felt a secret desire to teach her. To help her learn. He pushed it out of his mind. He was there for Daniel.

“This stall is included in our property permit,” she announced as Wes approached her. “But we do not have a horse to store here.”

“Do you live in one of these huts?” Wes asked, gesturing towards the crescent of small homes.

“They aren’t huts!” The girl snapped as she stood up to her full height. She poked a finger into his chest hard. “My home has two whole rooms, I’ll have you know, and a privy in the back! I don’t live in one of those little hovels in the south district!”

“It is as you say,” Wes conceded, and tugged on the brim of his hat in apology. “I have never been here before so I didn’t know there were houses smaller than yours.”

The girl growled in annoyance, and thrust her finger in the direction of a small house at the end of the row. It was positioned directly alongside the stables.

“Does my house look small to you?” Wes said nothing. It was not worth the lie. She glared at him for a moment, then when she realized he wouldn’t respond, she held her hand out between them and showed him her open palm. “Let’s see what you’re offering for this stable.”

Wes looked past her toward the stall, and considered. It was small, only allowing his mare enough room to turn around in, but he hoped he didn’t have to keep her there too long. It also had a canopy of crude timber overhead to offer her some protection from the elements. Two small fireboxes burned just outside the stables, and were a part of those that lined the streets so they would hopefully be lit every evening. It would have to do. The area was relatively quiet, being at the end of a street, and the other horses seemed indifferent to their surroundings as they rested. Wes looked back to the girl.

“My horse is the nicest of the lot here. What guarantee do I have that she won’t be stolen?”

Again, the girl glared at him as though he just insulted her mother. It seemed like everything Wes said made her more and more angry with him. After the initial shock of his apparent insult, her face went hard, and her eyes burned like fire. She spoke softly through clenched teeth.

“You dare imply that my people would actually steal from each other?”

“I reckon so,” Wes said as he looked down on her. She was like a fox backed in a corner. “But I mean you no disrespect.”

“Mean no disrespect!” The girl stepped up to him, and actually jumped so that she could catch hold of the collar on his jacket. She used it to force him to bend forward, and brought his face level with hers. “You have done nothing but disrespect me this night.”

“You can’t slip in and out of darkness like you do, and not be a thief,” Wes said defensively. Even though this girl was furiously angry, Wes found that he was surprisingly calm. His anger no longer plagued him since Sassy rooted the seed of evil out of him. At least for the time being.

“I would never steal from my own kind! We steal from the coffers! From the guild masters! From the city itself! Not those that struggle to live inside its walls!” Her voice rose, and soon she was shouting at him. It was the last straw for Wes’ poor mare. In one swift jerk, she pulled her tether free from his hand, and reared up on her back legs as she screamed out her objections. Wes dashed forward, the girl too startled to hold him, and raced to get control of his horse before she ran.

“Easy! Easy!” Wes called to her, and thank the Lord he managed to snatch up her lead as it swung across her neck. The mare dropped back down hard, driving her hooves deep into the soft earth of the street, and danced in place as she tried to regroup her footing. She backed away, putting the full weight of her body into her earnest desire to break free from Wes’ grasp. It was all he could do to hold onto her tether. “Help me get her inside the stall!”

The girl fell in beside him, grabbing for the bridle, and gave a little squeak when the mare tried to bite her. They got hold of the horse, and with some maneuvering, Wes guided her over to the stall while the girl opened its gate to receive the animal. The mare took one look at the cramped quarters, and made another attempt to run. Wes pulled her, growling through the strain, and the horse glared at him with large wild eyes as she tried to slip out of her bridle. Behind her, the girl pushed at her flank.

“Mind her legs!” Wes shouted but it was too late. The mare landed a square kick into the girl's thigh and she staggered backwards, before falling hard on her rump. The kick was the last gesture of resistance his horse had in her, and she stepped forward meekly into the stall. As soon as she was inside, Wes threw the gate closed, then leaned over it panting. He looked up to see the girl staring at him, still sprawled on the ground, as they both fought to catch their breath. Then, without reason, they both broke into fits of laughter.

“Tell me your name,” Wes said when he was able to catch his breath, and the girl managed to get back on her feet.

“Palto,” she replied as she brushed dust from her backside. Then she pointed a finger at him, but the mirth did not leave her eyes. “You owe extra for pain and suffering!”

“Of course I do,” Wes said with another laugh. How long has it been since he laughed like that? “Well I’m Wes. Thank you for lending me the use of this stable. I should only need it a day or two.”

"You can store your saddle over there," Palto said, pointing, then indicated a row of shelves at the end of the stable. "And there are lockers over there for your personal things." Of course she noticed his pack. Wes tended to his horse, calming her further, then removed her saddle with precision spawned out of routine. Leaning on the railing, Palto watched him with a mix of indifference and acute curiosity.

"Sorry about your leg," Wes said, gesturing toward where his mare kicked her.

"You think I'm too weak to withstand a horse kick?" Palto asked, suspiciously, and Wes shook his head, laughing again. Lord, he really liked this girl. It amazed him that even in this horrible place, flowers could still grow.

"I beg your pardon," he said, removing his hat and bowing theatrically, then returned to brushing his horse.

"It's fine," she conceded, then squinted at him suspiciously. "Why do you cover your head with that cloth? The color isn't affiliated with any guild or labor unions. Is it a private club marking?"

Wes chastised himself for being careless. He forgot he was there to find his own child, not adopt a new one. He considered his words carefully, to avoid having yonder bucket thrown at his head.

"I...don't want others to see the whole of my face," he replied, but this only made her more curious. She leaned over the railing with her head tilted to the side, so she might get a better look at his forehead. Curls of red hair dangled from her hood.

"Surely you haven't come down with the ooze. You're nowhere near that far along. I haven't looked so untarnished since I was three."

So young! Far too young an age to learn the wage of sin.

"Thank you for waiting on me," he said, changing the subject. "I needed to tend to her before I could compensate you." Palto forgot all about Wes' mysterious face, as he grabbed his pack, and stepped through the stall door. She looked up at him eagerly, and in that moment, she was every bit a child. Wes couldn't help but smile.

"I will take good care of her," she said while she watched Wes kneel down and open his pack. "Equal work for equal pay as they say."

"I hope that my offering will buy a little more from you than this," he said as he rummaged about.

"Oh..." Palto said, hesitating, "yes, I have many talents. I can clean your clothes. I can shop. I can give you information."

Wes' hand closed over the relic he kept stored in his pack, then stilled. He kept his head down, letting his hat hide his face, and tried to sound casual when he spoke.

“I do seek information, now that you mention it. Have you seen a boy, possibly on his own; about thirteen years of age, with sandy blonde hair, and a scar that runs the length of his face?” He snuck a glance up at her from under the brim of his hat to see if any signs of recognition crossed her expression. She only looked confused.

“I don’t remember seeing a boy with a scar like that before. When did you last see him? If the sin sickness had spread enough, it might have covered the scar.” Wes frowned. He had not considered that possibility. He knew Daniel would not look like the boy he was at five. But what if he looked like Benji’s mother? What if he hid in the shadows of those small alleyways, and avoided the fireboxes at night? Would Wes ever be able to find him?

“Perhaps I can walk around,” he thought aloud, as he withdrew an item wrapped in linen from his pack. He straightened, then looked out over the street. Sassy said he needed to find Daniel, but he never thought to ask her how.

“Don’t be so hasty,” Palto offered, and when Wes turned to look at her, he noticed her eyes darting between his face and his occupied hand. He wondered about the life she had to live to be so enticed by wealth. “I might be able to help you find this boy you’re looking for. I know the head of the slavers union.”

“No,” Wes said.

“But if he’s a child on his own, it’s unlikely he will be anywhere else.”

“No,” Wes repeated. He did not want to think for a moment that his son was in some way a slave.

“Of course, mister,” Palto said to appease him. Then she gave him the sweetest smile, and held out her open hand again. “If I have something of value, I can find out all sorts of things about this boy for you.”

Wes offered her a smile in return, but doubted it was so sweet, then placed the item into her hand. As soon as Palto received it, she held her hand out and admired the wrapped item. Without even opening it, she was so happy that in her hand was something she actually owned. Sadly, Wes could see a hint of greedy wickedness in her smile. She was so young. Daniel was even younger.

Palto pulled back the linen wrapping, then brought her hand to eye level to examine the item more closely. Gently, she plucked up the chain in between two fingers, and allowed the relic to hang suspended on the other end.

“What is it?” she asked, breathless and mesmerized.

“It’s a relic from the Before,” Wes explained. “It survived through the Damnation, although I don’t know how it works or for why. It’s called a pocket watch. It belonged to my father-in-law.”

“An actual relic!” Palto looked in awe at the watch spinning lazily on its chain. Then she abruptly snatched it into her fist, and clutched it to her chest. She looked up at Wes, her eyes wide with excitement, and startled him by squealing in delight. She danced around the clearing, clapping and shouting and spinning about, and Wes’ mare rolled her eyes in Palto’s direction. He quickly stuffed a wedge of hay into her feed trough before she got any ideas.

“Thank you so much!” Palto cried out as she returned to Wes, and threw her arms around him. His mind reeled over the quick change act she kept throwing at him. He didn’t know what was true, and what was trickery. Again she shifted, from delight to reverence. Palto pressed her face against Wes’ chest and slid her arms around his waist. “You don’t know what this means to me, mister. For something this valuable, I will give you anything. I will *do* anything.”

“Still your tongue,” Wes scolded and firmly pushed her off of him. Her shoulders felt bony and frail in his hands.

“I don’t understand. Perhaps you want someone older? My mother is very beautiful in the lantern light.”

“Be still, be still,” Wes groaned. “I will hear no more of this.” He felt like his skin was crawling. It was only made worse by how hurt she looked.

“But...this is all I have to offer a man.”

“Listen to me, Palto,” Wes said, and leaned over so that he could catch her eye. “I might ask you to do a few errands for me, tend to my horse, and yes, give me information. But I will not ask anything like that. There is only one more thing I want from you for the price of this relic.”

“Anything,” Palto said, her face a reflection of her determination.

“Be sincere.”

“What?”

“Be sincere with me. No more trickery. No more shows. No more sweet smiles. Just be yourself. For I want to trust you, and I’ll never trust you if I don’t know who you are.”

“Alright, mister,” Palto said, “I will try.” Wes put his pack into one of the lockers Palto offered, then adjusted his jacket to ensure it still covered his revolver after the way Palto leaped on him.

“I plan to look around. Maybe I will get lucky, Lord willing.” He only took a few steps before Palto fell in beside him.

“Where do you plan to go?”

"Well, to start, I reckon I'll go find the Guardian Son," Wes said, and Palto gaped up at him.

"The...what?" She asked weakly.

"The Guardian Son," Wes repeated. "To inquire about the location of the boy I told you about. If anyone knows where he is, surely it will be this Guardian Son who is in charge of the city."

"Shut your mouth, mister," Palto said, her eyes wide with urgency, "Don't speak that name out loud. You just invite trouble when you talk about the Elders or about...him."

"I hear you," he said to her, "and I'll do as you say. But I don't understand why."

"There are other ways to find your lost child without getting a rope tied around your neck," Palto said gravely. Then she gestured back toward the center of town.

"Come with me. I know the guy who runs that tavern at the end of the street. It never gets too crowded in there, so if we keep our voices down, not one will listen in. I'll tell you anything you want to know about the capital. I can even help you find your lost boy! Just as long as we don't talk about...him."

"Very well," Wes agreed and together they walked back to the heart of the city. Palto took the opportunity, and pulled her hand away from her chest to sneak a peak at the pocket watch again. She smiled to herself, a motherly look coming over her face, then she caught sight of something and dipped her head to inspect it closer.

"You said you haven't been to the capital before," Palto said as she looked up at Wes with newfound suspicion.

"I haven't."

"Then why do you have a watch with Old Father's mark upon it?"

"What do you mean?" Wes asked as he stopped walking, and turned to her. Palto held up the watch, and indicated what she found. On the back plate of the watch, the letters J.C. were scratched crudely into the surface.

"J.C. was the mark of Old Father, may he live forever in the realm beyond. If you have proof this scribe came directly from Old Father himself, this watch will be priceless! Do you bear a certificate, mister? Perhaps a letter of record?"

Wes stopped listening. A cool feeling of dread raised the hair on his head and numbed his feet.

He had to admit, he wasn't even surprised. Ever since he spoke with Chancy, and first heard the name Guardian Son, he had known. It was the knowing that came from being a father. Daniel's father. Of course Jethro was this 'Old Father' for he was a cunning man.

If there was power to grasp, he would not hesitate to grab it. Years of his life revealed itself to Wes in an instant. Jethro was Old Father. And Daniel was the Guardian Son.

"Are you alright, mister?" Palto asked, and Wes suddenly felt dizzy. He stumbled, and would have fallen if Palto did not manage to hold him up. He held on to her, his hands on her shoulders, as he took a few steady breaths, and his vision cleared.

"I know now what must be done, Palto," he said, hoarsely. "Take me to this Tavern. Then tell me all that you know about the Guardian Son."

Chapter Seventeen

But the wicked are like the troubled sea,
when it cannot rest, whose waters cast up mire and dirt.
There is no peace, saith my God, to the wicked.
-Isaiah 57:20-21 KJV

"This isn't going to work," Palto declared, then swallowed the contents of her cup in a single gulp. She brought him into the tavern they were outside earlier, and true to her word the place had only a few patrons. A smattering of people sat about, either in front of the bar or at one of the few tables the place provided. The owner himself stood behind the bar looking sallow and stooped; regretting the geographical placement of his enterprise.

Palto led Wes to the far end of the narrow room, where there was a row of unoccupied tables, and sat across from him at the farthest one. They looked like two people that didn't want to be heard, but Wes hoped everyone would just assume she was working over a trick. Palto bought them both a drink, which Wes was grateful for as he was terribly thirsty, but after the first sip, he let the elixir rest between his hands.

"How do you reckon?" he asked, as he examined the reddish liquid in his glass. He spun it slowly around with his fingertips, and watched how it refracted starbursts of light on the table. Palto looked over her shoulder, and examined the room conspicuously, then lowered her voice.

"No one sees *him*," she explained, referring to the Guardian Son. Her fox-like face wore a grim expression. "Not without a formal declaration from one of the guilds, a permit from the masters, or a sigil mark from one of the four barracks."

"The four barracks," Wes repeated, sounding out the words. It seemed to him like Palto was speaking another language with all these titles, labels, rules, and permissions.

"Yes, the four Barracks, stationed at the four corners of the world: north, south, east, and west. Do you know nothing, mister?" Palto glared at him like he was daft. He had much to learn. "My point is, you're not able to get into the Divine Hall, so don't even try."

"The Divine Hall," Wes repeated, again sounding out the words which suggested religious meaning. He thought back to those effigies in the one store display: The portraits of the Christ child. Again he wondered if these people still followed some form of the Word. Palto groaned, raking fingers through her hair, and letting the curls fall around her face. Her other hand still clutched the pocket watch to her chest.

"Do you have to repeat everything I say?"

"Beg your pardon," Wes said, with a quick tug of the hat. "I've not heard these titles before. Will you tell me about this...Divine Hall?"

"It's that big building in the center of the city," Palto said as she waved her hand to the owner, and pointed out her empty glass, "It's where *he* resides with his twenty four Elders. Old Father resided there too once, may he live forever in the world beyond."

"Does the Guardian Son govern the capital by himself?" Wes asked, and Palto looked around nervously. Perhaps he should lower his voice a little more for her sake.

"He is the exalted one, mister Wes. Everything he says will be, must be."

"Exalted one," Wes repeated to himself. He looked down at the smooth red liquid in the glass he held. "How is he exalted?"

"By the Disciples mostly," Palto said with an uncomfortable shrug. "The greater part of the city tries to avoid them, but there is no denying they are closely connected to the Divine Hall."

"Do they have a shop in the center of town? I saw a window display selling portraits of a young boy."

"Yes, those are paintings of...well, everyone likes to think of him as the child he was. I think half the houses in the capital have similar ones on their walls. Whenever we see him now, it's because there's about to be an execution." The bartender brought a bottle over to fill Palto's glass, and she stopped talking the moment he approached. She sat back, and watched as he poured her drink, then asked him to bring her some food as well.

"You plan to pay me this time," the sallow man said, and Palto smiled up at him. He shook his head as he shuffled away. Wes watched their interaction distantly, but his mind was elsewhere. He let out a heavy sigh. He thought the portrait was of the Christ, but sadly God no longer lived in the walls of this city. Instead of exalting the Lord, they have decided to exalt a man instead. Or more accurately, a boy. Wes' son.

Wes stared deeply into his drink, rolling the glass through his fingertips. Things were far more complicated than he could have imagined. But if Daniel was worshiped by these people, perhaps he was protected by them as well. Wes liked to think this was the case, but feared it only made the situation worse.

"He is only a child," Wes said sadly, thinking back to that portrait painting in the shop window. It was no wonder he mistook it for the Christ. He did not recall Daniel ever looking so...flawless. Palto looked up from her drink, but her confusion only lasted a moment.

"He is the most holy," she replied, picking up the conversation. Wes scrutinized her closely.

"Is that what you think? Do you revere him as well?" Again, Palto glanced around; her small black-scaled hand a tight fist around the relic held to her chest.

"Of course!" She said, her tone a little too forced. "Everyone praises the holy child." A young woman approached them, and Palto sat up a little in anticipation.

"I don't know why he keeps trusting you," the woman said flatly, as she placed a large bowl in front of Palto.

"It's because I always pay him back," Palto responded with a wide grin. "I can honor the cost."

The woman shook her head, disapproving, but she did not argue the point further. She turned, and left them to their meal which appeared to be a stew full of root vegetables and beef. Palto snatched up a potato, and popped it into her mouth. She then puffed her cheeks out and blew through her pursed lips to cool the piping hot morsel.

Wes had to wonder how she intended to cover the cost of her food and drink when she seemed unable to part with the watch she held. Palto gulped down the potato, wincing against the heat, then plucked up a chuck of meat to repeat the process. She ate like a girl who had not seen food for a long time. Wes returned to staring at the red liquid swirling around the glass in his hands.

How could a girl so young be forced to struggle so much? The sin on her face; the black scales that spread up her arms, Wes remembered a time when this was not commonplace. When he was a child, not much younger than Palto, all of the children in his village had faces and hands unmarked by sin. They all prayed for salvation from the Lord.

"Tell me something, Palto," Wes said softly, "do you ever pray?"

"What's that?" Palto asked around a mouthful of food.

"It's what you do when you want to talk to God." Palto lifted her head and met Wes' eye. She stopped chewing her food and for a moment, they just looked at one another. Then she shrugged, and turned her attention back to her meal.

"The Guardian Son only listens to donations."

As soon as she said the words, the young woman appeared beside them with a fresh drink in her hand.

"What did you just say?" She asked, but Palto snatched the drink away from her, and gulped half of it down. Wes offered the woman a small smile.

"Thank you, ma'am. I think we have what we need here." The serving woman scowled as she walked away.

"We should leave," Palto said, glancing over her shoulder at the woman as she retreated through a door into the kitchen.

"If the Guardian Son accepts donations, how does he receive them?" Wes asked, ignoring her worry, for he saw a possibility.

"I don't really get mixed up in all that worship stuff," Palto said, and used her sleeve to clean her face. "You'll need to talk to the Disciples to get the answers you're after."

So much for her getting him any information he needed. It was just as well. Even if Palto knew the answers to his questions, he still wanted to visit the Disciples on his own. Milling over all he learned, Wes looked over the handful of other patrons in the tavern. Some were huddled in pairs, but most of them were alone. All had drinks in hand. One called out, asking when his food was going to arrive.

"Where is that blasted woman?"

All of them were covered in scales to some degree. On their hands and over most of their faces. Some were painted, others weren't. The costumes were a little less elaborate here. Still they tried to decorate themselves and be presentable in other ways. They wore adornments on their faces, their ears, draped over their heads, or wrapped around their fingers. So many inventive ways to conceal the blackness underneath.

The nature of these urban dwellers made Wes nervous. He expected to see sin on full display in this city, but what he did not expect was how indifferent they were to it. He recalled how Palto questioned whether his forehead was oozing and he thought of Benji's mother. This was not a nightmare to avoid for them, but instead an inevitable fate.

What also bothered Wes was how little attention they paid to those of them that showed advanced stages of deformity. Wes saw a man sitting hunched at the bar, and the shape of his face was all wrong. His lower jaw jutted out; his teeth jagged and skewed. His nose sunk into the slope of his face and only open nostrils like vacant sockets remained.

How long before the madness took hold of that one? Days? A week at most? What will happen to him, when madness tears apart his mind?

Yet no one seemed to notice him sitting there. No one saw the threat that grew within him. Wes turned his focus back to Palto, and her fox-like features.

"These Disciples you speak of...do they resemble that man over there?" He tilted his head in the direction of where the deformed man sat, and Palto looked over his shoulder. Her glass was empty again.

"No, not usually," she said with a shrug. "The Elders would never interact with someone like him. Even if it was for an offering. They strive for perfection, you see. They wish they all looked like *him*."

"So what will happen to that man?" Wes asked as he leaned forward to catch Palto's eye. "Is there no madness for the wicked in this city?" Palto glanced over his shoulder again, to the man sitting at the bar.

"Madness hides in the dark alleys where no light touches them, mister. Even in the day, the light is not strong enough to dispel the shadows. No one likes to speak of those places, and no one ever ventures there. No matter how you enter them, it leads to death."

"Why don't you try to flush them out? Exile the wicked, and eliminate the risk." Wes kept his voice low, but he could sense the deformed man listening to him. Palto met his eyes with a grimness he had not seen in her before.

"Why take the risk of getting poisoned just to eliminate the damned, when all of us are damned and will join them in the alleys soon enough." She leaned back, and gestured for another drink.

There is nothing worth living for here. Hope already died upon their doorsteps.

The room went silent, and an anxious energy hung on the stillness in the air. Palto winced from the tension, and reached across the table to snatch Wes' drink away from him. Over her shoulder, Wes saw a tall man step into the room. He was barely more than a boy, not yet able to shave, but carried himself as a man all the same.

He was one of those black clad figures Wes saw lighting the fireboxes, and later on patrol around the city. His uniform was clean and trim, with broad shoulders on the jacket, a slim belted waist, and fanned out trousers tucked into polished boots. His hat, round with a flat top, had a brim like a duck bill which was only in the front and bent downward to cast shadow on his eyes. Wes focused his attention on the long club that was hooked on one side of the man's belt, and a slim sword sheathed on the other. Wes never saw a man dressed in this way, but he had no doubt that it indicated a position of authority. Behind the guard, the serving woman slipped inside, and scampered back into the kitchen like the rat she was.

"It will be as it should be," Wes said softly, as the man in black scanned the room, then approached their table. Palto groaned, and took a long draw from Wes' drink.

"I should have known it was you causing all this trouble," the man growled when he reached their table. He glared at Palto, and she glared at her drink. When she did not respond, the man lifted a black gloved fist, and pounded it once on the table. As though this were a cue, all the other patrons in the bar got up, and quickly exited out the door. The owner was resigned as he watched them leave, then calmly retreated through the same door as the serving woman. Palto looked up at the guard, and acted surprised.

"Oh...hello Jack, I didn't see you there."

"Don't play games, Palto. You're in a lot of trouble. I have a signed affidavit accusing you of heresy."

"Heresy?" Palto almost squeaked the word. Her face went pale except for her flushed cheeks; a result of the drink.

"When you say heresy," Wes interjected, "are you referring to her speaking the name of the Guardian Son?" Both Palto and Jack slowly turned to look at him. Palto, her eyes wide and horrified, and Jack in utter disbelief. His nostrils flared, as he scowled.

"H-he's not f-from around here," Palto stuttered, her voice high pitched and unnatural. Her eyes danced wildly between the two of them.

Oh, Palto. This battle is not for you, dear girl.

"What is your name, mister?" Jack asked as he leaned over the table. Wes met fellas like him before. Jack was used to getting his way.

"I'm Wes."

"Well, Wes. Palto here says you aren't from around here. So I will educate you regarding section eighty-five of capital law: no one beneath the High Council is permitted to speak the name of our great lord. An offense punishable by death."

"When you refer to my naming your great lord," Wes said as he peered at the boy from under the brim of his hat, "am I not permitted to call him Guardian Son, or Daniel."

Palto lifted the glass from the table and downed the remainder of what it contained. Jack's eyes popped with outrage, and without looking, he grabbed the glass out of her hand, and smashed it on the floor by his feet; a sudden starburst of tiny sharp prisms. For a brief moment, Wes examined its remains, and marveled on how something created remained beautiful even after it was torn apart.

"I don't know this man," Palto cried out, nearly hysterical. "I just met him tonight!"

"Look at that," Jack said as he turned from Wes, and sneered at Palto. "Not much has changed, if betrayal is still your second nature"

Palto was on her feet in an instant. She broke away from the table, turning to run for the door, but Jack managed to grab onto the hood of her tunic, and used it to pull her back. He wrenched her towards him, and Palto was too small to put up any sort of fight. She flailed, lost her footing, and Jack slammed her harshly onto the floor. The impact knocked the wind out of her, and Palto gasped, then coughed as she rolled onto her side, and curled into a ball. This was not the first time she was forced into this situation. She knew how to best protect herself.

"Is this all you're good for?" Jack shouted down at her, "Deceiving men out of their hearts!" He planted a swift kick directly into her ribs, and Palto made her body smaller. She covered her head with one slim hand, while the other one continued to clutch that stupid watch against her chest.

"That's enough," Wes commanded, and calmly got to his feet. He might be slow to anger, but this boy had him furious. Wes was under no illusions that he might win in a fight against this giant, but he also knew something neither of them knew. Jack was a bully, which meant he was a coward. The tall guard turned his head just enough to glare at Wes from the corner of his eye.

"And what do you think you're going to do to me, mister Wes? When I can just call out and bring a dozen guards down on your head."

Wes had not considered this possibility.

"He's just a country rube," Palto said, as she cautiously sat up. "He doesn't know what he's saying. Just a rube..." Wes was amazed she was willing to speak in his defense, considering what Jack was capable of doing to her. Indeed, as soon as she tried to defend him, Jack turned on her; his cold anger burning hot again.

"Shut your harlot mouth!" Jack shouted, and struck her face with the back of his hand. Palto crumpled, and the watch flew from her grasp.

"No!" She cried out, but Jack scooped it up before she could retrieve it.

"What is this?" He asked, suspending the watch in its chain the way Palto first had. A darkness fell over her eyes, and Palto lunged at Jack with a screech. She tried to grab the watch out of his hand, desperate to get it back. With one fluid motion, Jack grabbed hold of Palto's neck, then shoved her hard against the table so that he pressed her face into the wood. He held her there, unaffected by her struggling, and turned his attention to Wes.

"Is this...a relic?" he asked Wes instead of Palto. When Wes did not respond, the guard held his hand open and examined the watch again where it rested in his meaty palm. "It looks like this belonged to Old Father."

"I reckon so," Wes said gruffly. He looked at Palto splayed over the table; her face squished under the guard's palm, and slipped the leather strap off of the grip on his revolver. Jack leaned over Palto, leering as he spoke; his breath hot against her face.

"Did you steal this, thief?" Palto looked up to Wes, then the light went out of her eyes. She knew getting caught with this relic sealed her fate. Hope left her in a heartbeat.

"The watch was mine," Wes said, his voice hard as iron. "I used it to pay her for her help." He glared up at the younger man as he fought to remain calm, but Wes had a long history under the control of a bully. He remembered how it felt when Jethro struck his wife. He felt small and inadequate. He would not feel that way again. A fire bloomed inside of him, and whispers sprung up in his mind; tempting him to sin.

Wouldn't it feel good to drive a fist into that square jaw? Wouldn't it feel good to empty your gun into that smug guard's belly? Wouldn't it feel good to bury your knife into the side of his neck?

A fire burned behind Wes' eyes, and the longer the guard glared at him, the more uncertain he grew.

"I don't see blackness on your tongue," he said skeptically, "but that doesn't mean you aren't trying to trick me."

"Why would I bother, when you're just a beast that bullies little girls?" Uncertainty was swallowed by rage. Perhaps Wes went too far.

"I have had enough of your mouth, mister," Jack growled with a spray of spittle through clenched teeth. He released Palto, and used that snake-like quickness to wrap a fist around the lapel of Wes' jacket. He pulled Wes close so that his red snarling face filled his vision. "I am placing you under arrest, and will rejoice when you hang!"

"I will go nowhere with you, unless you plan to take me to see the Guardian Son," Wes insisted. He knew that he was poking a bear long after the beast was already awake, but his own fire was up, and those sinful voices were pushing him to take things further. He almost welcomed the first blow. His hand was a breath away from his knife and his gun.

"You will not talk to me this way," The guard growled, giving Wes' jacket a hard jerk. Wes leaned into the man, and even though Jack was a hand taller than him, Wes sneered up at him. Within his mind, the voices of his sin were frothing, and half crazed by his fury.

"You are not my keeper," Wes growled, then spat square into the taller man's face. Jack was so fast, Wes hardly saw his hand move until he felt the fist land on his jaw. His hat fell from his head, but Wes held his ground, and managed to stay on his feet. He glared up at the guard, but Jack gave him no time to recover. Another fist connected under his eye, and this one took Wes to the floor.

He was dazed, unable to react before the guard fell upon him. He caught sight of the blind fury on the other man's face, and knew he had little time to act. Soon the fists would come, pummeling him until consciousness escaped him. Jack might keep going until he killed Wes outright. But Wes couldn't help himself. He was far too angry to stop goading the younger man. He flashed a wolfish grin, as he floundered to retrieve a weapon. It was his hunting knife he located fist, and quickly pulled it from its sheath.

Jack hoisted his club into his hand, then grabbed Wes by the hair with the intent to hold him in place while he hammered blows down upon him. But when he pulled Wes up, the cloth on his forehead slipped down around his neck. Wes gripped the knife, about to plunge it into the guard, when there was a sudden gasp, and Jack scrambled to get off of him. Wes shook his head to get his hair out of his eyes. The haze of anger still had hold of his mind, and Wes fought against the impulse to lunge at Jack and sink his knife into the other man's thigh. His breath was heavy as he blinked to clear his vision, and look up at the guard standing over him.

Jack was utterly stunned; all the fire of his anger extinguished in an instant. He stared at Wes with his eyes wide, but not a word escaped him. Palto however, took one look at Wes and screamed.

"Please, Jack! I swear to you, I didn't know! I would have told you or...I would never have spoken to him in the first place!" Wes could not understand the sudden look of horror on her face, and she hid behind Jack. The guard looked just as fearful, his face a ghostly shade of white. Wes ran fingers through his hair, pushing it off his forehead, then worked his jaw to make sure the thing wasn't broken.

"Your name's Jack, correct?" Wes asked and the guard nodded numbly. Behind him, Palto started to quietly cry. Wes sighed, then got to his feet. He bent, and brushed the dust from his pants and jacket.

"I'm sorry," Jack said, and his voice sounded so small. Wes saw past the man he wanted to be, for the child he still was. He couldn't be a day over eighteen. Backed into a corner, Palto slid to the floor behind Jack, and covered her head. She keened softly in her terror. Wes picked up his hat, and smacked dust from its brim. He peered up at Jack as he placed his hat back on his head.

"Why do you both fear me all of a sudden?"

"The prophecy," Palto called out.

"Be quiet, girl," Jack snapped at her from over his shoulder. Then he turned back to Wes, and moved to put himself between Wes, and Palto. Was he actually trying to protect her?

"Explain this to me," Wes demanded, suddenly annoyed with how things turned against him. "What prophecy?"

"I can't," Jack said, shaking his head; his eyes pleading for Wes to not demand more of him. Frustration fanned the fading coals of his rage, and Wes lashed out; grabbing hold of one of the chairs, and throwing it across the room.

"You will answer me!" He shouted, and Palto broke into sobs. She covered her face with trembling hands. Wes never saw a child so terrified, and it disgusted him to know that he was to blame. Jack watched him solemnly, and looked as though he was fighting back his own tears.

"If they see your face..."

"Who are they?"

"If they find out what I did to you..."

"They won't find out. You have my word. Who are they?" Wes demanded, and Jack's shoulders slumped. He looked down at the pocket watch he still held in his hand.

"You must meet with the Disciples. They can tell you about the prophecy." Ah. Again, the Lord seemed to be pointing Wes in a solitary direction. Still, he could not help but try one last time.

"Can't you take me to the Guardian Son instead?" he asked and Jack winced.

"I am not a member of the Guard Watch Elite. They will execute me if I try." It was just as well. While Wes was growing increasingly more desperate to reconnect with Daniel, he needed to know what this prophecy was about; especially if it involved him.

"How do I get in touch with these Disciples?"

"There is an alley that runs alongside their storefront," Jack explained, "It leads into a courtyard which is how you reach their hall of worship." Jack gave Wes a quick miserable glance, then dropped his eyes again respectfully. "Please, mister...my mother is a member of the Disciple guild. Please don't harm her."

"Stop this nonsense," Wes growled. He did not like the way they behaved towards him. Palto was trying to get herself under control, but looked no less terrified. Wes hoped to catch her eye, but she would not look at him. He stepped forward, and plucked the pocket watch out of Jack's hand.

"How will I know which door is theirs?" Wes asked, assuming the courtyard was shared. He looked up at Jack from under the brim of his hat, but Jack tried very hard not to meet his eye.

"They have painted it in the holy color, great one," Jack said. "The door to their hall is white."

"Look at me, Jack," Wes commanded, and Jack hesitantly lifted his eyes to meet Wes'.

"If you want what happened to remain between us, then I expect you back here at the next sunset. Do you understand?" Jack winced, made a soft groan in the back of his throat, but nodded all the same.

"It will be as you say, great one."

"Good," Wes said, nodding to himself. "And stop calling me that. You may leave now." He wasn't sure yet what he planned to do, but thought that Jack might be useful all the same, so he leaned into this new position he found himself in, and gave out his command.

Jack hesitated, glancing over at Palto who still sat curled against the far wall, then gave Wes a quick salute, and stomped out of the tavern. As soon as he was out of sight, Palto started sobbing again. Wes approached her slowly, but when he reached to comfort her, she recoiled as though she was struck. She slid away from him on her backside, and moved to the farthest corner so that she put as much distance between them as she could.

"Palto," Wes began, but she grabbed her hood, and pulled it over her face. Wes sighed again. This night left him utterly exhausted. He eased himself onto the floor, and sat against the same wall as Palto, but on the other end of the room. He leaned back, closed his eyes, and they sat together in silence. Outside, Wes could hear the voices of people as they returned to their homes. The nightlife was waning, morning was on its way. Even the city had its own kind of birdsong.

"What do you want from me?" Palto asked after some time. She would not turn to look at him. "Why me? What have I done to deserve any of this?" Wes did not respond. Instead, he removed his hat and carefully retied the scrap of blue cloth over his forehead. Then he gently placed the pocket watch on the floor between them. Palto lifted her head, and peeked past her arm to examine the watch. Then she looked up at Wes.

"What do you want from me, mister?" She asked again.

"I want to trust you," Wes said sincerely. He desperately needed an ally in this strange place. "And I want you to trust me."

"But you're the one from the prophecy! You must be!"

"What prophecy, Palto? What does it say about me?"

"I...I heard things a long time ago," Palto said as she wiped her tears away. Wes was relieved to see a little of her true self returning. "Only one thing, really. And I never learned to read so when the Disciples hand out those little booklets, I use them as fodder for my fire. But I've heard their talks on the street corners in the middle of the night. They talked of prophecies about a man dressed in black traveling from outside the city. A man with a pure face, untouched by sin." She glanced over at him, then down to the watch again. "Of course you would be related to Old Father."

"What else did they say? Can you remember anything?" Wes didn't know how much stock to put in a random prophecy, but knowing what Ruth was capable of, not to mention Sassy and of course Eve, he had to at least consider there was truth to this apparent legend. Maybe he could use this prophecy to his advantage to gain an audience with his son.

"I can't remember," Palto said, growing anxious. "Something about light and a dragon..."

"Dragon?" Wes sat up, staring at Palto in alarm, and she instantly shied away from him.

"I don't know. I don't know anything else!" she whined desperately, and Wes had no desire to push her. He leaned forward, and got to his feet. Then he bent to pick up the pocket watch, and placed it directly in front of Palto.

"The sun will soon find us," he said gently. "Get back home. You may find me sleeping by my horse a little later. But first, I must go see these Disciples." He made his way to the other side of the tavern, and was about to leave when he heard Palto call out to him. She looked so small, curled up in the corner as she was. Her arms hugged her knees as a form of meager protection, but Wes was pleased to see that she no longer looked afraid of him.

"I didn't hear what you said," he called to her.

"I said be careful," Palto responded, her green eyes studying him from across the room. Wes offered her a smile, and a nod. Then he stepped out into the predawn light.

Chapter Eighteen

So the great dragon was cast out,
that serpent of old, called the Devil and Satan,
who deceives the whole world; he was cast to the earth,
and his angels were cast out with him.
-Revelations 12:9 (NKJV)

Since the prayer in the woods at Sassy's home, the dreams Wes had were often of Peter. Knowing this, Wes found every reason to avoid sleep, even when he felt heavy weariness in his bones, and burning behind his eyes. Sensibility told him to find a corner in the stable to sleep in, but instead he made his way to the little shop with effigies in the window.

Wes examined the boy portrait again, and saw the resemblance to Daniel in the light of day. The boy looked older than Wes' memory of him, but he could not mistake those haunted blue eyes. They were dark and murky like the sky during the last light of day. Wes also noticed the lack of scar on the boy's face, and he had to wonder if the portrait was artistic liberty, or a representation of truth?

Wes stared at the portrait so intently, he didn't immediately notice the short balding man standing behind the window display. His smile was easy, and he pointed to his right where an alley led alongside the building just like how Jack described. Wes took the gesture as an invitation, and ventured back the dim alley which led into a garden courtyard. The area was enclosed by surrounding buildings full of hollow windows and closed off doors, but Wes quickly located the white painted door that Jack described. It was open just a crack; an invitation for him to go inside.

Wes hesitated, feeling a sense of unease, but he was determined to learn what he could about this prophecy and how to reach his son. He cautiously pushed his way inside, and entered a long hallway with barren walls, and a wooden floor worn smooth from years of foot traffic. The only furniture occupying the space was a bench farther down the hall, and a pedestal holding an empty bowl beside the door. Along the left outer wall of the hallway, a row of windows displayed a view of the garden outside.

"Welcome sir, welcome!" The small man from behind the window came into view at the far end of the hallway. He walked briskly towards Wes, his feet kicking the hem of his long coarse robe, and Wes noted that he wore a decorative jacket over the robe that ended in twin points below his waist. His dark hair, thinning on the crown, was slicked back with oil, and Wes noted black scales that fanned out from his forehead into his hairline. He had an olive complexion, with high cheekbones, and a hawkish nose.

"What is this place?" Wes asked. The man offered a disarming smile.

"Well sir, this is the Church of Pure Waters, brothers and sisters in worship to his holy creation the Guardian Son." He gave an exaggerated bow.

"You don't whisper when you say his name. Aren't you afraid of getting hanged?" Wes asked, and that disarming smile never wavered.

"I assure you, sir. All the necessary permits are in order."

"Have you ever met with the Guardian Son?" This question startled the man.

"Never, sir! None of us are worthy. No, not one." If this man was a Disciple, they might not be able to help him after all. Wes bit his lip, thinking.

"Are you...a Disciple?" He asked after a moment. The smile returned as the man nodded.

"Yes, sir. I have committed my life to the Guardian Son, may he live forever."

The man's eyes went distant in his reverence, and Wes realized he was not exactly sober. He smelled a strange sour sweetness in the air, similar to what he smelled out in the street the night before, and recalled the woman unconscious on her porch. She held a strange thin pipe in her hand. Were these people smoking something other than tobacco leaves?

"So if you don't see the Guardian Son, is it the Elders you have your dealings with?"

"Dealings?" The small man's smile faltered slightly, then returned.

"When you give your donations."

"I see," he said cautiously. A glint of suspicion came into his eye. "We do give offerings to the Guardian Son, may he live forever. But so do the Guilds and the masters. We are no exception."

“But when you go, you have dealings with the Elders, correct?” Wes asked, trying to be patient.

“We have dealings with one Elder, sir,” the man’s suspicions grew, but he was still willing to answer Wes’ questions.

“Does this one Elder come here?” he asked, and the man laughed.

“Oh, by the Divine Hall, no sir. One as great as him would not come to this lowly place.” He scratched at his arms, absently. The scales there appeared old and brittle.

“So how do these offerings go from your hands to the Elders?” Wes asked and the other man’s eyes slid away from him. He moved with a deliberate slowness to stand by the row of windows. The sun was just starting to reveal itself, and in the daylight, the capital lacked its teeth. All the same, the man kept a safe distance away from the soft rays shining through the windows.

“Dear sir, please don’t consider me rude. You ask many questions, and such infor mation...it can be offered to you, yes. But only at a cost, sir. An offering, if you would.”

Wes felt disgusted. Even here, wealth was an oil to lubricate. The man lifted a black scaled hand, and idly ran fingers along the edge of the empty bowl poised on its pedestal.

“I have no coins to offer,” Wes admitted, but of course the short man already knew that. He peered over at Wes, then his eyes fell to Wes’ hip.

“There are other prices that can be paid, sir,” he said slowly, and Wes pulled open his jacket to reveal his revolver. This man thought he was a fool to swindle. No information was worth such a price. Wes sighed. Why did everything have to be so difficult with these city folk? He lifted his hat off of his head and examined it in his hands.

“I reckon you already figured I’m not from around here,” he said as he picked at something on his hat. The small man smiled, and nodded patiently.

“Well, I’ve managed to learn a thing or two since coming to your lovely city. Like with these prophecies I keep hearing about.” The smile vanished from the man's face. Maybe he will finally take Wes seriously. Wes raised an eyebrow in feigned surprise. “Oh, you know of them?”

“Of course I do, sir!” the small man retorted. He looked offended as he turned his attention from the window back to Wes. Wes smiled, allowing himself a sliver of satisfaction for irking the man.

“I’m a little skeptical, but I’ll admit I haven’t heard much. Do you know all the prophecies this city holds?”

"I wouldn't be a Disciple if I didn't!" The small man said, lifting his chin with indignant pride. Spots of red bloomed in his cheeks. "I have memorized the prophetic canon of Elder Strupple, as well as the tellings of Old Father!"

Old Father. Jethro inserted himself into Wes' life again. Watching the man's eyes, Wes lifted a hand to his brow, and pulled the strip of cloth off of his forehead.

"Then I don't need to explain to you why I must reach the Guardian Son." Wes took pleasure in the way the small man's face transformed as understanding sunk into his bones. The color seemed to drain out of him, as he stammered through his words.

"Oh...sir...I..." His lips trembled as words died upon them. Then he sank to the floor, pitched forward, and prostrated himself at Wes' feet.

"Light Keeper!" He cried out and Wes stepped back, startled. The man's shouts filled the high ceilings. "I rejoice in your coming! Guardian to the Lord of the Sun! Harbinger to the Child of Promise! The forerunner to he who cleanses with light! Utter destruction is carried in your wake!"

"Stop this!" Wes yelled, mainly to be heard over all the shouting. "Quiet yourself and get on your feet. I can't speak to you like this."

"It is as you wish, sir," the small man said with an abrupt and eerie calm. He got to his feet with practiced fluidity, and while his face was placid, his cheeks were streaked with tears. Wes turned away, not wanting to see a grown man's shame; weeping as he did. He looked out the window instead. Outside, the towers of the Divine Hall were bathed in sunlight.

"Will you help me to get into the Divine Hall? I must find my...the Guardian Son."

"The Hall is not something we have access to, sir," the small man admitted sadly. "We never go past the offering house. But...We can get you there at least. Past the initial gate. We can get you to the offering house doors, which is directly adjoined to the greater Hall."

"That will have to do," Wes said, not revealing his excitement. Finally! A chance! "Tell me what I must do."

The man turned and slowly stretched a hand to point at the Divine Hall.

"Do you see that archway on the side there?" Wes stood next to the man and looked to where he pointed.

"The one with the statue of a woman looking down at the entrance?"

"Yes, Mother of the Guardian Son, that's the one sir. During our times of worship, a guard comes to escort one of our flock to deliver our offering into the hands of Elder Collins, the Keeper of the Coin. It's a very high honor to be selected to go. But we can send you instead. This means I will take active part in the prophecy! Oh..." The small man groaned in his rapture, and Wes winced.

"Can't I just show them my face? They should allow my entry if they see who I am."

"Not all will welcome you, Light Keeper," the other man said as he stole quick glances at Wes' face.

"When Elder Strupple spoke of his visions, it put the Elders in an uproar. Some rejoiced but many did not. Some called for his execution! An Elder! It is better you reach the Guardian Son before they know of you or your purpose."

"Will some of your...congregation be opposed to my purpose as well?" Wes didn't want to find an unexpected knife in his ribs.

"Divine Hall, no! We don't seek out the indulgences of the Elder class. Our lives are humble ones. We eagerly await our cleansing from the Bringer of Light."

Wes recalled the whispers in the night. They also called Benji the Bringer of Light. Wes thought these prophecies had to do with Daniel and with him. But it seemed that they were tied to Benji as well.

"When is your next time of worship?" he asked, and the short man smiled at him. He reached under his jacket, into the pocket of his robes, and produced a small slender pipe. Same as the woman on the porch just as Wes suspected.

"The time turns in your favor, sir. We happen to have a service this very evening." The man brought the pipe to rest between his teeth and lit it with a lighter less impressive than Chancy's. "When the last of the sun leaves the sky, we gather all that we can for the offering. Return to us then, and we will celebrate your coming. We will send you, sir. With the offering and with our blessing. But oh..." The man bit the end of his pipe, worry creasing his face.

"What is it?" Wes asked.

"I forgot the guard escort! The guards know the faces of all those blessed to deliver the offering. They will be suspicious of you."

"Don't worry about that," Wes said with a small prayer of thanks to the Lord. "I know a guard who will help me."

"Truly you are blessed, sir!" The man sang out, and Wes shrugged uncomfortably. He wanted to be gone from this place.

"Very well," he said. "I will return to you later." Wes turned, reached for the door, but the small man extended a hand and tugged at his sleeve. He stared up at Wes as he spoke hushed words.

"Tell me, sir, for I know the prophecies well... have you yet kissed the fingers of the Bringer of Light?"

Wes stared at this strange small man with his deep set eyes. Eyes that carried a mix of longing, fear, and desperation. Wes felt captivated. He felt compelled. He felt a desire to share what he knew.

"I have," he whispered, just as softly; caught up in the other man's reverence of the boy he's grown so attached to. He perceived why the wicked longed to extinguish his absolute light.

"Ah," the man sighed, and released Wes' sleeve. He slid away from Wes, and languidly turned to look back out the window. "Then it has truly begun." Wes waited for the man to say more, but when the silence stretched on, he grew frustrated.

"Explain this to me. Tell me some of your prophecies." The man took another draw of smoke from his pipe, then closed his eyes as he recited his prophecy like he was reading from the Word.

"The foretelling of Elder Strupple: The New Prophecy of Fate for the Guardian Son. The Bringer of Light will arrive in the wake of the Light Keepers coming. For he is the forerunner to the dawn. He will light the way for the Guardian Son, and when he comes, the Son must come. Where he goes, the Son must go. For the Keeper will crumble the Temple of the Dragon, its walls will be ground to dust, and reformed like clay into something new. A new temple where all will be cleansed! Washed in light and made clean all by the grace and mighty mercy of the Bringer of Light!" By the end of his retelling, the small man was shouting again. He trembled in a strange sort of ecstasy, and Wes backed away from him. He knew madness when he saw it.

"What you claim is not why I'm here," he argued, but a worm of doubt squirmed through his mind. How much of his path was already seen by the scribes of fate? Both Sassy and Eve told him that he needed to take his son home if he wanted to save him, but what exactly was involved in the saving?

"*For the Keeper will crumble the Temple of the Dragon, its walls will be ground to dust, and reformed like clay into something new.*"

Still trembling, the small man returned his attention to the Divine Hall and his Guardian Son. His lips moved in silent prayer as his hands gently caressed the slender pipe they held. Wes wanted to be away from this madness. He swung the door open with a swift jerk, and stepped outside. He paused to draw in a deep breath, and appreciate the freshness of the air. The sun was high, and the day unseasonably warm.

Knowing he could avoid it no longer, he returned to the stables and checked on his mare. She dozed, but her ears twitched when he approached. Taking his saddle and blanket off the rack, Wes used them as bed and pillow to sleep outside her stall.

In spite of his reluctance to face his dreams, sleep took him the moment he settled into a comfortable position, and the nightmare started anew. Peter crying out as the mare took off running.

Wes seeing his son fall;

Wes hearing the sound of his little head cracking against the stones.

His recollection would never be as vivid as his dreams. Every detail of Peter's face was revealed to Wes. The fear in his eyes. The scream that could not escape him when his head hit...

Wes groaned; grinding out his suffering through clenched teeth, but he refused to wake. He needed this sleep for the night to come. He would endure, for he had to endure.

His son fell.

His small arms outstretched; hoping to grab hold of something.

Salvation.

His son's head hitting the stones with a dull thud.

Wes could hear his own breathing. In that moment, before everything fell apart, he was oddly calm. If he didn't move; if he didn't drop the corn; if he didn't run to where his son fell, Peter would still be alive. Peter would still be breathing. In his dreams, Peter would stay alive.

But the day rewound, and started anew. He looked up in time to see his son coming out of the barn on the back of his mare once more. But this time it wasn't Peter looking terrified. It was the boy in the painting at the Disciples store window. It was Daniel. Wes heard a soft keening sound coming from his own throat, but he did not speak. He did not move. He just stood, and watched as Daniel let go of the horse.

Arms outstretched;

Falling;

Landing;

Dying.

Then the day rewound, and started anew. Wes wanted to scream. He wanted to cry. He wanted to beg forgiveness from all of his children that he let down. This was his Hell, and Wes bore the key to his cage.

When Wes woke, Palto was sitting in front of him, watching him while he slept. She quickly looked away when their eyes met, and moved to get to her feet.

"Don't go," he said. She froze for a moment, then settled back on the ground. She looked at him cautiously.

"You said you want to trust me," she remarked. Wes noticed her hand was balled up in her tunic pocket. It seems she still carried the watch.

"Aye, I do."

"And you expect me to trust you." She sounded a little indignant. Wes watched her as he nodded.

"Then answer a question for me. Tell the truth," She declared, "and I will try my best to trust you." Wes sat up, nursing the ache in his neck, and lifted his hat off the stall post to place it back on his head.

"If this be a barter, then I deserve a question as well."

"Alight," Palto said with a nod. She reached out, and poked Wes on the nose.

"Tell me why you want to see *him* so badly," she demanded. Wes studied her for a moment, then sighed. It was hard to trust.

"He's my son."

Whatever answer Palto expected, it was not this. She stared at Wes, dumbfounded. Then she gave his revelation some thought, and nodded to herself.

"I understand. It makes a lot more sense now. I thought you were going mad, the way you kept throwing around his name, knowing it might get you hung. We all do foolish things for the ones we love." Palto was still a child, but sometimes wisdom sprouted from her like a new blossom on the stem. He wanted to ask her who it was that she loved so much to risk her life for.

"It's my turn," he said, and leaned over to tap a finger alongside Palto's nose. "Why are you holding on to that pocket watch instead of just selling it?" He looked pointedly at her pocket, and Palto quickly stuffed a bit of chain out of sight.

"I know what I'm doing. I need it for something specific."

"For what."

"I already answered your question."

"Trust, Palto." Palto glared at Wes, then lowered her gaze to the pocket that held her treasure.

"I plan to give it to a smuggler in payment for transport," She said softly, and peered up at him. "But not until you leave. I will not swindle you, mister, for you hired me squarely.

"Where do you plan to get smuggled?" Wes asked.

"Out of the capital," Palto declared, lifting her chin.

"Can't you just leave?"

"Not without a permit. Or a writ of worship. Or a slave master's mining pass."

"Can't you use the watch to get one of these...permits or whatever?"

"You're asking a lot of questions," Palto said, her eyes sharp.

"Help me to understand." Wes never dealt with a smuggler, but he has dealt with their type, and a young girl like Palto would not likely reach whatever destination she was intending to go to. He worried about her, for he liked her. But her eyes turned cold. She was not yet ready to fully trust.

"All you need to know is that my watch will buy one ticket out of this Hell. With luck, I'll make that purchase the moment you're gone from this city."

It might have been fear for his life that brought Jack back to the entrance of that small tavern in the town square, but Wes liked to believe he was just good to his word. Either way, he looked miserable, and he glanced at Wes ruefully, before dropping his eyes to his feet.

"What do you want from me now?" he asked of his boots. His jaw rippled muscle as he clenched his teeth. Wes left his spot leaning against the sallow man's tavern, and got closer to Jack so they wouldn't be overheard.

"Well, to start, I want you to go back to yonder Hall, find out who is assigned to escort the Disciple transporting the night's offering, and volunteer to take their place."

"What? Why would I do that?"

"Because I am telling you to!" Wes said sternly. He had little patience for this pouting guard who liked to kick girls laying on the ground.

"What will I say? How will I explain the transfer?"

"Tell them you're sweet on someone among the Disciples. Tell them you're doing it for your mother. I don't really care, just do it and return to me here."

Jack's face turned a dark red from his irritation, but he gave Wes a curt nod, and stomped back toward the Divine Hall. Wes watched him as he thought through his plan, then turned back to the tavern only to find a small girl staring up at him from where she sat under the tavern window. It was the same girl Palto shooed away the day before. How much had she heard?

Wes stared at her, unsure what to do. Her eyes were enormous as she gaped up at him. She looked horribly thin, and with how malnourished she was, she could have been five or fifteen. Her hair was wispy and the color of corn silk; it hung around her face like curtains concealing the scales of her sin. She was very pale, even her lips, and shivered from the cold with her sack dress offering little protection.

"Can you spare some food, mister?" Her voice was high and unsteady. Her large eyes never shifted from his face.

Her eyes are like Benji's.

"I don't have any food with me," he had to admit. He could return to his pack, but then he'd miss Jack's returning. The girl lowered her gaze, looking a bit crestfallen, and Wes pitied her. Jack returned a moment later, and glanced down at her dismissively.

"They had not assigned the task to the roster yet," he reported, "so I was able to request the job without rousing any suspicion."

"Well done," Wes said with a small nod, then looked back at the girl by his feet. "What is your name?"

"Clem." She sounded like a timid bird.

"I'll remember you, Clem," Wes told her gently. "When I have food again." He turned from her, rejoined Jack, and made his way up the street toward the Disciple's building. All around them, the inhabitants of the city were just starting their nightly activities. They wandered the streets looking for something to entertain themselves with. Desire, desperation, and hunger swirled around Wes in a haze of need. How can a girl like Clem survive in a place where people only cared for themselves?

"What is your plan, mister," Jack said softly at his shoulder.

"I struck a deal with the Disciples to allow me to transport their offering from this evening's collection. So you see why I needed your assistance to escort me?"

"I do see. Such a good plan," Jack said then looked down at Wes with a smug half smile. "And what will you do after you get past the offering gate, oh wise one?"

"Something will come to me," Wes replied, feeling stubbornly determined. Jack wasn't done goading him. He seemed to have lost his fear.

“Do you plan to just go through the Mother’s entrance, storm the collectors house, and demand to see the great lord? They’ll be sure to drop everything and serve you.”

“I don’t need to be served,” Wes replied, “My Lord is with me. He will make a way.”

"You sound like them," Jack said with a scoff and gestured toward the familiar store front as they approached it. The alley alongside the building had a handful of fireboxes burning low and illuminating the way. Wes approached the alley’s mouth, but Jack hesitated.

"I'll wait for you here," he announced as he looked warily down the alleyway.

"Didn't you say that your mother was among the Disciples? What do you have to fear?"

"I'm not afraid!" Jack snapped, then again looked back at the alley. "I just... gave all this up."

"Alright. I reckon you don't need to be there for this part of the plan. Wait for me here." Jack nodded, looking relieved, and leaned up against an adjacent stone building that shared the alleyway entrance.

Wes stepped into the alley, and was assaulted by the sickly sweet smell of pipe smoke. He also noticed a soft thrumming of drums that grew louder with each step he took. When the court yard came into view, Wes was surprised to find it full of people.

All around were women and men in robes dancing, shouting, playing instruments, or hammering upon drums. The whole area rested under a haze of smoke that choked the lungs and burned the eyes. Wes wondered if Jack had the right idea, waiting out in the street.

Is this some sort of Jubilee?

Wes pushed into the crowd, looking for the small man he met before, and quickly found him sitting on an ornate chair like a throne. All around him, people were gathered to hear him speak.

“And then I said to him: ‘Light Keeper! Does this mean you have already kissed the fingers of the Bringer of Light?’ And that man, he turned to me, his eyes as cold as stone, and this he said: ‘I have.’” Many of the people listening moaned and swayed when they heard his words. The small man caught sight of Wes, and he lifted his hands in greeting. Or perhaps in reverence.

“Hark! Here he stands, Disciples! He has come to lay claim to the Guardian Son!” All eyes fell upon Wes. The drums and instruments faded, and the dancing slowed, then stopped. Wes took in the eerie stillness of the Disciples, then turned his attention back on the small man. He disliked being the central focus of so many people.

“You have an offering for me,” Wes asked, wanting to be done with their transaction quickly. At the sound of his voice, many around him moaned and swayed. They dropped to their knees and reached for him. Gentle fingers brushed his legs; his boots; his jacket. Wes had an overwhelming desire to bathe. He was no Messiah! These people just needed the Word!

"Show us your face!"

"The pureness of your skin!"

“Yes, Light Keeper," the small man said, "we hold our offering for the Guardian Son, may he live forever."

“Bless us Light Keeper!”

“Heal my sight!”

"But before you go, sir," the small man continued as he hoisted a small wooden box onto his lap, "perhaps you will show the others what you have shown me?"

"I don't understand," Wes said as he jerked away from a man stroking his arm.

“Take my sin from my skin!”

“Cleanse me and make me new!”

"The lack of mark, sir," the small man said and pointed to his own sinful forehead. "Let them see the full splendor of the Keeper of Light."

Wes looked at the many faces of Disciples in reverence and worship. They all looked at him. So many misguided souls. If only he had more time to explain things to them; to show them that the true way to salvation was through the Lord. With a deep shame he did not fully understand, Wes pulled the cloth and hat from his head. The whole group of them breathed in as one, then let out a long sigh of universal relief.

"Salvation!"

"Sanctuary!"

"Redemption!"

Wes took the offering box the small man offered to him. It felt heavy in his hands.

“That's enough,” announced the small man to his Disciples. “The Light Keeper has his purpose, and we have ours. Go, sir. By the blessing of the Guardian Son."

“Thank you,” Wes said, moving toward the alley, anxious to be free from these strange people and their smoke filled courtyard.

“One more thing,” the small man called to him, and got to his feet. He picked up a loaf of bread the length of his arm and approached Wes.

“There is something you must know,” he said, lowering his voice. “Three times you will find yourself backed in a corner. Three times, you will have no options for possible escape. Seek us out in those moments, sir. We will be able to assist you when no others can." The small man placed the loaf on top of the offer box in Wes' hands, and smiled. "No matter the cost."

"I'll remember," Wes said. He started to feel dizzy from all the smoke. "But, I never got your name." The small man's smile widened to show a row of tiny rotten teeth.

"I don't have one, sir. We give all that we have to the Guardian Son.

Chapter Nineteen

Watch and pray,
that ye enter not into temptation:
the spirit indeed is willing,
but the flesh is weak. -Matthew 26:41 KJV

"How did it go?" Jack asked when he caught sight of Wes exiting the alley. Wes only shook his head. He didn't want to ever interact with those strange people again

"I got what I came for. Let's move on from this place." They walked back up the street together toward the Divine Hall that towered in the distance. Jack glanced over at Wes as they went, and snorted out a laugh.

"Do you hope to barter your way in with bread?" He asked, and Wes looked down at the long loaf in his hand. He had not eaten so much food as this in many days, and part of him would have loved to devour the whole thing on the spot. But the nameless Disciple gave it to him for a specific reason, and it needed no explanation.

When they reached the city square, Wes diverted from Jack long enough to approach the girl named Clem, still huddled against the tavern wall. Wes bent and placed the bread in her small hands. She lifted her head, and blinked in confusion.

"I kept my word. Off with you, now." Clem sprung to her feet, clutching the bread to her chest, and vanished down a side street. Wes smiled as her corn silk hair vanished out of sight.

"She isn't what you think she is," the young guard said as he rejoined Wes. He watched the girl flee with little emotion.

"Regardless of who she is, I'm glad that I was able to offer her this little mercy," Wes replied, then met Jack's eye. "Not that you know much about mercy."

"If you're referring to Palto, you don't know her like I do. You don't know what she's capable of," Jack said, his eyes hard and defensive. "For someone destined to destroy the world, you certainly have a high opinion of yourself."

Wes glared at Jack, unwilling to show his surprise. Destined to destroy the world? Jack did not explain further, but instead pointed toward a large gate in the distance.

"There's your entrance. The Mother's gate. I'll get you through it, but after that I hope to never see hat or backside of you again."

"Very well," Wes said with a nod, "thank you." Both men continued toward the Divine Hall, and the closer they came the more of the lower part of the building came into view. The Hall was fashioned out of large gray stones, fused together with impressive precision. It extended four stories at its lowest points, and had three towers that jutted up at different corners of the sprawling building.

Of course it showed some decay, for even things from the Before died with time, but the occasional broken shingle or missing lattice failed to dull the Hall's majesty. The building was so vast, Wes had to wonder how anyone could live there without getting constantly lost.

Surrounding the Divine Hall, a stone wall towered over their heads, and was broken by two different archways placed on either side, as well as a grander one in the front. All three gates held a statue over the entrance that was green in color. Wes did not recognize the people immortalized there. They too were relics from long before the Damnation. The woman over the northernmost gate was definitely not Daniel's mother.

"You might get lucky," Jack said under his breath. "It looks like the Elders are hosting this evening."

"Hosting?" Wes repeated, looking up at the guard.

"Don't look at me!" Jack hissed under his breath, and Wes dropped his eyes in a semblance of humility.

"It looks like they are hosting people from the capital. Ones selected specifically to entertain them. You might not stand out among their ilk." Jack scrutinized Wes for a moment. "No, you'll still stand out."

"That is gracious of them to host the public," Wes acknowledged appreciatively, but Jack scoffed.

"Very gracious," he replied

As they approached the Mother's gate, two other guards dressed identical to Jack, rose from where they were sitting, and studied Wes with immediate suspicion. Wes made a show of holding out the box in his hands, and they both seemed to relax a little.

"You're early, Disciple," the one said.

"Dressed funny too," replied the other.

"I brought an offering to give for the Guardian Son," declared Wes. His weapons were concealed under his jacket, but there was not much he could do to make his attire less suspicious. He refused to wear one of those crude robes.

"You sound funny," the first guard said, with narrowed eyes. "You have a strange accent."

"I've recently arrived in the capital," Wes explained, "but am assisting the Disciples in their duties." Wes preferred honesty, even if it made circumstances harder to navigate through. The two guards studied him for a long time. Then, Jack sighed and reached over Wes to open the box in his hands.

"These country rubes have no idea how things run around here," Jack said, shaking his head. They all chuckled at the idiocy of one country rube.

"You vouch for him then," the second guard said, "as his escort." Jack placed a few coins from the box into each of the guards hands. Then glanced over at Wes dismissively.

"Everything he said is the truth." The first guard smiled at the coins in his hand, then reached up, and knocked twice on a small shuttered window built into the wall. Immediately the metal gate started to swing inward on chains.

"Off with you then, rube!" Jack gave his shoulder a firm shove, but Wes leered up at the taller man and tried to convey his false authority in his glare.

"Until we meet again," he said softly, and before Jack could respond, he walked through the open gate. He had no idea if they would ever actually meet again, but it irked him how relieved Jack was to be rid of him. Let the guard chew on Wes' parting words for a while.

As soon as Wes passed through the gate, the chains rattled and the heavy doors swung shut once more. He looked around, and took in the vast courtyard of the Divine Hall. The open expanse of grass wrapped around both sides of the large building and was decorated by different statues and shrubbery. During the summer when the flowers were in bloom, it was probably a wondrous sight. Wes stood at the Mothers gate, with the main entrance to his left, and a series of gardens to his right. Before him, a narrow path led directly to a small stone structure butting up against the larger Hall. This must be the location of the collector of offerings, for the door hung open. It clung to the Hall like a parasite.

As Wes walked toward the open door, he took in the grand sweeping architecture that gave beauty to every aspect of this ancient building. It was hard not to gawk. Was this really the place where his son resided?

There was light flickering from inside the open door, so Wes accepted the invitation, and entered. The area within was cramped and warm. There were piles of paper, scrolls, and boxes strewn about on tables, and shelves.

Behind a large desk, a round man with a flabby chin sat back in a vast plush chair while he smoked a slender pipe. He looked up as Wes entered the room, then sat up attentively, and placed his pipe on a wooden stand.

“It’s about time they sent me some entertainment,” the soft man said, “I like the costume. You’ll do just fine.” Wes tried not to stare at the man, but it was hard. His soft hands and painted nails, his painted lips and powered face, and it looked like he had hair placed on his head that was not his own. He wore white, which told Wes all he needed to know about the man’s intentions, but the white was silky and fashioned into a billowing dress that draped over his massive girth and puddled around his plump feet. Wes never saw such decadence on display before. He was stunned, and lost coherency.

“Um...I have... I brought...an offering. It’s...From... the Disciples,” he managed, and was embarrassed at how sheepish he felt under the man's scrutiny. The soft man smiled like a cat with a mouse in his paw. He leaned forward, sliding long lacquered fingers over his desk, and batted his eyes at Wes.

“I would rather take you as an offering, handsome,” he said and his grin grew wicked. Wes stared, and words failed him anew. No one had ever spoken to him in this way before, and he never expected to hear such things from another man. He was so baffled, he couldn’t seem to find his voice. He just stood there, staring as the large man rose, and glided around the desk with an outstretched hand.

“It’s been a while since I’ve seen such pure skin. I can’t wait to touch it. We will have to do something about this beard but...” Wes ducked away from the man's outstretched fingers, and managed to break free from whatever spell he was under. He rushed out the door, stopped, returned long enough to place the offering box into the pudgy man’s hands, and escaped for good.

“Come back my sweet prince!” The soft man called, but Wes didn’t slow his pace. He shivered at the thought.

“Oh, Daniel, what have you gotten yourself into?” Wes looked to the Mother’s gate, and saw her guards were occupied talking to others that came with offerings. He took the opportunity to make his way to the front of the Hall while they were distracted. He hoped he might find a way inside from there.

The main entrance to the Hall was massive with large wooden doors that would need two people to open and close. Guests in elaborate costumes filtered in and out of the entrance, but they were all examined by a pair of foreboding guards. These guards were dressed in black, but their uniforms were adorned in braids of silver. Their duck bill hats had white feather plumes sticking out of them. Wes imagined these guards were a representation of the Guard Watch Elite.

Some of the guests wore a myriad of colors, while others were dressed only in white. None of them wore black as Wes did. None but the guards and servants. No wonder Jack was amused by his optimism. How was he ever going to get inside?

Wes examined the other guests in the courtyard. Some staggered about, while others wandered in a daze. Smells of alcohol and sickly-sweet smoke overpowered the more unpleasant smells of the city. He considered finding a patron similar in size to him and nabbing his outfit, but struggled with the idea of wearing something so ridiculous. He looked around. Maybe he could find another entrance less guarded.

"You look lost."

Wes turned and saw a young woman swaying as she approached him. She had a wide smile on her face, and half hooded eyes. She was quite beautiful, with raven dark hair, sharp facial features, and full lips. Her shoes dangled from one finger by their straps, and her sleeveless dress barely reached the middle of her thigh. Her body was a road map of seduction and sin. Wes averted his gaze.

"I reckon so," he said gruffly, and tugged at the corner of his hat in greeting. The woman giggled at him. Her smile was as bright as a mirror in the sun. She couldn't be a day over twenty.

"You're so lovely," she purred as she wrapped both arms around one of his. "So handsome and lovely."

"Would you help me get inside?" Wes asked, as he glanced over at the guards by the door.

"It's so stuffy in there!" The woman whined. "But I'll go in, if I'm there with you. What's your name?"

"Wes," he said, and offered her a small smile. She smiled back at him, sunshine cutting through a cloud filled day.

"Wes," she said, imitating the gruffness of his voice. Then she laughed. "I'm Clara. You're not from around here, are you Wes?"

"I reckon not," Wes said vaguely, then gestured toward the entrance to the Divine Hall. "Is this a Jubilee?"

"A what?" The young woman wrinkled her nose in confusion.

"Never mind," he said, and let her lead him toward the door.

"You talk funny," Clara purred as she rubbed her face against his jacket. Face powder smeared with the dust of the road. She seemed a lot more intoxicated than what a few glasses of alcohol would render. She might have smoked from one of those strange pipes, but even the Disciples didn't seem so...wanting. She fed on the sin of her desires. They walked together, and approached the grand entrance to the Divine Hall. Clara staggered about, singing and leaning on Wes, and the guards looked them over.

"Who is this man with you, Clara," one of the guards asked, and the woman waved him off.

"I'm entitled to bring guests if I choose to," she said, and they said nothing further. But the guard that spoke glared at Wes with an edge of jealousy. Wes kept his head down and his eyes diverted. He felt them watching him as he entered.

Just inside, the Hall opened into a foyer filled with colored costumes alongside men and women in black uniforms. The black clad ones were taking jackets from all their guests. The woman on Wes' arm did not have a jacket, let alone a scrap of cloth she could safely remove, but one of them reached for his jacket, and he waved them away with a polite smile. He dared not uncover the gun he had hidden underneath. But his black jacket and hat drew attention from the other guests in the room.

"Who is this man, Clara?"

"Can I share with you?"

"My he is handsome. And look at his skin!"

"Perhaps he can tell us the name of his Healer!"

They all laughed at this, a joke that Wes did not understand, and Clara waved at each of them as she pulled forward into another room. Her lithe, vibrant body glowed in the firelight as the two of them bled into a smaller antechamber where blue globes covered the fireboxes and cast the room in hazy light. Clara did not pause in this location either. She doggedly half led and half clung to Wes as she pulled him past a handful of curious onlookers. She brought him to a smaller door, and through it into an adjacent room that was surprisingly vacant. It appeared to be the size of Sassy's cabin. Clara stumbled into the room on Wes' heel, and immediately closed the door behind them. The sounds of people from the adjacent rooms cut to a dull hum, and Wes let out a long breath.

“That was an intense odyssey” he muttered to himself as much as to Clara, but the moment he lifted his head to look at her, she pressed her lips to his. Her kiss was hungry, needful, and desperate; an act crucial to survive. Wes pushed her away from him, trying to catch his breath, but she immediately lunged forward and kissed him again. Her hands were all over him at once. She pulled at his jacket; his shirt; slid fingers along his skin, inching closer to his gun. Wes grabbed Clara’s arms, shoving her away, but it seemed to only embolden her. She was breathing heavy, her face red with her lust.

“Come on, stranger, have some fun with me,” she pouted, then she was on him again, knocking off his hat, snaking her hands into his hair, and running her tongue along his neck.

“Drinks,” Wes said, then cleared his throat to get the roughness out of his voice. He grabbed Clara’s wrist, more gently this time, and pulled her away from him. “Why don’t I get drinks for us.”

Clara smiled at this offering, and turned to sit on a soft plush armchair. She looked up at Wes hungrily, and for a moment Wes saw a different face overlapping her own. It was the face of a weasel, but deformed and covered in wet putrid scales. Wes immediately looked away. He did not want to think on which face was the one that kissed him. Any heat she might have lit inside of him winked out in an instant.

“Don’t keep me waiting long,” Clara said, looking at him from under her lashes. Wes smiled at her, gave a little wave, then snatched up his hat and placed it back on his head. He stepped out into the antechamber, and scanned the room until he located a set of unoccupied chairs placed against the wall. He took one, and jammed it under the doorknob to the room Clara was in. Satisfied it was secured, he looked up, and saw a thin young man watching him.

“Interesting,” was all he said, and then he smiled. Wes considered asking the man where he could find the Guardian Son, but decided against it. Best to not attract any more unwanted attention. Instead, he smiled back at the man, feigned a knowing wink, and ventured further into the Divine Hall. Past the blue lit antechamber, the area opened into a massive hallway that seemed oddly empty. Directly in front of Wes, was a great elaborate archway covered by a red veil.

The veil concealed what lay beyond, but Wes could just make out movement on the other side. There were also noises; so many noises he couldn’t quite identify, that gave him a sense that many people were doing ...something, behind that curtain. Wes had a strong sense of wrongness about these people and their noises. He felt a sinking feeling, and knew the Lord was telling him not to go any further. There was something on the other side of that curtain, he did not want to see.

But what if Daniel is in there?

Wes edged forward, walking softly on hunters feet, and approached one side of the entrance. He pressed his back against the wall alongside the curtain, and tried to take control of his fear. He knew he stood on the precipice of something dark, evil, and otherworldly, yet he could not help but look inside.

Wes closed his eyes. He took one long breath, then another, then he turned, and carefully lifted a corner of the curtain to peek into the large room beyond.

"Dear God!" Wes jerked back from the curtain as if burned. He stumbled in his urgency, and fell against the wall opposite to the large entrance. He stood there, feeling the coolness of the stone against his fingers, and willed his mind to forget what he just saw.

It was only a glimpse, but that solitary instant bored a hole into all the memories he had that were innocent, pleasant, and kind. Every time a child cried out, every time a man laughed, every time a woman screamed, the sounds of this place would return to his ears, and with it, visions of the nightmare he just beheld. Those sounds were no longer a mystery to him.

Lord, please!

Wes stood very still. He focused solely on the sound of his own breathing. All other sounds fell away one by one, until Wes could only hear his shaky breath, and the steady thrumming of his heart.

Lord, please burn this memory from my mind!

Even Peter's death was the choice fodder for his nightmares.

Let Daniel not be a part of this. Please, dear God in Heaven, please tell me he's been spared.

Wes closed his eyes, and turned his head to press his face into the coolness of the stone. He fought to slow his breathing, and with it his racing heart. He truly did not think it possible to have so much wickedness in one place. Men and women seeking pleasure at the expense of others suffering. Food spilling out from all sorts of containers and being smashed dismissively on the floor. And those poor children...

Everyone in that room was growing fat from suckling on their indulgences. Everyone in that room took delight in controlling those put there to entertain them. Of the little clothing he saw, all of it was white. Of the few faces Wes glimpsed, every one of them wore a wicked grin.

Wes knew he could go no further. If he forced himself to endure that room, he would surely go mad. If he forced himself to witness those children's suffering, he would kill as many of the wicked as he could. It was tempting, but he would not survive long enough to enjoy the satisfaction. It wouldn't help Daniel, and Wes was determined to get his son away from this horrible place.

His hands trembled as he pulled the cloth from his forehead down to cover his eyes instead. He adjusted the tie in the back to snug the wrap, and the world vanished behind his own curtain. He reached into his jacket pockets, hoping to find a way to plug his ears, but he felt something else instead. As soon as he touched it, he knew what it was. Benji's broken wishbone. The memory flashed through Wes' mind of the boy praying over the bones in his pocket, but he quickly let it go. He did not want to think of Benji in this place. Wes gave a quick prayer with the wishbone in his hand, not believing in its magic, but desperate enough to want to.

Lord, help me get through this vipers nest. Guide my footsteps, and lead me to my son.

Suddenly, Wes felt his body shift and spin as if the floor was giving way around him. A cool breeze swept across his face, sending a chill throughout his body. Wes smelled the crisp air of a brisk autumn day. Then he tumbled off the precipice of reality, and down into a hole tethered to his past.

Chapter Twenty

I will make your oppressors eat their own flesh,
and they shall be drunk with their own blood as with wine.
Then all flesh shall know that I am the Lord your Savior,
and your Redeemer, the Mighty One of Jacob.
-Isaiah 49:26 ESV

Across the barren field, the crows circled and landed around something in the distance. What was laying out there? It appeared to be a mound of something dark, but Wes could not define it beyond that. He considered walking over to see what it might be, but before he could, he felt her there. Hands ran slowly up his back, and Wes knew it was Ruth.

"I'm so close to him, Ruth. But I don't know how to reach him. How do I find what I can't look for?" Ruth's hand stroked his cheek; wisps of her hair tickled his eyelashes; causing them to flutter. Wes closed his eyes, a momentary reflex, but suddenly felt Ruth's lips upon his own. Wes leaned into her, yearning for more, but she left him as quickly as she came. His hands grasped only air.

Wesley.

He could almost hear her voice. He yearned to hear her say his name out loud.

Wesley open your eyes.

Wes did as Ruth instructed, and he was back in that hallway, on the outside of that wicked red veil. Even though he knew the blindfold was still in place, somehow Wes was able to see beyond it. His vision saw only darkness, and yet the edges of walls and floors seemed to glow like stars in the night. Wes looked around, taking in this new way of seeing, and realized he could peer past the curtain, past the walls, past the Divine Hall itself. All around him, blurry visions of light moved with a fullness of life. They reminded Wes of lost summer days, when he was a boy catching fish in the stream. He would glimpse the fish as hazy visions deep in the cooler water. They swam in and out of clarity with the water's current. Each burst of light moved through the cooler waters of a vast abyss stretching as far as Wes could see.

What is this?

Wes stepped away from the wall, and slowly turned in a circle to examine the world around him. Through the dull shapes and outline of walls, an ocean of darkness housed swarms of bright fish. Something must have happened to Wes when he encountered Ruth in his memory spell. Or maybe it wasn't a memory spell at all.

Is this what you used to see, Ruth? Is this the second sight?

The impossible was made possible with God. With this strange new way of seeing, Wes might be able to navigate through the large room beyond the curtain. He just needed to not look closely at the banquet they were having. He knew in some strange way that Daniel existed past the festivities. Wes took a few steps, trying to grow familiar with moving through a world he could not properly see. The more he moved about, the easier it was to recognize outlines as furniture, or doors, or even windows. The fish that swam around them, or through them were people that numbered in the hundreds, and dotted the distance like stars. Turning to the curtain, and seeing past it to the room beyond, Wes also saw deeper colors intertwined with the light. Rich shades of burgundy red that almost took shape before his eye.

Help me get through this, Ruth.

Wes stepped forward, pulled the veil aside, and entered into the heart of Hell. His senses were assaulted by sounds and smells that his mind tried to comprehend. Such horrible heavy sounds!

Thumping.

Slashing.

Groaning.

Pleading.

And the smells. Lord! A wretched pungent mixture of food, of alcohol, of vomit, of drugs, of blood. Wes stilled his thoughts, and focused his mind.

He will not listen. He will not smell.

He will not allow his mind to discern what he could not see.

Cries of pain and delight; torture and ecstasy. Laughing and weeping, wanting and begging. Smells of meat, of fruit, of rot, of decay. The briny smell of bodies rich with sweat. Wes opened his mouth, and started to sing. His voice shook like a leaf in the wind.

"I'm just a poor Wayfaring stranger
traveling through this world below..."

His eyes beheld without seeing, and he knew he was at the top of a sweeping staircase, overlooking two long tables that were filled with activity. A banquet hall in the thick of hosting a feast for the damned. The sweetness from smoke pipes hung in the air, and Wes clung to that smell as the least offensive to endure.

"There is no sickness, toil, nor danger
In that bright world to which I go."

He could see without seeing that there were at least fifty people in the room. He didn't look under the water too long though. He did not want to see the nature of what swam there. Or the larger fish consuming the smaller fish. Or those most vulnerable fish floating belly-up at the bottom.

Wes didn't know any more words to the song Solomon once sang, so he started it anew.

"I'm just a poor wayfaring stranger..."

Wes heard a scream, and turned reflexively toward its source. A burst of light. A woman being held down on a lounge chair. The light flickering; fading. Wes quickly looked away. He heard a child crying; begging for her mother. Wes swallowed down the grief swelling up in his throat.

"Traveling through this world below..."

Wes peered past the banquet tables, and noticed three doors at the far end of the room. Daniel was behind the door in the middle. So close. Wes just needed to wade through the outer darkness to reach him. He pushed forward, and down the stairs he went. He focused on the doors, keeping those glowing outlines in his sight, and tried to see nothing else. He was taken by surprise when a large man stepped in front of him, and blocked his way.

Wes lifted his head, old habits guiding his actions, but as soon as he beheld the man's face, he quickly looked away again. He tugged the brim of his hat in greeting, trying to hide his revulsion. For in that brief moment of seeing, Wes looked past the glow of the man, and beheld the dark red monster coiled up inside of him. It was a massive insect-like creature, with many long legs tucked under the swell of its body. It lounged in a nest in the pit of the man's large stomach. When Wes tried to step around the man, he turned and looked at Wes. At the same time, the monster lifted its head, and looked at Wes as well.

It was all he could do not to scream.

"What do we have here?" The man asked, and reached out to tug the blindfold away from Wes' eyes. Wes was able to sidestep his grasp, and just managed to squeak past him. The man appeared as though he intended to stop Wes, but found the cries of someone else distracting, and blended back into the chaos.

Wes quickly realized that this was not the only person who carried a monster inside of him. He tried so hard not to see beyond what he had to see, but the monsters often shone brighter than the bodies they were coiled inside. Some were small, but many others were massive. Some towered over him in twisted and distorted ways. They had dark ugly faces, and strange bodies bent in ways that defied God's creation. But these beings were not formed by God's hand. They were born of the defiance towards him.

Forgetting his place, Wes restarted the song.

"I'm just a poor Wayfaring stranger..."

He tried to slip through the enclave, but it was impossible to go unnoticed. He was one of the few people clothed, in black instead of white no less, but he also couldn't disguise his misery. He did not blend in with those enjoying themselves, nor with those that endured that enjoyment.

One of the creatures rose up from a chair where it was just devouring something Wes willed himself not to consider. The beast had long thin arms that ended in sweeping massive hooks. They dripped with spoil. Its face was a bald monstrous thing with warts and scales, drooping jowls, and a jagged black beak. The monster and the vessel that contained it turned in unison and smiled at him.

"My, you are handsome." Wes was horrified to realize this creature was a woman. "But what is this thing over your eyes?" She reached for him with one of her angry looking hooks. Wes backed away, avoiding her grasp, and then skirted around her while she observed him with passive curiosity. Her attention was limited, and it did not take long for her to return to her indulgences.

"Traveling through this world below..."

Wes felt sick. His stomach churned from the smells and his mouth filled with saliva as his body threatened to vomit what little was in him. It was so hard to see without seeing. He kept his eyes on the floor as much as he could, but even there he saw signs of sin. How could anyone live this way? How are they not consumed by madness, or burnt up in the firelight? Something was unnatural about the way they were able to thrive in their vices. Wicked things were welcome here.

"There... is no... sickness, toil... nor danger..."

"Look, everyone! We have a visitor! Is he from one of the Barracks?" Wes ignored the voice and continued forward. The row of three doors were still so far away. The room seemed vast now that he was in the middle of it, and he attracted more attention with each passing moment. He could feel their eyes upon him like a layer of slime on his skin. They might make an attempt to apprehend him, or worse, they might strip away the cloth from his eyes. Even the monsters he could see paled in comparison to the realities in this room.

"Look at his clothes. Surely, he must be from the Barracks."

"Will you not join us, attractive Barracks man?" Laughter came from many. Wes tried to move quickly but dare not run, for surely running would only entice the monsters to pounce. He was almost out of time.

"in the...land...where...I..."

"Looks like he's ignoring us, Bruce. What a snob!"

"I've never seen him before, and I have visited all the Barracks during my vacations last spring." Wes stepped around a body laying motionless on the floor. He could not afford it a glance. He was more than halfway through the room, yet there was still so much misery and longing around him. So many huddled forms that lacked monsters coiled inside of them. Fodder for the sport of the evening.

"He isn't a spy, is he?"

"A spy from where? Nothing lies beyond the four corners! Nothing but desolation!"

"Maybe an assassin then? There have been spots of unrest in the city."

"If you call drunken brawls a form of unrest!"

"Sir! I say, take off that blindfold and face us. Are you playing some sort of new game?"

"Oh! A game! I do so love a good game!"

Wes gritted his teeth to stifle the groan that wanted to escape his throat. These people were horrible! They spoke so casually in the middle of such profound suffering. A figure stumbled toward him, deformed with long spider-like legs and dripping fangs. Wes rushed past it; feeling its eyes upon him.

How were you able to stand this second sight, Ruth? How can Eve stand it now? Lord, I hope she doesn't have to see such things as this.

Wes had to wonder if everyone looked like this on the inside or was it reserved to the unique group of individuals in this room. He wondered what his own soul looked like. What sort of monster did his body contain? The very idea that one of these creatures might be housed in his own stomach was all Wes could take. He stumbled forward, slipping on a slick of blood, and vomited onto the floor.

"Oh, look, the poor fellow is sick."

"Too much of the drink, I gather. Maybe he was enjoying one of the private rooms."

"Perhaps it was something he ate."

"We all regret the things we eat from time to time."

Laughter. So much laughter that it drowned out all the sounds of misery in the room.

Lord, save me from this madness!

Wes got to his feet, and lunged forward until his hand felt the cool smoothness of polished stone. He had finally reached the other side of the banquet hall. The three doors were spaced evenly along the wall beside him. He could feel Daniel behind the door in the middle.

Wes reached for it, fumbling nervously with the handle, then he paused, and took a steadying breath. No matter what he beheld, Wes knew that he was about to face his son. He opened the door, and stepped into the room beyond. Voices called to him from the banquet hall, and Wes shut the door with an urgency that caused it to slam hard in its frame. All the noise of the outer room fell away, and Wes sighed in relief. He felt better already. Knowing he could delay no further, Wes turned from the door, and took in his surroundings.

The second sight made an outline of the room for his mind's eye. It was a sketch scrawled on dark paper, but clear enough to navigate. The room was much smaller than the banquet hall, and sparse in décor. Only a few chairs lined the wall, and a much grander lounge chair rested in the middle of the area. Behind the lounge, two figures stood at attention, waiting until needed, but Wes could only focus on the chair itself where his son sat.

"Daniel," Wes whispered, for his voice failed him. The second sight was cruel. It lent no disguise to reality. Before Wes sat an aberration that carried a black scaled muzzle filled with jagged teeth, hands curled with long talons, and two enormous bat-like wings.

Oh Ruth, how right you were.

Wes pulled the cloth from his eyes, no longer wanting to see the truth of what his son had become. He winced a little, unaccustomed to the light, but when his son came into focus, Wes was amazed by what he saw.

Daniel was beautiful. He was not simply dashing, or handsome, or attractive, but truly beautiful. His hair, wavy and fine, encircled his head like a soft honey halo. His pale vibrant skin had rose blossoms high on his cheeks, and he still carried a round child's face. His large eyes, the color of sapphire, looked upon Wes without expression, but Wes was certain that recognition settled deep within them.

The boy was dressed in robes of rich black, adorned by rows of fluffy gray feathers. The fabric looked thin, clinging to him, and hung off his shoulders so that his chest was left exposed. That subtle act told Wes all he needed to know about the situation his son was in. After the room he just vacated, there was no doubt in his mind what his boy was forced to endure. This filled him with such profound sadness, that Wes didn't know what to do. He didn't know how to face the things his son has been doing; those ways he entertained and was entertained. Wes collapsed to his knees, and felt the weight of despair like a boulder on his back. He wanted to curl into a ball like Palto did, to protect himself from the truth behind his son's perfect face.

Instead, he stared at Daniel, crushed by his own hopelessness, and his son turned away from him in shame. Behind Daniel, two young boys reacted to the shift in his mood. They stepped forward and stood protectively to either side of him. They were dressed in black, servants there to serve, but they also seemed fond of Daniel.

"Is this a caller from the party? He's really early," said the one boy as he moved to stand between Wes and his son. The lad was far too young to have to use his body as protection.

"I do not recognize him as an Elder, my lord," the other responded, looking concerned. His hands worried the hem of his jacket. Wes imagined he was no older than ten.

"No, he is not an Elder," Daniel said, his voice guarded. He didn't look at Wes still, but Wes couldn't help but feel warmth in his heart after hearing his son's voice for the first time in eight years.

"But the fellow seems to know you, my lord," said the first boy, bolder but shorter than the other, with large ears that made him look like a rascal.

"He looks sad when he beholds you," the taller boy observed. The threads looked bare at the hem of his jacket from how often he rubbed at it nervously.

"Is he one of your Disciples?" asked the first. Wes wondered if these boys understood what was going on in the room beyond these walls. Did they hear the other children crying, and painfully dying? Wes put the two lads out of his mind, and forced himself to wrestle down the sadness he felt when he looked upon his son.

In spite of his provocative dress, and the creature nested inside him, Daniel didn't appear to have a mark of sin upon him. Even his fingers were free of blackness. He looked as pure as Benji. His scar from the fall in the barn was gone as well, as if it never existed. Not a single mark upon him. Daniel was completely flawless. How in heaven could this possibly be? It had to be some kind of deception.

For a brief sinful moment, Wes secretly hoped that he was being tricked. That this boy with his wet lips, hazy drug glazed eyes, and painted nails and face was not actually his son.

But the second sight confirmed what Wes did not want to see. This was indeed Daniel. This was his son. Wes felt like he was drowning in a strange unexplained grief. Voices of sin whispered for him to abandon this effort. He should just leave his son behind, and break the promise he made to his wife. She was dead anyway.

Daniel lifted his chin, finding strength within himself, and met Wes' eye. Wes knew he could not hide his despair from his face, but Daniel must have mistook it for disappointment. His shame quickly shifted to self righteous anger. Wes couldn't blame his son. It was easier to get angry as opposed to facing what he's become. Daniel looked down his nose upon Wes with cold calculation. Then he stood, gracefully pulling his robe tighter around his body, and smiled down at one of the two boys.

"No," he said, his voice so much different than what Wes imagined it to be. He reached out and brushed gentle fingers against the boy's upturned face. "No, this one is different. He is more... special."

He peered at Wes from the corner of his eye, and a small cunning smile curled the edge of his mouth. At that moment, Wes saw Jethro reflected in his son. He sighed, and looked to the floor. How could he ever convince this boy to leave his indulgences, and go back home?

Wes remembered how Ruth said that their son was lost to them. He didn't want to believe her. He thought maybe Jethro confused her mind. But seeing Daniel as he was in his garish robe, pretty paints, and flawless face; seeing the usurper that slept inside of him, Wes felt that Daniel was lost to him as well.

Wes slowly got to his feet, then turned a cold stare upon his son. Immediately, the two boys sprung forward to block him with their bodies.

"What are you doing, sir?" The one said, "Your glare is a direct challenge toward the Guardian Son!" The shorter boy broke away and grabbed at a pull rope hanging alongside the lounge chair. Wes had not noticed it before.

"I'll call for the guard!" The boy warned, but Wes ignored him. He confronted his son just as he confronted the ache in his own heart.

"Do my boys have cause to worry? Have you come to kill me?" Daniel asked and the boy pulled the rope before Wes could respond. Somewhere from far above them, a bell rang.

"I'm not here to kill you," Wes assured him.

"I see you brought your gun."

"I would never," Wes replied softly, as he studied the many emotions that were revealed on his son's face. Shame, determination, anger, and just the smallest hint of disappointment.

Part of him wanted me to kill him.

In that moment; in that very instant, Wes chose to no longer be sad for the son who was no more. He wasn't there to condemn Daniel for the sins of his past. He was there to save him.

"I would never hurt you," Wes said, louder than before. "I would protect you with my life."

"I'm not sure that I can return the sentiment," Daniel responded; his voice was hard but contradicting the pain in his eyes. Wes understood his son, for the damage had already been done. In truth, Wes wasn't able to protect him at all.

"I must speak with you in private," Wes said just as the door burst open and a handful of guards ran into the room. One of them came up alongside Wes, and drove the butt of his club into his temple. Wes staggered from the blow; flashes of light overtaking his sight. His hat fell from his head, and toppled across the stone floor.

"Don't hurt him," Daniel commanded. Fortunately, the guards obeyed. They hooked their arms in his, securing him in place, and Wes blinked up at Daniel as he waited for his vision to clear.

"What is going on?" One of the enclave wandered into the room. Wes managed to stifle his groan.

"I have a visitor," Daniel announced, and his face lost all expression the moment the others entered the room.

"You know this man, great lord?" A woman asked, "He was wandering around the room earlier with a silly blindfold over his eyes."

"We thought he was playing a game," a man added.

"Your escort sounded the alarm. Did he try to hurt you, great lord?"

"We will gladly see to his punishment," a man called out, eagerly.

"No one is to touch this man," Daniel commanded, and his voice was hard as iron. "Take him to an unoccupied room. I'm sure there's a few in the upper quarters. See that he is fed and made comfortable, but keep him on guard. I don't want him wandering about the place, and getting himself in trouble." There was some laughter at this.

"Who is he, great lord? I've never seen you take such interest in our guests before." Wes hoped this meant Daniel didn't do the things the rest of them did.

"He is not your guest, Carthidge. He is mine. This man...he's my father." Voices erupted all around them but Wes did not want to look. Instead he stared at where his hat fell on the floor.

"Surely, you're joking, great lord!"

"The Dragon is your father!"

"He does resemble you in the eyes, Guardian Son."

"I thought Old Father was your father, great lord!"

"I always thought you killed your father then fled to the capital."

Wes glanced over to Daniel, and his son was smiling smugly at his group of followers. Someone had placed a long slender pipe in his hand. Wes wondered if Daniel's smiles were ever sincere.

"If he is your father," said a soft female voice, "why does he avoid looking at us, great lord?"

"He's afraid of you," Daniel announced with a flare of grandiosity.

"If he is your father," said another of the enclave, "why does he avoid looking at you, great lord?"

"Because," Daniel said, his voice carefully even, "he's also afraid of me." Even though this was untrue, Wes still felt a stab of shame.

He thinks I'm weak.

"Afraid? But why? Surely, none of us would harm another Elder."

"HE IS NOT AN ELDER!" Daniel's sudden anger was astounding. Wes lifted his head, and stared at his son in the same stunned silence as the rest of the room. Behind his son's shout, Wes heard another voice. A twin voice, echoing his son's words just a beat behind. A demon's voice.

Oh, Lord, no.

The silence that followed was pregnant with foreboding. No one knew how to react. Then Daniel forced out a long laugh, and everyone cautiously joined in. Wes just watched his son miserably. He did not understand the relationship Daniel had with these people. They called him great lord as though they followed him, but Daniel did not dress like a leader. He dressed like a child who didn't understand abuse.

Wes yearned to speak with his son. His son! After so many years, his child was standing before him holding himself with an authority that Wes couldn't help but feel a small amount of pride for. This beautiful boy had a presence about him that compelled others to want to listen to his every word. Even dressed as he was, he seemed strong. But Wes saw the vulnerability in his eyes; that secret part of him that glimpsed potential freedom on the receiving end of a gun. Stepping forward, Daniel scooped up Wes' hat and smiled at it in his hands. The curl of his lips never brought mirth to his eyes.

"Once, long ago, I climbed up on the shelf and got my hands on this hat of yours. I never understood why you never wanted to wear it when you worked out in the sun. I put it on my head, and pretended I was just like you. Just like you." Daniel lifted the hat, poised to put it on his head, but then lowered his hands again. He approached Wes, and placed the hat carefully back on his head instead. Wes stared at Daniel, both fascinated and confused by his words.

"You look awfully beat up," Daniel said, and the small half smile he gave Wes was gentle. It warmed Wes' heart and filled his chest full of all the words he wished he could say to his son. That he loved him. That he missed him. That he regretted everything that happened between them. Daniel reached tentative fingers towards the slight swell below Wes' eye where Jack struck him the second time. Then he let his hand fall with a sigh, and turned to walk back to his lounge chair.

Wes glanced over to where the other party guest stood, what he had to assume were Elders, and saw that all of them were watching him. They looked more human than he thought possible. The sin barely impacted their hands or faces. Where scales appeared, they each used paints to camouflage them against their skin. Many of them looked at him with open surprise. Some looked with calculating thoughtfulness. A few of them glared at him with seething jealousy. Wes cleared his throat, and tried to choose his words carefully.

"Daniel...perhaps we could go somewhere else to..."

"That is not my name," Daniel said coldly. His back was to Wes, but there was a hint of warning in his voice. "You will address me as Guardian Son."

"But that's not who you are to me," Wes argued. He was hoping to remind Daniel of their connection, that Daniel was his son in more than just name, but he knew immediately that it was the wrong thing to say. Beside him, Elders gasped, and whispered to one another. The guards tightened their grip on his arms. Daniel whirled around, and there was a fire in his eyes.

"You will address me as Guardian Son, or you will leave!" Daniel shouted, his anger rekindled anew. The way his emotions shifted reminded Wes a little of Palto. Beside them, the Elders kept whispering, and many of them looked from Daniel to Wes.

He doesn't want to be seen as weak. He doesn't want them to think he's like me.

"Begging your pardon," Wes said with a bow of his head. "I only wish to speak with you privately, Guardian Son."

The fire winked out of Daniel, and he nodded in satisfaction. But Wes could see the uncertainty in his eyes. He looked vulnerable, and scared. He looked like a child. He turned, and addressed the guards in the room.

"Take him away as I commanded. The best room available, mind you. Leave him to rest for a while." The guards immediately drug Wes to the door.

"Wait!" He called out, desperate to spend time with his son, but Daniel just quietly looked at him. Their eyes met, for a brief moment Daniel held his gaze, then Wes was pulled out of the room, and out of Daniel's sight.

They drug Wes down an array of hallways filled with old furniture, tapestries, and uniform doors. They led him up two sets of stairs, as grand as the rest of the building, and down another call in the opposite direction. The Divine Hall was vast and disorienting, but after some time, Wes was finally led into a lavish room housing a large bed, ornate table with chairs, and a well stocked fireplace. The walls were painted in rich shades of blue, and a set of windows on the far wall were decorated with colored strips of cloth. They waved about in a slow breeze from outside.

Wes was thrust forward, and turned to glare at the guards that released him, but they didn't even glance at him as they exited the room. They didn't speak a word as they left, and the hard click of a lock sounded after their exit. Strange that they were willing to guard the door, but cared little of the window that was left open. They also allowed him to stay armed. Was this a mistake on the guards part, or were they simply following Daniel's orders, and it was something his son overlooked? Wes turned to the window, shoved the cloth strips out of the way, and took stock of his location. He was on the third floor, a long drop to the ground beneath him, but a quick examination of the building showed some areas that he could use as a foothold. There was a path to the left that led to an area of the Hall that wasn't as tall, and had a rooftop Wes could easily slide down onto.

He looped his leg over the windowsill, and pulled his hunting knife from its sheath. He stuck it in his teeth, the blunt end of the blade snug against his lips, and reached to hoist himself onto the window ledge. He sat crouched there for a moment, poised and looking to where his foot should go, then realized what he was doing. What was he planning to do? For surely he could not leave without his son. Wes crawled back into the room, and returned his knife to its sheath.

Maybe Daniel didn't overlook anything. He already knew that Wes wasn't going to leave until they at least talked to one another. There was no need to put him in a cage lined with bars when Daniel knew he would do just as well in a cage with open windows.

Feeling the sudden weight of his exhaustion, Wes staggered over to the bed and sank down onto the floor. He leaned back against the foot of the bed, and pulled his hat down to shade his eyes. In his mind, he remembered the look of his son. The way his chest was bare. The way he slipped in and out of anger like it was a pair of gloves. The sound of the second voice that came out when he was angry. The usurper demon inside his stomach. Wes had to conclude the monster he saw was the demon he heard. The dragon that Ruth told him about. He thought about those black webbed wings that flapped and fanned out behind his little boy. Those ugly jagged teeth that overtook his son's mouth. Wes thought of Daniel when he was a young boy of six, and tried to remember what his voice sounded like. He tried to remember the way Daniel looked when he laughed. All of it slipped through his hands like watery mud. Time robbing him again of his sacred things.

"What happened to you, Daniel?" Wes asked miserably. He allowed himself one final moment to mourn the boy he once knew. There were so many things he wished he had done differently. Everything just kept happening, and misery piled atop misery. It was so much easier to not think about what happened to his son, when he could put his head down, and focus on the tasks on his farm.

Wes pulled his knees up, and rested his forehead against them as he closed his eyes. He did not want to sleep because he dreaded his dreams, but the events of the night left him exhausted far beyond what a day's labor ever caused. He sank down into a mire of despondency; unable to envision a way out of this mess.

Chapter Twenty-One

When thou sittest to eat with a ruler,
consider diligently what is before thee:
And put a knife to thy throat,
If thou be a man given to appetite.
Be not desirous of his dainties:
for they are deceitful meat. -Proverbs 23:1-3 KJV

When sleep overtook him, Wes was prepared to endure seeing Peter on his mare. Or maybe a view of his field with a gathering of crows. Or even a recollection of the banquet he endured; hungry monsters ready to devour him in his dreams. So he was surprised to be standing in that familiar little cabin tucked away in the hills. This place that Benji called home.

As he looked around, he almost wished he could go back in time. Everything was similar to when he last stayed there. Empty bowls of once eaten stew still cluttered the table, a dwindling fire huddled over its fodder, and he spied soft leather boots arranged alongside the door. They were just the right size for a young boy. But while it was familiar, the cabin also felt eerily uninhabited; like a replica of the original, yet devoid of life.

"You shouldn't have come here." The voice startled him, and Wes looked to the loft where Eve stood exactly in the place he last saw her; a scowl distorting her pretty face. She had let her hair out of her braids, and looked much older than what Wes remembered her to be.

"Am I here? Truly?"

"Somehow, yes. You are," Eve said dubiously. She was strangely cautious towards him.

"This must be Ruth's doing," Wes explained. Her influence was fading from his mind, but perhaps enough remained to bring him to this home. "Her second sight was lent to me, by the grace of God."

Eve stepped away from the banister, folding into the darkness behind her, then suddenly reappeared standing directly in front of Wes. He drew away from her, startled by her strange bending of space. He knew this place existed outside of his dreams, similar in feeling to his farmhouse on the hill, yet somehow Eve was able to still distort reality.

"Why are you here?" She demanded, her annoyance plain upon her face.

"I don't know...I didn't expect to come. I just fell asleep, then I was here." Eve's eyes went unfocused as she considered this revelation. Then she turned suddenly, and peered up at the darkness of the loft.

"Perhaps your coming here was no fault of your own."

"Is Benji here?" Wes asked, as he turned to the loft as well. He would love to see the lad again, and appreciate his hugs. Eve's eyes were sharp when she faced him, and she spoke loudly so even loft-dwelling ears would hear her.

"That boy gets ahead of himself, brother Wes. A horrible student, if you ask me. He insists he needs to be with you. Won't hear a word to the wiser."

"I would love to see him," Wes said, "but he can't come to the capital. You must make him understand that."

"I say what you say, but I could be talking to the trees for all the good it does. When are you coming back? He listens to you."

"I'm not sure. I managed to find Daniel, but I think he's holding me prisoner. I don't know how much longer this will take. Should I be worried?"

Eve hesitated, then shrugged.

"It will be as the Lord wills it, brother. Do what you must to see your promise kept. I will contain the child for as long as I can."

"*Please* don't let him out of your sight," Wes implored. "I don't want him to ever see the things I've seen."

"It will be as the Lord wills it," Eve repeated stubbornly, "Now enough of this talk. You need to go. All things evil surround the darkness of this place. They hunger, and I struggle to keep us hidden. You put us at risk with your presence here."

"I understand," Wes said solemnly. He was not surprised that the night searched for the boy.

"Forget how you got here," Eve said, then lifted her hand, and pressed it gently against his forehead. Wes bolted awake with a gasp. He looked around, startled at the abrupt transition, but quickly identified his gilded cage. He remained locked away in the belly of the Divine Hall.

Food was brought to him on silver platters. Decadent cakes, chunks of aged cheese, and strange fruit Wes never saw before. He avoided the slices of meat and skewers of sausage. He could not forget those things that men and women devoured the night before, and meat made his stomach weak. He decided on a hunk of bread along with some cheese. His eyes lingered, and after a moment he snatched up one of the round fruits as well. Wes was amazed at how much food they offered him. It was enough to feed ten men instead of one. He thought of Clem with her body as thin as a reed, and wondered if there were many children like her: begging to be fed. When a servant returned for his tray, Wes got to his feet and approached the aging woman.

"Beg your pardon," he said and tugged at the corner of his hat. "What are your intentions for all this food?" The woman glanced up at him, confused, then quickly lowered her eyes to the tray in her hands.

"I assure you high lord, we will dispose of everything properly."

"Dispose? I hardly touched this food and you'll just waste it?" Again the woman glanced up at him, confused, then back to her tray.

"All edicts are honored, high lord. The rules are addressed."

"Look me in the eye, woman," Wes demanded, and she surely tried, but after a moment she looked away again. "What is your name?"

"I am Agatha, high lord" she said softly, and her hands started to tremble. Cups rattled against bottles of untouched wine.

"Agatha, I am not a high lord, and I can not command you, but I reckon I would be a little upset if you threw all this food away instead of giving it to the hungry." Agatha stared at him, too stunned to adhere to the demure expectation of her position.

"But..." her hands trembled more, and one of the fruits fell from its platter.

"Maybe not the meat. Give that to the dogs. But there must be children begging outside the Hall. You could give them some of those sweet cakes."

"High lord!" Agatha said, as her whole body trembled. Wes was surprised to see how horrified she looked. "What game is this, then? Have you poisoned the pastries? Drugged them somehow? I don't want to take part in your entertainment, sir. I beg you, please don't make me." Wes stared at her, dumbfounded, then a deep gut-wrenching disgust overtook him. He turned his back to her.

"Get out of here," he growled, and Agatha fled from the room. The renegade fruit fell from the tray in her haste, and she left it abandoned to roll across the floor. When she was gone, Wes plucked it up and held the fruit in his hand.

"This place has so much cruelty, she could not fathom an act of charity. She thought it was a trick contrived by a monster." He placed the fruit on his table, then sat at the foot of the bed, and stared at it as time passed him by; marked by the lengthy shadows on the wall.

The more he sat there, staring at the fruit, the more Wes realized the conundrum he was in. There were many obstacles in his way. First, he was not sure he could even convince Daniel to go. If he accomplished that much, he was certain the Elders would not be willing to *let* Daniel go. So they would have to escape somehow. But Wes didn't know how to navigate the labyrinth that made up the interior of the Hall. He could attempt his window escape, but dare he risk Daniel falling from such a height? Maybe Daniel knew of a way to slip out of the Divine Hall undetected, but then they had to navigate through the city. When he first arrived, Wes noted how guarded the entrance was to the capital, but he was too distracted by all the people, and the buildings, and the colors, and the sin. If Palto was willing to forfeit something as valuable as a pocket watch relic that once belonged to Old Father just to pay a smuggler to oust her from the city, Wes knew that he and Daniel wouldn't be able to leave by simply walking out into the wilds. Daniel might be able to acquire a permit, or one of the other things Palto mentioned, but what would they do about Wes' mare? If he was able to secure her, would she attract unwanted attention? Elders roamed the streets alongside the residents. They might be able to go during the day, but then they could not blend into the crowds. They could abandon the mare and go on foot, but how would they be able to carry enough provisions to survive the time it would take to walk home. Not to mention the Elders would certainly hunt them down the moment they realized Daniel was gone. Wes might be able to hide Daniel from them, but not if any one of them carried the second sight. Not with that monster glowing brightly inside of his son. Would they drag Daniel back to the capital, or just kill him right there and let his body lie crumpled in the dust?

Wes sighed, and rubbed moisture back into his eyes.

"We look forward to meeting you, father of the Guardian Son!" A woman shouted outside of his door, and two other women giggled alongside her. Wes lifted his head, and stared at the lock but it didn't click open, and the laughing women moved further down the hall. Feeling restless, Wes got to his feet, and started to pace about the room. His mind replayed back all the obstacles that he faced. First, he was not sure he could even convince Daniel to go...

The sun took its journey across the sky, and as it started to sink in the west, the activity increased inside the Divine Hall. Voices calling to one another, asking about plans and attire, and if there was a theme for the evening, and what the entertainment would be. Wes wondered if he was far enough away from the banquet hall that he wouldn't hear all the screams.

When the sun sank far enough to cast the yard of the Hall in shadows, Wes heard a voice calling out his name. He stepped cautiously to the threshold of his open window, and peered down into the gloom below. There was a worn patrol path that ran the length of the perimeter wall, and in the middle of it, a solitary figure stood looking up at him.

"Why are *you* here?" Wes asked, for he didn't expect to encounter Jack again. The tall guard tucked his duck bill hat under his arm, and looked about nervously. When he spoke, it was just loud enough to be heard.

"I have been called to serve."

"By the guards?"

"No!" Jack's head swiveled as he looked up and down the path, then he turned his glare upon Wes. "The Disciples wish to serve you, oh great Light Keeper."

"You do the bidding of the Disciples then?" Wes asked, noting Jack's sarcasm.

"No!" Again he looked about, then lowered his voice. "I do the bidding of my mother."

"Your mother wants you to serve me, Jack?" Wes asked and couldn't help but smile. He was in no position to tease the lad, yet he found himself doing just that. He had to admit this smart-mouthed guard was kind of growing on him.

"My mother wants me to remember my commitment to the flock," Jack said, looking miserable. Wes nodded, knowing he was given a greater understanding of who Jack was and who he used to be.

"So you are called to serve, but why are you here?" Wes asked and Jack stared at him dumbly.

"I'm here to help you escape!"

"Escape? But why?"

"Why? Do you plan to just rot away in there?" Jack was incredulous, and no longer whispered. Voices called to each other in the distance, and he slipped deeper into the shadows against the wall. Wes leaned out the window to see him better, and could just make out the glint of Jack's eyes glaring up at him. "The Disciples have eyes and ears all over this place. They know that the great lord tossed you in there, and threw away the key."

"He didn't do that! He...just hasn't had a chance to come speak with me," Wes said, feeling defensive.

"Even if that's true, the moment the Elder's find out who you are, they will have you killed!"

Wes stared at Jack as he bit his lower lip. This thought already occurred to him, but it wasn't death that he feared. It was the idea of Daniel spending the rest of his life in this place that terrified him.

"I have to go, mister. What are your orders for me?"

"Orders?"

"I have been called to serve." Jack said with a flourish and a bow. Wes considered his options.

"Are you able to smuggle people out of the city?"

"The Disciples are already preparing to extract you from the city."

"I will need passage for three people," Wes said, then reconsidered Jack. "Maybe four."

"They will gladly move mountains for you, Light Keeper," Jack said, with another bow and flourish. It seemed that he liked to use Wes' supposed title every time he wanted to be a little sardonic. "Is there anything else his lordship desires?"

"Yes," Wes said as thoughts circled each other in his mind. "I need you to bring a friend to speak with me."

"Which friend?" Jack asked with narrowed eyes, and Wes smiled a little.

"I reckon you're already familiar with Palto."

"No."

"You have been called to serve," Wes reminded him. He didn't know what the history was between the two of them, but it seemed that Jack held the greater grudge. All the same, Wes needed to speak with Palto, and saw no other way. "Bring her here at the same time tomorrow."

"There is no way I can sneak a girl inside the Divine Hall. Especially *that* girl!"

"If you can't sneak her in, how do you expect to sneak me out?" Wes asked, and Jack stared silently up at him with a grim frown.

"Same time tomorrow," Wes said with a small wave, then ducked back into his room.

Night fell upon the capital and the festivities began anew. Wes remained captive, and spent his time listening to faint lines of music from the street, when it drifted high enough to reach his window. More food was brought to him, a man holding the tray this time, but one look at his face told Wes that he had developed a dastardly reputation with the kitchen staff. They might decide to poison the food before it arrived to his room. The tray was placed upon his table, and Wes eyed it dubiously after the servant made his hasty exit.

Outside his window, Wes heard the trill of a piano, a woman's laughter, and a lone child wailing into the night. The capital never slept; its residents had no reason to dream. The night stretched just as the day did, and Wes returned to his pacing. His mind circled back to the problems he faced, incorporating in his potential aid. Long before the birdsong that eluded him in the city, he heard the lock click open on his door. Wes turned from his window, and was surprised to see Daniel stroll majestically into the room. He was like that large male turkey Wes saw with Benji in the wilds. The one who strutted as he led his flock to graze.

Daniel was dressed in a gallant black uniform, with gold braiding around the cuffs and lapels. The length of his jacket was cut short, and tapered at the waist. His black boots went to his knees and his tight fitting trousers tucked into them without a crease. He knew how dashing he looked, for he put on a good show of it.

"Hello father," he announced grandly, but there was a notable slur to his words. His eyes were hooded, and occasionally closed for a few seconds before drifting open again. Regardless of his intoxication, he did not look happy. He looked like he was there to pick a fight. The tall boy and the boy with the big ears slipped quietly into the room behind him, but lingered by the door.

"I'm glad you came," Wes said warmly, and smiled at his son. Daniel stopped short, and the cool grin slipped from his face. He looked surprised; uncertain; doubting, but then turned from Wes and focused instead on his platter full of food.

"You aren't eating," he commented as he picked up the solitary piece of fruit that rested in front of the ornate tray.

"I've eaten enough," Wes replied carefully. He needed to guard his words. If he told Daniel that he feared the food was poisoned, his son might decide to replace the entire kitchen staff, or worse one of the Elders might have them killed. Wes moved closer to stand next to his son, and was surprised to see how short Daniel was. No matter how much he liked to pretend, he was still a boy. When Daniel saw how close Wes was, he turned his back to his father, and approached his two boy guards.

“Do you boys remember the stories I told you about the man who is supposed to come one day and take me away?”

“Are you talking about the prophecies?” Wes asked, and Daniel turned to look intently at him from over his shoulder.

“Stories,” he corrected with deliberate conviction, then returned his attention to his guards. “Do you remember?”

Both the boys nodded up at him eagerly. There was an excitement in their eyes. They enjoyed hearing his tales.

“Then you’ll remember how, in my story, the man that comes doesn’t have any markings on his face. No scales, no blackness, no sickness.”

“Just like you,” the tall boy said, nodding. Daniel gave him a small but tender smile.

“Yes. Just like me.”

“You said that the Elders will hunt down such a man,” said the smaller boy with the ears and Daniel nodded at him, exaggerating how impressed he seemed to be.

“That’s right. Exactly right. Such a man would be foolish to let Elders face him.”

“And what about you,” Wes asked, feeling suddenly frustrated. He spent hours trapped in this room waiting to talk to his son. Now Daniel wants to play this foolish game with a couple of children. “Will you not face me either?”

Daniel turned, and stared up at Wes with an expression he couldn’t quite discern.

“You’re not thinking clearly about why I am here,” he said flatly, and his patronizing tone caused Wes’ frustration to grow into anger. He charged forward, confronting the boy head-on.

“And *you’re* not thinking clearly about why I’m here!” He snapped, then tilted his head as he leaned close to his son’s face. “Do you think I care a lick about your stories? Do you think I care about everyone calling me the Keeper of Light?”

Behind them, the two boy guards gasped in unison. Daniel stared up at Wes, but did not respond right away. His mouth worked over words left unspoken, then Wes noticed how his lower lip trembled and he blinked in surprise.

“Daniel...” But what should he say? Was he too harsh in his anger? Was his son truly so sensitive? Daniel glanced back at the two boy guards who both appeared to be terrified. Then he let out a sigh, and looked up at Wes with a small smile affixed to his face.

“So why are you here, father? All this time, I was nothing but an afterthought to you. Now you stand before me, spewing your vitriol, and expecting to be heard. Well you have earned my attention. So please tell me why you are in my life again!”

Daniel's anger was not the blazing furnace Wes experienced when they first met. Instead it was cold and tempered, like a steel blade after quenching; its edge being honed with each clipped word. The things he said stung, but it was his anger that left Wes feeling breathless. He studied his son's face, strikingly beautiful, and fumbled through what he intended to say.

"I came...I'm here because of your mother."

"Mom?" Daniel said, and instantly his face softened. His cold anger shed away like an outgrown skin. "Wh...what do you mean? What about her?"

Wes could not stand the look in his son's eyes; the mix of hope and dread. He shifted his attention to the fireplace and let the flames help bring focus to his mind. This was not the way he wanted to break the news to his son. He wanted to hug Daniel the way he did with Benji, but everything was so strange between them. Every step he took was the wrong one. He forced himself to meet his son's eyes, knowing he was about to break his heart.

"She crossed beyond the veil, son," Wes said, his voice as coarse as his words. "Your mother is dead."

"She's...dead?" Daniel was stunned, and his voice trembled like the music outside Wes' window. He stared at Wes, waiting to be told it was all a stupid farce, but when the words did not come, his eyes went unfocused. Wes watched as his thirteen-year-old son came to realize that the first love of his life was gone. He struggled to find something he could say to ease his son's pain even if only a little.

"She loved you dearly, son. I know how hard it is to lose her."

"To lose her?" Daniel said, and his eyes came back into focus. He looked up at his father, then scoffed. "To lose *her*? Do you think she's the only thing that I loved and lost?"

"I didn't mean to say..."

"Everything!" Daniel said as he leaned toward his father and bared his teeth. "Everything that I loved, I have lost."

"I'm sorry, I..." Daniel lifted his gloved hand, placing it directly between the two of them, and stared past it as he tugged at his fingers.

"You've had the pleasure of witnessing one of the Elder's parties. They have so many. And when they grow tired of all the ways they find pleasure, they come up with new inventive methods to hurt me."

"Daniel, can't we talk about..."

"Listen to me!" Daniel shouted, and Wes heard the second voice echo a step behind. The dragon. The usurper. Daniel stripped the glove from his hand, then placed pale fingers against the breast pocket of his uniform jacket. He opened the button as he went on.

"When they ran out of ways to cause physical pleasure, or physical pain, they discovered a new way to worship me. They gave me something to love."

Daniel pulled the pocket flap free from its button, then lifted it to reach inside.

"They produced a puppy from somewhere, poor thing. She was a sweet little brown dog with a stubby tail." Daniel smiled in his recollection, then extracted a small velvet pouch from his pocket. He pulled at its strings to open it.

"They insisted I name her, but I was so afraid to. I knew that if I named her, I would love her and of course I did. Her name was Misery." Behind him, one of the boys started to cry. Wes watched, horrified without understanding why, as Daniel turned from him, and approached the two boy guards by the door.

"Love was far crueler than any whip or blade. Love showed me all the things I can't ever have." He stood before his two guards, and rested his hand against the shorter one's face. The boy smiled up at him even though there were tears in his eyes. Daniel held out the pouch, and he took it into his hands. Daniel turned his head, peering back at Wes from the corner of his eye.

"So you came all this way to tell me that my mother is dead?"

"And to take you home," Wes said, his voice muted and pathetic. "To pay your respects to her."

"Back home," Daniel said as the small boy pulled something from the pouch and placed it into his mouth. Then he handed the pouch to the taller boy who repeated the same action. "So the prophecies are true."

"I reckon they might be."

"Does this mean you have met the Bringer of Light?"

"Yes," Wes said softly as tears stung at his eyes. "Yes, Daniel, I have."

"Great lord!" The shorter boy gasped, and Daniel reached for him with such gentle tenderness. The boy collapsed into his arms, and Daniel eased down to the floor, while cradling the child against him.

"Hush now. It's alright. All will be well."

"It was an honor sir," said the older boy as he sank down alongside the other, and Daniel pulled him close as well. "An honor to serve you."

"Stop it," Wes whispered, but tears filled his eyes, and choked the words in his throat. He didn't want to comprehend what he was seeing, but could not will himself to turn away. The small boy smiled up at Daniel, and fought so hard to not cry.

"Don't be scared," Daniel said softly, and bent over to kiss the boy's forehead. His voice wavered with heartache. "You're just going to sleep for a while." The taller boy reached for him, and Daniel took his hand. He looked down at the boy, and smiled at him sadly. "No one will serve me better than you did."

The tall boy gave Daniel a wide joyful smile. He looked so happy; so at peace, then his eyes rolled, and he pitched forward. Daniel grabbed hold of him, and pulled him in closer. He sat with both boys cradled in his arms, and buried his face in their hair.

"What have you done?" Wes gasped. He was utterly appalled.

"This is not the first time love has ripped open my heart," Daniel said as he gently laid each still child onto the floor. "But it never gets easier to endure."

"You speak of love with your tongue while you murder with your actions. Why do this wicked thing?"

"Because I had to," Daniel said. His face was hard as he raised his chin, and turned cold eyes on his father.

"But why?" Wes cried out, mortified by his son.

"Because I love you more!" Daniel shouted back. He got to his feet, leaving the boys limp bodies discarded on the floor like clothes. He glared at Wes as his anger grew in heat. The blade was sharp; precisely honed. His anger was ready to slide effortlessly into a man's heart. "Did you not see the fear in their eyes? They *knew* you. They knew what you represented, and it terrified them, father! *You* terrified them! So what would happen to them after we left this room? What would the Elders do with two boys that suddenly had fear in their eyes? They would not be able to guard their hearts. They have not lost all that *I* have! The Elders would take them from me. Have them drugged, and abused, and tortured for information. They would die horribly, and painfully, and confess *one* name as their breath left their broken bodies..."

"Daniel!"

"Light Keeper!" Daniel stepped forward to stand before his father and sneered up at Wes with menace.

"I don't want to hear this," Wes pleaded.

"They would say your name, and the Elders would learn who you truly are. You can't imagine all the ways they would hurt you. And when they saw how much that hurt me...our suffering would be immeasurable."

"Those boys are dead because of me," Wes said, too stunned to feel the full grief of what happened. But that would come later. Another burden to add to his nightmares. Daniel stepped back, his face growing placid as he reigned in his fury.

"No, father. They are dead because of me. They both knew this would happen one day. It's the price everyone pays, for loving me."

Chapter Twenty-Two

Take no part in the unfruitful works of darkness,
but instead expose them.
For it is shameful even to speak of the things
that they do in secret.
But when anything is exposed by the light,
it becomes visible,
for anything that becomes visible is light.
- Ephesians 5:11-14 ESV

Wes paced by the open window, waiting for Jack to return, and occasionally looked out over the capital to gauge the time of day. Not much longer. He wanted to push on with his plans, no matter how flimsy they might seem. After what Daniel told him, his strongest desire was to be free from the Divine Hall and the city that contained it.

Time moved in step with the shadows which grew, blended, and merged. Wes started to think Jack wasn't returning. He leaned out the window, checking for signs of movement in the yard below, but was left wanting. When twilight found him, the city came alive again. Every night, the damned marched about in unison while they searched for an ounce or pint of the happiness that eluded them.

Wes watched their progression, then his eye caught sight of a flickering firebox, turned low to avoid attention. It was floating above the pathway that ran the perimeter wall. He ducked back into the room, and waited, for he dare not assume it was Jack, and wanted to avoid attention. Wes listened to boots crunching over the stones outside his window, then a familiar voice came to his ear and made him smile.

"You better be true to the coin you offered me. They will kill me if I am caught in here."

"Keep your voice down then! I thought maybe you *wanted* to die."

"I'm glad you came back," Wes said softly as he returned to his window. Twin pale faces turned to look up at him, and Palto's eyes grew wide with recognition.

"What are you doing up there?" She hissed with her hands raised in exasperation. "And why am I down here?"

Jack's words came right on her heels: "Mister, if you ever ask me to herd this wild animal again, I will refuse you, my soul be damned."

"I appreciate the effort you made to get her here, Jack. And Palto, it is good to see you again." Palto dropped her arms, and tilted her head as she stared at him with wide-eyed confusion. She resembled a bird trying to make sense of a caterpillar when she expected to see a worm.

"I needed to see you, Palto, so you knew the words came from me. You see, I need your help again."

"Oh, no," Palto said with a shake of her head, "No, no, no. I'm not getting involved in any of this Divine Hall nonsense. Find yourself another stooge." She turned back the way she came, and looked as though she might run, but Jack clamped a large hand onto the back of her neck and held her in place.

"Don't hurt her," Wes warned, but Palto lifted her leg, and drove her heel down on Jack's foot. He yelped before he could stop himself, then released her to turn and limp through the pain. Wes burst into laughter, and Palto peered up at him with a challenge in her eye.

"You'll be laughing all the way to the gallows, you rube."

"I can't help it," Wes said, still chuckling, "you make me laugh."

"Is that some way of insulting me?" Palto asked, a little heated.

"No, Palto. I just like you, that's all." Palto's face took on an expression of guarded appreciation. She considered Wes, while Jack got himself under control, and returned to her side. He glared down at her but kept his hands to himself.

"What do you want me to do, mister?" Palto said, having made up her mind.

"I need you to get my horse ready to ride for tomorrow. She must be saddled by nightfall for I plan to leave in a hurry. Walk her a little to get her legs stretched, and make sure she is brushed and well fed. Will you do this for me?"

"Yes, mister. I will do what I've been hired to do." Wes liked to think she would do it even if he hadn't hired her. He knelt by his window and leaned out of it so he might see her face better. The firebox resting at their feet worked against him.

"Palto, I'm fixing to leave and take my son home, but I'm willing to take you with me. I'll get you out of the city, no need for you to pay. And after we're free of this place, you're welcome to stay or go as you wish. Will you follow me?" Palto stared at Wes, stunned by his gesture, then her shoulders sagged and she looked away.

"I can't."

"What? But why?" This was not the answer Wes expected. Palto glanced over to Jack, who studied her intently, then turned her face up to Wes once more.

"I...don't want to be around...*him*. Don't worry about me, mister. I'll find my own way." Wes was sad to hear her refuse. He hoped he might convince her to stay with him for a while. He didn't understand the issue she had with Daniel any more than he understood the issue Jack had with her.

"Alright, tend to my horse then," he said, and Palto seemed to relax.

"It will be as you say, mister."

"And you were able to get here unseen?" Wes asked, turning his attention to Jack.

"I found a way. But it's good you plan to go tomorrow. The other guards will catch on sooner than later, and I can't see another way to get two of you out of here."

"Are you really going to kidnap the Guardian Son?" Palto asked; too amazed to guard her words.

"Only if he wants to go. But I think he will. I hope he will."

"Speaking of going," Jack said, and tapped Palto's arm with the back of his hand. She picked up the firebox, ready to leave and Jack peered up at Wes again. "Am I meeting you here tomorrow night?"

"I'll meet you over there," Wes said, pointing toward the base of the Hall's lower area which had a pitched roof starting high against the wall and sloping down until it reached an overhang that was only about five feet off the ground.

"Do you plan to jump out the window and land like a cat?" Palto asked.

"I plan to follow this ledge here, then climb down yonder," Wes said as they all took a moment to trace the course with their eyes.

"Is there anything you can't do, oh great and powerful Light Keeper?" Jack said, sarcastically, but Wes ignored his baiting.

"Come in the later part of the evening, when everyone is intoxicated by their indulgences. Hopefully they won't notice us when they can barely keep their eyes open."

"Alright, mister. I'll be back tomorrow to get you out of here. But I hope you know what you're doing." Wes gave him a nod, unwilling to speak a lie, and Jack turned to leave. He had no idea what he was doing, but he hoped that God did.

Wes watched the two of them fade into a forming fog. Clouds were gathering overhead; the air wet with cold mist. He closed his eyes, feeling the damp as a layer on his skin, then was surprised to hear the click of an opening lock. He stepped back, turning from the window, just as Daniel staggered into the room.

There was no grand entrance this time; no entourage of expendable boys in his wake. Daniel wore a flimsy frock that flowed around him like a cloud. The door closed behind him, unseen hands working the mechanism of the lock, as Daniel pushed forward on unsteady feet. His eyes were half hooded and unfocused. His hair was tousled, sticking up awkwardly on his head, and in his hand he held one of those long slender pipes. Daniel's eyes remained focused on the floor, yet he still stumbled over his own feet. He pitched forward, and grabbed the table to regain his balance. The contents of Wes' untouched tray rattled in objection.

Wes moved to Daniel's side, hoping to assist him, but as soon as his son turned from the table his legs gave out under him. Wes lunged forward, caught his son, then lifted him up into his arms and carried him over to his bed. Daniel felt so thin, and Wes wondered if all boys his age were as small as he was. He gently placed Daniel on the edge of his bed, then pulled the untouched blankets back from the overstuffed mattress. Daniel turned his head slightly, examining the inviting pillow, then leaned towards it, but he needed Wes' help to reach it. Wes pulled the blanket over his son's body, and noticed Daniel was shivering as he grabbed hold of it.

Wes lifted his eyes to the window. He supposed it was a little cool in this room. He never thought about it, being familiar with sleeping in the wilds alongside a spindly fire. He went to the window and pulled it closed, then gave the fire attention; feeding it to give it more life. Feeling the warmth of the room, he stripped his jacket off, and draped it over the foot of the bed as he returned to his son. He was surprised to see Daniel's eyes were open, and as he watched Wes approach, his attention momentarily went to Wes' gun.

The fire caught on, and cast the room in dancing light. Wes had a better view of his son's face and as he sat down on the floor next to him, he noticed a bruise high on his cheekbone. He brushed back his son's hair to examine it more closely, then realized there was also a row of bruises like fingerprints running down Daniel's neck. Wes pulled the blanket away, driven by his outrage, and observed through the thin material of Daniel's clothes, a large purple stain upon his ribs, as well as other large bruises on his arms and legs. What level of brutality was this to cause a child to bruise so intensely in such a short period of time.

Daniel reached for the blanket Wes held, and wrapped it around his body again. He looked exhausted, but in his eyes Wes could also see a bitter deep shame.

"Daniel, what have they done to you?" Wes asked, dreading to hear what his son might tell him, but also desperate to connect with him in some way.

"Nothing I didn't deserve," Daniel replied thickly, as his eyes drifted closed. Wes' heart ached for his son.

Oh, my sweet boy. No one deserves this.

"Daniel...are you happy here?" Wes reached tentatively for his son, and gently smoothed down his hair.

"It was better when Old Father was alive," Daniel said with a yawn. "He made use of me as a means to control, but with him gone...it's been chaos."

"Then leave this place," Wes said desperately. He placed his coarse hand upon the soft skin of his son's face, and Daniel opened his eyes. "Come with me. Tomorrow night. We'll go visit your mother's grave, then we can start a new life together. You and I. You can be free from this place."

"That sounds wonderful, father." Daniel seemed to speak without expression, yet tears welled up in his doll-like eyes, and slid down the bruises on his face. "But I can't go with you."

"You...But why?" Wes said, and used his sleeve to gently dab at Daniel's tears. "Why can't you go with me?"

"The Dragon," said his son with complete indifference. Then he yawned and closed his eyes again. Wes felt a chill, hearing the name of the monster that wore Daniel like a garment. The usurper. The demon. The Dragon. Daniel's breathing got heavy. He was slipping into sleep. Wes reached out, and desperately shook him awake.

"What about the Dragon? I don't understand. Please explain this to me!" Daniel yawned again but didn't respond, and Wes could only stare at him helplessly. He wanted so much to reach for his son; to hold him and care for him, and protect him from all the things that have hurt him. But Daniel felt so far away from him, even though they were mere inches apart. Wes watched him, certain that he was asleep, but then Daniel spoke in a soft whisper as though his spirit called to Wes from within his dreams.

"If I don't fend off the Dragon, the Dragon will turn on me."

Wes stared at Daniel sleeping as he tried to make sense of his words. The Dragon will turn on him? What future was in store for his son?

Wes fell asleep leaning against the bed next to Daniel, and Ruth appeared in his dreams. He was at his homestead, but instead of seeing barren fields, the air was thick with summer heat. Ruth stood before him; young, and pregnant with their first son. She danced about their grassy hill as she laughed and sang. She looked so beautiful, and even though she was never this happy in her life, Wes still felt his heart quicken when he saw her this way. She was so captivating, he never understood what she saw in him when she could have had anyone in their village.

Admiring his wife, Wes saw movement from the corner of his eye, and turned in the direction of the barn. Someone was in there. He abandoned Ruth, and approached the barn as he peered into its dim interior. He was surprised to see that the barn was empty. There weren't even animals stabled there.

Wes glanced over his shoulder at Ruth who continued to spin and to laugh as though she were condemned to this eerie cycle. Wes stepped cautiously into the barn, and felt the wrongness of the place.

"Hello?" He called out as he tilted his head and examined the vacant hayloft. Where were the animals? Where was Jethro? Movement caught his eye again, and Wes looked back to the barn's entrance where the outside world was bathed in sun. A silhouette of a boy stepped into the doorway, and turned toward Wes who squinted against daylight to make out his face.

"Benji?"

A loud bang suddenly jolted Wes awake, and he immediately moved to protect the bed only to find it was vacant. Daniel was gone; the blanket he used, discarded as a heap on the pillow. Wes tried to move; tried to stand, but everything seemed to swim around his consciousness as though the room was shaken by an unseen force. His head was full of cobwebs, and his mouth was incredibly dry. The darkness outside was like a blot of ink upon his window. Did he sleep through the entire day? Wes wondered if Daniel drugged him somehow, but was not able to think too long on the matter, for the door flew open, and a small group of guards spilled into the room. One of them stepped forward; a hard no-nonsense sort of fellow, and he looked over Wes sprawled out on the floor.

"You need to come with us, sir," he said, and Wes took in the stern faces of all the guards in the room. No sign of Jack, but of course he was not part of the Guard Watch Elite. If these men caught wind of his intent to escape somehow...

"Water," Wes rasped, thinking to buy a little time to allow his head to clear. One of the other guards reached for a pewter cup and pitcher resting on the table. Wes tested the water on his tongue and did not taste anything bitter. No tingling or numbness either. Resolving to consider it free of poison, Wes downed the whole cup in one gulp; holding it out for more.

"No more delays," said No-nonsense, and smacked the cup out of Wes' hands. Wes felt his head clearing, and he regarded the main guard with deliberate sternness.

"Where is the Guardian Son?" he demanded, and No-nonsense gave a quick bow of his head.

"We have been ordered to deliver you to him, sir. So you'll find that out on your own." This relaxed Wes a little. He got to his feet, brushed at his pants, then tried to retrieve his jacket.

"Allow me," No-nonsense said, stepping in Wes' way. He snatched up the jacket from where it was still draped at the foot of the bed, and approached Wes. His eyes never wavered from Wes' as he reached out to pluck his gun from its holster. The weapon caught, strapped in as it was, but the guard managed to figure out the loop of leather that held it in place. Wes didn't try to stop him, but wondered if the guard was simply being cautious, seeing the gun that Wes failed to conceal, or was this another order from Wes' son. No-nonsense slipped Wes' hunting knife out of its sheath as well, and held the two weapons together in his one large fist. He then surprised Wes by reaching out, and snatching his hat off of his head. Wes pulled at the blue cloth still tied around his neck, thinking to use it to cover his forehead, but the main guard stopped him.

"Our orders were clear sir," was all he said as he pushed Wes' jacket into his chest. Wes glared at the guard, but wisely remained quiet. If they knew that his face was unmarked, then they must know the nature of who he was in relation to their prophecies. Wes urgently wanted to reach Daniel and make sure that he was alright. When Daniel was at his most vulnerable, it was Wes that he sought out. Wes had to believe they still had a connection that meant something to his son.

All things are possible with God.

"Follow me, sir," No-nonsense commanded, and when he turned to exit the room, Wes fell in behind him. He quickly realized that the remaining guards intended to surround him. One walked on either side of him and two flanked a few feet behind. He tried not to worry about what this meant, but he couldn't deny that he truly felt like a prisoner. If they got hold of Jack, or worse Palto...

If they did to them all those things Daniel said they were capable of doing...

As they led him down the hall, Wes memorized the path they went. It might prove useful to know. They snaked through uniform hallways and down large stone stairways that echoed their footsteps. When they reached the main floor, the hallways widened, and the walls were decorated with old tapestries and an array of paintings. Among them, Wes saw a boy portrait similar to the one that the Disciples were selling in their store front. His eyes lingered on it as they passed.

A few Elders caught sight of Wes being ushered down the hall, and they fell in behind his entourage as though they were forming a bizarre parade of prisoner, captor, and spectator.

"Is this really the boy's father?" He heard one of them whisper.

"Don't let our great lord hear you calling him a boy."

"Maybe our great lord will let us have a taste after he's done playing with him."

"Surely his face cannot be so pure naturally. He must have a great concealer."

"Or a great Healer."

"If we drink his blood, will our faces look as good as his?"

Wes quietly grieved over the burden of his own hearing. These creatures talked so much, yet said nothing worth listening to. He thought back to the song that Solomon sang with Benji and his sister, and hummed it softly to expel their chatter from his mind; the cacophony of the damned.

They approached the banquet hall as they continued along their path, and Wes held his breath until they passed it. Thank the Lord they were not taking him there. Instead they took him to the hall's other end which led to a set of double wooden doors, ornately carved with rows of some long forgotten flower. An old green sash with small hand-sewn livery on it, draped across the top of the door and ran down either side. All of this beauty, created by men of the Before, and ignored by everyone who bore witness to it every day.

They confronted the door, and No-nonsense held up his hand to call a halt to their procession. The Elders that followed behind, fluttered past them in elaborate white outfits, and opened the one door only wide enough to slip inside.

Wes tilted his head, trying to look into the room beyond, but the guards on either side of him grabbed hold of his shoulders and pitched him forward. He had to crane his neck to glare up at No-nonsense with his hair in his eyes. The main guard gave him a small half smile, then turned and hammered a fist on the door.

"Respected Elders, herald to the great Guardian Son, Sir Wes of the Outlands stands before you!"

"You may enter!" A voice called from within. The guards on either side of Wes continued to hold him in place, but the ones that flanked him strode up to the doors and pushed them in unison. As soon as the way was made clear, the lead guard moved ahead of them, but Wes was given an opportunity to take in the room, bent forward awkwardly as he was.

The first thing he saw were many rows of books positioned on shelves lining the full length of both walls. The room was more long than wide, extending about fifty feet to the other end, and both sides were lined from top to bottom with books. Wes had no idea that so many existed in this world. Books of different sizes and colors and widths. There had to be hundreds or possibly thousands! Surely, they couldn't all be copies of the Word. Wes couldn't help but wonder what they contained.

When No-nonsense was a good distance into the room, the two guards that held Wes in place, pulled him back upright, and guided him forward. He twisted out of their grasp, turning to glare at them both, and caught sight of the flanking guards closing the doors behind them. They remained in the hallway, no doubt taking place on either side of the doors, but Wes did not hear the lock clicking into place. A useful thing to know. He turned his attention back to the room full of books, and was grateful his two guard escorts settled on standing at either side of him, instead of manhandling him forward.

Taking in the rest of the room, Wes turned his attention away from all the books, and noted two rows of ornate armchairs made of plush, leather, and wood. They were evenly spaced in front of the bookshelves, and faced inward toward a long red carpet upon which Wes stood. Each chair was inhabited with men and women that were indifferent to the tomes that loomed over them. They were dressed in lavish white garments full of lace, tassels, and plumes, and reminded Wes of a room full of roosters sizing each other up; determined to pick a fight. But instead of looking at one another, all of them were staring at Wes.

Feeling uneasy, he ran his fingers through his hair, unaccustomed to it falling over his eyes, and noted the ripple of gasps and whispers he caused. In the corner of his eye, the faces of his spectators morphed into vile creatures that bent reality around them. If Wes tried to turn away from one, another would shift in his peripheral sight. With no place safe to look, he stared at the red carpet which felt spongy under his feet. His eyes followed the path it took down the center of the room, and at the far end he saw No-nonsense placing his hat, his gun, and his knife on a large white glossy desk. When the guard stepped to the side, taking his place next to one of two large statues positioned at the end of the bookshelves, Wes realized that a solitary figure stood behind the desk examining his spoil. A word left him in a soft burst of breath.

"Daniel."

"Thank you for joining us, Father," Daniel announced in a booming, grandiose way. There was no warmth to his words, and while Wes told himself that his son was putting on a show, he couldn't ignore the sinking feeling that he was walking into a trap. Even from such a great distance, Wes could tell that Daniel looked...hurt.

What is going on here?

The guards on either side of him urged him forward, and Wes focused numbly on the function of his legs. His movement was a catalyst, spurring the Elders to speak.

"Look at his face!"

"You were right, not a single mark upon him."

"Even the bruises have healed. The Hall is doing its work."

"Is he truly the one spoken of by Elder Strupple?"

"Oh, this is a disaster! Our Guardian Son will be destroyed!"

"Don't let the great lord hear you say that!"

"He is too handsome to be so evil."

Daniel looked odd dressed in black among so much white. He opted for a uniform again, but this one had a lacy ruffle that splashed across his throat and dripped down his hands. So much darkness only accented the paleness of his skin.

"I would like to get to know him before we kill him."

"The Light Keeper in the flesh. The harbinger of the world's destruction."

"Not a single spot upon his face."

"Such a lovely face for one so horribly cruel."

Wes wanted to scream at them. Evil? Cruel? Him? After what he observed these people doing, the very idea that they would brand him with these words was infuriating. He looked at Daniel, and his face made plain the thoughts of his mind. He was *betrayed*! Was it Daniel that told these Elders that he was the Light Keeper? Was this information forced from his son in ways that inflicted large bruises all over his body? Wes wanted to believe the boy wouldn't willingly give over such information, considering all he said was at stake, but when Daniel met his eyes, Wes saw his own look of betrayal mirrored back at him. He stopped, confusion stunting his progression, but the guards allowed him no delay.

"Do you think he will really crumble the Temple of the Dragon?"

"Ground to dust and made like clay into something new."

"Not if we stop him! Not if we kill him!"

"And what of the Light Bringer?"

"Can such a creature exist?"

"One devoid of all sin? Impossible. Impossible!"

"Don't let the Guardian Son hear you say that."

The desk stretched before Wes, only a few feet away, and he took in the shape of the bronze statues on either side of it. Both of them were of women in flowing robes with large sweeping wings. They looked angelic, and again Wes took note of how the Word seemed to cast ripples and echoes throughout the city. It was as if people took scraps of fabric and tried to form a garment based on the account of a memory. At some point in the history of the city, they tried to reinvent something they didn't have a pattern for, and forced the leftover scraps of cloth into the spaces they were unable to fill. The Elders in the room were the descendants of those people that ripped the word of the Lord apart. All that remained were shadows of the truth and decorative statues that had no meaning.

"Look! His hands are black! Are you sure he's the Light Keeper?"

"We could strip him down, and see how far the stain stretches."

"Yes! Strip him down! Tear everything away!"

"His death would upset the Strupple prophecy."

"No need to worry then."

"No cleansing light."

"No destruction."

"Father, come sit with me please." Daniel gestured to an empty chair placed directly in front of his desk, and Wes examined it warily. There was a chance that this revelation of his title didn't come from Daniel at all. There was still the possibility of Jack. Or Palto. Were they already dead? Wes hoped this wasn't the case. He approached the chair, and moved to sit upon it as requested.

"Look how slim he is."

"Slim? He appears half starved!"

"Too bad he didn't dine with us on that first night."

"If I was there that night, I would have stopped him before he got halfway into the room!"

"You would have been too busy playing with your dinner, Elder Thoss."

Hearty laughs came from many in the room.

This is Hell. I have been swallowed up by Hell itself.

When Wes sat down, Daniel raised his fist into the air, and the room went blessedly still. The guards moved to stand on either side of Wes; resting firm hands on his shoulders to hold him in place. Daniel studied him for a moment, then turned his attention to the items laid out on the desk.

"I remember watching you every morning," he said softly, as his fingertips glided over Wes' revolver, "cleaning this thing. Taking out the bullets, putting the bullets back in. I watched you so often, I could probably do it myself. Is this the part you press to make the thing fire?"

"Something so dangerous shouldn't be toyed with," Wes said, just as softly. He wanted to lean over and take the gun away from his son, but the guards did not allow him the opportunity.

"And this old filthy thing," Daniel said, ignoring Wes' words as he turned his attention to his hat. "I should have a new one crafted for you. This one is about to fall apart."

"Why am I here?" Wes asked, feeling Daniel was toying with him the way he toyed with his gun. Daniel met his eyes, appeared as though he wanted to say something, but instead looked away again and shifted his attention back to the gun. He pushed the hat and knife to the side, and slid the gun to the middle of the desk.

"All the years you had this, I never saw you fire it once. I wonder if the thing even works."

"It works."

"A weapon you never intended to use. Yet it still got ten times the attention you allotted for me."

Wes didn't know what to say to that. Words failed him as Daniel flicked the grip of the revolver and let it spin in a circle on the table. The barrel turned around and around like the hands of Palto's pocket watch. First it pointed to Wes, then it pointed to Daniel, then it rolled back around to Wes again. Wes could stand it no longer.

"Please, Daniel, don't play with that gun."

"Do not call me that name!" Daniel hissed in a whisper. He leaned over the desk and peeled back his lips from his teeth. "Not here. Not now." Wes heard the Elders gossiping behind him.

"What are they talking about?"

"Does this father have a permit for all those relics he possesses?"

"It would be grounds to have him hanged if he does not."

"Simple solution to an unwanted problem."

"Where is the wine? I have an unquenchable thirst!"

"Doesn't the great lord look exceptionally handsome this evening."

"Enough!" Daniel called out and the room went silent once more. As Wes watched his son, standing over him and examining the Elders in the room, he realized that the bruise on the side of his face was gone. It hadn't even faded, it was completely gone.

Daniel reached into his jacket pocket and extracted a long slender pipe. Wes looked away, unwilling to watch his son drug himself.

"He avoids looking at his son."

"He won't look at us either."

"Does he think he is lesser than us?"

"The Guardian Son's father is weak."

"I will kill you where you sit if you speak another word!" Daniel's words seemed to hang in the air. A casual declaration of murder.

"What happened to you?" Wes asked, astonished, and Daniel gave one of his small joyless smiles, then pulled a long draw of smoke into his lungs.

"Tell me, father, how many bullets remain in your gun?"

"Three," Wes responded immediately. Three bullets. The same number that he carried since his father placed the gun into his hands. Things would have turned out so different if he used one of those bullets on Jethro. It mattered not. Not anymore. Wes knew it wasn't his will that was done, but God's.

Wes looked at his revolver, and saw the black eye of the barrel looking back at him. Daniel drew from his pipe a second time, then placed it on his desk as he leaned over to open one of the drawers. He extracted a small black box, and circled around the desk with it cradled in his hands. He stopped directly in front of Wes, leaning casually against the desk behind him, and held the box out as an offering.

"I have a gift for you!" He announced, and placed the box into Wes' hands. Wes hesitated, then cautiously opened the lid to reveal a row of six shiny new casings in the caliber of his revolver. Wes studied them for a moment, then tilted his head up to peer at Daniel through his hair.

"You look so strange this way," Daniel remarked, and tenderly brushed Wes' hair out of his eyes. He plucked the hat up from the desk behind him, and placed it awkwardly atop Wes' head. Daniel seemed nervous under his scrutiny. He cleared his throat, and lifted up the revolver awkwardly into his hands. He glanced at Wes, and rolled his eyes.

"Oh, *do* let go of him," he commanded the guards, and Wes felt their hands obediently fall away from his shoulders. Daniel placed the revolver carefully atop the open box of ammunition in Wes' hands, then leaned against the desk in front of him.

"Load it," he commanded, and whispers arose from many of the Elders in the room.

"What do you plan to do with this?" Wes asked, hesitating. Daniel did not turn from his father, but lifted his hand and slapped it on his desk. The sound cut through the whispers; the rooms energy pulled as taut as a bowstring. Wes worked the release on his revolver, and with a practiced jerk of the wrist, the gun cylinder flopped to the side. He tilted it and allowed the old bullets to tumble soundlessly onto the carpet before reaching into the box, and loading a new bullet into every vacant hole of the cylinder. When done, Wes stared down at the circle of shiny casings, and considered his odds of escaping with Daniel if he unloaded them into the crowd behind him. He slapped the cylinder back into place, and returned the revolver to the desk. When he glanced up at Daniel, he saw that his son's lips were parted in a mirthless grin. He really was a beautiful boy.

"The Guardian Son is so delightful." A voice murmured from among the onlookers.

"I long to enjoy him once more."

"Well then, let us move on," Daniel said with a clap of his hands and almost sounded jovial. He snatched the empty box away from Wes and tossed it back into his desk drawer. Then he scooped up his pipe, and brought a lighter to the bowl. Wes wondered if any of this was genuine. He reached up, and adjusted his hat to fit properly on his head.

"So much is happening tonight!"

"This is all so very exciting!"

"I thought the Guardian Son was going to make his father shoot at us."

"That would have been interesting to see!"

"Would his face turn black before our eyes? Or does he warrant the Hall's protection?"

"I think it's time for us to meet our special guest," Daniel announced, cutting through the conversation in the room, and many of the elders cheered.

"I'm so excited!"

"At last, our real entertainment!"

"If the rumors are true..."

"I hope they are true!"

"They can't possibly be true!"

"All our fears, gone in an instant!"

"If it's true, if it's true!"

Daniel took in a long pull of smoke, then held it in his lungs as he closed his eyes. The Elders cheered and chattered and speculated on their esteemed guest.

"Nothing can stop the course of fate," Daniel said softly, then opened his eyes and looked at Wes. He looked so weary, burdened by the pain in his heart, and Wes knew he was seeing his son's true emotions for the first time that night. "They are not stories, father. They are prophecies."

Daniel pounded his fist against his desk in a steady rhythm, and soon all the Elders were doing the same. Pounding fists to chairs as they called out and whistled.

"Bring him forth!"

"Let our dear brother rejoin his counsel!"

Brother? As in another Elder? Wes looked around, confused. Was it possible they did not know of Jack or of Palto?

Next to one of the angelic statues, Wes caught sight of the wall as it seemed to break away and sway inward. It was a disguised door. He only had a moment to comprehend this, when a man ducked his head, and stepped into the room. When he looked up, his eyes met Wes' and he smiled. It was bizarre, but the flash of his white teeth caused Wes to picture his barn back home, with a boy's silhouette framed in its doorway.

"Lord," was all he was able to say, and noticed that Daniel was studying him intently.

"Father, I've heard that you already met our Elder Chancy." Chancy dipped his head toward Wes in polite greeting, then raised his voice to address the crowded room.

"I've returned, brothers and sisters! And I brought with me a great surprise!"

Chapter Twenty-Three

For we are not fighting against flesh-and-bone enemies,
But against evil rulers and authorities of the unseen world,
Against mighty powers in this dark world,
And against evil spirits in heavenly places.
-Ephesians 6:12 NLT

Chancy appeared largely unchanged from the last time Wes had to face him; on that day when he mounted his horse and bid them farewell. He was dressed more for the occasion, with a slim fitting tailcoat, shawl collar vest, and lacy ascot all in white. He left behind the flat-top hat, and gathered his hair at the nape of his neck with a cord. But when he entered the room, Wes immediately noticed the thin rope he had wrapped around his hand. A rope that was tethered to a small boy.

"Benji!" Wes exclaimed, and the boy lifted his head to stare with large moon eyes. He was dressed in the same shirt, leather vest, and tan hide pants Wes last saw him in, but his face was dirty and his hair rumpled. His hands were bound at the wrists, and secured to the leash Chancy used to control him. As soon as their eyes met, Benji's filled with tears. Everyone seemed to all speak at once, including Wes.

"The Light Bringer!"

"Is it truly him?"

"Benji, don't look at them!"

"How can we trust Brother Chancy, you know he's a liar!"

"He's so small! So beautiful!"

"Benji, don't listen to what they are saying!"

"What are we going to do with him?"

"What are we going to do?"

"Look at his face! Look at his eyes!"

Look at his eyes indeed. So many emotions were revealed there. Fear, shame, frustration, relief, but above all else, love. Pure, innocent love.

"Benji, close your eyes!"

"Wuh!"

"Enough!" Daniel shouted, and the voices died away, "I can't think with all this noise!"

"Benji!" Wes pushed forward in a rush, too desperate to heed the order from his son, "mind me, now. Close your eyes and turn from this place. Hum, or pray, or wail if you have to, but blind your senses from everything in this..."

The slap was hard across his face. No-nonsense making his presence known. Wes tried to shake the stars from his eyes. He looked to Benji just as the boy closed his eyes, and lowered his head. He lifted his bound hands, pressing them to his chest, and leaned into prayer. Good lad.

Wes turned his attention back to Daniel, and their eyes met while his son stood over him; his face a portrait of his lamentation. Chancy moved to stand next to Daniel, and pulled Benji along with him.

"How did you find him?" One of the Elder's called out and Chancy smiled his victory.

"It was quite astounding how events transpired, Elder Agatha. I'm truly certain my path was laid out by the Lord Dragon himself!"

"Nonsense!"

"Listen!" Chancy called out with a hand raised, then bowed his head respectfully, and turned to peer down at Daniel with a small smile on his lips. "With your permission, great lord."

"I want to hear how the Dragon guided your journey, Elder," Daniel replied, and Wes could not tell if there was anger or indifference in his son's words. Chancy's gaze swept over all the Elder's in the room and he seemed to glow from all the attention. Standing beside him, Benji was a vision of supplication.

"Ladies, and gentlemen!" Chancy began with grand, theatrical movements. "Brothers and sisters! Let me tell you of a new tale that will surely be passed down in the records of history!"

"Here, here!"

"Another great performance, Chancy?"

"As you know, I stood before you all a few weeks ago, and requested a permit to leave the capital. This was not due to a strong desire to sample the Barrick's cuisine."

A few laughs from the spectators behind Wes. His gaze switched between Benji and Daniel as he noted how his son wasn't watching Chancy like the others. He was staring at Benji; his expression cloudy with a heavy unnamed mood.

"I wasn't sure why I wanted to leave, to tell you the truth, I just felt that I needed to go. But the day before my planned departure, I was standing on the balcony to my quarters. The servants were working to clear the mess in my room from the night before, and needed a cigarette to...settle my nerves."

"We have all been there, brother."

"Many times, in fact!"

More laughter.

"It was on that balcony that a voice came into my head," Chancy recounted, and Wes' eyes sought him out. Chancy glanced at Daniel with another small smile. "A voice proclaiming himself to be our Great Lord."

"Are you sure it wasn't too much morphine?"

"Or the results of a sour stomach?"

Almost all of them were laughing. Wes noted how Chancy navigated around the misgivings his peers had for him, and got them to laugh; delighting in his tale. Chancy was a dangerously cunning man.

"So I packed what I needed, said my goodbyes," another quick glance at Daniel, "and headed to the east without knowing why."

"Remarkable!"

"What did the Great Lord sound like? I want to hear him too!"

Chancy snaked a hand over Benji's shoulder, and Wes wanted to strike at him.

Keep your filthy hands off of him!

He knew though that the guards would restrain him. He needed to bide his time; awaiting the right moment.

"So I rode through the later part of day, and well into the night, all the while feeling the path laid out before me. It was like the ground seemed to shine underneath me, guiding me onward until I saw a small campfire in the distance and knew that was where I needed to go."

"All this coming from the Great Lord himself?" Daniel asked, scrutinizing Chancy. "Quite remarkable indeed."

"The man at the fire was sick with fever," Chancy went on, his eyes connecting with Wes'. "But he doesn't matter to me in the least. It was the boy that sat alongside him that caught my attention right away. They were all cuddled up together; the boy fretting over the man's sickly state."

"Is the boy a pet of the Keeper, then?"

"A pet on a leash."

"So the Great Lord spoke to you and led you to apprehend the Bringer of Light?"

"Yes, Elder Thoss," Chancy went on eagerly, "and I knew it was him from the moment I saw him. A boy well beyond his testing years, and with no mark upon him. A lamb without spot or blemish."

"Not even on the tips of his fingers."

"Not a freckle of sin."

"What are we going to do with him? What are we going to do?"

Benji's lips twitched with the unspoken words of his prayer. Daniel's mouth twisted as he watched.

"I offered to buy him, but this man refused," Chancy said, chanting out the words.

"You should have offered more."

"I offered to give him a writ of sale in case he changed his mind, but again the man flatly refused."

"You should have killed him the moment his fever put him to sleep."

"I dare not separate them by force!" Chancy lifted his chin defensively, and spoke over the shouting in the room. "It might have affected the prophecies if I took the boy that way. I dare not risk altering such things without the advice of someone like Elder Thoss."

"Here, here!"

"Brother Chancy is very smart."

"You seem quite fond of Elder Thoss." This was from Daniel; his words guarded.

"Elder Thoss, will you not share your thoughts, brother?"

"When the sun started to rise," Chancy continued; guiding the performance to its end, "I knew I needed to push on so I did not burn from exposure. I said goodbye to them both, rode off, and found a place under a canopy of trees, where I observed them from a distance. They got ready to leave, mounted that sack-of-bones for a horse, and rode to the west. I was on their tail in a matter of minutes but remained out of sight."

"You're such a spy, Elder Chancy!"

"I like a man who has his wits about him. We should dine together one of these nights."

"You're wasting your breath, Elder Estella! Chancy only has eyes for our Guardian Son."

“How did you separate Bringer from Keeper?” Daniel asked as he looked up at the tall lanky man. Endeared by his passive interest, Chancy smiled down at him warmly.

“I didn’t even have to. They did that part on their own. Unfortunately, the Light Keeper housed the boy in a place I could not reach. I saw it there, like a hazy mirage on the horizon, but could not ever get close enough to touch it let alone find its door. During the day, I hid in the woods nearby, but every time I thought I caught sight of him, I would turn and the mirage would dissolve before my eyes. It felt...uncanny. But I didn’t sense the presence of our Great Lord’s legion. Something was controlling what I was able to see. Something powerful.”

Eve.

Wes suppressed a smile. He wished he had her wisdom in that room. Maybe she could show him a way to protect both of these boys and allow them all to escape. Benji remained quiescent; deep inside his prayer, but Daniel was quite the opposite. He was full of guarded nervous energy, and snatched up his pipe to fill its bowl with oil.

“So what did you do, brother? What trap did you set?”

“No trap needed, Elder Sensa, for I can charm even the most sinister of snakes. I simply waited, and eventually the boy came out to me. I lifted my head, and there he was looking down at me. It was as though he wanted to be with me all along.”

Wes thought of Eve and how she warned him that Benji was hard to control. He wasn’t listening to her, and was determined to leave. What was the boy thinking, pairing up with Chancy like he did? He had enough sense to be terrified of the man when they first met, yet somehow forgot that those things viewed as safe in this world amounted to a piddling.

“What if this was the Light Bringers intention all along?”

“Did he plan to come here?”

“Does he plan to execute his cleansing light?”

“What are we going to do with him? What are we going to do?”

“*You* aren’t going to do anything!” Chancy said with a touch of cocky confidence, and the commotion of the room fell off sharply. Wes looked up at him, and saw Chancy was unconcerned by the shift in mood. “You forget that this boy belongs to me. I acquired him, and thus he is mine. Only *I* decide what to do with him, and it is my intention to offer him back to the very source that urged me to seek him out in the first place. I am giving his custody over to the Guardian Son.”

With that, Chancy uncoiled the leash from his hand and placed it gently in one of Daniel’s. Daniel gawked at the leash lying limply on his palm, lifted his eyes to the boy he suddenly owned, then looked up at Chancy with his tender smiles.

Wes' eyes blazed as he took in this exchange, then shifted to examine his knife upon the desk; lying naked of its sheath. His anger burned enticingly in his mind, and while he fought to get it under control, the flames were catching. He was not blind nor deaf to the words said from the Elder's behind him. It was obvious that Chancy was in love with his son. A man fifteen years his senior, and Daniel a child. The truth of these Elders stating this as fact without an ounce of abhorrence, only made the actuality of it all the more appalling.

Wes' focus was solely on controlling his anger, so he didn't notice at first the way the silence stretched on in the room. These Elders never remained quiet for long unless they were ordered to. Since the guards on either side of him seemed resolute but permitting, he risked a glance over his shoulder, and scanned the Elders in the room. All of them had turned from Chancy's storytelling, and were instead focused on a solitary Elder who stood in the middle of them all. The man was very old; stooped over a cane, and shorter than most of the women in the room. His white garment, a simple set of loose pants and smock, hung from him like over-sized curtains. He had a long white mustache that extended past his jawline, and white thin hair pulled up into a knot on the back of his head. As he stood, he seemed to contemplate the top of his cane.

"Elder Thoss," Chancy said curiously, and Wes could hear the apprehension in his voice. "I usually don't see you rise unless there are children running about the room."

No one laughed. Chancy's previous tactic was ineffective.

"I see a solution to our dilemmas," Elder Thoss announced to his cane, or perhaps the floor beyond it.

None of the Elders spoke. All remained captivated by Thoss.

"What dilemma?" Daniel asked with genuine interest, and Elder Thoss slowly shifted to blink cloudy eyes at Daniel

"Not one dilemma, but two," he said and held up two gnarled black fingers. "First, we can stop the progression of Strupple's New Prophecy of Fate. We can thwart the Bringer of Light."

"Remarkable," one of the Elders whispered, and another drove a stiff elbow into her ribs.

"Second, we can correct the passage of time. Reweave the unraveling of the past."

"Well...that sounds like an astounding proposition, Elder Thoss," Daniel said, condescendingly, "Do you care to share how we might accomplish this?"

"There is no *might!*" Elder Thoss screeched. He sounded like a leathery old bird, and his words made Wes' hackles rise. Thoss stepped out of the line of Elders, and made his way to the front of the room.

"There is no might," he repeated. "All of you tried to ignore me, but I've seen the future! I know the truth! Time is unraveling outside of these walls. You content yourselves, despicable louts, inside your cages of pleasure. You blind your eyes to the building that burns around you! Time is unraveling! And the unraveling grows closer! Memories forgotten swiftly, and in abundance! When will you listen? When will you see that you too will feel the consequence of our ruin!" Elder Thoss lifted his head, and blinked at the two guards on either side of Wes. The two men glanced at him nervously, then to each other, but before he could react, Thoss lifted a knotted hand and pressed his fingers upon the guard to his left. The guard collapsed instantly.

Many of the Elders in the room gasped, and the guard to Wes' right shrank back before turning and running from the room entirely. Thoss stepped forward, the path made clear, and leaned over next to Wes while he examined Benji and Daniel.

"Don't worry, he's only sleeping," he said softly, intending to reassure Wes for some reason, then straightened once more. He went on raucously, but no less parched. "Time is unraveling; the threads plucked apart upon our doorstep. When the past crumbles, the present will follow. Everything will unweave until the ground itself breaks apart and the dead will walk among us once more. Nothing can be done if it reaches this place. No turning back when chaos is born."

"All is lost!" One of the Elders broke out in a wail. Many of the others joined with her; crying and wailing and mourning the loss of their existence.

"We are doomed!"

"Surely this can be stopped somehow," Daniel said, a little breathless. "You spoke of solutions to our dilemmas." Chancy reached for him, offering a comforting hand, but Daniel pushed him away; oblivious to his wounded look.

"You see what is in front of your nose, but I see all there is to see. I know what the Great Lord sent Brother Chancy to do." More gasps in the room; Elders whispering to one another with rushed words. Elder Thoss allowed them their moment to speculate as he stroked his mustache and studied Benji.

"Are you going to share what you know?" Chancy asked; vexed to have lost the attention of the crowd.

"I'm surprised you haven't seen it for yourself," said Thoss, lifting his eyes to examine Chancy's apparent displeasure.

"I don't see what you mean."

"You brought the very creature prophesied to destroy us directly into our Hall," said Thoss, his voice rising with a surprising amount of anger, "are you claiming to have drug him unwillingly into the very nest of his enemy with no consideration on how he might harm us? Are you really so stupid to reveal this boy to the very people that fear him?"

"We fear no boy!"

"We fear no slave!"

"Foolishness!" Thoss snarled, as he tottered forward to stand at the edge of the desk and point his cane at Chancy. "Why were his words wasted on you?"

"I could have done things better."

"I want to hear the Dragon's voice too!"

"He chose me because he saw my potential," Chancy objected, his face clouded by his rising anger. "Maybe you should ask why he didn't choose you!"

"You came here with a plan to give the boy as an offering to the great lord," Thoss said, not rising to Chancy's challenge.

"I think I made my intentions plain."

"What do you think this *boy* is going to do with him?" Thoss asked with a dismissive gesture at Daniel. Even Wes could see the blatant insult in his gesture. "How is he going to protect us from the child's light?"

"You forget yourself, Elder Thoss," Daniel said with a dangerous coolness.

"I forget nothing!" Thoss screeched, far louder than before, and everyone winced. He shifted away from Chancy and jabbed his cane in Daniel's direction. "You are not strong enough to contain the Bringer of Light! You betrayed us the moment you kept the Light Keeper from us, and you will no doubt betray us again!"

"Blasphemy!" Chancy shouted, reaching for Daniel, but the boy only stared at Thoss. Realization swept over Daniel's face, extinguishing his rage, and left him looking terrified. Seeing the wide fearful look in his eyes caused a chill to sweep through Wes. He leaned forward, and snatched his hunting knife off of the desk.

"Your mistake was offering the boy to your great lord," Thoss continued, "instead of the true Great Lord that lives within him. The Dragon!"

"The Dragon!"

"Our Great Lord, most divine!"

"What are you saying?" Daniel asked, but the words were prosaic; the answer was already known.

"You were a suitable vessel for our Great Lord, boy. But sadly, you grow old. Soon, your body will falter. Degrade. If we don't have a vessel to replace you, our Great Lord will convert back to what he once was."

"We can't go back!"

"Don't let him go back to what he was!"

"We have already begun our efforts to locate a new, young, more...alluring vessel. But such a child has thus far eluded us. Even if this boy wasn't who he is, I would have demanded his confiscation. A lamb free of speckle and spot. A perfect sacrifice for the altar. But knowing him as the Bringer of Light, we *must* give him over to the Great Lord directly! If our Lord Dragon is handed such power as this, he will surely be able to accomplish anything including the repair of time itself!"

Silence.

Wes turned in his chair and watched the Elders shift from shock, to understanding, to acceptance, then to wicked excitement. They looked at one another, then all of them turned to look at Daniel.

"Well," Daniel said, and his voice broke. He swallowed, cleared his throat, and lifted his chin. "Well, if this is what has to happen, then let it be done."

He moved past Chancy to stand next to Benji, then put a lighter to his pipe and pulled smoke from the flame.

"I respect your willingness to move forward with this considering the agonizing death you will surely be forced to endure," Elder Thoss said with an appreciative nod. Daniel appeared unfazed by this revelation. Thoss turned his attention to Chancy. "I must also show you my appreciation, Elder Chancy. For while you were too much a fool to see the danger you put us all in, if not for you I would have never realized the true potential of the Bringer of Light. We will honor you tonight when we dine in the house of our new Guardian Son."

"New Guardian Son?" one Elder whispered. Elder Thoss glanced at Benji one last time, a secret smile curling the corners of his mouth, then he turned and shambled back toward his seat.

"I am promised suffering, and have no doubt that he will suffer as well," Daniel said softly, then drew in smoke from his burning pipe. He shifted to lean over Benji, grabbed a handful of his hair, and tilted his head so that he faced the ceiling. He bent close to the boy, and slowly exhaled the smoke into his face.

"What are you doing?" Wes demanded, and got to his feet. With his guards no longer holding him in place, Wes looked to where No-nonsense stood but noticed the large guard had left his station to help Thoss back to his seat. He was almost doubled over, speaking to the much smaller Thoss, their words too low to be heard.

"My intentions are without malice," Daniel said, and pulled another long draw of smoke from his bowl. As he blew it upon Benji's face he spoke his words into the swirling haze. "I offer him a balm for the Dragon is quite...excruciating."

"Great lord, this is madness," Chancy said softly as he leaned closer to Daniel so that the Elder's could not hear them. Many of them were speaking to Thoss as he walked, and some of them were whispering to each other as they glanced at their current and new Guardian Sons. Among them, another Elder was getting to his feet. He offered Thoss a quick bow, then lifted his head to gaze in Daniel's direction. He was tall with dark skin and ice clear eyes. He stood like a proud bull; imperious and demanding as he waited for Thoss to pass, then strode toward the desk.

"Elder Maxwell will see to this matter."

"He is skillful in the transfer of vessels."

"I'll make my way to the vault below."

"We will meet you there Elder Jay."

"Let's get this over with. I'm ready to enjoy the new Guardian Son."

"The new Guardian Son!"

"THE NEW GUARDIAN SON!"

"Great lord! Please, we have to get out of here," Chancy said, all grandiosity wiped clean from his face. Wes made his way to the end of the desk, his focus on Benji.

"Daniel, please, stop doing that to him!"

"He'll thank me later," Daniel snapped as he glared up at Wes, "if I'm even alive to hear it."

These words were like a knife to the chest. Wes didn't know what to do. What to do? What to do? Chancy grabbed Daniel's arm, hoping to urge him into the room beyond the secret door, but Daniel jerked away from him.

"Great lord, they intend to kill you!"

"And how do I know you aren't a part of all their planning?" Daniel countered, and the fire of betrayal burned hot in his eyes. He pulled away from the older man and back toward the middle of his desk.

"Don't be stupid! I would never *do* such a thing. I didn't mean for this to..." Chancy's words trailed off as Daniel's hand closed over the grip of Wes' revolver.

"There will be no exchange if there is no vessel," he said, his voice shaking like the gun in his hand. He glanced at Wes, the message clearly for him, then back to Chancy. Behind them, Maxwell continued his swift progression as the Elders rose to make their way out of the room. On to the next bit of entertainment; a meander through a dungeon meant for torture. Wes placed his knife back in its sheath and bent to quickly untie Benji's wrists, freeing him of his leash.

"Guardian Son," Chancy said, his hands outstretched and imploring.

"I'm no longer your Guardian Son," Daniel replied, and pointed the gun at Chancy. Some of the Elders in the room called attention to the exchange and No-nonsense abandoned Thoss as he made haste back to the front.

"Daniel, please," Chancy said as his eyes shifted from Daniel's face to the gun in his hand. "We will find a way out of this. Please...I love you."

Finally getting the ropes loose, Wes pulled them from Benji's wrists, then lifted the boy into his arms. Elder Maxwell was almost upon them. Daniel smiled at Chancy with the tenderness he once showed his two guard boys.

"You knew this would happen one day. It's the price everyone pays, for loving me."

The gun went off in Daniel's hand, and the room erupted in chaos. His hand was weak, and he was unaccustomed to the double-action, so the first shot hit Chancy low, but he had no time to react before two more bullets sealed his fate. Then Daniel turned, pointing the weapon into the crowd, but Wes didn't need to see anymore. He held Benji to his chest, and ducked into the side door Chancy tried to use. If it was good enough for Chancy, then it meant an exit awaited Wes somewhere on the other side.

When he cleared the door, he turned to push it closed behind him, and caught a glimpse of No-nonsense glaring at him from the middle of the room. He set the door back in place and threw the bolt into its cradle; locking it there. He doubted it would delay No-nonsense very long. Wes needed to move.

He scanned the room, which appeared to be a private sitting area, and quickly located a door on the opposite wall. He dashed over to it, worked it open, and entered into another room, much larger, but thankfully unoccupied. A quick scan again revealed a door to his left, and Wes carried Benji through it without hesitation. He scanned the room again, realized where he was, and his feet faltered. He was standing in the midst of the vacant banquet hall.

The food was gone, the corpses were removed, but most of the floors still carried stains. The walls, the tables, the chairs, all of it showed shadow stains from blood. The air smelled stale and metallic, like meat left in the sun too long. The memories of all he saw that first night came rushing back into his mind, and Wes lost himself in the nightmare.

The boy is in danger! Stop staring, and get out of here!

Wes blinked, coming back to himself, then tilted his head toward the voice in his mind.

"Ruth?"

Run!

Wes ran.

He dashed through the banquet room, his eyes fixated on the curtain at the other end, then he scaled the staircase and lurched through it into the hallway beyond. He looked to his left, saw that all the activity was mostly at the far end of the hall, and ran in the opposite direction before he was noticed.

He looked down at Benji, and realized the lad was staring up at him with clouded eyes.

"Mind me, boy. Keep those eyes shut for now." Benji did as he was told.

The sound of hysterical laughter reverberated down the hallway. It lingered in the ribbed vaults, turning bitter to Wes' ears. God, he hoped it wasn't from Daniel. Benji covered his ears with cupped hands.

Wes continued to run, ignoring the sounds of shouts and screams; for it was impossible to know their origin with all the echoes in the hallway. When Benji grew too heavy to carry, Wes slung the boy over his shoulder like a sack. Benji emitted a soft wordless keening, and continued to cover his ears. This was fine, as long as he didn't open his eyes. If Benji had the second sight that Eve claimed he did, Wes didn't want to risk him seeing the Elders or the things the Elder's contained.

Wes ignored all other possible options for escape, and instead focused on the plan already set in place. He hoped that Jack was still there. All he could do was keep Benji safe, then find another way to help Daniel later.

Wes made his way toward the room he occupied over the past few days, for he remembered the way. He dashed down hallways, up stairs, and down hallways again. The door to his room appeared abruptly, and Wes burst through the opening into the room beyond. Everything remained as it was: the tray of untouched food, the rumpled blanket discarded on his pillow, and the window showing a skyline shadowed by the night. He still had time. Benji continued to softly keen, so Wes dashed over and laid the lad on the bed. He then returned to the door, closing it, but found he was unable to secure it from the inside. Looking around the room, he located a large armoire placed against an adjacent wall. He pulled at its one side, wrenching it free, and it screeched over the floor as he strained to drag the heavy closet away from the wall. He fought to place it so that it ran parallel to the door, and paused for a moment to listen to the shout of guards in the distance. He must have been seen.

Wes managed to get the armoire where he wanted it, panting from the effort, then moved to the back end of the lumbering furniture and used his back to push his weight into it. His boots skidded over the floor tile; the armoire giving its last cry of resistance, then it finally gave over; pitching forward to crash against the door with a deafening bang. Immediately, Benji started to scream.

"It's alright lad! It's just me. It's alright!" Wes tried to console Benji, but the boy kept his eyes pinched shut, and slapped at his head repeatedly as he cried and screamed. Wes reached for him, smoothing his hair, and stroking his cheek.

"Benji, look at me. Please, open your eyes. It's safe now. Look at me, Benji. Please!" He tried to sit Benji up at the edge of the bed, but the boy jerked away from him, and lunged across it in an effort to get away from something; anything; everything. Shouts echoed from somewhere down the hall, growing louder, getting closer. Wes could make out the sound of running boots. He glanced at the door, feeling hopelessness well up inside of him.

"No," he growled, refusing to give in, and grabbed hold of Benji's legs to drag him back off the bed.

"Benji, open your eyes. Now, Benji! Right now!"

Benji abruptly opened his eyes. His screaming abated, and while he didn't remove his hands from his ears, he was looking at Wes. His eyes looked flat and distant; his senses dull. He was trembling, and his breath hitched in his throat. He blinked, and tried to focus on Wes.

The drugs have taken hold of you, lad.

"Benji," Wes sighed, then managed to flaunt a half smile. "It's so good to see you again." Tears clouded Benji's vision, but he managed to restrain himself. He reached for Wes, hands desperate to grab hold of some sort of stability, and Wes did not hesitate. He pulled Benji into a hug. It was hard to believe they were together again. It was impossible to fathom all that led to this reunion taking place. Wes didn't care. He was just happy to be near Benji and know he was safe.

"Benji, I..." A fist slammed against the outside of the door, causing both of them to jump, and Wes turned to see the door inch open a little before it reached the armoire obstruction. Wes knew it wouldn't postpone them long. He had to move quickly, for their time was all but up.

Chapter Twenty-Four

But the path of the just is like the shining sun,
That shines ever brighter unto the perfect day.
The way of the wicked is like darkness;
They do not know what makes them stumble.
-Proverbs 4:18-19 NKJV

Benji's fingers reached, searching for Wes' face, as he drifted along the edge of sleep.

"Benji, we have to go. I need you to hold on to me, can you do that?"

"Wuh," Benji said, the word almost a sigh, and his eyes drifted closed. A shoulder slammed into the door, and the loud boom jolted Benji awake. He looked up at Wes with eyes wide, then his face fell. His lip started to quiver. He was going to cry again.

"We don't have time for this," Wes said, impatiently. The door boomed from the force of the guards' conviction, and Benji keened as he covered his ears. "You need to climb onto my back, Benji."

"Wuh! Wuh!"

"Listen to me!" The door gained a few inches of ground. A hand snaked around and grabbed hold of the armoire obstruction. "We have to get out of here right now. Do you understand?"

Benji jerked out of Wes' grasp, but tottered and Wes took hold of him. He pivoted on his knee, and showed Benji his back.

"Climb onto me," he instructed, then felt Benji's arm snake around his neck. "Hold on tightly."Wes rose, settled Benji into a better position, and went to his window. The fireplace from his room splashed a puddle of light on the ground outside, and when Wes opened the window, he saw Jack's upturned face.

"Where have you been?" Jack hissed under his breath, "This whole place is going crazy!"

"Why are you here? This is not where I told you to meet me," Wes countered. He lifted a leg and stretched it over the sill until he felt the stone ledge that ran the full length of the wall under his window. The guards at his door argued on how to best bypass their tenuous blockade.

"I waited where you told me to for over an hour!" Jack rebutted, "then I remembered how old you are, and thought you got confused or forgot what your plans even were." Wes chuckled and shook his head. Jack was a lunkhead, and quick to use his fists, but Wes still liked the lad. God found function even in the flawed.

As soon as his other foot cleared the window opening, a loud bang came from inside the room. The armoire screeched as it slid a few inches on the tile floor. Jack's face went blank with fear.

"What *was* that?" he asked, straining for a better view of the room. Wes got to his feet, stood on quivering legs, and examined his footing. It was just wide enough for him to walk with Benji on his back. Nevermind the drop beside him, or how a sudden move from Benji might hurtle them both off the ledge.

"A party of Guard Watch Elite are trying to break into the room," Wes said with a serenity he did not feel. Jack's reaction was truly warranted.

"Calamity! You have brought this upon us! We have to go now, we..." Jack's words trailed off as Wes started his precarious path along the ledge. The air was damp, an afterthought of the rain that fell most of the night, and the stone was slick under his feet. He stepped through hazy reflections of firelight, allowing him just enough to see by, and as the light swept across his profile, Jack saw Benji draped over his back.

"Is that *him*?" He asked, as he followed alongside Wes on the ground below, "he's much younger than I thought he would be."

"This isn't your great lord," Wes said through clenched teeth. Benji was like a millstone wrapped around his neck. It was hard to breathe let alone speak, not to mention the rising dread Wes felt strangling the breath out of him every time he glanced down at Jack. The drop seemed far greater when balanced precariously on a narrow ledge.

"I don't understand. I thought you were going to escape with the Great Lord. Who is this boy?"

"Enough," Wes growled, and eyed the set of roofs as he approached them. The one that reached just shy of the ledge, had a gentle slope that extended down to the lower area of the Hall where it blended into a gable roof with a flat peak that ran the length of the auxiliary building. The slope of the gable was far more severe, but Wes would worry about that after he arrived there.

When Wes reached the first roof, he swallowed down his nerves, and crouched down carefully. The roof came to a point just beneath the ledge, so Wes shifted his weight and lowered himself to his knees to better examine it. The slope seemed a lot sharper, now that he was balanced over it. He tried to determine the safest way down, but another crash came from his vacated room, and Wes heard the distinct thud of an ax. No more time for hesitation. Wes dropped a leg down over the ledge, and struggled to find purchase on the smooth steel rooftop.

He slid, balanced on his stomach, and eased the other leg over. Dangling for a moment, he thought he could continue to slide down on his stomach to keep Benji secured against his back. It was as good a plan as any.

Lord give me the strength for what I'm about to do, and Ruth...don't come get me just yet.

Wes allowed himself no time to think, and thus no time to reconsider his plan. He let go of the ledge, and flopped onto the roof. He began as he thought he would, but his speed increased rapidly and with it, he lost control.

There was no time to recalculate or even react. Wes' body pitched to the side, and Benji broke away from him. He lost sight of the lad as he tumbled and rolled the remaining few feet onto the gable roof. It rose up to meet him, and Wes landed hard on his back; half sprawled across the peak for the gable. A moment later, Benji flopped on top of him, and drove the breath out of him in a grunt.

"Mister Wes?" Jack called to him from somewhere outside of his pain.

Wes groaned, as he fought against bewilderment. Everything was blurry, and he felt the sting of hot blood working into his right eye. What happened? Where was he?

"Wuh!" The panic in Benji's voice had Wes react before he could make sense of what was happening. He lunged forward, seizing the lad as he was starting to fall down the deeper pitch of the gable roof. But when Wes grabbed hold of Benji, he sacrificed his position on the flat peak, and was no longer able to stop the course of his own fall. Wes had just enough time to pull Benji close to him and wrap himself around the boy as best he could. They slid down together, and launched off the side of the roof. Wes' impact with the gravel was both harsh and unforgiving.

"Ah!" He bellowed, unable to stop himself, and guards called out, alerted to the noise.

"What are you doing? How are you supposed to escape if you break every bone in your body?" Jack asked as he helped Wes to sit up.

"Things didn't go exactly as planned," Wes muttered, and sought out Benji, who lay near him on the ground. He appeared thankfully unbroken, since Wes took the brunt of their fall.

"You alerted the entire patrol with all the noise you made. If we don't move now, you won't get out of here tonight. Can you stand?" Wes tried to push himself to his feet, then hissed as pain radiated up the length of his arm. He lifted his hand into the light, and realized that it bulged in an unnatural way at the wrist. Two of his fingers were also bent at an odd angle. As soon as Jack saw it, he started to retch and turned his head away.

"No time to worry about such things," Wes said, then clenched his teeth as he used his left hand to get to his feet. His body was a chorus of pain singing out in unison. The moment he put weight on his ankle, it felt like a blade twisting in his bone, but it functioned as it should. Nothing else seemed to be broken, except maybe a rib or two. "I can't pick up the lad. Hand him to me, please."

"What's wrong with him?" Jack asked as he bent to scoop up Benji. "He slept through that whole thing." Wes drew Benji into his arms, and while cradling the boy clumsily, he examined his tranquil face. There was a scrape on his forehead, and his cheek might bruise, but indeed he looked to be sleeping.

"They drugged him right before we made our escape. Blew some kind of smoke in his face."

"I see. Well, if that's all it is, he should come around soon enough. The effect never lasts long." Without warning, a bell chimed overhead, and both men turned to stare up at the spires of the Divine Hall.

"No more delay! Come with me now!" Jack turned, and dashed into the darkness opposite the main entrance with its three gates. He produced a firebox, lighting it as he moved, but only made it bright enough to guide their way. He followed along the outer wall, and Wes managed to keep up with him, but couldn't avoid limping. The pain was difficult to endure.

Nearing the back corner of the wall, Jack moved in closer and his firebox revealed a break in the stone where a low doorway possessed an iron gate that was held ajar.

"A guard friend of mine knows how to pick the lock on this gate," Jack said as he bent down by the opening, "He uses it to sneak women into his quarters when he's off duty. Made me agree to cover two whole shifts to leave it open for me."

"Well, I'm grateful," Wes said sincerely, as he hobbled through the opening.

"I am here to serve," Jack responded, with only a hint of cynicism.

"You risked your life for me, and stayed with me when I reckon many wouldn't. I hope this will repay you." Wes said, as he watched Jack ease the gate closed between them. "I'm going to convince Palto to leave the city."

"What makes you think I care," Jack scoffed.

"I might be this rube you all like to call me, but I am not naive. I saw the way you looked at her when Palto talked of leaving the capital. I know now that you're a man in love." Jack stared at Wes for a moment, unwilling or unable to find the right words to say, then he looked back the way he came.

"I have to go. If I don't respond to the bell-call, they'll have me hung. But...thank you. Truly. Just keep her safe."

"If she goes, will you join her?" Wes asked, even though he knew the answer.

"You know I can't do that. What about you? Will you flee this place while you can?" Jack countered and again their eyes met. Much was spoken in the silence between them: an exchange of duty, determination, and the need to do what needed to be done to protect the ones they loved. Then Jack turned from him, and vanished back the way he came.

Wes moved away from the small doorway, and stepped into the light of the empty street. Getting his bearings, he limped in the direction of the town square with intentions of seeking out the familiar path to where Palto lived. He took a few steps, wincing from the pain, but the throbbing in his wrist grew too great to ignore. Benji was like an anchor in his arms.

"Benji, can you hear me," Wes said, leaning in close to his ear. He was surprised to see the lad open his eyes, and squint up at him. "I can't carry you like this. I...hurt my arm a little." He decided to omit the sprained ankle, broken ribs, and dislocated fingers. "Can you get on my back and hold onto me again?"

Benji moved slowly, shifting his body to stand, but his legs buckled the moment he tried to put weight on them. He leaned into Wes, wrapping arms around his neck, and Wes lurched to his feet. He held Benji in place with his good arm, and Benji rested his head on Wes' back with a sigh.

"That's right. Hold onto me. That's a good lad." Wes heard guards calling to each other as they formed groups and left the Divine Hall to filter out into the city. They must have determined he was no longer in the building. Seeing the black uniforms blending into the garish colors of the locals, Wes realized how much he would stand out in the crowd. He already knew his attire drew attention, but he was also carrying a child on his back. In a city where few children walked the streets, he would certainly be noticed. Would they feel drawn to Benji the way the sinners of the wild were? Even though he was outside the Hall,

Wes was acutely aware of how trapped he still was. He had to reach his horse, and find his path from there.

The central part of the city was not an option, so Wes moved in the opposite direction. Being that the area was a residential district, the streets remained bare of activity. As Wes moved along the outside of the Hall, he came upon an illuminated path to his left. It was wider than an alleyway, but provided him an alternate route to the next street. Wes took it, moving further away from the Hall, and when he got to the next street over, he was not surprised to find it unfamiliar. Wes figured Palto's house to be at least one more street over, or more likely two.

Even though the fireboxes kept the worst of the darkness away, Wes started to feel a growing menace in the shadows around him. Eyes unseen and yet watching as he passed. Claws stretched out, and bodies shifted as monsters rose to trail behind him. Wes lost all track of the time, but surely the hour of the birdsong was upon him. This was usually the safest time to travel at night, so when the whispers came, Wes knew it was all because of Benji.

"The Light Bringer!"

"He's come! He's here!"

"Taste him, feel him!"

"Smell him, want him!"

"Vanquish the light!"

"Benji? Can you hear me?" Wes said, as he tried to look everywhere all at once. He spotted another illuminated side street and headed for it. A man walked past them, focused on the activities in the center of town, but as their paths crossed, he slowed. He turned to watch them, and soon stopped all together.

"Benji?" Wes couldn't keep his anxiety out of his voice.

"Wuh." The word was weighted with lead.

"Benji, I want you to hum that song Solomon taught you. Do what I say, now." Benji did. Slowly, dreamily, he hummed under his breath.

I'm just a poor wayfaring stranger...

Wes limped into the side street, and was dismayed to see the man following behind him. Soon, he crossed paths with two more city residents, who also stopped to watch him. They followed along as well.

"God help me," Wes whispered as his heart thrummed in rhythm to Benji's song.

"What do you want?" He called out to the forming crowd, but none of them responded to him. They looked dazed; their eyes transfixed on Benji. He limped into the next street which ran directly beside Palto's, but his heart sank when he found no cross street that would take him to her home and his mare. Wes looked toward the center of town, and saw the group of onlookers had grown. They numbered eight in total, and seemed to loaf around like scavengers awaiting his demise. He noted a group of guards forming at the entrance to the street, and walked in the opposite direction.

"Keep humming, Benji," he said nervously, and tried not to glance over his shoulder. A creature both half-human and half-monster became visible at the very edge of the firebox light. It tilted its head, examining Benji closely, and Wes shifted his path to veer away from the beast.

"Please, Light Keeper," the creature said as it trailed Wes in the shadows. "Please command the Light Bringer to free me of my sin."

"Off with you," Wes snapped. He didn't need cause for more attention. The crowd that followed him whispered softly to one another; repeating the monster's words.

"Light Keeper, please! I have a child as well, you see. Have mercy on her, if not on me!"

"Light Keeper?" a woman called from the crowd, "can it be?"

Wes walked faster. He winced through his pain, which pulsated in sequence to his racing heart. His eyes swept over the street before him, and he became aware of a much narrower path to his left. It was a shroud of darkness, and seemed to consume all the light surrounding it. As soon as he saw it, Wes knew exactly where he was, for he had seen this alleyway before.

"They come!" One of the spectators called out, and Wes peered back the way he came to see a row of guards heading in his direction. Some of them already took notice of the forming crowd. In the shadows alongside him, Half-and-Half's excitement grew.

"Light Keeper!" He whispered in eager urgency, "I will help you! Give me the child, then you can escape! I will take care of him. I promise I will. V-v-vanquish! Vanquish the light!"

"Vanquish the light!" The spectators echoed in unison; caught up in the monster's frenzy.

"Quiet! All of you!" Wes snapped, and eyed the alley with wary apprehension.

"Your thoughts are madness!" One of the spectators shouted at him. She must have the second sight. She sounded terrified. The guards were looking at him as they pointed and talked to one another.

"Light Keeper...please..."

Wes ducked into the alley, and the darkness swallowed him whole. He blinked, trying to adjust his eyes as he staggered forward. As light from the road dissolved behind him, another path grew more visible just ahead: the exit to this nightmare. Benji continued to hum softly by Wes' ear.

"Keep singing, lad. That's a good boy." Wes's voice shook like a willow. It was impossible to bury his fear when so much hunger and longing dwelt in the unseen. He felt the wicked all around him. They seemed to be...sleeping, or rather...waiting. Being surrounded by them, Wes could tell that these creatures had lost all ability for human thought. Only madness remained, driven on by hunger. But with no cohesive understanding on how to hunt out a meal, they were left to live in this pit of hopelessness. Condemned to feed on one another, until they were fed upon. Into this night stepped a phantom of what once was. A man and a child, unchanged by the taint of sin. Not *just* a man and a child, but the Keeper and Bringer of Light!

The night groaned, and Wes felt his skin crawl. It was a cry of desperation. Of *need*. A sudden sound came to Wes' ears like the flapping of wings or the shuffle of feet. He looked toward the light, his beacon of salvation, and saw it cloud over with the shadows of many creatures returning to their nest. They must have responded to the cry from their dying companions.

"Oh God..." Wes whispered, and clumsily pulled his hunting knife into his left hand. He held Benji in place with his other hand, but the pressure on his shattered arm was excruciating. No time to think about the implications of that. No time to think at all. There were dozens of monsters surrounding him, and Wes looked desperately upon the light of the distant street.

He was over halfway through the alley, when the first creature rose up to challenge him. He had a moment to see its long neck full of rippling insect arms, then he lashed out with his knife. Let these monsters know that the Keeper also has teeth. The creature recoiled with an unearthly screech, but Wes was under no illusion that he could kill any of them with a mere hunting knife.

He clenched his teeth, trying his hardest to work through the pain, and picked up his pace. If he was fast enough, he might still make it through before they rallied to enclose him.

In the distance, the dull light of the fireboxes seemed to float ethereally in the darkness like a mirage. Wes could hear Benji, heavily draped on his back, slow in his humming. It grew soft, and he could only hear a few notes.

Wes despaired over the pain he was in, but dare not slow down, for shortly after the insect creature retreated, two more monsters inched forward to take its place. Knowing he had no way to defend against both of them, Wes broke into a shambling run. He willed the light to be closer. He could make it. If he was fast enough, he could. Benji's humming ceased for his sleep was deep.

A hand lashed out from places unseen, and grabbed at the boy, but Wes' reflexes were wound tight like a pressed spring. He dodged the creature, only he didn't account for his newly acquired limitations, and stumbled when he tried to pivot on his injured ankle. He tried desperately to regain his footing, but when he shifted, Benji's arms came loose, and he fell away from Wes'.

"Benji!" Wes called out, yet the boy was unresponsive. He twisted around in time to clumsily catch Benji in his arms, and was forced to abandon his knife in the process. Wes knew that if he lost contact with Benji, living darkness would surely drag him away, and tear him apart.

They were surrounded by eager voices that hissed and chattered. They keened and hummed with glee. Wes cradled Benji in his arms and used his ruined hand to pull the boy close to his chest. The light at the end of the alley was still too far away. He already knew he was not going to make it. Still, he had to try.

Wes defended Benji as best he could, while he labored to get on his feet again. He managed to half limp and half run toward the alley's exit, but the effort was futile. Creatures laughed as they moved to overtake him.

"Now is our chance!"

"We shall taste eternity!"

"But first, the Light Keeper must die!"

The wilder ones, too far gone for speech, just moaned or screamed. Their hunger was suffocating. Sudden pain blazed up the back of Wes' leg as an unseen force severed his Achilles. His foot flopped, now ineffective, and Wes collapsed to his knees. Something sharp slid between his ribs, and Wes couldn't help but cry out. His suffering was seen as ecstasy for the attentive, and many of them moaned with elation.

Blood spilled from the wound; a red flower blooming on his jacket, but it was the poison burning deep inside his chest that told him this would be the place of his death. Unable to go any further, Wes shook Benji hard in desperation.

"Benji! Run!" Something struck Wes on his back, and he fell forward. He lost his grip, and Benji tumbled out of his arms; falling in a heap on the ground before him. The drug's sleep-spell still had hold of him, and he showed no sign of waking. Wes crawled over to him frantically, and immediately covered the boy with his body; cocooning him as best he could.

The smell of his blood permeated the air, and the monsters grew delirious with their desire. They fell upon him with claws and teeth, and pain overtook all conscious thought. His body was an inferno. Voices of sin roared out in his mind; inviting him to join in on the fray. Wes felt his body being pulled off of Benji as he was consumed in this gale of malevolence. He reached desperately, and his blood stained fingers brushed against Benji's open hand. Wes closed his eyes, knowing that all he had left was prayer.

Lord! Lord, please...Please don't let him suffer.

Then there was light. A sudden flash so radiant, Wes was forced to squint even though his eyes were already closed. The alley became a chorus of screams. Dozens of voices sang out all at once in their agony, and Wes joined in with their song.

Pain.

So much pain.

An eternity of fire that scorched away skin and muscle until all he had was bone. It scraped away his insides until he was hollow, then filled him up with the white solid light of the cleansed. All existence lived inside the high-pitched ringing that overtook his mind, and caused his teeth to ache. Wes knew he was screaming, yet did not hear a sound.

Then the light was gone. It blinked out as quickly as it set upon him, and Wes became aware of distant screaming. It sounded like it was many streets over, but the alley he occupied was completely still. Wes cautiously opened his eyes, but only saw blackness. After-image flashed like starbursts across his vision, but when he lifted his head, he could just make out the alley's opening and escape. Wes crawled to Benji, and was surprised to feel no pain in the effort. He reached for the lad, and could hardly believe he was still sleeping. So much transpired, and he was completely unaware of it. Somewhere far away a woman was crying. Guards were shouting.

What just happened?

Wes got to his knees, testing the function of his feet, then lifted his right hand and was amazed to see his fingers were all intact; the swelling vanished completely. He examined his body and sure enough there were dozens of places where the fabric of his clothing was torn open from attack but the skin underneath was clean and unbroken. It was as though all events over the past hour were completely undone.

What just happened?!

The darkness around them was like an empty tomb. The hunger, the longing; all of it gone. The alley was utterly devoid of all that was once living, and assumed dead. Shouting guards, and running boots brought Wes out of his stupor. He reached for Benji, and the back of his hand brushed against something cool and smooth. His hunting knife. He plucked it up, wiped its edge against his pant leg, then slipped it back into its sheath. He then picked up Benji, and got to his feet with a flexibility that's been absent for years.

Was this...a miracle?

Wes carried Benji in his arms even though the boy was limp and weighted like a stone. Feeling his newfound strength, he had no difficulty running. People called to one another, asking for the location of the unexplained light, while others directed the guards where to go.

"Guards!"

"Over here!"

"It was in this alley!"

"A wicked flash of light!"

"Oh, Vanquish! Vanquish!"

When Wes reached the end of the alley, his desire to be free of the place dominated his sensibility for caution. He raced out into the open, and rushed into a small crowd of curious onlookers. Wes originally thought he and Benji might find refuge in the horse stable, but with so much attention drawn to the area, this was no longer feasible. He could not let them see him go to Palto's door.

"You better run! He might do it again!" Wes shouted, and they scattered as he hoped they would. He had no time to be evasive with the guard actively seeking him out. Wes took in the familiar surroundings, relieved to find he was exactly where he hoped to be, and ran across the street toward the horse's stable. He took a quick glance at his mare, pleased to see her freshly brushed and saddled, but had no time to do more. He was desperate to hide, and he focused on Palto's home.

Wes ran up to her door, and pounded on it with a heavy fist. In the distance, he heard the guards announcing that they found the area the thief was last seen in. He had no doubt as to who they were referring to. Moments passed as he listened to the guards gather together, then he heard boots uniformly advancing at a run.

Wes knocked harder. He glanced around for potential witnesses, but the street was stripped of all activity. The occupants elected to remain indoors.

"Search the houses!" One of the guards called out, and Wes felt like he was walking into a snare. If he was backed into a corner, was it wise to pull Palto with him? Wes looked up the street, and saw half a dozen guards advancing toward him. His breath caught in his throat as panic welled up from within.

What should he do?

Where should he go?

The door drifted inward a few inches, and Palto's green eyes came into view. She looked up at Wes, then over to the row of approaching guards. Confusion evolved into understanding, and she immediately tried to close the door again. Wes didn't have time to appeal to her. He threw his shoulder against the door, being sure to avoid Benji's head, and plowed through Palto's reluctance. She glared at him, her mouth agape in her outrage, but she recovered quickly and eased the door shut behind him.

"What do you think you're doing?" She growled, "You're going to get us killed!"

"Only if they think you're housing a fugitive," Wes countered. "Better for you if you hide me somewhere."

"You are a wretched man, mister!" Palto declared with ire. "I should open this door right now and call for the guards to..." Then she saw Benji, and her face softened.

"If they find me, they will hurt him," Wes said desperately. His urgency forgoing any finesse. Palto bolted her door, then moved to confront Wes; her eyes sharp and penetrating. Outside the walls of the cramped room, he could hear a commanding guard ordering the others to divide and search the row of homes.

"You shield yourself behind children," Palto berated, which Wes was quick to deny.

"He is more a son than a shield." Palto intended a retort, but the pounding of fist on door caused both their heads to turn. It was not yet Palto's home, but close. She looked to Wes with keen scrutiny.

"Still trying to decide if you can trust me?" Wes asked with a weak smile, and Palto scoffed.

"Alright, follow me," she said, and led Wes through a doorway. "But don't you dare get me in trouble!"

"I'll do my best," Wes assured her, as he took in the adjacent room. It was dim, with the only light coming from the slats of a cook stove. There was a tiny table with two leaning chairs, and a narrow bed that was tucked against the back wall like an afterthought. "Do you live here alone?"

"Mind your own business, mister!" Palto warned, then kicked an old thread-worn carpet off of the floorboards. The sound of knocking was louder; much closer than before. Wes watched as Palto kneeled down, stretched out her fingers, and grabbed hold of one of the floorboards. She lifted it from its joist, set it to the side, then reached for another. Her front door rattled under the force of the fist upon it, and both of them froze as they looked at each other.

"Get over here," Palto whispered as she urgently pulled another two floorboards out of their places. Wes approached, and peered down into the hole she formed which revealed an earthy crawlspace a few feet beneath. She gestured for him to climb in. "Quickly!"

Another knock on the outside door, followed by the shout of a guard, and Palto called out that she was coming. Her eyes were wide, and her nerves drawn tight like a bowstring. Wes wanted to tell her to calm down, or she might give away that she was hiding something, but there was no time.

He eased himself into the hole, and sat on his backside with Benji on his lap. The position gave him just enough clearance to lean over the boy with his head bowed. As soon as he was in place, Palto replaced the boards and covered the area with the old rug; blanketing Wes in abrupt darkness. He tried not to draw comparisons to the nightmare alleyway he just fled from.

Palto rushed to open her door, and while Wes couldn't make out what the guards were saying to her, they were obviously angry. He heard Palto's voice, discerned she was trying to explain her delay, then a hard crack of hand to skin stilled her tongue. A soft gasp resonated from somewhere in front of him, and Wes lifted his head. It was far too dark to see anything, but it was evident that he and Benji were not alone.

Booted footsteps thumped through the home as a small group of guards crowded into the room overhead. Wes closed his eyes, and tried to focus on what he was hearing. One of the guards moved to stand directly over him.

"We will not be delayed further. Conduct a sweep! Find that thief and his pearl!"

Wes felt a sudden jolt in his arms, and recognized that the guard startled Benji awake. The boy was alarmed from not knowing who was holding him, or why he was in complete darkness. Wes quickly put a hand over his mouth, then leaned close to whisper in his ear.

"Hush now." His voice allayed Benji at once.

"We have witnesses saying they saw you conversing with a person matching the description of the accused." The guard over Wes declared. The other guards soon rejoined him, surrounding Palto. There were so few places for them to search.

"He hired me to stable his horse," Palto replied, and sounded quite indifferent if one didn't know her well. But Wes heard how her voice was strained, and knew her nerves were on edge.

"How many are licensed to reside in this dwelling?" asked the overhead guard.

"Two sir. A teenager, age sixteen, and her mother, aged forty-four." A female voice responded.

"So where is the mother, then?" the guard asked slyly; thinking he uncovered a cunning scheme. "Did she find herself a new Outlander boyfriend?"

"She's working," Palto responded a little too quickly. Wes prayed she didn't let her nerves get the best of her. He glanced over to the place where he heard the gasp. Was it Palto's mother hiding over there?

"Her profession isn't logged in our records," the woman guard commented.

"Does that have anything to do with me?" Palto disputed, growing impatient.

Careful girl, you're far too eager for them to leave.

"Does your mother have records from her place of employment?" Another male voice chimed in, his words casual and friendly. "Perhaps this is a location that warrants further investigation."

"You should know that my mother's a whore, or do you usually forget the women you lay upon?" Palto snapped.

"You dare speak to me that way?" The friendly tone vanished in an instant. Wes wondered if they would strike her again, or this time worse. He considered his options while Benji quietly breathed evenly against his cheek.

"Enough! We don't have time for this."

Wes looked up in the darkness. That voice belonged to Jack. As soon as he spoke, the tension seemed to drain out of the room. Boots scuffed as they walked, and guards filed out of the house.

"Next time, you better watch your tongue, child," the third guard warned but his friendly tone was back in place. "If we weren't in such a hurry, I would see you beaten for speaking to me that way."

"Sorry, sir," Palto replied, sounding chastened.

"If you're following in your mother's line of work. Come to the guards gate of the Hall. I'm sure we can find use for your services." The door closed, latching into place, then all was silent overhead. Wes waited, Benji waited, the presence in the darkness waited, and Palto waited. The guards did not return. Palto rushed back into the small bedroom and pulled away the dusty rug.

She lifted the boards out of their appropriate spots, and Wes looked up at her when she reached for him. He helped Benji to grab her hand, and after she pulled him out of the crawlspace, Wes was able to stand and climb out on his own. He stole a final quick glance into the gloom under the floorboards, and could just make out a small shape curled up in the shadows.

As soon as he cleared the opening, Benji fell upon him in one of those wild hugs that Wes grew to love. Everything he just endured was worth that moment. He stroked the boy's hair, while Benji rubbed his face against Wes to wipe his tears away.

"It's good to see you, Benji. It's so good to know that you're okay."

"I hate to do this, mister, but I need you to leave," Palto abruptly declared. Wes looked up at her, and Benji turned to look at her as well. She tried to appear stern with her hands on her hips; her resolution a dour expression upon her face, but she was still just a scared child trying to be brave. Wes chose a careful approach.

"Do you wish for Benji to leave as well?" Benji's face instantly transformed into moon-eyed innocence, and Palto bit her lip, hesitating.

"No... I don't but..."

Benji pulled away from Wes, and crawled over to the edge of the opening in the floor. He laid down on his stomach, and extended his arm into the hole, hand outstretched, waiting.

"If this is about your mother," Wes said, following Benji's cue, "I already know she was hiding down there with us. I heard her gasp when you were struck. You don't need to make us leave just to keep her hidden."

Palto stared at him, stunned. Then as Benji pushed himself up, holding fast to a small hand gripped in his, she cried out.

"Lilly! You were supposed to be quiet!"

A small red-headed child allowed Benji to pull her free from the crawlspace, while she stared at him with dumbfounded fascination. She wore a pale yellow dress, and her strawberry hair hung down her back straight as an arrow. Her eyes, green like Palto's, were as large as Benji's, and soaked up the scene with intense curiosity.

Benji stood before her, did a small kick-step dance that he must have learned from Solomon, then bent over in a theatrical bow. Lilly stared at him for a moment, transfixed with fascination, then suddenly she smiled. It was like a gleam of sunlight.

"Incredible," Wes remarked, and Palto dropped to her knees beside the child.

"Please, mister! Please don't tell anyone about Lilly! They'll take her from me if they find out!" Palto started to bawl. This drew Lilly's attention, and the small girl crawled onto her lap, and patted at her face with a tiny hand. Was she Palto's sister? She couldn't be a day older than three.

"I will never betray her to anyone," Wes said, "you have my word." Palto smiled at him weakly, then turned her attention to Lilly. She ran a hand over the girl's dusty hair to smooth it down, then tucked the strands behind her ear. Wes watched how she doted on the child and realized that Lilly was physically devoid of sin. A lamb without spot or blemish, just like Benji.

How was such a thing possible in this city? Especially when Elder Thoss and his men were actively searching for such a child to be a new vessel to their demon dragon. Benji, also watching the exchange, crawled over to be closer to Lilly. When she saw him approach, she smiled again.

"Take care with her, I'm the only person she's ever known," Palto told Benji and he nodded without taking his eyes off Lilly. This puzzled Wes, for he didn't recall Benji making such an effort for Eve or Solomon, but then Palto's words caused revelation, and he focused on her instead. She said that she was the only person Lilly's ever known. This meant that Palto's mother was not Lilly's.

"Before she was born, I kept hoping I would have a son," Palto said, and looked up at Wes. "I didn't want her to live the life my mother had. The life I had. A life of stealing, and begging, and selling whatever you had to sell. Even your own child." She fiddled with Lilly's hair, absently smoothing it in place. Benji puffed out his cheeks and crossed his eyes, and Lilly let out a soft laugh. It was a lovely sound. It reminded Wes of something from his past. A boy in the grass? He couldn't remember.

"With a boy, I could have donated him to the guard or offered him to the Disciples. He might have had a chance if he was smart enough and strong enough. I would never know him as my son, but I would at least know he was alive. That he was safe. But when Lilly was born...my heart couldn't contain the love I felt for her. I refused to give her over to the monsters, but I couldn't afford the cost of a parenting permit. So I decided to keep her hidden, and spare her from all of it." Palto made a sweeping gesture to indicate the whole of the city. Wes leaned forward to examine the girl more closely, and she turned her large moon-eyes from Benji to him. She looked at him with apprehensive fascination.

"She doesn't have a mark of sin upon her," he confirmed, amazed.

"Neither does your boy," Palto replied, and Wes couldn't decide how best to explain Benji's unusual circumstances.

"This is not a common phenomenon," he relented, "Have you seen other children like Lilly in this city? Ones that have no sickness."

"I see very few children," Palto said, shaking her head, "most parents can't afford the permits. They either get surrendered to the Elders or killed or worse...this is no place for a child to live."

"This city sullies the innocent," Wes agreed.

"This house and these walls are all she's ever known. She has never seen the sun. She's never known the wind on her face. If I continue to hide her here, she never will. The older she gets without the sickness, the more desirable she will be. This room is the only safe place for her in the city."

"What about your mother? Does she know about your child?"

"My mother hasn't been home for months," Palto said bitterly. "But on those rare nights in the past when she did stumble back home, she was too intoxicated to realize Lilly was in the room. She always thought my daughter was a ghost or a dream. No, even she didn't know about Lilly's existence. Until now, she was always just mine."

Wes looked at Palto, and thought of her as a thirteen-year-old girl, the same age as Daniel, but pregnant with a daughter. He thought about her hiding her pregnancy from everyone including her own mother. Did she even understand what was happening to her? How did she manage it on her own without being terrified? He thought of her giving birth, alone in a dark room, while her mother fed her indulgence with drugs and men. Palto was right. This was no place for a child to live. She just never thought that included herself.

Wes felt the Lord working within him, and knew what he needed to do. He remembered how Palto wanted to smuggle someone out of the city, and he just assumed she was talking about herself. He realized that she was actually trying to smuggle out Lilly. Did she really think her daughter would be better off out in the wilds if that meant she couldn't have her mother with her? He had to get them both out of the capital. He needed to be sure they stayed together.

Wes looked to Benji, and was surprised to find the boy staring at him with that same strange knowing look he's had before. Exactly how strong was his second sight? How much did he know, when he walked outside of that cabin, and approached Chancy in the woods? Did he come here to be with Wes, or did he come because he knew he needed to guide Palto and Lilly back to Sassy's home?

"I think we have a lot to talk about, you and I," Wes said to Palto. "I ask that you allow me to stay."

"I have no choice but to trust you now," Palto said with a cautious smile, "My whole heart is laid bare for you to see. Tell me what you need to say."

"There will be time for that later," Wes said as he got to his feet. He walked over to the bed in the corner and drew back the blanket. "But it's very late, and the sun will be rising soon. Little ones should be asleep."

Benji got to his feet without complaint, and took hold of Lilly's hand. He guided her over to the small bed, crawled in first, then Lilly joined him. Benji looked at Wes expectantly.

"Wuh!" he said in a huff, and Wes somehow understood in their strange second language exactly what the boy was saying.

"I agree, a story would help you both fall asleep," Wes said as he sat down beside the bed. "But I don't know many stories from the Word by heart. Ah, but I reckon there's one story I know well enough. Settle in, and I'll tell you what I know about a man named Noah."

Chapter Twenty-Five

Have compassion on me,
Lord for I am weak.
Heal me, Lord, for my bones are in agony.
Psalms 6:2 NLT

Wes recalled a time, when Daniel was almost six, and Ruth read to him about Noah with his ark of many animals. Even when Daniel grew bored with the verses, Ruth still read them aloud, and explained their deeper meaning.

"What lesson is gained from this story?" Daniel asked of Noah. His inflection reflected his bravado. Ruth looked up from her book, and the smile she gave him was serene.

"When the Lord tells you to follow him, then you must follow him no matter the cost."

"Why does God need us to do things for him, when he can do anything he wants for himself?" Daniel asked, skeptically.

"God doesn't *need* us to do things, my dear son, but to believe in Him means we must serve Him. It's how we show our faith. Where the Lord leads, we follow."

"Well, does he give you anything in return for doing what he says?" Daniel asked, and Ruth laughed. She reached over, and tousled Daniel's hair. It was one of the last endearing moments they shared together.

"You gain his compassion, dear Daniel, and in this cruel world, compassion is something worth striving for."

The sound of the front door woke Wes abruptly. He rose, halfway reaching for a gun he no longer had, when Palto appeared at the threshold, and slipped inside her home. She was soaked with rain, her thick tunic sodden and dripping, as her boots sloshed with each step. She saw that he was watching her, and tossed an apple in his direction.

"I brought plenty for all of us," she said as she walked past him, and into the adjoined room. Wes didn't ask how she acquired this surplus of food. His hunger overshadowed his creed. He rose with an agility he was still not accustomed to, and followed behind Palto.

"Mama!" Lilly called out from her perch next to the cook stove. She reached for Palto to pick her up, then noticed how wet she was, and settled on an apple instead.

"There's a few for each of us. A good way to gain strength for travel."

"Don't eat the core," Wes advised Benji who sampled his apple, then proceeded to inhale it like air. Palto laughed for she found Benji both amusing and understandable. Unlike the Elders, starvation was not a foreign concept for any of them.

"You'll quickly grow to love Benji if you don't already," Wes said with a fond smile. "I'm grateful he has you as a companion on his journey back home." Something Wes said got Benji's attention, but Palto just chuckled.

"Well it's not like we have many options. It would be only a matter of time before Lilly got discovered, and besides...it's nice to hear her laugh." Palto wrestled out of her hooded tunic, spraying rain drops that hissed against the iron of the cook stove, then draped the soggy garment over one of the chairs. Dressed in thin dark pants and shirt, she kicked off her boots and held her hands over the stove to warm them.

"It's cold out there!" She said with a shiver. "The sun is covered by the storm, which usually gets people out on the streets, but not today. Too cold and far too wet." Without her thick tunic, Wes could clearly see how distinct each of her ribs were. He wondered how many meals she skipped so that there was enough for her daughter to eat. Palto suddenly turned hard eyes on him, as though she sensed his pity and was poised to pick a fight.

"Did you see a lot of guards?" he asked, diverting her intentions. She shook her head.

"I saw a few...about five different patrols of three, but it was easy to avoid them. The chill has fogged the streets."

"Then I should go," decided Wes, "and take advantage of the weather the Lord has blessed me with."

"Don't be foolish, you can still be seen," Palto countered with a flick of her wet hair. "One guard can bring twenty more down on your head, and you can't outrun the entire Guard Watch Elite."

"I'll be careful," Wes said, finishing his apple. Benji rose, with the small bits of apple he couldn't manage to eat, and collected all the other cores from each of them.

"Are you careful enough to go completely unseen? For if anyone takes one look at the way you're dressed, they're going to call the guard." Palto made a sweeping gesture to incorporate Wes' full attire. His clothes were covered in rips and tears. Dark spots of dried blood stood out all over his body. Only his hat remained intact, and it drew its own attention being that no one else wore such a thing; let alone in black.

"There's little I can do about it," Wes grumbled, though he was willing to admit she had a good point.

"I...think I can help you," Palto said, suddenly uneasy. She glanced at the two children watching her intently, and guarded her words. "My mother...well. She's never brought her work home with her. Except this one time, there was a man that came into town one night. No idea where from. No name given. Just a man who needed a place to stay, and she let him stay here. She...left him here." Palto shrugged, not meeting Wes' eye, and he dreaded the story behind the one she told.

"Did he hurt you?" he asked, but Palto quickly shook her head.

"One of the few that didn't. But...it was a cold night, mister. Colder than the rain out there today. And I was shivering so. I wanted to...well, he was warm, you see. I expected to pay him for keeping me from shivering, but he took nothing. He was like you. He never named a price to pay. When I woke, he was gone, but he left something behind that he draped over me."

Palto padded out of the room on bare feet, and Wes glanced over to Benji. The boy stood with a pile of used-up apples, and looked at Wes when he noticed Wes looking at him. His eyes were twin wells. Any emotion within them was hidden at the very bottom. Palto returned a moment later, carrying a long leather duster draped over her arm.

"It might fit," she said, holding it out to Wes without meeting his eye. "The man...well, you remind me a lot of him."

Wes took the duster into his hands and examined it. It was well cared for. The leather was oiled to endure rainy conditions, and Wes had to wonder about the nature of the man that owned it. A kind of man that blows into a town with a duster but not a name. He slipped off his trim jacket, eased into the duster, and it hugged him like a lover.

"It's a little snug, but will serve its purpose." It covered the worst parts of his mangled clothing. Wes picked up his hat, placing it just so on his head.

"Wuh," Benji said, and stepped forward to give Wes the pile of apple bits he held in his hands. Wes took them and was puzzled, but responded all the same.

"Thank you."

"Off with you then," Palto commanded, then plucked up his jacket with a sour expression on her face. "I'll try to mend your jacket while you're gone. Maybe I can get some of the blood out as well."

"Much obliged," said Wes, and turned for the door.

"Be careful," Lilly called out, and Wes watched as she walked over and wrapped her small arms around his leg. She blinked up at him with the large eyes of the innocent. "Come back soon."

Wes gave her a nod, then stepped out into the dreary day. He drew in a long breath of the cool crisp air. Palto was right, it was a bitter day, and the rain came down like a waterfall. He stepped off of Palto's stoop and was instantly submerged in the thick of it. It was the kind of rain one didn't bother rushing through, for it left you soaked the moment you stepped into it. He noticed his mare watching him, and approached her as Benji's intentions became clear.

"I reckon you have a friend," he said, and held out Benji's offering. She plucked up the apples with gentle lips, and blinked her appreciation at Wes. She was a good horse.

"It's past time we gave you a name," he said as he scratched behind her ear.

The streets were mostly devoid of life. A few bony animals slunk in and out of trash bins, and a bleary-eyed drunkard staggered his way home. A hazy mist hung like a weighted cloud, brought about by the rain, and shrouded Wes as much as it did the streets around him. He peered out from under the brim of his hat, sweeping the landscape for signs of spectators while he trudged toward the center of town and his eventual destination.

He needed to speak to the Disciples, for he saw no other way to get the three children safely out of the city. They went to great lengths to try to help Wes before, he just hoped they would still be willing when they learned he didn't have Daniel with him. They were so focused on worshiping their Guardian Son.

The rain drowned out all sound, and paired with the fog, there was no way of knowing if he was truly alone. He followed the familiar path back to the Disciple's church while he wondered how Palto was able to even see the guards that she did. He worried he might not be as stealthy as he thought.

Lord, hide me away for just a little while longer.

Wes passed by the storefront with nary a glance, and went through the adjoining alley into the garden clearing. While the day was overcast, it was still brighter than Palto's dim little home. So when Wes lifted his hand to knock on the Disciple's church door, he truly noticed it for the first time since he fled that dark alleyway. He stared at his hand, for he was too stunned to do anything else, and marveled at the untarnished skin of his fingers. Wes raised his other hand, and again was awestruck at the lack of sin upon it. He pulled back the sleeves of the duster as much as he could, and the wrists were bare of black scales as well. It was all just... gone. All of it, *gone*! He was... *cleansed*. Cleansed in the light.

"Benji," Wes whispered, and in that moment, the boy felt too immense for him to perceive. This child was outside of Wes' comprehension, and could do things beyond rational understanding. Wes might have ignored other signs that lent to this fact, but the evidence of it was unavoidable upon his hands. It choked his breath, and staggered his feet.

He was so mesmerized by this apparent miracle, he wasn't aware of the door opening until he heard the strangled cry of alarm. In the doorway stood a man barely older than a boy whose face was half consumed by sin. Wes peered past the rain toward the man, and the awestruck terror in his eyes was reflected back at him as they both examined Wes' stainless hands. Then the young man ducked out of sight, and Wes saw him run down the hall through the windows.

"Wait," Wes tried to call out, but the word choked in his throat. Nothing seemed real.

His voice wasn't real.

The rain wasn't real.

His hands weren't real.

The only thing that existed in actuality was the thrumming of his heart, and the image of Benji in his mind. He was just a boy. A child unable to speak. A child of a whore mother that lost herself to her sin. How was he able to do these things?

"Light Keeper," a voice said, and Wes stopped the prolonged groan that escaped his lips. He blinked, and focused on the small man who stood in the doorway.

"He's just a boy," Wes whispered, as his hands trembled before him.

"C...Come inside, sir," the man said as his hooded eyes went wide at the sight of Wes' miracle. When Wes remained rooted, the small man grabbed hold of his arm and guided him inside.

"You are utterly soaked, sir! You will catch a sickness dressed as you are. Towels!" He shouted as he shut the door behind them, "and a warm robe! Hurry!"

"I didn't know he did this. I didn't see it until just now...I..."

"Speak sense, sir. I must understand how this happened."

"There was this moment. In the alley."

"Are you the one the guards are seeking, sir?" the small man asked, and behind him many robed Disciples ran down the hall with bundles in their hands.

"I am," Wes said, as he stared at his fingers, captivated. The crowd suddenly encircled him. They put towels to his duster, his boots, his hat, his face.

"So you are the source of the great light many bore witness to the night before?" Hands pulled at his duster, trying to strip him of it, but Wes shied away from them and backed up against the wall.

"No, I wasn't the source. But..."

"But you were there," The small man said, no hint of a question. He peered at Wes intently; his muddy eyes sparkling with growing excitement. Many people pressed upon Wes, with towels and hands and fervent eyes.

"I was there," he cried out; too stunned to evade the truth. Yes, he was there, and he was *cleansed*.

The Disciples all around him gasped and looked to one another. Then they regrouped and focused their efforts. When they grabbed at his damp leather duster, Wes relinquished it to them. The moment his clothes were exposed, the Disciples were touching him again. Probing into the bloodied tears. Wes couldn't get away from them.

"Look at his shirt! See the blood there?"

"His skin is unbroken. His body is healed!"

"Look at his fingers! Look at his hands!"

"His sin is cleansed! Cleansed!"

"Get off of me!" Wes growled, for it felt too familiar. His mind flashed back to that dark alleyway, and the dozens of monsters that tore into him with fervent delight. Panic rose up in his throat, and threatened to expel itself in a scream. His body felt the pain of the burning sin inside him, and he knew it wasn't there. He *knew* it wasn't there! But it took his breath away all the same. Hands grabbed at his clothes, and tore them away from his skin. The Disciples shouted to him, telling him to calm down, be still, stop fighting, they were trying to help him! But Wes' ears rang and his hair fell into his eyes as his hat was pulled from him, and all he could think was that he couldn't breathe. He needed to breathe!

"Enough!" The small man said, and all hands fell away. Wes stood, chest bare, and realized that the strangled, rapid gasping sound was coming from him. The small man parted his Disciples like the sea, and leaned in closer to Wes while he peered up at him.

"Tell me, Light Keeper, what terrifies you so." His voice was soft, and soothing. Wes clung to the sound for an ounce of stability.

"The damned," he gasped, as the room went dark around him. He was going to faint.

"Where were these damned?"

"In the...alley...they were...upon me... so many...so many...they tore at me...they hurt me..."

Breathe.

Breathe.

Breathe!

"He's panicking!"

"He's terrified!"

"What happened to them, sir? Where did the damned go?"

"Vanished," Wes whispered.

Breathe.

Breathe.

"How did they vanish?"

"Vanquished...by the light."

"Impossible!"

"Can it be?"

"Light Keeper," the small man whispered, "Has the Light Bringer come to our city?"

Wes no longer gasped to breathe. His body was wet with rain and sweat, but air filled his lungs unfettered once more. His vision cleared, and he stared into the large mud-brown eyes of one nameless Disciple.

"The Light Bringer is in the city."

"Take the rest of the clothes. Find suitable replacements. Give him that robe. He must stand before the flock!" The small man stepped away and hands were upon Wes once more. No mercy was given for the sake of his fear. But he was suddenly too exhausted to notice. The panic that filled him left him hollow; a void of both emotion and thought. He stared at the boy who was no older than twenty, and let the others take all that remained on his body.

What was happening to him? Why was he so acutely scared?

Wes dreaded to think he made a terrible mistake. It was hard to trust, and these radicals made it no easier. But the boy stepped forward when the others were done, and gently placed a robe over Wes' shoulders.

"Have you seen enough?" Wes spit as he glared at them in turn. They said he could seek them out three times and they would help him no matter the cost. Yet there he was, stripped bare and shivering while they ran off with the shredded remains of his clothing. Even the small man was gone. Only the boy remained. Wes closed the robe over his shame.

"Come, sir!" The young man said, turning.

"Where are we going?"

"To the Assembly." The boy led Wes up the same hall the others went, and guided him to a place where twin doors opened into a large room filled with people. They were all dressed in the same gray robe he wore, and standing in tightly packed rows from wall to aisle. The room was suffocating for how full it seemed.

"Our numbers have doubled today," the boy with the sin-filled face said beside him, "after reports of the light."

Wes saw that the small man stood at the far end of the room upon a low stage. He gestured Wes forward, and motioned to the others in the room.

"Disciples new and old! We have one who comes with his testimony! He is here cleansed by the Bringers light! He offers forth proof of salvation!"

"Oh Guardian Son! We are saved!"

"He is the Keeper! He is a walking God!"

"Give us your testimony! Show us your cleansing!"

"Come along," the young man said with an encouraging smile, and Wes was too numb of mind to render a valid way to refuse. He followed the boy who led him to the stage, then he was standing in front of hundreds of people; packed into a place of desperation and heat. All their eyes were upon him.

"The Keeper has been cleansed!" The small man shouted, arms outstretched, and the others cried out or sang praise. Hands raised, palms facing where Wes stood.

"The prophecies are being fulfilled!"

"The cleansing light is realized!"

"Our time of salvation is coming!"

"Why have you come, Light Keeper?" the small man asked, as his flock gaped. Wes saw no other way but forward.

"I need your help to get some children out of the capital."

"How many children?" Asked someone in the crowd.

"Three," Wes said, glancing around, "one is a teenager, but the other two are just kids."

"Are any of the three the Guardian Son?" The small man asked, and Wes peered at him.

"No," he admitted.

"Are any of the three the Bringer of Light?" someone in the crowd asked, and Wes let his eyes sweep over the sea of upturned faces.

"Yes." Many voices spoke at once. A jumble of noise and senseless words.

"Do you intend to go with them, sir?" The small man asked over the throng, and all fell silent to await Wes' answer.

"I made a promise I intend to keep. My purpose stands alongside the Guardian Son."

"The prophecy realized," someone in the crowd said softly; reverently.

"Then we will gladly help you, sir," the small man said with a smile. "Bring the children here tomorrow, just before the lighting of the lanterns. We'll withdraw them from the city that very night."

"How do you reckon I move three children through the capital without them being seen?" Wes asked, slightly vexed. He felt like he was being pulled along a sea of emotions and staring faces. He didn't have time to think, and he was losing control of the plan.

"We will supply you with a horse and cart," said the small man.

"I have the horse I want them to use."

"Then we will supply you with just a cart as well as provisions," said the small man.

"And I'm to bring them here to you?"

"Just as you say. A wise plan," he said, sweeping his hands to incorporate the assembly. "We will do this for you, Light Keeper. But first you must do something for us."

Wes stared at the man, confused. "You said you would help me, no matter the cost."

"And we will, sir," replied the small man with his placid smile, "but even compassion has its price."

All around them, the flock of Disciples started to hum. It was soft at first, but grew quickly louder, as the whole of the assembly was spellbound in their veneration.

"What do you want of me," Wes demanded as he observed this strange shift in the crowd. He felt like his lungs were slowly being squeezed in a vice of panic that he couldn't shake. The small man took his arm and pulled him to the front of the stage directly in its center. Lights were placed around him to illuminate him from all sides. The humming of the crowd grew so bold that it overtook his thoughts, and Wes forced himself not to cover his ears. But then the small man lifted a fist into the air, and the sound ceased in an instant.

"We want a demonstration, sir." The small man's voice could barely be heard over the ringing in Wes' ears and he turned to the crowd. They swayed as they reached for him, a sea of gray robes and equally gray faces.

"Show us the victory!"

"Show us the salvation!"

"Show us the healing!"

"Show us, sir, what the Bringer can do. Show us the cleansing of his merciful light. Then you will have everything we can offer you."

Wes looked upon the small man, watching him expectantly. He scanned the crowd of faces, gazing at him reverently, and saw the young man with half his face consumed by sin, and realized he looked no different than the rest of them.

Is this your will as well, Lord?

Wes opened his robe, and let it fall.

Chapter Twenty-Six

Have mercy on me, O God,
because of your unfailing love.
Because of your great compassion,
blot out the stains of my sins. -Psalms 51:1 NLT

"Where have you been?" Palto asked when Wes returned to her home. "and what are you wearing?" Wes glanced down at the dark trousers, and gray washed tunic that replaced what once was. He held a small sack in his hands, along with the damp duster draped over his arm and his father's hat secured in his grasp. There was no need to put them back on when they were so wet. The rain had stopped while he was busy dealing with...

No. Don't think on it now.

"I secured your passage out of the city," Wes said, ignoring Palto's questions.

"You've been gone for hours. Did everything go alright?" As soon as Palto spoke, Benji dashed past her and wrapped his arms around Wes.

"I was given a small cart to use for transporting the little ones. They promised to load it with provisions for your travel. We can secure it to my mare...or rather your mare. I want her to be the one to take you, for she knows Benji, and he knows how to handle her."

"Why won't you answer my questions? What's wrong with you?" Palto asked, and Wes looked at her miserably. Something in his eyes altered the expression on her face, and she quickly changed the subject. "Benji's been hitting himself for the past hour. He kept saying 'wuh,wuh,wuh'. Can't he speak, mister?"

"He speaks in his own way," Wes said, offering the lad a wan smile, but Benji just stared at him, concern clouding his eyes, and Wes resisted the urge to look away.

"How am I supposed to know what's got him all upset if he can't tell me with words," Palto complained.

"His eyes, mama," Lilly said, as she tottered into the room. "He talks with his eyes."

Benji looked over to her, and smiled tenderly.

"We won't have much time," Wes said to Palto. "You'll need to gather anything you want to take with you, and we should all get some rest before your journey tomorrow with the Disciples."

"Is it really safe?" Palto asked, "They won't try to kidnap us, or sell us, or sacrifice us, or whatever they do out in the wilderness?"

"It's safe," Wes assured her.

"They won't expect us to repay them somehow?"

"The cost has already been paid," Wes professed, and Benji looked up at him worried.

"I can't believe this is actually happening," Palto said, a little breathless. She looked down at Lilly and a cautious smile came across her face.

"Well the Disciples asked that we come before tomorrow's lighting of the fireboxes or...lanterns, I reckon. In the meantime, they gave us a sample of the provisions they aim to provide." Wes lifted the sack to show the weight of all it contained. "Benji, will you do the honors?"

Benji grabbed the sack and ran into the other room with Lilly on his heels. She squealed in delight as she followed him, and the sound made Palto laugh.

"It's so good to see her playing with another child," she said, and gave Wes a smile.

"Palto, I want to ask you something," Wes said, hesitantly, and her smile fell from her face. "What did Jack mean when he said I was destined to destroy the world? What prophecy were you reluctant to share with me before?"

Palto stared at him for a moment, then snorted a bitter laugh and looked back to the children. Wes moved to stand beside her and listened as she spoke delicately.

"We used to tell each other stories when we were little. Jack, me, and a few others. It was just a stupid way to scare everyone. We used to say 'look out! The Keeper will eat you up if you don't avoid the light!' You're nothing like what I imagined you would be." She glanced at him from the corner of her eye, then they both turned when Benji made a wordless humming sound to express his joy. In his hand was a small bag of colored glass balls. Something one of the Disciples must have slipped in the sack for the children.

"Why am I a thing that children fear?" Wes asked, and Palto sighed.

"Only the Disciples know all the prophecies, and maybe a few of the Elders. But there are a few things that all of us know, and there is one line from the Prophetic Canon that everyone knows by heart." The children broke chunks away from a loaf of bread, then proceeded to eat them while they scattered the glass balls over the floor for closer inspection.

"Tell me," Wes said, watching Palto instead of the younger children. "Please."

"Beware the Keepers' compassion, for it will destroy the world."

"Nonsense," Wes muttered, but frowned all the same.

"You don't sound convinced," Palto remarked, her smile returning.

"I think some of your prophecies are true, at least in part, and it scares me," Wes admitted. He tossed the duster on the back of the one chair, and reached for his jacket which Palto was kind enough to patch and quickly clean.

"What has you so convinced they are true," she asked, and Wes lifted his hands before her. The Disciples were gracious enough to give him a set of riding gloves, which he stripped away from each of his hands, and revealed the unfettered skin free of sin.

"How?" Palto gasped, her eyes wide with the same fear Wes felt before. Benji lifted his head, sensing the shift in mood and Wes quickly tucked his hands behind his back. He wasn't sure if Benji knew what had happened, or how he would react if he found out. Palto followed Wes' gaze, and offered Benji an awkward smile. Then Lilly squealed again, and drew his attention away.

"Great Guardian Son!" She whispered.

"I don't think he's deserving of your praise."

"Are you crazy!" Palto hissed, and that old familiar fire was back in her eyes. "You want me to wander into the wilderness with the actual Bringer of Light?"

"He's not the Bringer of Light, he's Benji."

"He's apparently both," she corrected, glancing over at the lad. "And now he scares me."

"Don't let him," Wes said, worried over how the world was going to treat his lost boy. Benji wouldn't want people to fear him, would he? No, Wes refused to doubt the truth of who Benji was. "He's just a child, and he needs people like you and me to love him for who he is."

Palto stared at Wes for a long time. He could see her mind working through the things he already had when he stood before the flock of Disciples, exposed and naked, and listened to them glorify him as a holy shrine to pray upon. Benji was capable of doing things that no one would ever understand, but he was still a child who desperately wanted to be loved. Turning from him in fear would be profoundly painful for him, and so Wes chose not to fear him at all. That didn't mean it was an easy thing to do.

"Alright," Palto said with a nod, then let out a sigh. "I will love him for who he is. Because I love him for who he is to Lilly. I better get to packing, mister." Palto left Wes to gather the few things she owned, and Wes eased into one of the table chairs where he could watch Benji and Lilly. Benji ran up to him, offered him some bread and cheese, then gave him a hug after Wes took the food. Hard to believe such a child had the power that he did. Maybe Wes mistook the whole incident, and the flash of light didn't come from Benji at all. All the same, he focused on his food and savored the freshness of the bread.

She said my compassion was going to destroy the world. I dread to think she meant my compassion toward Benji.

They all slept, for they knew that they should. Hours passed with Palto and Lilly resting in their bed, and Benji laying his head on Wes' lap on the floor beside them. While the three children managed to sleep unimpeded by their dreams, Wes woke often and with a feeling of sudden panic. Every time sleep took him, dreams of many hands upon him tearing into his flesh brought him back to the small room with the lowly burning cook stove.

Wes took off his hat, and found his brow damp with sweat. He wiped at it with his fingers, then marveled at the reacquired sensation of touch to his fingertips. A small hand slipped into his own, and Wes looked down at Benji looking up at him.

"Wuh," he said softly, and Wes shook his head.

"I just can't sleep. It's alright."

"Wuh."

"Nightmares. I keep having nightmares about...well, it doesn't matter what they are about."

"Wuh."

"I'm going to miss you too, Benji. I have no doubt that Sassy will be overjoyed to see you again, but I think you'll have to make amends with Eve."

Benji winced at this, and pulled his hand from Wes'.

"Benji..." Benji looked to Wes with his deep profound eyes, and waited for there to be more. "Nevermind. Get some sleep."

Doing as he was told, Benji turned his head away from Wes and closed his eyes. Wes ran his fingers gently through Benji's hair and stared at the fire licking its fodder through the narrow slats of the cook stove.

Benji...are you the Messiah?

When the day faded into the soft glow of twilight, Wes knew it was time. He made ready his plow horse, strapping the small cart behind her, and she settled into the feel of it like it was an old friend. He then signaled for Palto who watched him from the shadows of her open door, and she led Benji and Lilly over to the stables. Lilly's eyes were everywhere at once, but Benji was mindful to usher her along and get into the cart quickly. Good lad.

"The Disciples have given you a useful gift," Palto commented as she examined the cart. It wasn't large, only suitable for hauling potatoes or perhaps a couple of concealed children, but it would do for them.

"Aye, this solves many issues when it comes to traveling through the wilds." Benji guided Lilly into the cart then climbed in after her. Afterwards, Palto draped a saddle blanket over the two of them and covered them both with the leather duster. They settled into a small shapeless mound and went relatively still. Palto smiled but worry still creased her brow and when she reached for the horse's tether, her hands shook.

"You're scared," Wes commented and Palto laughed dryly.

"Terrified," she admitted. "This situation is so much bigger than either of us. And now I'm running off to the wilds with no idea on how I'll survive it. This city is horrible, but it is all I've ever known."

"Benji knows the way you need to go," Wes said, "And if he happens to get lost, I know that Eve will find you." Palto looked at Wes, frowning, but did not argue. He explained to her all he could about Sassy and her grandchildren, although she was only half convinced he wasn't making the whole thing up.

"Alright, I think we're ready. Not a sound, Lilly. Not until I say you can," Palto instructed then glanced at Wes. "She's very good at keeping quiet."

"So is Benji," Wes said with a sly smile, and Palto snorted a laugh. Wes reached for his mare and gave her nose a quick stroke. "Time for you to get out of this place. Be good for them while I'm gone."

Palto pulled at the tether, and Wes' mare obliged her. They walked along together for one final time, for soon Wes needed to distance himself so as to not attract attention. Soon, but not yet. For the moment he broke away from the three children, he would no longer be part of them. He will be alone once more.

"I can't believe this is actually happening," Palto said with a shake of her head. "After spending so much of my life struggling just to get by, you come along and show me that people can actually do things just because they care."

"God wants us all to show compassion to each other. But I'm glad I was able to do this for you."

"Compassion," Palto replied with a wary scrutiny; then shook her head.. "I'd like to hear more about this God of yours."

"Sassy can explain everything to you," Wes replied. "She can show you the path to salvation."

"Well, I can't thank you enough for all you've done and...I want you to have this. I don't think I'll be needing it anymore."

Palto reached over to place Jethro's pocket watch back in Wes' hand. He looked at it, then to her, and she smiled at him. He knew it was her way of saying goodbye.

"Alright then," Wes replied, placing the watch into his jacket pocket, he stepped away from her and pushed ahead of the cart. They talked about this during the early morning hours while the children slept on in a tangle of arms and legs. Palto knew where to go, and Wes felt it would be safer for her to get there without him beside her. If he happened to get spotted by the guard, it was imperative they didn't recover Benji as well. This was the safest way to ensure that didn't happen.

Wes was able to reach the familiar alley long before his mare and her cart, and while the sun was only an afterthought in the sky, the fireboxes had not yet found their fire. Some other residents wandered the streets, taking in the damp evening after the heavy rain of the day, but Wes was not given more than a passing glance.

Entering the alley and the adjacent courtyard behind it caused a bitter taste to form in his mouth, but Wes pushed away any temptation to remember his last encounter with the people that lingered there. He glanced behind him, noted that he wasn't being followed, and approached the familiar door.

"Light Keeper," a small woman said, her voice like a spoken whisper. She stood in the doorway, answering his knock, and stared up at him with an awestruck expression. "Please, come inside."

"I'll wait out here, if it suits you," he said, stepping back from the door. "I need to speak with your leader."

"There are no leaders among the flock," the woman softly said, spreading her arms in a shrug.

"Well none of you have names so how can I ask for him?"

"I have a name," she replied, unblinking. "I am called Sorrow. For my river runs deep." She lifted the sleeve of her gray robe to reveal to Wes the length of her sin, but also how it strangely twisted and weaved around the large angry scars that ran the length of her forearm.

"Who would do such a thing?" Wes breathed, horrified by the layers of cuts that showed a legacy of wounds that healed then were cut open anew.

"I did it to myself, Light Keeper," the woman said, "to release the poison and gain relief."

"Don't mind her, sir," a voice called out, and the small man gently led the woman out of the doorway. "She's new to our flock."

"Is she alright? Some of those cuts look new," Wes said, and noticed the woman peering out at him from the shadows of the hallway.

"She will be alright. Like I said, she is new. But she is one of us now."

"I see...do you have everything in order?" Wes asked, and the small man stepped out into the evening to stand alongside him.

"See for yourself," he said with a smooth gesture and Wes watched as a dozen gray robed Disciples filed out of the building. Many of them carried parcels that Wes assumed were the promised provisions.

"How do you plan to get them past the guards at the perimeter of the city?" Wes asked, but the small man looked distracted.

"The permits are in order, sir. Um, excuse me..." the small man moved to intercept one of the Disciples and ordered the man to obtain horse feed from their stores.

"Keeper," the soft-spoken woman said, and Wes turned to see that she was standing beside him again. She looked shy, her eyes fixated on the ground, and she reached up to tuck a lock of her dark hair behind her ear.

"What can I offer you?" Wes asked and the woman named Sorrow smiled.

"Thank you for the blessing you gave us, Keeper. Seeing the way the Bringer healed you, and how you no longer carry the blackness of sin, it was...inspiring." She tucked her hair behind her ear again, and immediately half of it tumbled back into her face. Wes watched the Disciples as they got into a line and allowed the small man to inspect each of their parcels in turn while another Disciple marked on a slate an inventory report.

"It didn't feel inspiring," Wes admitted, half distracted, "I felt overwhelmed." Wes remembered how Benji put the apple cores in his hands. Did he notice the change in them then? Did he notice the change when they woke from sleep and Benji held his hand? Did he even understand the significance of what it meant?

“Oh, but you were wonderful, Keeper! Just…wonderful,” Sorrow said, her hair shrouding her face, “you took my breath away.”

“Hush now,” Wes muttered, embarrassed.

“Do you think…well, is it possible that the Bringer…will you ask him to heal me too?” She looked up at Wes, her expression one of hopeful devotion. Their eyes met, then the distinct sound of clopping hooves alerted them all that the children had arrived.

“They come!” One of the Disciples called out, and more of the gray robed followers poured out of their church into the courtyard.

“Is the Light Bringer with them?”

“I want to see him!”

“Will he speak to us at all?”

“Everyone! Prepare to add provisions to the cart,” said the small man, “but be careful of the cargo already there.” He smiled as Wes’ mare came into view with Palto in the lead. She looked over the group of Disciples with visible apprehension, then her eyes found Wes. She turned the horse toward him, but she only went a few more feet before the Disciples approached with their various parcels.

“Let them be,” Wes said to Palto when she moved to block their approach, “they have provisions for your journey.” Wes felt the young woman’s eyes on him, her dark hair obscured her face in waves. When the small man approached him, Sorrow backed away from Wes and joined the other spectators in front of the horse.

“She seems to have taken an interest in you,” he remarked with hazy indifference as he watched her go. Wes glanced at the small man then returned his attention to the cart.

“I am grateful for all you have done,” he said and the small man gave him a thin smile.

“I am grateful to you as well, for paying the recommended price.”

“Provisions secure!” One of the Disciples announced, “Ready to depart! Turn the…” A sudden whining interrupted the man’s orders and all the Disciples looked to one another then to the cart they just carefully loaded. Benji sat up, and his appearance was so abrupt, that some of the Disciples staggered back in shock.

Benji was visibly upset, and looked all around him at the upturned faces of the flock, but then he caught sight of Wes, and climbed over the parcels to jump off the side of the cart.

“The boy!” Said the small man.

“Wuh! Wuh!” Benji cried out, his face contorted with emotion.

“Benji, what…” the boy flung himself at Wes and pulled him into a hug. All around them, the courtyard came alive with shouting.

"It's him! It must be him!"

"Oh, glory be! The Light is upon us!"

"The son of promise has shown us his face!"

"What a beautiful boy. So young, so pure!"

"He will cleanse us all! Burn the evil from the world!"

"Tell them to stop this!" Wes snapped at the small man, who urgently tried to placate the other Disciples, but they seemed to not even see him. All they saw was Benji. They circled around Wes, holding out hands in longing, and called for the Light.

"The son of promise!"

"The Bringer of Light!"

Wes worried all the shouting might frighten Benji, but was surprised to see that the boy was just calmly watching him. His eyes carried no passion, but instead were a murky abyss that eluded to a profound intelligence that had no evident meaning. They were two large windows that revealed an outer darkness full of a vastness but also emptiness.

"Please, Light Bringer, make me clean again," Sorrow pleaded from among the crowd, but Benji must not have heard.

"He doesn't know your prophecies," Wes shouted to the rabble, hoping to stop them from moving any closer, "he doesn't understand your expectations nor your names."

"Light Bringer!" Someone groaned and Benji looked at him. He then pointed to the man and stepped forward to place fingers on Wes' lips."Ignore him," Wes said, pulling his hand away. "Your name is Benji." Again Benji pointed at the man, an added force behind his gesture, and placed fingers against Wes' lips. Wes leaned forward, pressing against those tiny fingers and took hold of Benji's hand.

"Benji," he repeated, his eyes sharp as he stared down at Benji, for he wanted the lad to know that it didn't matter what these Disciples called him or what the world promised him to be. He would always be who he was, and there was only one name his mother gave to him.

"B-E-N-J-I."

Wes didn't know what to expect from Benji as a response, but it certainly wasn't the large smile the boy gave him. He grabbed hold of Wes' jacket, and rubbed his face against it in his strange affectionate way.

"Benji, you know it's time for you to go," Wes said, gently.

The boy nodded.

"Then why did you jump out of the cart and run over here? The way you ran up to me, I thought you were going to demand I let you stay." Benji gave Wes a half smile and a look that seemed to say *don't be so foolish.*

"Then...why?" The smile faded from Benji's face. He lifted a hand, fingers splayed, and gave Wes a quick wave.

"You wanted to say goodbye?" Wes asked, and when Benji nodded, he looked away. "I'm not good with this stuff."

Benji approached him, grabbed hold of his jacket again and pulled down on it. Wes got down on one knee, following the boy's lead, and looked up at him when Benji cupped Wes' face in his hands. He stared at Wes, and his eyes consumed all of Wes' vision. Everything around them fell behind a curtain of silence and all that remained was Wes and Benji.

Goodbye.

The thought was as clear as a spoken word, but the message was conveyed through Benji's eyes. Wes blinked in surprise, but the boy just smiled.

"I understand you," Wes whispered, "and I want you to have this." Impulsively, he bent and first removed his hunting knife then unhooked its sheath. He tied the sheath to Benji's hip, working the straps into the loops at his pants, and then slid the knife back into place.

"I think it's past time I gave this to you," Wes said as he appreciated the look of it on Benji's hip. He hated saying goodbye. He tried to avoid it whenever he could.

"Good bye, Benji," Wes said, knowing that he was not sure if he would ever see the boy again. "I love you."

Benji looked at him, his eyes wide with surprise, then he bowed his head, closed his moon eyes, and gently took Wes' hands in his own. Together, they prayed for safety, for protection, and to one day be reunited again. Then Benji turned, and waved to Palto. He dashed away from Wes, without another glance, and as he passed Sorrow, he reached out and gave her a gentle pat on the cheek.

"Turn the horse and exit the alley!" The Disciple said, completing his orders. The group moved to take the tether from Palto and fall in around the cart and horse. She looked to Wes one last time, gave him a nod of unspoken promises to keep the children safe, then followed the others to the alley's exit.

Wes lifted a hand, giving the cart a final wave as Benji climbed in, and tried to not let the ache in his heart show on his face.

"We will get them out, do not worry, sir." Wes turned to see the small man looking at him with a placid smile. "I am so glad to have laid eyes upon the Bringer of Light. I look forward to his return."

"He's never coming back here," Wes objected but the small man only shrugged.

"The prophecies are not guides, sir. They are promises." Then he turned and raised his arms to the jumble of onlookers still watching the cart go.

"Come all, we will spend the night in prayer. We will ask the Guardian Son to protect our sojourning children on their journey into the east. Pray with me for their safe deliverance from the night!"

"Pray for the light!" Many called out in response, and all that remained made their way to the door. As they went, Sorrow broke away from them and approached Wes with her downcast eyes.

"Did you see him touch me?" she asked.

"I did," Wes said, and glanced at her hands curiously. They were still black with sin.

"It's alright," she said, seeing his gaze. "I don't care that he didn't heal me." She smiled, but she looked so sad that Wes could understand her strange name.

"Here," he said, reaching into his pocket. He pulled out the old watch and gently placed it into her hand. "It's not much, but all I have to give. I hope it makes you feel a little better."

Sorrow looked at the pocket watch, then up to Wes in amazement.

"Oh, thank you, Light Keeper. I will pay you back for your kindness somehow!"

"Don't even think of it," Wes said with a shake of his head. "Compassion isn't rewarded. It's supposed to be given freely. This is what God teaches us to do."

"God," Sorrow whispered. "The only God I see is you."

Wes backed away from her, stunned and unable to think of what to say. She stood transfixed as he turned from her and made his way to the alley. He glanced back at her before he stepped into the shadows of the short passage, and she looked like a statue in the deepening night.

Wes exited the alley, anxious to be away from her, and looked up the street where he could just make out the procession of Disciples guiding the cart to the edge of the capital. He thought to follow them, and make sure they got out safely, but decided not to take the chance.

This won't be the end for us, lad. I swear I'll return to you.

Wes looked toward the Divine Hall as a thought lingered in his mind: a word conveyed by a boy he was destined to forget.

Goodbye.

Chapter Twenty-Seven

'In the last days,' God says,
"I will pour out my Spirit upon all people.
Your sons and daughters will prophesy.
Your young men will see visions,
and your old men will dream dreams. -Acts 2:17 NLT

Leaning against the outside of the tavern he once visited with Palto, Wes watched as dark clad servants lit fireboxes one by one. The residents of the capital stepped out into the night, and braved the thick mud of the rain soaked streets. Wes watched them comb the city like ants in a nest, while he contemplated his next course of action. Of course he needed to reunite with Daniel, but he wasn't sure exactly how. Considering how complicated an effort it was before, he doubted he could just approach the guard and demand an audience with the Guardian Son. He also dreaded asking for help from the Disciples, when there was potential for a different solution.

"Hello, mister," said a small voice, and Wes glanced down to see Clem standing beside him.

"Lovely evening," he said, with a tug on the brim of his hat, and Clem smiled. Even though the rain had moved on, it was anything but a lovely evening. The whole area stank of mud and filth. People trudged through the slop and tracked it wherever they went. Moisture clung to the air, and caused a chill to sink into the bones. Wes let his eyes sweep over the city, while his mind worked over his issue.

"Why are you here?" Clem asked, and leaned against the wall beside him. She was in the same thin dress that left her arms and legs bare, and Wes wondered how she wasn't shivering.

"I am trying to figure out the solution to a puzzle."

"What kind of puzzle?" asked Clem with a tilt of her head.

"I'm trying to get in there." Wes pointed a finger toward the Divine Hall.

"The Elder castle?" Clem asked in her soft voice, and craned her neck to see the spires of the Hall.

"There's someone in there that's precious to me and I need to find him."

"Oh, well that's easy, mister," Clem said with a wave of her hand, and Wes peered down at her curiously.

"What do you mean?"

"I go there all the time," she replied and her voice seemed to change. It grew bolder. "I entertain the guards for tips."

"You entertain the guards," Wes repeated, and raised an eyebrow in confusion.

"I can show you. I owe you a favor anyway, and no one is going to notice me standing in this muck." Clem wrinkled her nose at her muddy bare feet, then pushed off the wall. "Wait here."

She slipped out of sight down a side street, and Wes returned to watching his surroundings. He noticed the residents weren't wearing their best costumes considering all the mud. Most of them were in stiff muted colors that Wes blended into well.

The rain makes us all a little more humble it seems.

"Do you know how to play the fiddle?" Clem asked, suddenly reappearing, and when Wes faced her, his mouth fell open. With all traces of mud removed, Clem stood before him in a pair of trim breeches, mid-length boots, and a flashy green coat cut to the waist. Her straw-colored hair was freshly combed, and pulled back into a bun at the nap of her neck. Atop her head, she placed a small conical cap, and in her hand she held a bow and fiddle. "Well? Do you?"

"What? Oh. No, I don't," Wes admitted after he found his voice.

"Pity," Clem said, looked down at her fiddle, then shrugged. "It's alright. I'll still get you in."

"What are you planning?" Wes asked, as he considered the risk of trusting a girl who was so masterful at deception.

"I'm *planning* to go inside the Elder castle!" Clem declared impatiently, "are you coming or not?" It was like she was a completely different person. Her look, her personality, her voice, all of it changed in an instant. Wes wasn't pleased with his options, but had very few of them.

"I'll come."

With a nod, Clem turned on her heel and led the way through the city square. Instead of approaching the main gate of the Hall, or the mother's gate where he went before, she veered to the left and approached the southern gate.

"This is the guard's entrance," Clem said over her shoulder as she trotted along. Her lithe frame leapt between the worst offenses of the street, and she remained relatively clean. Wes lifted his eyes to take in the full height of the arching gate. Upon it's crest, a bearded man sculpted and green with age, stared accusingly at all who ventured inside. Not wanting to appear out of place, Wes let his gaze fall back to the ground.

"It's right up here," Clem said, her fiddle tucked under her arm. Wes remained close to her, growing hopeful in her confidence, and when they approached the guards stationed at the gates entrance, she lifted her arm in a wave.

"Hello, fellas!" She called in a boisterous voice, no longer the wayward child begging in the street.

"Hey it's Clem!" One of the guards exclaimed, and a wide smile spread over his face, "come to give us a show?"

"No other reason to visit your sorry lot," Clem said with a bit of snark.

"You're a bit early," the other guard remarked, with narrowed eyes. "And who's that fella you have with you?"

"It's too dirty to be out in the streets. I'll get my fiddle all muddy!" Clem said as she lofted the instrument into the air. "Somewhere warm and dry is a better place for me."

"And you thought of us? I'm touched," said the first guard, still smiling, but the other guard remained skeptical.

"Still didn't explain who that fella is behind you."

"Well," Clem said, as she strode closer with all the confidence of a queen, "the last time I came here, you were all so deep in the drink, that some of you lost track of your hands. So I brought along my friend here to keep said hands off my person." Clem smiled fondly up at Wes while the skeptical guard eyed him up and down.

"A bodyguard to guard you from the guard!" The smiling one said with a laugh.

"That's right," Clem replied with a deep bow.

"You got a name, body guard?"

"I didn't pay him to talk," Clem interjected, and Wes obediently closed his mouth.

"Oh, let her in," the smiling guard said, "I want to hear her playing. Our shift is ending soon. We can actually see her show."

"Fine," the older guard said, his eyes on Wes, "no one is stupid enough to try something in the middle of a guard barracks anyway." Clem grinned in victory as she proceeded through the gate. Wes obediently followed behind her, but wondered if that guard had a point. He was closer to Daniel, but still very far away.

They walked a pathway that led directly to an auxiliary building which mirrored the one he fell off of before. The doors were propped open, revealing a well lit common area inside, and as they approached, Clem placed her fiddle on her shoulder and tore into it with her bow. The jig was fast and lively, and faces appeared at the entrance, all of them showing grins. She approached them, and men raced to push tables and chairs out of the way, allowing an open space for Clem as she stepped inside.

"Hello boys!" she called out as she pulled the fiddle away from her chin and broke into a dance. Wes never saw anything like it. She kicked her legs, hopped around, and shuffled her feet all over the floorboards. It was mesmerizing and for a moment, Wes forgot why he was there. He got caught up in the show and clapped alongside the guards as they shouted and cheered for Clem. She made a final leap into the air, put her fiddle to her chin, and broke into another song the moment she landed. The whole room erupted in cheers.

Wes realized that everyone was captivated by the show, and knew he needed to make his exit. Knowing how hard it was to enter through the main doors, he didn't want to return to the yard outside, but he noticed a set of doors that led deeper into the Hall at the opposite end of the room. He made his way toward them, but it was not an easy endeavor. Everyone danced around enjoying the fiddle music, and some coins were tossed at Clem's feet where she stopped long enough to fluidly scoop them into her pocket. Watching her, Wes was distracted and didn't notice a new guard run into the room until he collided with him. The guard staggered, but held his footing while Wes was not so fortunate, and found himself knocked flat on his backside.

"The Elite! The Elite!" The guard cried, and everyone moved at once. They dashed about in a sort of unified chaos as they rushed to hide Clem, hide drinks, and eventually form into two uniform rows. One of the guards stumbled over Wes in his urgency and knocked his hat off of his head. As Wes stretched across the floor to retrieve the thing before it got trampled, the room went abruptly still. Wes replaced his hat, then turned toward the entrance and instantly locked eyes with No-nonsense himself. The massive guard stood at the front of a group of Guard Watch Elite, and glared down at Wes first in surprise, then in recognition. His face softened and a slow wicked smile curled his lips.

"I suppose you won't consider taking me to the Guardian Son," Wes offered, returning the guards smile with one of his own. No-nonsense's fist connected to his eye like a hammer to an anvil. The world vanished behind a brilliant burst of light, and Wes crumpled to the floor. The darkness of oblivion beckoned to him, and wrapped him in unconsciousness like the embrace of an old friend.

Wes looked around, startled by the shift in location, and strained to recognize where he was. The hill was stark and cold; all things once growing had long since died. In the distance, crows danced about a field and seemed to linger over a dark form there, but Wes couldn't determine what it was. Glancing over his shoulder, he saw a small dark house looming on a hill. Its windows were black like eye sockets and its crooked porch stairs resembled teeth.

What was this place? He remembered it from somewhere.

The past is unraveling.

The voice came from within him, but it was not his own. Wes looked around, trying to see what could not be seen. For the voice was that of a woman, but she was not there with him. He was alone.

"Is this the past?" he asked out loud, hoping the woman would answer. The sound of her voice was comforting to him. He waited while the winds howled past his ears and chilled his nose. Then the voice came alive again in his mind.

No, Wesley, this is not the past, but it is of the past. You must remember this place. You must find your way home.

"I don't understand," Wes said miserably. Everything around him seemed so familiar and yet so unfamiliar. His mind felt foggy. All thoughts slipped through his hands like muddy water.

You must remember! I will help you remember!

"I want to remember everything!" Wes agreed, "It's all so jumbled in my head. Why can't I recall this place when it's so familiar to me? And you! I can't remember who you are!"

Soon...you will.

The voice was fading; drifting away.

"When?" Wes asked, and looked around again to try to catch sight of the woman that was speaking through his mind.

When you stand at the edge of the veil and peer through it. Then you will remember all that you have lost.

"Wake up!" The harsh voice was accented with a splash of what Wes hoped to be water on his face. He sat up, sputtering, and looked around. He quickly realized that he was in a prison cell, but it was more of a crude hole cut out of stone with a set of bars blocking its opening. There were no windows; no views of the outside, and Wes was not sure how long he was unconscious or what time of day it was. He wiped at his face with his sleeve, and numbly looked at his hands.

"Wake up, I said!" The voice demanded, and Wes lifted his head to meet the gaze of a giant man looming on the other side of the bars. He was massive, his bare chest covered in scars and muscle, and his arms were coated in sin. He was also bald, his head covered in scales, and his sunken dark eyes glittered under a protruding brow. Wes blinked up at him, his mind still in the thick of a sleepy haze.

"Have you come to take me to my son?" he asked, but the man didn't bother to answer him. He released the secured latch of the barred door, and a section of the bars slid to the side.

"On your feet," he demanded, and Wes numbly complied, though he swayed a little upon standing. His head pounded, and his eye throbbed where he was struck. He adjusted his hat, then peered up at the bald guard who seemed to only know how to scowl. Wes meekly exited his cell into the hallway. It was dim with only a few low burning fireboxes, and he saw how it was also carved out of stone. There was a stale dampness clinging to the air, and everything smelled of rotting hay and filth.

We must be underground.

Wes noted a row of six cells, paired in twos, and all facing one another. The light in the hallway was unable to reach the back of the cells where the deepest shadows lingered, but Wes could sense other people there. When the large guard turned and gestured for Wes to follow, he felt their eyes on him, watching him as he passed. He hoped Daniel was instructing the guard to remove him from this place. He didn't want to stay long in the heart of so much misery.

While they walked, Wes was able to study the bald guard more closely. The length of the man's sin started just above his eyes and cloaked his bald head, stretching all the way down to the rolls of skin at the base of the man's neck. The sin in his hands completely eclipsed his arms in black, and tendrils of the sickness intertwined with the scales on his head, forming strange patterns across his shoulders. His back was covered in scars from a whip, and when he glanced at Wes to ensure he was following him, Wes saw that his nose had been broken more than once. The sin sickness did its part to make him look intimidating, and Wes committed to cooperate. His head hurt too much to be on the receiving end of another giant's ire.

The bald man led him into a room with a solitary table that had two buckets tucked underneath. The windowless walls were thick with mold, and the two fireboxes on the table did little to illuminate the area. The bald man entered the room, and turned to Wes.

"Strip," he demanded, and Wes acquiesced to the command without hesitation. After standing naked in front of the entire Disciple flock, what was one other man? He peeled away his clothing, both old and new, and placed them on the table as the guard indicated for him to do. The last thing he removed was his father's hat which he gently placed on top of the tidy pile. He started to shiver, with no defense from the cold, and noticed the guard examining him. If he was at all impressed by the lack of sin on Wes' body, he gave no indication of it. After a moment, he turned his attention to the pile of clothing where he proceeded to examine each one in turn.

"Any weapons?" he asked, his low voice like a bear's growl. His tongue wasn't black, and Wes had to wonder on the nature of his extensive sin.

"No weapons," he replied, and endured the bald man's scrutiny.

Good thing I gave that knife away, right Ruth?

Wes blinked. Who was Ruth? The moment he tried to recall a face to match the name, his thoughts turned thin and watery. He knew the memory was there, but it just slipped through his hands.

"What's this?" the guard asked; his hand still poised in a jacket pocket. With his dark eyes on Wes, he removed his plump fist and opened it to reveal pieces of a broken wishbone.

Benji.

Wes couldn't remember how those bones got into his pocket, but he was certain Benji was involved. He didn't know why they were so significant to him, but even there, freezing and naked in the middle of a prison, Wes wished he could have those pieces back. The bald man studied him, waiting for an explanation, and Wes gave him a shrug.

"A trinket. For...luck."

The guard frowned at his open hand, then tossed the bones against a wall where they got lost in the darkness. He searched a little further, but there was nothing else to be found.

“Time for a bath,” he announced, and Wes lifted an eyebrow. All efforts of recollection vanished from his mind when the giant picked up one of the buckets and tossed its contents onto him. Wes gasped, for the water was freezing, and wiped it from his eyes. When he brushed against the swollen place high on his cheekbone where No-nonsense struck him, he winced.

The bald man made a circular motion with his finger, indicating Wes needed to turn around. Wes complied, knowing fully what was about to happen, but the second bucket was a shock to his senses all the same. His whole body spasmed with the force of his shivering. He couldn’t stop his teeth from chattering.

“Follow me,” the oaf grumbled, and lumbered out of the room. Wes glared at his back, and conjured dark thoughts of the man with his skull split open after slipping in the water he so callously threw. But Wes followed behind him obediently, while his body shivered, chattered, and ached.

On the way back to Wes’ squat cell, the bald guard paused to collect a bundle of folded cloth off of a low shelf, then continued on without bothering to check if Wes was following him. He thought that Wes was properly cowed, and considering that he was wet, cold, and naked, the guard wasn’t wrong.

This was beyond what he expected. He knew he might be captured the moment he agreed to follow Clem, and understood he might even be imprisoned, but he didn’t expect to endure this. It was a foolish assumption on his part to think they would return him to the room he occupied before.

They approached the end of the hall, and Wes could see the yawning cell door, waiting to welcome him back inside. He knew he had little time left, and had to at least try to find out what Daniel knew.

“Beg your pardon,” Wes said, as he stood in the other man's shadow, “do you know if word of my capture was passed on to the Guardian Son?” The guard acted as though he didn’t hear a word. He ducked low to step inside the cell, and examined the meager offerings for stashed contraband. Wes watched as he inspected the privy bucket, and kicked at the soggy mound of straw; scattering it all over the ground. When he was satisfied that nothing was hidden there, he returned to the hallway and peered down at Wes.

“Get in,” he commanded, and Wes craned his neck to meet the man’s eye.

“Has the Guardian Son been informed of my arrest?” he asked. The words quivered because of his body shivering, but his eyes never wavered. The bald man bent close to Wes, twisted his head to the side, and peeled back his lips to reveal rows of yellow broken teeth.

"Oh sure, mister. Why, the first thing we did after dragging your sorry lot in here was run off and tell the great lord all about the low-life we just bagged. Now get in that cell before I ram my fist into your pretty face."

Wes got into his cell. The bald man shoved the cloth bundle into his hands, and pulled the cell door back into place. It clicked into its lock, and Wes studied the bundle while he listened to the guard's heavy footfalls fading down the hallway. He knew the bundle contained clothing, but his skin was still wet, and with how damp everything felt, he might get sick if he got his clothing wet as well.

Wes set down the bundle, and while he rubbed at his skin, trying to warm himself with the friction, he examined the cell around him. The ceiling sloped down at the back, making it impossible to stand at his full height unless he stood next to the door. Much of the straw was damp and moldy, and provided little comfort if he laid upon it. With few options, he remained by the cell door, and waited through an eternity for his body to dry.

Rubbing his skin, Wes realized how thin he's become. He could feel his ribs, similar to Palto's thin frame, and the sunken abdomen underneath. His hands were still free of all sin, and when a sudden memory bubbled to the surface of his mind, he turned to examine his left bicep where Benji's mother scratched him. The puckered scar was completely gone.

Wes stared at the unbroken skin, puzzled. She *did* scratch him there, didn't she? Yes, he remembered clearly how it festered, and in spite of his efforts, the sin sickness got into his blood. It left a scar and Sassy said the taint would never fully leave his body. He wondered if that was still the case. After the light in the alley, were all the scars of his past erased? Wes pressed his fingers to his eyes. A headache was forming there.

"Is that ye, friend?" A voice called, and Wes lifted his head to peer across the hall. In the cell sitting opposite his own, he could just make out a huddled shape half concealed by shadow. Wes reached for his bundle of clothing, no longer wanting to be so exposed.

"Do I know you?" he asked. The shape moved, elongated, and slowly rose to reveal itself as a man. He stepped forward, stooped and hobbled, and as he came to stand at the bars of his prison, the dim light defined his features enough for Wes to recognize him as Gad. He stared in amazement, for while he was certain the man was Gad, the sin sickness spread significantly since their last meeting. Exactly how long ago did they last meet? Wes tried to recall, but his memory would not allow him to retrace those steps.

"It is ye, friend. I thought it so." Gad's voice sounded strange and distorted.

"Gad? I thought you fled the capital. How did you end up back here?" The scales of sin, once only on half of his face, consumed the whole of it in black. His sunken eyes were also black like twin inky pools, and stared at Wes, vacant of all emotion. His jaw jutted out, and his teeth were jagged like a fish. The rapid transformation was shocking.

"Oh, friend, the Lord was good to ye. Look at yer skin! But sadly, we both have reached our end here. This is where ye wait to be hung." Gad shook his head woefully, as he scratched at the scales on his cheek.

"That's not possible," Wes argued, unwilling to believe Daniel would permit his death. "Enough talk of death, tell me what happened to you. How did you end up here?" Wes unwrapped the bundle of cloth and found that it contained a thin brown blanket made of coarse wool, and a crude burlap set of shirt and tunic with drawstrings at the waist. They had black stripes running their length, and looked dingy and overused. Wes put on the clothing while he listened to Gad explain what happened after they parted ways.

He traveled to the east, and eventually encountered a barracks that he described to be at the end of the world. It sat up on a hill, and with Gad being hungry, weary, and desperate for safety from the night, the place looked like sanctuary. Upon entering, he was greeted and taken to the central magistrate. He begged for kindness before their tribunal, and was given a warm bed, two meals a day, and a minor scrap of income in exchange for hard labor on a retention wall.

Gad agreed without hesitation, was shown to his bunk, and offered a meal. That same night, they discovered him in the magistrate office, trying to pry open the money box stored there. He saw it the moment he was brought before them, and knew he needed to have whatever it contained. He was promptly arrested, and when a previous warrant was discovered for theft from the Guardian Son's garden, Gad was brought back to the capital to be hung.

"I thought you were stealing to feed yourself. That you only did it out of need," Wes remarked as he spread out the thin blanket and sat upon the floor.

"Precisely, friend! I *needed* that money to feed myself. I was only stealing out of need."

"But they offered to feed you and give you a place to sleep. You had what you needed. I don't see the justification."

"God sees!" Gad declared while pointing a gnarled finger toward the sky. His unblinking eyes lent to his fish-like face. "God understands my need."

"I reckon it's plain on your face what the Lord thinks of your need," Wes said, disapproving.

"Well enough about me then," Gad said, flicking a dismissive hand. "I want to talk about ye, friend. Tell me why ye were asking that big fella about the Guardian Son."

"That's no business of yours," Wes said, narrowing his eyes.

"Here's how I see it," Gad went on, as he grabbed hold of the bars to his cage. He wore the same burlap outfit as Wes. "Ye were comin' here to locate a boy. A boy with a scar like this," he turned and ran a thumb down the side of his face. Wes remained silent, and frowned.

"Now, here we are, and ye were askin'for yer son. Now yer askin' for that Guardian Son lad to be told of yer...de-tain-ment." Gad savored the word like an exotic dish. "So what I thinks is that ye might know this Guardian Son a little more than ye be wanting to tell ol' Gad. I'm thinkin' that ye might be old Gad's ticket out of here."

Again Wes did not respond, for he refused to lie, but didn't want to tell the truth either. His silence was confirmation enough to Gad, and he pressed his leering face between the bars of his cell as far as it would go. He grinned at Wes with his jagged gray fish teeth.

"I reckon this boy might be yer son. And surely a son won't hang his own father, right friend?" Gad pushed his face farther through the bars so that his eerie black skin stretched against his skull in a grotesque way. It split open in some places; the dark bile oozing slowly down his cheeks.

"You're mad!" Wes declared, and stepped back to distance himself from the man.

"They plan to hang me, friend," Gad said, his voice a high-pitched whisper, "Right out there in front of everyone, they plan to see me swing." His voice dropped into a low growl. "Surely ye will be spared from such a fate, will ye not ask for mercy for old Gad as well?"

"You think I can work miracles," Wes scoffed, and silently wondered if he had any of the sway Gad thought he did. It was demeaning to be stripped and dowsed in freezing water.

"Talk to yer son for me. Tell him I'm a man of the Word. Ye will help me, won't ye, friend? I will pray for ye. For ye and for he. Just get me out of this mess, will ye?" The more Gad spoke, the stranger his voice became. His lifeless eyes grew wide, and he licked his trembling lips, as he quivered in his need. The sin sickness was at work in his mind.

Wes shifted his thin blanket, finding a smoother place on the stone wall to lean against, then settled in for a very long wait. He missed his hat, and the comfort it gave him when he laid it over his eyes. He wrapped his arms around his body in an effort to stay warm, and turned away from Gad. The other man eventually extracted himself from his prison bars, but continued to plead for his rescue. He sank down to the floor, leaning against the bars, and his voice, with its peaks and valleys, rambled on into the darkness.

"I'm a Godly man."

"I'll share my moneybox with ye. Plenty for us to split."

"I'm strong in the belief; diligent in the prayer."

“If the Guardian Son knew, he would spare Gad from the rope.”

“Please, friend, speak on Gad’s behalf, will ye?”

Wes closed his eyes, and thought on the name Ruth. Why did he think of that name? He strained to figure out who she was, but nothing came to his mind. Behind him, Gad laughed. It was a dry raspy sound that shifted into sobbing.

Wes did his best to ignore it, but he suddenly felt terribly alone. He had to believe Daniel wouldn’t leave him in such a horrible place, which meant he didn’t know that Wes was there. Did he think Wes abandoned him? And if he did, was it at all a surprise? Allowing himself to acknowledge his own despair, Wes drew his legs to his chest, and wrapped his arms around them. He rested his head on his knees; an unpleasant pillow.

“Do ye hear me, friend?” Gad asked, his sanity temporarily restored. The question went unanswered, and he eventually gave up and slunk back into the shadows of his cell. He laid down on the straw, and whispered to himself softly. The sounds did not form words, but were impossible to ignore all the same. Wes could close his eyes but not his ears. There was nowhere to escape.

I wonder if Benji is warm. I wonder if the Disciples are keeping him safe.

Wes didn’t think he would find sleep in that cold cell, and was surprised to be sitting on the same hill that overlooked a barren field. If he could just lift the fog in his mind, these familiar places might become clear to him again.

You will remember. You must remember.

That same voice of a woman in his mind. Wes looked around, intending to seek its source, but instead he saw a boy standing behind him, further up the hill. When Wes spotted him, he shifted in a way that looked like he might run, but hesitantly the boy held ground instead. He lifted his chin in an effort to solidify his confidence, and met Wes’ eyes with his own.

“Benji?” Wes asked, for the boy looked much older than the lad Wes knew, but the eyes were the same and the way he looked at Wes hadn’t changed.

“Are you really here?” Wes asked as he pushed himself up and got to his feet. “Or are you a part of my dream?” Benji shook his head as he laughed to himself, then offered Wes a sheepish smile. Wes approached him, cautious in his confusion, but the smile fell away as Benji abruptly jerked his head skyward. A look of fear entered his eyes, and all at once the world around them twisted; melted; bled away as Wes felt himself being pulled by a great force that dragged him into a new reality. He took in his surroundings, and vaguely recognized the small cabin with its low burning fire.

"What have you done!" A voice shouted, and Wes turned to see a young dark-skinned girl glaring at him from across the room. A name manifested in his mind. Eve.

"I.." Wes began, confused, but Eve spoke over him; past him.

"Answer me! What do you have to say for yourself?" Her anger was an inferno that burned deep within her eyes, and Wes turned to see Benji, much smaller than before, lingering near the cabin door. Guilt hung over him like a cloud, and his eyes remained fixated on the floor.

"I know your thoughts," Eve said, her anger softening a little, "I hear your words. But he walks on God's path, not yours. If he forgets you, then it is the Lord's will that he should. This does not give you the right to ignore the rules of what is forbidden!"

"I'm not going to forget you, Benji," Wes assured the lad, but Benji just shook his head. Eve concentrated on Wes and spoke to him for the first time.

"Madness has its claim on you, brother." Her voice was harsh and unyielding. "A parasite possessing its host. I pray you find the light on the other end of this forest, but it's God that sees your path clearly, not I."

"I'm not mad," Wes argued but Eve was unconvinced. Her eyes didn't look upon his, but instead into them and past them; peering upon his very soul.

"Don't come back here, for you will poison this well, brother. You have madness as your bedfellow. I ask God to harden your heart, and blind you from the spirits that haunt your dreams. Benji can't stop breaking the rules because he wants to see you. Well I am telling you now, brother, this is the last time you'll be dreaming of him. Your dreams are not your own anymore."

"Wuh!" Benji cried out, his voice a mix of urgency and despair, but when Wes turned to look at him, Eve lunged forward and drove her shoulder into his stomach.

Wes gasped as he was startled awake, and took in his surroundings. His mind spun, disoriented from the lack of sky, but the pain and stiffness of enduring the cold was enough to solidify reality. The chill sank into his bones, and everything ached.

Gad mumbled in his sleep, calling out to the phantoms of his dreams, and Wes froze until he was sure the other man wasn't going to wake. He eased back against the stone wall, and tried to remember what he was dreaming about since it caused him to wake so abruptly. He recalled thoughts of madness, but it all seemed so insignificant when compared to the overpowering feeling that he just lost something precious to him. Mumbling under his breath, Wes sifted through his thoughts, and probed at all the holes that were left behind.

Chapter Twenty-Eight

I searched everywhere, determined to find wisdom
and to understand the reason of things.
I was determined to prove myself
that wickedness is stupid
and that foolishness is madness.
-Ecclesiastes 7:25 NLT

Time passed.

Time passed.

Time passed.

All the while, Gad never stopped talking.

Wes jerked awake, and laid on the straw in the dark, as his mind corkscrewed around the concept of reality. Again he dreamed something that caused him to wake up in a panic.

His heart thrummed in his ears,

his body was covered in a thin slime of oily sweat,

his breathing was shallow and rapid,

but his mind was empty.

He felt both indifferent and desperate, and lacked any understanding as to why.

Over time, he avoided sleep entirely.

Wes wished he had two blankets. With the option of only one, he used it as a barrier between himself and Gad instead of its intended purpose.

It was a scrap of privacy to hide behind.

It was unable to stop Gad from speaking.

Gad begged Wes to talk to his son, and ask to let them both go free.

Gad suggested Wes help him escape, by finding a way to kill the guard.

Gad threatened Wes' son, saying he would kill the boy if Wes didn't help him.

Gad suspected Wes was involved in the barracks knowing of his warrant to the capital.

Gad believed Wes was the reason he was arrested there.

Gad accused Wes of bringing him back to the capital because he wanted Gad to be hung.

Gad believed Wes was the one who stole from the Father's garden in the first place.

Gad knew Wes was a demon, he had no doubt.

Gad never stopped talking.

Time no longer mattered. Wes stayed awake as much as he could, but when he slept he could not tell if it was for a moment or for days. Bowls of oats mixed with water were served at intervals that seemed random to him. A small cup of water served with it. Wes shoveled it all into his greedy mouth with eager fingers. He felt like an animal because he was one. He felt like a demon because he was one. Gad said so. Gad who knows everything, and speaks everything all the time.

"I know the source of sin," Gad whispered from behind the blanket, "it's in the eyes. My eyes see the truth even when I don't want them to."

Wes whispered to his wicked eyes, while Gad wept harshly.

Wes could no longer remember what he looked like, but he remembered what Gad looked like. The brief glimpses that he caught of the other man showed how deformed he's become. His gray lips sagged and drooled as he roamed about his cell. His clothing split apart in places where his body twisted or bulged. He dragged himself around like a half discarded husk, while he whispered and cried in twin voices that made Wes shiver. Wes curled into a ball behind the protection of his blanket, and trembled through the depths of his fear.

"If thy right eye offends thee..." Wes opened his eyes. Words floated in the darkness. The sound of shale scraping under foot. He reached. Fingers trembled. Brushed the length of cloth in front of his face. His blanket. His protection.

"If thy right eye offends thee..." His stomach hurt. His head hurt. His teeth hurt. His thoughts hurt. His memories hurt. His dreams hurt. His eyes hurt.

"If thy right eye offends thee..." How long has it been? How much longer will it be? Why was he there? How did he get there? This was all he knew. All he has ever known. Everything else was a dream. A fantasy. A mirage. Something he wished he could have. Something he wished he never had to see again.

"If thy right eye offends thee..."

"Pluck it out," Wes whispered, and closed his eyes.

The sound of boots. Wes opened his eyes. His face pressed to the cold stone floor. He reached, searching for a bowl. A cup. A way to ease the pain in his stomach for another day.

"Here he is."

"You're joking."

"I never joke. There's another one over here."

Someone yanked the blanket away from his prison bars. Light from the hall stung his eyes. He scuttled back into the shadows of his cell.

"You don't have anyone else?"

"Only this one over here, and you don't want to parade him in front of the Elders."

"Wait... bring up the light. I want a better look at them."

The light grew brighter, and Wes recoiled. No longer able to hide in the shadows, he squinted as he staggered to his feet. He had to stoop, with how low the roof of his cell was, but this was something his body had grown accustomed to.

"By the Elders, look at him!"

"Aye, I didn't know he was this bad. It's a wonder he's got any sense left in him."

"How do you know he's not mad?"

"He's not trying to attack us. Those black eyes are considering. Calculating."

"Prisoner! My name is Captain Ashter. I'm here with a proposition."

Wes shuffled closer to the bars as his eyes adjusted to the light. In the hallway he identified the bald guard who occasionally brought him food, but the other man was a new face to him.

"Captain Ashter," Wes repeated, sounding out the words. The lanky tall man turned from Gad, and looked him over with sharp hawkish eyes.

"Ah, that's better. Here I thought you were already lost to the madness."

"I can't guarantee that I'm not," Wes admitted, "But the mind bends long before it breaks." It was strange to hear his own voice after so long. It sounded funny to his ears, and he wheezed out an arid laugh. He scratched absently at his coarse beard.

"So you claim to be of sound mind, more or less," replied the captain, contemplating. "Yet I see scratches alongside your right eye. Scratches that appear to be self-inflicted."

"A failed attempt to remedy a problem," Wes said with a shrug. The result of darker days when he couldn't escape his mind. Ashter studied Wes for a long time, then he smiled.

"You fascinate me, prisoner" he said with a tilt of his head, then focused his attention across the aisle to Gad who was tucked back against the wall, "and I think I have an idea. One that would provide both of you with a chance at freedom. I wish to have you fight one another in front of the High Counsel. A means to entertain them during their celebration day."

"What are they celebrating?" Wes asked, his tongue clumsy with the words. Ashter glanced over at him. His smile looked sincere.

"Old Father. His day of birth is a few days away. We originally planned on a hanging to honor him, but watching a fight would be so much better."

"No hanging?" The gravelly voice drew all of their attention. Slowly, the shape in the other cell uncoiled, and crawled toward the bars. Wes was used to Gad's appearance, but Ashter gasped, flinching away from the cell with his hand over his mouth.

"I will do whatever ye ask," Gad said with a horrifying smile; his voice like tumbling rocks, "for a chance to be free."

"And what of you," Ashter asked into his hand as he glanced over to Wes. "Do you wish to be free as well?"

"I wish for nothing," Wes replied, and said no more.

I wish for nothing I think of nothing I hope for nothing I am nothing.

"Get them both cleaned up," Ashter ordered, turning and striding up the hallway. The bald guard followed behind him obediently. "Leave the monster here until I can find him suitable accommodations, but take the other into the old prison area. Find him clothing. Only the best! And get our tailors to work on the beastly one. Weapons! Gather different kinds. The High Counsel won't have a simple hanging. This is going to be a major event!"

Wes glanced over to the boy in guard attire, but the child kept his head turned away. He was clearly disgusted by Wes, and while a small part of his mind was shamed by this, Wes couldn't stop himself. The table was covered in platters of food, and Wes wanted all of it in his stomach. He ate with a frenzy that he could not control. He got sick once already, vomiting everything he took in all over the floor, but returned to the food with the same manic focus. He didn't know what the food was nor did he even taste it. He just needed to eat it.

Eat it.

Eat it.

Eat it all.

Wes grabbed the pitcher full of water, and tipped it over his gaping maw. No need for a cup. No need to pause long enough to chew. Wes fought against his bodies desire to stop. He needed to eat. He must eat all of it. For he didn't know when he would be fed again.

"I was told to wash him."

"He isn't finished...eating."

"Is that what he's doing?"

"Like a ravenous dog."

"He's filthy! How am I supposed to clean all that?"

"Captain said he's got to look like one of the Elite."

"How long was he locked up to get like this?"

"Over two weeks. Spent the whole time next to the fish."

"Two weeks," Wes repeated, and the two boys jumped as they turned to face him. Wes took in their plain black uniforms and downy cheeks. Then he looked at his hands, filthy and covered in food, and the carnage on the table he ate from. He fought to not sick up again.

Two weeks.

What has he become in that time?

Inside his mind, a quivering tangle of threads pulsed and threatened to overtake all logical thought. It was a powerful force, stained black with the taint of madness, but Wes found in him the strength to keep it contained.

"What are your names?" he asked of his guards, and both boys glanced at each other nervously.

"I'm Patrick," said the first one, "but everyone calls me Pip. This is Kenner. He's the Elder's wash boy."

"They called for the best because of you being in such a state, prisoner," Kenner said proudly. "Said they never saw anyone as filthy as you. But I'll get you clean."

"Then I reckon it's time we get started," Wes said, and as he watched the boy get to work, he probed the bundle of black string in his mind. It swelled for a moment, and he pushed it back into place. He wondered if it would always be with him. A clump of madness to fill in all the holes in his head.

Wes never took a bath before. The large copper tub, filled with water warmed over a small stove, eased a little of the ache in his bones. He stretched his back, and tried not to slouch. The ceiling was no longer pressing down upon him.

The pit is comfort.

The pit is where I belong.

"What is this place?" Wes asked Kenner as he looked around the room. It was a bathhouse adjoined to the mess hall he was just in, and both led into a larger hallway full of prison cells. There had to be two dozen or more empty cells.

"This is the old prison. We used to house criminals here, but have no use for it now that everyone arrested is found guilty, and all the guilty are eventually hung."

"That doesn't explain why everyone was moved to...that other place."

The dark place.

Kenner picked up soap and cloth, and took to scrubbing the grime from Wes' neck.

"Old Father. He...well you see, prisoner, the other cells down in the pit; the ones you and the fish were in...people say that they push the sickness along. Makes monsters out of people. Old Father liked to hang them after they changed 'cause it took longer for them to die. Old Father...he likes..."

"I don't want to hear anymore," Wes said, disgusted. The bundle of knots and string pulsed in his mind. A result of Old Father's entertainment choices. Wes didn't know the man but loathed him still.

"Things seem to be coming along," a voice announced, and Kenner jumped to his feet. Wes smiled up at Captain Ashter who stood with Pip a step behind.

"Being clean does a lot for a man's constitution."

I wear sanity as a disguise.

"It's a wonder you came out of the pit looking as you do, prisoner. Not a scrap of black on you. Remarkable." Wes lifted his hand out of the water, and examined the shriveled tips of his fingers; untouched by sin. Kenner, standing at attention beside him, had black scales up to his wrists and along the tips of his ears. Was this boy more wicked than him?

"Is this why you've come?" Wes asked with an arched eyebrow. In truth, he wanted to shift the subject away from things he didn't understand.

"I came to let you know that the banquet will be held three days from now. Considering the rarity of the event, I received a permit to grant access for the entire capital to attend. For the first time since Old Father's passing, we will open all three gates to the city. Everyone will want to come watch you fight against your friend. You'll be famous, prisoner!"

"I'll be dead," Wes muttered, for he was under no illusion that he stood a chance against a monster of the night.

"I'm not so sure," Ashter countered with a quizzical expression. "You seem to look at the world as I do: with a cunning eye and a calculating mind. That will take you far against one as thoughtless and irrational as the fish. But you can't rely on your wits alone. Come over to this mirror, prisoner, I want you to see something."

"I'm not going to stand here exposed in front of the boys," Wes said, grimly determined.

"Why not?" Ashter asked with an incredulous laugh, "Kenner bathes the Elders every day, and Pip shares a bunk in the barracks. They have seen the flesh of men before."

"I understand your ways may not be akin to my own," Wes replied coolly, "But that does little to change the way I feel, and no boy should be forced to observe the full nature of a man's sin."

"Sin," Ashter replied dreamily. His eyes distant as he considered the word. "I remember a time when such things mattered here." Then he shook his head, and let out an uneasy laugh. He turned his hawkish eyes upon Kenner and Pip, and gestured them toward the hall.

"Out with you then," he commanded and the boys cast a mistrustful glance towards Wes before dashing out of the room.

"What an odd thing to see," Ashter said as he sat on the edge of Wes' tub. "You've only just met, and already you play the roles of the protective father and the unruly sons."

"Father," Wes scoffed and pondered the word.

Am I a father?

Am I anything at all?

"Back to the task at hand," Ashter said, and got to his feet. "Come over here, prisoner, look into this mirror." He strode across the room to where a full length mirror leaned in its floor stand.

"I have a name," Wes said as he climbed out of the tub, dripping from head to toe.

"Not to me, you don't. You are 'prisoner' and will remain 'prisoner' until you face judgment." Ashter's words weren't harsh. He was just stating fact. Wes eyed him with apprehension, and strode over to stand before his own reflection.

"What do you see?" Ashter asked and Wes examined the man who he no longer knew. A man with a thin frail body, overgrown beard, and haunted wet eyes. His face held an expression like he was just alarmed by something, except the look never seemed to go away. He was always alarmed; always on the cusp of being terrified.

"I see a husk," Wes said, and his reflection's lips moved in unison.

"I see someone who is weak," Ashter said at his shoulder, "and needs to be strong."

"I'm weak," Wes agreed, nodding.

"Not in spirit," Ashter argued, then left Wes to stride silently to the other end of the room. "Just in body. But you can change that! You have three days to get stronger." He snatched up a large towel draped by the stove and returned to embrace Wes in it. "You have been broken down, but the bits and pieces are all still there. Build them up again. Fortify the foundation. Face the fish head on."

"That sounds very heroic," Wes said, wrapping the towel around his shoulders. He peered at Ashter through the mirror's reflection. "Do you see that person in me?"

“I want to believe I do,” Ashter replied, and Wes marveled on how this was the man who led the very people that locked him away in darkness in the first place. He should hate Ashter. He should hate Pip and Kenner. They all knew the nature of what that place did to a man's mind, and left him there for two weeks anyway.

“Is there anything I can get for you to help you in your recovery?” Ashter asked, and Wes saw in his eyes a ransom's worth of guilt for his part in Wes' ruin.

“I reckon there is,” he replied, for in his mind there was a memory of something held precious to him. “If you're able, there's something I'd like for you to find.”

There are no enemies in this place, only actions and consequences.

Over the next three days, Wes focused on getting stronger. Ashter was right in saying he had grown weak. His skin hung loose in places where muscle atrophied. His endurance was that of a toddler learning to crawl. His lungs wheezed from the weeks of dampness, and often he started his morning in a fit of coughing. The tangle in his mind pulsed and pressed against him, but Wes grew familiar with the constant struggle to keep his madness contained.

He woke at twilight, for this was when his guard was with him. They consisted of all children which made evident how little of a threat he posed, and aside from keeping the barred gate that led to the outside world secure, Wes had free reign of the entire prison. They knew he wouldn't escape. He had nowhere to go. No destination. No home.

A small window, high on his prison cell wall, did not allot him a glimpse of the outside world, but he could at least see sunlight and judge the passing of time. He often laid on his cot and watched the sun stretch her rays at different angles along the ceiling while he probed the holes in his mind. Every evening he woke up in a panic, not understanding why.

Kenner washed Wes, cut his hair, and trimmed his beard. He and Pip spent a lot of time with Wes, and took to telling him about all their hopes and all their dreams. Wes listened, attentive to every word, but had nothing to give in return. He had no hopes. He could not remember his dreams.

His mind was adrift on the black waves of vacancy.

Wes looked in the mirror as he buttoned his coat. He was given a uniform of the lower guard, but Wes refused their round hat with its lowly bent brim. He turned down the tops of the uniform's black boots so that they only went above the ankle, and the trim pants bunched against their tops, instead of getting tucked inside. His black jacket was altered by the guard tailor to fit him perfectly, and Wes requested they change the high neck collar to a slim peak lapel. He vaguely recalled owning a jacket cut like that before. His reflection looked incredibly thin, but Wes was stronger, and felt alive in his own presence. The only thing missing was a relic covered in cobwebs that still lingered in the corner of his mind.

"Well, look at you," Ashter said when he appeared at the bathhouse entrance. The man walked without sound, like a cat.

"It's been a while," Wes said, a wry smile not quite reaching his eyes. He knew how haunted he still looked, but he hoped the smile softened the stare.

"I've been working nonstop transforming the front of the Hall into a vast arena. But I think we will have it ready in time for the trial tomorrow."

"Trial?" Wes asked, turning from the mirror.

"Well, let's not forget you were imprisoned for a reason," Ashter laughed. "But the trial is more a performance for the crowd. Try to imagine it: 'the hero and the fish!' That's how we are going to approach it, but worried the public might not relate to a man with no sin on his body. If we convict you as a criminal, they will cheer you on as one of them! You'll be talked about for years to come!"

"I could just cover my hands," Wes argued, for he didn't like the idea of being a hero to the city. "Wear gloves and maybe a hat."

"You most *certainly* will wear gloves and a hat!" Ashter replied with mock indignation. "You won't look nearly so dashing without them! But we also want to take all precautions. If the crowd thinks you're flawless and innocent, they will start to compare you to the great lord himself. Or worse, they'll start spouting about prophecies and Keepers and Bringers and Light. I thank the Elders that the Disciples wanted nothing to do with our event, and refused to attend."

"It all sounds very complicated," Wes said and Ashter rolled his eyes.

"So you say, and so it is! But enough of all that, I came to give you a gift."

"Did you find it?" Wes asked, as a small smile curved the corners of his mouth. Ashter gestured toward the door, and Pip ran over carrying a parcel. He presented it to his captain, and Ashter lifted the box out of his hands.

"You look amazing, mister," Pip said to Wes while Ashter was distracted. "like a real hero."

"Thank you, lad," Wes replied and his smile grew, for Pip was a good boy, and had big dreams.

"You may go now," Ashter said, and Pip gave him a quick salute. He smiled at Wes, then retreated out of the room.

"It took years to train that boy," Ashter sighed as he peeled back the box's flaps, "and you undo all of it in a few days."

"Where did you find it?" Wes asked as Ashter pulled out his gambler's hat.

"Some fool Disciple was worshiping it of all things," Ashter said with a cocky laugh. "He was quite sad to give it up."

Wes examined the hat, and noticed it was well cared for. It looked freshly cleaned and brushed, no longer resembling the battered relic of his memory, but Wes had no doubt that it was his hat. The hat that once belonged to his father. His last ties to his past.

"Thank you," he whispered as he lifted the hat, and placed it just-so on his head. A tranquility fell over him the moment it settled into place, and Wes let out a long sigh. He closed his eyes, and offered up a prayer.

Lord, thank you for this day. Thank you for this gift. Thank you for this memory.

"Are you alright?" Ashter asked, and Wes opened his eyes.

"I'm just praying."

"To the Guardian Son?" Ashter asked, surprised, "I didn't peg you for a Disciple." His dark hawkish eyes were bright with curiosity.

"To God. The one true God. For if I survive this fight it will be by his mercy, and not my own strength."

"God?" Ashter asked, his eyes wide with incredulity. "Who *are* you?"

Who am I?

Who am I?

Who am I?

It's time, Wesley. It's time for us to say goodbye.

Wes cried out when he woke, and Kenner fled from his prison cell. A moment later, he poked his head around the corner and watched from a distance. It took Wes a moment to get his breathing under control. His heart thrummed in his ears and his body was clammy with sweat in spite of the cool air.

"You were watching me sleep," he managed to say after regaining some control.

"I was just guarding you," Kenner said from the entrance.

"Don't lie, boy. You risk a blackened tongue for foolish reasons."

"I...was sent to get you dressed. The captain will be coming soon to take you to your trial."

"I see," Wes said. The small window showed enough of the sky for him to know it was twilight.

"I didn't want to tell you," Kenner said as he wrestled to conceal his sadness. "I don't want you to go."

"Come in here," Wes said, and Kenner did as he was told. He was dressed in his guard uniform, and Wes noted the tops of his boots were folded over at the ankle. He slumped onto the old prison cot next to Wes. "I want you to do something, and I reckon you better let Pip know as well."

Kenner looked up at him, blinking his large moon-sized eyes, and Wes smiled gently. It was a familiar gesture.

"When I go out there, I don't know what will happen to me. I will fight the hardest I can, for you and for Pip..."

"And for Captain Ashter?"

"And for Captain Ashter," Wes agreed. As if on cue, the captain appeared at the entrance to the cell. He took in the scene, then his eyes met Wes', and he slipped back out of sight. It would embarrass Kenner for his captain to see him being so vulnerable with a prisoner he was supposed to tend to, and guard.

"I reckon I'll be out there fighting my hardest for all of you. But my hardest might not be enough." The light faded from Kenner's eyes, and Wes pushed on in a rush. "I want you to promise me that you won't watch the fight. Pip as well. Play that hopping game you two invented, or one of the many other games you know, but don't watch me fight the fish."

"But...why?" Kenner whined, his eyes large and wet and showing his hurt. "Pip and I were gonna cheer for you!"

"Listen to me lad. The monster you know as the fish, is a man I know as Gad. I spent two weeks with him, and in that time, he blamed all of his hardships on me. Given the chance, I have no doubt he will tear me apart. If he's successful, the last thing I want as I lay dying, is to see you two boys watching. I will try my best to do what needs to be done. But please do this for me. Just in case my best is not enough in the eyes of God."

"Kenner? Are you in there?" Ashter called out from down the hall, and Kenner quickly got to his feet while he scrubbed at his eyes.

"I-I'm here. I'm helping the prisoner prepare."

Ashter appeared at the entrance a moment later, and examined Kenner like a hawk watching a rabbit graze.

"I'm dragging my feet a little," Wes said in defense of Kenner's delay. It was also the truth.

"Go on, lad," Ashter said, dismissing Kenner with a wave. "I'll help him with his dressing."

Kenner looked to his captain, then to Wes, and quickly gave them both a salute.

"I'll do what you asked, mister! I promise!"

"Kenner..." Ashter warned but the boy was already running out of the cell. Ashter watched him go, then shook his head sadly. "Two perfectly capable guards ruined by one kindhearted convict."

"Children shouldn't ever be capable guards," Wes grumbled.

"Oh? Better for them to work in the mines?" Ashter asked, a sharp edge of challenge entering his eyes, "better as fodder for Elder fancy?" Wes saw in the man an energy that explained his position as captain. He felt the ranking was warranted.

"I'm sorry," he conceded, and Ashter sighed. The words tamping his fury.

"What's done is done, and they are a problem for another day. You're our guest of honor tonight! We need to make sure you look your best. Come, prisoner! We shall get you dressed."

"Why offer to dress me? I'm capable enough to do it myself," Wes argued. He stripped off his night shirt, then strode over to a small basin in the corner where he could wash the sweat from his skin.

"Don't you think I know that already?" Ashter asked, his voice playful and yet careful at the same time, "which would lend to the true question you have yet to ask me."

Wes looked over his shoulder, and scrutinized Ashter curiously. "Why are you really here?"

"That's the right question!" Ashter declared, and moved to stand directly in front of Wes. With the two of them clustered into the corner of the cell, Wes felt the sting of panic for he was no longer comfortable with small enclosed places. It reminded him of the pit; the ball of tangles and string rippled in his mind. Ashter's lips curled into a smile. "Why am I really here?"

Wes had to lift his chin to glare at Ashter, for while the man was only a few inches taller, it was evident when they stood so close to one another. Wes wanted to back away. He wanted to sidestep around Ashter and feel the ease of the more open space. Instead, he grabbed hold of his madness, squeezed it down into acute focus, and leaned towards the other man.

"It may come as a disappointment to you," he said softly, his eyes cold and in control, "but I am not of the disposition to desire another man."

Ashter's composure shattered. He broke into fits of laughter, and stumbled backwards. With his eyes squeezed shut, he tripped over the edge of the cot, cartwheeled through the air, and sprawled onto the floor. This in turn caused Wes to laugh as well. He laughed so hard he fought to breathe. In his mind, a young girl's laughing face flashed into his forethought then vanished a moment later. It sobered him enough that he was able to catch his breath.

"I've grown quite fond of you, prisoner," Ashter declared as he wiped a tear from his eye, "Under different circumstances, I'd like to think you and I would have been good friends."

"I like to think we are friends all the same," Wes replied as he turned his attention to putting on his hero's uniform.

"I would like that as well," Ashter said, as he got to his feet. "But I don't even know your name."

"I thought you said I would always be 'prisoner' until I faced judgment," Wes said, with feigned innocence, and Ashter frowned.

"If you expect me to beg, I'd rather ram a fist in your ribs," he grumbled. Wes just laughed.

"My name is Wesley," he said, meeting Ashter's eye, "but I prefer Wes."

"Wes," Ashter repeated, then smiled. "I never heard that name before, but I like it. Well, you asked why I'm really here, and now I'll tell you. For I know you put faith in your God, but I put my faith in the double-cross. Listen to me closely, dear friend. I have found a way to give you a fighting chance."

Chapter Twenty-Nine

And you, son of man, will you judge,
will you judge the bloody city?
Then declare to her all her abominations.
-Ezekiel 22:2 ESV

Ashter brought Wes out of the confines of his prison, and delivered him into the hands of two Guard Watch Elite. They were strangers to him, but judging by their grim expressions, Wes was no mystery to them.

"I am needed elsewhere, but these are capable men. Follow their direction and they will get you to the steps of the Hall unseen."

"Is that where you will be?" Wes asked, and Ashter smiled.

"That's where I will be." He gave a nod to his two men, then vanished into the world that lived beyond Wes' sight. The two guards approached Wes, eyeing him up and down.

"Looks like we're moving the captain's fancy man," said the larger of the two.

"A fancy man that only needs to be guarded by the gentle hands of little boys," said the other guard and they both grinned at Wes. He smiled back at them.

"When I was in the pit, with the fish and the madness as friends, I tried to dig out my own eyes. Compared to that torment, your words matter not." The guards found little joy in teasing him after that.

They bound his hands, and holding him between them, guided him to a narrow stairwell. Wes looked up as they approached the stairs, and saw a set of doors propped open at the top. Beyond that entrance, he had a glorious view of the night sky. He couldn't help but stare as he was led along, for the sky was beautifully clear, with millions of stars decorating the canopy. If anyone ever doubted the existence of God, they merely needed to look up.

As Wes was drawn upward, ascending the stairs into the world beyond, and he felt as though he were being reborn. Reality surrounded him with bitter sensation. The cool air stung at his eyes and burned his lungs. Smells overwhelmed him, and his body shivered from the abrupt temperature shift. Wes savored every sensation while the madness in his mind quivered and twitched. Every experience calcified his existence.

But when his eyes swept his surroundings, his smile faded. The yard of the Divine Hall, an area that appeared to be in the back of the vast building, was sequestered by dozens of guards. In the middle of their perimeter, and directly in front of where Wes stood, was a strange decorated box. It had broad wooden polls strapped to its sides, and a small door that stood open like a yawning maw. Wes jerked his arms, trying to break free from the guards grasp, but their conviction was firm.

"What is this?" he asked as his eyes danced over the surface of the vessel. It was about the size of the cell he once thought was his home. The dark place. Dark like the opening to his tomb.

"It's a palanquin," one of the guards said in his ear.

"It's how we're going to get you to your trial without attracting public attention."

Wes laughed as spider legs of madness skittered in his mind. The guards exchanged worried expressions, and guided him forward.

"No!" Wes gasped.

No.

Keep it together.

Keep it together.

"I'm trying," he whined as he twisted against his restraint. Some of the other guards approached; their well practiced eyes seeing potential for trouble. Wes hardly noticed them, with the menacing box, painted dark like an ugly coffin, growing closer with each passing moment. He could almost feel it reaching for him, ready to drag him back underground.

"Don't put me in there!" he cried out, panting through his rising panic, when suddenly his madness broke free. Wes screamed, and thrashed against the men holding him. His actions provoked the guards' reactions, and they grabbed hold of him; the iron grip of authority pulling at his arms and body and legs. He was hoisted off of the ground, squealing like a pig tied to the spit, and madness battered his mind with razor threads. Rational thought evaded comprehension.

"Gag him before he attracts the whole city!"

"What's wrong with him?"

"I don't know, we were trying to put him in the palanquin and he panicked."

"He's crazy! He's as crazy as the fish!"

It's the pit! It's the pit! I'm going back into the hole. Into the dark place. Into the cold. Into the wet. Gad will speak again and never stop. NEVER STOP! The nightmare made real all over again! Again! Again!

"Again!" Wes screamed, and a cloth was shoved in place to silence him. He was tossed, squirming and writhing, into the greedy mouth of the wicked box, and it swallowed him down into its stomach. He screamed into his gag until tears clouded his eyes. He knew it did little good, but he didn't care.

"Let me talk to him."

"He's crazy!"

"I know, I know. Let me try to calm him down."

"You're a fool if you think you'll reach him."

"And you're a fool if you think you can transport him when he's thrashing around like that."

The door opened. Wes caught a glimpse of the open sky. He lunged his body forward, desperate to get out, but hands grabbed his shoulders and placed him firmly onto a seat.

Thrash! Thrash! Thrash!

"Stop it! STOP!"

Wes tried to stand again but an arm like a rod of iron slammed into his chest and pinned him against the side of the coffin. He groaned. He cried out. He laughed.

"Open your eyes! *Look* at me! Open your eyes, old man!"

Wes' eyes opened wide with terror. Madness tore at his mind. Madness made his body tremble.

"Mister Wes! Pull yourself together! Here..." The sound of something sliding, and a window appeared in his cell. In his *coffin*. Wes viewed the night. His eyes tried to swallow up the sky.

He stared, and he breathed.

He stared, and he breathed.

He was not in the pit.

The dark place.

In his mind, massive clouds shaped like hands enclosed the madness within them. The storm raged on, but was contained in a prison of its own.

Wes blinked up at the sky, then regarded the young guard leaning over him. They tried to seek out answers in each other's eyes, then the guard eased his arm away from Wes' neck. He settled onto the bench opposite of Wes and watched him carefully.

"Proceed!" he called to his companions, and Wes could hear the crunch of boots on gravel. He looked out the small window, and saw guards lining up alongside the polls and using them to lift the box off of the ground. More guards formed a barrier around the entire apparatus, and orders were called out to drive the entourage forward. Wes slid to the other end of the bench, and used his nose to work open the shutter on that side as well. Leaning against the coffin wall, he blinked watery eyes up at the sky.

"What happened to you?" The guard asked softly. Wes knew the man was watching him, but kept his eyes on the stars. They calmed him. They soothed the sting of madness on his mind.

The guard leaned forward and gently worked lose the knots that bound Wes' wrists and secured the gag in his mouth. "I haven't seen you in weeks, and now here you are acting nuts. Is this some kind of scheme you put together with your son?"

"My...son?" Wes asked after he was free of his gag. He brushed at his clothing, trying to put himself back in order while he spoke. "I think you have me confused with someone else."

"What?" The guard looked stunned. "What are you talking about? Look, whatever you're planning, this isn't the time or place. The whole of the Hall is crawling with guards. They plan to have some sort of fight for the Elders to enjoy."

"I know," Wes said hoarsely, but his mind was elsewhere. The way he lost himself to the madness really scared him. He thought he had it under better control.

"Well if you know so much, what are you doing here? This palanquin was meant to transport the prisoner. Are you playing understudy again?"

"Wes."

"What?"

"The prisoner has a name."

"I *know* he has a name."

"And it's Wes."

The guard stared at him for a long time. The palanquin rolled and shifted as they went. Outside the window, Wes saw a large arched gate with its doors open to the city beyond. Hundreds of people filed in and out of that entrance, many of them watching the procession of guards curiously.

"Do you remember the face of your son?" the guard asked softly.

"I have no son."

"Do you remember what happened to that little boy you carried out of the Hall?"

Wes turned from the window, and peered at the guard suspiciously. "I did no such thing."

"Mister Wes, do you remember ever seeing me before?" Wes stared at the young guard for a moment and had to admit the man looked...familiar. Then he felt the bottom of the coffin scrape against something and turned his attention back to the world outside.

They placed him upon a platform which rested at the base of a large staircase. From where he sat, Wes had a good view of the entire arena, roped off and patrolled by guards. It was no more than a clearing in the yard, but fanned out from the stairs which led up to the main entrance of the Divine Hall.

"Where is the fish?" Wes asked as he looked around.

"They have him in a pen on the other side. Drugged him with morphine to keep him quiet. It won't last very long." The way the guard clenched his jaw grazed fingertips against a memory. Wes stared at him, waiting to discover more, but when nothing came, he put it all out of his mind. There were bigger things to concern himself with.

In the center of the clearing, two women were introduced by a gaudy announcer in a striped suit. When he stepped out of the way, they lunged at each other in a savage fight. Both women looked haggard, with hollowed out cheeks and missing teeth. They screamed with gaping mouths like black hungry cavities ready to receive anything the other would give.

They reminded Wes of Gad, and he forced them from his mind. He instead craned his neck to look up the steps to the entrance of the Hall. Upon the landing at the top, Wes could see a long banquet table full of food. Facing out to the arena yard was an array of men and women dressed in outlandish white outfits. Each outfit was more extravagant than the last, and all of them had silver crowns of various shapes and sizes atop their heads.

"Who are they?" Wes asked of his guard companion while he watched with fascination.

"Those are the Elders," replied the guard; his expression ambiguous. Wes noticed an empty chair, ornate and overbearing, sitting directly in the middle of the group.

"Who sits in that middle chair, yonder."

"I can't see what you're looking at, but I imagine you're referring to the chair that seats the Guardian Son. They should announce him soon."

"Guardian Son," Wes whispered, and felt a sudden sharp pain behind his eyes. He squeezed them shut and rubbed at them with his gloved hands.

You're starting to remember.

Wes looked up at the guard, bewildered by the voice he just heard in his mind. Mistaking his expression for something akin to grief, the guard leaned toward him and spoke with tenderness in his voice.

"I'm sure he will find a way to get you out of this mess. He's clever enough to, and if the rumors are true, he's been miserable since you disappeared. You're not going to be forced to fight that monster."

"You keep speaking like that," Wes said with a hint of a smile, "your tongue will turn black."

He turned his back on the voice in his mind.

Best to avoid those doorways into madness.

"The great lord will help you," the guard said desperately. "He has to."

"Your great lord is just another one of the many that locked me in a hole where they expected me to lose my mind."

The women concluded their fight. Servants clad in black swept dust over the blood they left behind.

"Ladies and gentlemen!" the announcer called out as he rushed to stand in the middle of the arena, "We thank you all for being here tonight in honor of our great Old Father!" He paused for applause. Wes counted hundreds among the mass of observers. He didn't know so many people existed in the world. "Before we continue with our entertainment, I want to welcome our honored High Counsel for joining us this evening!" More applause from the drove. "You might have noticed the vacant chair of our great lord, and wondered if he might grace us with his presence tonight. It has been over a year since his last public appearance, and we yearn to see him again."

"We love you great lord!" Someone called out in the sea of faces. Wes pressed his own face against the window to get a better look.

"Indeed we do! And all can rejoice, for I am here to call him out to join us tonight!" The crowd clapped and cheered. People shouted out their love of the Guardian Son. The announcer let their cheering go on for some time, then raised his hands to quiet them down once more. "Ladies and gentlemen, I am thrilled to announce the arrival of our Lord of the Sun; the great ruler of our land, the humble, the beautiful, the powerful Guardian Son!"

The cheers silenced all other sounds in Wes' ears. Even the madness took second seat to the prominence of the crowd's applause. Wes covered his ears against the reverberation in his tiny box, and craned his neck to see. Pounding outside the door.

"Jack! We need you on the line!"

"I need to leave you," the guard said, and Wes glanced over at him.

"Thank you for spending time with me," he replied sincerely, "your captain is honored to have such a loyal guard."

"Right," the young man said, looking oddly ashamed, and he exited out of the palanquin. The cheering of the crowd swelled, their excitement growing, and Wes looked out his window to see a young boy dressed in an extravagant black uniform stride gracefully down the stairs. He paid little attention to the crowd cheering him on, and swiftly joined the others sitting at the banquet table. His face was beautiful; unmarked by sin, but he looked distant and sad. There was a tightness around his eyes that made Wes feel sorry for him.

"He's so young," he whispered, but no one was there to hear him. All the guards were outside his coffin.

"Great lord, Guardian Son, thank you for coming this evening, we are so humbled to stand in the presence of a God! Please! Enjoy some of our offerings, and let us show you more of our entertainment!"

Everyone cheered their excitement, while the announcer gestured for a small group of people to come to the middle of the arena. They all faced the High Counsel, and lifted their voices in song. Wes sat back, and closed his eyes to better appreciate their singing. He might as well.

I'm going to die either way.

After a few of the songs, Wes peeked out of his box to observe the Guardian Son, and noticed that the boy wasn't eating his food. He frowned at his plate miserably, and poked the food idly with a fork. Wes watched from the shadows like a spy.

"I want to see the monster!" Someone said among the crowd of spectators.

"Show us the fish!" More shouts joined the others as the crowd grew impatient. The singers tried to continue, but eventually faltered and stopped. They looked about, defeated, and Wes sunk back into the shadows of his prison.

"I could run," he said to himself, and another laugh bubbled out of his throat. "I could run through one of those gates. No one would notice. I'm fast. No one would catch me." But if he ran, who would they place before the fish instead? The guard who sat with him? The captain? The boy at the top of the steps who poked listlessly at his food? Wes bit his lip, but he didn't move.

"I'm finished with this," the boy in black declared, pushing at his plate. "Clear everything away."

"Great lord, you hardly ate anything at all."

"You have grown so thin."

"Get rid of it!" The boy snapped, and Wes felt a yearning in his heart he didn't understand. He leaned forward, fingers grasping the bottom ledge of his tiny view of the world, and gazed upon the sadness of one teenage boy.

Daniel.

Servants rushed to take trays away, and the boy stopped them from retreating back into the Hall. "Give it all to them," he commanded with a sweep of his hand over a crowd that cheered his name.

"Great lord, it is unwise to share wealth of any kind with those in need," said one Elder loud enough for Wes to hear.

"They'll start to get ideas," another agreed.

"This is a day of celebration," the boy said, and turned to face them with a cold smile on his lips, and a challenge in his eyes. He was beautiful, and tragic. And *familiar.*

"On with the show," the boy cried out, and the Elders conceded their objections. Servants struggled to navigate the crowds as eager hands reached for anything and everything including the platters themselves. Their hunger reminded Wes of his own when he first left the pit. The announcer distracted him from that dark place in his mind. The stripe-suited man raised his hands as he entered the arena, and called out to the masses.

"Residents of our *great* city, it is time for our main event: the battle of the hero and the fish!" Many cheered, bits of food spraying from open mouths, and Wes saw Ashter come into view. The Captain was dressed in his black uniform, decorated like the Guard Watch Elite, but with a silver falcon in flight pinned to his jacket. He strode over to the box Wes was in, and positioned himself next to the door.

"I could run," Wes whispered. "Right out that open gate and into the city. I could run."

"Today marks the birthday of our beloved Old Father," the announcer went on, "And to celebrate this day, we want to enjoy one of his favorite occasions: trial and execution!"

Cheers from the crowd. Delight from the masses.

"Like many of us, our hero is also a criminal. But he was caught! Arrested! Imprisoned! Now he stands before you dressed in the color of the owned, about to face his trial at the hands of our great lord. When he is convicted, for he *will* be..."

Laughs from the crowd. Joy from the masses.

"When he is convicted...there will be judgment!"

Everyone cheered. Wes cheered as well.

Madness has robbed me of my past. The joy of others will rob me of my future.

"It's now time to bring out our honored guest!"

It is time for me to go beyond the veil.

Wes closed his eyes and offered up a prayer to the Lord. He wondered if it would be heard over the noisy rabble.

"Ladies and Gentlemen, I give you, the hero!"

They cheered. They whistled. They shouted. Not for Wes, but for the promise of his demise. The door opened. Ashter peered in at him, and his eyes grew wide. Wes did not struggle. He was being set free. He coasted, glided, hands leading him and pulling him. He smiled at the captain. But Ashter didn't smile back. He looked worried. He looked ashamed. Wes spread open his arms and spun around as he took in the people who cheered or shouted or booed or haggled.

All of it, an offering to him. All of their faces, exactly the same. Jubilation from the masses.

Lanterns dotted the crowd, but it was the large braziers of burning wood in each of the corners that brought illumination to the whole of the arena. Wes examined the area, and imagined fighting a monster there. The announcer turned his attention to the top of the stairs.

"High Counsel Elders, Guardian Son, we are graced with your authority and wisdom! We humbly implore you to condemn the wicked.Convict this man, and force his hand to face judgment by combat!"

"Get on with it then!" One of the Elders called out, as he flagged down a servant for a goblet of wine. Most of them busied themselves with obtaining drinks, but the Guardian Son stood and watched Wes who in turn was watching the rowdy crowd.

"I want to see a fight!"

"I want to see bloodshed!"

"It's time for the great lord to render judgment!"

The crowd cheered and demanded Wes' price be paid in blood. Elation from the masses.

Thy will be done.

Thy Guardian Son.

"Let the trial begin!" the announcer shouted when he saw the boy nod. The crowd cheered and danced about in their excitement. High in the spires of the Divine Hall, a bell chimed. Wes turned from the drove, his eyes following the noise to its source, but he quickly realized that all the Elders were staring at him.

A row of placid faces, examining him collectively.

Wes on a stage, naked and determined.

Eyes upon his vulnerable body.

A memory.

The first clear memory to exist in his mind. Wes poked at it inquisitively, as it established itself in one of many vacant spaces.

"Great residents of the capital! We shall now hear the verdict from our great lord!" They all cheered for the boy in the black uniform who was a head shorter than the men and women all gathered around him. The crowd adored him. Reverence from the masses!

Am I headed to Hell? Or am I already there?

Be still!

Wes glanced at Ashter to see if the other man could hear the woman's voice in his mind.

"Before I determine a verdict," the boy announced in a strong voice that cut through the cheers from the crowd, "I would like to hear the prisoner's charges. I would also like to...observe him more closely. He is a hero, after all." Wes laughed, and some in the crowd did as well, but mostly everyone just watched and waited. The Elders settled into their seats, and sought out smoking pipes or goblets to drink from. The boy remained standing. He stared at Wes with growing disbelief.

"How would you like to observe him, great lord?" Ashter called out, and the boy bit at his lip. Then he raised his head and spoke.

"Bring him to stand before me."

"Great lord, this isn't safe."

"He's already guilty, no need for all these theatrics!"

"Do as I say," the boy insisted, and Ashter placed a hand on Wes' shoulder. He numbly followed the captain's lead, and together they approached the staircase. As they climbed it, the Guardian Son intently watched their slow assent.

"Are you alright?" Ashter asked softly, speaking through barely moving lips. "Your eyes look...turbulent."

"It's hard sometimes to keep the madness under control," Wes admitted, for Ashter was his friend.

"Keep it together. Don't forget what I told you."

"I won't forget," Wes assured him, and managed to stifle his laughter.

"Judge him!" Shouted the mob.

"Kill him!"

"Let him be ripped apart!"

"Bring out the fish!"

As they approached the table, the boy's eyes grew wider. He looked confused. He looked terrified.

"Well, let's get a look at him then," said one of the Elders.

"Wait, that hat looks familiar."

"Actually, now that you mention it..."

"Take off that hat, man. Let's have a look at your face!"

Wes pulled the hat from his head, and studied the many stunned expressions of the High Counsel.

"Wait...isn't that your father, great lord?"

Wes glanced over to the thin woman with a pinched face who spoke, then back to the boy who stood before him. Father? Him?

"Why is he here?" the boy asked, his voice shaking. He turned his head slightly, addressing the Elders around him, but his large eyes never left Wes' face. The Elders all seemed to speak at once.

"We thought he fled the city!"

"He ran off with the..."

"Don't say it! Not here!"

"But that means he's the..."

"Hush!"

"We must kill him! Now! Right now!"

"Don't let the Guardian Son hear you say that!"

"WHY ARE YOU HERE?" The boy shouted. He pounded a fist on the table, causing more than one goblet to spill its swill, and he glared down at Wes. Silence pressed upon them like a sodden blanket. Somewhere in the crowd of observers, a child softly cried.

Ashter nudged him, and Wes glanced at the captain then back to the boy. "I'm here to die," he replied and the crowd cheered their agreement. The surprise on the boy's face changed to alarm. He stared at Wes for a long time as the crowd continued to express their elation.

"Great lord," a small pudgy Elder offered with a nervous titter, "we are here for a trial."

The boy looked at the man, horror of understanding evident on his face.

"I can't," he said, too softly for the crowd to hear.

"The Guardian Son wishes to hear the crimes of the arrested!" Another Elder announced, and Captain Ashter cleared his throat as he produced a booklet filled with his written hand.

"His known crime is that of trespass. Suspected attempt of assassination, and if he is who you identify him to be, he is also accused of..." pages flipped as Ashter searched his ledger. Upon finding the page he was seeking, he read over it, then looked at Wes. "Theft from the High Counsel."

"Grounds for death!" Called out one of the Elders and many of the spectators cheered.

"But wait!" Another Elder interjected. Her painted red lips a sharp contrast to her high-necked white jacket. "If he is judged, how will we ever recover...the property he stole?"

All the Elders went silent, thinking, then turned to one another to discuss how to approach this new issue. The boy continued to stare at Wes. His eyes conveying a mixture of confusion, surprise, anger, fear, and strangely: joy.

"What happened to you?" he asked quietly, "I barely recognize you. You're so thin, and that beard! You... you just look so... empty. I...thought you fled. I thought...I thought you left me."

"You thought I fled, now I'll soon be dead." Wes chuckled at his little rhyme. Thin wisps of madness tickled his brain. It filled in the holes, and Wes forgot all about what he lost.

"I...don't understand," the boy said and Ashter cleared his throat.

"If you'll allow me to speak sir...yes. This man was arrested when he was discovered attempting to infiltrate the Hall. He's been...imprisoned in the pit, you see. For over two weeks."

"What? That place causes people to go insane!" The boy's emotions were eclipsed by outrage. "Why was I not informed of his capture? How did this go on for so long?"

"We didn't know who he was," the captain explained, shrugging, "we accused him of being an assassin, but in truth I just figured he was a petty thief."

"This can't happen," the boy said, turning to the Elders. "He didn't commit a crime, he was trying to return to me. If he's forced to face this monster you told me about, he will be torn apart!"

"And *we* will be torn apart if we don't give them a show," one of the Elders said, pointing at the crowd.

"Then make someone else do it! Get another prisoner and put them in his place!"

"We have no other prisoners," Ashter said anxiously, and Wes noticed he was growing pale. "The past week has been a jubilee in celebration of Old Father. All arrests were acquitted."

"Enough!" the boy shouted and pounded the table again with his small fist. He stared at his hand, then raised his eyes to look upon Wes. He calmed his words; his patience a thin wire he tried his best to balance upon. "Find someone else. Anyone else. Offer them food. Gold. I don't care. Just please! Don't make me watch my father die!"

"Weakness," hissed an Elder and the boy turned to glare at him.

"An unworthy vessel," said the oldest among them. His eyes were closed but his head was nodding in agreement.

"Then replace me if you can," the boy snarled with teeth bared. He glared fire at the old man, but the Elder remained placid with his eyes closed.

"We will cast crowns," the woman with the pinched face announced. "Usurping you *is* our right. For all those in favor of death, a crown will be cast."

"Let it be done," another Elder agreed, and they all rose in unison from their seats. They turned their backs on the Guardian Son, and circled around the table to its front. As they passed between Wes and the boy, each of them plucked their crown off of their head, and tossed them one by one at the boy's feet. Every single crown got cast. None were left behind. As they returned to their respective seats, the boy looked up at Wes with a face of utter despair.

"Don't be sad, great lord. I am prepared to face this battle today."

"If you get so much as a scratch from that monster you will die," the boy said with tears in his eyes, and Wes smiled.

"Better for it to be me than someone else who has something to live for."

"Something to live for?" the boy said, incredulous, then understanding softened his face.

"He doesn't remember who you are," one of the Elders said; something the boy already realized.

"He doesn't remember who he is either," said another, laughing. The boy did not scold him. He just stared at Wes, and tears made his eyes look like pools of water reflecting the moonlight.

It is almost time, Wesley.

"The trial has concluded!" One of the Elders cried out when the silence stretched on too long, and the crowd cheered.

"Is it really wise to send a person of the prophecies to his death?"

"Is it wise to kill the only person who can deliver the vessel of Light back to us?"

"You cast your crown just like the rest of us."

"I only did it because everyone else did!"

“Alright everyone! Silence as the verdict is declared!” Called out the announcer and the crowd obeyed. The Elders obeyed as well. Wes glanced to his left where he could just make out the top of a gate with its doors held open; welcoming someone to run through.

All among him seemed to universally lean forward in eager anticipation of the one word they all wanted to hear. The word that they *must* hear.

Always convicted.

Never innocent.

Never set free.

All eyes rested upon the Guardian Son. The Guardian Son only had eyes for Wes.

“It’s going to be okay,” Wes said softly, and smiled.

“Guilty,” the boy replied and everyone sighed.

Hallelujah.

Rapture from the masses.

It’s almost time, Wesley. It’s almost time.

Chapter Thirty

Moses said this about the tribe of Gad:
"Blessed is the one who enlarges Gad's territory!
Gad is poised there like a lion to tear off an arm
or a head." -Deuteronomy 33:20 NLT

"What is this?" Wes asked, holding up the small vial of liquid. Ashter, leaning against the wall of his prison cell, watched him carefully. Being the captain of the guard, he was risking much to aid one convict.

"It's a bottle of morphine."

"What am I to do with this?" Wes asked, and Ashter shifted his hawkish gaze to watch the hall outside of his cell.

"Before your fight against the fish, we will show you an array of weapons for you to choose from. Knowing the greatest risk to your life comes from the claw or the bite, I suspect the halberd would be your best choice for attack."

"I will do as you say," Wes said as he rolled the small vial along his fingertips, "if you think it will help."

"It truly is your best chance to hurt that monster without getting hurt yourself. Putting my strongest poison on the blade should help as well. At least I hope it will."

"You want me to put morphine on the blade?" Wes asked, indicating the vial. Ashter pushed off the wall and approached Wes. He leaned in, and his ardent eyes conveyed the extent of his misgivings.

"The poison is already on the blade. This morphine is for you, my friend, in case the poison fails. A scratch from a monster is a horrible way to die. If you drink down the whole of that vial, it will not only ease the pain, but will also eliminate your desire to breathe."

"We will now judge the accused!" the Guardian Son called out to the cheering crowd, yet sadness clouded his eyes. "Our hero will face judgment by combat against the accursed: the creature known as the fish!"

"The accused and the accursed!" Shouted the crowd.

"The hero and the fish!"

"Place your final bets now! Hurry! Hurry!"

"Betting closes before the weapon is chosen!"

The Guardian Son looked to him, but the pain in the boy's eyes meant little. Wes descended the stairs, Ashter at his side, and followed the captain's lead to a table, resting at the base of the stairs, and covered in a red cloth.

"Bring out the accursed!"

"Bring out the fish!"

Soon you'll remember, Wesley. It is soon time.

"Great High Counsel! Esteemed guests!" Called the announcer from the center of the empty arena, "We will now allow our hero to pick his weapon!" Ashter gave the crowd an embellished bow, then yanked the cloth from the table. Wes focused on the array of weapons before him. Some of them he recognized, while others were entirely new. Blades and clubs and maces and spears. A long bow with quiver that made his fingers twitch, and yes there was a halberd. Similar to a spear, it had a staff and a long curved blade on its end, which was topped with a spike.

"Make your choice!" One of the Elders shouted down at him, and the crowd howled impatiently. The anticipation stirred them into a frenzy, and the noise of it swelled until it overtook the whole of the arena.

There was a sudden unearthly roar that rose up, and overshadowed the cheers. All present fell silent as they listened in cautious curiosity for the sound to come again. For it was a sound that baffled the mind. The cries of a monster.

The howl came again, and Wes felt the hair rise on the back of his neck. The wrongness of the sound was profound, and all eyes shifted to examine a large metal box tucked against the side of the stairs. It appeared to be a relic from the Before, and used to sit on wheels. It was long and tall, potentially once used to transport animals like horses, and had a barred window on its flank. It was to that window that everyone looked when the whole of the container shuddered. The creature within screamed out his fury as he threw his body against the wall.

"Choose!" Ashter demanded urgently, and Wes hefted the halberd, testing the balance and weight of it in his hands. It was indeed the best choice on the table, even without the poison, but Wes could only hope it was enough.

"Release the fish!" the announcer called out, and Ashter exchanged a final glance at Wes before retreating to join a group of off-duty guards. Wes carried his halberd to the center of the arena, crossing paths with the announcer in his fancy suit who took to fleeing into the crowd as well.

Standing alone, Wes tossed the halberd from hand to hand, getting a feel for its function, as he waited to see what he was about to face. Guards lined up along both sides of the metal box, clubs in hand, and one of them cautiously reached out to pull a latch free. The whole back of the metal box flopped open like a broken jaw, and revealed shadows that shrouded the space within.

The crowd leaned forward, necks craning for a glimpse of the monster, but the creature wouldn't reveal itself. One of the guards hesitantly stepped into the opening, hoping to lure the creature out of hiding, but didn't realize that Gad was lightning quick. His body, no longer human, lunged on four beastly legs. Leather pants that fit like small-clothes, covered his groin and the upper part of his legs, but the rest of his distorted body was left bare so that every twisted inch could be observed with revulsion. His skin, gray and covered in boils, looked slick and clotted like jelly but his resemblance to a fish, reached no further.

Gad's head bulged at the skull, and his jaw was retracted into his chin so that his lips sagged like flaccid flaps of skin. Long brown trails of mucus dangled from his mouth, dripping globs upon the dusty earth. His hands, twisted into massive paws, had claws the length of a man's finger and glistened in the firelight. He used those paws to grab hold of the young guard's head, and crushed his skull with a twist of the wrist. It sounded like a snapping twig.

A women screamed, and the crowd scattered in panic. The Elders' got to their feet, some of them casting glances to the door of their Hall. The creature turned, long black spikes bristling on his back, and he stepped into a pool of light. Wes was amazed to see that he was entirely unaffected by the firelight. His skin didn't burn. He didn't recoil in pain. A monster immune to fire. A nightmare walking in reality. Gad faced the dissipating guards, and his strange lips parted in a roar. He was about to bathe himself in their blood.

“Gad!” The monster turned at the sound of his name, and Wes was horrified to see that his eyes were gone. He looked around as though eyes still existed, but only black vacant sockets remained. he peeled back his gray lips to reveal the top row of black teeth in some semblance of a smile.

“Weeellll...helllooo frieeennnddd.” Gad said, moving his mouth in strange ways to create the words he still knew, for he somehow had not lost himself to the madness of his sin. He recognized Wes which meant his mind was intact even if his body wasn’t.

“Your fight isn’t with these folks,” Wes called across the vast space between them, but with how silent the spectators were, his words were easily heard. He stepped sideways, and readied himself to spring away.

“Isss it wiitthh yeee?” Gad hissed, and Wes hefted the halberd in his hand. He held it out level, pointing its long spike at Gad’s vacant eye socket.

“I reckon it is, if I’m the reason you’re here.” Wes knew that Gad blamed him for his capture, so his words had their desired effect on the beast. Gad unleashed a gruesome cry of voice echoing voice, and charged at Wes. Expecting this response, Wes planned to dash to the side at the last moment, and swing his halberd so that it slashed into Gads gut, but Gad was far faster than he anticipated. One moment he approached at a distance, then time seemed to skip ahead, and Gad towered over Wes. Before Wes was able to react, Gad crashed into him with the full force of his lumbering body. Wes felt his feet lift off the ground. He flew backwards, then crashed back down onto the earth where he rolled, end over end, until the momentum of the impact expended itself and he came to rest flat on his back.

“Ow,” Wes grunted, as he stared up at the sky in a daze. Gad roared again, the demon voice a whisper behind his own, and pushed himself up to stand awkwardly on his hind legs. The man was massive; twice the size of his previous state. He stood like Goliath, towering over Wes, and stared down with empty black sockets. Seeing the dread on Wes’ face, Gad stretched his skin, forming his painful looking grin.

“I heeear theee voiiicceee ooofff Gooooddd innssiiidee meee,” Gad hissed, his words growing clearer. “It wantsss meee to raaakkee yer soft belllllyyy open withhh meee claawwws. Feellll the heaaattt of yeeerr guts on meee armsss. Buttt I donnn’tt wannnt to kill yeeee so easilyyyy. I waannt tooo savoorrr yeerrr pain slowwwly. Savvoorrr theee feaaarrr innn yeeerrr eyessss.” Gad flexed his claws; the long black quills on his back bristled, and Wes found his feet as he broke into a run. The crowd started a new cheer, as their numbers swelled once more.

Gad was indifferent to their fervor, as he dropped down on all four legs, and moved to intercept Wes. Before he could, Wes reached the halberd he lost in the force of Gad's initial attack, and paused long enough to pick it up. He stumbled, tripping over his footing, and his oafish behavior bolstered Gad. He rushed forward, hungry to hurt the man he grew to hate, and Gad was so fast. Far too fast for his broken, deformed body. But Wes was prepared this time.

The moment Gad was almost upon him, he shifted himself; no longer tripping over his footing. He dropped down on one knee, and braced the hilt of the halberd against the earth as he pointed it directly at Gad. The monster put too much force behind his assault and was not able to avoid the weapon. He shifted his body just enough so that the poisoned blade didn't sink directly into his heart, but connected with his right shoulder instead. Gad screamed as his momentum propelled him forward, and the halberd snapped just under the blade. He collided with the earth, the blade still embedded within him, and slid to a halt a few feet from where Wes sat panting. The crowd broke into wild cheers, and many of the Elder's cheered as well. The hero and the fish were putting on a good show.

Wes groaned as he rolled, got to his feet, and limped toward the staircase leading up to the Hall and the Elder's table. They watched him approach, eyes cold and calculating, but when Gad let out a groan, Wes put the Elders' out of his mind and instead picked up his pace toward his destination. He stole a quick glance over his shoulder and was dismayed to see Gad trying to push himself up, but fortunately collapsed a moment later. Was the poison working? Wes hoped it was so.

A furious growl emitted from Gad's throat, and the cheers of the crowd died away. Finding his footing, he pushed himself up another time, and rose to his full height. He sought out Wes, and his empty sockets seemed to glow in his desire for retribution. He reached, and yanked the broken halberd out of his body with a wet slurping sound. Black bile spilled out over his bare blistered chest, as he held up the halberd to examine it, then hurled it at the steps of the High Counsel. The Guardian Son rose, excused himself, and stepped away from the table the others remained at. Wes could not watch the boy further, for Gad had turned his focus back to him.

"Oh Lord," Wes grumbled, and pushed his pained body to sprint. He was under no illusion that he could outrun Gad, but had to instead focus on what he could change which was his lack of a weapon. He could feel Gad's overpowering hunger, knowing the man wanted to cause him immeasurable pain, and scrambled to reach the table that held his weapon options. Wes' eyes scanned over the variety, and grabbed the first thing that seemed promising: a club the length of his arm with a ball full of sharp points on one end: a spiked mace. It took only a moment, but already Wes was out of time.

Just as Gad was about to overtake him, Wes wheeled around, gripping the mace in both of his hands, and swung it with all the force he could muster. Sadly, three days of intense training was not enough to regain all his strength. Gad grabbed hold of the mace in the middle of its swing, and ripped it out of Wes' hands with little effort at all. He threw it down, and sprung on Wes so that they both tumbled onto the ground.

Wes could no longer hear the crowd. No longer was he the spectacle of a show. Under the weight of this massive beast, Wes felt the crippling panic that came from enclosed places, and it was all he could do not to scream. Gad hovered over him, slobber dripping onto Wes' face, and panted heavily as he peeled back lips to reveal rows of teeth. They looked like black daggers, each one tipped with a sharp razor point, and Gad lunged directly at Wes' throat. Wes was loosing control of the panic welling up inside of him, so it was God's will that he managed to move out of the way just in time. The teeth snapped together next to his ear with a forceful click.

Black bile from Gad's wound splattered across Wes' face causing it to burn. Gad growled in frustration, and reared back to try again. His dagger teeth parted, jaw quivering, and Wes could already feel them sinking into his throat.

Wesley! Remember!

Wes felt his mind seize; enthralled by the sight of his own demise, the sharp sting of panic rose up in his throat. He flailed his hands, desperate for escape, and felt the smooth handle of the spiked mace alongside his head. Just as Gad dove to tear into him, Wes hoisted the weapon and rammed its spikes into the soft tissue of his vacant eye socket.

The monster screamed, rearing back from Wes to grab at his face, and Wes took the opening to roll onto his stomach and crawl out from under the beast. He scampered toward the table of weapons. He reached, grabbed, fingers brushed the hilt of something, then an iron grip closed around his ankle and dragged Wes away. Gad flopped Wes onto his back, and immediately shoved an arm hard against his throat. He leaned hard into Wes, cutting off his air supply, and grinned his black grin with his black empty eye sockets.

Black ooze dribbled out of the eyeless void, and burned Wes' skin. He grunted through clenched teeth, and Gad leaned close to him, pressing his arm down more on his throat. A ringing sound grew in Wes' ears as he gasped and groped for the air denied to him. The world around him faded to black until Wes looked out from one end of a dark tunnel, and saw nothing but Gad's wicked smile on the other side. Gripping the hilt of the weapon in his hand, Wes drove the dagger into Gad's side over and over again, but it had no effect.

Remember!

Wes struggled to find a way out. The dagger was utterly ineffective. No weapon, no strength, no air, and no way out from under this monster which drove his panic into a frenzy. The ringing in his ears turned into a wordless roar.

"We willll buurrrnn innn Heellll togeetthhherr, frieeend," Gad growled as Wes' eyes rolled. His vision went black. His body burned for air. "I willll heellpppp yeee geeettt theeeerrreeee!"

His twin voices were unified; demon and man made into one, and Gad opened his mouth wide. He worked his jaw in an unnatural way, and his mouth fell open fully; revealing endless rows of jagged black teeth.

Remember your children, Wesley!

The mouth expanded; Gad stretching his gray lips until they split, and his mouth was made massive. Like a snake, Gad intended to swallow Wes whole.

"Stop!" Wes wheezed helplessly but no one could hear. Unconsciousness rose up to grab hold of him.

Remember your son!

Sound exploded above his head, cutting past the ringing in his ears, and Wes immediately recognized it as a firing gun. In the same instant Gad pitched back, then flopped to the side. His arm no longer barred Wes' throat, and he sucked air into his hungry lungs gratefully. This was his last coherent thought however, as Gad's hot blood splattered all over his face and neck. The blood was tainted and brought sudden pain that was so intense, Wes threw back his head and screamed. His face, his throat, his eyes; he felt like he was set on fire. The pain was so paralyzing, screaming was all he could do. Then water was splashed over his face, giving him the slightest relief. Wes coughed and spit as water mingled with blood. Everything burned. Everything burned! He opened his eyes, but they stung and tears flooded into his vision. Everything looked blurry. Someone dragged Gad off of him, but he hardly noticed for Wes was consumed with pain.

The Guardian Son demanded a Healer be called. He screamed for a stretcher. The crowd shouted their opinions, calling the Guardian Son a hero, or claimed him to be an infiltrator and a fraud. They demanded an execution. The Elders also spoke up, seemingly all at once. They asked why the great lord risked his life. Why was he holding onto his father's gun? What on earth did he think he was doing shooting the fish like he did?

More water was splashed on Wes, and he coughed.

"Over here with that stretcher! Quickly! We must get him inside while he still breathes!"

Daniel...

The woman sighed in his mind.

"Daniel..." Wes croaked. His throat felt like he swallowed a handful of wasps. He stretched a hand toward the boy's voice, but something cool and hard slid underneath him.

Wes was hoisted into the air, opened his eyes as much as he could endure, and looked for the boy through his tears. Elders surrounded their Guardian Son as they leaned over to whisper in his ear or to each other. They peered down their noses at Wes, and tried to lead the boy away.

"Keep him alive, or it will be your neck in a noose," the boy snapped at one of the people tending to Wes, then pushed past the Elder's to take Wes' gloved hand in both of his. His perfect face blurred in Wes' vision; his eyes full of dread.

Remember our son, Wesley. Our sweet boy. Our Daniel.

"Come back to me, father," the boy said softly, then pressed his cheek against Wes' outstretched hand. A black smudge marred his perfect face. Tears wet his eyes.

Daniel...

Wes opened his mouth, wanting to speak, wanting to say the name, slowly realizing what it meant, but no sound would come. Suddenly, he couldn't breath. His chest was on fire!

"Great lord, we must take him now!"

Wes was moving, gasping, burning, dying. He writhed against the straps that secured him. He heard his heart thrumming in his own ears, faster, faster, faster! Then it abruptly went still along with the rest of the world. Wes sank down into the deep well of his muddled mind.

It was a hot and humid late afternoon, as the sun rippled behind a thick haze of muggy heat. In the surrounding forest, Wes could hear birds calling to one another from deep within the lush trees. He wiped his arm against the sweat running down his brow, and smiled at the boy reaching for him.

"Again! Again!" Daniel cried. He was only two, but almost three. Almost safe. And he was such a strong boy! Wes knew his son would be a leader.

"Alright, lad. One more time." He scooped the boy up into his arms, then threw him as high as he could into the air. Daniel squealed with delight as he rose higher and higher, and for a brief moment he was suspended above the world. Somehow Wes knew that every time Daniel reached that split-second of suspension, he was deeply afraid. For while he faced this moment many times before, he convinced himself that one of these times, he would not come back down. He would just rise higher and higher, unable to stop. Then the moment would pass, and as he dropped Wes caught him. The rising was fated to cause a flicker of fear inside Daniel, but the falling didn't scare him at all. Wes always caught him. Wes always would.

Daniel's favorite part came right after Wes caught him when he leaned over Daniel, and burrowed his nose in the boy's soft belly. It made Daniel laugh wildly, and he took such delight in having his father's attention. Wes never knew that about his son, but in the remembering, he was somehow certain that this was Daniel's oldest and fondest memory. It was one he carried with him still. Wes threw Daniel into the air, then nuzzled his stomach after catching him again.

He loves you so much.

"I know that now, Ruth," Wes said as he pulled young Daniel close to him, and lovingly stroked the boy's hair. Daniel looked up at him, and his smile was like sunshine. How did Wes ever forget this moment, and all the moments like it? He seemed to remember the many ways he failed Daniel, but not these moments of love between them from their past.

Don't drop him, Wesley. Never drop our boy. Now go to him. Bring our son back home.

Wes breathed in, filling his lungs even though it burned; Lord, how it burned. He couldn't open his eyes. His face felt tight and heavy.

"What happened? What are you doing?"

Daniel!

Wes tried to move, but his body would not cooperate with his yearning. He groaned and noticed how different his voice sounded in his ears. His lungs were an inferno; his tongue thick and swollen. There were people shouting all around him. Where was he? What happened to him?

"His heart stopped, great lord. Fortunately we were able to revive him."

"Where are you taking him?" A voice shouted in the distance

“We want an execution!” Another called.

“Judgment!” Other called out and a chorus of boos joined in.

“We need to get out of here, great lord!” A voice closer to Wes.

“They will riot without a show!”

Wes could feel himself being lifted again on the surface he was strapped to. The water splashed on him had long since dried, and his skin burned with a searing intensity. His eyes throbbed. His throat pulsed its pain with each of his heartbeats. His face felt tight like a drum-head and on the verge of splitting open. If he could, he would cry, for he never knew such agony.

“Burn the body of the fish,” Daniel said. “That will give them something to look at.”

“Yes, sir!”

“Where do you expect the servants to take him, great lord?” So many voices both near and far, but Wes only knew his son’s voice.

“To the Lord Healer Elite,” Daniel replied.

“Why are we treating him? He’s been convicted! The accused must be executed!”

“To Hell with your execution!” Daniel snapped. “I’ll refuse to let my father die that way.” A cool cloth pressed against Wes’ face. He breathed slow in an effort to control the pain.

“We must hurry, great lord, he aspirated some of the blood and his breathing is highly erratic.”

“We suspect his lungs are swelling like his face.”

“Faster!” Daniel ordered, and Wes felt his body shifting about under his restraints. The sound of the crowd faded, replaced by the more intimate sounds of an enclosed space.

“Great lord, we can’t make exceptions for the accused once they are condemned. It sets a dangerous precedent.”

“He stole a child that was deemed your property! Any theft from the High Counsel would warrant a hanging!”

“Not just any child!”

“He was to be ours!”

“Our new Guardian Son!”

“I wanted to taste the Bringer of Light!”

“Enough!” Daniel shouted and all voices went still. Footfalls echoed down the corridor; perhaps a hallway. Wes drew in his careful breath to help with the pain. He opened his eyes just enough to see the light of fireboxes above him, but the light caused a flash of stinging pain in his eyes and Wes was forced to shy away. He was afraid of losing his sight, but so much of what was happening to him he didn't fully understand. A new set of footfalls ran down the hallway to join the rest of the group.

"Great lord! The commoners are starting to riot! They demand an execution!"

"Then find someone to execute!" Daniel shouted, frustrated.

"The cells are empty! We need a trial for an execution!"

"If there are those that dare to riot, then there are those that are willing to be hung," Daniel growled, "Find five of the worst offenders, and let them swing at the gallows. Forget about their need for a trial! Your arguments are forfeit!"

"Yes, sir," the reporting guard declared, and ran back the way he came. Orders needed to be carried out. People needed to be killed. Daniel's anger was ruthless.

"The Disciples will not like this, great lord."

"This is not the way things are done."

"They will like it a lot less when a riot turns up at their doorstep. We will deal with them. But right now, we need to save my father."

"This assassin? This thief of children?"

"You know those accusations aren't true."

"The past is unraveling. Perhaps what you remember is not what occurred."

"The unraveling doesn't alter what we remember, it just erases it."

"The way this man doesn't even remember you? How can you save a man who can't remember that you're his son?"

I remember now! I remember!

"It was the pit that robbed that from him. My own prison stole him from me!" Daniel sounded deeply mournful. Wes tried to lift a hand. To comfort his son. But he couldn't move. Why couldn't he move?

"Great lord, he's barely breathing! His heart might seize again!"

"Hurry!" Daniel said, and the sound of their footsteps shifted into a run.

Is it time to go, Daniel? Then show me the path that leads us home.

Chapter Thirty-One

The wicked build houses as fragile as a spider's web,
as flimsy as a shelter made of branches.
The wicked go to bed rich,
but wake to find that all their wealth is gone.
Terror overwhelms them like a flood,
and they are blown away in the storms of the night.
-Job 27:18-20 NLT

Wes opened his eyes to the sound of a child's laughter. He suddenly felt so young and strong! There was no pain, no suffering, no burning of his eyes, his face, his lungs. He stretched out his arms, savoring the feel in his muscles, and took in his surroundings.

He was standing upon the porch of his homestead, overlooking countless rows of corn ready for harvest in his field. Ruth was singing to herself as she hung bed linen to dry on the line. Beyond the sheets rolling in the wind, Wes saw a boy's bare feet spread out in the lush grass of late summer. A moment later, the boy laughed as he threw a burst of maple tree seeds into the air.

For a moment, Wes was confused by what he saw. For he recalled clearly how Sassy helped him to let this particular memory go. He did so reluctantly, but knew it was necessary to set poor Ruth free. So why was he there? What had changed?

The world flickered, and for an instant all of the crops vanished, leaving behind the broken stumps of shorn stalks. In the middle of the field, a group of crows gathered around a mound of something black. Then the laughter returned; the corn was brought back to life, and it was summer again. Wes felt immediately drawn again to those bare feet waving back and forth in the yard.

"Peter." he said aloud, and recognition bloomed a tapestry of memories in his mind. Oh dear, sweet Peter. The Lord was cruel for allowing Wes to forget his youngest son. He felt a sudden need to see the boy's face. The desire was so overpowering, he couldn't seem to think of anything else. He knew that if he was able to see his son's smiling face, then his dying wouldn't be so hard to accept. For Wes was certain that he was indeed dying.

While he stood before Ruth and Peter, he was also somewhere else struggling to stay alive. The knowing did not frighten him, for if Wes called any place the first step toward Heaven, it would surely be this place and this moment in time. When he stepped off of the porch, the memory didn't crumble the way it always had before. Bolstered by this realization, Wes did what he wished he could have done a hundred times over. He ignored the corn of his field, and instead approached his son.

This farm mattered not. The summer and the sun and the call to tend to it all mattered not. Wes just wanted to embrace his little boy. He wanted to see Peter's pudgy round face. He approached those bare feet, winking in and out of view behind the bed linen making lazy waves on the breeze, but after a few steps, Ruth suddenly appeared in front of him, blocking his path.

"Please step aside, Ruth. I must see him," Wes pleaded with his wife without giving her a glance. He tried to go around her, but she barred his way, and held him back again. He craned his neck to look past her, desperate to see his son. Little feet danced. Little hands grabbed maple seeds and tossed them into the sky. Wes remembered how Peter had freckles; a fact that was previously stolen from his mind. What he would give to see those freckles again. To count each one while Peter smiled up at him.

"Not yet, my love. This is not yet your time."

"Please Ruth! Let me just look at him. I just want to see that he's okay. I want to see that he's happy. I want to know that he's still..."

That he's still alive.

Cold frail hands closed around his own, and when Wes lifted his head again, it was as though he were seeing Ruth for the first time. No longer the sweet girl he once knew, nor the ailing wife he left behind with a promise to return, *this* Ruth looked like she was already dead. Her skin was gray and paper thin. Her eyes peered at Wes dully from sunken sockets, and all that remained of her hair was a few sparse strands that did little to cover the large patches of her bare skull. Part of her left ear was ripped away as though an animal had chewed it off. She was a skeleton draped in loose sagging skin and it was starting to slough off the bone. Seeing her as she was, Wes recoiled from her touch, horrified.

"Listen!" Ruth demanded, and Wes winced hearing his wife's voice coming out of the nightmare before him. Ruth sighed through her frustration. "Wesley, I don't have much time left on this side of the veil, and neither will you if you don't listen to me."

Wes found it hard to look at Ruth, and the allure of Peter was far too great to ignore. He craned his neck again to see past the wraith in front of him, and smiled at the boy off in yonder yard.

"You will listen to me!" Ruth snapped, and stamped her foot in frustration. The evidence of her exasperation was so familiar to the woman Wes once knew, that a warm fondness overtook him. For he still loved Ruth deeply, and knew she deserved his full attention if she sought it. He forced himself to look into her vapid milky eyes.

"Alright, Ruth," Wes sighed, playing his role in the decades-long performance between them, "I'm listening."

"You can't stay here, Wesley, you have to return. We will all still be here waiting for when your time comes, but you must turn your focus to Daniel. For he needs you right now. It is imperative that Daniel return to our home. You *must* take him home! This will not be possible if you choose to remain here."

"He claims he can't go with me," Wes argued, "that the demon inside him won't let him."

"He listens to the Father of Lies and believes he speaks the truth. But I have seen a thousand futures, Wesley, and the problem is far greater than you or me or Daniel. There is only one way to repair the unraveling of time, and that is with Daniel returning home. For he *must* return home, just as Benji *must* stand and face the self-proclaimed Elders of the capital. Both of which will not occur, unless you are by their sides."

Wes stared at Ruth grimly. Compared to all she just said, his desire to hold Peter seemed vastly insignificant. Duty bound him to the tasks at hand, and he had to let go of his longing for his youngest son.

"What do I need to do, Ruth?"

"You need to return. Return to the fallen world with full knowledge of who you are and all you have once forgotten."

"Breathe!"

"What?" Wes looked around for the source of the unfamiliar voice. The world grew drab, as color drained out of everything around him. All faded into shades of lifeless gray.

"Our time is up far too soon," Ruth said with a tired looking smile, "Goodbye, Wesley, I love you."

"Breathe!"

"Ruth?" The grays flattened, blending into one lifeless color which spread over everything Wes could see.

"He's breathing unassisted, sir!"

"Alright everyone, give him some space. Allow him to rest, then we will see where we stand." The grayness solidified, and grew into an oppressive mist that swallowed all that it interacted with. Peter vanished, along with the linen on the line, and the house on the hill. Ruth started to fade as well, a visual reminder of all that was taken from him.

"Ruth! Don't go! I don't know what I'm supposed to do," Wes said desperately.

"Our time is up, my love," Ruth replied sadly, "Follow the path God leads you down. I'll see you again one day, on the other side of the veil." She vanished before him, absorbed into the mist along with the rest of the world. Wes looked down at his sinless hands, and watched as they too melded into the mist, turning gray alongside everything around him: a neutralizer to this place between life and death.

"Goodbye Ruth!" Wes called into the void, "I love you both so much and will be with you again one day! I promise I will."

Wes tumbled through an unseen realm, as his consciousness drifted in and out of newfound memories. There were so many memories; countless in number. Dreams, and recollections, and remembrances, and flashbacks. The painful, the divine, the sweet, and the ones best left forgotten. Everything lost to the madness in the pit, to the unraveling of time, and to his own human limitations were restored to him in full. He couldn't comprehend how so much thought was able to be cataloged and sequenced in his mind, yet somehow it all was. A tableau of every life experience congealed into reality. It was overwhelming, it was captivating, and it worked to fill in all the holes in his mind.

The madness that had occupied those spaces vanished fully. Wes observed his entire life, seeing it for what it truly was, and felt complete. When the work was done, and all wounds mended, Wes sank down into the heart of his being, and felt the weight of his body surrounding him. Exhausted, he gave over thought to dreams. He slept for two days.

When at last Wes rose to the surface of tranquility, where sleep had little effect on awareness, he felt the depths of his physical pain. It seemed less than before, when he first endured the effects of Gad's bile upon his skin. Consciousness made Wes aware that he was unable to see, but he felt the soft embrace of a bed beneath him, and heard the breathing of others quietly present in the same room. He winced as he tried to sit up for the bones of his chest ached and joined the multitude of other pains in his body. Pain layered upon pain. Wes raised a hand to touch the tender place over his heart.

"He's starting to rouse. Should I give him more morphine, great lord?"

"No, don't give him anything yet. I wish to speak with him, and the drugs will only put him to sleep again." Wes recognized Daniel's voice, and reached a weak hand toward his son. His body felt...strange. It felt like he was stranded on an island, and all around him were waves of pain in his eyes, his throat, his lungs, his chest. The waves rose and fell; crashed and waned, but never touched his bare feet in the sand. Daniel's voice also seemed to dance among the waves, while Wes watched everything with distant apathy, on this island of numbness behind his closed eyes. Even without the help of morphine, his body started to sink into the warm embrace of sleep.

"Father, can you hear me?" The voice drifted through the darkness alongside him, and Wes cautiously opened his mouth to respond.

"Yes, Daniel." The words were slurred and unnatural. His tongue was like a bloated fish beached on his island's shore. His throat was like the withering trees: parched and brittle in the scalding sun.

"There is swelling in the larynx," said a man on the opposite side of the bed from Daniel, "he will not be able to speak or eat very well. I would like to give him a few vials of water to test his ability to swallow without choking. May I proceed, great lord?"

"Of course," Daniel replied, "Thank you, Healer. Father, I must speak with you. A lot has happened since you took on the fish."

"A lot certainly has!" Interjected another voice. One that Wes assumed belonged to an Elder. "My lord, if I may speak freely, these past few days have been madness. The initial riots were quelled rather quickly, but when the Disciples learned of who we tried to...um, who was involved in our...entertainment...My point is, while you've locked yourself away in this room, great lord, the city has turned to looting and destruction. The zealot fools stand outside our walls and shout all night long; demanding retribution for the Keeper, and are recruiting the commoners in droves. Great lord, if we don't appease the Disciples, anarchy is a real possibility!"

"And who is to shoulder the blame for this mess, Elder Bruce? Who do we hold responsible? My father for not dying like you wanted him to? Me for using his gun on that monster? The Disciples for their part in spreading prophecy like it was madness? Maybe that strange light that occurred so many weeks ago could be the cause? But I suspect that we should blame the Elders themselves. For the many years you indulged yourself at the expense of those so-called commoners you despise!"

"Great lord, I regret to say that I must concur with Elder Bruce," another man interjected and Wes recognized Ashter's voice. "If we provide the Disciples with proof that the

Keeper is alive and well, it will go a long way to quell the unrest that is roosting outside of our gates."

Hands gently guided Wes to sit up, causing him to wince, and pillows were pushed behind him. He coughed as the thick mucus in his throat moved with the shift in his body. He felt the weight of cloth wraps covering his eyes and face but didn't have the strength to remove them. A man spoke softly near his ear.

"I'm pressing a small vial to your lips, sir. Please try to swallow the water it contains." Wes felt the coolness of a glass vial press against his lower lip, and opened his mouth, greedily accepting the liquid like a baby bird.

"Since the captain has resolved the crisis you insisted on interrupting me for, may I please continue Elder Bruce? For I would like to speak to the lot of you as well as to my father regarding what I learned in the time you claim I did nothing but sit here and watch him sleep. Over the past few days, while his body struggled to keep his mind alive, I was visited often by Elder Jay. From what he's told me, I now know that we no longer have the luxury of heated debates that amount to nothing. Actions must be made! We must urgently retrieve the Son of Promise!"

"Our true Guardian Son!"

"The great Bringer of Light!"

"The Lord Dragon has gone silent," Daniel continued, "he does not speak to any of you and he no longer speaks to me as well. I still feel him deep within, but he seems to be...sleeping. He rests and he waits for his time of need. The last time I heard his voice was when the boy stood before all of us and Elder Thoss made his bold claims. In that moment, our Lord called the boy the Son of Promise. He said 'if I had control of the Son of Promise, I could repair time itself.'"

"Then we must go retrieve the boy! We must bring him back to us!" Cried out a woman Elder.

"A wonderful idea!" Daniel retorted, his words entwined with cynicism. "And where is he, exactly? Even if we find him, based on Chancy's testimony, the only reason he was able to return with the child at all was because the Son of Promise approached him directly. How long do you anticipate this retrieval effort will take? Who among you are willing to leave the power of the Divine Hall to chase down a seed on a beach full of sand?" The room went very still, and Wes could sense a mix of emotions among the onlookers: fear, apprehension, expectation, curiosity. Daniel rested a hand atop his own, and Wes turned his head in the direction of his son's voice.

"Father, do you know where the Son of Promise is located?"

“Yes,” Wes replied carefully.

“And do you remember why you came here in the first place?”

“I remember everything,” Wes whispered.

“For the others in this room, I’ll say that you came to ask me to return to our home with you for the sake of my mom who recently died. You wanted me to...what was it called?”

“Pay your respects,” Wes agreed. It was an old term; an honored tradition.

“If I go with you, and do as you ask, will you return to the Divine Hall with the Son of Promise?”

“No,” Wes replied stubbornly. He meant what he said: that he remembered everything. This included Ruth telling him that Benji needed to face the Elders with Wes at his side, but he didn’t care. He refused to bring the boy back to this twisted place. Daniel didn’t seem surprised by this response, but all the Elders started to speak at once.

“Quiet!” Daniel snapped, and all present complied with his command, except for one. A small voice called out from the other end of the room.

“Great lord, if you make this deal, and if you go with the Keeper, how do you plan to survive?”

“My survival is no longer relevant,” Daniel replied with a sigh. “Go on, Elder Jay, tell the others what you told me. It’s alright. Tell them.”

“Well,” Elder Jay began nervously. A healer pressed another vial to his lips, and Wes drank as he listened. “During the celebration of Old Father, a messenger came to me with grave news from the northern barracks."

"Yes...I recall hearing of how you were conducting experiments in the four barracks."

"Oh! Experiments are so entertaining!”

"Go on, Elder Jay," Daniel said patiently and the Elder nervously cleared his throat.

"As some of you may know, I have been questioning the residents in each of the barracks on the four corners of the world, for they are the farthest from this central point of the Divine Hall. I wanted to establish significant memories for each person, then see how quickly those memories are forgotten. We have been following the trends of how memories are influenced by the unraveling of time for months now.”

"Get to the point, man! What does all of this mean?"

"The evidence the messenger provided was grave but irrefutable: the decaying of time is accelerating. We also learned that sometimes when a prominent memory is forgotten by one, it is forgotten by everyone who experienced it. This indicates that, at least in part, entire moments are being erased from the collective timeline.”

"Surely this can't be the case!"

"Elder Jay, tell them the last thing you said to me," Daniel said, "when we met the other day."

"Unfortunately," the Elder continued, "the worsening memory loss, from the start of my research to the present day, proves that the unraveling of the past has increased. More-so, it has become evident that days are no longer uniform, as some are confirmed to be longer than others, and the nights seem to sometimes be endless. The unraveling is no longer affecting just the past. It is bleeding into the present as well."

"Surely this isn't affecting us!"

"The barracks are a week's ride away!"

"It *is* affecting us," Elder Jay concluded. "For I regrettably must admit that citizens of the city are starting to forget things as well."

"Foolishness!" A woman cried out.

"The commoners are fools! This will never reach us! We will not be affected!"

"If that is so," Daniel interjected, "can someone please tell me how Old Father died?"

Silence.

Stillness.

Dread.

"The world is ending!"

"My collections! I don't want to forget my precious things!"

"What shall become of us if we can't remember all that we enjoy?"

"I don't want to forget all the delightful things I've done!"

"Listen to me!" Daniel demanded. Another vial of water was pressed to Wes' lips, and he drank it down hungrily. It tasted bitter on his swollen tongue.

"Now that you know what's at stake, you know why urgency is needed. But I know my father, and if he made a promise to my mother, he's going to do everything to keep that promise. Do you want me to go with you father, back to our farm?"

"Yes," Wes replied, his voice stronger from the water.

"This is suicide," someone whined; no one disagreed.

"And knowing what you now know, the things Elder Jay shared, if I go with you, will you return here with the Son of Promise?"

"So you can sacrifice him to a demon?"

"The Dragon is going to save the world!" One of the Elders called out.

"So you say," Wes laughed and then coughed.

"Answer the question, father," Daniel demanded and Wes could sense them all watching him.

“If I say no, will you still go with me?” he asked.

“Never,” Daniel replied without hesitation.

"Here, here!" One of the Elders commemorated.

Wes understood the fine line Daniel walked with these Elders that only respected him for the parasite inside him. The *usurper*. But he could not ignore Ruth’s words. She told him that Daniel must go home, and that Benji must face the Elders. He didn’t like any of it, but knew that if she said this, there was no other way.

“I will do as you say,” Wes conceded. “With or without you, I will bring him back to the Divine Hall. You have my word.”

“He has no sin on his body! He must be telling the truth.”

"Weren't his entire hands covered in black scales when he last met him?"

"It terrifies me to admit that I can't remember!"

“Then the matter is settled,” Daniel declared and his hand fell away from Wes’ as he got to his feet. “Healer, how long do you think before my father’s able to ride.”

“Preferably another week,” the Healer said, “but knowing you, great lord, I will try to have him ready in another two days.”

“Very well,” Daniel said calmly, “Captain, please stretch two of our good horses and ready them to ride in two days. The Divine Hall is doing its work on him. He should recover in that time and when he does, we will go east. Be happy! For you will regain custody of your Light Bringer. I just am grateful I won’t be here to witness it.”

Silence stretched on between the Elders as they considered Daniel’s words. Wes didn’t fully understand why Daniel thought this journey was a death sentence, but he liked to believe that his son was mistaken. Eve and Sassy and Ruth all told Wes in their own ways that Daniel needed to return home, so that was where he was determined to take the boy.

“Great lord,” one of the Elders said at last. A timid man who had not spoken before. “If you leave, what will happen to all of us? What will we do without the Dragon’s protection?”

“You see how far his protection goes,” Daniel said with a bitter laugh, “we risk losing ourselves every time we leave the Hall grounds. Our position grows weaker every day, and now our own people have turned against us in the streets! We don’t have the liberty to hesitate anymore, Elder Spry. Even if I don’t survive, the Dragon will. He always finds a way. He will be ready when a vessel is opened to him. Just as he was ready when I was made open to him. Now please, all of you, I wish to be alone with my father.” Wes listened to the Elders as they each made their way out of the room. The Healer offered him another vial of bitter water, then he too left along with the others. The last Elder to leave paused at the door, and turned to address her Guardian Son.

"You are...so beautiful, great lord." Her words trembled as though she were close to tears. "I hope to never forget your face as you are sitting here today."

"I'm touched, Elder Agatha, truly. But my father almost died. It's by the grace of the Hall itself that he remains with us today. Please allow me this time alone with him. I'll make an effort to visit your quarters later."

"Yes, great lord. Of course," the Elder responded, and Wes heard her step out of the room as she pulled the door closed. At last they were alone together. Wes expected Daniel might have something to say to him, but the silence stretched on between them. He thought to speak instead, but realized that he could think of nothing to say that would make the situation seem any better.

Daniel took Wes' hand in his own, and clutched it with a fervent desperation he concealed when there were others in the room. When Wes caught the soft sounds of his son's private tears, he mustered his strength, and reached over to pull Daniel into a hug. Even with his mind full of memories, he didn't know the right thing to say to ease his son's pain. He guided Daniel to lean against his shoulder, and allowed his son to give over to his despair. Wes leaned close to him, and drew in the scent of Daniel's hair.

"I'll pray for you," Wes whispered, and felt the bitter sting of helplessness. "I'll pray for us both."

Chapter Thirty-Two

Once a message came quietly,
so quietly I could hardly hear it.
Like a nightmare it disturbed my sleep.
I trembled and shuddered; my whole book shook with fear.
A light breeze touched my face,
and my skin crawled with fright.
-Job 4:12-15 GNT

Wes woke abruptly, gasping from the weight of his panic. Hazy visions swam through his mind; memories of dreams he could not fully recall. Terror seemed to follow him into the waking world. His eyes, still covered in strips of cloth, camouflaged the day, and left him feeling like he was in a daze. Or perhaps there was more to this shroud that covered his mind. He suspected that the Healer must have put drugs in the water they offered to him.

Wes tried to sit up, but his arms felt heavy and numb; his muscles were not working as they should. Hoping to ease the turmoil in his mind and get his bearings, he sank back against his pillows, and reached for the bandages covering his eyes.

"Please don't touch those, sir, you might cause harm to your vision." Wes turned to face the direction where he heard the woman speaking. Her voice sounded familiar.

"I'm feeling out of sorts...a side effect of a dream I can't seem to remember," he said hoarsely. A cup was pressed to his lips, and he took a careful sip. The water was cool, and lacked the sharp bitter taste like the water he had before. Wes enclosed the woman's hands with his own, and guided her to tilt the cup further while he drank down the remaining water with greedy gulps. When it was drained fully, he collapsed back on his pillows, breathless from the effort.

"Are you an Elder?" Wes asked, unable to place her voice.

"I am a Disciple," the woman replied, the words soft and airy. Wes searched his tableau of memories and a name of a conflicted woman came to his mind.

"Sorrow?"

"I have no name. I gave it as an offering to the... Guardian Son," she whispered in reply.

"What are you doing here?" Wes asked, trying again to sit up. Sorrow leaned over him and adjusted his pillows. She propped him upright, then sat facing him on his bed.

"I was sent here by the other Disciples as a part of the treaty formed with the High Council. I am here to assist in your care and ensure you are not mistreated any further. It was horrible what they did to you, sir. They don't know how to properly treat a God."

"Well, I appreciate your help," Wes said, feeling a little uncomfortable with her proclamation, and paused to drink the water she offered him. "I'm sure as a new Disciple you would prefer to be among your flock."

"Oh, not at all, sir," Sorrow replied in her breathless way, "I'm honored to be chosen to serve you. Most of my kind prefer to worship from a distance, and while they thought it was necessary for one of us to come, none volunteered aside from me. That makes me special."

"Indeed you are," Wes conceded, and chose his words carefully. "Why did you agree to do something none of the other Disciples were willing to do?"

"Oh, sir," Sorrow sighed, and slipped her small cool hand into his, "It was such an honor to receive a gift from you, Keeper. I am here to worship and rejoice in your presence. I am here to give gratitude to my God."

"I am not a God," Wes offered forth in protest into the space hidden from his closed eyes. He could hear Sorrow's soft breathing. She removed her hand from his, and Wes felt her fingertips skim the edge of his beard. He pulled away from her touch.

"I'm tasked to change your dressings," Sorrow breathed, and retracted her hand, "so I need you to keep your eyes closed while I remove the old dressings and replace them with new. They need to rest so they can heal."

"I'll keep them closed," Wes assured her, and listened attentively to the rustle of her movements. She rose from beside him, and moved to a different side of the room. Wes hoped she would return with more water. His tongue felt shriveled and sore.

Sleep took him like the snuff of a candle's light, and when something was pressed to his lips, Wes jerked awake.

"Be still," Sorrow whispered as she stroked his arm with gentle fingers. Wes gulped down the water she offered him again. Only after he emptied the cup did he realize how bitter it tasted. Wes eased back on the pillows, sighing under the heavy weight of exhaustion while Sorrow worked the dressings loose around his head.

"I have heard much about you, Light Keeper" she said softly as she worked on her task.

"Tell me," Wes murmured. A warm tranquility spread over him, and he knew with certainty that the bitterness in the water was a drug. Morphine.

"There are lots of things," Sorrow said as she finished removing the old wraps of cloth, then used cool water to help soften and remove the old gauze laid over his skin. It was dried and crusted from his skin weeping, but Sorrow was gentle and Wes only felt the occasional sting of pain.

"I want to hear what you heard," Wes said, and carefully listened inside the enfolding embrace of his hazy mind.

"I heard that you were born from the God of old, and he cursed you to never lie. I heard you rendered the fish blind during your battle, then lured him into a trap so that our great lord could execute him. I heard you draw strength from fire, and your eyes glow in the sun. Also...I heard you have never known a woman, sir."

"All foolish gossip," Wes mumbled; his words slurred.

"Is any of it true? Have you...known a woman, Light Keeper?" Wes' comprehension roamed in and out of clarity.

"What else have you heard?"

"I heard that you are the true father of our...Guardian Son. I heard that he cured your sin and not the light in the alleyway. When you embraced him, your sin fell away like flakes of dry mud. I...also heard that... you are lovers with the Captain of the Guard."

"Nonsense," Wes sighed as he sank into the bed. Down he went, while it enclosed him with secret spiderwebs. He was cocooned in the soft welcoming embrace of just existing. Sorrow cleaned his face with gentle strokes, and removed the coils of gauze that covered Wes' eyes. He obediently kept them closed. He lacked the strength to open them anyway.

"Sit still, sir," the young Disciple said, her voice delicate like lace, and she cradled his face in her hand. The cloth she used was cool; soothing him while she dabbed at the corners of his eyes.

"How bad does it look?" Wes asked sleepily; vaguely aware of how close Sorrow was to him.

"The Healers told me that you sustained burns to the whole of your face as well as your neck and chest. You also sustained burns in your mouth and lungs, and both of your eyes of course."

"You didn't answer my question," Wes said with a small smile.

"And you didn't answer mine," Sorrow replied, a heartbeat later.

"What question was that?" His words tumbled through his vacant mind, and Wes fought to stay awake; to think clearly; to focus on this girl who was touching his face. Morphine collided with him like waves; ebbing and flowing.

"If you've known a woman, sir." Sorrow sounded carefully impassive.

"Why do you ask such things?" Wes let out a long sigh when Sorrow tenderly placed a cooling gel on his skin. Blessed relief.

"I have seen the full of you, Light Keeper, for I cleaned you while you slept, and I can say with full certainty that there is no part of you that has known the taint of sin. It's so incredible to see. Pappa...he always told me it was women that led men to sin. Do you avoid women for this reason, Keeper? Would I lead you to sin?" Her fingers slowed, turning the process of her application into more of a caress, and Wes fought against the pull of sleep.

"I've known the cost of sin," he muttered, "and I knew my wife before the Lord took her from me." Sorrow placed gauze over Wes' moistened skin.

"Yet not a mark upon you to show for it. You are spotless. Perfection. Just like the...Guardian Son. Forgive me, I am not used to saying his name." She unrolled strips of cloth and wrapped it around Wes' face from the nose up. When she finished with her task, Sorrow's fingers glided down Wes' cheek, and she ran a gentle thumb across his lower lip.

"What are you doing, Sorrow?" he whispered. He was too weak to push her away. He was barely clinging to his own consciousness. His words floated in the air; an undesired illusion. It felt like a dream. His dreams felt like reality.

"That is no longer my name, sir, but I am thinking about kissing you." Words came to his ears. A moment later, his mind gave them meaning.

"Why would you do such a thing?"

"To see if it makes your skin turn black."

"You're far too young to be kissing an old man like me," Wes said, and a moment later wondered if the words were just considered, or fully spoken.

"I'm sorry...We...You're just so...handsome...Guardian Son." Wes tried to focus on what this woman was saying, but sleep kept grabbing at him and pulling him down into the void where his dreams always found him.

"Iwonbehansumanymore," Wes mumbled, a breath above a sigh, "wickedbludburnmyface."

"The Divine Hall is a sacred place, Light Keeper," Sorrow said, her face so close that Wes could feet her breath upon his exposed skin, "it strips away the burden of injury."

"How?" Wes asked, the word was barely more than a thought formed upon his lips.

"That I don't know, but I'll tell you everything I *do* know...if you let me kiss you."

"Takeyourpricefrommethen," Wes managed to reply, and so she did. Her lips pressed against his own, then she pulled away from him and sat back down on the chair. She spoke until sleep took Wes fully, but from her explanation, he understood why the Elders were reluctant to leave the building. He understood why they all grieved over Daniel's resignation to go. Alas, Wes finally understood that if the two of them left together, Daniel would probably not survive long enough to return.

For his first meal, Wes was fed a bland broth, and for that he was grateful. He had little interest in food and didn't seem to feel the pain of his own hunger. Eating was a chore only made worse when he was fed by someone else. He still had swelling in his throat, and the Healers that came to examine him worried that any solid food wouldn't go down so well.

Obediently slurping the broth one spoonful at a time, Wes reflected on what he learned of the Divine Hall. After hearing what Sorrow said of the place, he asked anyone who visited him about the strange qualities of this ancient building. One of the Elders, while visiting Wes, told him about the day they first met Daniel. As a small boy, he had sin staining the length of his arms, and an angry scar running down the side of his face. The Elder fondly recounted how the scar twisted the corner of his mouth, giving him a cocky half grin. They all found that smile endearing, and couldn't resist the boy. It was Old Father that showed them the path to the Dragon. The Healers took away Daniel's scar, but it was the Dragon who took away his sin sickness. It was the first of many miracles that their Great Lord performed.

When Elder Jay visited him, Wes recalled the man's scientific nature, and asked if he ever did research regarding the Halls healing properties, or how that dungeon under the Hall was able to accelerate people to the brink of madness without them tipping over. Elder Jay admitted to conducting experiments on many reluctant locals in his past, but was unable to draw conclusions from them. He eventually abandoned his efforts to focus his attention on the current state of time. He explained that while the Hall quickened the healing process, and even held off most sicknesses, it was also once impervious to the unraveling of time as well. His revelation that this was no longer the case has caused great turmoil among the High Council. The Elders feared that the Hall's other protections were no longer a guarantee.

Wes also learned that the Elders used to be able to leave the Hall for weeks at a time and not be affected by the progression of their ongoing sin.

"I think the longest anyone stayed beyond these walls was nearly a month," said a bold woman's voice with an air of authority to her, "But that was nearly a decade ago."

Wes listened to it all while blinking heavy lids over glazed eyes, and fathomed concepts of time. How quickly will the black scales of sin show on Daniel's hands and face? How quickly will it evolve into something more? What kind of horrible creature will he become in the end?

Seeing the process with Gad first hand, Wes was under no illusion that Daniel will suffer immensely. His body will deform before Wes' eyes, and the whole process was dreadfully painful. It will be hard enough to just exist, but Daniel also needs to travel across the wilds and seek out his redemption at their old home. Maybe it wouldn't be that bad. Gad was under the strange influence of those dark places under the Divine Hall, and Daniel would not be. Wes wanted to believe that God would spare Daniel. He *had* to believe this. Everyone was pointing him down this path, but Wes couldn't bear to think that he was leading his son toward his own destruction.

Wes only realized he had fallen asleep again when he woke up. The room was silent, vacant of life, and he felt both isolated, and exceptionally useless. He could hear the noise of engagement in the places beyond his corner of the Hall. Laughter and screams. Happiness and despair. Wes looked to the Lord and silently prayed.

Lord, I know thy will be done, but please spare my son from the agony of his choices. He's just a boy, God, and while he's done some wicked things, I pray that you show him your mercy. Don't let him suffer like Gad did. Show me the way to get him home safely, God. Guide me down the path I must go.

"Amen."

“You’re awake.” Wes turned his head toward the sound of Daniel’s voice. His son was lingering next to the open door. He seemed hesitant to enter.

“I was praying,” Wes replied, and pushed himself to sit up in his bed. He groped about, looking for what he knew was there, and located a small table where a cup was placed for him. He lifted it to his lips, and took one long sip, then carefully replaced it on the table.

“You’re not drinking more?”

“It’s drugged,” Wes said, and Daniel scoffed.

“Of course it is.”

“Will you come sit with me?” Daniel didn’t respond, and still he hesitated. After some time, Wes heard the click of the door closing. He thought for a moment that Daniel had left him, but then heard the creaking wood from the chair placed on the right of his bed, and knew his son had settled into it. Wes faced the direction of the sound and spoke again.

“Tell me why you are so upset.” He didn’t need the second sight to know such things about his own son. Wes could clearly discern that something was troubling him. He reached for his boy, and felt Daniel take hold of his hand.

“What makes you think I’m upset?” His voice was tactfully neutral, but Wes was not deceived. There was something in the way he spoke that seemed off, and when Wes gave it some thought, he realized that Daniel was speaking through his teeth as though he didn’t want to move his jaw. Wes leaned forward, reaching with his other hand to seek out his son’s face. Daniel tried to pull away from him, but Wes grabbed hold of his arm to hold him in place. Fingers probed his son’s down-turned face, and it didn’t take long for Wes to find the hard lump that formed along his jawline. There was swelling around the eye, and a cut on his lip. He was struck on his cheek, high on his forehead, and a large lump was hidden in his hair. When Wes touched a cut alongside Daniel’s mouth, he sucked air through his teeth and turned his face away. The damage was not just reserved to his face either. Wes realized that his clothing was torn, and he seemed to carry a sour smell to his skin.

“What have they done to you?” Wes breathed. He knew he was furious, but the drugs muffled his mind and left him feeling hollow.

“It’s... not a big deal. Just a little... sport.” Daniel sounded raw and exposed, making the sting of his paltry words bite deeper. “Some of the Elders they...since I’m leaving they wanted to...play...a game...with...me.”

Wes never felt as feeble as he did in that moment. He saw the helplessness of his son’s circumstance and while he knew the solution involved escaping it, the world on the outside would be no kinder to him. This was Daniel. This was his *son*. And while

Wes could admit he held a deep desire to take hold of those perpetrators that assaulted his boy, and do the same wicked unto them in kind, the application of this desire was currently impossible. He has been rendered an invalid, and his son, who needed him desperately, was left alone to fend against the ire of his wretched Elders. He was still so young, barely thirteen, and used in ways even adults shouldn't be forced to endure. His face was branded, and his body decorated in black: the color this city chose for its slaves.

Wes didn't think it was possible for him to feel a new kind of pain. He thought he already experienced all the cruelty this world had to offer. He evidently was wrong. Helpless anger made him feel frustrated and restless. He should do something! He needed retribution for his son!

"If I had my gun," Wes growled, and Daniel surprised him by laughing.

"And what would you do exactly? Would the great Light Keeper have some sport of his own then? Not likely for a man of inaction, who blames his cowardice on the laws of his supposed God!"

Wes opened his mouth, but couldn't find the right words to say. This always seemed to be the way between them: Daniel, abruptly overcome with anger, slinging barbs at Wes with his tongue, and Wes, befuddled by the truth of his words, staring dumbfounded and devoid of response. He felt blind in more ways than just his sight, and suddenly yearned for their relationship to be easier.

"I will be fully healed in a few days and so will you," Daniel went on, pulling away from Wes, and getting to his feet, "you're already able to sit up on your own, so I have no doubt you'll be ready to leave at that time. Until then, let's see what your God does for you."

"Wait," Wes said, desperate to hold onto these brief moments they kept having together. Daniel always seemed to be running away from him, or running toward him, but never just being present with him. Wes reached, wanting to feel Daniel take his hand again, but already his son was moving to the exit.

Don't go! Please come back! Stay with me.

Daniel slipped out of the room without either of them saying another word, and left Wes to sit, still facing the door. He waited for a long time, listening to the sounds outside of his room, and willed the door to open, indicating his son's return. When the festivities of the evening quieted down as its own form of birdsong, Wes took it as indication of the upcoming day. He snatched up the cup from its table and gulped down the water it contained in hopes to stifle the acute pain gripping his heart. Let the morphine silence the turmoil of his misery.

I am a coward.

Wes found the comfort of drug induced sleep.

It was dim; hard to see. Wes reached and felt the familiar thin blanket tied to his bars. Recognizing his prison cell, a strange acceptance overtook his mind. Of course he was there. Of course he was.

"If thy right eye offends thee..."

"No." Wes cupped his hands to his ears and curled into a ball on the cold earthy floor.

"If thy right eye offends thee..."

"No!" Wes shouted for his hands failed to defend his hearing.

"YE DARE DEFY THE WILL OF GOD?" roared the beast, and Wes felt the force of his rage. Metal screamed against his ire as the fish ripped his way out of the cage that contained him.

"Ye think ye are free of yer madness?" He growled as he slammed his hulking form into the bars of Wes' cell.

"No, no, no!" Wes whined as he drug his morphine laced husk into the back corner of his cell: this place where he conjured his worst ideas. It didn't matter. Let the madness come if it kept him away from that monster and his endless teeth!

"Madness never leaves ye, friend. It hides in the eyes. It forever lingers in the corners of yer sight!" The fish slammed up against the bars again and the whole metal frame broke free from the stone it was lodged up against.

Wes raised his hands, desperate to ward off this nightmare, but the beast was on him in an instant. His arm, blistering and wet with ooze, pressed against Wes' throat; crushing him into the floor, and cutting off any hope of air. Trapped as he was, Wes was seized with panic. He stared, eyes wide with terror, as the fish peeled back his flaccid lips, and bared his black dagger teeth.

"I'll pluck the madness out for ye, friend," The monster's voice cooed next to his ear, and Wes opened his mouth in a soundless scream.

He felt a hand grab hold of his shoulder; an impossible feat considering he was pressed flat against the stone floor, but true all the same. He was pulled directly into the earth itself. Reality reformed around him, and a cool breeze chilled his face. Wes sucked in a long breath of crisp air, as he sat up and realized the fish was gone. The sun was warm upon his skin, and Wes found himself sitting at the edge of his field overlooking the spent stalks of harvested corn.

He shivered, and pulled his father's jacket tighter around his gaunt body. In the distance, he watched those familiar crows circling around a black form in the field. He could sense he wasn't alone though, and put the birds out of his mind. Looking over his shoulder, he turned his attention to the farmhouse looming on the hill.

"Ruth?" Wes called out, but was not surprised when she failed to respond. He knew she was in a place where he could no longer reach her, but hoped she might be able to hear him still.

"I'm bringing him home to you, Ruth," Wes called up to the farmhouse, "but you failed to tell me about the cost."

Another breeze brushed past him, and a scattering of leaves danced through the air. Wes watched as they tumbled and collected against the crude stairs that led up to his porch. As he studied their course, he caught a flicker of movement, and realized something pushed closed the front door of his home.

Madness forever lingers in the corners of yer sight!

"Hey! Wait!" Wes called out, ignoring the monster taunting in his mind, but when he got to his feet, a deep mist overtook him. It swirled up out of nowhere, blotting out the sun, and carried with it a strange sound like a thousand buzzing insect wings. Wes tried to push forward, into the mist itself, but felt the force of something shove against his chest hard. He fell backwards, and tumbled into a gray void of vacancy.

Wes sat up, gasping in panic, and listened to the thrum of his racing heart. Whatever dream put him in such a state, he lacked all recollection of it. He was frustrated, always waking up this way, but was unsure whether his dreams eluding him were a curse or a blessing. Wes felt around, recognized his familiar bed, and relaxed in knowing he was still in his room in the Divine Hall. For some reason, he feared he was back in that prison with no concept of days or time.

Back in the pit. Down in the dark place.

"Hello?" Wes called out, and after a moment, he felt something shift at the foot of his bed. "Who's there?"

A tentative part of him hoped it might be Daniel, but the voice that responded was not his son's.

"Did I wake you?" it whispered softly, and Wes sat up.

"No, not you. I keep having these...dreams I can't seem to remember. Come sit up here with me." He felt movement as someone slid off the foot of the bed, and then the familiar squeak of the chair Daniel occupied earlier. A moment later, the seat on the other side of the bed creaked as well. So, two visitors then.

"Speak up now," Wes said with growing curiosity, "tell me why you're here."

"We...we were worried about you, Mister Wes," said the voice to his right, and Wes immediately recognized it as Pip's.

"We heard all about your fight, Mister Wes. It sounded amazing!" Kenner chimed in, "we love hearing our guard brothers tell the tale. The way you drove that halberd into the fish monster... kapow! It's incredible! Everyone wants to be trained on the halberd now."

"He almost died," Pip scolded but could not deflate Kenner's gusto.

"But he didn't! He'll be alright, Pip, Healer Bostwick said so. They wouldn't even let us in here if he wasn't going to be okay."

"I'm glad you came to see me, boys," Wes said fondly, "but I'm also glad you didn't watch the fight."

"I'm glad we didn't see it too!" said Pip. "Other guards that are...younger like us, well...a lot of them keep having nightmares about the fish."

"Did he really have a thousand teeth?" Kenner asked.

"Of course he didn't! Right, Mister Wes? But I'm sure he was still really scary," Pip said, "I'm so glad you're going to be alright."

"Yes, I'll be alright," Wes agreed.

"Will you tell us about the fight?" Kenner perked up, "tell us how you took down the fish!"

"I will, but first I want to ask you something. Does your captain know you're here?"

Silence.

"Will you get in trouble if he finds out you're here?"

Silence still.

"I think you two better go for now. Get permission from your captain, and please come back to visit me soon. I want to see you again before I have to leave the city."

"You're going away?" Kenner whined, making evident his deep disappointment.

"I have something I need to do for the sake of my son."

"Will you come back when you're done?" Pip asked and Wes sighed.

"Yes, I'll come back when I'm done. I just don't know exactly when that will be. But no more chatter from you two. If you aren't supposed to be here, then you best be on your way."

"Alright, Mister Wes, we were about to leave anyway," Pip said, "we have to sneak back to our bunks before morning call."

"Goodbye, boys, and be careful," Wes said as he reached for them both.

"Feel better soon!" offered Kenner as the two boys leaned in and gave Wes a quick hug. He listened to their footsteps as they shuffled quickly out of the room, and eased back in his bed when he heard them close the door. Alone again, Wes reached for his cup and found it empty. No water. No morphine. He flopped back with another sigh. He wanted the morphine more than the water. It might help him to no longer feel the weight of worthlessness pressing down upon him.

"Will I always be this helpless?" Wes asked of the darkness that shrouded both his eyes and his room. He laid there contemplating a way out of the mess he found himself in. It took a long time for him to fall back to sleep.

Chapter Thirty-Three

My heart beats wildly, my strength fails,
Am I going blind?
My loved ones and friends stay away, fearing my disease.
Even my own family stands at a distance.
-Psalms 38:10-11 NLT

The following evening, just as the sun sank low enough to cast long shadows in the streets, a man entered Wes' room. He introduced himself as Healer Bostwick, and determined that it was safe for Wes to have his dressings removed.

The process took little effort, which was a wonder considering how careful Sorrow needed to be the night before. Bostwick removed his dressings, peeled back Wes' eyelids to examine his eyes, and declared him medically cleared.

"I will send for the guard tailor as he needs to get started on your attire immediately. You certainly can't travel in bedclothes, and I suspect the Guardian Son will want to leave tomorrow."

"I understand, but everything is still so blurry," Wes said, as he blinked at the dark complected man standing over him, "will this improve at all?"

"Based on your progress, I expect your vision to be as restored as it possibly can be by the night's end," replied the Healer as he rummaged in the pockets of his coat. "I will leave this for you to take at your discretion, in case they continue to cause you some level of discomfort."

He walked over to a long narrow table that hugged the wall opposite Wes' bed, and pulled out a small bottle which he placed next to a cup and water pitcher.

"Thank you, Healer," Wes said softly as he studied the bottle with its silent invitation. Another chance to feel nothing. Another chance to escape all that tormented his mind. Noticing none of this, Bostwick nodded to him absently, and strolled out of the room.

The guard tailor seemed very interested in Wes' choices for attire; nodding eagerly and jotting down many notes. He was willing to dress Wes in anything he desired, and while Wes wished he still had his father's clothes, he would at least get something similar. The tailor was just jotting down the last of his measurements when Ashter strolled into the room.

"Well look at you," exclaimed the captain, and Wes couldn't help his smile. "fresh out of bed, and already setting the next fashion trends among my men."

"You speak nonsense," Wes muttered, and watched as the stooped tailor bowed to them both, and hastily fled the room. "Ah, look. You scared him off."

"I doubt that greatly," Ashter said with a laugh. "He's probably just in a hurry to get started. After your last grand appearance half the city wanted to copy your look. The demands for alterations were overwhelming, and our dear tailor made enough money to keep both his wife *and* his mistress happy for at least a year."

"I don't like all these people making such a fuss over me," Wes grumbled, but softened his scowl as Ashter approached him. "Still, I'm glad you're here."

"A sight for sore eyes, I'm sure," Ashter teased and rubbed a knuckle against the corner of his eye.

"As you say, my vision is not fully recovered," Wes admitted, then flashed the captain a wolfish grin, "the Lord has blessed me, for I am unable to clearly see your face."

"Wes, I'm wounded! I'll have you know, I am reputed to be the most dashing; most handsome; most roguish devil in the city! Or at least I used to be. All everyone wants to talk about lately is you." Ashter sighed, and gave Wes' shoulder a quick squeeze. "All the same, it's good to see you recovering quickly, and I'm sorry I didn't come sooner. It was hard to see you hurt...knowing I was involved in your attack. I just...I couldn't bring myself to come, I fear. Call me a coward if you want, but at least I am here now."

"There's no need for so much fuss," Wes said with a quick laugh. He moved past Ashter so he could sit on the edge of his bed. All the posing and measuring he did for the tailor left him feeling exhausted.

"Well then enough about me," Ashter said with a wave of dismissal. "I'd rather talk about you. Look at you! When did you last eat? You're nothing but skin, bones, and a beard! If your vision isn't up to snuff, I insist on shaving that thing off for you!"

"I *am* growing tired of this scruff on my face," Wes conceded, with an absent scratch to his chin.

"Then I consider the matter settled! I'll have the handmaid bring in a tray for you and I insist you eat all of it. Meanwhile I'm going to collect my personal razor to shave your face. No half dulled edge will be used to butcher you today, no sir."

"You don't have to do all this," Wes tried to argue, but Ashter wouldn't be dissuaded.

"I choose to ignore everything you say if it isn't what I want to hear!" He declared, then strolled out of the room. A moment later, a woman entered with a tray in her hands.

"Sorrow?" Wes asked, blinking at her blurry face.

"No, she isn't returning until the morning," said the woman coolly.

"I just want broth," Wes insisted when she bent to set the tray on his lap.

"Orders from the captain say you are to eat more," the woman scolded, hands on her hips. Wes let out a sigh.

"I'll try to eat some fruit as well," he conceded. When she was finally satisfied enough to leave him, Wes said a prayer. He thanked God that he was at least able to feed himself again, then tucked into the thin soup. He managed to eat the fill of the bowl, and a cluster of small tart fruits, then looked for a place to set the remaining tray. Wes' eyes slid over to the table across the room.

The table with the water pitcher, the cup, and the little glass bottle. Wes itched absently at his arm as he hesitated to walk his tray over there. Already that evening he drank two glasses of water laced with oil from that bottle, yet the drug didn't seem as effective anymore. It no longer provided that full escape from his racing thoughts like it once had. He wondered if this was the result of him using it so frequently, or if it meant he needed to increase the dose. The Healer gave him no instruction about such things.

Wes eased out of bed, and approached the table to set down his tray. He lifted the pitcher, filling the cup with its cool liquid, then plucked up the bottle. He placed a few healthy drops of the drug into the cup, added a few more, then stowed the bottle under some cleaning cloths to keep it out of sight. Cup in hand, Wes went to return to his bed but was surprised to find someone watching him from the doorway. The man was tall and broad in the shoulders, so Wes knew immediately that it wasn't Ashter nor Daniel, and the relief he felt made him ashamed. His shame in turn made him defensive, and Wes narrowed his eyes at the man whose face he couldn't clearly see.

"State your business here," he demanded, and the man, dressed as a guard but absent the hat, let his eyes fall to the floor. He seemed...embarrassed and Wes regretted his approach.

"I'm sorry," he relented, softening his tone, "I can't see very well and I don't like being caught off guard. I see you there, but I can't clearly make out your face. Do I know you?"

"You knew me once, but I really can't say if you know me now," the man replied sadly, and Wes felt the sting of regret. Nothing from the past eluded him anymore, so Wes clearly remembered the last time he encountered this young man. He was a very different person then.

"Jack," he sighed, and grabbed hold of the table as a wave of dizziness swept over him. Jack rushed over to offer him support, and while a little of his water sloshed onto his hand, Wes was able to catch himself before falling.

"Are you alright, old man?"

"I'm alright," Wes said as he waited for the dizziness to subside, "just a little weak still."

"You look very thin. I thought you were thin when I first met you. Then I thought you were half starved on the day of your trial, but seeing you like this..."

"I don't have much of an appetite lately."

"Will you get back in bed before you fall over?" Jack scolded and Wes peered up at him with a challenge in his eyes.

"I am not a sickly grandfather, I can handle myself."

"Not from my point of view," Jack retorted. Wes knew it was in his nature not to let things go easily, and he had no desire to argue with the arrogant boy. Instead, he relented and shuffled across the room with a sigh. He desired the comfort of his bed anyway. Taking a long draw from his cup, Wes placed it on the side table, and regarded Jack who took the chair next to his bed.

"I'm glad you came," Wes said with a smile, "I'm doing much better since the last time we met."

"What happened to you?" Jack asked abruptly, and the smile faded from Wes' lips.

"I assumed you knew. I was wounded during my fight with the fish. When he spilled his vile blood, it burned me terribly."

"I'm not talking about then, old man, I'm talking about now."

"I reckon I don't understand what you mean." Wes said with guarded tongue and narrowed eyes, but Jack just scoffed contemptuously.

"I come here and find you frail, weak, practically falling over, and lapping up morphine like a dog..."

"It's for my pain," Wes objected meekly, but felt the burn of the lie on his tongue.

"You were more yourself when you were screaming from your madness inside the palanquin."

"I never thought madness was one of my better qualities," Wes said bitterly, and scratched at his arm again.

"At least back then you put up a fight instead of rolling over and showing your belly," Jack shot back at him, "the man I know wouldn't back down from a challenge, then greet me with a warm smile."

"Why are you here exactly?" Wes snapped with a scowl, and the indignant anger seemed to drain out of Jack. He looked away from Wes and sighed.

"We're always getting on the wrong foot with each other," he mumbled.

"Too late to worry about that now," Wes sneered, for his anger was still kindled; fueled by the truth of Jack's words. He didn't like feeling ashamed of himself, and the idea that he appeared to Jack like a dog lapping up morphine appalled Wes. He looked at the cup he had resting within reach of his longing, then turned his back on the desire to take the easier path towards escape.

"Well I might as well get to the point," Jack sighed, and glanced up at Wes.

"If you're done trying to make me mad."

"I'm not...I just...worry about you."

"Tell me why you're here," Wes pressed for Jack looked strangely nervous.

"Knowing you remember me now, do you also remember the night I helped you escape?"

"Of course," Wes replied.

"Do my ears deceive me?" Both men turned to see the cat-footed Ashter standing in the doorway with a bundle in his hands and fire in his hawkish eyes. Jack leapt to his feet, and snapped off a quick salute.

"Sir!" He called out, standing at attention, but Ashter was not appeased. He strode across the room and squared off in front of the much larger Jack who seemed to shrink in his presence.

"You helped him escape?" Ashter asked, incredulous as he glared up at Jack, "It was that night he climbed out his window like some wild raccoon, wasn't it? It drove me crazy trying to figure out how he slipped past us. Here it was you! Traitor to your brothers!"

"Hey, easy," Wes said, and Ashter turned his ire on him.

"Four of my men were flogged that night for allowing you to escape! Two men by my own hand! Explain yourself!" he demanded, turning his sharp eyes back on Jack. The guard shied away from his captain's scrutiny, and stared wide-eyed at the floor. When he failed to respond, his captain's anger only grew into a white-hot rage that honed the edge of his indignation. "You *dare* to defy me, boy?"

"If he defies you," Wes interjected calmly, "then who do *you* defy, my friend?"

"Stay out of this, Wes!" Ashter snapped, not looking away from his cowed guard, but Wes pushed on anyway.

"If there is a crime in helping me escape, then surely there is a crime in helping me win in a battle I was meant to lose by putting poison on a certain halberd."

"You poisoned the halberd?" Jack asked, lifting his head to look at Ashter.

"Not that it did him any good!" the captain snapped then pointed a finger at Wes. "I *said* stay out of this!"

"Either way," Wes went on as he picked up his cup of water, then set it down again, "if I was captive then, I don't seem to be captive now. I am under no guard, I am not in any confinement, and the intention is for me to leave the capital tomorrow without ceremony or trial.

So, I reckon you don't have a whole lot to argue about here." The two men stared at Wes, then turned and looked at each other.

"Why did you put poison on the halberd?" Jack asked, and Ashter gave an uneasy shrug.

"I grew to like Wes, and I didn't want to see him get ripped to shreds without a fighting chance. Of course that was before I started to rub off on him. Now he's becoming as cocky as me! The poison didn't seem to touch that monster anyway so all my effort was for naught."

"I don't think I would have had the drive to take on that beast if I didn't have you as an ally," Wes confessed, and Ashter gave him a quick smile, before returning his scrutiny to Jack.

"So why did you help him escape in the first place?"

"He's the Light Keeper," Jack declared with a shrug, "and acquired the loyalty of the Disciples. So you see, my mother…well…"

"Your mother," Ashter said thoughtfully. He tapped a finger to his chin for a moment, then strode over to sit in the chair to Wes' right. The wood didn't make a sound when he settled into it. "I think I recall in my youth, when I was a low rank guard much like yourself, the day your mother brought you here. She was simple, but with kind eyes. She seemed extremely distraught about giving you over to the guard. If I recall, the captain took pity on her and gave her quite a large sum of money for you."

"I don't want to talk about *her*," Jack warned.

"Did she join the Disciples to atone for her actions towards you; selling you into slavery and everything?"

"I don't want to talk about getting sold off by that woman!" Jack snapped at his captain, forgetting his position, but Ashter did not waver. He pressed Jack like a bird seeking out its worm.

"You don't want to talk about her, yet your loyalty to her supersedes that of your Hall and your comrades. I insist on an explanation!" Jack's zeal left him when he knew his confession was inevitable. He collapsed back onto his chair, with a sigh.

"My mother is not the woman who gave me over to be a guard. She's had no real love of me since birth, so that makes it easier somehow to endure her. But she took advantage of my situation. Spurred on by her brethren, she insisted I aid the Keeper in his escape."

"In exchange for what?" Wes asked, and Jack looked at him intently

"In exchange for the truth. Which is something she has yet to provide."

"I suspect there is more to this story," Ashter said, getting to his feet to fill a cup of water for himself. "On with it then! For I will have my explanation."

"Ashter," Wes spoke up, "Can you please pour me a fresh drink as well? The water in this cup has gone stale."

Chapter Thirty-Four

The grave wrapped its ropes around me;
death laid a trap in my path.
But in my distress, I cried out to the Lord;
yes, I prayed to my God for help.
He heard me from his sanctuary;
my cry to him reached his ears. - Psalms 18:5-6

"Life lost all joy, the day you were born." Jack's mother said that to him often. He was not something she anticipated, a product of her profession, and one she would have gotten rid of if not for her closest friend and roommate. Aunty was what Jack called her, but she was half a decade younger than his mother, and begged to keep Jack the moment she laid eyes upon him.

"This city is such a cruel place," Aunty said to him, one of his oldest memories, "but seeing you smiling at me, makes it worth living in." While Jack's mother was either cold and distant, or red-faced, angry, and abusive, Aunty always showed him compassion. She was the one that wiped his tears away after his mother was done with him, or slipped him extra scraps of food to quell the pain of his stomach.

"I don't know if it was the best life for a child, but it wasn't much different than many in the city," Jack reflected while Ashter prepared to give Wes a shave.

Everything changed when Aunty realized she was pregnant with a child of her own. This caused Jack's mother to turn bitter towards her.

"You better hope it's a boy," his mother warned; wiggling her finger in front of Aunty, "at least then we can get them working in the mines in a few more years."

"What if it's a girl?" Aunty asked as she protectively cradled her belly.

"You know what will happen if it's a girl," Jack's mother sneered. "She'll become just like us, selling whatever she has to give, or she'll die from starvation because we don't bring home enough to feed her."

"I can steal to feed them both," Aunty suggested.

"Then you'll surely get caught, and they will hang you for it!" Jack's mother snapped. "Don't think I'll care for these vermin with you gone!"

Life loved irony, for it gave Aunty a girl. Jack was captivated the moment he saw her. He remembered just wanting to stare at her all the time while Aunty whispered stories to him about the grand lives they would live together when they grew up.

"One day, sweet Palto will be a great princess of the Divine Hall, and you will be her loyal guard!"

"I want to be the captain!" Jack declared, and Aunty took on a serious expression.

"No matter what happens, I need you to protect her for me. Can you do that, Jack?" Of course Jack agreed, not knowing the weight of what it all meant, but learned far sooner than he should, for neither woman was able to make enough to feed the four of them. The night Jack's mother came home and announced that Aunty had been arrested for stealing in the market, he remembered it was wretchedly cold.

"Now you'll both starve," she declared with her lip curled in disgust. That night when she abandoned them to pursue her nightly ventures, she didn't bother with lighting their woodstove, and left them hungry and shivering in the cold.

Jack was desperate to protect Palto, and knew they wouldn't survive without Aunty to care for them. He wrapped her little body as best he could to keep her warm, and took her to the west gate in hopes of appealing to the guards there. It was desperation that drove him into the bitter night, but he already knew it was a foolish effort. His life never gave him cause to hope.

"This cruelty is a large reason why they implemented the parenting permits," Ashter remarked as he lathered Wes' neck, "there were far too many children abandoned to starve in the streets or worse."

"We certainly looked the part," Jack agreed. He was only three and Palto was barely six months old. They were both small and underfed, and while the guards at the gate tried to send them away, Jack was so scared of Aunty being executed, he started to sob. Palto immediately joined him, and they raised such a ruckus, it drew the attention of the captain.

"You remember our Captain Strupple, don't you, captain?"

"Of course I remember Strupple," Ashter replied, half distracted as his attention was divided between Jack and running the edge of a sharp razor against Wes' neck. "He was quite the imposing force. A hard and impatient fellow. I endured his intolerance for years before he became an Elder."

"Yes, I know he had a reputation as a hard captain, that he was mean with an iron heart, but he took notice of Palto and I that night, and was strangely willing to let Aunty go. He had us bathed and fed, then released the three of us the following day."

"That's impossible," Ashter said dismissively. "Strupple never released a prisoner. Never." But Jack insisted his story was true. Unfortunately, after he let Aunty go, she wasn't the same. She looked at both Jack and Palto strangely, rarely engaged with Jack, and left most of Palto's care to him. Often, she argued with Jack's mother but their fighting was no longer loud. The arguing occurred in hushed whispers with side glances at the children.

Jack didn't understand what happened with Aunty, or how to fix the strangeness in the home, so he decided it would resolve on its own eventually, and focused completely on Palto. It didn't take long for Aunty to abandon him. A few weeks later, or maybe a month at most.

With his mother's consent, Aunty took hold of Jack's hand and while she smiled at him for the first time since her release, he also saw that she was sad. That sadness turned to despair eventually, and she cried openly when she handed him over to the guard, but she didn't change her mind. She sold him into their fold, pocketed the few coins she received from enslaving him, and vanished into the city once more. Seeing her go, Jack felt the harsh sting of betrayal for the first time. The pain was sharp and penetrating, and Jack cried quietly in his barrack's bunk thinking he would never see Palto again. He didn't protect her. He was a failure.

A few years passed with Jack unable to enter the city as he was deep in his training, but was visited one day by Captain Strupple himself. The man insisted that Jack go and locate Palto and her mother and offer his protection to her once more.

"If you made a promise to protect that girl, you should keep it."

"I'm not going to humor this tale of yours if you are going to lie!" Ashter scolded while he pointed the wet blade of his straight razor at Jack. "Strupple would never had allowed you to enter the capital streets for personal reasons. Certainly not to humor some childhood promise! You are a fool if you think I'll believe that!"

"I'm telling the truth," Jack said, his face red with indignation, "but believe it or not, it doesn't matter. Just know that I entered the city to find Palto and her mother."

He went to their old home, and learned that his mother sold it shortly after she agreed to sell him. He wasn't sure how to find her; he was only a child after all, so he returned to the guard house unsuccessful. When Strupple discovered Jack's failure, he grew angry and demanded Jack try to find them again.

"If you can't find where she lives, go to the places where she works."

Jack, following his captain's orders, sought out the woman who once sold him in all those places where she sold herself. He looked in all the taverns until he eventually found her high on opium, and asleep at a table occupied by two men. On the lap of one of those men, sat Palto. She was almost seven at this point and the haunted look in her eyes told Jack all he needed to know about how well she was being protected.

Even then, Jack was tall for his age, and in his guard uniform, he wore an intimidating presence. The men looked like they didn't want any trouble. They saw his uniform, and eased Palto onto the floor, but Jack's mother was an angry woman and her blood also ran in him. He drove the thick heel of his boot into the one man's shin, and threw a hard right into the other man's eye. Before they could recover, he snatched up Palto, and fled into the night.

With nowhere else to go, he returned to his captain with Palto draped over his back. She was exhausted, starving, dirty, and terrified of all adults. But she clung to Jack with silent desperation, and shivered in the early spring chill. Captain Strupple showed her kindness by having the Hall servants clean her, dress her, and allow her to sleep in the prison for a few nights. Eventually, he told Jack that he acquired access to one of the pauper's huts on the outer regions of the city for her to stay in. With Jack's help, she did well there on her own, but eventually her mother tracked her down and convinced Palto to let her move in as well.

As for Jack, he was allowed to see her often and was with her almost every day. He worked twice as hard as his peers to keep up with his training for he feared his captain might take this unique privilege from him otherwise, and while the other children of the guard grew to despise him for his differential treatment, he didn't care. All the fighting just made him stronger, and a good outlet for all his anger and frustration. For he loved Palto long before he understood what love was, and was furious with himself for failing her.

Palto grew to love him as well, when she was able to trust again, and it was she that taught Jack the ways of a man and a woman. Jack was only sixteen; almost seventeen, but developed a profound understanding of his situation. He was a slave. He was *just* a slave. Slaves were never able to get married, or own property, or work for wages, or love. He had nothing he could give her, for he didn't even have an identity he could claim as his own. The more he wanted of her, the deeper his bitterness grew toward himself.

He thought it was due to this ongoing struggle he had, that Palto suddenly stopped talking to him. One moment she was there, eyes bright, face smiling, and the next, she ducked into alleys every time she saw him, and went out of her way to avoid him. He went to her home to confront her, but he was so hurt and angry that he immediately lashed out the moment her drunken mother answered the door. They both shouted at one another, saying all the things they wanted to say before; hurtful words that rewarded no joy when spoken.

Aunty forbade Jack from ever visiting their home again, and when he returned to the guard house angry and flustered, his captain abruptly ordered him to no longer seek out Palto. Jack demanded an explanation, emboldened by the fire of his anger, but Strupple's charity only extended so far, and Jack sadly had a sharp tongue. He was ordered to Hall restriction for a year.

Strupple didn't need to give a reason for the restriction just as he gave no reason for allowing the relationship in the first place. This was in his right to do, but without lack of understanding, Jack was constantly tormented with regret and heartache. It caused him to grow angry with Palto, and took his cruelty out on others around him. It isolated him, and he wore his misery like shackles. He had to endure it though, for the alternative would be insubordination and could get him killed.

"I returned to the capital eventually, but Palto never came into my view. She got better at hiding while I was locked away yearning for her. When I was called into the tavern on that night I met you, mister Wes, it was the first time Palto didn't run from me. It was also the first time she spoke to me since she broke my heart. Her casual nature, and the way she acted like I was of no significance to her...it infuriated me. I...I regret what I did, and how I treated both her and you, but understand that my actions were the result of my training. When she dismissed me, I returned to just being another guard."

"I appreciate your willingness to share this with me," Wes said as he took a towel to his freshly shaved face. The skin was remarkably smooth; unscarred by all the burns he endured, "but I imagine you didn't share all this simply to apologize."

"No, I didn't," Jack agreed as he lifted his head to look at Wes for the first time since he began.

"And so we come to the point," Ashter mused as he idly cleared away his tools.

"When...when I saw you that night...the night of the trial and the fight...everything that I thought happened was brought to question. You said you would get Palto safely out of the city. You said you would return to address the great lord. When you didn't return right away, I assumed you were escorting Palto someplace safe with intentions of coming back eventually. I never imagined you were imprisoned that whole time. As soon as I saw you, fighting to stay out of the palanquin and screaming about how they were putting you in a coffin, well...I am ashamed to admit that all I could think about was what happened to Palto? Did she escape? Since that night, I had time to wonder about a lot of things. Like what exactly happened to you. Your hands are free of sin! And I think I recall you breaking a bone or two when you fell off that roof."

"You fell off a roof?" Ashter asked, looking amused.

"Not everyone strives to be a cat," Wes grumbled.

"I also wondered about that boy you were carrying when you escaped. There was something...compelling about him. I worried he was in danger and you were too insane to even remember where he was."

"When you say 'boy'," Ashter interjected, "are you referring to the actual Bringer of Light? Property of the High Counsel!"

"Hush your mouth," Wes said much like Sassy would, and met Ashter's eyes, "If you're willing to make that claim, then you don't know a thing about their intentions for that boy. Go on, Jack."

"With how badly the pit broke down your mind," Jack said with a nervous glance at his scowling captain, "I knew I wasn't going to get the answers I needed from you. So I decided to approach the Disciples again to find out if they were able to help you. I confronted my mother, demanding to have answers to these questions because she failed to tell me anything about Palto from my helping her before, and she led me to speak to a little rat-like fellow who smiled too much. That was when I learned of the great escape, and how the Disciples smuggled the actual Bringer of Light out of the city. He was so proud of this, it was almost an afterthought to mention that the boy was joined by a teenage girl who had to be Palto and...."

Jack paused as his voice broke. He swallowed, cleared his throat, and tried to get his emotions under control. When he spoke again, it was in a much softer voice. One that quivered with each word. "And...a small girl. A child that couldn't be older than two, and with hair the color of newly formed rust. He said that she was very pale and thin but looked so excited to go."

"She has the largest eyes," Wes said as he recalled his time with Lilly, "they are the color of spring moss, and carry such a vast curiosity it's almost as if she wants to perceive the whole world in a glance."

"A young girl with her presumed mother, yet I don't recall the name 'Palto' on our roster of parenting permits," Ashter remarked thoughtfully when Jack didn't immediately respond.

"Do you really think she'd be able to afford one?" Wes asked and Ashter let out a long whistle through his teeth.

"Are you saying she conceived this child and gave birth to her completely in secret?"

"And raised her in a home the size of this room for two years without Lilly ever seeing the world outside, or that outside world seeing her." Jack got to his feet; restless rambling thoughts staggering his actions, and he steadied himself on the table.

"You...you said her name was..."

"Lilly," Wes repeated, and Jack met his eyes. There was pain on the younger man's face that Wes was all too familiar with. The pain of a father filled with regret.

"Lilly," Jack said, his voice hoarse. He cleared his throat and pressed on. "Lilly was my mother's name."

"So Palto named her daughter to honor your mother?" Wes asked, confused but Jack shook his head.

"My mother gave her name to the great lord when she became a Disciple. This happened long before we...before she...before Lilly was born. But I know Palto, and I have to believe that she used this name as a message to me. If something happened to her, and it was discovered she had a daughter named Lilly, I would have known what that meant. I would have known she was telling me who I was to this girl."

"She certainly couldn't tell you while she was concealing such a secret," Ashter added, "imagine your position as a guard if you knew your own child was being concealed in the city. She was protecting her daughter and herself, but I think she was also protecting you."

"All this time," Jack breathed, tears dancing in his eyes, "I thought she shut me out of her life because she stopped loving me."

"It sounds to me like she loved you more than you knew," Ashter lamented.

"She just had someone else who needed her love more," Wes concluded, and grew sad as he thought about Daniel. The morphine would help quell his haunting memories, but no. He was done running from all his mistakes.

The door suddenly burst open, drawing the three men out of their quiet melancholy. Two young boys ran into the room, distraught and focused solely on Wes, they ignored the other men including their own captain as they threw themselves on him , and hugged him from both sides of the bed.

"Mister Wes! It's a calamity!"

"We heard people talking!"

"They are sending out orders to come and collect you!"

"That horrible great lord wishes to leave this very night!"

"Easy boys!" Wes soothed as he tried to coax Pip and Kenner to calm down.

"You make very strange alliances," Jack remarked with mild amusement, but Ashter rose from his chair looking far more alarmed.

"Who did you hear this from? When? Why was I not informed?" He demanded.

"Maybe...maybe they couldn't find you," Kenner said without looking at his captain, and Wes immediately knew he was lying.

"I need to look into this. I don't understand who is pushing for this sudden urgency. You don't even have suitable clothing to wear! I need to find out where all this is coming from," Ashter collected his things and made for the door.

"I'll return as soon as I can, but if this proves to be true, I have much to do in the meantime. Please, all of you remain here. I need an honor guard if we are to escort him. I refuse to let him be seen as weak!"

"Thank you," was all Wes could think to say but the depth of his gratitude extended beyond simple gestures of good faith. His gratitude for Ashter and even Jack and Pip and Kenner was immeasurable. They were all good men in a lost world that gave little to hope for. After Ashter slipped out of the room, Wes focused on getting the two boys under control.

"Alright Pip. Kenner. Dry your tears now. Spend some time with me while I'm here, for if I am called to go tonight, then I will do what must be done. We have time now, though. Spend it with me instead of in your own sadness." With a few sniffs and bashful scrubbing of wet cheeks, Pip and Kenner stopped with their sniveling. Pip moved to take the seat Ashter vacated, but Kenner chose to remain on the bed with Wes.

"You look funny," he said in his soft-natured way, and poked Wes on the cheek.

"What do you mean?" Wes asked, then touched his face, and stared at Kenner in wide-eyed shock. "Where did my beard go?"

Both of the boys laughed; the best remedy for childhood sadness, and even Jack seemed to collect himself. He returned to his seat and studied Wes.

"You seem calm," he observed.

"I'm resigned to what will be," Wes corrected, for the last thing he felt was calm.

"You can barely see, mister," Jack argued, "so how do you expect to navigate your way back home?"

"I will find my way back home," Wes assured him. He didn't need his eyes for that.

"Mister Wes, will you tell us a story?" Pip interjected, and Jack looked insulted.

"Act your position instead of your age," he snapped, and the boys had enough sense to at least *look* ashamed.

"We're sorry sir," grumbled Kenner, for Jack was their superior officer.

"Can you tell us where you found out about this sudden change in plans?" Wes asked, and Kenner turned his head to share a look with Pip. There were secrets there.

"I...don't remember," Kenner said, glancing over at Jack.

"Honesty will not harm you as much as a lie will," Wes scolded, and let out a sigh. "If you don't want to tell us, just say so. All the same, I suppose we can only sit and wait for your captain to return. I might as well tell you a story or two."

"Will you tell us about the battle with the fish?" Pip asked, perking up.

"Will you tell us about the strange flash of light in the city streets?" Kenner asked, catching Jack's attention.

"Tonight seems to be a night of confessions," Wes said, glancing at Jack, "So I will tell you all that I have time to do. Maybe, you will be willing to confess something as well, when you know it's safe for you to do so."

"Start with the fish! I want to hear about the battle again," Kenner said, sitting at the foot of the bed and bouncing excitedly.

"It will be as you say, but I cannot start there. Like I said, tonight is a night of confessions, and I want to start by telling you a story that's important for you all to know."

"What on earth would that be?" Jack asked and all three of them seemed to lean in with a rapt attention that only existed in the young.

"I want to tell you about your *horrible* great lord. The Guardian Son," Wes replied with a doleful smile, "for once upon a time, he was just a boy like the two of you, and his name was Daniel."

As time marched onward, it also stood still. For in a small dimly-lit room somewhere in the heart of the Divine Hall, Wes felt suspended in a past he yearned to relive. He told the guards all he could about his son. Daniel's laughter, his inquisitive nature, his boldness, and his skepticism. He told them about the night that Daniel left and fled to the capital with Jethro, and how hard it's been between them since Wes entered back into his life. By the time his tale was over, both Pip and Kenner laid their heads on him and Jack had moved his chair closer so he could place a hand on Wes' arm. All of them grieved for the boy behind the mask of the Guardian Son. Then Wes decided to move on.

He talked about Benji, how they met, the strange encounter with Benji's mother, and everything leading up to the moment he met Lilly. Wes thought it was important to include her so that Jack could have a glimpse of his daughter as a person, and not just a name. He wanted them also to know Benji as a person and not just the Bringer of Light.

At last he told them all about the battle of the fish, and found it was far more enjoyable in the telling than it was in the living. He was deep into the heart of the battle when Ashter finally returned, but concluded it quickly to allow for the captain to give his report. Ashter looked frazzled, frustrated, and exhausted. His dark hair was a wild halo around his face, there were sweat stains on his shirt and his jacket was removed completely. In his arms he carried a large basket full of clothing, and panted as though he just ran the whole length of the Hall.

"This place is utter chaos," he declared when he knew he had their attention.

"Captain," Jack announced, and all three of them reflexively rose to give him a salute. Ashter looked them over, set the basket down, and came to sit next to Kenner at the foot of the bed.

"My guard gets more lax by the second," he mumbled, noting the delay in their regard, but Wes suspected Ashter was far too distracted to presently care much about rank.

"What's going on in the Hall?" Wes asked, in response to Ashter's declaration.

"People are running everywhere. Elders rushing to get dressed and look presentable, guards and servants scrambling to collect provisions...I had to issue countless orders, and everything should have been done hours ago! Fortunately, I had a list of supplies already determined so I didn't have to oversee all of that, but it was important to make a statement to the city itself. Imagine if the Guardian Son fled in the night without a word to the people who both looked to him for direction and at times even worshiped him as a god. We needed to secure transportation and form an honor guard to take you out of the city limits. Not to mention us here; for we are now the honor guard to the Father of the Guardian Son; the Keeper of Light. In truth, no one expected this sudden exodus. Not the Elders, and certainly not the guard. This new order came directly from the great lord himself."

"He requested this?" Wes asked.

"That appears to be the case."

"But why?" The silence that followed was like a vacuum.

"Should we leave so you can get ready?" Jack asked after some time and Wes reached for his hand.

"In a moment. But first, I have something I want to ask of all of you." Wes paused to look at each of them, as they all watched him intently in turn. He knew that they would agree to anything he asked of them, for this was the cost of true friendship.

"I am destined to return here, and when I do, I will bring with me the Bringer of Light. I don't know what this means for this city. For he might carry the blessing of the Lord to heal that which is broken," Wes stretched his once-broken fingers and wrist in front of Jack's eyes; the unspoken made clear, "or he might carry the blessing of the Lord to destroy all that is wicked in this world."

"Beware the Keepers' compassion, for it will destroy the world," Jack said, quietly quoting the prophecies.

"Until I return, I want you all to look out for each other. All of you have shown me you have integrity, and are honorable men. I want to leave here comforted in knowing that each of you will have the protection and support of each other while I'm gone. Will you do this for me?"

"You have my word, on my honor," Ashter declared without hesitation. The man who had the most to lose by allying with his own guards was also the first to proclaim his allegiance to them.

"I suppose someone needs to look out for these brats and keep them in line," Jack said, and reached over to ruffle Kenner's hair.

"You can count on us!" Kenner agreed but Pip, slumped in his chair, remained quiet.

"Pip?" Wes asked, and the boy met his eyes.

"Tonight is a night of confessions," he said, and glanced over at Kenner. "We have something we need to say."

"We didn't mean any harm!" Kenner said, looking a little scared.

"Tell us," Jack insisted, and Pip got to his feet.

"It's about the great lord. Daniel. We didn't know then all that we know now about him, mister Wes, we thought he was a bad person."

"He's always so mean and angry all the time," Kenner said, and looked miserable.

"We understand why now, at least a little, but we didn't earlier today and...well we happened to be too loud for his liking when we passed his quarters."

"He came out and yelled at us! He looked really scary."

"And we got mad. I know he's supposed to be our leader, but he's the same size as us."

"We didn't know he was thirteen. He's so small and thin," added Kenner.

"What did you do?" Ashter asked, cutting to the point, and Pip winced. He looked down at his hands.

"We...got an idea."

"A bad one," added Kenner.

"We got some black ink and brushes from the scribe's office and went back to his quarters."

"He was sleeping. He smoked from one of those funny looking pipes."

"We...painted his fingers with the ink."

"Oh, Pip," Wes said, for he already could imagine the outcome of this horrible child prank.

"We didn't stay in his room, but we were working nearby," Kenner said.

"So when he woke up, and...when he screamed..."

"Everyone heard it. It sounded scary, like there were two people screaming at the same time."

"Some of the Guard Watch ran into the room and..."

"We heard him make the order that he had to leave tonight," Kenner concluded.

"You have to leave because of us," Pip said sadly.

"I think that's the least of Wes' worries at this point," Ashter said, his irritation evident. "Our alliance does not excuse you from punishment, and I will determine suitable recourse for the two of you."

Jack shook his head, and laughed. "You foolish boys."

"We're sorry, mister Wes," Pip said sincerely, and Wes considered the situation.

"I must ask you all to do one more thing for me," he said at last, "I want to pray for my son and I'd like for you all to join me."

"Pray? To the Lord Dragon?" Ashter asked.

"Never," Wes scoffed, and smiled at his friend. "I pray to the one true God. The Lord of the Before. The Father of Creation. My salvation from sin."

"Does such a thing exist?" asked Pip, wide-eyed and confused.

"Is that how you were cleansed of sin?" Jack asked, looking equally amazed.

"Is that how you survived your injuries from the fish?" Kenner asked from the foot of the bed.

"The Lord is with me in all things. When I pray, I give thanks, and ask him to show mercy to those around me. Tonight, Daniel desperately needs my prayer and if you all join in with me, the Lord might hear it a little better."

"Well, I'm willing to give anything a try at least once," Ashter said with a wry smile. "Tell us what we must do to pray."

"Close your eyes, show God your spirit, and ask him to guide you so that you can better serve him. I'll start with my prayer, then any of you can add your own prayers if you want. I'd like to see how God can move in each of you." Wes closed his eyes, took a steadying breath, then raised his voice to God. In this deepest den of wickedness, where even the just have forgotten His name, four guards prayed to a God they didn't know existed, and Wes showed them the way.

Chapter Thirty-Five

Unleash the fury of your wrath,
Look at all who are proud and bring them low
Look at all who are proud and humble them,
Crush the wicked where they stand. -Job 40:11-12 NLT

Ashter helped Wes dress, and he had to admit the tailor did wonderful work in the little time he was given. His jacket was slim in fit, mid-length, with a thin shawl lapel. Underneath, he wore a gray wool tweed vest with a high neck, and under that he had on a collarless white shirt with loose airy sleeves that buttoned at the wrists. He wore pants that were altered to remove the high waist of the guard uniform, and instead they rested lower to the hip. Ashter also brought him his father's hat which he kept stowed away while Wes was recovering along with his revolver and holster. Having his gun slung back on his leg had Wes feeling like an empty part of him was filled. He decided to keep the same guard issued boots for they served their purpose and were comfortable when he folded down the tops at the ankle; a style that even Ashter adopted.

"For someone who cares little about his appearance, you surely know how to look dashing," Ashter remarked as he placed the hat back on Wes' head. Wes quickly adjusted it so it fit just-so, and gave Ashter a wry smile.

"An unfortunate side effect, I assure you."

"It's a pity," Ashter mused, "When you return, I fear we might find ourselves on opposite sides."

"I reckon we might," Wes agreed, "you'll have to help the others understand that. Each of you has sworn to protect your home, and I gave an oath to protect the Light Bringer. Whether we are friend or foe will be determined by the choice others make."

"Whatever happens, it was an honor to know you, and it will be a privilege if I see you again," Ashter concluded and they embraced. For the world was cruel, and even with best intentions, they might not ever meet again. When Ashter opened the door, Wes followed him into the hall.

In the past, the guard led Wes like he was a prisoner, and while his friends surrounded him, the way they walked with him was different. There was pride in their step instead of veiled hostility. Ashter called it an honor guard, and since he adored the dramatic, Wes knew they were putting on a great show.

To his left, Jack put the turmoil of his situation out of his mind and held himself to the full height of his imposing stature. Wes knew he was leaving Jack with so many unanswered questions, but he hoped that there was some way this father might reunite one day with the daughter he didn't know he had.

Pip and Kenner, walked on either side of his flank, their backs straight and their chins held high. They caught the eye of many guards around their age and Wes saw respect in the eyes of the observers. They will have many stories of their own to share soon.

Captain Ashter elected to walk to Wes' right; the highest position among the honor guard. He took the time to comb his hair, and slicked it back in a distinguished way. His jacket was brushed and buttoned to the throat, and while he looked commanding, he still sauntered like a rogue. Together, they appeared to be an imposing site, and it was impossible for them to go unnoticed.

Guards, servants, guests, and even a few Disciples watched in amazement as the honor guard passed with Wes at its core. Every time they swept past a new person, that person was compelled to fall in behind them and follow along. In this way, they formed a strange impulsive parade of people curious to see what was happening. By the time they reached the grand stairway outside the main entrance of the Divine Hall, Wes' honor guard became a small army. He looked down, feeling the power of his position, and observed the well of Elders clustered with their servants and Guard Watch Elite. They seemed small and insignificant to him. At their core, the Guardian Son was the smallest of all. Wes' eyes could not clearly make out Daniel's face, but he sensed his son's mood. He was terrified.

"He's coming!" One of their number shouted, and all heads turned upward to see Wes at the top of the steps.

"The Keeper of the Light approaches!" Wes took the stairs casually in spite of the thrumming of his heart, and watched Daniel throughout his descent. The boy was dressed in his black uniform with high-neck and gloves. He seemed to want to cover every inch that he could with black cloth, revealing only his face which appeared as pale as the moon.

"Oh, look how handsome he is!" An Elder called out, and Wes was surprised to realize they weren't talking about Daniel, but him.

"I like him better without the beard."

"I regret not having the chance to play with him."

"Plenty of time for that when he comes back."

"I'll be too distracted by the little treat he's bringing back with him."

"Don't let him hear you say that!"

"Stop talking," Daniel snapped and some of the Elders peered over at him as though they forgot he was even there. A discarded toy, no longer shiny and new, that no one wanted to play with anymore. They only wanted to break him and throw him away.

Wes approached them in the same yard where he fought the fish just a few days before. Off to their left, a row of guards stood at attention next to a covered wagon that was saddled up to two restless horses, ready to run. Behind them, he could see the gates were closed against a swell of spectators from the city. They clung to the bars and cried out their allegiance to their great lord. The city dwellers seemed to show little interest for the Elders and could Wes truly blame them? It was impossible to ignore how these white clad monsters treated members of their own city. They didn't seem to notice the lack of reverence from the capital. They were too busy eyeing each other.

Their Guardian Son, no longer held in a place of adoration, stood alone among them; pedestaled by the remains of his dignity. Wes approached him, and noticed the fear that he sensed before, was replaced with something more cold and calculating.

"You look impressive," Daniel remarked casually. The Elders whispered to each other in low voices and watched Wes with hungry, curious, predatory eyes. Knowing the precarious position his son was in, Wes made a point of removing his hat and mimicked Ashter with a deep flourishing bow.

"I am here to serve *you*, Guardian Son," he declared and was pleased to see the reaction it caused in the Elders. Many of them looked at Daniel with a respect they didn't have a moment before. Daniel, for his part, acted as though Wes' behavior was expected and lifted his chin in a way that he could peer down at his father while still having to look up at him.

Ah, Daniel. You disguise yourself so well.

"Is our wagon ready for departure?" demanded the Guardian Son.

"Yes, great lord!" Called a member of the guard.

"We assembled an honor guard to escort you out of the city, great lord," Ashter spoke up at Wes' side.

"I expect you will join them," Daniel said, without giving the captain a glance.

"It will be an honor, sir," Ashter concluded, then the four of them moved to join the row of others by the wagon.

"Great lord," a woman spoke up, "perhaps a few guards on horseback should accompany you on your venture. A means of protection during your travels. I'm sure a dozen or so would benefit your safety."

"Tell me, Elder Estella," Daniel said with a sort of condescending patience that made anyone he targeted feel abysmally stupid, "how much time do you think I have before I am lost fully to my sickness?"

"I...don't know, great lord. Possibly a week. Yes, hopefully a week."

"And how long do you think it will take for a three day journey to be completed when you incorporate an entourage of guards that get hungry, and ride on horses that get hungry, and all of which need shelter from the sun, and consistent sleep?" Daniel's words were so shrewd and berating that Wes almost felt sorry for the poor red-faced Elder. Then he remembered the things these people did to his son, and all his pity withered.

"I only wanted to protect you, great lord!" Estella simpered.

"Open your jacket," Daniel demanded, and turned to look at Wes.

"I...beg your pardon?" Wes asked, confused. Daniel took hold of his arm, and guided Wes to face Estella alongside her companions. He then pulled the front of Wes' jacket to the side like a curtain, and revealed the revolver he had holstered underneath.

Estella gasped at the sight of a weapon capable of executing an Elder or a monster in an instant. Wes realized that Daniel was looking at him and when their eyes met, his son showed him a wide but humorless smile.

"I could tell by your gait that you were carrying your gun again," he said softly.

"Great lord! What are you doing?" Elder Estella cried out, but Daniel continued to hold Wes' gaze.

"Care for a little sport, father?"

"Daniel..."

"Kill her!" Daniel shouted, and Wes had to believe that his son's intentions were not to make his father gun down a woman in cold blood. The gun was in his hand in an instant and Wes pointed it directly at the Elder named Estella.

"Great lord!" She cried out, hands raised defensively. In the distance, the citizens of the city reacted with shouts, screams, and cheers.

"Wait!" Daniel commanded, and stepped forward. Wes held the gun poised, barrel aimed at Estella's eye, while Daniel confronted her.

“I don’t need an escort, Elder Estella,” he said softly; condescendingly, “I already have one.”

“G-great lord...” Estella whimpered, but Daniel turned his back on her.

“We ride!” He shouted to the spectating crowd and of course they cheered. Daniel pushed past the group surrounding him, and strode over to the wagon with Wes following behind. He holstered his gun, and glanced over to his friends. They stood with their brothers, ready to escort him out of the city, and Wes was grateful to share this last moment with them.

“It’s a home on wheels, father,” Daniel mused as he examined the wagon. He ran a gloved hand along the canopy. “It carries plenty of provisions, but also allows me a place to shelter from the sun. Isn’t it wonderful?”

“I suppose so,” Wes admitted, but was apprehensive of the unfamiliar vessel as he climbed the two iron steps into a seat built into the front of the wagon. Daniel climbed up behind him, his step limber in his youth, and gallantly turned to face the crowds. He raised his hands in a gesture of victory and while many cheered his bravado, the Elders did not. Wes could not see their faces clearly, but knew them to be quietly considering; calculating the best way to approach this sudden void in power. It mattered not. Let them vie for small squares of land. Daniel and Wes had a world to experience.

“Esteemed High Counsel,” Daniel began, and paused to allow the crowds to quiet in anticipation. “Divine Hall servants and valiant guards, glorious citizens of the capital, and all of our guests, I am leaving you today. We leave on a quest to ensure the prophecies are fulfilled, and the unraveling of time is thwarted. We do this by returning with a new Guardian Son!” He waited for a new round of cheers to subside, then continued, “The *new* Guardian Son will restore our past, protect our present, and ensure our futures!”

“We believe in you great lord!” Cheered a crowd that had yet to realize Daniel was no longer in the position he once was.

“We eagerly await your return!”

“Our Guardian Son will repair time itself!”

“He will restore us to glory!”

Cheers came from all around; even some of the Elder’s joined in. One of the Elders appeared to be weeping. Daniel scooped up the horse's reins and faced the crowd one last time. As he spoke, guards rushed to open the Hall’s front gate, while the honor guard took their places around the wagon to keep all pedestrians out of the way. Ashter and Jack brought the boys over to walk along Wes’ side of the wagon.

"Elders! Guards! Servants, citizens and guests, I am leaving today as your leader. But the Light Bringer will return your hero!"

Cheers rose up although many still did not understand what was happening. They were all simply caught up in the moment and the excitement of the departure. Daniel gave the reins a jerk of his wrist and the eager horses lurched forward. The guards strolled around them, pushing back any spectator that got too close, but Daniel did not temper the energy of the horses pulling them along. They rushed forward, being overwhelmed by the crowds, and soon the guards had to jog to keep up.

"Daniel, perhaps we..." Wes began, thinking to encourage prudence to avoid damaging anything before their journey even began, but one look showed him that Daniel was on the verge of falling apart. All his gallant posturing and confidence left him the moment his wide eyes took in the massive expanse of the wilderness beyond the city.

"Daniel?" Wes asked, getting to his feet, and his son turned to him.

"Help me," he whispered, and his haunted wide-eyed expression was all Wes needed to see.

"Get in the back," he said, taking the reins, and Daniel did as instructed without question. He curled up with his knees to his chest, and leaned against the back wall of the driver's seat. Wes looked down at Ashter and the captain caught his eye.

"I'm sorry for any trouble I cause you tonight," he said and as Ashter looked at him in confusion he added, "I reckon this is goodbye."

He whipped the reins, spurring the already restless horses into action, and they burst forth in a full run. The wagon broke away from its honor guard in an instant, leaving a flurry of shouts in its wake, but Wes thanked the Lord when he saw that most of the spectators already cleared the street and the remaining few were able to jump out of the way unscathed. Unfamiliar with such a lumbering load, Wes side-swiped a vendor stand, but was otherwise able to push the caravan into the depth of the wilds without causing any other damage.

"That was amazing!" Daniel screamed over the roar of the wagon wheels. Wes studied the way his son leaned over the back of the driver's seat and peered out into the night. He looked vibrant and excited, but at the same time his eyes were wet with tears. Wes tightened his grip on the reins; thinking he'd stop the horses so that Daniel could collect himself, but his son grabbed onto the sleeve of his jacket, and restrained him from commanding the animals to slow.

"No, don't stop. Keep going. Just keep going." Wes did as he was told, driving the wagon into the early light of an oncoming day, and while Daniel continued to watch a horizon he was unable to see for years, Wes listened and tried to determine if his son was laughing, crying, or both.

Chapter Thirty-Six

Look at all their evil deeds, Lord.
Punish them, as you have punished me for all my sins.
My groans are many,
and I am sick at heart. -Lamentations 1:22 NLT

Wes closed his eyes, and breathed in the dry air of the wilds. There was a silent stillness all around him, the sun brushed lazy fingers of warmth across his face, and Wes felt as though he just woke up from a nightmare of eternal night. Daniel had fallen asleep behind him before the sun even crested the horizon, and he laid on his side curled into a ball with a bedroll for a pillow. It was hard to believe he was actually there. Against so many odds, Wes was able to extract him from that horrible city. Knowing they would get to spend some time alone together, Wes hoped they might actually grow to better understand one another. Whatever else happened, he would deal with it somehow.

The day stretched on, but Wes took advantage of the light and the well worn road to press the horses. He knew time was limited if what that Elder said proved true, so he was hopeful to reach the point where the highway took that sweeping turn toward the north by the end of day.

Pressing the animals as he was, Wes was so focused on the road ahead of him that he didn't at first realize something was wrong with Daniel. His vision was still blurry, and might not ever fully recover, so it was hard to see his son when he was no more than a shadow within the deeper shadows of the covered wagon. In spite of this, Wes could tell that he was in pain. He occasionally heard a sharp intake of breath, or a soft groan often drowned out by the sounds of horses and wagon, but he was certain his son was suffering all the same.

"Daniel?" He said softly, unwilling to wake his son to quell his nagging worry, and the boy didn't respond. Wes tried to not let it overtake his thoughts, and instead put his focus on the task at hand.

Even though he slept most of the past few days, Wes felt drained. He lacked the energy he once had before all the weight loss and his prolonged time in bed. He also felt sick to his stomach, which he attributed to a lack of food, but worried it might be caused by a lack of the drug as well

He was ashamed at how often he thought about morphine and its appeal to the restless mind. Everything was much easier to endure when morphine was covering up the rawest parts of understanding. He idly considered searching the supplies for one of the tiny vials of the elixir but quickly pushed the idea from his mind. He seemed to almost thirst for its bitterness and the need caused his body to ooze a clammy sweat that clung like oil to his skin.

"I reckon I've got myself in a fine mess," Wes muttered in disgust, and tried to focus on the rolling hills. He found himself looking north, and soon he spotted the low stretch of mountains broken in two along the horizon and knew that was the path that led to Benji. If Benji was even there. Another thing to add to his worries.

"Enough," Wes commanded his traitorous mind. "Just be still."

At last he saw the place where the highway turned, and a much smaller path extended forward. There was still an hour or so before the sun fell below the mountains behind him, but Wes needed time to allow the horses to drink, find food for both the animals, Daniel, and himself, and collect the wood needed to get a fire started. Wes reigned in the horses by the familiar campsite alongside the road, and remembered when he and Benji were last there. They argued over which direction to take, but that was before Wes started to see that there was more to Benji than he originally understood. The well of second sight that boy drew from ran deep.

It took little effort to draw the horses to a halt. They were exhausted from the long relentless drive. Wes climbed out of the wagon, sore from the way it shifted him about on the unforgiving wooden seat, and enjoyed a long stretch before he got to work. He unyoked the horses, allowing them to shake the frothy sweat from their fur, and tied them each to a tree with a rope long enough to let them graze.

Keeping an eye on the sun, Wes fell into the routines of travel which always seemed to relax him. He collected enough to burn for the night, and rummaged in the wagon as quietly as he could for supplies. From there he recovered a hatchet, along with flint, and a loop of striker steel. He also found some dried fruit, bread, and dried strips of meat to enjoy by the fire. Without the morphine dulling his senses, his appetite returned with a fury.

Wes had just got the fire lit in the twilight hours of the day when he heard noise from the wagon, and knew that Daniel was awake. He did not sound happy, and Wes could only sigh. Sensing another conflict was brewing, he eased down to sit upon the earth and wait for the onslaught to come.

"What are you doing?" Daniel growled the moment his feet touched the earth. He strode over to the lowly campfire, and jabbed a finger toward the east. "We need to keep going!"

"We can't drive the horses through the night. They need time to rest and if we run them in the dark, they will go lame, or the wagon will."

"We don't have time for this!" Daniel shouted. Wes, understanding the meaning behind his frustrated insistence on urgency, tried to appease him.

"Relax son, we'll get there when we get there. Come, sit and break bread with me."

Daniel frowned down at Wes, as he considered whether to push the issue further. Seeing that the horses were already settled into a doze, he decided to concede the point. He went to the wagon and retrieved a roll of bedding to sit upon, then joined Wes at the fire.

"You seem angry," Wes remarked of Daniel's evident scowl. He presented a small loaf of crusted bread, and his son snatched it out of his hands.

"I *am* angry," he said, fuming.

"Are you mad at me?" Wes asked, wondering what pitfall he fell in this time.

"I'm not mad at you," Daniel snapped. He bit into his bread, grimaced, then let out a long sigh. "I'm not mad at you. I'm just angry at the world."

"Why?" Wes asked as he gnawed on a strip of dried meat.

"Because I thought I might be somehow spared from this wretched sickness," Daniel said, suddenly tempered. He stared down at his gloved hands. "That I was in some way special. What a foolish notion."

"Daniel..." Wes hesitated, but reminded himself that there was little his son could do to the boy guards of the capital anymore, "The black on your fingers... it was ink put on there by a couple of boys while you were sleeping. It was meant as a joke, although a cruel one."

"Do you think I'm stupid, father?" Daniel asked, and the low burning coals of his anger were fueled anew.

"I don't understand."

"Do you really think I can't tell the difference between sin sickness and writing ink?" The utter indignation on Daniel's face left Wes to feel inept before his son yet again.

"What are you saying?" He asked, and Daniel leaned over him in a way that his face, contorted by the harsh shade of the firelight, twisted into an ugly sneer.

"It didn't all wash off, father. It didn't all wash away."

"Let me see," Wes said, reaching for Daniel's hand, but his son recoiled. Dropping the bread he held, Daniel stepped back and cradled his hands to his chest.

"I can't."

"You have nothing to hide from out here," Wes said with a frustrated laugh, "the birds and rodents don't care about the nature of your sin."

"Can't you see that I'm scared?" Daniel shouted in a flash of fury, but in an instant his anger crumbled like a house made of playing cards. All that remained was raw, unrestrained fear. "I don't want to see what they look like. I don't want to know!"

"Daniel," Wes said, gently, "we all bear the burden of our sins. You are not an exception, you've just been wearing a disguise. Take off your gloves, and be free of this fear that binds you."

"These gloves do indeed bind me," Daniel said, looking down at his hands. "Everything I have ever worn for these past many years of my miserable life have bound me. For I am marked with the color of my servitude." Determination overtook him, and Daniel plucked at the fingers of his first glove, working it free. "I have grown to detest the color black!"

He ripped the glove from his hand, and threw it into the fire. He then worked open the buttons of his uniform jacket and yanked his arms free of it as well.

"The city has no claim on you out here," Wes said, encouraging his son's impulsive liberation, "the cage you now know is locked from the inside."

"For so long, I've endured cruelty at the hands of those who were supposed to take care of me. For so long I've been tempted and manipulated by the demon inside of me! I am tired of these shackles that have bound me to a life of both luxury and misery. There is nothing there for me! There is nothing *left* of me!" Daniel threw his refined jacket directly into the fire with no hesitation. His other glove followed the first, and he stripped away his thick lined undershirt that was also black. Beneath the layers he had a thin honey-colored sleeveless shirt that would have once been a defiance of his position. Out in the wilds, it was just an indicator that he was going to be cold. Daniel barely noticed the chill of the night for his fire was up and seeing his clothing burn brought him to a zenith of indignation. He threw back his head and roared his anger into the night.

The fire, emboldened by the new fodder, danced wild shadows across his thin body, but when Daniel doubled over, panting from the effort of his anger, Wes worried he might faint. He reached for his son, hoping to offer him support, but Daniel recoiled from his touch.

"Hush now, be still," Wes said reassuringly, but Daniel continued to struggle against him, and unwittingly ended up striking him in the face.

"Oh! Oh no..." he said, his anger once more dissolving into a fear that was transparent in his wide eyes. He staggered back from Wes, and spread his hands defensively. "I didn't mean to do that. Please, don't hurt me!"

Daniel's words were like a blade to his heart. For Wes understood that the lad wasn't specifically fearful of him, but more so he was fearful of everyone in his past. His actions were the direct effect of years of abuse.

Wes wanted to hug Daniel. He wanted to smooth his hair and tell him that the monsters in his life were gone. Yet they still seemed to haunt his son, so maybe this wasn't entirely true. Without the need to put on a face of arrogant confidence, his son seemed to be falling apart.

"Daniel, look at your hands," Wes said, hoping to distract him from his misery. He stepped forward and drew Daniels hands into his own. Holding them in his palms, he allowed his son to see what he's already seen. The skin, still wearing faded stains from the ink, showed clear signs of sin forming on the fingertips. None of it expanded past the first knuckle of each finger and Wes didn't see any black scales anywhere else. "Most children have sin like this by the time they turn four. From what I hear, you had it all the way up your arms when you arrived in the capital."

"I don't care about that place anymore," Daniel growled, and looked past Wes to where the capital glowed at the base of the distant mountain ridge.

"You hear me, you selfish lot of vermin? I DON'T CARE! I will no longer be your vessel to fill! Your bowl to tarnish and polish as you see fit!"

"Daniel...you shouldn't shout so much," Wes said as he looked around nervously, "you're going to attract attention if you haven't already. The monsters that dwell in darkness always come seeking those that dwell in the light."

"Don't worry, father, nothing from the dark will harm you as long as I'm here," Daniel said and yanked his hands from Wes' grasp. His mood shifted again, and a cool cunning returned to his face. It wasn't the first time Wes was left to wonder if he even knew his true son at all.

“Does madness itself fear you?” Wes asked skeptically while Daniel slipped deeper into the shadows of their camp to rummage in the wagon supplies.

“Madness reveres me.” He returned to the fire with a small pack in his hands. “They watch from the dark and yearns for me to join them. Do you think I should go, father?”

“Certainly not!” Wes said, indignant at the absurdity of the question, but Daniel just laughed. Then he winced.

“Are you alright?” Wes asked and Daniel shook his head.

“Every so often this sharp intense pain just runs through me from head to toe. I am used to pain, but it’s this sudden unpredictable intensity that catches me off guard. From what I’ve been told, the pain will only get worse. I have brought morphine for when that time comes.”

He opened his pack, and pulled at a brown woven sweater that looked thick and inviting. He also removed a long sleeved shirt in the same muddy color.

“Contraband,” he mused, offering Wes a smile that looked both guilty and innocent. “It was an offering given to me by an old Disciple years ago. The Elders ordered to have it burned but I hid it away. I liked to wear it sometimes when I was alone. My little secret defiance against my monstrous tyranny.”

He put on the shirt, then pulled the thick sweater over his head and sighed. “I will choose what colors I want to wear. I will be free to at least choose that.” He smiled to himself and watched the remains of his old clothing burn. Both men fell into a comfortable silence, and without awareness, Wes found himself turning to look toward the north. Benji was a half day's ride away from him. Would he know that Wes was nearby? Wes thought about how nice it would be to see Benji again. To hug him and for it to be warmly received instead of recoiled from.

Things are so much easier when they’re younger.

“Tell me father,” Daniel said, breaking the long silence between them, “do you really intend to return to the capital with that boy? This...Son of Promise?”

“I said that I would,” Wes replied although he did not specify when. He still silently hoped he might get Daniel back home then return to this very place and head north with his son. Benji might be able to heal Daniel the way he did with Wes. He would take Daniel north immediately, if not for Ruth’s words. He had to trust that she knew what was best for their son.

“You're willing to throw him to the wolves? I’m surprised.”

“He isn't like other lambs," Wes said with a smile, for he had to wonder if the Elders truly posed such a dire threat to one small Bringer of Light.

“So where did this boy come from? How did you acquire him?” Daniel asked as he picked up the bread he previously discarded and settled onto the bedroll to listen.

“How did I acquire him,” Wes repeated, while he considered the question. He wasn't quite sure how to explain their strange first encounter, for he didn't fully understand it himself. “It’s a lot to get into.”

“Oh. Well I do love a good story,” Daniel said with a sly smile. Wes watched his son bring bread to his lips, and noticed that the black scales were beyond the first knuckle. Black flecks were also forming along his temples. The world wasted no time filling in the gaps that the Divine Hall's influence chose to ignore. Hopefully the progression will slow over time, but Wes refused to speculate a timeline.

“I reckon it all started when I left home to come and get you. For I was only two days into my journey when I felt the presence of something in the night watching me. She was hunting me specifically, but I didn't know why." Wes proceeded to share everything he could with his son. The encounter with Benji's mother, and the way he attacked her then tracked her down to finish her, but found her waiting for him with her son.

He talked fondly about how horrible Benji was when they first met, how he fought against every step they took, but how he slowly grew more comfortable with Wes, and eventually they found an attachment with each other similar to the one he had with Daniel. What Wes didn't tell Daniel, was the strange looks that Benji sometimes gave him, the way he seemed to often understand what Wes was thinking, the unexplained flash of light in the alley, and the way he immediately attached to Lilly. There was so much about Benji that Wes didn't understand but thought should be kept secret from everyone including his own son.

“This mother you mentioned," Daniel said, bringing Wes out of his thoughts, "You said she was on the verge of succumbing to her madness?”

“That’s why she offered Benji to me.”

“Do you know how long before she would have lost her mind? Or is it possible that they never really give over to the madness fully. Perhaps there is some part of them that remains and remembers who they once were."

"Absolutely not," Wes said with a shiver, for it wasn't Benji's mother that came to his mind but the countless wanton monsters of the alley that exuded a never-ending and overpowering need to devour and consume.

"So there is no hope for me," Daniel said sadly, staring at the fire; once again tempered between them. Wes berated himself silently for stumbling over that bramble on the path. He bit at his lip, and studied his son's drawn and melancholy expression.

"There's always hope," he offered at last, "when you ask God to share the weight of your burden."

"Oh please, father!" Daniel said and shot a scathing look at Wes, "let's just stop with the make-believe magicians in the sky."

Wes frowned, feeling the sting of his son's insult, but felt something holding him back from pressing his way into another argument. Instead, he got to his feet. Stretching, he reached for his bedroll, and opened it to spread over the ground.

"What are you doing?" Daniel asked, suddenly anxious.

"I am going to sleep. When the birdsong wakes me, you can seek out your shaded wagon again, and I will continue to take the path east."

"You're sleeping out here?" Daniel asked, looking around at the imposing darkness.

"That is the plan. Don't worry, the fire will last as long as it needs to. And of course, the madness reveres you anyway."

"No, I just...I mean...." Daniel stared at the fire for a moment, then his gaze shifted back to Wes. "Can we sleep in the wagon instead?"

"You plan to join me to sleep? You've been asleep all day."

"I'm not very tired, but my bones ache. I just want to rest."

"Rest might benefit you," Wes agreed, and picked up his bedroll to smack away the dust that clung to it. He turned to the wagon, intending to light one of the fireboxes they provided, and Daniel followed behind him sheepishly for all his previous bravado. Wes was able to fumble around in the dim light of the adjacent fire and lit a firebox just bright enough to keep them from complete darkness. It was more a comfort for him than Daniel as his son seemed convinced that they didn't need protection from the night.

"I told you there is nothing to be afraid of, the night creatures keep their distance from me," Daniel commented as though he knew Wes' thoughts, and the arrogance in his voice struck Wes with a burst of irritation.

"If there is nothing to fear, why are you in this wagon?" he countered, and the way Daniel's face fell made him regret the words immediately. He spread his bedroll out for his son, then located stacks of blankets which he used as a cushion to sit upon. He offered one to Daniel as well. A peace offering for this minor battle in their war.

Wes sat on the blankets with his back against the wall of the wagon and leaned into the canopy which was surprisingly comfortable. He had grown soft on all the lush beds of the Divine Hall and appreciated this simpler form of comfort. He closed his eyes, bleary from a day riding into the sun, placed his hat over his face, and settled in as he waited for sleep to take him. The silence caught his attention, for Daniel had not made any effort to lay down, and after a while, Wes lifted his hat to peer over at his son who was watching him.

"What do you need, son?" he asked, and watched as Daniel hesitantly spread his bedroll out alongside Wes, unfolded his blanket, and eased onto his side with his head resting against Wes' leg. He did this once before in the Divine Hall, and it immediately reminded Wes of Benji. But deeper memories revealed themselves to him on the tapestry in his mind. Memories of Daniel, in the few months leading up to his fourth birthday, falling asleep often this way on Wes' lap. In the hottest of the summer days where the heat drove a man to sleep off the worst parts of the day, Wes would wake to find Daniel curled up beside him in this same way.

"You used to lay like this when you were little," Wes reflected as he marveled on the ways things changed over the years and how they sometimes remained the same. He absently stroked Daniel's hair as his mind drifted through his recollection."On hot days, I used to lean up against that big old maple tree in our yard, and you would often curl up beside me and rest your head on my leg just like this."

"That sounds like a nice memory," Daniel said softly, and Wes listened to his steady slow breathing. He hoped that Daniel was able to relax finally, and let go of this strange fear he was carrying. He always tried so hard to be in control of himself and show that he was brave, but Wes wondered if Daniel was simply afraid to be the thirteen year old boy that he was.

"I cherish every memory I have of you," he replied, and Daniel again went quiet for a while. Wes closed his eyes, sleep rose up to claim him, then Daniel spoke again.

"It must be hard," he said mournfully, "to love such a son as me."

"I never found it hard to love you, I just find it hard to not make you mad," Wes admitted with a dry chuckle. His fingers mapped lazy strokes through Daniel's hair. Lord, he was tired.

"Well then, tell me this, father," Daniel said, and his voice sounded bright and friendly. His constantly shifting of mood drained the authenticity from his words. "That boy of yours...did he remind you of me? You know, back when I was young and naive and not so easily angered."

"No...," Wes replied, hesitantly, for he feared he was stumbling into another pitfall. "Benji did not remind me of you. Actually, when I first laid eyes upon him, I thought he was Peter."

"Peter?" Daniel sat up, and looked at Wes. "Who is that?"

"Oh..." At first Wes thought that maybe Daniel lost his memories of his brother, but clarity came with the realization that Daniel had left their lives before Peter was even born. He left before the loss of his sisters, and that small one that they found in the bed. He left before Ruth turned into the person she was at the end of her long life of suffering. Daniel knew nothing of the pain in his own family.

"Oh? Oh, what?" Daniel asked, suddenly anxious.

"Peter...," Wes began, but had to pause for the death was still new, and the wound was closed with the most delicate of skin. "Daniel...Peter was your brother."

"Oh." Daniel fell silent again. Wes yawned and closed his burning eyes. He had little desire to explain how Peter lived for it always ended with how Peter died.

"Perhaps we can continue this conversation after we get some rest," he suggested, and Daniel seemed to quietly concede. He settled back on Wes' leg, and bundled into his blanket without a word. Wes sighed. He might still have an hour of sleep before the birdsong woke him as it always seemed to do. Thinking of all those morning tasks that needed done when he woke, Wes sank down to the edge of sleep and drifted against unconsciousness where dreams formed out of horses, knots, and wagon ties.

"Father," Daniel said unexpectedly, and Wes jerked awake. "Will we see Peter when we return back home? Are people caring for him there?"

"Neh, son," Wes said through a yawn. "Peter is dead." The words carried more weight to him than they ever would for Daniel. But why should they? He never knew Peter existed until the moment before learning that Peter died.

"Ah, I see." Daniel said, more curious than forlorn. He quickly decided he wanted to know more. "Did the taint of the world take him? I heard this is a thing that often occurs with children in the wilds."

"No. Not with him." Wes admitted. "It was an accident. A stupid accident. And it wouldn't have occurred if not for me."

"So you killed him?" Daniel lifted his head again, but Wes didn't open his eyes. He didn't want to discern the meaning in his son's expression.

"Yes... I suppose I did." he was reluctant to say. Regardless of all the assurances from people like Sassy and Ruth, Wes knew in his heart that Daniel's words were the purest form of honesty. Wes' guilt compounded his grief in a way that seemed crippling at times. He now realized he would never be free from it either. Every time he thought the edge of his pain was growing dull, despair washed over him anew like the waves of an ocean. The pain of his grief; always ebbing and flowing; ebbing and flowing in his mind. If he felt like he was growing used to the feeling, a sudden giant surge would envelop him, overwhelm him, and rob him of the ability to breathe. *Of course* he killed his son. *Of course* he did. For no other death endured hurt him so.

"You're a murderer," Daniel mused with a bit of bite to his words. "First you tell me how you killed that boy's mother, and now you speak of a brother I'll never know."

"I'm afraid so," Wes said solemnly. He thought his son was cruel for challenging him in this way, but in truth, he was too tired to care. The weight of his raw-rubbed grief took what remained of his spirit out of him, leaving only exhaustion.

"A murderer and yet not a mark on you," Daniel said softly. "You must share this secret with me."

"I don't understand it much more than you do," Wes mumbled as he coasted along the edge of sleep.

"You have no idea? None at all?" There was an edge of desperation in Daniel's voice and Wes understood that his words, while painful to hear, were not meant to maim. His son was simply trying to understand the difference between Wes and him. He was trying to find a way out of his supposed fate. Wes draped an arm over Daniel's shoulder and gave his arm a gentle squeeze.

"Nothing is certain, but I know where we can start," he said softly as he stroked his son's hair. It felt thinner than before. "We can start with a prayer."

Chapter Thirty-Seven

Trust in the Lord with all your heart;
do not depend on your own understanding.
Seek his will in all you do,
and he will show you which path to take.
- Proverbs 3:5-6 NLT

Wes jerked awake with a gasp, and listened to the thrumming of his heart. Again, his dreams left him feeling desperate with no understanding as to why. It both worried and frustrated him for he seemed to remember everything from his past, yet couldn't remember anything from his dreams.

The flaps of the wagon canopy were drawn, but there was a large enough gap to show Wes that the sun was about to rise. It was time to move on. Wes eased out from under his sleeping son blindly, and made to exit the wagon. He couldn't see Daniel in the gloom; the firebox having spent its oil at some point in the night, but Wes was able to pick his way through the clutter to climb out without waking him.

He allowed himself a nice long stretch to ease the ache in his back, then settled into the comfortable process of addressing the tasks at hand. Working with his hands always seemed to quell the turmoil in his mind, but he knew he was just avoiding the things he couldn't accept or change. Wes checked on the horses, who were still shaking off the dew of the morning, and led them some distance off the main path to where a dense copse of greenery painted a stripe of life through the desert wasteland. It was easy to find water in places where so little of it existed.

By the time he returned with the horses well watered, the sun was already peeking over the horizon in the east. He made quick work of tethering the two horses to the wagon's yoke, kicked dust over the remains of the fire, then climbed into the driver's seat to take up the reins. He commanded the horses forward but at a slower pace than before as the path they traveled was far less used. Fortunately, it was still wide enough for the wagon to avoid potential snares, and Wes kept his focus on the horizon where a long stretch of forest came into view. It had taken him days to travel this far when he was heading west, but Wes had to remind himself that the circumstances were much different then.

"Soon, we'll get him back home, Ruth. Soon you'll see your boy again."

After some time, Wes could hear the sounds of his son thumping about in the wagon. It was still very early for him, for the sun was only reaching its zenith in the sky, and Wes listened with curiosity; trying to discern the meaning to all the noises he was hearing. It sounded like his son was just wandering around aimlessly.

"Daniel? Are you doing alright back there?"

"What do you think?" Daniel snapped, and Wes tried not to wince. Again his son was angry and poised to take it out on his father, but Wes would not be dissuaded.

"Can I help you somehow?"

"Oh gee, Father, it never occurred to me you might be able to come back here and help me, considering you're the one driving the wagon."

"You don't have to be so vicious," Wes growled. He was growing tired of his son's condescending attitude.

"Well, I'm sorry that I'm in horrible pain and haven't paused to consider *your* feelings," Daniel snapped back at him; emboldened by unwarranted hostility.

"I didn't know you were in pain," Wes countered, and tried to peer into the shadows of the wagon, "what are you doing exactly?"

"I'm looking for something."

"Are you already seeking comfort in your pipe and your drugs?" Wes asked for he didn't think Daniel was in pain, as much as he was looking for escape.

"Oh, *spare* me your sense of moral high ground, father. I know *all* about your own tendency to indulge during your recovery."

Wes glowered hotly at the road in front of him. He was not proud of those moments during his confusion and blindness after his fight with Gad. During that time, there were so many things he struggled with: his restored memories, the reality of his madness, the strange tension with his son, not to mention all the pain and difficulty with his physical recovery. When Wes realized that a steady stream of morphine kept all the torment in his mind muffled to a low hum, he gave over to the ease of escape without hesitation. It was far from one of his finest moments.

"Are you looking for your pipe or not?" he asked, and tried to soften his tone.

"No, I have my pipe," Daniel growled as he continued to rummage and search, "what I don't have is my lighter. I can't find it anywhere."

"Oh," Wes said, and his hand went to the jacket pocket where a lighter was contained. After he fumbled with the firebox the night before, he must have tucked it into his jacket without thinking. He dreaded admitting this to Daniel, and chastised himself for being so nervous about speaking to his own son.

"I wish you mentioned this sooner," Wes said, trying to sound casual, "I happen to have a lighter in my pocket here."

There was a pause; a stillness inside the wagon, then Wes heard Daniel rush forward, and he jutted his palm into view through the canopy flaps.

"Give it to me!" he growled, and Wes couldn't help but gasp. Not only was Daniel's hand and arm completely covered in scales, the fingers themselves were bent and deformed into curled paws with long glossy black claws. The canopy of the wagon shaded them both significantly, but the day was bright and even in the shade, Daniel had to withdraw his hand a moment later with a soft hiss of pain.

"Here," Wes said with a heaviness that eluded to all that he was feeling. He stuck the lighter through the canopy opening, and felt Daniel pluck it out of his hand. Wes continued to push the horses onward, staring blankly at the open road, while his son whimpered and fumbled in the dark behind him. Wes tried not to speculate. He tried not to think about anything at all. Soon the familiar sweet smell of morphine permeated the air around him, and Wes tried to put that out of his mind as well.

"Oh, God," Wes whispered. The progression of the sin sickness in Daniel was so much worse than anything he'd ever seen before.

No, better to not think on it.

If that was how his hand looked, Wes dreaded seeing Daniel's face.

You can not let him see the fear in your eyes.

Wes understood that this was clearly a time for strength as he needed to take responsibility for his son in his time of weakness. Knowing this, and understanding what he was about to face, Wes allowed himself a solitary moment to close his eyes, and grieve over the son he no longer had. That vibrant boy in his youth, and even that cruel but beautiful teenager always dressed in black. Daniel was so proud, but his constant polarizing emotions made even that much seem like a facade.

He was strong yet weak.

Angry yet amused.

Impulsive yet calculating.

This was how Wes saw his son, yet still he loved him deeply. Knowing that Daniel might have only a few days instead of the projected week they hoped for, revealed to Wes the deep well of despair he tried to always keep covered. The murky waters within rippled their greeting and invited Wes to slip into its chilly embrace, for there was some strange security in the clutches of misery. He stuffed all he was feeling into the farthest corner of his mind and focused on the needs of the present. There will be plenty of time for despair later. He needed to just focus on getting his son home in order to save him and save the world they knew. What any of that meant exactly, Wes couldn't say.

"Daniel, are you feeling better?" he ventured to ask.

"No, father," his son responded softly, for the morphine drained all the heat from his words, "I will never feel better again. But I'm no longer in pain."

"The sun is behind us now. Come sit with me," Wes offered even though he partly dreaded the monster he would be forced to see. "I want to show you something." Daniel shuffled around behind him, and soon climbed out to sit by his side. At first, Wes didn't look at Daniel, for his son's companionship was bittersweet.

Push down the pain.

Bury it away.

Time for that later.

Time for that all too soon.

"Do you see that patch of woods yonder?" Wes asked as he gestured to the strip of trees in the distance.

"I do," Daniel replied calmly, his words laden with drugs.

"With time pressing upon us, we don't have the ability to go around that forest. We will have to follow this path and cut directly through it. Just know that the last time I encountered this place, it nearly cost me my life."

"How did that happen?" Daniel asked. He sat huddled, hugging himself, and seemed to generate his own darkness.

"It carries an old witchcraft which has grown evil, and spread to corrupt everything. The trees themselves cry with voices from your past. They entice you off your course, and while you wander through your directionless mind, in reality you might stumble through the forest for hours or for days."

"Like a memory spell?"

"Similar, but also far worse. One can usually shake a memory spell from their skin the way these horses shake away their sweat, but this miasma is unabating."

"Will it kill us?" Daniel asked, and his young voice sounded both wary but also, sadly, resigned.

"Neh. Not unless we succumb to the miasma and lose sight of those monsters that linger in the forest underbrush. When night falls, the monsters of the shadows will come into the open and tear me apart. When the day returns..."

"I'll burn up in the sun," Daniel concluded. "So this miasma brings back the dead?"

"It might," Wes had to admit. "But none of it is real. It's all just a trick of the mind. You must avoid all deeper thoughts that might amplify your past. The forest will blind you with your own memories, and it is difficult to shake from their grasp."

"I don't waste my time dwelling in the past," Daniel said boldly, but Wes could tell that he was lying. Very few walked the earth free from thinking of their regret.

"Well with luck, we can push through to the other end within an hour or two. Truly, I'm just worried about the wagon. The earth might rise up to claim a wheel or snap an axle if we are too distracted to avoid the worst of it."

"Nothing is ever simple," Daniel grumbled, "What does this stupid forest have against us anyway? We didn't do anything to harm it!" Wes marveled at how Daniel sounded his age at the strangest of times.

"I reckon that sometimes evil exists just to exist, son. There isn't always a reason for what we must endure, but we still have to endure it." When the sun sank low, offering dimmer light to the remaining day, Daniel held out his hand to take the reins.

"I'd like to guide the horses for a while." Handing them over, Wes glanced at Daniel's face but quickly looked away again. He tried not to see all that has changed.

"Is it so bad?" Daniel asked, and Wes never felt more compelled to lie.

"It's bad."

"I feel the scales all over my face. My skin burns and itches. I also think my jaw is...shifting somehow. It aches like a cutting tooth. Does my jaw look different to you?" Daniel asked, but Wes couldn't bring himself to look at his son.

"Yes," he managed to say hoarsely. "Your face seems to be growing longer, and your teeth..."

Endless rows of tiny black daggers.

"I see," Daniel replied softly, and leaned over, shivering as he clutched the reins.

"You're cold," Wes observed and glanced into the wagon bed, "Do you have something warmer to wear?"

"I have a heavy cloak stowed in the wagon, but I don't want to wear it."

"I don't want you to get sick from the cold. I can climb back there and get it if you don't want to stop the wagon."

"Father, I don't want it. It's black."

"Surely your comfort matters more than a color," Wes insisted.

"Will you stop?" Daniel shouted, instantly angry, and Wes could hear the second voice echoing a beat behind his own. The Dragon. The usurper. It had been dormant for so long, Wes almost forgot the monster was still in there. Hearing it again left him at a loss for words.

"I... I was just..."

"You might be my father, but don't think for a moment that you have any right to parent me. So stop trying to be my wet-nurse, and let me be!" Daniel's words cut like a whip, and Wes quietly turned his attention back to the forest ahead of them. They were less than an hour's ride to the campsite Wes once shared with Gad at the forest edge, but he would have to hurry to avoid tending to the evening duties in the thick of night. Silently, he formed a list of tasks that needed done in his mind. It was easier to feel useful in these things, for he wasn't very useful when it came to helping his son. Wes glanced over, and saw that Daniel was watching him.

"I shouldn't have said all that," Daniel said with a sigh, "I didn't mean any of it."

"I know you're trying to navigate your anger with everything you have to endure"

"I am angry," Daniel mused with a bitter scoff, "knowing that I'm going to die out here. A pointless death."

"We're nearing the edge of the forest," Wes said, avoiding his son's words. When Daniel lifted his head to examine their path, Wes noted that his black eyes seemed to have a reddish glow to them. The forest loomed sinisterly just ahead. It revealed none of the secrets nestled in its shadows, and the fading sun did little to penetrate the mysteries it contained.

"Our path appears to continue through the forest, but I am uncertain as to the condition of the road." Wes recalled the last time he entered these woods, and had lost his way completely. He was far wiser with this second effort. "While we have no choice but to cut through this forest, know that if we stray from the path, we may not find our way back to our wagon again."

"Can a bunch of trees really cause us to wander off like that?" Daniel asked.

"What I know I learned from the last time I came this way. It was by the grace of God that I found another traveler's firelight before the night took me."

"Must we stop?" Daniel pressed, "I can see well enough at night."

"You might," Wes said, glancing at his son's glowing red eyes again, "but the horses cannot. I also suspect the spell is stronger when the sun is absent from the sky."

"Very well," Daniel conceded, and Wes showed him where to guide the horses so that they pulled the wagon up alongside the small campsite with its remnants of past fires spanning over the years. Seeing Gad in this place felt like a lifetime ago. When the wagon came to a stop, Wes stepped down from the driver's seat and stretched out the weariness of the day's ride. He then turned his attention to the horses and it took him a minute to realize that Daniel was moving much slower than before. His arms and legs were unwilling to cooperate the way they once had. He bared his teeth, grunting through the pain of his efforts, and Wes turned his attention back to the horses; plodding through his chore with spiritless intent.

"Do you need your pipe again?" he asked as he worked to loosen a strap.

"In a moment," Daniel replied, and shambled toward the forest. "Right now, I just want to be alone."

"Don't stray too far into the woods," Wes warned, unable to stop himself.

"What would an *idiot* like me ever do without your constant reminders to follow common sense?" Daniel replied, but there was no heat in his snark.

Wes briefly watched as his son lumbered into the woods, then returned his focus to the horses. Time to despair later. There was too much to do in the now. He took a moment to brush down the horses fur, then found a place close by that had bushes still clinging to life in spite of the late season to tether them. He spent the rest of the day gathering and preparing for a fire as he had done so many times before.

Just as the sun slipped out of sight, Daniel returned to their campsite. He lingered at the edge of the firelight and stared vacantly at the low burning flames. The fire's glow only highlighted the red already burning in his eyes. Wes raised a hand, offering his son some of the cheese he recovered out of the wagon, and noticed how unnerving those eyes looked when they shifted in his direction. Daniel stepped forward, grabbed at the cheese clumsily, and shoved it past his rows of teeth.

While he ate, Wes watched long enough to ensure his son wouldn't choke. Daniel managed well enough, and as he chewed, his teeth nested haphazardly within each other. Wes wondered when the madness would start to show, and *how* would it show. Would Daniel turn on him the way Gad had? He didn't know how he could endure such heartache, but he would for he *had* to. Daniel's eyes shifted from the fire again, caught Wes staring at him, and discarded the remains of a half eaten loaf of bread into the flames.

He eased down to the ground, pitched forward, and laid on his stomach with his face half buried in the dirt.

"Do you want a blanket?" Wes asked.

"In a minute," Daniel mumbled in reply.

"Is the fire too strong? Does the light bother you?" Wes asked.

"Not really, but I'm too tired to care either way."

"Why were you gone for so long?" Wes asked, as he took off his hat and let his hands work nervously around its brim.

"I was thinking," Daniel replied.

"What were you thinking about?" Wes asked and moved to sit next to his son.

"Father, tell me about Peter."

"Peter?"

"Tell me about the brother I never got to know," Daniel's black eyes shifted to look up at Wes again.

"Alright, son, I'll tell you about Peter," Wes replied, and so he did. He told Daniel everything he could about his brother. Peter's gentle nature, his hesitation to try new things, and his easy laugh that came out at the most unexpected times. He shared the way Peter asked so many questions, but never seemed satisfied with a simple answer. He explained how Peter often cried because his mother didn't pay attention to him in the ways that a mother should, and how he wished he had comforted his son in those moments instead of growing frustrated with him.

Wes couldn't help but smile when he pictured that bright-eyed boy with mud-colored hair. He reflected Wes the way Daniel resembled Ruth. Wes found himself talking also of the two sisters Daniel never knew as well. Two perfect babies that were both too weak to take on the weight of the world. He did not mention the little one that they found dead in the bed. He didn't know if Daniel would understand the heartache that it caused.

Finally, when nothing else could be said, Wes told Daniel about the day that Peter died: about the mare and the fall. He talked about the way Ruth reacted when she touched her dead son, and even told Daniel about that dark moment when he sat on his porch and hoped that something would come and drag him into the night. Wes' voice broke from the emotion of the telling, but he refused to hold anything back. For this was a moment between them that could be counted among only a few, and he felt like every moment needed to count for something. Wes told Daniel about Ruth's rapid decline, and his ultimate decision to leave. He admitted for the first time aloud that while his intention was to go and find Daniel, in truth he was running from the reality that he would have to watch Ruth slowly die should he remain.

With that last revelation concluded, Wes snatched up his waterskin, and drained its contents in a single go. He gulped greedily as water trickled down his chin, then wiped at his face with his sleeve as he let out a long sigh. The telling was hard, but it was good. He felt a peace he had not known before. Silence clung to the moment for some time, then Daniel slowly shifted, spreading his hands over the earth, and pushed himself into a sitting position. He could have said a dozen scathing things about Wes in that moment, but what he said was nothing Wes ever expected to hear.

"I regret leaving our home."

"If we could all drape ourselves in our regrets, we would never be cold," Wes said cynically, and took in a view of Daniel's glowing red eyes.

"Will you run from me, the way you ran from mother, when my time comes?" Daniel asked, and tilted his head as though he expected a blow to the chin.

"What is the point of regret unless we learn from it? I will not run again," Wes concluded, then got to his feet. It was past time he closed his eyes for a while.

"I need to get some rest to prepare for the push ahead. Do you want to rest as well? It might help to ease your pain."

"Yes," Daniel replied, his face smeared with dirt, "to ease the pain."

Wes watched as Daniel fumbled with his pipe, pulling it out from the sleeve of his sweater, and struggled to hold it between his thinning lips. Daniel lifted his hand, which shook as he struggled to work the mechanism of the lighter, and Wes could not bear to watch him any further. Instead, he turned and looked to the west where the faintest glow of the capital was still visible on the horizon.

"Daniel...what if we went back?" Wes heard himself ask. Of course he knew it to be a foolish desperate plight, for he did not doubt Ruth's words to him about the importance of this journey, but his lovely wife never disclosed to him exactly how hard this journey was going to be. Seeing his son tortured in this way; unable to ease his suffering, Wes thought it preferable to return him to the capital where he might find healing. Maybe the damage could be undone. Maybe his suffering would end.

"Don't be stupid," Daniel grumbled, "You know what's at stake. The prophecies, the unraveling of time, the loss of memories, all of it. If we returned as we are...I can only speculate what they would do to us if we lacked possession of the Son of Promise."

Perhaps it was due to the adjacent miasma, but Daniel's strange name for Benji immediately conjured memories of the lad in Wes' mind. Of all the things to remember, Wes recalled the look on Benji's face when he was in his deep sleep that night in the alley a moment before the monsters were about to overtake them, and the strange light liberated them from their dismal fate. In that brief moment, Benji's tranquil face looked so normal; just a boy asleep dreaming innocent dreams. If that strange light truly came from Benji as it seemed to, Wes had to believe Benji would be able to do the same thing for Daniel. The problem was, Daniel wasn't saved. For while Wes was cleansed of his sin, all the wicked that swarmed around him that night were obliterated completely. The alley was swept clean. Could the same thing happen to his son?

"Father," Daniel said, and Wes blinked as he looked around, disoriented. The miasma influenced him already. Daniel sat next to a fire that appeared to be reduced to embers and coals. Exactly how long had he been standing there?

"Yes, Daniel...what is it?"

"Can you help me into the wagon? I want to be near you while you sleep."

"Yes. Of course." Wes was not sure what to think of his son's sudden attachment to him. He tried to ignore the foreboding rising up like bile in his throat and reached for his boy. He helped Daniel to his feet, and together they turned toward the wagon. Daniel left like stone and moved like sacks of sand, but he was able to limp and stagger to the wagon with little support from Wes. Climbing inside was another matter, and every limitation that revealed itself was another dagger thrust into Wes' heart. His boy. His poor poor boy.

When Wes got into the wagon, he took up his same position leaning against the side, and helped Daniel stretch out the bedding alongside him. He slipped into the same familiar position next to his father and rested his head on his leg. Wes closed his eyes, and traced his fingers along the lumps on Daniel's head like he was plotting constellations.

"I wish there was more I could do for you. I hate to see you suffer like this," Wes confessed, and looked through the opening between the flaps of the wagon canopy to examine the glow of the night's eye balanced among the stars.

"Sadly, my suffering is unavoidable," Daniel mumbled, his words heavy with weariness.

"Your dragon takes too much from you."

"Even so, the cost has yet to be paid in full."

"You can give yourself over to the Lord," Wes ventured, "Let him help carry the burden of your sin. I can explain to you how..."

"You never stop, do you?" Daniel snapped, suddenly full of indignation. Wes' hand froze on his head.

"I...don't understand."

"Of course you don't," Daniel said, and sat up to glare his anger with glowing red eyes. "You and mother and your *stupid* book. Always telling your *stories* and sharing your *life lessons* but what has it gotten you? A legacy of dead children and a wife who lost her mind before she lost her life. All that suffering, and in the end your prayers and your faith did nothing to protect you from the cruelty of this world! But look at all I had, father! Look at what the *Dragon* gave me! I was beautiful! Powerful! Worshiped by hundreds!"

"You were abused, manipulated, and stripped of everything you loved," Wes rebutted calmly. Daniel's anger always seemed to lash out like an unseen snake, and Wes clearly heard the second voice lurking just behind Daniel's own. That secret voice that only presented itself when he was angry. The voice of the usurper. If this dragon creature gave so much, what exactly did he take in return?

"Those things that happened to me were the result of the people around me and not the Dragon's influence. Can you say the same, father? Who else can shoulder the blame of your suffering besides your supposed God?"

"There is much you don't understand," Wes said solemnly, for the Word never proclaimed God would spare those around him of the suffering they faced. The agonies of Job were a testament to that. The path the Lord offers was not easier, just more righteous. It promised something beyond the suffering of the present. But what will happen to Daniel if he comes to face the veil without salvation waiting for him on the other side?

"What I understand is that I have little time left, and I get to spend it enduring endless wisdom from *you*. I don't need your God to tell me that I'm *dying*."

"You sound hoarse," Wes said, reaching for a full canteen. "I can't recall the last time you drank anything."

"When will you be ready to listen?" Daniel muttered, obviously frustrated. Wes brought the spout of the canteen to Daniel's mouth, and his son gulped the liquid clumsily; spilling half of it on the wagon bed. He broke away, gasping and drained, and flopped back down with his head on Wes' leg once more.

"I'm sorry I said what I did. I didn't mean it. I'm glad I am with you, father," Daniel mumbled, and again Wes closed his eyes. Was Daniel's bouts of sudden anger a result of his circumstance, or the start of an inevitable madness that could not be thwarted?

"I should have chased you down that night you left," Wes confessed, and hearing himself say those words stung his eyes and caused his nose to burn. Giving Daniel over to the fate of his actions was one of the deepest regrets Wes possessed, and for some reason he felt compelled to share everything with his son. That night played over in his mind a hundred times as Wes picked apart all the ways he failed the boy. After Daniel left, Wes told himself he would go check on his son as soon as he had an opportunity to do so, but he had to manage the toils of the farm on his own, and with Ruth's instability, the many children they brought into the world, and his own cowardice, Wes never left. The distance between father and son only widened with every passing day.

"If I had known...if I was aware of everything you were going through..." Wes couldn't find the words, for nothing he said mattered anymore. If he had known what they were doing to Daniel, what would he have done? Would he have found enough strength to locate his son or would he find another reason to remain right where he was on that farm?

"Oh, don't be so hard on yourself. You wouldn't have been able to convince me to go back home no matter how hard you tried. If you drug me away kicking and screaming, I would have just run away again. The world was far too big to ignore. The capital was too exciting not to be a part of. I hardly even gave my old life a thought until that day you walked through my doors like you were some kind of honored guest and laid the burden of my past at my feet. I still can't believe you were able to reach me so easily." Daniel laughed at this, but the sound was half-hearted and weary."I'm sorry I keep dwelling on the past. It must be this miasma. It pulls at the mind strongly during the night, but with hope, it will be easier to ignore in the morning."

"It's okay, you don't have to apologize, but father... I'm really tired," Daniel said, and Wes realized how exhausted he sounded.

"I understand. Get some rest," he said as he ran fingers along the ridges of his son's head. "I'll take care of everything in the morning."

Wes took a moment to look around, and while the campsite appeared to be in order, it also seemed strangely different than before. The whole area was lit with a glow that was neither sunlight nor firelight, and was just simply there. The entire area was motionless and artificial; a replica of reality.

"Daniel?" Wes called out, then realized that the wagon and Daniel were gone. He made a slow circle as he took in his surroundings, but was unable to locate his son for as far as he could see.

"Daniel!" He shouted, but his voice didn't seem to carry at all. It was as though this strange place swallowed up sound along with life. Growing worried, he tried shouting again. "Daniel! Where are you?"

"Hush now, brother, no need to get all excited."

"Sassy?" Wes turned in the direction of her familiar voice. "I can't see you!"

"I'm not so strong to manifest myself in a place I've never been to, but wherever you are, the veil is thin there and I am able to at least *speak* to you on your dreams." Her voice seemed to be coming from somewhere within the forest, but there were far more important things to consider than the nature of her strange supernatural abilities.

"Did Benji find you, Sassy? Is he okay?"

"Oh yes, brother. He's with us alright, and we all sure do know it. That boy's been half crazed with anger; stompin' around like a bear with a mouthful of bees since he got here. I only just recently found out why."

"Tell me what happened," Wes urged, but was too relieved knowing that Benji was safe to be concerned over why he was presently so mad.

"Eve; my dear granddaughter, she means well, brother. But she overstepped her place and made a choice to take action without thinking things through."

"I don't understand," Wes said, as his eyes scanned the forest's shadows for some indication as to the source of Sassy's voice.

"Turns out the lad was visiting your dreams. Checking on you and the like. But there is great danger in treading through another man's mind. Benji was warned of this, and he stubbornly ignored those warnings. He's just a boy, so I forgive him for his good intentions. But Eve is not used to having her teaching ignored. She grew quite furious with him, and acted in her anger before she knew what she was even doing. She tied your mind up with a knot that the lad can't work apart. She claimed she saw a madness in you, although I don't see it now. But she also had good intentions so I ask for you to forgive her as well."

"What do you mean when you say she tied my mind up with a knot? What kind of knot?"

"The kind that binds your mind shut, and causes you to forget the nature of your dreams. That particular part is an unfortunate side effect, but not a detrimental one. What Eve discovered though, and what she kept from me until recently, was that she *also* doesn't know how to work apart the knot she made. The lad is furious, both with her and with his own inability to do what she can't. He's been beating against the locked door of your mind with such a ferocity, it leaves him exhausted when he wakes in the morning. He's desperate to reach you. He thinks there's a question you've been wanting to ask him."

"Could he reach me here? Can I speak with him now?" Wes asked, for if Benji was desperate to connect with him, he was just as desperate to talk to Benji.

"If he discovered you were here, I'm sure he would have tried, but there's danger in bringing him to a place where the veil is so thin."

"But if he needs to see me..."

"More like *you* need to see *him* and he be knowing it. But the knot is still tied, so why put him through the heartache when you won't remember anyway."

"Then what do I do? I don't want him to struggle with all of this."

"That's exactly why I'm here, brother. So you can ask your question to me." Wes narrowed his eyes at Sassy's words.

"I reckon I don't understand..."

"We don't have much time left, brother. A darkness is brewing. Ask what you want to ask and be quick about it. What did you want to ask Benji?"

"If I'm doing the right thing," Wes said without fully understanding that yes, this was exactly what he would ask Benji if he saw him. "Am I doing the right thing forcing Daniel to go back home?"

"Ah, yes. That is a very good question. So, tell me the answer."

"If I knew the answer, why would I ask the question?" Wes demanded, growing frustrated.

"Because you're desperate," Sassy replied without hesitation, "and would rather a child make the decision instead of taking ownership of the choice yourself."

"You don't need to be cruel," Wes grumbled, for Benji was more than just a child, and Sassy knew it.

"What did Ruth tell you?" Sassy pressed, unphased. Wes didn't bother to question how she knew this particular conversation occurred.

"Ruth said the only way our world will have a future is if Daniel returns home, and if Benji faces the Elders with me at his side."

"Then the burden of the decision was already taken from you, brother, for your wife has told you all that you need to know. I will make sure Benji knows so he can find peace until he's able to see you again."

"And will *I* have peace, Sassy? Will I remember any of this when I wake up again?" Wes could already feel a slow panic growing in his chest.

"Far greater issues await you upon your waking," Sassy said and her voice sounded right next to his ear, "but I will pray for you to somehow find the peace you seek, knowing you have no choice but to take your son back home, no matter the cost."

"What cost?" Wes began, but the moment he spoke, screams pierced the stillness of his dreamscape, and jolted him awake.

He reached for his gun reflexively, unnerved by the wretched sound he heard, but quickly realized the cries were coming from Daniel. It was too dark to see him, but Wes could hear his son thrashing around on the wagon floor, and knew he was in the throes of a nightmare. Wes was instantly teleported back to those nights when he sat up watching Ruth struggle through her own nightmares. Shaking free the weight of his recollection, Wes pushed himself up, and groped at the darkness until he laid hands upon his son. Something struck him across the face, a result of his son's thrashing, but Wes didn't hesitate to pull Daniel into his arms and rock the boy back and forth gently.

"Hush now," he soothed, "It was just a nightmare. Daniel, wake up. Everything is alright. Hush. Hush." Daniel's whole body trembled as he raised his hands to protect his face.

"No! Don't hurt me!" He cried, and struggled to get away, but Wes stroked his head soothingly and continued to rock him. The ridges and lumps on his son's head were forming points.

"No one will hurt you. You're alright now. You're safe. It was just a dream. Nothing can hurt you here. Just a dream." Eventually, Daniel stopped crying, and simply laid limply in Wes' arms while he rocked his son back and forth; back and forth.

"Just a dream," Wes soothed as he stared blankly into the fullness of night, "you're safe now. Just a dream. Just a dream."

"Everyone was crying out to me," Daniel keened; his voice quivering with fear, "All those that have died by my complacency or by my own hand. The countless faces of those I've seen slaughtered for little or no reason haunt me, and sing to me in my dreams."

"What do they sing?" Wes asked as he cradled this creature who was once a boy, but still his son.

"They sing of a veil growing thin. Of time unraveling. Father...father...they said the dead will soon walk the earth. They called me the Harbinger of Destruction. The beginning and the end."

"Don't listen to such nonsense. This is all a result of the forest and its miasma. The old evil has come to torment you."

"What if it's true? If the dead come to walk the earth, they will surely come for me. *Chancy* will come for me. Oh, my head! I feel like I'm losing my mind!"

"Hush! Hush now. It's just the old witchcraft of the forest. It must be growing stronger."

Of course it's stronger, if the veil is thinning.

“I hear the birdsong,” Wes said, for indeed the morning birds were starting their daily routine, “stay here and I’ll get us out of this place. Once the forest is behind us, you’ll feel much better. No more nightmares when we’re free. Hang in there, son, you’ll see.”

“Yes, father,” Daniel whimpered, but at least he no longer trembled in fear.

“Stay with me, in the present. No more sleeping and no more dreaming,” Wes warned, “and no morphine; not until we are free from this place. For it will only make you easier to influence.”

“Yes, father. Thank you.”

Wes pulled Daniel close to him again and hugged his son for a long time. Even with all the changes to his appearance, he was still far too small for his age. A creature that was once a boy, but hasn’t known the joys of being a child for a long time. After a while, Wes forced himself to release Daniel, and slipped out of the wagon into the chilly early hours of a new day. The miasma was a constant yoke on his shoulders but tasks would help distract the mind.

Wes retrieved the horses, who seemed completely unaffected by the forest nearby, and secured them to the wagon. He then eyed the overgrown trail that stretched into the forest and determined that it was clear enough for the wagon to safely traverse through. Although Wes could not be certain of those areas that remained unseen. He decided to focus his full attention on the road, determined to avoid any potential snares to both hoof and wagon wheel, and strived to put everything else out of his mind. Whispering a prayer for the Lord to help guide him through to the other side, Wes used the reins to urge the horses forward on a path shrouded in the shadows of the forest’s canopy.

Chapter Thirty-Eight

This is why we never give up.
Though our bodies are dying,
Our spirits are being renewed every day.
- 2 Corinthians 4:16 NLT

Wes approached a small camp with a fire burning low in its ring of stones. Glancing to the sky, he was surprised to see that he had wandered through the forest far past nightfall without any source of light. He was lucky to still be alive.

A blanket was neatly folded next to the burning scraps of timber, so Wes hunkered close, and lifted chilled hands to warm them by the flames. He caught movement at the corner of his eye, and turned to see Benji sitting next to him. This confused him at first, but when the lad smiled at him, he only felt relief.

"Benji, it's good to see you."

"I'm glad to be here," Benji replied as he spread his arms in a long languid stretch. Wes immediately saw the deception for what it was. The forest miasma must have custody of his mind.

"Who are you?" Wes demanded, and Benji looked wounded.

"You don't know who I am?"

"The real Benji can't speak, and even if he could, I reckon he wouldn't sound like Daniel."

"Do I though?" Benji asked with feigned innocence, then his easy-going smile returned. "Do I sound like Daniel, or does that supposed *Guardian Son* sound like me?"

"Usurper," Wes growled, and the boy's eyes flashed red; a confirmation to his claim.

“Call me what you like, Light Keeper, it makes no difference to me,” he said with a shrug, but the fire didn’t leave his eyes.

“How are you even here? You share no part of my memories, so how do you have hold of my mind?”

“The veil is growing thin, and the veil is thinnest right here.” The usurper pointed at the fire pit.

“But what purpose do you have with me? And why do you wear Benji as a disguise?”

“Oh, I thought I would try him out, see how he feels,” said the demon as he examined his arms and patted hands against his small torso. “Since he will be mine one day.”

“He will *never* be yours,” Wes sneered; grimacing in disgust.

“A bold claim, Keeper, but a useless one,” the demon replied. He leaned in, a small smile playing over his lips, and spoke to Wes in a secretive whisper. “I always get what I want, and I *want* this boy.”

Wes heard a scream. The night and its fire, along with Benji’s smiling face turned to vapor in front of his eyes. Wes found himself sitting on the wagon, and realized that while it was still day, the horses stopped moving forward; they were all suspended in time. The horses stomped and danced about impatiently, and Wes wondered how long he left them standing there.

Daniel cried out again, and Wes put the thought out of his mind. He climbed over the back of the seat into the wagon bed, and pulled the canopy closed behind him.

“Daniel? Are you alright? Are you...” A powerful blow struck Wes high on his cheek and he staggered as bursts of light danced across his vision.

“Stay away from me, vermin!” Daniel growled, and Wes was stunned by how inhuman he sounded.“I will rip out your throat if you try to touch me again!”

“Daniel, stop! You’re seeing phantoms! None of it is real!”

“My life isn’t real!” Daniel cried, then struck himself in the head again and again.

“No! Daniel, stop it! Don’t hit yourself! Stop hurting yourself!” Wes rushed forward to restrain Daniel’s hands, but immediately his son lunged at him. He swiped the air between them with ready claws, but by God’s mercy Wes was able to stay out of his reach.

“I’ll rip you open! I’ll cut you down with my teeth!” Hearing Daniel say these horrible loathsome words in this strange new bestial voice; Wes no longer recognized his son.

The madness has hold of him. He is lost to me now.

“No,” Wes growled, “I made a promise, and we *will* be keeping it.”

Wes scanned the wagon's interior, and located a length of rope that he slung over his arm. He regarded Daniel who appeared to be bent over, crouching as though he were poised to charge. Seeing him that way, Wes couldn't help but think of Gad.

No.

Gad with his sallow fish lips and endless rows of razor black teeth.

No!

Gad with his whispers in the hole. He never stopped speaking in that dark place. The coffin. Wes' portion of hell where Gad was always whispering. Always tempting.

"If thy right eye offends thee..."

Not again!

Gad with his lust for blood that clouded his eyes and stretched his rubbery skin into a hungry smile. Wes had no doubt the monster wouldn't stop until he cut him down. Gad's blood will spill and burn like an inferno upon Wes' skin and eyes and lungs. The *pain* it will cause. The endless searing *pain*!

"I will not be overtaken by you again!" Wes roared, and lunged at the other man. Gad shifted, not expecting the sudden assault, and Wes was able to overtake him easily. He drove the broadside of his arm against Gad's neck, shoved him to the floor, and managed to pin him there. The rope was in his hands in an instant, and he made quick work of tying the beast up as though he were a pig. Wes' mind, focused and directed, gave over to the determination of his survival. He knew what was at stake. He knew how this was destined to end. With Gad secured, Wes pulled his revolver free from its holster, and placed the barrel against the monster's head.

"Father!"

Wes gasped as reality struck him like a punch in the gut. He dropped his weapon as though it scalded him, and fled from the actions he was about to take.

"I'm sorry...I'm sorry...I thought you were...I thought Gad was..." Wes stammered as he stumbled over his feet to get to the rear of the wagon.

"Don't say the name," Daniel warned, "I know your mind wasn't your own. Neither was mine. I thought you were...nevermind. Just untie me please."

"Yes...I'm sorry. O-of course," Wes said clumsily, and crawled closer to his son. He dared not dwell on what he was about to do. Not here. But the lack of control he had horrified him. Wes reached out a trembling hand, and numbly worked loose the knots he made to bind Daniel's ankles to his wrists. When Daniel was free, he sat up and retrieved Wes' gun.

"You should take this back," he said, holding out the revolver, but Wes' initial reaction was to throw the thing out of the wagon and never touch it again.

"I don't want it," he said, scowling at the weapon as though it betrayed him.

"Don't be foolish. This is the only advantage you have against the evil of this world. Take it. Please. Then I think you need to tie me up again. Just a little more comfortably this time."

"I don't understand," Wes said, as he warily returned the revolver to its holster.

"If the forest tricks my mind again...I don't want to risk hurting you or forcing you to hurt me. It will be safer if I am restrained until we get out of this place. Please, just hurry and get this done so we can keep moving." Wes did as Daniel requested. He secured his son's wrists with an overhand knot and looped the rope around one of the canopy's metal ribs. He wouldn't escape easily.

"I forgive you for hitting me," Wes said as he stepped back and examined his work. Daniel sat with his back against the wall of the wagon and his arm pulled tight over his head with minimal slack for his wrists.

"I forgive you for trying to kill me," he replied with a wry smile. "Get us out of here, father."

Wes gave a nod, and left his son to get the wagon moving again. The horses were poised to move on, and so Wes took up the reins and obliged them. They sprung forth eagerly, and Wes focused his attention on both the path and the woods surrounding him. The stillness of the area made him nervous. Even Daniel was silent. Wes could no longer see an opening in the trees where they entered, nor could he see the exit he needed to reach. The trees cocooned him, and any sort of progress felt like a mirage. The little bit of light that cascaded through the branches indicated that it was still day, but without the sun as a guide, Wes had no idea how close they were to nightfall. He abruptly pushed the thought away. Even though it wasn't a memory, there was risk in ever letting his mind wander. Forward they went, treading this ancient path back home, and onward time went even though it seemed to not move at all.

Daniel let out a strange high-pitched whine that reminded Wes of a time when he happened upon a fox in the woods near his farm. The thing had wedged his paw in a snarl of roots, and went lame in his fervent madness to escape. When Wes found him, the fox was exhausted from struggling for so long, and laid limply on the forest floor. But when Wes tried to pull at the roots in an effort to free his paw, the fox lunged at Wes' hand and tried to bite with feral teeth. This animal was more willing to die trapped, than risk trusting something he didn't understand. With night approaching and the fox refusing to cooperate, Wes had no choice but to abandon the animal to his fate. It was almost fully night when he finally returned to the farm.

The farm. A brutal, unforgiving place that showed him the pain of living. Nothing ever just *rested* there. Everything required that something else be done. Wes hardly kept up with it on his own, but when Ruth was doing well, she made all the effort easier. Her energy, her smile, her little songs she liked to sing while she worked...

Ah Ruth. She was such a sweet and beautiful girl. In spite of her second sight, she never used it to take advantage of Wes or the other children in town when they played together. She never complained. When they teased her for her limitations, she just smiled and said she would do better next time.

"Wake up, Wesley!"

Wes lifted his head as reality returned. His mouth was dry, and his stomach rolled with hunger. The wagon crept through open barren fields, as the horses meandered idly forward. Craning his neck, Wes leaned to the side, and examined the way he just came. The forest was only a few minutes' ride behind him, but already his mind was so much clearer. Praise the Lord, they made it out unscathed! He also recognized these fields, and knew they were almost back home.

"Daniel, we made it! We're free from that horrible place. Daniel, are you awake?" Wes got to his feet, and pulled back the canopy flap. The dim orange glow of the late afternoon sun revealed the wagon's interior was absent his son. A pile of frayed rope eluded to his chewing through them. Daniel was gone.

"Oh...Lord..." Wes breathed, as his eyes lifted again to the sky where the sun just touched the top of the treeline. He had time. Not much, but he had time. He dare not waste it turning the wagon around. Climbing out of the seat, he threw back the rear canopy flaps and rummaged around until he was able to locate a ground stake. He silently thanked Ashter for considering everything, as he rushed to free one of the horses from the wagon yoke. He drove the stake right into the trail, gave it a few solid strokes from a shoeing mallet, and used it as a way to tether the remaining horse in place. The other horse that he liberated, had a bridle with a short rein but the gelding lacked a saddle.

It had been a long time since Wes pulled himself onto a horse without the aid of a pummel and stirrups. Any other time he would have ended up spilled over the ground, but his blood was running hot over worry for his boy, and Wes seated the horse on the first go. He whipped the reins, drove his heels into the gelding's ribs, and the horse charged forward with a toss of head and snort of indignation.

“If you help me get my son out of these wretched woods, I’ll give you a fill of oats once we reach my farm,” Wes said encouragingly, and onward they raced together. As they slipped into the shadow of the trees, Wes took a final glance at the open sky. An hour. Maybe he had an hour.

The cool day only grew colder when Wes reentered the forest. The day was almost gone, and the miasma would only get stronger with each passing moment. Wes needed to keep his focus. He needed to avoid all distraction so he could get Daniel and get out while he still had time. He tugged at the reins, urging his horse to slow, and scanned the area as he strained to listen for any indication of his son's presence. Somewhere deeper into the forest to his left, Wes heard someone crying.

“Daniel!”

“Father?”

Wes climbed down from his horse, his heart thrumming in his ears, and they both continued forward on foot.

“Daniel, where are you? Keep talking so I can find you!”

“Papa?”

Wes’ head whipped to the right, and he froze mid-step. The shadows mocked his limited vision, but there was no doubt of what he heard.

“How?” Wes whispered, “you’re dead.”

“No! Stay away from me! You’re not real!” Wes’ attention was drawn back to the left. Daniel seemed close. Somewhere just inside all that gloom.

“It’s going to be alright, son,” Wes called out, “I’m going to get you out of here.” Alongside the path, Wes spotted a tree that had the stump of a broken branch within reach. He slipped the gelding’s reins over it, securing him in place, then stepped off the path into the denser forest, and for his son again.

“Shut up! Shut up! SHUT UP!” Daniel howled through his sobs. From the path it was clear the direction that he was in, but by stepping directly into the mouth of this hungry forest, Wes felt enveloped in an encroaching silence that skewed the senses and distorted direction. Fortunately, Daniel seemed close and if Wes didn’t go too far he was sure he’d be able to get back. He picked his way carefully through shrubs and the remains of things that clung to life in this colder weather. Eventually, he stumbled through a dense patch of bramble, and into a small clearing where he immediately located his son. Daniel was curled into a ball on the forest floor.

“Daniel,” Wes sighed with relief; knowing that his son appeared to be alright, but when Wes approached him, Daniel let out a terrified scream.

"Get away from me! You aren't real! YOU AREN'T REAL!"

"Easy, easy." Wes showed his open palms. "Don't let the miasma take hold of your senses. I'm real and I'm here to get you out."

"They haunt me from every shadow and every tree. Everyone is dead. The dead are alive again! Soon I'll join them. Soon I'll haunt the earth too!" Daniel rolled around on the ground as he wailed.

"Stop that now," Wes said urgently, and when he reached for his son, Daniel looked up at him with a pitiful desperate hope.

"Are you truly real, father?"

"If I was part of the miasma, I'd be convincing you to stay here, not urging you to go." Daniel slowly nodded, and sanity seemed to return to his haunted eyes. He let Wes help him to his feet.

"Get me out of this hell."

Wes took hold of his son's hand, and guided him toward the bramble patch. Daniel's fingers felt cold, and with the area growing darker, the chill would only worsen. Fortunately, Wes could see a brighter area ahead of them, and knew it was the trail that would guide them to freedom.

"I'm dead and this is hell," Daniel whimpered, "I'm dead and this is hell."

"Stop saying such nonsense," Wes chided, and his shoulders slumped.

"I'm sorry," he cried, "I'm so sorry. It's hard to stop seeing and hearing and knowing. Oh, this horrible place!"

"Papa? Is that you?" Wes froze the moment he broke free from the dense forest canopy, and stood with one foot on the path that led home. A few feet away, the gelding watched him quietly, while Wes' mind was arrested by the effort to understand what he was hearing. It was the miasma...or was it? The usurper claimed the veil was thinnest in these woods. Was Wes hearing Peter calling to him from the other side?

"Father?" Daniel asked and Wes glanced absently at his still-living son.

"Just...just the miasma," he said, sounding a little breathless. He tried to push himself forward, but his legs refused to work. Part of him wished to remain; suspended in a place where he could be allowed to believe he still had a chance to reconnect with his lost boy.

"Papa? Are you there?"

"What are you looking at?" Daniel asked, suddenly standing next to him, and Wes jumped a little. He needed to get away from Peter's voice calling to him or he would soon be joining his youngest son.

"It's nothing," he assured Daniel, and led him over to where the horse waited for them. He got down on one knee and offered a hand to his son. "Step on my leg here and hoist yourself up on his back."

Daniel did as instructed, and with Wes' help, he managed to steady himself by holding the reins. The gelding stomped his hooves and rolled his eyes. He was unaccustomed to the change in the boy's smell, so Wes didn't allow him an ounce of control; guiding him back up the path with a firm hand.

"Papa! Where are you going?"

Everyone is dead. The dead are alive again.

"Did you hear something?" Daniel asked, turning his head in the direction of Peter's voice.

"Pay it no mind," Wes warned, then raised his voice to call into the forest. "If you're truly out there, seek out your mother. She'll tend to you until I can see you again."

"Father, are you talking to my brother? My *dead* brother?"

"Daniel, do you remember how to pray?" Wes asked as he scanned the trees for a decent glimpse of the sky. He lost all sight of the sun, but knew that his time was running out.

"Yes, I know what you and mamma taught me."

"Then pray, Daniel, for God to guide your brother back home," Wes urged as he stared out at the wagon and noted how the last rays of sunlight were illuminating the canopy. "I will get us out of here."

Wes navigated the remaining stretch of forest, all the while holding focus on that patch of sunlight spread across the canopy. When they finally broke free of the forest's grasp, and stepped out into the open field, Wes immediately felt his head clear. All that emotional torment that the miasma used as its weapon drained away from his mind until all that remained was exhaustion. But there was no time to feel weary. Wes gauged what light remained in the day, and picked up his pace to a jog.

"You've said that madness reveres you," Wes called up to Daniel breathlessly, "I suspect we'll be putting that claim to the test."

The gelding easily kept pace with Wes, so he was able to see that his son was sitting up and no longer seemed haunted by his own ghosts. Instead, he looked thoughtfully out at the open fields around them, and responded with a growing apprehension. "Father, I don't think it's wise to tempt the night."

"Explain what you mean," Wes replied as a strange unease caused sweat to dampen his brow.

"I...sense them. Out there. Waiting. Wanting. Dark *oily* things. I regret to say that the night no longer reveres me."

"How can this be?"

"I no longer harbor the Dragon's protection. They see that I am weak, and seek to liberate the spirit inside me."

"Are we not safe at all?" Wes panted as he shifted from a light jog to a brisk run.

"I fear we are not," Daniel replied, his red eyes scanning the expanse of barren land. He seemed strangely calm for someone who was about to get torn apart.

"We're not going to make it back in time," Wes despaired as he watched the sun's glow on the canopy convert into a tiny sliver.

"We have no choice," Daniel insisted and leaned down to offer Wes his hand. "Grab on, and I'll help you up." Both father and son gripped each other's forearms, and Daniel hauled Wes right off the ground with a growl, and a strength beyond what he should be capable of. He drug Wes over the horse's back until he slumped midway like a large sack full of feed. Wes was amazed by this strange new power his son possessed, but when he considered what Gad was capable of at the end of his time, he wasn't surprised. Holding his hat to avoid losing it, Wes lifted his head just as Daniel whipped the geldings reins and pushed him to go farther. The horse was able to run, but not as quickly as he did before.

"Faster, son. Make him go faster," Wes said, and Daniel leaned over him to cut down on any wind resistance. He then reached back and gave the geldings rump a firm smack. Wes could feel the animal push a little farther; giving everything he had left to give, and made that final charge toward their wagon. The cold air whipping into him caused Wes' eyes to blur. He blinked, trying to keep the wagon in his sight, and caught the last bit of sunlight on the canopy wink out like a snuffed candle. It was still light enough to see, but this would not deter the monsters from striking out at them.

"We will have to light lanterns," Daniel shouted over the sound of the horses' thundering hooves. "The moment we get there, we need light."

"Can you sense them?" Wes asked, "Are they coming?"

"They're coming," Daniel replied gravely. Their horse barreled toward the wagon, the distance dissolving between them, and as soon as they arrived, Daniel jerked the reins to cease their plight. The gelding screamed his protest, but didn't resort to rearing, and the moment his powerful legs countered their momentum and brought them to a halt, Wes pushed off of his back and slid onto the ground. He landed squarely, and reached for his son to help him down.

"Don't worry about me," Daniel growled, "get the lanterns started. Hurry."

"Get into the wagon when you can," Wes commanded as he rushed over to feel around in the gloom for the two fireboxes he knew were there. "Help me find the lighter."

Daniel climbed off the horse and landed hard on the ground, but recovered quickly. Just as Wes retrieved the canister of oil to fill the fireboxes' bellies, his son appeared next to him and lumbered over the edge of the wagon; rolling onto the floor with a loud thud. The threat of being torn apart by the madness of the night instilled urgency in them both, for even Wes could now sense the hunger of the beasts rapidly approaching. His hands shook as he drew the wick of the first firebox into view. He knew it wouldn't be long before his blood warmed the earth around his feet.

"They're close," Daniel said grimly as he appeared in front of Wes holding a lighter out in offering. Wes took it into his unsteady hand.

"Thank you," he said, and worked the wheel mechanism but the lighter barely produced a spark. In the stillness of deep twilight, Wes could hear the sound of dead grass being crushed underfoot, and the many urgent footfalls of large things drawing closer. He tried again to get the lighter to work, but his hands still shook and his clumsy attempt only produced a spark. He looked up into Daniel's glowing red eyes.

His son snatched the lighter out of his hands, and gave the wheel a practiced flick so that a small flame sprung to life instantly. Wes cranked the knob of the firebox so that the tongue of the wick grew longer just as he touched the lighter to it. The entire wick was instantly cloaked in flame; a mini inferno crafted in near darkness, it washed the entire area in light. Daniel hissed as he stumbled over himself trying to get to the other end of the wagon, and the reaction behind Wes was similar. Hisses and howls; keening and curses came from at least half a dozen voices. He made quick work of getting the second firebox filled and lit before one of the beasts grew clever enough to risk cutting him down at the knee from underneath the wagon.

"How many are out there do you think?" Wes asked as he raised this second firebox over his head. All around him, the world was still.

"Eight. We are fortunate to be out in the open. With no place to hide during the day, they had to travel a short distance to get here. If they had been any closer..."

"Try not to dwell on it. I must tend to the horses then I'll join you. Look for something for us to eat while I'm gone." Pulling the wick back a little, Wes hooked the first firebox onto a metal peg at the rear of the wagon, and carried the second one with him as he approached the gelding and brought him back over to his mud-colored companion. The gelding was covered in frothy sweat and his chest still heaved from the run. It was far too late to address all this in the moment, and already Wes was forming a list of things to do in the morning.

"I won't forget my promise regarding the oats" Wes said to the gelding as he clipped a tether to his bridle and used it to secure him to the stake where his companion was already tied. Satisfied they were both secured, Wes returned to the back of the wagon. He extinguished his firebox, and climbed in to rejoin his son.

"Are there any more of those small bread loaves?" Wes asked, but realized that Daniel was quietly wiping tears from his face. "What's wrong?"

"I'm just overwhelmed. How can you do this all the time?" Daniel asked with a disbelieving shake of his head. "Every moment we spend out here in this awful wilderness involves us facing some sort of impossible challenge, many of which could easily result in one or both of us dying! I feel like I'm constantly dreading the things that are about to come, and meanwhile you're idly talking about food and asking if there's any more bread."

"It's true, we've had our share of challenges, but it isn't always as hard as this. Either way, it's easier knowing that I have God looking out for me." Daniel sighed in annoyance and Wes added, "Son, I know you're sick of hearing all this, but you must understand that my faith is at the heart of everything I do. I approach every challenge with my faith as my guide, and if I don't speak about such things, well...I reckon I'd be pretending just so I don't offend you."

"I never thought about it that way," Daniel admitted, "I don't know why, but I find myself growing more and more annoyed every time you bring up your God."

"That's the demon inside you whispering in your ear. They lose all power in the Lord's unyielding light, so of course the wicked want to lure people away."

"Well the way I see things, it wasn't God or even the Dragon that pulled me out of those woods today. The only person I owe my gratitude to is you, father." Daniel's eyes lowered as he watched his hands fidget nervously. "This day has been abysmal, and somehow you were able to remain so strong. You have always had my affection, father, but today you have earned my respect as well."

"Does that mean you won't get angry with me anymore?" Wes asked with a small smile. His son's heartfelt confession was unforeseen, and Wes wished he had something far more meaningful to say in return.

"It's the price everyone pays, for loving me," Daniel said with a laugh, then winced.

"What's wrong?"

“I fear I must ask yet again for you to help me,” Daniel replied with a mix of emotions that highlighted his disgust with his growing limitations.

“I’ll gladly help you. Tell me what you need.”

“I need you to help me get these boots off my feet. They hurt so much, but I’m too tired to do it myself. I’m tired all the time lately.” Wes studied Daniel’s weary face for a moment, then smiled.

“Of course.” He bent over the boots, and noticed that they were bulging out around the toes. He unlaced each of them, but when he tried to pull the first one free, it didn’t budge. He pulled and wrestled with it for a while, but only when Daniel grabbed onto the edge of the wagon and Wes put all his weight into yanking on the boot was he able to wiggle it free. He cried out the moment the boot slipped off his foot, but insisted Wes not stop and offered his other foot to his father. The second one was harder to remove than the first, causing Daniel to groan and silently cry from the effort, but eventually it came free as well, and both father and son were left panting and exhausted.

Wes examined Daniel’s black scaled feet, looking for any sign of injury. They were twisted out of shape, longer in the middle, and somehow his five human toes transformed into three elongated toes that had thick black nails forming on them.

“Do they hurt?” Wes asked, eyeing the feet with a mix of horror and fascination.

“Not anymore,” Daniel said with a sigh. “Thank you.” He wiggled his three long toes and Wes couldn’t suppress his shiver. He lifted his gaze and for the first time since his son started his transformation, Wes took in the full scope of what Daniel had become. His once beautiful face was deformed into the shape of a lizard. His forehead elongated while his nose flattened, and along his bald head, ridges formed rows of small horns like a crown. His body also changed shape with his torso growing longer, but his arms and legs seeming to be shorter. The clothing he wore was stretched in some places and sagging in others. There were many spots where the seams split open, exposing black scales underneath. His brown sweater which he secretly cherished for so long appeared to be unraveling in a dozen different places.

It was hard to believe that this creature was once a boy. It wasn’t hard to know that this creature was still his son. But it was so much easier to see past the reality of the situation when Wes was busy with work that needed done. Being that he was trapped in this place, surrounded by the night, he had no choice but to acknowledge what his son has been trying to tell him for the past few days. The thing he was unwilling to hear.

The understanding of it fell upon him like an oppressive and suffocating vapor: Daniel was dying. There will be no reuniting with Benji the way Wes had hoped. No cleansing light. No restoration to the boy he once was. Daniel was dying, and in knowing this, Wes immediately started to bargain with God.

He was willing to care for Daniel as long as his son was able to pay respects to his mother's grave. He was willing to stay by his son and watch him breathe his final breath, as long as he wasn't suffering when he died. He was willing to bury his son, as long as he could rest alongside the rest of his family. He was willing to endure all of it, if God helped guide Daniel back to the Word and the faith.

"Daniel...I'm ready to listen now," Wes said, but when he lifted his eyes, he saw that his son was slumped over a mound of blankets and bedrolls, asleep. Wes smiled sadly at his exhausted boy, and moved to sit against the wagon next to him. Gently, he guided Daniel towards him, and laid his head on his shoulder.

"Everything's going to be alright," Wes whispered to no one in particular. He closed his eyes, his exhaustion deep, and fell asleep thinking of little Peter calling out to him from the shadows beneath the trees. When he woke again, it was the start of birdsong, and for the first time in what felt like forever, Wes didn't wake to the feeling of unexplainable panic. The transition back into reality was as gentle as the distant bird's singing.

The firebox barely gave off a flicker, having spent all its oil in the night, but Wes knew it was too late for the creatures of darkness to seek them out anyway. Listening to his son's soft breathing, Wes let out a contented sigh, and turned his attention to the east in anticipation of the coming sun. He sat that way for some time, just enjoying the stillness of the moment and the weight of his son leaning against him, but movement caught his eye in the grass beyond their dozing horses and what Wes saw amazed him.

"Daniel," he said softly as he shook his son to wake him. "Daniel, look over there."

His son sat up, groggy from his sleep, and rubbed his one eye with the palm of his hand. "What is it? Is something wrong?"

"No, not at all. Look, son, in the grass over there," Wes said, and pointed toward the place where he saw movement. After a moment, Daniel caught sight of it as well and his dark eyes looked puzzled.

"Are they...animals?"

"Foxes," Wes replied, "haven't seen the like since I stumbled upon a lame one in the woods well over ten years ago."

"What are they doing?"

"Playing, I reckon. Looks like a parent and cub running around chasing each other's tails."

"Ah," Daniel sighed. He leaned back against his father and the two of them watched as the foxes played. "Is the bigger one a father fox or a mamma fox?"

"I can't say one way or the other from here," Wes admitted, "but I have no doubt that the bigger one is a parent to the smaller. Even though they are playing, lessons are being learned about what makes a fox a fox. The bigger one is teaching the smaller one how to survive."

"Then I'd like to think it's a father fox," Daniel replied. They sat together for some time quietly watching the foxes play. The small smile that curved the corners of Daniel's lips remained in place long after he drifted back to sleep.

Chapter Thirty-Nine

The greater my wisdom, the greater my grief.
To increase knowledge only increases sorrow.
-Ecclesiastes 1:18 (NLT)

Wes sat upon a barren yard which overlooked his fallow field. Feeling content in the recognition, he laid back upon the slope, and felt himself sinking deep into the warm earth until it surrounded him; swallowed him; consumed all that he was. It discarded him out into the outer darkness, where nothing could reach him except for brief glimpses of memories.

"Father?"

Wes jolted awake and took in his surroundings. Whatever his dream was, it caused him to sleep far too deeply; a dangerous thing considering he was the one guiding their horses. While the hour was growing late, he was fortunate to see it was still day and the path still laid before them.

"Forgive me," he mumbled, as he searched for the horse's reins, "I somehow managed to fall asleep."

"This journey has us both exhausted," Daniel noted from the shadows of the wagon bed, "I hope you had dreams and not nightmares."

"I can't seem to remember them anyway," Wes replied, distracted by Daniel's voice. It seemed off somehow. A strangeness in the ear. "How are you feeling?"

"Better now that we're away from that forest. If I never return there, it would be too soon. If I never see another tree, I wouldn't complain. But I still feel a deep pain in my bones," Daniel admitted, "and my stomach..."

"What about your stomach?"

"It feels...unsettled. Unpleasant. Maybe I just need to eat something."

"The sun sits low and shouldn't cause you any harm. Why don't you gather some food from our rations and come sit with me." Daniel didn't reply, but Wes could hear him rummage around the wagon in search of food. After a few minutes, his face appeared between the canopy flaps, but one look at the sky caused him to retreat back into the bed again.

"Does the light hurt you?" Wes asked as he tried to catch sight of his son in the shadows.

"Just my eyes. I need to give them more time to adjust to it. They are meant for the darkness now." Eventually, Daniel did reappear, and climbed over the back of the driver's seat with more agility than he managed the day before. Wes noted that Daniel was moving about as an animal would: using his arms as though they were legs. After sitting, he revealed a small parcel that contained strips of jerky, and some hard cheese.

"A feast for a king," Wes said, smiling at his son, and picked up a piece of jerky. Beside him, Daniel's attention was fully focused on utilizing his uncooperative hands to lift food into his mouth. After a few failed attempts, he gave up the effort and instead leaned over to pluck up the meat with his teeth. His face was unreadable as he methodically chewed; staring out at the distant trees to the east.

Wes searched his mind; yearning to put words into the space they occupied. How could he explain to Daniel that, while he understood death was inevitable, it did not mean Wes was any less terrified of the moment his son would be taken from him? A goodbye with no hope of future greeting. Wes felt so desperate to *do* something; *be* something; *say* something that meant something *more*. But there was a chasm of silence between them Wes could never seem to cross, ever since Daniel was a little boy. His tongue remained still; his lips unmoving.

"What are you thinking about?" Daniel asked, and when their eyes met, Wes quickly looked away.

"I was thinking about you." Daniel grunted and returned his attention to the east.

"A waste of valuable time." Suddenly, Daniel bent over with a groan and wrapped arms around his stomach.

"What's wrong?" Wes asked; anxiety weighing down each word. Daniel reached into a tattered sleeve and pulled free his pipe.

"The food didn't help. If anything I feel worse," Daniel growled and Wes suddenly realized why his voice sounded so strange. It wasn't actually Daniel's voice that changed, but instead that second voice inside of him. The one of the usurper. The beast not only lingered upon everything Daniel said, he was no longer an echo. Instead, it was a mere breath behind Daniel's own. It anticipated every word in lockstep to his son. This strange creature was dormant for days, but when Daniel complained of pain in his stomach, this so-called *dragon* was evident in all of his words. Wes had to speculate that the two were related.

"Maybe the medicine will give you relief. Do you need my help?" Wes was not pleased that he might need to assist his son in drugging himself, but anything was better than watching Daniel in pain.

"Yes. Please. And can you help me with this as well?" Daniel handed a vial of oil over to Wes. It was very small, but still relatively full. Wes pulled the cork from its mouth and poured a few drops into the pipe's bowl. He managed to get the lighter to cooperate as well, and touched its flame to the bowl's opening. Daniel drew in the sweet-smelling smoke a few times, and eventually pushed it away as he sagged back against the wagon with a sigh.

"Thank you," Daniel said, looking down at his open palms which rested on either side of him, "I have such useless hands."

"Wouldn't it be easier for you to drink the oil instead of burning it?" Wes asked. "That's what I was directed to do during my recovery."

"The morphine you were given was far less potent than the oil in that vial. If I take too much of that at one time, I'll go to sleep and never wake up again." Wes recalled a time when Ashter handed him a similar bottle right before he had to face Gad. It was a contingency plan, in case Wes failed to take down the monster; a way to ease his suffering by ending his life. He quietly returned the vial and lighter back into his son's care who tucked them up his sleeve.

"I feel much better now thanks to you, father," Daniel said, "thank you for helping me."

"Its the least I can do," Wes said awkwardly, and gave the reins a soft snap of encouragement. The last thing he felt was helpful.

"Well with that settled, can you tell me what we're in store for when we get over there?" Daniel asked, gesturing toward the forest in front of them.

"I don't understand."

"Oh, I'm just anticipating the next challenge we're going to be forced to face. What will it be this time? Venomous snakes dropping on us out of the trees? Impossible puzzles to unlock mysterious entrances? Whatever it is, I'm willing to face it as long as I don't have to endure another one of those horrible miasmas."

"The only challenge we face in the forest up ahead, is having to abandon the wagon at the narrow path that will lead us home."

"Are we that close?" Daniel asked with nervous excitement. "Will we reach the farm before the next sunrise?"

"Probably...but we have to travel through the night which is unpredictable. We're also leaving the wagon which means you run the risk of being exposed to the sun if I miscalculated the distance."

"I don't want to delay this further," Daniel insisted, "if we are faced with a situation like that, I'm sure you'll figure something out."

"The path we're taking ventures toward the south. When we reach its opening, we can rest until nightfall. Lord willing, we'll travel the rest of the way without any difficulty. And if so, we should arrive home in plenty of time."

"Home," Daniel repeated with little enthusiasm.

"You should take the gelding," Wes added as he mapped out the distance in his mind. "He's familiar with your smell now, and hopefully he will not put up a fight. It will save time."

"Whatever you think is best," Daniel replied, flatly. Wes glanced over at his son, and the look he saw in the lad's eyes was far too similar to the way Ruth looked when she gave up on trying in life. Wes buried the thought in his mind. Daniel was just a little emotional about going back to his old home. Wes raised his hand, and pointed to the stretch of forest before them.

"There, lad. Up yonder where the trees bend toward each other. Do you see the gap beneath them? Yes, that's it son. Well done spotting it. That is where we need to go. That is the path that will lead us home."

"Easy, easy," Wes soothed, stroking the horse's nose as Daniel climbed with weary slowness onto his saddle. Wes had already lit a firebox, anticipating that night would overtake them quickly beneath the canopy of massive ancient trees, and by the time Daniel found a way to sit in the saddle comfortably, it was well past when they could still rely on the sunlight's protection. In the rising gloom, Wes eyed the southern trail with nervous apprehension.

"Do you see something?" Daniel asked, and Wes steered his focus back to his son. It seemed that the memories haunting this place manifested their own sort of miasma.

"Nothing to worry over," he replied and hefted up a long stick that resembled the handle of a broom. He carried it with him as he approached the mud-colored mare.

"What are you doing with that?" Daniel asked. He watched as Wes secured the firebox to one end of his stick with the remnants of their shredded rope.

"I plan to give the horses a little light. So they can avoid potential snares. Neither of them are good to us with a broken ankle." Wes gave the mare a smile as he stroked her coarse fur, "and let's not forget the monsters will be less likely to attack us inside this light."

"You always think of everything," Daniel said as he frowned down at his hands holding the horse's reins.

"Only because I've learned the consequences of not doing so." Wes hoisted himself on the mare's saddle, "are you ready?"

When Daniel nodded, Wes urged his mare with a soft kick to her ribs and she sprang into action. Daniel was only a breath behind, and kept Wes' pace easily enough. Good lad. Wes extended his arm, and held the firebox steady on its branch a few feet above the ground; illuminating a path for the horses.

The surrounding night concealed the passage of time; its only evidence shown through their progression. In this dark stillness, both father and son fell into their own silent reveries. Wes succumbed to an enchantment of his own making. It was a place so bittersweet; where he could pretend that the two of them were simply returning back to a house full of light and homecoming, instead of a tomb. It was an imaginary place where Wes could actually talk freely with his son and not second guess everything he wanted to convey. Where death had yet to stroke their lives with its cold, unforgiving hand.

"How much farther?" Wes glanced over at his son, and focused on the dark reality around them. It seemed like the night had also sapped Daniel of his reprieve for he appeared to be slumped over and hugging his stomach.

"It's hard to say with such limited light," Wes replied, "but I reckon in another hour or maybe two, we will be home."

"Home," Daniel said, again repeating the word, but rode on in silence. It didn't take long for Wes to get drawn back into his wandering thoughts. Ignoring the progression of time, he was caught off guard when a sudden shift of light captured his attention. Wes immediately turned his eyes to the sky. Surely it was still too soon to harbor a new day.

The trees spread their arms wide, obstructing most of the space above him, so Wes was unable to see the eastern horizon. He knew it was too early; the lack of birdsong confirming it so, but there still seemed to be a wrongness about the place that unsettled Wes. His eyes reflexively drifted toward those deeper shadows that huddled beneath the trees.

"We're close now, son," Wes said apprehensively, for he recognized the trees around them. The shapes of their branches were like unchanging fossils that guided him back home. "Very close."

Daniel didn't respond, and Wes glanced over to see that he was draped over the gelding's neck; face pressed against his mane. His eyes were closed and he looked calm. Somehow, he managed to fall asleep. Wes considered waking him, but then caught sight of open grassland through the trees. There it was. After all this time, and all he endured, Wes was home.

He decided to allow Daniel his reprieve, and planned to lead the horses up the sloping hill of his yard on foot. Extinguishing the firebox, he slid down from his horse, and grabbed the reins of both animals. He guided them along the trail as it opened up and led out of the forest, and just as he cleared the last few trees, the start of birdsong reached his ear. He still thought it was too soon, but nature knew its own business far better than he ever could. If the birdsong was a testament to timeline, Wes should have enough of it to tend to the horses, and to see Daniel safely indoors. He guided them forward as the birds rejoiced around him, and when the full expanse of his farm came into view, Wes stopped and stared.

"It means nothing," he muttered, yet continued to study his old home. He had no doubt of how long it's been since he left the place, yet the dark foreboding structure looked as though it's been fallow for years. The sky overhead was turning a soft shade of gray, yet the windows remained inky black like open mouths devouring the light; black eyes with jagged glass teeth. With the crooked staircase leading up to the porch, the whole structure resembled an old decrepit skull, and the thing appeared to be grinning at him. "It means nothing at all."

Wes forced his eyes away from the dismal farmhouse, and instead focused on what needed tending to. He approached his barn, and hitched the gelding outside before leading the mare within. The tools housed in the barn looked picked through, with many missing, but he wasn't surprised. There was little charity in this world and his neighbors needed to survive as well. The whole place smelled stale; unoccupied; devoid of life, but Wes saw that there was still a little alfalfa hay, and that was all he needed. He led the mare into one of the open stables, and worked free the leather strap of her saddle before a rustling sound pulled at his attention.

"Hello?" Wes called out, and quietly wondered if there was a monster hiding somewhere in the deeper shadows of the barn. Oddly though, his eyes weren't drawn to those shadowy spaces, and he instead found himself staring at the open barn door. For some reason, he half expected to see the silhouette of a young boy standing there.

"Focus!" Wes growled, shaking his head to free the cobwebs in his mind. He slid the saddle off of his mare, and she sighed in relief. He fell into the old routines of horse care, and mused on how animals were much easier to handle than children. He gave the mare a quick brush, and placed a wedge of alfalfa into her trough. She ate gracefully but her silent desperation made it evident to him how hungry she was. He looked around, wondering if any of his oats were left behind, when he heard the heavy thud of Daniel falling off his horse.

"Foolish old man," Wes chided to himself, and rushed out of the barn to see to his son. He gave the sky a quick glance, saw that he had spent far too much time tending to his horse, and for the first time in his life, hated the sun for rising. The Gelding would have to wait; he needed to get Daniel indoors immediately.

"Daniel, come on. Get up, son. That's it lad. We need to get you inside. Come now. Inside." Daniel opened hazy eyes, and slowly pushed his ungainly form up onto his back feet. He immediately staggered, lost his balance, and dropped down onto all fours. He proceeded forward in this way; walking as an animal would, and Wes anxiously lingered at his side.

"I overdid the morphine," Daniel mumbled with slurred words. Wes couldn't recall when Daniel even smoked his pipe last, and had to conclude that Daniel was keeping it secret because he knew he was doing too much. He glanced nervously to the East.

"The sun might crest the trees at any moment. We won't make it inside with the pace you're keeping. Here, let me carry you like I did before." Wes tried to lift Daniel into his arms but the weight of his son was staggering. The moment he lifted him, he stumbled, and both of them fell in a heap on the ground. Impossible as it seemed, Daniel's weight doubled overnight. It was no wonder he moved so slowly.

"I'm sorry, let me try again," Wes insisted, but Daniel snarled at him like a dog. His eyes looked wild; hostile from desperation, and Wes shied away from him immediately. The way his mood shifted was nothing new, but it was the glint in his eyes that Wes found so unsettling, for he knew the look of madness when he saw it.

Nestled in their silent moments, Wes' mind circled around the same simple hopes of Daniel somehow finding peace. He knew it was foolish to hope for, but he still thought about it many times every day. But when Wes saw hints of madness in his son, it was brutally evident that all hope was lost. The idea that Daniel might die in a state where he no longer knew who he was or who Wes was, it was too dreadful to even consider. Wes closed his eyes, and took a moment to again bargain with God.

Please, Lord, protect him from this madness. Let there be limits to his suffering.

"Come on, Daniel," Wes said, refocusing on the task at hand, "Come now. Inside. We have to get you away from the sun." Daniel didn't growl or lash out at him when Wes reached for him, and so he helped his son up onto his feet. Daniel allowed Wes to support him, and together they climbed the porch steps, then approached the front door.

Wes placed his hand on the door latch, but for a brief moment was seized with the thought that he might find Ruth laying on her bed; decomposing, yet somehow still alive. She would look up at him with watery yellow eyes sunken deep into crepe-paper skin. Wes pushed the thought away, unwilling to let it seize him, and forced his hand. The latch lifted stiffly, and the door swung open on raw noisy hinges. The gloom beyond seemed impenetrable.

"It's smaller than I remembered," Daniel murmured; his red glowing eyes revealing things that Wes could not see. But even without the advantage of light, he could not agree with the boy's sentiment. The farm *used* to feel small to him in the past, but seeing it in this fossilized state, it looked like a hulking monster. It overshadowed him, glaring its inky-black eyes, and haunted his mind with decaying memories. The last thing it felt like was home.

As they entered, the darkness within was pregnant with foreboding, and Wes wondered if the house would collapse upon them; devouring them; a marker of rubble for their eternal tomb. But his eyes started to adjust, and soon he could make out the barren interior. The place appeared stripped clean of anything worth taking, but the bed was still there, and thank the Lord; Ruth was not in it.

"Over here, son," Wes said as he guided his son to the bed, which housed a cobweb of old dusty memories. Some of his best moments involved that bed but also some of the worst. Wes wanted to believe these moments with his son would not add to the latter. He watched while Daniel climbed into the nest of all those memories, and brushed the cobwebs to the side.

He groaned in relief to be off his feet, and slumped onto his side so exhausted that sleep nipped at his heels. He closed his eyes, and drifted away from the outside world in minutes. Wes found the old chair he used to sit in when Ruth was having a bad night, and placed it alongside the bed where it sat so many times in the past. He rested there for a while, watching Daniel sleep, and appreciated how peaceful he looked.

"I hope you have dreams and not nightmares," Wes said softly, then stood before despair overwhelmed him. He returned to the open door, and looked out upon the world beyond. At least he had work to do.

Wes covered Daniel with one of Ruth's hand-woven blankets, then stepped out onto the porch. He closed the winter shutters to cut down on light from the outside, and returned his attention to the horses.

As Wes approached the gelding, the sun broke over the horizon, and bathed him in the warmth of a new morning. Pausing to appreciate the moment, all he could feel was relief to be away from his son, and hated himself for it. Craving these periods of normalcy felt like betrayal. He should yearn to be present in every second that his son still breathed on this earth, but in truth, it was so *exhausting*. Part of him just wished it would be over, but most of him dreaded the moment that it was.

Wes turned his face away from the sun's caress, and formed a list of chores to tend to in his mind. There was always work to be done, whether Daniel was dying or not. He started with the horses: tending to the gelding the way he did with the mare, and made sure they had ample food and water with a small scoop of oats scraped together for them both. From there, he drifted into other jobs that needed done while his mind wandered through imaginary lands. Places where he and Daniel were able to rebuild this farm together. Wes didn't mind doing most of the work, at least until his son was well, and maybe he could introduce Daniel to the neighbor's daughter. She was a few years older than him, but she was sweet, and she would give Daniel something to smile about again. Wes spent most of the day working while he daydreamed about a life he could never have, but the sun was not compassionate and soon started its descent in the west.

Reality was knowing he would have to rejoin Daniel soon, and Wes needed a little more time to be vulnerable. He walked to the edge of his yard where a gentle slope overlooked his barren field, and it was there that Wes located a row of graves. Two of them were fairly new, and the one closest to where he stood was the only one he didn't dig himself. Wes noticed they placed a crude wooden marker at the head of her grave with the name 'Ruth' carved into it. It was a nice touch he never considered doing for other ones that rested there. He knew their names without a marker to remind him.

"I did what I promised, Ruth. I brought him home to you. I remember how you said that he was lost to us forever. I hope you didn't mean that. I hope I can still reach him here in this place." Wes squinted at the low hanging sun, which warmed the sky in deep orange. The moment was still and beautiful. The world at peace, allowed all living things to rest for a spell. "He's dying, Ruth. I reckon you knew that was going to happen. I reckon he knew it too when he left that horrible city." Wes plucked up a maple leaf that lay browning on Ruth's grave and slowly pulled it apart in his hands.

"But he's in *so much* pain. He tries to hide it, but I *see* it and I feel *so* useless to help him. He's such a strong boy, Ruth. Lord, you should have seen him when he stood above all those people in the capital. Every time he entered a room it was like the sun just spread over the sky. But even then, he was in pain; just a different kind. I wish...it would have been nice to have more time with him. To get to know him better." Wes' tossed the ribs of the leaf onto the ground, and caught sight of something jutting up from the earth. He reached for it, and plucked up a small black feather; a crow's feather. Wes twirled it between his fingers, examining the black glossy vanes, then rested it atop of Ruth's marker.

"It's going to be your turn soon. Look after our boy, Ruth. Introduce him to his kin. Bring him home. Help him to not hurt anymore." Slowly, Wes trudged up the hill toward the farmhouse; his feet feeling heavier with each step. The sun was all but gone from the sky as time warped around his being. When Wes at last pushed open the front door, the inside was obscured, but fraught with misery.

"Daniel?" Wes called out as he stepped into the shadows. He fumbled, hands outstretched, and located the firebox he placed on the kitchen table earlier. He already filled its belly, and made quick work of getting it lit, but kept the flame low for his son's sake. With that done, Wes focused on the bed; half dreading what he might find.

Daniel was curled up, but looked as though he had not moved all day. He was so still, Wes immediately believed he was dead. He *knew* it would be a mercy for his boy, but with the moment upon him, death dug thick claws of dread into Wes' throat, and strangled his breath out of his voice.

He wasn't ready for this!

He needed more time!

"Daniel!" Wes shouted; grief causing his voice to sound strange, and when Wes caught sight of Daniel's leg moving, he almost collapsed in relief. He still had time. He still had time.

Daniel groaned, despairing over the waking world, and Wes felt woefully guilty for not wanting to let his son go. Was this the same as the hold he once had on Ruth? Was Wes content to allow his family to suffer if it meant he could hide a little longer from his own fear? Eventually, time would no longer pause for him. Eventually, Wes had to say goodbye. He reached for Daniel's pipe and vial. "It's alright, son. Let me help you take away the pain."

Daniel shifted his head, and one glowing eye peered out to examine the contents of Wes' hands, and he pushed through the arduous task of sitting up in bed. Nothing was left of the thirteen-year-old boy that he once was, and Wes was sure most of his appearance was the effect of the usurper inside him, but at least his mind was still his own. At least he reacted to his own name.

He readied the pipe, and Daniel clutched it in his teeth as Wes worked the lighter for its flame. It was much easier to use with all the practice he was getting. After a few draws of smoke, Daniel's shoulders relaxed, and he eventually pushed the pipe away. Wes sat perched on his chair, watching his son ease back onto the bed, and waited. There was plenty of time for sadness later. Plenty of time.

"Father?" Daniel said slowly as he waded through his fatigue and sedation, "are you alright?"

"Yes, son," Wes cleared the hoarseness from his throat. "I'm alright."

"You look sad."

"This place is full of memories."

"Is this where she died?" Daniel asked; his voice not large enough to fill the tiny room.

"I reckon so," Wes replied, and they both were silent for a moment as each of them remembered Ruth as either a mother or a wife.

"I would like to see her grave," Daniel said at last, his voice all his own. Wes knew the creature before him was still and would always be his son, but also a boy who carried the fate of the world asleep inside his stomach.

"Soon," Wes said, "for night has just fallen. It's best we wait until that time right before the new dawn. It's less dangerous that way. We will visit your mother's grave then, and do what needs to be done."

"That's when we'll say goodbye?" Daniel asked, and Wes smiled at him sadly.

"That's when we'll say goodbye."

They both could sense time slipping through their fingers, and while Daniel didn't have the strength to stay awake, Wes knew if he also slept, his devotion would be a fraud. He needed to stay present in case Daniel required something of him. He needed to stay present in case Daniel died. Until then, every moment they shared together, created a tapestry of lasts. The last smile, the last bread broken between them, the last time Wes would be able to hold his son's hand. Each moment was both heartbreaking and precious; dreaded and revered. They all carried a weight of significance, and Wes was determined to never let any of them fade in his mind. Each moment was its own small goodbye.

Wes watched him fall asleep, and saw the exact moment when dreams took his boy and covered him in soft peace. This might be the last time he could watch his son the way he used to when they all shared a bed together so many years ago. Wes yearned for more. He hungered for some kind of meaningful connection between them. He thought this bond was imperative, but didn't know how to cultivate it, and his desperation for a solution left him exhausted.

Without conscious awareness, Wes' eyes drifted shut, failing his vigil, and bitter resentment followed him into his dreams. There, he found himself laying in that same bed dying. In his dream the chair was empty; no one was there to watch over him, or offer him comforting words, or hold his hand. He cried out in his final moments, but no one was there to hear him. His own small goodbye lingering in those vacant places where fears were born.

When Wes opened his eyes, he saw that the bed was empty. He sat up, alarmed, but immediately located Daniel, who was standing by the farm's open door, and peering out into the world beyond.

"Daniel?" Wes beckoned, and his son turned to look at him. His glowing eyes had an eerie vacancy as though he were seeing a thousand things all at once, or absolutely nothing at all.

"Something calls me," he said dully; almost trance-like. His black, forked tongue darted over jagged teeth.

"I don't understand," Wes said, although he suspected he knew exactly what Daniel was saying. Madness had come for a visit.

"I hear something. A voice in my mind. Telling me to go. Telling me to find the shadows. Telling me to rip open the flesh and feast with the fallen."

"Enough of that," Wes got to his feet and reached for Daniel. "It's madness you hear, son. Don't listen to it."

"Don't touch me!" Daniel sneered, and Wes could clearly hear the usurper: his words eclipsing that of his host. The boy snarled like a monster; his eyes devoid of all recognition.

"Daniel, please." Wes implored; desperate to regain an ounce of what existed between them, and through God's mercy his words seemed to somehow reach his son. Daniel brought a hand to his head and staggered back from the doorway.

"I'm sorry, I..." his voice was familiar once again, and he looked horrified as he stared at the floor between them. Wes reached for him, and gently lifted Daniel's face to meet his eye.

"You're alright," he said, though his tongue burned from the lie. "It's going to be alright."

"I think enough time has passed," Daniel said as he turned his attention back to the world outside, "please take me to my mother."

With a firebox in hand, Wes followed Daniel out into the night, and helped him down the porch steps. Daniel refused to walk on four legs, even though it would be easier for him to do so, and so he limped along slowly as Wes guided him down the slope of the yard to where that familiar spot overlooked the field. Daniel winced with each step he took, but remained silent. He seemed tired, resigned, and overcome.

"She is just over here, son. They were all buried together with a nice view of the field." The place seemed to cause Wes a strange anxiety brought about from a memory he didn't quite recognize, but he pushed the thought away. This was his home, and in this place memories compounded memories until some got pushed to the bottom. Daniel focused on his feet as he walked. They were swollen, with the leathery skin split open in some places. Black bile oozed with each step he took. Wes ignored what he didn't want to see.

"Just over here, son. Just over here." He wrapped his arm around Daniel, and led him over to Ruth's grave. Daniel looked down upon the freshly turned earth, then sank to the ground with Wes alongside him. "Here she is, Daniel, here's your mother."

Wes placed the firebox nearby to ward off anything that might be observing them, and watched as Daniel reached out a black-scaled hand, and placed it on the mound of dirt. He closed his eyes and leaned into Wes, turning his head so that his muzzle pressed against his father's shoulder. Daniel no longer carried the familiar scent that was once uniquely his, and as Wes held his son, he contemplated this new small goodbye.

"Hello again, Ruth," Wes said, guiding Daniel along, "I brought our boy to you, dear wife. He's come to say goodbye."

"Uh...hello, mom," Daniel said, trying to sound casual, but obviously uncomfortable. He cleared his throat and went on. As he spoke, Wes closed his eyes, and willed his mind to memorize the sound of his son's voice. "I know you've been worrying about me. I...I shouldn't have left like I did. I'm sorry about that, mom. I know I messed up. I messed up a lot. And it's been really tough. It's been so tough without you. I...I wish..." Daniel's voice broke, and the tears he fought to hold back, spilled over. Wes held him as he wept, and in this moment, he could simply be a boy grieving for his mother. "Please, mom, please forgive me for leaving you. Please forgive me for letting you die."

"No, lad, don't blame yourself for that. There were so many things your mother endured after you left. She lacked the strength to remain with the living. But she wanted you to come home. It means a lot to her, knowing you're here."

"I'd like to sit with her for a little longer," Daniel said as he rubbed away his tears with the back of his hands. Wes remained with him, feeling the weight of his family together in this strange way, and eventually Daniel fell asleep in his arms. He held onto his son, and thought about the person that dwelt under each mound of earth before him. The firebox started to burn low, and a quick glance at the sky told Wes it was time for this moment to end as well.

"Come on, Daniel. Let's get you back inside to rest." Daniel groaned softly as he came out of his sleep, and sat up without much effort. Wes got to his feet, guiding his son up as well, and Daniel took a final look at his mother's grave. He turned from her without another word, and they toiled back up the slope toward the farmhouse together. Wes never left Daniel's side.

"It's just a short walk," he said with an earnest smile, "it's not far at all."

"I'm glad she's not here to see me like this," Daniel said as they went, "I don't want her to know what I've become."

"You're still her son. She loved you long after you left, and will continue to love you even though she died. Besides, your appearance on earth matters little to the spirit you take with you to the other side of the veil."

"There is nothing for me after I die. Not my spirit, not the veil, and not my mother. I'll never see her again."

"We're at the porch steps. Here, Daniel, lift your foot onto that first one there."

"But if there is something after I die, and I do have a spirit that isn't black with sin and monstrous to behold, I'd like to think I'll see her waiting for me. Something to hope for. I want to see her again. I'd like to meet Peter as well. I always wanted a brother."

"We'll talk about all that later. Here, through the door. That's good. Lay down, and I'll close out the sun."

"Wait," Daniel said, placing a hand on Wes' arm, "Let me stand here for a moment. I...I want to see the night become day." Wes reluctantly released the door latch and stepped out of the way so that Daniel could see the world outside.

"Won't it hurt?" He asked, unable to cloak his worry.

"Probably."

"Daniel..."

"Just for a moment, father. It's been so many years since I was able to stand outside during the day." From within the gloom of the farmhouse, they watched as the sky slowly turned a hazy blue-gray. Soon, the sun reached out from beyond the horizon to bathe the earth in a new light. Daniel was already wincing from the brightness, and Wes reached for the door.

"Please Daniel, back away before it gets too bright outside."

"You know...I could end all this misery right now," Daniel said softly, and Wes peered at his son anxiously. "All I need to do is take a step forward, and walk out into the light."

"Stop talking such nonsense," Wes scolded, and guided his son away from the door. "Here, take your pipe. Ease your pain so you can sleep. Rest up, son, and I'll take care of everything around here. Just rest and save your strength. We will decide on what to do next when you wake up again."

"Yes. What to do next," Daniel echoed as he shuffled numbly toward the bed, "when I wake up again."

Chapter Forty

The righteous detest the dishonest;
The wicked detest the upright.
-Proverbs 29:27 NIV

The sun could only do so much to keep the chill out of the air, and Wes felt it settling in his bones. He spent most of the morning tending to the horses, but when he sat down on his porch steps to take a break, he lacked the desire to get up again.

Time moved.

Time stood still.

None of it seemed to matter anymore.

Day and night, night and day; they all bled together when everything was overshadowed by fear, heartache, and longing. Inside, Daniel sat in the darkness and spoke to the shadows. Just like Gad, he was always whispering. Always whispering.

"Madness takes residency just out of sight," Wes muttered to the sky, "we think we're free, but it never really leaves the mind. Not his and not mine."He closed his eyes, and offered a quick prayer to the Lord, for he knew that God could do wondrous things. Without his mercy, Daniel would only continue to get worse.

Oh God in Heaven, please release my son from this burden. Let the madness fall away and allow him to have these last moments of peace. I beg for your mercy, Lord. Amen.

"Stop dragging your heels, old man," Wes grumbled to himself, "Get on in there and help the boy." He stood and stretched the chill out of his muscles, then forced himself to climb up the porch stairs, to warily enter his old home.

"Daniel, I've come to help you. Do you want your pipe? I can help if you need to ease your pain." Wes stepped into the gloom, and was immediately struck by the stench in the room. Daniel smelled wrong. He smelled of death.

"Morphine steals all thought away. Only the wicked. Only the wicked remain." Daniel's voice made Wes' skin crawl. He put the lighter and small vial into his pocket, and cautiously approached the bed with the pipe in his hand.

"Here, Daniel, I have your-" Daniel's hand was a blur of motion as he smacked the pipe from Wes' grasp. Wes' first reaction was to follow its trajectory to where it landed. While cautious, he was not at all guarded. Not in the presence of his son. Thus he was caught completely off guard when Daniel lunged forward and rammed his shoulder squarely into Wes with the force of a grizzly bear. Wes was lifted off the ground, and a moment later slammed hard against the wall on the other end of the room.

He crumpled into a heap on the floor, and wheezed as he desperately tried to draw air back into his quivering lungs. He laid discarded like a doll, his body alarming all over in pain, as he stared up at the creature who was once his son. Daniel looked to Wes like a predator examining his prey, and Wes felt he could only stare helplessly as he fought against the blackness clouding over his vision.

"Tear the flesh, render the bone, vanquish the light," Daniel growled as he drew closer. His glowing red eyes were overcome with madness. Wes stared, stupefied by those rows of black jagged teeth.

"Daniel, please," he pleaded. His son suddenly dashed forward, graceful on all four legs, and Wes knew he had to escape. He managed to sit up just as the beast grabbed hold of his shoulder and shoved him hard against the wall. Wes squeezed his eyes shut, and waited for the inevitable pain as teeth cut into flesh. His body trembled like a mouse feeling the hot breath of a hungry cat upon his face. But the bite never came, and abruptly Daniel pulled away from him with a groan. He made a sound in his throat; tormented by the hijacking of his mind, and reared up on his back legs. Towering over Wes, Daniel glared down at him with anguish in his red eyes.

"If thy right eye offends thee," he hissed, then raked claws down the length of his face. His right eye popped like a taut grape, and black bile splattered over Wes' face; burning his skin. Daniel screamed with the voice of two, and Wes stumbled over his feet putting some distance between them.

"Lord..." Wes whispered, his voice trembling with fear, "please save my son from this misery!"

"Don't be stupid!" Daniel growled, and drove his balled fist into Ruth's old rocking chair, causing it to crumble into a useless pile. "Only *you* can save me from my misery. You and that gun of yours."

"I will never do that to you," Wes insisted, horrified, and Daniel lunged for him. He was small, but his presence seemed massive as he shoved Wes against the wall again.

"Then you will die by my teeth and my madness," he growled with his face inches away from Wes. Wes looked at the vacant space where his right eye used to be and felt a calmness overcome him that could only come from God.

"The Lord will protect us both, son, so you can take your place by your mother's side."

"Stupid!" Daniel hissed, and twisted away from Wes. He struck himself in the head, overwhelmed in his frustration, and collapsed onto the bed heavily. "If you knew the things I hungered for; the ways I yearn to hurt you, I don't think you would want me near mom. I mean look at me. I've become the monster I always deserved to be."

"Nay, son." Wes forced himself forward on trembling legs to retrieve a scrap of cloth out of Ruth's old dresser and bring it to dab at the black fluid oozing down Daniel's face. The cuts didn't look too deep, but his eye was ruined. "This body you wear is no different than the black clothes you were shackled to. You won't take your sin with you when you die. You'll shed your body like old snake-skin. Your soul will be free of these earthly burdens, and with God's grace, it can be washed clean for your path into Heaven."

"So what's the secret," Daniel asked, and turned to look at Wes with his remaining eye. Against all reason, Wes saw clarity there, and was amazed. God performed a miracle, cleansing Daniel of the madness in his mind, even if it might be temporary.

"I don't understand," Wes said, sounding a little awestruck, and watched the way Daniel earnestly searched his face.

"Tell me the secret to get God to accept me into Heaven. I don't want to look like this when I die. I want to be clean like you said. I want to see mom again and be the person I used to be. I want to be her son."

"You want to know how to be saved?" Wes asked, stunned, and Daniel let out a dry laugh at the look on his face.

"I know how to be saved. Mom explained all that to me. I remember everything she taught me from the Word, but I just can't see the truth in it. I need to see proof. A sign like when God parted the sea or made fire rain from the sky."

"Proof?" Wes asked, confused, "but God shows proof of his existence every day we're alive."

"Now it's my turn not to understand." Daniel managed a weak smile that looked menacing on his mutated and scarred face. Wes had hoped for a chance like this to speak truth into the face of his son's doubt, but that didn't make him less nervous; knowing what was at stake.

Daniel knew of the gospel and the stories in the Word that guide the message of God, yet he still doubted the existence of God's mercy. Worse, in those moments that he allowed himself to believe there might be something waiting for him on the other side of the veil, he didn't think he deserved to be allowed to go there. He felt shackled by the wages of his own sin, and didn't believe in the transformation God provided when the bill was laid at his feet. The transformation of life and spirit wasn't a condition of salvation, but a side effect of it.

Wes cleared his throat, and looked down at his son who sat huddled on the edge of the bed; seeming both vulnerable and dangerous at the same time. The weight of what was at stake was not lost to him, and Wes understood what Eve and Ruth had been telling him this whole time. He was glad he brought Daniel home.

"I told you before how I act in faith, knowing God will guide me down the right path," Wes began and Daniel quietly nodded. "I trust in God when my path brings me through moments of good along with moments of bad, because everything that has happened to me gives purpose for the things to come. Think on all the choices you have made and all the things that occurred in your life, Daniel. Even the painful moments that caused you horrible suffering, and yes I grieve for those moments, but did they not lead you down a path of purpose? Would you be sitting here today if anything in your life transpired differently? We have been forged in flame, our steel honed into a weapon wielded by God. All that happened in your life led you to this moment, and this moment is leading you back home to Him."

"But that's just how life is. This thing happens then that thing happens. Everything just happens and if something seems tied to something else, it's just a coincidence."

"Words like 'luck', 'coincidence', and 'happenstance' were emboldened by the faithless. They exist simply to discredit the Lord's work. Consider, just for a moment, removing these concepts of chaos from the progression of your life. If you can't attribute things to chance, what do you have left? When I opened that door to you in the Divine Hall, was it coincidence? And if not, what was it? When I came out of the clutches of the prison to stand before you during my trial, was that happenstance? And if not, what was it? When I managed to find you in the forest miasma and get you back to safety before the night took us, was it luck? And if not, what was it? When you remove all those notions from your mind, you create a space for God to move into. He knows the nature of your heart, Daniel. He sees purpose in the upright and potential in the wicked. All have a place in his kingdom."

"How can you be so sure?" Daniel asked, and Wes was surprised to see that he was crying. "How can you possibly know that God is behind all these situations? The Dragon carries power that I have seen with my own eyes! All the Elders worship him without hesitation!"

"Has your dragon ever done anything that did not benefit him directly? You might reap rewards from his effort, but that doesn't mean he is doing anything for your sake. In the end, you are expendable, and your Elders worship a demon that uses up children and discards them when they are too weak to endure him anymore. God might not yet have purpose for you, son, but he will never discard you, and he will not abandon you when you're at your weakest. He's proven that to us both today." Wes reached for Daniel's hand, and looked him intently in the eye. "I have prayed for you, Daniel. I prayed for God to free you from your madness so that you could know me and know yourself in those moments before you died. You wanted a sign. You wanted a miracle. Well *you* are the miracle Daniel. For the madness no longer has its hold on you. Can you say that anything similar happened in any of the other Fallen you've encountered? Is this luck? Is this a coincidence? Is it just happenstance that you decided to ask me about your salvation the moment your sanity returned to you? Was it just some spontaneous request that carried no meaning? Surely, you must see there is more purpose to life than this. There is more meaning to the choices you make every day that extends beyond yourself. We are here to serve, son. We have no choice in this matter. But our choice lies in *who* we serve. And as for me, I serve the Lord."

"I believe you," Daniel said softly, sounding a little breathless, "because I've never known you to lie, and because there is no other explanation as to why I am having a conversation with you now. The voices that have tormented me for days...they are suddenly absent from my mind. A miracle. It's so strange feeling this way. I feel so...at peace. Is it odd, father, to be overjoyed when I'm about to die?"

"God is blessing you today," Wes said, and rubbed away the sting in his eyes. "If you're ready to surrender yourself to him, I can show you how. All it takes is prayer and we can do it together. It will be a first for us."

And a last.

"I'm ready. Show me what to do," Daniel replied, and watched Wes demonstrate holding his hands in prayer. After fumbling a little with his clumsy paws, Daniel eventually managed a semblance of Wes' posture, so the both of them bowed their heads and closed their eyes together.

"Daniel, I'm going to say the prayer of salvation. It's a prayer my father told me and his father told him. It's a prayer that's been passed down through years spanning all the way back to the beginning of known time. It's our commitment to God and our way of knowing that we are saved by Him. I'm going to say it aloud, and I need you to repeat every line after me."

"Alright," Daniel said with a voice so vulnerable, Wes yearned to embrace him. Instead he spoke out the prayer he knew by heart, and true to his word, Daniel repeated every line.

"Lord, I know that I'm a sinner. I know that I am a flawed lamb.
But I also know that you have given everything to me, Lord, so that I can be saved by you.
Your mercy. Your compassion. Your son.
Christ, who was given and died on the cross for me.
I know that my blessings could be named by you, oh Lord.
For each has been given by you as a gift unto me.
I submit myself as your servant.
My ransom paid, my soul washed clean,
I am forever yours, in knowing your son has died for me.
Thank you, Lord, and Amen."

Night had fallen upon them like a blanket, and both father and son leaned into the hushed stillness of the moment. Without thought, Daniel reached out, and Wes took hold of his hand. The world beyond their home was absent from their minds. The usurper in Daniel's stomach, powerless under the will of God. Wes was so proud of Daniel for coming so far from that boy he reunited with those many weeks ago. The love he felt for his son was overwhelming, and Wes was compelled to voice it into the stillness of this moment.

"Daniel, I-"

"Father, I'm ready to go see mom now," Daniel said abruptly, and let go of Wes' hand.

"You...want to see her grave?" Wes asked, confused, but Daniel shook his head solemnly.

"No, father, I'm ready to see her in Heaven. My body...I feel it shutting down, and I'm so tired. I want to go see mom now."

"What can I do?" Wes asked because he knew he could avoid this no longer. He just hoped Daniel was as sincere as he seemed regarding his salvation. Considering how difficult everything had been between them, this seemed far too easy. "How can I help?

"Help by taking me outside, father," Daniel replied as he struggled to get to his feet. "I want to see the sunrise."

Wes lit one of the fireboxes with the last of their oil, and led Daniel out into the night. Darkness still commanded the world, but Wes could see the start of grey at the edges of the sky. In spite of the pre-dawn, Wes could still sense the eyes of monstrous things that came forth from the woods and all the places beyond. The amount of them caused the force of their hunger to overwhelm and skew their numbers. Wes worried that one firebox would not be enough. They couldn't simply be there to observe the passage of a father and his son.

"How many are there do you think?" Wes asked as he squinted into the night.

"Twenty...maybe thirty...hard to say. More are coming."

"Do they intend to hurt you?" Wes asked, raising the firebox in feeble warning. His other hand was occupied with supporting his son.

"They only want to watch," Daniel said, his voice flat with the weight of his exhaustion. "Besides, nothing can hurt me anymore. I have God now, and soon I'll have mom too." He sounded so confident that Wes couldn't imagine he was wrong. He supported Daniel as his son limped through the yard, down the sloping path to Ruth's grave, then past her resting place as he continued on into the field.

"Where are we going?" Wes asked, glancing over at Daniel in confusion.

"Out into the field. I want to be clear of the trees and their shadows. I want to feel the sun on my skin."

"It will burn you, Daniel, you know this."

"Nothing can hurt me anymore," Daniel repeated. "Please, father. Come sit with me. Let me lean against you. I want to be near you this last time." Wes did as his son requested, ignoring how the words were like a knife twisting in his heart, and sat down upon the earth. When Daniel lowered himself to the ground in front of Wes and leaned against him, Wes realized that he was shivering. He regretted not bringing Daniel's heavy cloak, but the fool boy wouldn't have worn it anyway; the thing was black. Wes wrapped his arms around Daniel's misshapen frame and leaned over him as best he could. Anything to help him stay warm.

"How long do we have to wait?" Daniel asked, his voice soft. That second voice was completely gone.

"Soon, I think, but I won't know for sure until I hear the birdsong."

"Will the sun be warm? I'm so cold."

"It will be warm." Wes rubbed at Daniel's arms. The boy felt as chilled as a stone.

"Will Heaven be warm?" Daniel sounded dreamy. He was falling asleep again. Next to them, Wes noticed the firebox sputter, then dim, and finally it winked out.

"It will be warm," he said again. If it was anything other than warm, it wouldn't be Heaven. As they waited, Wes looked around, and examined the deeper places where the darkness was rich with occupancy. The situation would have him terrified on any other night, but sitting in the cold, holding his dying son in his arms, Wes didn't feel anything at all. All his emotions were wrung from him over the past few days, leaving him scooped out; empty; hollow.

The early song of the bird reached his ear and Wes knew they were heralding in a new day. One by one, he felt the monsters slipping away, and their hunger and curiosity ebbed. Whatever drew them together, Wes couldn't say, but in a strange way, they somehow knew to come and pay homage to a fallen king. They came to witness the death of the great Dragon. There was little left to see. Wes lifted his head, and he sought out the sun. Off to the east, the darkness of the night was budding into the brilliance of a new day.

"Daniel," Wes said gently. He unwrapped his arms, and gave his son a gentle shake of his shoulders. "The sun is coming. Wake up so you can see it."

Daniel didn't move. His body felt stiff; cold...lifeless. Wes was instantly overcome with desperate panic.

"Daniel! Look! Look to the east! The sun is coming, you have to see it, son. Look!"

Daniel opened his one eye, and blinked a few times until it came into focus. When he looked up, it was Wes he looked at and not the sun. He tried to smile, and lifted a weak paw, claws outstretched, until Wes took hold of it and held it in his hand. Daniel's touch was icy cold. It burned his skin, but he refused to pull away.

"It's the start of a new day, son. Look, off to the east." Wes said tenderly and pointed. Daniel's eye slid toward the eastern horizon. His chest hardly moved; his breath so shallow, it was barely there. So little of him remained in this world. The birds grew louder, more joining into the morning song.

"Daniel, please don't go," Wes said miserably, as he rocked his boy back and forth. "You'll miss the sunrise."

"Father," Daniel whispered, and his eyes were full of wonder as he stared at the brilliant colors to the east; a celebration of the coming sun. "Father...I love you."

The sun broke over the horizon, and spread its rays, like outstretched hands, over the two of them. Wes closed his eyes, savoring the warmth of those rays on his skin, and held onto this final moment between the two of them. A final goodbye.

"I love you too," Wes whispered but knew the words came too late. He felt the moment Daniel expelled his last breath. He knew that his son was already gone. Still, Wes didn't want to let him go just yet. This strange creature in his arms was all that remained of the brief but vibrant time they spent together. He couldn't help but remember the moments they shared, both good and bad; usually challenging, but sometimes simple.

The understanding that there would be no more moments between them; no more small goodbyes, overwhelmed Wes and made it hard for him to breathe. His grief surged up and towered over him like a tidal wave which threatened to crash down upon him. He would drown instantly in the undertow. He sat, unmoving, but gasping for breath until he was certain he was about to lose himself fully in his own despair. Then a strange sound came to his ear and Wes opened his eyes to see that a crow had landed a few feet away from them and peered at him inquisitively.

"Shoo," Wes scolded, and used his hat to spook the bird by waving it around near where the crow sat. The crow spread its large wings, used them to propel into the air, only to coast a few feet farther away from Wes, and land in the field again. The crow tilted his head to examine Wes, and a moment later, another crow joined the first. Then a third came and landed on Wes' other side. Wes watched them watching him, but remained in place, cradling his son.

What is this? What are these birds doing here?

Wes was suddenly startled by a subtle movement of his son's body in his arms. At first, he had hoped that maybe he was mistaken about Daniel dying, but one look at his son's vacant face and clouded eye told Wes otherwise. He forced Daniel's eye closed with trembling fingers, and two more crows landed to observe the exchange.

Daniel's body jerked again, more apparently than before, and the movement was done in a way that seemed unnatural; not a way a living person would move. It was as though he were propelled by a strange force from within. Wes stared, horrified by the cruel defilement of his son's body, then Daniel suddenly erupted in spasms. Terrified, Wes dropped his son, and scrambled to get away from this strange supernatural possession. He tripped clumsily over his numb feet, but Wes managed to regain momentum, and retreated a few feet away, while never taking his eyes off of the nightmare before him.

As the sun burned the frost from the ground, it also illuminated the scene Wes was forced to endure as Daniel's body came alive again. His feet and hands jerked and tapped against the ground as his arms and legs flopped like waterless fish. Soon, his whole body spasmed in a strange seizure, as though he were fighting against the shadows of a fever dream. His chest swelled bizarrely, and the pressure expelled out of Daniel as his lips abruptly parted, and a high pitched wheeze escaped him from somewhere deep within his throat. The sound was enough to invite an instant return of madness to Wes' mind. He covered his ears to try to silence the noise, but he couldn't avert his eyes. He was hypnotized by the belief that there had to be an explanation to what he was seeing. His heart thrummed heavily in his ears, but he could still hear the disquieting sounds coming from his son. Beyond that, two dozen crows flapped their wings; lifting, flying, landing, as they raised their heads to the sky and trumpeted their tribute: "Caw! Caw! Caw!"

Daniel's mouth stretched open, and his tongue bulged out through his many rows of jagged teeth. But no, it actually wasn't his tongue at all. Somehow, a strange creature worked its way up Daniel's throat and out of his body. Wet and writhing, it struggled to break free from its prison, but eventually managed to drag itself clear of Daniel's mouth and collapsed exhausted upon his unmoving chest. The moment the creature escaped him, Daniel's body went still once more. The crows were elated with what they saw, and heralded in their new king: "Caw! Caw!"

"Wicked spawn of Hell," Wes growled as he glared at the helpless panting creature. In the weeks and months to come, he will often reflect on this moment, and wonder why he didn't kill the wretched thing while he had the chance, but in turn he had to then admit that if he did so, he probably wouldn't have survived the night.

In that moment, he took no action, and instead sat stunned as he watched the creature take shape; its body drying under the sun, and eventually it rose up to spread open its damp glistening wings. It lifted its head to the sky, and opened its black beak in exclamation: "Caw!"

It was a crow, like the others. Not a dragon after all, but a usurper all the same. Wes felt evil hunger emanating from these birds, and it clung to him like oil on his skin. The more they flapped about; screeching and calling out for their king, the less safe he felt to be near them. He managed to stand in spite of his cold and numb legs, and stumbled woodenly back toward the farmhouse. He found comfort next to Ruth's grave, and sank down next to her resting place. He sat in silence for a long time while he looked out over his barren field, and watched the crows celebrate over Daniel's corpse. His son didn't deserve this. The cruelty of it broke Wes open, and his grief poured out.

"Why didn't I tell him that I love him when I had the chance?"

There was no reason to hold back the pain. Not anymore. The tears came hot and fast, and Wes leaned into the razor's edge of his despair. He wrapped himself in the agony of it; knowing it was the last connection he had to his eldest son. Wes squeezed his eyes shut and sobbed without restraint. His body gave over to his heartache fully, and his mourning left him gasping for air. All that he buried inside himself: the pain, the disappointment, the shame, the regret; it all spewed out of him through incoherent wailing grief. He cried for his wife, for his sons, for himself. He cried for all he lost, and all he had to endure. He despaired for so long, Wes no longer believed he was able to recover. How could he move on? What point was there to even try? There was no end to the deep cavern of sorrow that Wes wandered around in. The pain was far too great to overcome. Wes felt stripped down, stretched thin, and left out in the scorching sun until he was made brittle. Breakable. Useless.

He knew he should get up and bury his son. He knew he should get up and tend to the horses. He knew he should get up and decide on a plan. But Wes saw no point in any of it. Despair pulled at him, dragging him down into the earth, and Wes felt immobile. He was paralyzed by anguish and dirt. He stared up at the dimming sky, his body convulsing through tiny hiccups of breath, and felt the coolness of his tears as they slid back his face. He couldn't stop crying. He didn't want to stop crying. He lost everything. He had nothing left. He *was* nothing. Not anymore. Let him become the 'nothing' that he truly was. Let him dissolve into dust and return to the abyss where the Lord pulled him from. Let God ease the burden of his overtaxed lungs by ridding them of their function. Then he could be with his family again. Then he could be with his son. Then he could tell Daniel that he loved him too. Wes closed his eyes and prayed for God to end his existence. Anything was better than the pain of this grief. The pain he didn't want to end.

When sleep took him, Wes fled from his dreams. Dreams of his son convulsing; writhing, and creatures crawling out of him into the light. When he woke again, night had fallen upon him, and stole away his view of his son. Wes didn't care. He didn't want to see his son's body flailing and convulsing again. He wanted to see Daniel the way he was before. Wes wanted to see his soul washed clean. He might not have long to wait.

He felt the night monsters lingering nearby, and while he was unsure why they hesitated, he still anticipated an end by their tooth and claw. He imagined that moment of sharp blinding pain as his body succumbed to the night, and his mind was relieved of its torment; one form of pain extinguished by another. Still the tears continued to leak from his eyes.

Wes heard the shushed crackle of fallen leaves underfoot, and listened patiently as the first of the creatures approached him. It was close enough that he could hear its steady breath by his ear, and Wes waited to feel the keen cut of claw to skin. The creature eased closer still, but a sound came from over Wes' head like the flapping of wings.

"Caw! Caw! Caw!" Cried the crow, and the monsters all vanished deeper into the night.

“No!” Wes growled, frustrated at the intrusion, and sat up. He felt dizzy, having not eaten or drunk anything in more than a day, but was able to easily locate his intruder, for the crow peered at him from atop Ruth’s marker with a single glowing red eye. Seeing that eye glaring at him filled Wes with a white-hot fury he could barely contain.

“Get away from me! Let me be!” he snarled; each word full of contempt, but his demands were dismissed with an indifferent flap of wing and shift of foot. Wes flopped back onto the ground, unwilling to fight the beast any further, and glared instead at the countless stars overhead. He knew his anger was unwarranted, but couldn’t help himself. Anger was better than the pain. *Anything* was better than the pain. Wes closed his eyes, and felt the sting of tears returning. He endured for he had to, and waited for sleep to claim him once more.

Wes woke to the sounds of the birds and realized that he had slept through most of the night. A new day was dawning, and tasks needed to be done. He got up slowly, stiff from the cold settling in his bones, and sought out his crow sentry, but Ruth’s marker was bare. Putting the demon bird out of his mind, he made his way up to the barn and retrieved a shovel from within. He checked on the horses briefly, hoping to care for them more once this other task was done, and returned to the edge of the field. He stared solemnly at the black figure of his son’s body. The crows were all gone, discarding him now that his purpose was served, and Wes felt deeply ashamed that he left Daniel lay for so long. His son needed to return to the earth.

Wes tossed the shovel to the side, and trudged out into the field to retrieve him. He scooped Daniel into his arms delicately even though the lad was stiff and unyielding, and carried him back to his mother’s grave. As he approached, Wes paused when he saw that the solitary crow sentry had returned to his place on Ruth’s marker. He tilted his head, peering at Wes with his single red eye, and in the light of day, Wes could see three long jagged cuts that slashed down the bird's face where his right eye should have been.

“You’ve left your mark on my son, vermin, but I see he’s left his mark on you too,” Wes said with a wicked smile.

“Caw!” The crow replied, then spread his wings, and took to the sky.

I should have shot the thing dead.

It was too late to consider that option. Wes laid Daniel down next to his mother’s grave, and picked the shovel up once more. The ground was hard to cut into; the soil unforgiving and cold, but Wes worked on the strength of his determination and managed to carve out a shallow grave. He lifted Daniel, who seemed much lighter in death than he was near the end of his life, and laid him gently into the grave; his final resting place.

"Here you go, lad. You're next to your mother now." Wes stared at the corpse that was once his child, thinking on what words to say over his body, then quietly turned, and shoveled the dirt back into the hole again. He found the area where he once threw rocks when removing them from the field, and brought back handfuls to place them on the small dirt mound. The grave wasn't deep, and Wes didn't want to risk the intrusion of animals.

When at last the deed was done, he collapsed back onto the earth between the graves of his son and his wife. He would need to tend to the horses later. He was far too tired. Exhaustion robbed the little motivation he had in him, and Wes eased back into the comfortable cocoon of his despair. He knew he was taking this so much harder than any of the other losses he faced, but felt this was all due to not knowing if Daniel was truly saved. Did he understand the prayer he made? Did he feel the Holy Spirit breathe life into his soul? Wes should have asked him these things. If he knew for certain that Daniel was safe with his mother, this wouldn't be so hard to endure. The despair would be a little less somehow.

Wes' stomach twisted in hunger but he didn't care. When he realized he was running his fingers along the hilt of his gun, Wes pushed his hands down into his pockets to contain their longing. His fingers brushed against something, and Wes withdrew a tiny vial of morphine. The liquid inside was yellow and thick. It rolled around and glowed invitingly in the sunlight. Wes closed his hand around the vial just as he closed his eyes. The tears were starting to form again.

Wes woke, not realizing he had fallen asleep, and tried to determine if it was night or day. Was the sun coming or going? Time became malleable like clay. He worked it into whatever he wanted it to be.

Weary, hurting, and delirious from dehydration, Wes turned toward Ruth's marker, and sure enough that same one-eyed crow was glaring down at him. Wes' hand itched for his revolver, but he then noticed he was still holding on to the little vial. Daniel's morphine. A drug that helped make all pain fade away. It was half empty. It was half full. The thick golden liquid slid around as Wes rolled the vial in his fingers.

He didn't give much thought to his actions. He was not seeking death, but he did not yearn for life either. In truth, what he wanted more than anything was an ending. An ending to his struggle, his pain, his grief, his regret. He longed for an ending so intensely that he could not see a place for a beginning. He uncorked the vial cradled in between his fingertips, and emptied it into his mouth. The liquid was strong and bitter. It burned his parchment tongue and stung his eyes. Wes couldn't work up the saliva to swallow the liquid down, but it already seemed to be taking hold. Behind him, the usurper cawed out his objections. At least Wes wasn't entirely alone.

He let the vial fall and turned his attention to the sky. It only took a few minutes for the pain to fade from his body. It only took a little longer for the anguish to leave his mind. Nothing could hurt him anymore. The crow's squalling was swallowed by a steady humming in his ears.

Wes took in a breath, and realized that he had stopped breathing. The effort to breathe became a conscious one, and each time was harder than the last. Deep in his mind, he could feel a rising panic but the drug held it at bay. Giving over to the tranquility, Wes closed his eyes and succumbed to the seduction of sleep.

"You foolish, foolish man!" When Wes opened his eyes again, he saw that he was sitting at the edge of his yard overlooking the field. It was not too far from where he fell asleep, yet that could have been another lifetime for how transformed the place looked. The fields were full of sweet corn, the lush grass teased at his nose, and the soft breeze caressing his face was warm. In front of him, Wes was pleased to see Ruth pacing the length of the yard; kicking skirts with each step.

"It's good to see you too, dear wife," Wes said with a teasing smile.

"You aren't supposed to be here!" Ruth stopped pacing long enough to stab a finger at him. "You stupid *stupid* man! What were you thinking?"

"I...wasn't," Wes had to admit. He didn't see past his actions to the potential consequences. He was far too overwhelmed by the pain.

"I know you grieve husband," Ruth said and her sad smile made her even more beautiful. "I know that you have suffered greatly."

"It was the hardest thing I ever endured." Wes' eyes burned from the remembering, but he refused to cry in front of his wife.

"So you thought to come here to escape your pain?"

"I reckon so. But I also would give anything to see him again."

"You can't see him," Ruth said with a shake of her head, "not here."

"But...I didn't tell him that I love him."

"Oh, dear one. He knows you love him."

"I didn't get to say goodbye."

"You hate saying goodbye," Ruth said with a chuckle. "You know that, Wesley."

"If he's not here, how will I know if he's saved? What if I didn't explain things well enough? What if I failed him somehow?"

"Be still, husband," Ruth said and knelt down in front of him. She cupped his face in her hands and her beauty left him feeling breathless. Ruth wiped at tears that Wes wasn't aware of, and shook her head. "I've never *seen* you like this. You look exhausted, and my Lord! You're so thin!"

"Ruth...please tell me what happened to Daniel."

"You know more than anyone that being a servant of God means that you must serve. Because of you, Daniel found his path to salvation, but even in death he is no exception. He is needed just as much as you are. Which is why it is so *frustrating* that you are here! How can you be so foolish? You know what's at stake!"

Ruth stood, her anger rekindled, and resumed her pacing. Wes watched her warily for he knew his wife's temper well.

"I... don't understand," he ventured at last, and Ruth turned to glare at him.

"You're not allowed to claim ignorance, Wesley. Not this time. You *know* you are duty-bound to the Light Bringer!"

"Benji?" Wes stared at Ruth, dumbfounded. Somehow, in the depth of his despair, he forgot Benji even existed. This surprised him at first, but then he recalled the way he leaned into his grief. He was paralyzed by his sorrow. He couldn't see beyond the field in front of him, so of course he didn't think about Benji.

"All things *must* serve the Bringer of Light. That includes you, Wesley, and that includes our son."

"Daniel?" Wes tried to get up, but his body felt thick and formless. He moved like sap in the snow. "What does Daniel have to do with Benji?"

"You will know the answer to that when you need to know it. Right now, you just need to focus on yourself. You must fight, dear husband. Find the way out of this maze of misery you created for yourself. You must go to the boy urgently, for the dead are rising, time is thinning, and dreams are transforming into nightmares. All things must serve the Bringer of Light. That includes us as well."

"How am I supposed to serve him? What am I supposed to do?"

"You'll know when you need to know, Wesley. Look to your dreams to guide you."

"I can't remember my dreams anymore," Wes said, frustrated, and Ruth knelt down next to him again. She looked worried, and urged him to lay back upon the soft summer grass.

"We are out of time. You can not stay here any longer. I have mended what was fractured in your mind. Your dreams are your own once more. Now go, and face the consequences of all you have done."

Wes opened his mouth to speak; to ask; to try to understand, but he felt the heel of Ruth's palm thrust into his soft unguarded gut, and he immediately rolled onto his side to vomit up the meager contents of his stomach. His body heaved long after there was nothing left for it to give, and when Wes regained some control, he realized he had returned to the bitter cold of the present world. He laid for some time, panting and taking stock of his condition. His mind felt hazy from the drugs, but he was breathing without effort at least. His throat was raw; desperate for water, and Wes imagined the horses felt much the same way. Still, it was so tempting to give over to his despair again; to wrap himself in it, and refuse to face the oncoming day. But he heard birdsong, and it drove him forward.

"Alright, Ruth. I'll do as you say." With great effort, Wes got onto his knees, then eventually got to his feet. He glanced at Ruth's marker but its usual occupant was gone. So he stumbled up the hill, one foot at a time, and staggered into his farmhouse where he ate all that he could find. Little remained of their provisions but there would be more in the wagon if it was where they left it.

The food didn't sit well inside him, and Wes struggled to keep it down. Still, he didn't have time to allow himself some reprieve. As soon as he could move without losing everything he just ate, Wes made his way over to the barn to tend to the neglected horses.

As he cared for the animals, Wes' nausea slowly abated, and his head cleared. He gathered what he could from the home he spent the majority of his life in, including a few things of Ruth's that weren't stolen, and packed everything into the horse's saddlebags. Just as he finished, the sun spread over the land, and gave Wes a view of his farm. He took a moment to look it over one last time, then walked down to the graves of his family.

"Thank you for all the wonderful years we had together," he said as he looked over the row of everyone he's lost. "I'll cherish all the good memories, and carry with me the bad ones as well. You won't be forgotten. Even when time itself crumbles at my feet."

A soft sound of feather drew Wes' eye to the trees overhead, and he saw a solitary crow perched upon the barren branches. This crow was not the usurper for both of his eyes were intact, but Wes called up to him anyway.

"She said that all must serve the Bringer of Light, so I know where your master must be. Go to him and give him my warning. Tell him that he better behave, 'cause I'm coming to join him, and I reckon I'll be there to stand in his way."

The crow took to the sky the moment the words were spoken, and Wes put the usurper out of his mind. That was a problem for another day, and Wes needed to saddle his horse. It was time to ride out into the world beyond this cemetery.

Soon, he will reach that familiar highway, and make his way northwest. He'll seek out a special place nestled in the low hills; full of secret homesteads. He will come upon an empty rocking chair sitting in the middle of the road, and he already knew the moment he got there, he will see a small boy running toward him from out of the scrubland; skinny legs kicking up dust behind him.

Wes knew this as surely as he knew that he was bound to that boy's destiny. For Wes felt the Lord guiding him as he did from the moment he bid his dying wife goodbye with a promise of return laid upon his kiss. Every moment was woven together into this complex tapestry that included both Wes, and also the rest of mankind. God had brought him this far, and Wes trusted Him to lead wherever he's meant to go. For Wes was one of the upright. A believer in the Word. And God was guiding him exactly to where he needed to be.

All must serve the Bringer of Light.

He didn't see the Bringer of Light, he just saw Benji: a boy who made a home of his own inside Wes' heart.

Ephesians 5: 8-14 NLT

For once you were full of darkness, but now you have light from the Lord.
So live as people of light!
For this light within you produces only what is good and right and true.
Carefully determine what pleases the Lord.
Take no part in the worthless deeds of evil and darkness; instead, expose them.
It is shameful even to talk about the things that ungodly people do in secret.
But their evil intentions will be exposed when the light shines on them,
For the light makes everything visible. This is why it is said,

"Awake, O Sleeper,
Rise up from the dead,
And Christ will give you light!"

About the author:

Sarah Wallis resides with her husband in Lebanon Pennsylvania and has three adult children and a young son with special needs. She worked as a registered nurse in Hospice as well as Mental Health. She was saved in 2016 and continues to find joy in her journey with God. This is her first novel.

If you would like to write to her about how this book might have impacted your life or opened a door for your own salvation story, please write to her at: Sarah Wallis PO Box 221 Lebanon PA 17042.

Gratitude from the author:

Thank you, Nate, for your eternal patience in me.

Thank you, Russ, for cheering me all the way to the finish line.

Thank you, Liv, for your keen eye and smart opinions.

Thank you, Lincoln, for showing me the small joys tucked inside this thing called autism.

And Thank you God, for being at my side every step of the way.

www.ingramcontent.com/pod-product-compliance
Lightning Source LLC
Chambersburg PA
CBHW020945310726
48980CB00001B/61
* 9 7 9 8 9 9 4 1 7 4 1 2 8 *